ENCYCLOPEDIA

Star Wars: Guides and Resource Materials
Published by Ballantine Books

Star Wars Encyclopedia

Star Wars Technical Journal

A Guide to the Star Wars Universe

Star Wars:
The Essential Guide to Characters

Star Wars:
The Essential Guide to Vehicles and Vessels

Star Wars:
The Essential Guide to Weapons and Technology

Star Wars:
The Essential Guide to Planets and Moons*

Star Wars:
The Essential Guide to Droids*

**Forthcoming*

ENCYCLOPEDIA

Stephen J. Sansweet

With an introduction by Timothy Zahn

The Ballantine Publishing Group • New York

A Del Rey® Book
Published by The Ballantine Publishing Group

http://www.randomhouse.com/delrey/
http://www.starwars.com

Library of Congress Cataloging-in-Publication Data

Sansweet, Stephen J., 1945-
Star wars encyclopedia / Stephen Sansweet. — 1st ed.
p. cm.
"A Del Rey book."
Includes bibliographical references
ISBN 0-345-40227-8
1. Star Wars films—Dictionaries. I. Title.
PN1995.9.S695S24 1997
791.43'75—dc21 97-15066
CIP

Manufactured in the United States of America

Interior and Jacket design by Michaelis/Carpelis Design Assoc. Inc.

First Edition: July 1998

10 9 8 7 6 5 4 3 2 1

To George Lucas,
for inspiring creativity in an entire generation,
and to the Star Wars *generation itself,*
for providing so many friends in the Force.

Introduction

What's it like working in the Star Wars universe?

It's a question I've been asked a lot since *Heir to the Empire* came out in 1991. And depending on how things are going on any particular day, there are a lot of possible answers I can give. It's an honor and a privilege; it's a challenge and a responsibility; it's a high compliment and a lot of work. But for me there's always one answer that underlies all the others.

It's a lot of fun.

It really is. Whether flying alongside Wedge Antilles and Rogue Squadron, standing behind Luke as he faces down trouble with drawn lightsaber, or trading wisecracks with Han and Leia in that special relationship they have, there's something uniquely satisfying about visiting this immensely rich cosmos George Lucas created more than twenty years ago.

But whereas *Star Wars* began as the vision of a single man, over the past few years it has grown into an impressively intricate group effort. Large and, on occasion, just a tad bit unwieldy.

I sometimes think of it as a huge, multi-course banquet that's in the process of being created for all of us *Star Wars* fans. We have the fiction writers off in the corners in their individual kitchens, whipping up main dishes, hors d'oeuvres, and desserts. The artists create place settings, design tableware to complement the chefs' selections, paint portraits of the banquet's main guests, and sculpt some absolutely stunning centerpieces for the tables.

Off in the next room, the various comics writers and artists have set up an impressive buffet with the same great spread, only in bite-sized portions. One room over, the game designers have come up with a selection of cookbooks for those who want to prepare their own version of the banquet for a few friends at home. Across that room, the toymakers, collectibles creators, and card designers are busy with souvenirs and mementos we can play with or simply take home to help remind us of all the fun we've had.

It really is a great time we're having. The only problem is that it's *such* a huge party that it's becoming increasingly hard for any of us to keep track of everything that's going on. There's a touch of some elusive spice in this dish over here, for example; but I think I caught a whiff of it across the table, too, and I'd really like to know what that spice is, where it came from, and maybe other ways it can be used. Or else I've heard rumors of a chocolate-macadamia combination and want to know where else it may be found.

How do I go about keeping track, finding everything I want (even need)?

It's very simple. I consult the book. *This* book.

Because while there have been limited compendiums of *Star Wars* material before, this is the first one to pull it *all* together. Here you'll find the heroes and villains of *Star Wars*; the spaceships of *Star Wars*; the weapons and vehicles and worlds and aliens and creatures and droids and everything else that makes the universe of *Star Wars* the wonderful place that it is.

Frankly, I stand in awe of Steve Sansweet. I've done my fair share of paging through multitudinous reference books in search of some elusive *Star Wars* fact or name or gadget that I *know* I've seen somewhere. I know how much work even a limited search can be. For Steve to have even tackled a project like this—let alone to have pulled it off—is an accomplishment far beyond my abilities and patience.

But it's finished, it's here, and it's terrific. For all of us, writers and fans alike, it's the perfect solution to the where-is-it/what-is-it/who-is-it syndrome. Though like eating salted peanuts you'll probably find you can't stop at consulting just a single entry, but will end up searching and cross-referencing and browsing for a pleasant hour or two. I wish I'd had this book a couple of years ago; but I have it now, and I'm very grateful.

And Steve, I'm also grateful that you permitted me to add this little note to your work. It was an honor and a privilege, a challenge and a responsibility, a high compliment and, yes, a certain amount of work.

It was also a lot of fun.

TIMOTHY ZAHN

About this Book

Many Bothans died to bring you the information in this book.

Well, not really. But if you aren't exactly sure who the Bothans are, or why they might have died, then this book is for you.

If you do know, prepare to delve even deeper into the *Star Wars* mythos. Although the line about the Bothans was uttered by Rebel Alliance leader Mon Mothma in *Return of the Jedi*, it was subsequent novels, comics, and even video games that provided the "back story" of who the Bothans are and what they did in the *Star Wars* universe.

Many fans and admirers of the universe that George Lucas created have watched it grow with a great deal of admiration, and just a bit of trepidation. After all, how do you keep track of everything? Since the universe is so interconnected, an event that transpires in the Outer Rim may have major consequences years later in the Inner Core. Suppose you've missed a novel or an issue of the comics? How does a character in a customizable card game fit in? Just who is that mysterious figure in the latest hot CD-ROM game? Personally, I've long wanted to have an encyclopedia covering the entire *Star Wars* oeuvre.

Well, you know what they say about being careful what you wish for.

The "conceit" behind this *Star Wars* encyclopedia is that it was compiled by a group of scholars about twenty-five or so standard years after the Battle of Endor. Naturally, there's a bit of a New Republic spin on entries; it's impossible to be morally ambiguous about the depredations inflicted on untold billions of sentient beings by the Empire. And while much information about the Empire and the Old and New Republics has become available to the scholars, there still are mysteries to be resolved and people, places, and events yet to be uncovered.

There always has been more information than could be included in the original trio of two-hour films. In fact, the novelization of *Star Wars* that appeared nearly nine months before the first film opened contained detail that never reached the screen. There were also comic books and radio dramatizations that told the same general story, but in fuller detail and with more history. And much of the expanded universe dates from Timothy Zahn's groundbreaking and exciting Grand Admiral Thrawn trilogy (starting with *Heir to the Empire* in 1991).

Which brings us to the often-asked question: Just what is Star Wars canon, and what is not? The one sure answer: The Star Wars Trilogy Special Edition—the three films themselves as executive-produced, and in the case of Star Wars written and directed, by George Lucas, are canon. Coming in a close second we have the authorized adaptations of the films: the novels, radio dramas, and comics.

After that, almost everything falls into a category of "quasi-canon."

The creative folks at Lucasfilm spend a great deal of time and effort to ensure that everything published fits together. There's a lot of discussion between and among the authors of the various books and comics. That's why a minor planet casually mentioned once in a past novel may become an important site in a current or future one, or the spirit of a towering figure who "died" 4,000 years before the Battle of Yavin comes back to play a major role in the life of Luke Skywalker.

The *Encyclopedia* dates events as they occurred in relation to the Battle of Yavin. Thus "year zero" is marked by the first all-out victory for the Rebel Alliance and the destruction of the first Death Star, events portrayed in the film *Star Wars: A New Hope*. Every attempt has been made to guide readers with cross-references and a source code to indicate where to turn for even more information and a fuller story about individuals, creatures, planets, vehicles, and the like.

This book began, at its core, with the comprehensive second edition of the *Guide to the Star Wars Universe* by Bill Slavicsek. It makes full use of several other major resources including *The Essential Guide to Vehicles and Vessels* by Bill Smith and *The Essential Guide to Characters* by Andy Mangels. It could not have been completed without the generous help of fan-turned-author Dan Wallace, who let me use copious amounts of his planet guide, versions of which he put on the World Wide Web for access by all. The book depends, of course, on the writings and imaginations of scores of authors, artists, and game designers, who are credited in the bibliography (with source codes) at the beginning of this book.

Special thanks must go to the entire gang at West End Games. They were there first, way back in 1987, and have contributed more new people, planets, creatures, vehicles, weapons, and stories than anyone.

Even with eighteen months of time devoted to this book, I could not have completed it without the able assistance of my panel of first-readers: Tom Nelson, Josh Ling, Les David, Catherine Springer, Anna Bies, Kevin Stevens, Dan Vebber, and Lance Worth. At Lucasfilm, my thanks go to my editor and good friend Sue Rostoni, who tried very hard to keep me on deadline and provided both help and a handy shoulder. Thanks also to Allan Kausch, Lucasfilm's other continuity editor, and Lucy Wilson, director of publishing, with whom I first discussed the idea for this book in 1991. Besides Sue Rostoni, I received invaluable editing and fact-checking help from the aforementioned Dan Wallace and from Pablo Hidalgo, a West End Games author whose eighty pages of small-type notes prevented me from making numerous errors.

A special thanks to Stephen Stanley, Dan Burns, and Warren Holland of Decipher Inc., for the generous use of so many of the great computer-enhanced images that appear on the cards of Decipher's *Star Wars* Customizable Card Game; to Sean Tierney and Rich Young of Dark Horse Comics and the Dark Horse Service Bureau for similar assistance; to Halina Krukowski, photo librarian at Lucasfilm; to Stacy Mollema, Athena Portillo, and Cara Evangelista in Lucas Licensing; and to the other artists whose sketches and illustrations fill in where photos just don't exist.

At Del Rey, copious thanks to editor Steve Saffel, a long-time believer in this project, who pushed, cajoled, and didn't lose his cool very often despite some extenuating circumstances. Thanks also to Fred Dodnick, Sylvain Michaelis, Ellen Scordato, and Elizabeth Zack, who shepherded the illustrations and design of the *Encyclopedia*.

Finally, the biggest thanks of all to George Lucas, without whom countless lives would be considerably duller.

The author, of course, is solely responsible for any errors or misinterpretations amongst the entries. And while every attempt has been made to get the latest information into this book, the fact that the *Star Wars* universe is so alive and dynamic means that we'll always be playing at least a bit of catch-up.

Stephen J. Sansweet

Stephen J. Sansweet
Los Angeles

Star Wars Timeline of Key Events

NOTE: The Timeline is based on the Battle of Yavin being Standard Year Zero (the film *Star Wars: A New Hope*). Events take place BBY (before the Battle of Yavin) and ABY (after the Battle of Yavin).

5,000–4,990 BBY
Pioneering hyperspace explorers Gav and Jori Daragon stumble upon the mighty Sith Empire, which is ruled by Dark Lords of the Sith and thrives on dark-side Force powers. This eventually leads to a major battle between the Old Republic and the Sith Empire.

4,000–3,998 BBY
The Jedi Knights act as guardians for the Old Republic. Two in particular stand out, Ulic Qel-Droma—who helps to end a planetary civil war—and Nomi Sunrider. They team up during the Freedon Nadd uprising.

3,997–3,996 BBY
The Sith threat returns as Dark Lord Exar Kun seduces dozens of Jedi Knights to the dark side, including Ulic Qel-Droma. Kun is destroyed as a Jedi army invades his base on Yavin 4, but his spirit remains trapped for millennia.

896 BBY
Jedi Master Yoda is born.

200 BBY
The Wookiee Chewbacca is born on the planet Kashyyyk.

60 BBY
Ben "Obi-Wan" Kenobi is born.

41 BBY
Anakin Skywalker is born.

32 BBY
Emperor Palpatine begins his rise to power.

29 BBY
Han Solo is born.

22–20 BBY
Anakin Skywalker is seduced by the dark side of the Force and becomes Darth Vader.

18 BBY
Luke Skywalker and his twin sister Leia are born.

10 BBY

A teenage Han Solo develops into a hotshot pilot and smuggler, and eventually wins the *Millennium Falcon* from the gambler Lando Calrissian.

10–5 BBY

The droid companions C-3PO and R2-D2 are involved in a series of harrowing adventures in the service of several different owners.

5–2 BBY

Han Solo and his first mate Chewbacca take part in a series of exploits in the Corporate Sector.

1–0 BBY

Rebel agent Kyle Katarn steals the Empire's Death Star plans.

0

The Imperial Senate is dissolved and Emperor Palpatine declares a New Order. Luke Skywalker, Ben Kenobi, Han Solo, and Chewbacca save Princess Leia, confront Darth Vader, and help destroy the Death Star at the Battle of Yavin, but not before it is used to destroy Leia's adopted planet of Alderaan. Kenobi lets himself be struck down by Vader and becomes one with the Force.

0+ ABY

Luke and Leia search for the Kaiburr crystal, which contains great Force powers, and encounter Darth Vader. The Rebel base on Yavin 4 is evacuated and a search is begun for another, eventually ending on the planet Hoth. The Rebel Alliance heroes encounter bounty hunters on the planet Ord Mantell.

3 ABY

The Empire strikes back, routing the Rebel Alliance during the Battle of Hoth. Luke Skywalker goes to Dagobah to train under Jedi Master Yoda. Leia, Han, Chewbacca, and C-3PO are captured by Darth Vader on Bespin's Cloud City and held as bait for young Skywalker. Solo is frozen in carbonite and given to bounty hunter Boba Fett for delivery to crime lord Jabba the Hutt. Luke confronts Vader, who claims to be Luke's father, and Luke loses his hand and lightsaber, but is rescued by Leia and Lando Calrissian.

3+ ABY

Young Cindel Towani and her family crash on the forest moon of Endor. They are helped by a tribe of native Ewoks.

3.5 ABY

Prince Xizor, head of the Black Sun criminal organization, plots to discredit Vader and become the Emperor's second-in-command by having

Luke Skywalker assassinated. Instead, it is Xizor who is terminated. Luke builds his own lightsaber.

4 ABY

Luke Skywalker destroys Jabba the Hutt and rescues Han Solo. Returning to Dagobah, he finds Yoda's life force ebbing. There Luke learns that Vader is truly his father, and Leia is his sister. On a moon of Endor, with the help of the Ewoks, Han and Leia destroy a shield generator that had been protecting a new, more powerful orbiting Death Star, which is destroyed by Lando and X-wing pilot Wedge Antilles during the Battle of Endor. Vader saves his son Luke from certain death at the hands of the Emperor, but is killed destroying Palpatine.

4+ ABY

Just days after the victory at Endor, the Rebels have to team up with Imperial forces to defeat the reptilian Ssi-ruuk under a truce at Bakura.

4.5 ABY

Rogue Squadron's X-wing pilots begin a systematic retaking of the galaxy, planet by planet.

5 ABY

Various attempts to lead the tattered Empire include one by the three-eyed mutant known as Trioculus. Young Jedi Prince Ken emerges from isolation in the underground Lost City of the Jedi.

6.5–7.5 ABY

Rogue Squadron, under the leadership of Wedge Antilles, liberates the Imperial capital planet of Coruscant and engages the former head of Imperial Intelligence in a fierce struggle over the galaxy's supply of curative bacta.

8 ABY

Han Solo and Princess Leia Organa finally get married, but only after Solo "kidnaps" Leia and takes her to the planet Dathomir.

9 ABY

Imperial Grand Admiral Thrawn returns from the far reaches of the galaxy and becomes a major threat to the New Republic, though ultimately he is killed by his own bodyguard. Leia Solo gives birth to twins, Jaina and Jacen.

10 ABY

Two different clones of Emperor Palpatine, backed by forces wielding new super-weapons such as the Galaxy Gun and World Devastators, bring chaos to the New Republic, and Luke nearly succumbs to the dark side. Imperial forces briefly regain Coruscant. Leia gives birth to her third child, whom she names Anakin.

11 ABY

Luke establishes a Jedi training academy on Yavin 4, but is nearly killed by the reawakened spirit of ancient Dark Lord Exar Kun.

12–13 ABY

Luke has an epic—but ultimately unfulfilled—romance with one-time Jedi Knight Callista, as he is trapped aboard an old Imperial battle moon, battles a Hutt crime lord, and deals with a mysterious outbreak of a deadly plague.

14 ABY

Leia and Han's three children are kidnapped by a one-time Imperial official who has established an "Empire Reborn" movement.

15 ABY

Luke Skywalker achieves the ability to cloak objects.

16–17 ABY

The New Republic is threatened by the cruel and xenophobic Yevethan species. Luke searches for clues about his mother. Wedge Antilles becomes a general.

17 ABY

Kueller, a one-time pupil at the Jedi academy, becomes a dark-side menace, even as bombs he planted endanger the New Republic.

18 ABY

Thracken Sal-Solo, Han's nearly identical cousin, leads a brutal revolutionary army intent on ruling the Corellian sector. The Solo children help to stop him by disabling Sal-Solo's star-busting weapon.

22–23 ABY

Anakin Solo begins his instruction at the Jedi academy.

23–24 ABY

Jaina and Jacen Solo train at the Jedi academy and help to take on the evil Second Imperium.

Source Codes and Bibliography

AC—
Ambush at Corellia, volume 1 of The Corellian Trilogy, Roger MacBride Allen, Bantam Books, 1995.

AIR—
Alliance Intelligence Reports, Bill Smith, West End Games (WEG), 1995.

AS—
Assault at Selonia, volume 2 of The Corellian Trilogy, Roger MacBride Allen, Bantam Books, 1995.

BF—
Boba Fett, one-shot and limited-series comics, Dark Horse Comics, 1995–1997.

BFE—
Ewoks: The Battle for Endor, MGM/UA, 1986.

BGS—
Battle for the Golden Sun, Douglas Kaufman, WEG, 1988.

BI—
Black Ice, Paul Murphy and Bill Slavicsek, WEG, 1990.

BTS—
Before the Storm, volume 1 of The Black Fleet Crisis, Michael P. Kube-McDowell, Bantam Books, 1996.

BW—
The Bacta War, volume 4 of the X-wing series, Michael Stackpole, Bantam Books, 1997.

CCC—
Crisis on Cloud City, Christopher Kubasik, WEG, 1989.

CCG—
Star Wars customizable card game, Decipher, 1995–1997.

CLC—
Classic Campaigns, Bill Smith, editor, WEG, 1995.

COF—
Champions of the Force, volume 3 of The Jedi Academy Trilogy, Kevin J. Anderson, Bantam Books, 1994.

COG—
Creatures of the Galaxy, Phil Brucato et al., WEG, 1994.

COJ—
Children of the Jedi, Barbara Hambly, Bantam Books, 1995.

CP—
Star Wars Campaign Pack, Paul Murphy, WEG, 1988.

CPL—
The Courtship of Princess Leia, Dave Wolverton, Bantam Books, 1994.

CRFG—
Cracken's Rebel Field Guide, Christopher Kubasik, WEG, 1991.

CRO—
Cracken's Rebel Operatives, Bill Smith, WEG, 1994.

CS—
The Crystal Star, Vonda McIntyre, Bantam Books, 1994.

CSSB—
Han Solo & the Corporate Sector Sourcebook, Michael Allen Horne, WEG, 1993.

CSW—
Classic Star Wars, issues 1–20, Archie Goodwin & Al Williamson, Dark Horse Comics, 1992–1994.

D—
Droids, series and specials, Dark Horse Comics, 1994–1995.

DA—
Dark Apprentice, volume 2 of The Jedi Academy Trilogy, Kevin J. Anderson, Bantam Books, 1994.

DE—
Star Wars: Dark Empire, 6-issue series, Tom Veitch and Cam Kennedy, Dark Horse Comics, 1991–1992.

DE2—
Star Wars: Dark Empire 2, 6-issue series, Tom Veitch and Cam Kennedy, Dark Horse Comics, 1994–1995.

DESB—
Star Wars: Dark Empire Sourcebook, Michael Allen Horne, WEG, 1993.

DF—
Dark Forces PC game, LucasArts, 1995.

DFR—
Dark Force Rising, volume 2 of The Thrawn Trilogy, Timothy Zahn, Bantam Spectra Books, 1992.

DFRSB—
Dark Force Rising Sourcebook, Bill Slavicsek, WEG, 1992.

DLS—
Tales of the Jedi: Dark Lords of the Sith, Tom Veitch and Kevin J. Anderson, 12 issues, Dark Horse Comics, 1994–1995.

DOE—
Domain of Evil, Jim Bambra, WEG, 1991.

DS—
Darksaber, Kevin J. Anderson, Bantam Books, 1995.

DSC—
The DarkStryder Campaign, Peter Schweighofer et al., WEG, 1995.

DSTC—
Death Star Technical Companion, Bill Slavicsek, WEG, 1991, 1993.

DTV—
Droids animated television shows, episodes 1–13, Nelvana, 1985.

DU—
Death in the Undercity, Michael Nystul, WEG, 1990.

EA—
The Ewok Adventure (Caravan of Courage), MGM/UA, 1984.

EE—
Empire's End, 2-issue series, Tom Veitch & Jim Baikie, Dark Horse Comics, 1995.

ESB, ESBN—
The Empire Strikes Back film, 20th Century Fox, 1980; novelization, Donald F. Glut, Del Rey Books, 1980.

ESBR—
The Empire Strikes Back, National Public Radio dramatization, Brian Daley, 1983; published by Del Rey Books, 1995.

ESBSB—
See **GG3**, revised and expanded by Pablo Hidalgo, 1996.

ETV—
Ewoks animated television show, episodes 1–26, Nelvana, 1985–86.

FNU—
The Freedon Nadd Uprising, 2-issue series, Tom Veitch et al., Dark Horse Comics, 1994.

FP—
The Farlander Papers, as reprinted and continued in *X-wing: The Official Strategy Guide,* Rusel DeMaria, Prima Publishing, 1993.

FT—
Fantastic Technology, Rick D. Stuart, WEG, 1995.

GA—
Graveyard of Alderaan, Bill Slavicsek, WEG, 1991.

GDV—
The Glove of Darth Vader, Paul and Hollace Davids, Bantam Skylark Books, 1992.

GG1—
Galaxy Guide 1: A New Hope, Grant Boucher, WEG, 1989.

GG2—
Galaxy Guide 2: Yavin and Bespin, Jonathan Caspian et al., WEG, 1989.

GG3—
Galaxy Guide 3: The Empire Strikes Back, Michael Stern, WEG, 1989.

GG4—
Galaxy Guide 4: Alien Races, Troy Denning, WEG, 1989.

GG5—
Galaxy Guide 5: Return of the Jedi, Michael Stern, WEG, 1990.

GG6—
Galaxy Guide 6: Tramp Freighters, Mark Rein-Hagen and Stewart Wieck, WEG, 1990.

GG7—
Galaxy Guide 7: Mos Eisley, Martin Wixted, WEG, 1993.

GG8—
Galaxy Guide 8: Scouts, Bill Olmesdahl and Bill Smith, WEG, 1993.

GG9—
Galaxy Guide 9: Fragments from the Rim, Simon Smith and Eric Trautmann, WEG, 1993.

GG10—
Galaxy Guide 10: Bounty Hunters, Rick D. Stuart, WEG, 1993.

GG11—
Galaxy Guide 11: Criminal Organizations, Rick D. Stuart, WEG, 1993.

GG12—
Galaxy Guide 12: Aliens: Enemies and Allies, Bill Smith, editor, WEG, 1995.

GOR—
Goroth, Nigel D. Findley, WEG, 1995.

GQ—
Game Chambers of Questal, Robert Kern, WEG, 1990.

GSWU—
A Guide to the Star Wars Universe, Raymond L. Velasco, Del Rey Books, 1984; second edition, Bill Slavicsek, 1994.

HE—
Heir to the Empire, volume 1 in The Thrawn Trilogy, Timothy Zahn, Bantam Spectra Books, 1991.

HESB—
Heir to the Empire Sourcebook, Bill Slavicsek, WEG, 1992.

HLL—
Han Solo and the Lost Legacy, Brian Daley, Del Rey Books, 1980.

HSE—
Han Solo at Stars' End, Brian Daley, Del Rey Books, 1979.

HSR—
Han Solo's Revenge, Brian Daley, Del Rey Books, 1979.

IC—
The Isis Coordinates, Christopher Kubasik, WEG, 1990.

ISB—
Imperial Sourcebook, Greg Gorden, WEG, 1989.

ISWU—
The Illustrated Star Wars Universe, Kevin J. Anderson and Ralph McQuarrie, Bantam, 1995.

JAB—
Jabba the Hutt, specials, Jim Woodrig and Steve Bissete, Dark Horse Comics, 1995.

JASB—
Jedi Academy Sourcebook, Paul Sudlow, WEG, 1996.

JH—
Jedi's Honor, Troy Denning, WEG, 1990.

JJK—
The Golden Globe, Lyric's World, Promises, first three volumes of *Junior Jedi Knights,* Nancy Richardson, Berkley Books, 1995.

JS—
Jedi Search, volume 1 of *Jedi Academy,* Kevin J. Anderson, Bantam Books, 1994.

KT—
The Krytos Trap, volume 3 of the X-wing series, Michael Stackpole, Bantam Books, 1996.

LC—
The Last Command, volume 3 of the Thrawn Trilogy, Timothy Zahn, Bantam Spectra Books, 1993.

LCSB—
The Last Command Sourcebook, Eric Trautmann, WEG, 1994.

LCF—
Lando Calrissian and the Flamewind of Oseon, L. Neil Smith, Del Rey Books, 1983.

LCJ—
The Lost City of the Jedi, Paul and Hollace Davids, Bantam Skylark Books, 1992.

LCM—
Lando Calrissian and the Mindharp of Sharu, L. Neil Smith, Del Rey Books, 1983.

LCS—
Lando Calrissian and the Starcave of ThonBoka, L. Neil Smith, Del Rey Books, 1983.

ML—
Mission to Lianna, Joanne E. Wyrick, WEG, 1992.

MMY—
Mission from Mount Yoda, Paul and Hollace Davids, Bantam Skylark Books, 1993.

MTS—
Movie Trilogy Sourcebook, Greg Farshtey and Bill Smith, WEG, 1993.

NR—
The New Rebellion, Kristine Kathryn Rusch, Bantam Books, 1996.

OS—
Otherspace, Bill Slavicsek, WEG, 1989.

OS2—
Otherspace II: Invasion, Douglas Kaufman, WEG, 1989.

PC—
The Politics of Contraband, Gary Haynes et al., WEG, 1992.

PDS—
Prophets of the Dark Side, Paul and Hollace Davids, Bantam Skylark Books, 1993.

PM—
Planet of the Mist, Nigel Findley, WEG, 1992.

POG—
Planets of the Galaxy: Volume One, Grant Boucher et al., WEG, 1991; *Volume Two,* John Terra, WEG, 1992; *Volume Three,* Bill Smith, WEG, 1993.

POT—
Planet of Twilight, Barbara Hambly, Bantam, 1997.

PSG—
Platt's Starport Guide, Peter Schweighofer, WEG, 1995.

QE—
Queen of the Empire, Paul and Hollace Davids, Bantam Skylark Books, 1993.

RJ, RJN—
Return of the Jedi film, 20th Century Fox, 1983; novelization, James Kahn, Del Rey Books, 1983.

RM—
Riders of the Maelstrom, Ray Winninger, WEG, 1989.

ROC—
River of Chaos, Louise Simonson, 4 issues, Dark Horse Comics, 1995.

RS—
Rogue Squadron, volume 1 of the X-wing series, Michael Stackpole, Bantam Books, 1996.

RSB—
The Rebel Alliance Sourcebook, Paul Murphy, WEG, 1990.

SAC—
Showdown at Centerpoint, volume 3 of The Corellian Trilogy, Roger MacBride Allen, Bantam Books, 1995.

SF—
Starfall, Rob Jenkins and Michael Stern, WEG, 1989.

SFS—
Strike Force: Shantipole, Ken Rolston and Steve Gilbert, WEG, 1989.

SH—
Scavenger Hunt, Brad Freeman, WEG, 1989.

SL—
Scoundrel's Luck, Troy Denning, WEG, 1990.

SME—
Splinter of the Mind's Eye, Alan Dean Foster, Del Rey Books, 1978.

SN—
Supernova, Steven H. Lorenz et al., WEG, 1993.

SOL—
Shield of Lies, volume 2 of The Black Fleet Crisis, Michael P. Kube McDowell, Bantam Books, 1996.

SOTE—
Shadows of the Empire, Steve Perry, Bantam Books, 1996.

SOTEALB—
Shadows of the Empire CD liner notes, Varese Sarabande, 1996.

SW, SWN—
Star Wars: A New Hope film, 20th Century Fox, 1977; novelization, George Lucas, Del Rey Books, 1977.

SWAJ—
Star Wars Adventure Journal, quarterly, edited by Peter Schweighofer, WEG, 1994–1997.

SWCG—
Star Wars: The Essential Guide to Characters, Andy Mangels, Del Rey Books, 1995.

SWR—
Star Wars National Public Radio dramatizations, Brain Daley, episodes 1–13, 1981; published by Del Rey Books, 1994.

SWRPG—
Star Wars: The Roleplaying Game, Greg Costikyan, WEG, 1987.

SWRPG2—
Star Wars: The Roleplaying Game, Second Edition, Bill Smith, WEG, 1992.

SWSB—
Star Wars Sourcebook, Bill Slavicsek and Curtis Smith, WEG, 1987.

SWVG—
Star Wars: The Essential Guide to Vehicles and Vessels, Bill Smith, Del Rey Books, 1996.

SWWS—
Star Wars: The Wookiee Storybook, uncredited, Random House, 1979.

TA—
The Abduction of Crying Dawn Singer, Chuck Truett, WEG, 1992.

TAB—
The Truce at Bakura, Kathy Tyers, Bantam Books, 1994.

TBH—
Tales of the Bounty Hunters, edited by Kevin J. Anderson, Bantam Books, 1996.

TBSB—
Truce at Bakura Sourcebook, Kathy Tyers and Eric S. Trautmann, WEG, 1996.

TGH—
The Great Heep, animated television special, Nelvana, 1986.

TJP—
Tales from Jabba's Palace, edited by Kevin J. Anderson, Bantam Books, 1996.

TM—
Tatooine Manhunt, Bill Slavicsek and Daniel Greenberg, WEG, 1988.

TMEC—
Tales from the Mos Eisley Cantina, edited by Kevin J. Anderson, Bantam Books, 1995.

TOJ—
Tales of the Jedi, Tom Veitch, five issues, Dark Horse Comics, 1993–1994.

TRG—
The Red Ghost, Melinda Luke, Random House, 1986.

TSC—
The Stele Chronicles and its continuation in *TIE Fighter: The Official Strategy Guide,* Rusel DeMaria, David Wessman, and David Maxwell, Prima Publishing, 1994. Supplemented by TIE Fighter: The Collector's CD-ROM game by LucasArts, 1995.

TSK—
Twin Stars of Kira, Greg Farshtey, WEG, 1993.

TSW—
The Sith Wars, six issues, Kevin J. Anderson and Dario Carrasco, Jr., Dark Horse Comics, 1995–1996.

TT—
Tyrant's Test, volume 3 of The Black Fleet Crisis, Michael P. Kube-McDowell, Bantam Books, 1997.

TTSB—
Thrawn Trilogy Sourcebook, compilation by Bill Slavicsek and Eric S. Trautmann, WEG, 1996.

WC—
Wanted by Cracken, Louis J. Prosperi, WEG, 1993.

WG—
Wedge's Gamble, volume 1 of the X-wing series, Michael Stackpole, Bantam Books, 1996.

XW—
X-Wing Rogue Squadron, Dark Horse Comics, 1995–1997.

YJK—
Heirs to the Force, Shadow Academy, The Lost Ones, Lightsabers, Darkest Knight, Jedi Under Siege, volumes one to six of the Young Jedi Knights series, Kevin J. Anderson and Rebecca Moesta, Berkley Books, 1995–1996.

ZHR—
Zorba the Hutt's Revenge, Paul and Hollace Davids, Bantam Skylark Books, 1993.

ENCYCLOPEDIA

A-1 Deluxe Floater A luxury air speeder, it features automated steering and fine Corellian leather. It is manufactured by Mobquet Swoops and Speeders. [CCG]

A-3DO A multitalented service droid owned by Jedi Andur Sunrider, the robot was a crack mechanic and copilot who witnessed his master's death at the hands of a criminal gang headed by Great Bogga the Hutt some 4,000 years before the Battle of Yavin. Called ThreeDee for short, the droid then aided Andur's wife, Nomi, as she reluctantly trained to learn the ways of the Jedi. [TOJ]

A-1 Deluxe Floater

A-9 Vigilance Interceptor An Imperial starfighter, this short-range fighter was introduced about six years after the Battle of Endor, soon after Grand Admiral Thrawn's defeat. The A-9 Vigilance Interceptor gives up shields and hyperdrive for speed. Faster than TIE interceptors, it's about equal to the New Republic's A-wing fighters. Imperial forces use its forward-firing laser cannons for hit-and-run attacks on hardened Republic installations. However, overall performance is less than hoped for because of its limited maneuverability and relatively weak hull. [DE, SWVG]

Aalun, Syron One of a trio of famous Gand ruetsavii, or observers, who were sent to observe Rogue Squadron pilot Ooryl Qyrgg's life and determine his worthiness to become janwuine. The highest possible honor in the communal Gand society, janwuine involves the right of an individual to speak of himself in the first person and to use personal pronouns in conversation. The ruetsavii not only observed Qyrgg's activities but also participated fully in the squadron as fighter pilots and undercover operatives. [BW]

Aba The name young Jacen Solo gave to his Wookiee doll. [CS]

A'baht, General Etahn Assigned as commander of the New Republic's Fifth Fleet because of experience leading his native Dornean Navy against Imperial forces, A'baht had a leathery face that flushed purple and eye folds that swelled and fanned out. His flagship was the fleet carrier *Intrepid*, and he declared the fleet operational following the live-fire exercise Hammerblow. Defying specific orders from Princess Leia Organa to stay out of the unexplored Koornacht Cluster, he sent the survey ship *Astrolabe* to Doornik-1142, hoping to get good military intelligence. Yevethan forces, which had been roiling the sector and undertaking xenophobic extermination campaigns, destroyed the *Astrolabe*. Ambassador Nil Spaar, viceroy of the Duskhan League, declared the incident an act of aggression by the New Republic and prepared to go to war. General A'baht then led the deployment of the Fifth Fleet to the cluster and blockaded Doornik-319, where the Yevetha were mounting their forces. When the fleet came under withering attack, General A'baht was forced to withdraw. Princess Leia Organa Solo then relieved him of command and substituted her husband, Han Solo. [BTS]

Abano A poor farmer on Aruza, he was the father of Manaroo, a tat-

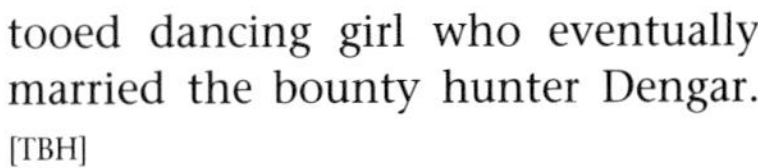

tooed dancing girl who eventually married the bounty hunter Dengar. [TBH]

Abbaji The planet where the famous 100-meter-tall firethorn trees grow in a single grove of the Irugian Rain Forest. Prince Xizor, head of the Black Sun criminal organization, was given a 600-year-old dwarf firethorn tree as a peace offering by a business rival. The tree, less than half a meter high, had been in the man's family for ten generations and was considered by Xizor to be one of his most prized possessions. [SOTE]

A-3DO

abo Old Imperial slang for native inhabitants of a planet, often used in a derogatory manner. [SME]

Abrax An aquamarine cognac with spicy vapors. The best vintages were produced during the Old Republic. [BW]

Abregado-rae A manufacturing and trade-oriented planet in the Abregado system, with a formerly primitive spaceport. Since the birth of the New Republic, the spaceport has cleaned up its act—at least to the untrained eye. Beneath the spit-shine and polish lies the heart of a smuggler, a spaceport where the galaxy's uncounted species mingle briefly, have wild and sometimes fatal flings, then head off again for parts unknown. An oppressive government allied to the New Republic rules the planet's population of 40 million. Some nine

A-9 Vigilance Interceptor

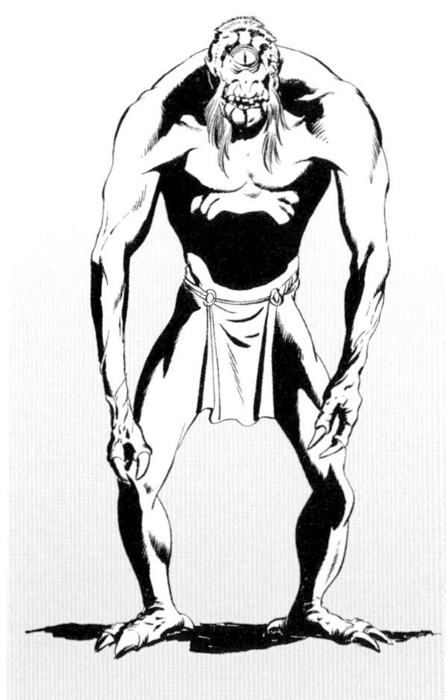
Abyssin

standard years after the Battle of Yavin, the leadership cut off all supplies to a clan of rebellious hill people, which created opportunities for ambitious smugglers. [HE, HESB, DFR]

Abregado system A planetary system located in the Borderland Regions—a militarized zone that separates the New Republic from the remnants of the Empire—it is controlled by neither but influenced by both. A vast and complex manufacturing infrastructure links the system's planets, and the goods produced there are vitally important to the well-being of the New Republic. [HE, HESB]

Abrion sector The location of the planet Ukio, one of the top five producers of foodstuffs in the New Republic. Grand Admiral Thrawn's capture of Ukio had serious repercussions in the sector. [LC]

Abyssin This primitive and violent species inhabits the occasionally fertile planet Byss in the binary star system of Byss and Abyss. (Byss has the same name as a distant planet that was used as a retreat by Emperor Palpatine). At about two meters tall, the hulking, humanoid Abyssin have long limbs and a single large eye dominating greenish-tan foreheads. Because they heal quickly and can regenerate any body part, this nomadic race condones a high degree of physical violence, since the consequences are short lasting. Off-world, they are often hired as petty thugs. [GG4]

Academy, the Under the Old Republic, this elite educational and training institution turned unseasoned youths into highly trained members of the Exploration, Military, and Merchant Services. Under Emperor Palpatine, the Academy slowly became a training ground for Imperial officers, especially Raithal Academy in the Core region. (The Academy's numerous campuses are spread across the galaxy.) Under the New Republic, the Academy is rebuilding to regain past glory. [SW, SWR, ISB]

acceleration compensator A device that generates a type of artificial gravity and helps neutralize the effects of accelerating to high speed aboard medium- and larger-sized spacecraft such as the *Millennium Falcon*. [HSE]

acceleration straps These passenger-safety harnesses are usually built into the seats of spacecraft to restrain passengers during takeoffs, landings, and violent maneuvers. [SW]

Access Chute The kilometers-long pathway snakes through a grid of decaying cities and tall docking towers on the spaceport moon Nar Shaddaa. Its entrance is masked by a bright advertising holoscreen, and the Chute leads to the repair facility of an old buddy of Han Solo, Shug Ninx. [DE]

Accuser *See Emancipator*

Ackbar, Admiral Born on the watery world of Mon Calamari, Ackbar has risen from humble beginnings to become a renowned military strategist. His championing of the Rebel Alliance—after conquering his own inbred caution—played a major role in the Rebels' defeat of Imperial forces during the Galactic Civil War. He prefers to personally lead major assaults, and his troops still affectionately call him Admiral even though he is now of higher rank.

Ackbar, who like other Mon Calamari has salmon-colored skin, large, bulbous yellow-orange eyes, and webbed hands and feet, was the leader of Coral Depths City when Imperial forces invaded and nearly destroyed his planet. Ackbar, one of the first to be enslaved, eventually became an interpreter for Grand Moff Tarkin. It was from Tarkin that Ackbar first heard rumblings of the Rebellion—as well as veiled references to a new super weapon that would crush the Rebels. Ackbar was rescued during a Rebel attempt to assassinate Tarkin and helped convince his species to actively support the Rebellion. Among the hardware that the Mon Calamari contributed to the Rebel cause were strikingly beautiful, organic-looking star cruisers.

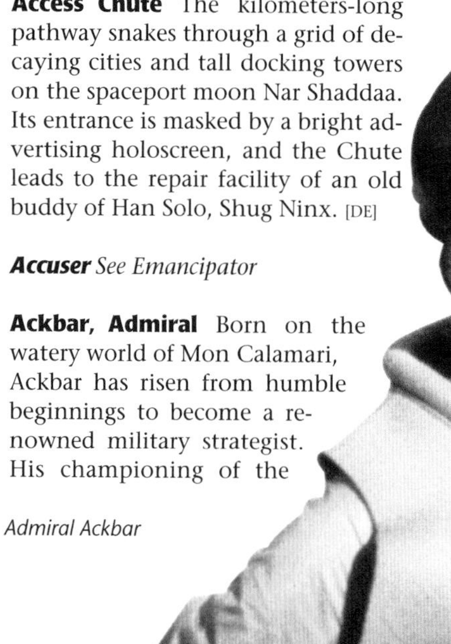
Admiral Ackbar

Made a commander, Ackbar helped develop the powerful two-pilot B-wing starfighter. After delivering several prototypes to the Rebels, he was promoted to Admiral by Alliance leader Mon Mothma. At the Battle of Endor, Ackbar at first called for a tactical withdrawal. After becoming convinced that the Rebels could succeed, he committed all of his forces in one of the bloodiest battles of the Rebellion. In the end, the Rebels destroyed the second Death Star.

Even after the establishment of the New Republic, remnants of the Empire and bold criminal gangs mounted major military challenges. The New Republic later faced an attack led by Grand Admiral Thrawn. In the midst of the onslaught, Ackbar faced a personal crisis. On the home front, Ackbar had been named a member of the Provisional Council and the ruling Inner Council of the New Republic, where he frequently clashed with Borsk Fey'lya, a Bothan leader. Based on what turned out to be false "evidence" planted by Thrawn in Ackbar's financial accounts, the commander was arrested on charges that he had embezzled New Republic funds. He was cleared in time to lead the New Republic fleet to victory over Thrawn's forces in the battle at the Bilbringi Shipyards.

Within days of Thrawn's defeat, survivors of the Emperor's ruling circle and six fleet commanders attacked and recaptured Coruscant, sending the New Republic fleeing to the fifth moon of Da Soocha. There, Ackbar and the others planned how to battle the clone of the Emperor Palpatine. After a few months on the space city of Nespis VIII, New Republic forces regained Coruscant.

Later, on a diplomatic mission to the windy planet Vortex with Princess Leia, Ackbar crashed his personal B-wing fighter into the planet's greatest artistic treasure, the towering crystalline Cathedral of Winds, killing 358 Vors. Later it was discovered that the commander's trusted chief mechanic had been turned into an Imperial operative and had sabotaged the ship. Before being cleared, Ackbar had to fend off an attack on Mon Calamari by the ruthless Admiral Daala.

Ackbar returned to Coruscant and reassumed his role in the New Republic. He asked Leia's aide, Winter, to join him on a trip to Vortex for a ceremony marking the rebuilding of the Cathedral of the Winds, and the two developed a close relationship. [SWCG, RJ, SWSB, SFS, HE, DFR, LC, DS, DA]

Adamant A New Republic bulk space cruiser, the *Adamant* was commanded by Admiral Ackbar. About twenty-three years after the Battle of Yavin, as it was shuttling a precious cargo of hyperdrive cores and turbolaser battery emplacements to the Kuat Drive Yards, the cruiser was attacked by a rump Imperial fleet within Coruscant's protected zone. The attack was led by one-time TIE fighter pilot Qorl, who had crashed in the jungles of Yavin 4 but survived until he was discovered by Jaina and Jacen Solo two decades later. He worked for the turncoat Jedi Brakiss. His modified assault shuttle was fitted with industrial-grade Corusca gems that enabled it to chew through the *Adamant*'s hull. After Qorl's crew boarded the ship, they jettisoned the New Republic crew in escape pods and made off with the cruiser and its cargo. [YJK]

Adamantine This New Republic escort cruiser visited the planet Nam Chorios. All of its personnel were killed and the ship lost after the Death Seed plague was unloosed. [POT]

Adega A star system located in the Outer Rim Territories, in ancient times it was the site of a major Jedi stronghold. It was also the source for powerful crystals used in making lightsabers. The planet Ossus orbits its two suns in a figure-eight trajectory. [DE]

Adegan crystals Ancient lightsabers most often used these precious crystals to throw off potent bursts of energy and light. Their force was unlocked when waves of the proper frequency were transmitted through them. They are also called Ilum crystals. [DE]

Adin A former Imperial stronghold, Adin is homeworld to Senator Meido, a former Imperial official who was elected to the New Republic senate thirteen years after the Battle of Endor. [NR]

Adjudicator This Imperial Star Destroyer was captured by the Rebel Alliance during the Battle of Endor. Repaired, refitted, and renamed the *Liberator*, it was shot down by resurgent Imperial forces over Imperial City on Coruscant on one of its first missions under the command of Luke Skywalker. As the mortally wounded ship plunged toward a crash landing, only a heroic effort by Skywalker saved the lives of the *Liberator*'s crew. [DE, DESB]

Adriana The third planet in the Tatoo system, the gas giant has rings of ice that are often mined and taken to the desert planet Tatooine for water. [GG7, CCG]

Af'El A large high-gravity world that is seldom visited, Af'El orbits the ultraviolet supergiant Ka'Dedus. Af'El's lack of an ozone layer allows ultraviolet light to pass freely to the surface, while other wavelengths are blocked by heavy atmospheric gases. Thus, all life-forms on Af'El can see only in ultraviolet light ranges. It is homeworld of the Defel, or "wraiths," whose bodies absorb visible light, giving them the appearance of shadows. The Defel live in underground cities to escape Af'El's violent storms. The planet's main export is the metal meleenium, which is used in durasteel and is known to exist only on Af'El. [GG4]

affect mind Using the Force, a Jedi Knight can employ this technique to change the perceptions of another person or creature. Affect mind can create illusions or stop the understanding of what's really happening by blocking the senses. It can also obliterate memories altogether or replace them with false ones. [SWRPG, SWRPG2, DFRSB]

Afit, Zeen A craggy-faced smuggler, Afit originally introduced Han Solo and Chewbacca to Smuggler's Run, an asteroid belt infamous as a smugglers' hideout. Afit was one of the smugglers Han encountered on the asteroid Skip One during his investigation into a bombing that rocked Senate Hall on Coruscant. [NR]

Afyon, Captain A native of Alderaan, Afyon heeded Princess Leia's call to join the Rebellion after the Empire

Cal Alder

destroyed his family, friends, and entire planet. A veteran of the Clone Wars, Captain Afyon served as first officer aboard a Corellian gunship and eventually earned his own command. At the age of fifty-two, some four years after the end of the Galactic Civil War, he was made captain of the escort frigate *Larkhess*, a warship that had been relegated to trade duty. The *Larkhess* transported cargo and hotshot braggart fighter pilots who never gave the "old man" captain his due. But during the Battle of Sluis Van, Afyon proved himself to be an excellent commander. When the *Larkhess* was boarded by stormtroopers, Afyon prepared to destroy his ship rather than surrender it. But the actions of a bunch of Rebel pilots, along with Luke Skywalker and Han Solo, made that ultimate sacrifice unnecessary. [HE, HESB]

Agamar Located in the Lahara sector of the Outer Rim, Agamar's towns include the large city of Calna Muun and the backwater of Tondatha, which was wiped out by the Empire for harboring Rebel collaborators. Binka trees are indigenous. A traditional Agamarian dish is mugruebe stew, made from bark, roots, and meat. The famous Rebel Alliance pilot Keyan Farlander was a native. [FP]

agee Tiny creatures, they exist in both flightless and winged varieties, the latter being particularly delicate. [NR]

Aggregator An Imperial Interdictor cruiser, it was owned by High Admiral Teradoc and leased by Ysanne Isard in her quest to crush Rogue Squadron. The ship was sent to the Graveyard of Alderaan to use its gravity-well projectors to prevent the X-wings from taking flight. Isard's scheme was working as planned until the unexpected appearance of the *Valiant*, a long-absent, droid-controlled Alderaan *Thranta*-class War Cruiser. The *Valiant* collapsed the *Aggregator*'s shields, and without awaiting further hull damage, the Imperial ship jumped to hyperspace, leaving behind its TIE fighters and escape pods. Admiral Teradoc was furious with Isard for nearly destroying his ship. [BW]

Agrilat An area on the planet Corellia, it is known for its crystal swamps, which contain hot springs with updrafts, geysers that spout boiling water, and sheer blades of crystalline underbrush. The bounty hunter Dengar was critically injured at Agrilat in a swoop bike race with Han Solo. After the race, Dengar was treated by Imperial physicians, then trained as an assassin. [MTS, TBH]

agrirobot A simple, inexpensive droid, it is programmed to perform one function in the cycle of producing food. Among the available models are agrirobots that plant, spray, harvest, and package such edibles as fruit, vegetables, and grain. [HSE]

Aguarl 3 The ocean-covered world of Aguarl 3 was home to a submerged Rebel base. The base was attacked by a wing of TIE bombers after the Empire learned its location from a Quarren spy. [ROC]

Ahazi A New Republic fleet tender, it was destroyed during the newly commissioned Fifth Fleet's live-fire training exercise code-named Hammerblow, killing all six aboard. [BTS]

Aida A lightly populated world formerly under Imperial control, Aida is located in the system of the same name near the Lomabu system. In an effort to trap Alliance agents, Io Desnand, Imperial governor of the system, shipped several hundred Wookiee females and cubs to the nearby planet of Lomabu III and planned to kill them during an attack that was designed to attract Rebel rescuers. The prisoners were eventually rescued by the bounty hunters Chenlambec and Tinian I'att. [TBH]

Aikhibba Located in the system of the same name, Aikhibba is home to crime lord Spadda the Hutt. The system is one of the minor stopping points on the smugglers' Gamor Run. Smuggler Lo Khan once delivered a cargo of spice to Spadda from the royal governor of the Thokosia system. [DESB]

airspeeder This small, wedge-shaped vehicle is designed to operate inside a planet's protective atmosphere. Mainly repulsorlift-powered, some airspeeders can soar more than 250 kilometers high at a speed of more than 900 kilometers an hour. Models such as the T-16 skyhopper are often bought as sport vehicles or for family transportation, but young people frequently turn them into souped-up "hot rods." The Rebel Alliance also modified them into specialized military vehicles such as snowspeeders and sandspeeders. [HLL, SWSB]

Akanah *See* Pell, Akanah Norand

Ak-Buz A Weequay, he was commander of Jabba the Hutt's sail barge. Ak-Buz was murdered by the Anzati Dannik Jerriko, who hid his body in a garbage heap. [TJP]

Akrit'tar The planet Akrit'tar houses a penal colony. One of Han Solo's former smuggling associates, Tregga, was imprisoned there and sentenced to life at hard labor after being caught with a smuggled cargo of chak-root. Rogue Squadron pilot Tycho Celchu was brainwashed and imprisoned by the Empire on the long-buried underground *Lusankya* Super Star Destroyer, then shipped to Akrit'tar. He escaped after three months. [HSR, WG]

Alder, Cal A top-notch scout for the Rebel Alliance, he is from Kal'Shebbol in the Kathol sector. Cal Alder served with Major Bren Derlin for many years and patrolled the outer perimeter of Echo Base on Hoth prior to the fierce battle with Imperial forces there. [CCG]

Alderaan A peaceful world, the planet was close to being the galaxy's paradise, and certainly was its heart.

Renowned poet Hari Seldona wrote of its "calm, vast skies...oceans of grass...lovely flying thrantas" in an elegy to her planet after Alderaan was destroyed in a demonstration of the power of the Empire.

It was a place of high culture and education, thanks to Alderaan University. The natives loved the land and worked with it or around it, rather than change or destroy it. Its vast plains supported more than 8,000 subspecies of grass and even more numerous wildflowers. Artists planted huge grass paintings up to dozens of kilometers square that could be seen only from flying observation boats.

Alderaan was famous for its cuisine, based on the delicious meat of grazers and nerfs along with native exotic herbs, flowers, and grain. The calm breezes carried large thrantas, which looked like flying manta rays and bore passengers safely strapped on top. Although there were no oceans, the planet had an ice-rimmed polar sea and thousands of lakes and gentle waterways plied by vacation barges. Among Alderaan's most imposing sights were the Castle Lands, towering abandoned cities made by a long-extinct species, the Killiks.

Ruled by the democratic Viceroy and First Chairman Bail Organa, the planet's population took to heart the horrors of the Clone Wars, which killed millions and devastated countless planets. After the wars ended, the people of Alderaan wholeheartedly adopted pacifism and banned all weapons from the planet's surface. All remaining super weapons were placed aboard a huge armory ship, *Another Chance*, which was programmed to jump through hyperspace continually unless called home by the Council of Elders.

As the New Order of Senator (soon Emperor) Palpatine took root, Alderaan supported the growing opposition to his rule. In fact, New Republic leader Mon Mothma gave Bail Organa credit for envisioning the overall structure of the Rebel Alliance. A tip from Organa let Mothma escape Palpatine's clutches with just minutes to spare. Giving up his own seat in the Senate and returning to Alderaan, Organa worked hard to convince his people to renounce their pacifism. His adopted daughter, Princess Leia Organa, also a senator, began to run secret missions for the Rebellion. But before Alderaan could fully prepare its defenses and officially join the Alliance, the Empire wiped out the planet in a flash with a single blast from its new super weapon, the Death Star, as a captive Leia looked on in horror. All that was left of the beauty and humanity that was Alderaan was an asteroid field, now fittingly called the Graveyard. [SW, SWSB, ISWU]

Alderaan Princess Leia Organa Solo named her personal starship after the destroyed planet where she grew up. [CS]

Aleema

Alderaan furry moth Now vanished from the galaxy along with the planet that nurtured it, the large-winged flying insect nested amid bushy flowers. The larvae of the Alderaan furry moth were armored caterpillars more than a meter long that burrowed under the ground and fed on swollen tubers. The caterpillars lived for a dozen years before sealing themselves in thick-walled cocoons and emerging transformed. [ISWU]

Aleema A direct descendant of the Empress Teta, Aleema was heir, with her cousin, Satal Keto, to the throne of the Empress Teta System some 4,000 years before the Battle of Yavin. She was too rich, too spoiled, and too bored with life. First for amusement, then in a lust for power, Aleema turned to the dark-side illusions of the ancient Sith magicians.

Alderaan

She helped murder her aunt, uncle, and others, and staged a coup to take over the system as coleader of the Krath dark-side cult. The spirit of the dark-side Jedi Freedon Nadd bestowed upon Aleema certain dark-side powers, including the ability to cast realistic illusions. Jedi Knight Ulic Qel-Droma traveled to the system in order to learn the Krath's dark-side secrets, but he succumbed to the dark side himself and helped Aleema defeat her enemies. Later, Aleema attempted to reassert her power over Krath forces by abandoning Qel-Droma during an attack on Coruscant, but he was rescued and eventually had Aleema killed. [TSW, DLS]

Algar A planet best known for a mood-enhancing drug, Algarine torve weed, Algar is also the base of operations for Wing Tip Theel, an expert computer slicer and former associate of Han Solo and Lando Calrissian. [POT]

Alien Combine Also known as the Alien League, this secret organization of nonhumanoid species was formed to protest unfair treatment and misconduct by Imperial forces on Coruscant after the Battle of Endor. The aliens were frightened because so many of their number were disappearing. They did not realize that forces of Imperial General Evir Derricote were rounding up aliens for experimental use on the Krytos project—a plan by the Director of Imperial Intelligence to infect the alien populace. She hoped to then bankrupt the Rebellion when it tried to buy enough bacta to cure them all. The Combine, reacting out of fear, suspected that Gavin Darklighter and his fellow Rogue Squadron members were out to harm them and brought the squadron members before the League for trial. Imperial forces attacked the hideout, and a bloody battle ensued. The Combine then realized that the Rogues were on their side, helped them to escape, and later joined the Rebel cause to liberate Coruscant. [BW]

Alien League *See* Alien Combine

Alima, Captain An Imperial officer from the planet Coruscant, he commanded the Star Destroyer *Conquest* in an attack against a herdship on the planet Ithor. A vicious man, he was an outcast among his own troopers and had been demoted to the rank of lieutenant. Alima had forced Ithorian High Priest Momaw Nadon to reveal secrets of his planet's technology to the Empire, and Nadon—who had no choice if he wanted to save the lives of his people—had been forced into exile. Years later, Nadon had his revenge by giving false testimony that resulted in one of Alima's superiors killing the lieutenant after making him the scapegoat for the escape of R2-D2 and C-3PO off of Tatooine. [TMEC]

Alkhara Centuries ago, this fierce bandit was the first usurper to occupy Tatooine's B'omarr monastery, in more recent times the palace of Jabba the Hutt. Alkhara once allied himself with the Tusken Raiders to wipe out a small police garrison, but then butchered the Sand People who had helped him, thereby kicking off the long-lasting blood feud between the Tusken Raiders and humans. Alkhara stayed for thirty-four years, expanding the monastery and adding dungeons and underground chambers. [ISWU]

Alk'Lellish III Homeworld of the ketrann, a dangerous carnivore. Governor Wilek Nereus of Bakura owned a set of the ketrann's four white fangs. [TAB]

Allegiance A Super Star Destroyer, it was the Imperial command ship at the Battle of Calamari. The *Allegiance*

All Terrain Armored Transport (AT-AT)

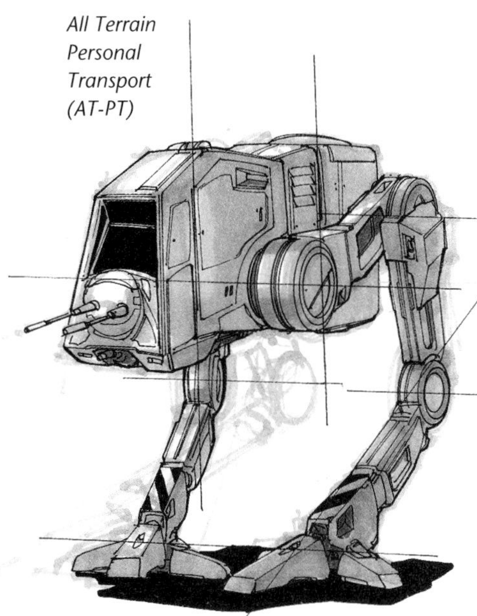

All Terrain Personal Transport (AT-PT)

was destroyed in an audacious maneuver by the *Emancipator,* a captured Star Destroyer commanded by Lando Calrissian. [DE]

Alliance High Command A top Rebel body that set important military policy in the early days of the New Republic, the Command consisted of General Jan Dodonna, General Carlist Rieekan, General Crix Madine, Admiral Ackbar, and Senator Garm Bel Iblis. The Alliance High Command emphasized flexibility, initiative, and speed of response. [JS, RSB]

Alliance masternav This computer system was developed to track the orbits of planets within known systems. Its reliability depends on the quality of its most recent software and updated data. [TAB]

All Terrain Armored Transport (AT-AT) A combat and transport vehicle—an Empire juggernaut—the immense four-legged "walker" is as much a psychological weapon of terror as an actual weapon of destruction. More than fifteen meters tall and twenty meters long, this nearly unstoppable behemoth looks like a giant legendary beast from the dark side. Despite its lumbering gait, it can stride across a flat battlefield at up to sixty kilometers an hour and lob heavy laser fire from the cannons mounted beneath its "chin" while providing supporting fire from two medium blasters on each side of its head. It can kneel to within three meters of the ground and offload forty heavily armed troopers and five speeder bikes—or other weapons—from rear assault ramps. The AT-AT is the Empire's ideal battlefield vehicle.

These heavy assault vehicles have both the heft and mechanics to march through most defenses. Their thick armor plating shields them from all but the heaviest of artillery fire. Their heads can rotate up to ninety degrees left and right and thirty degrees up and down, providing the commanding officer, pilot, and gunner with a sweeping view of any battlefield from the command deck. AT-ATs are usually among the first vehicles to enter a combat zone. Their heavy, stomping feet can cause the ground to shake even before they appear, frightening and demoralizing the enemy.

Based on ancient technology and at first derided by many Imperial officers, the AT-ATs have proved themselves on the battlefield. They were chiefly responsible for the rout of the Rebels during the Empire's assault on Hoth base. [ESB, SWSB, SWVG]

All Terrain Personal Transport (AT-PT) This small weapons system was the precursor of the modern Imperial walker. Developed by the Old Republic as a personal weapons platform for ground soldiers, it was ingeniously designed for its day and was intended to be a major component of Republic ground forces. However, nearly all the experimental AT-PTs were aboard the *Katana* Dreadnaughts when that fleet disappeared. The AT-PT project was canceled, although Imperial engineers copied many of its design features years later.

The two-legged walker was nearly three meters tall with a cramped central command pod housing one soldier, or two in an emergency. Its heavy armor made the pod nearly invulnerable to small-arms fire. Independent leg suspension let the walker climb up to forty-five-degree inclines and made it suitable for jungle and mountain terrain as well as urban areas. On open ground, it could move as quickly as sixty kilometers an hour. Its weapons typically included a twin-blaster cannon and a concussion grenade launcher.

Ironically, years after the project was abandoned, AT-PTs got their first real test under battle conditions. After the walkers were rediscovered along with the lost *Katana* fleet, Luke Skywalker and Han Solo used an old AT-PT to fight Grand Admiral Thrawn's clone stormtroopers. [DFR, DFRSB, SWVG]

All Terrain Scout Transport (AT-ST) These relatively lightweight and speedy vehicles are used by Imperial forces for reconnaissance and ground support for both troops and the larger AT-AT walkers. Although smaller than AT-ATs at about 8.6 meters tall, AT-STs are much speedier: On flat terrain they can move along at a ninety-kilometer-an-hour clip.

The two-legged "chicken" walker has a small but highly maneuverable armored command pod that houses a pilot and a gunner. Each leg has a sharp claw that can slice through natural or artificial obstacles. With just two legs and a gyro balance system that is highly susceptible to damage, the AT-ST is more prone to tipping over than the AT-AT, but its flexibility and fire power make it a strong addition to the battlefield.

Scout walkers are often used to lay down a blanket of covering fire for Imperial ground troops and to defend the flanks and somewhat vulnerable underbelly of AT-ATs. Its two-man crew enters and exits through a hatch atop the armor-plated command cabin. [ESB, RJ, SWVG]

All Terrain Scout Transport (AT-ST)

alluvial damper A unit that regulates the amount of thrust produced by a starship's hyperdrive, it moves a servomotor-controlled plate to block, bit by bit, the emission of ion particles. [ESB]

Allyuen Darth Vader ordered the planet Allyuen searched with recalibrated Imperial probe droids to scout for the new Rebel base. The planets Tokmia and Hoth were also probed. [ESBR]

Almania system A planetary system on the far reaches of the galaxy, it might have become part of the Old Republic but for its great distance from the center of the Republic's activities. The capital of the planet Almania—a large white and blue world surrounded by clouds—is Stonia. Almania has three smaller moons, the most famous of which is Pydyr, both for its exclusiveness and for its wealth. Almania considered itself loosely aligned with the Rebellion during the Galactic Civil War and later with the New Republic.

However, shortly after the New Republic defeated Grand Admiral Thrawn, the Je'har leadership on Almania changed. Some reports told of hideous brutality under the new regime, and communications from Almania to the New Republic stopped and the planet was forgotten. In fact, the Je'har had grown jealous of Pydyr's wealth and began ransacking the moon. During one raid, the parents of Dolph, a young Jedi trainee of Luke Skywalker, were killed in a particularly brutal fashion. Dolph returned home, let his anger turn him to the dark side, and undertook a holocaust even more terrible than the one he wanted to avenge. He adopted the name and death's-head mask of a long-ago despot named Kueller.

On a mission to investigate, Luke Skywalker crashed and was imprisoned by Kueller, who threatened to kill him and Princess Leia Organa Solo. The New Republic launched an offensive, the Battle of Almania, and Leia eventually killed a weakened Kueller with a blaster shot while he was battling Luke. [NR]

Alole A loyal aide to Princess Leia Organa Solo. [SOL, BIS]

Alpha Blue A mysterious, covert intelligence group within the New Republic's military and security hierarchy, it was headed by Admiral Drayson. [BTS, SOL]

Alpheridies Home planet of the Miraluka, who are born without eyes but see everything through the Force. [FNU]

Alsakan Now a heavily populated planet in the Galactic Core, Alsakan was settled millennia ago, before the foundation of the Old Republic, by colonists on the *Kuat Explorer*. The colossal battle cruisers of the ancient Alsakan Conflicts, first built about 3,000 years before the Galactic Civil War, inspired the *Invincible*-class Dreadnaughts. Alsakan was one of many planets that surrendered to Admiral Ackbar and the Alliance fleet in the years following the Battle of Endor. Imperial commander Titus Klev was born on Alsakan; his father was a Clone Wars veteran and his mother a member of a wealthy merchant family. Corporate Sector viceprex Mirkovig Hirken was also born on Alsakan, into one of the oldest families on the planet. [DESB, CSSB]

Altha protein drink A warm drink favored by Lando Calrissian. [NR]

Altis, Djinn This Jedi Master instructed his students, including Geith and Callista, from a Jedi training platform hidden in the clouds of the gas giant Bespin. [DS]

Altorian Two intelligent species inhabit hot, dry Altor 14. These Altorians hate each other, yet so far have failed to eliminate or subjugate each other. The primitive and lawless Avogwi, known off-world as the Altorian Birds, are a proud and savage species who place a low value on life. The Nuiwit, called the Altorian Lizards, have a highly structured and harmonious society and a desire to please visitors—except the Avogwi, for whom they are food. [GG4]

Alzoc III Home of the Talz species and source of the Alzoc pearl, the planet is in the Alzoc system in the Outer Rim. The moonless planet is covered with desolate, frozen plains, and its powerful sun glares harshly off the reflective snow. The Empire secretly placed a garrison on Alzoc III and forced the Talz to work as slaves in underground mines. The planet was never entered into the galactic registry, and the New Republic only learned of its existence after examining restricted corporate files. Imperial Commander Pter Thanas was assigned to the rim world of Bakura after refusing to destroy a village of Talz miners on Alzoc III. The Imperial battlemoon *Eye of Palpatine* stopped at the frozen planet to pick up a contingent of stormtroopers, but brought aboard a group of Talz instead. [TAB, GG4, COJ]

Amanaman A widely used nickname for a species of yellow-and-green-colored, long-armed beings with big hands. They are commonly called Head Hunters. They carry with them at all times a staff on which is strung

Altorian Lizard (Nuiwit)

Amanaman (Amanin)

a number of skulls, presumably obtained firsthand. The proper name for the species is Amanin. [RJ, GG12]

Amanin *See* Amanaman

Amanoa Queen of Onderon more than 4,000 years before the Galactic Civil War, she was also known as the Dark Queen because she dabbled in the remnants of Sith magic introduced four centuries earlier by the Dark Jedi Freedon Nadd. She was able to call upon dark-side forces to battle the Beast-Lords of Onderon. Her daughter, Galia, succeeded to the throne after Queen Amanoa's death. Amanoa was buried in a stone sarcophagus and eventually entombed on Onderon's closest moon, Dxun, near the body of Nadd. [TOJ, FNU]

ambori This liquid chemical fills a bacta tank and contains, in suspension, the bacteria particles essential to the tank's healing powers. [SWAJ]

Ambria A desolate and rugged ringed planet with several moons in the Stenness system, it was the location of Jedi Master Thon's training compound. The entire planet was once a repository for great dark-side forces, but they were driven into Lake Natth by Thon. [TOJ]

Ambrian wastes A large desert area on Ambria where Jedi Master Thon's house and training compound were located. [TOJ]

Amfar Amfar is a popular recreational world, and its beaches are always crowded. [SOL]

ammonia bombs Explosives that dispense ammonia in levels lethal to oxygen breathers, they are typically used by the ammonia-breathing Gands. [TBH]

Ammuud A planet with a rigid code of honor, Ammuud is known throughout the systems as being controlled by the Corporate Sector Authority. The code is enforced by the governing feudallike coalition of seven clans, which operate under a contract from the Authority. [HSR]

Ammuud clans Extended families such as House Reesbon and House Glayyd, the clans govern the planet Ammuud. Under Corporate Sector Authority orders, each clan must provide forces for port security. [HSR]

amphibion A moderately-armored hovercraft that can deliver twenty troops and all their gear into the heart of combat, the amphibion is quick and relatively safe. While primarily a water assault vehicle, an amphibion also can be used over flat terrain. It can travel up to 100 kilometers an hour. They have gained in popularity since their successful deployment during the Battle of Calamari.

The vehicle itself is lightly armored along its 7.3 meter length. Only the front pilot's cabin is fully enclosed. A gunner sits in the rear at the bottom of a rotating gun turret. The craft operates quietly, making it useful for stealthy commando raids. Many smaller hover engines are mounted along the bottom and sides. Slightly larger engines in the rear provide forward propulsion. [DE, DESB, SWVG]

Amanoa

Ampliquen A planet in the Meridian sector, it was the site of much activity nine years after the Battle of Endor when the New Republic cruisers *Caelus* and *Corbantis* were sent from the Orbital Station at Durren to investigate what was either a pirate attack on Ampliquen or a possible truce violation by the planet Budpock. At the same time, a revolt that was secretly supported by the Loronar Corporation broke out on Ampliquen. [POT]

Analysis Bureau The eggheads of Imperial Intelligence, Analysis Bureau members gathered data from tens of millions of sources to look for enemy activity. The bureau also searched for patterns or trends in social data that might be helpful to Imperial agents. Its branches included Media, which pored over every comlink transmission and holocast in the known galaxy; Signal, which examined the channels through which information was delivered; Cryptanalysis, which prided itself on

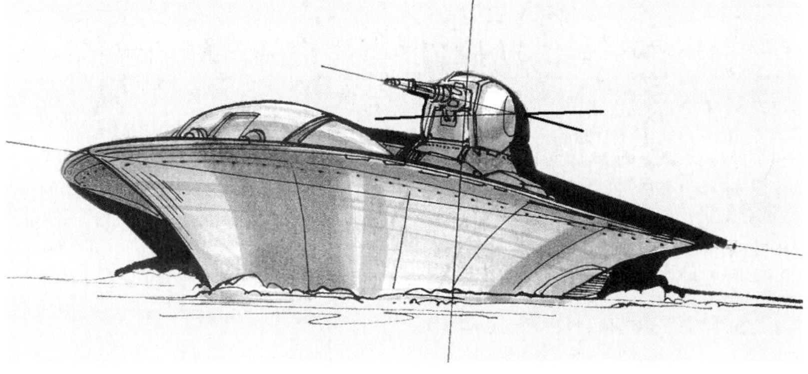
Amphibion

breaking even the most challenging codes; Tech, which broke down enemy hardware to determine how it worked, then provided superior devices to Imperial Intelligence; and Interrogation, which specialized in reprogramming captured Rebels and freeing them to become double-agents. [ISB]

Anchorhead A small community that is a central trading spot for moisture farmers, Anchorhead is on the desert flats at the edge of the Dune Sea on the desolate planet of Tatooine. The sleepy town sprang up eons ago around a deep well, frequented by pilgrims, that has long since dried up. Luke Skywalker, hero of the Rebellion, grew up on the moisture farm of Owen and Beru Lars on the outskirts of Anchorhead. As a youth, he spent much of his free time hanging out with friends in town, especially at Tosche Station, a power and water distribution complex. [SW, ISWU]

Anchoron Corellian hero Garm Bel Iblis was believed to have been killed on this planet. He actually survived but was forced to go underground, severing all ties with his former life and working in secret to bring down the Empire. The smuggler Talon Karrde posted men on Anchoron in an unsuccessful search for Grand Admiral Thrawn's traffic in clones, and Leia Organa Solo planted a false report stating that a Star Destroyer had been spotted near Anchoron in her attempts to locate an Imperial spy. [DFR, TLC]

Ando A watery planet with few solid land masses, Ando is home to the belligerent, walrus-faced Aqualish. The higher-class Aquala ("webbed" Aqualish) prefer to live on floating raft cities and large sailing ships, while the low-status Quara ("fingered" Aqualish) inhabit the larger islands of Ando. A sister planet in the same system has a blasted, uninhabitable surface, the apparent aftermath of an Aqualish war soon after the species discovered space travel. Ando mainly exports foodstuffs from its seas. The Jedi Master Jorus C'baoth was a member of the Ando Demilitarization Observation Group. Following his departure from Tatooine, the infamous criminal Dr. Evazan was sheltered on Ando in a well-guarded castle on a rocky isle. Ando was also targeted by Grand Admiral Thrawn as part of a multipronged attack intended to draw New Republic forces away from Ukio. [DFR, LC, GG4, TMEC]

Andona, Mari'ha An old friend of Han Solo, she ran flight control for a sector of the planet Coruscant. She could be counted on to bend the rules for Solo and would authorize his sometimes unorthodox flight plans. [TBH]

Andur A Coruscant bureaucrat, he was vice-chair of the orbital debris committee. [JS]

angler A spiderlike crustacean native to Yavin 4, the angler builds its home in the dangling aerial roots of majestic Massassi trees, which dip their tips in the slow-running rivers of the moon. Anglers have small bodies but long and sharp knobbed legs with a skeletal appearance. Camouflaged and motionless in the tree roots, an angler waits for a fish to drift near, then stabs down quickly and sharply, using its legs like a spear, and hungrily devours its meal. [ISWU]

animated metal sealant This special paste is essential for every spacer's tool kit. It crawls across the damaged area of a spacecraft, smoothes itself, then seals with a bond even stronger than the original hull. [YJK]

Annihilator A gladiator droid that was a member of Madam Atuarre's Roving Performers, at least to appearances—Annihilator was actually the droid Bollux. The droid was taking part in a scheme by Han Solo to deceive Viceprex Hirken and infiltrate the Corporate Sector Authority's secret penal colony, known as Stars' End, on the planet Mytus VII. [HSE]

Anoat system

Annoo An agricultural planet, Annoo was the stronghold of the gangster Sise Fromm in the early days of the Empire. Demma Moll and her daughter also had a farm there. [DTV]

Annoo-dat A species of reptilian humanoids from the planet Annoo, these creatures have heavy-lidded eyes, flat noses, and spotted faces. [DTV]

Anoat lizard-ants Small twelve-legged creatures from Anoat, they are best known for their tendency to swarm during mating season. [JS]

Anoat system Located in the backwater Ison Corridor, the system includes the planets Anoat, Gentes (the homeworld of the piglike Ugnaughts), and Deyer, a colony world. Animal life on Anoat includes the Anoat lizard-ant, which swarms in great numbers during mating season. Moff Rebus, a weapons specialist working for the Empire, had a hidden stronghold located under the sewage system of Anoat City. Rebus was captured by Alliance agent Kyle Katarn following the Battle of Yavin. After their evacuation from Hoth, Han Solo and Princess Leia found themselves near the Anoat system and decided to visit Bespin's Cloud City. [ESB, MTS, JS, DA, GG2, DF]

Anomid Born galactic tourists, the humanoid Anomids are native to the Yablari system. Anomids are technology wizards and wealthy enough to tour the galaxy even during times of upheaval. They are born without vocal cords, so when they deal with speaking species they wear elaborate vocalizer masks that produce synthesized sounds that serve as language. With these face-covering masks and the long, hooded robes they favor, Anomids' features are nearly 100 percent hidden—a perfect disguise that hasn't gone unnoticed by spies and agents. [RM]

Anoth A multiple planet orbiting a small white sun, Anoth consists of three parts that likely will collide and become space dust in the not too distant future. Anoth is unrecorded on any chart and was chosen by Luke Skywalker and Admiral Ackbar as the primary hiding place for Han and Leia Organa Solo's Jedi children, Jacen, Jaina, and Anakin. The two largest pieces of Anoth are close enough to scrape together, causing powerful static discharges between them that bathe the third fragment in sensor-masking electrical storms. The third piece orbits a safe distance from the other two and holds a breathable atmosphere in its valleys in spite of its relatively low gravity; it was the site of the stronghold where Leia's trusted aide, Winter, cared for the Solo children. An Imperial attack with MT-AT walkers led by Ambassador Furgan was launched against the Anoth stronghold in an unsuccessful attempt to kidnap young Anakin. The hidden base was repaired, and thirteen years after the Battle of Endor, Leia sent Winter and all three of her children there for their safety during the crisis at Almania. [JS, DA, COF, NR]

Another Chance Following the Clone Wars, all of Alderaan's weapons were placed aboard this huge armory ship. The uncrewed ship was programmed to jump through hyperspace until called by the Council of Elders. [SWSB]

Antar 4 Home to the Gotal species, Antar 4 is the fourth of six moons orbiting the gas giant Antar in the Prindaar system. Antar 4 has an unusual rotational pattern that makes seasonal climate changes very pronounced. The moon's orbital pattern around the gas giant also creates constantly changing day/night cycles. To help compensate for any absence of light, species on Antar 4 have developed organs and senses such as the Gotals' energy-sensing head cones, which aid them in sensing the moods of others and in hunting the native herds of quivry. Large head cones are considered an attractive feature by other Gotal, and those with small cones sometimes use artificial substitutes to help improve their appearances. Antar 4 has no organized government, but trades and otherwise interacts effectively with the rest of galactic society. The notorious bounty hunter Glott comes from Antar 4 and uses his head cones to predict what his enemies will do a split second before they can do it. Gotals are distrustful of droids, since their sensory cones are disturbed by the droids' electronic energy fields. [GG4, TMEC, ROC, POT]

Wedge Antilles

Antares sapphire A jewel so fabled for its healing powers that people were said to travel huge distances to touch it. It was stolen from its owner, the careless Dom Princina, by the droid 4-LOM while the two traveled aboard the *Kuari Princess* passenger liner. [TBH]

Antares Six One of two New Republic escort frigates that accompanied the *Millennium Falcon* to Coruscant to rescue the crew of the *Liberator*, the *Antares Six* saved Lando Calrissian and Wedge Antilles after their Star Destroyer, *Emancipator,* was destroyed by an Imperial World Devastator. [DE]

Anteevy A remote, lifeless, ice-covered world with at least one moon, Anteevy was the site of an Imperial robotics facility where the alloy phrik was refined and treated for use in armoring the Dark Troopers. Following the Battle of Yavin, Alliance agent Kyle Katarn disabled the facility with several sequencer charges. [DF]

Antemeridian sector Bordering the Meridian sector, it was once an Imperial satrapy. Heavy industry has a strong presence in the Antemeridian sector, and a trade artery passing through the sector is known as the Antemeridian Route. Following the death of the Emperor, Moff Getelles continued to rule the sector, backed by a strong naval force commanded by Admiral Larm. Nine years after the Battle of Endor, Getelles made a deal with Seti Ashgad of Nam Chorios to invade the Meridian sector and secure Nam Chorios for industrial development by the Loronar Corporation. But Admiral Larm was killed and his fleet defeated in the Battle of Nam Chorios. [POT]

Antemeridias A planet in the Antemeridian sector where the Loronar Corporation built a manufacturing facility to produce synthdroids and CCIR needle fighters. The facility was operated by Siefax, a dummy corporation for Loronar. [POT]

anticoncussion field A moderately protective magnetic shield, this field is used to protect buildings and space outposts from damage by solid objects such as space junk or small meteorites. However, an anticoncussion field offers little protection against concussion or energy weapons. [HSE]

antigrav A technique to counter the normal effects of gravity, it also refers to any mechanism that accomplishes that feat. The most common antigrav drive is the repulsorlift engine. Such drives work only when a large mass that produces gravity is nearby. [SW]

Antilles, Wedge With more lives than a recycled droid and more adventures than a Holocron could tell, as ferocious as a rancor in battle and as loyal as a befriended Wookiee, Wedge Antilles became the pilot ace of the Rebellion and now the New Republic.

Born and raised on outer Gus Treta, a spaceport in the Corellian system, Wedge Antilles was orphaned as a teenager when his parents were killed by fleeing pirates. With money from an insurance settlement, at the age of sixteen he bought a stock light freighter and tried to start a legitimate shipping business but was soon smuggling weapons for the Rebel Alliance. It didn't take long for Antilles to get behind the controls of an X-wing fighter and become a crack pilot.

During the battle to destroy the first Death Star, Antilles first teamed up with Luke Skywalker as a fellow member of Red Squadron; Wedge was Red Two to Luke's Red Five. Skywalker still kids his flying buddy about his first reaction to the Death Star: "Look at the size of that thing!" Antilles took out numerous gun towers and pulverized a TIE fighter that was on Luke's tail before his X-wing was hit and he had to pull away.

Antilles found a home with the renamed Rogue Squadron because it attracted some of the best hotshot pilots in the galaxy. During the Battle of Hoth, Antilles and other group members piloted snowspeeders against the Empire's huge AT-AT walkers. He and his gunner took out the first walker by tripping it with a strong cable.

With Skywalker away on other missions, Antilles was promoted to commander and assumed control of Rogue Squadron. He worked closely with Lando Calrissian under the guidance of Admiral Ackbar to plan the attack on the second Death Star. In the Battle of Endor, Antilles and his squadron took out an Imperial Star Destroyer that was being used as communications headquarters. Once the Death Star's shields were down, Antilles in his X-wing and Calrissian in the *Millennium Falcon* made a beeline for the reactor core, launching missiles and torpedoes that started a chain reaction explosion that destroyed the super weapon.

Just a day later, Skywalker had to rescue Antilles as the squadron leader attempted to defuse an explosive device on an Imperial drone ship. That encounter led to a mission to distant Bakura, where the Alliance helped defeat an invasion by the reptilian Ssi-ruuk. One of the greatest feats of Antilles and the squadron was the undercover work they did on Coruscant to bring down the planetary shields for a successful Alliance invasion. Five years after the Battle of Endor, the return of the long-absent Grand Admiral Thrawn led to battles that engaged Rogue Squadron at the Sluis Van shipyards, in the fight over the long-lost *Katana* Dreadnaught fleet, and finally in the decisive battle at the Bilbringi Shipyards.

After that, Antilles finally agreed to accept the rank of general, with the proviso that he could still lead Rogue Squadron. After some tough battlefield losses, Antilles acquitted himself with superb military tactics at the second Battle of Coruscant. He then became bodyguard and escort for the brilliant and beautiful scientist Qwi Xux, who was determined to destroy a new super weapon she had helped create for Imperial forces. The two grew closer, and as they spent time on the beautiful planets of Vortex and Ithor, they began to fall in love. But joy turned quickly to pain when one of Skywalker's Jedi trainees, drawn to the dark side of the Force, visited Xux during the night and performed a mindwipe, removing nearly all her memory.

Aqualish

In battle after battle, Antilles has proven to be all-action when needed. He is also capable of coming up with off-the-wall strategy if necessary, such as at the Battle of Almania when his flagship *Yavin* fired on its own forces to trick droid-piloted enemy ships. Antilles remains self-effacing and downplays his heroics, but he remains proud of his accomplishments and those of his squadron. [SW, ESB, RJ, HE, DFR, LC, DE, SWCG, DS, JS, DA, POT, TW, RS, WG, KT, BW]

Anton A front-desk attendant at the Lucky Despot hotel in Mos Eisley. [TJP]

ANY-20 active sensor transceiver A rectenna often used on YT-1300 transports, it provides ship-to-ship jamming capabilities as well as all required communications capabilities. [SWSB, CCG]

Anzati Closely resembling humans, this species has one addition to their anatomy that sets them apart and makes them almost mythological. Beside their nostrils, Anzati have fleshy pockets that hide a prehensile proboscis that can be uncoiled and inserted through victims' nostrils into their brains to suck out their life essence, or "soup," as the Anzati call it. [TMEC]

Aparo sector Together with the Wyl sector, it forms the inner border of the Corporate Sector. The Aparo sector was long ruled by Moff Wyrrhem. [CSSB]

approach vector A nav-computer-generated trajectory, this vector places a ship on an intercept course with another ship or a target for purposes of rendezvous or attack. [ESBR]

Aqualish A species of tusked, walrus-faced humanoids from the planet Ando, a world almost totally covered by water. On its few swampy islands and rocky outcroppings, the planet's Aquala and Quara races—distinguished by their different hands—have settled. Aqualish have a galaxy-wide reputation for being nasty, crude, and aggressive, although their basest instincts were tamed first by the Old Republic and later by the Empire. Many off-world Aqualish have become mercenaries, bounty hunters, and pirates. One Aqualish, Ponda Baba, a much-hunted murderer and thief, picked a fight with Luke Skywalker at the Mos Eisley cantina. Obi-Wan Kenobi tried to calm him and his partner in crime, Dr. Evazan, but they persisted. One swipe of a lightsaber later, Baba was short one right forearm. [SW, GG1, GG4, GDV, TMEC]

Aquaris A water-covered world that charts say is devoid of land masses, it is home to Silver Fyre's organization of former pirates and mercenaries, who call themselves Freeholders. The Freeholders inhabit an expansive underwater base accessible through a retractable landing platform, and pilot submersible aqua-skimmers when hunting the planet's local marine life. Among the many dangerous aquatic creatures in Aquaris's oceans is the enormous demonsquid. During Han Solo and Chewbacca's early adventures together, Fyre's pirates stole a valuable cargo of spice from them. Following the Battle of Yavin, Fyre and her Freeholders joined the Alliance during a conference with Princess Leia on Kabal. The princess and her companions visited Aquaris after leaving Kabal and were betrayed by Kraaken, Fyre's deputy commander. [CSW]

aqua-skimmer A vehicle used on Aquaris for underwater travel. [GW]

Arachnor A giant, spiderlike creature native to the planet Arzid, it spins especially sticky webs. [PDS]

Arakkus, Dr. The onetime director of an Imperial weapons development complex, he was contaminated in a radiation experiment. After that, Dr. Arakkus lived in an abandoned Imperial transport amidst a graveyard of ships circling a collapsing star. He was killed in an explosion after Han Solo ignited a negatron charge to free his *Millennium Falcon* from the gravitational pull of the star. [CSW]

Arakyd Viper probots These probe droids, manufactured under the supervision of Imperial Supervisor Gurdun, feature six segmented legs and flattened heads with multiple scanners. They were given sentience programming by the assassin droid IG-88 and, unbeknownst to the Empire, served as his scouts as he planned a galactic takeover. One of the probots discovered the Rebel base on the planet Hoth and obediently self-destructed when it came under fire from Han Solo and Chewbacca. The Viper is about 1.5 meters tall. It is spherical and curved to deflect sensor sweeps. The probots hover on repulsorlift engines. [TBH, ESBSB]

Aralia A small, tropical world in the Andron system, Aralia is home to both the planetary amusement park Project Aralia and the troublesome, semiintelligent Ranats. The Ranats (who call themselves Con Queecon or "the conquerors") evolved on the planet Rydar II, but came to Aralia when the spice-smuggling ship on which they had stowed away crashed in Aralia's jungles. Ranats live in tribes numbering around 100 and inhabit mazelike underground warrens. The Ranat population has expanded greatly since the crash, and they have taken over most areas of Aralia, including its grassy steppes and mountains. The Ranats' fierce appetites have led to a decline in most of Aralia's fauna, including the piglike roba. After Ranats interfered with the construction of Project Aralia, the builders tried to organize an extermination of the species. This led to an Imperial ruling that Ranats can be killed in self-defense, and they may not be armed under any circumstances. Some Ranats were drug- and mind-controlled by Emperor Palpatine and Darth Vader to serve as guards. [GG4, COJ]

Aramadia The consular ship of the Duskhan League. [BTS]

Arastide, Senator A New Republic Defense Council Member from the planet Gantho. [POT]

Arat Fraca Located two sectors away from Motexx, the planet is separated from Motexx by the Black Nebula in Parfadi. The starliner *Star Morning*, owned by the Fallanassi religious order, left Motexx a few weeks before the Battle of Endor with full cargo holds, bound for Gowdawl under a charter license. The liner then disappeared for 300 days, eventually showing up at Arat Fraca with empty cargo holds. [SOL]

Arbo Maze A natural feature on the forest moon of Endor, this overgrowth of trees is so dense and perplexing in its mazelike paths that most beings and creatures who enter it become hopelessly lost—even the native Ewoks who live in the trees. Arbo is also the name of a wise old Ewok legend-keeper. [ETV]

Arca *See* Jeth, Jedi Master Arca

Archimar, Dr. The surgeon aboard the *Intrepid*, the flagship of the New Republic's Fifth Fleet. [BTS]

Arcona Reptiles without scales, these creatures have humanoid body shapes and flat, anvil-shaped heads with clear, marblelike eyes. Their skin color ranges from mahogany to ebony. Arcona are native to Cona, a world where it is always hot, water is scarce, and the atmosphere is filled with ammonia vapor. Off-worlders used to

Arcona

trade water for mineral rights with them, but discovered that Arcona could become addicted to common salt; their eyes turned golden in the process. Traders therefore began importing large quantities of salt before Arcona communities outlawed such dealings. [GG4, TMEC]

Ardax An Imperial colonel, he led the assault team on Anoth to kidnap young Anakin Solo. [COF]

Ardele, Feylis A beautiful woman with a dazzling smile, blue eyes, and long blond hair worn in a thick braid, as one of the newer members of Rogue Squadron she is somewhat withdrawn and private about her background. Feylis Ardele is actually from an upper middle-class family on Commenor. Imperials wiped out the family after a business rival of Feylis's father accused him of being a Rebel sympathizer. She wasn't harmed because Imperial intelligence had been looking at her as a possible agent. Before they could recruit her, she vanished and later turned up on the Rebel side. [XW]

Ardos A white dwarf star orbited by Varl, it is the original homeworld of the Hutts. According to Hutt legend, Ardos was once a double star with Evona until Evona was drawn into a black hole. [GG4]

area illumination bank A group of high-powered lamps, also called an illumigrid, it contains enough candlepower to light up large public areas such as spaceports or arenas. [HLL]

Argazda Located in the Kanz sector, the planet was the site of a revolt against the Old Republic 4,000 years before the Battle of Yavin. Myrial, provisional governor of Argazda, declared the Kanz sector independent. Myrial began to enslave the other worlds of the sector, including Lorrd, and the preoccupied Republic did nothing to help. This period, which lasted for 300 years, is known as the Kanz Disorders. [CSSB]

Argon, Grand Moff An Imperial sector chief, he was conned out of 25,000 credits by the notorious Tonnika sisters and vowed to track them down wherever they went in the galaxy. [GG1, TMEC]

Arica An assumed name, it was used by the Emperor's hand, Mara Jade, when she went undercover as a dancer in the Tatooine palace of crime lord Jabba the Hutt. [TJP]

Aridus A backwater desert world, Aridus is home to short, lizardlike creatures called Chubbits, who cross the planet's sandy terrain in windrunners, wheeled vehicles with large sails. Animal life includes other large lizardlike creatures, which can be tamed and used as mounts. The natural interference from the Aridus atmosphere makes all long-range communications impossible, and after the Empire took control of the planet it built an immense Iron Tower to overcome the problem. The automated tower acted both as a signal amplifier and power transformer, allowing unrestricted communications and supplying energy to run Imperial hover trains. Hazardous lava pits were located in the region immediately surrounding the tower. Its powerful signals crippled the nervous systems of Chubbits, eventually killing many.

The Rebel Alliance supplied Chubbit resistance fighters with weapons. Following the Battle of Yavin, Darth Vader set a trap on the planet for Luke Skywalker by making it appear that Ben Kenobi had returned from the dead and was working with the Aridus resistance. The false Kenobi was actually a trained actor, altered by Imperial surgeons to resemble the dead Jedi. Skywalker managed to escape the trap, which also resulted in the partial destruction of the Iron Tower. [CSW]

Ariela An Alderaan native, she worked hard to build good relations between human moisture farmers and scavenging Jawa tribes on Tatooine. She even invited a Jawa clan to her wedding. At one point she was kidnapped by Tusken Raiders but was rescued. [TMEC]

Arkania A tundra world in the Colonies region, it is covered by diamond pits where miners extract melon-sized gems from the planet's crust. Jedi Master Arca Jeth established a Jedi training outpost in the wilderness of Arkania some 4,000 years before the Battle of Yavin. Centuries ago, the scientifically minded Arkanians began cyber-enhancing the brains of their primitive neighbors, the Yaka. Soon the stocky Yaka were one of the most intelligent and quick-minded species in the galaxy, with a bizarre sense of humor to match. Animal life on the planet includes the Arkanian dragon and jellyfish. [TOJ, FNU, DLS, DESB]

Arkanis sector Located on the border of the Mid-Rim and Outer Rim, the sector contains the Pii system. The forested worlds Pii 3 and 4 are sometimes called "Teeda's Eyes," after the fabled green eyes of the ancient Empress Teeda. The desert planet Tatooine is located in the Arkanis sector. [SWAJ]

armament rating A weapons rating assigned to all spacecraft, an armament grade depends on the level of offensive and defensive weaponry. Determining factors include the type and number of weapons aboard, maximum range, control mechanisms, and power-plant capabilities. The generally accepted categories are the following:

0—No weaponry.
1—Light defensive weapons only.
2—Light defensive and offensive capabilities.
3—Medium defensive and offensive weapons.
4—Heavy defensive and offensive weaponry.

[HSR, SWR]

armored defense platform These perimeter battle stations protect many planets and installations such as major shipyards from attack, but they sometimes offer only false security. Armored defense platforms are heavily armed with twenty-eight turbolaser batteries, five proton torpedo launchers, and six tractor beam projectors. The platforms are usually more than 1,200 meters long and have a crew of about 325. Because they are immobile—and thus sitting targets against full-blown offensives—much strategic planning goes into exactly where they are placed. They pay for themselves by handling such things as pirate raids or by catching smugglers trying to flee. [HE, HESB]

armored eel A creature discovered on Yavin 4 by the naturalist Dr'uun Unnh, it is well suited to the sluggish rivers that slice through the moon's overpowering jungle. Unnh observed and sketched the eel but didn't have time to record detailed characteristics before his death during the Battle of Yavin. [ISWU]

arrak snake Native to the planet Ithor, this reptile can sing. [TMEC]

arrol A semisentient poisonous cactus, it is native to the planet Ithor. [MEC]

Artesian space collage This form of artwork originates on the planet Artesia. [NR]

Artoo-Detoo *See* R2-D2

Aruza A peaceful, forested planet with five colorful moons, Aruza's major city is Bukeen. Native Aruzans are small, gentle people with blue skin, dark blue hair, and rounded heads. They keep neural interface jacks, called Attanni, beneath their ears to feel the emotions of others. They are tech-empathic and share a limited group mind. Imperial General Sinick Kritkeen was ordered to "reeducate" the populace and turn them into a fighting force for the Empire. Prior to the Battle of Hoth, the bounty hunter Dengar came to Aruza and assassinated Kritkeen, after which he escaped with the Aruzan woman Manaroo, whom he later married. [TBH]

Aryon, Governor Tour A key Imperial official, she was stationed at Bestine on Tatooine, where she was governor. [GG7, TJP]

asaari tree These waving trees cover the surface of the planet Bimmisaari. They constantly sway by moving

Asha

their leafy branches even when no wind is blowing. [HE, HESB]

Asha The long-lost older sister of the Ewok Princess Kneesaa, she was attacked by a terrifying hanadak when she, her sister, and their mother Ra-Lee were on an outing on Endor. By the time Kneesaa ran to the village and got help, Asha was missing and Ra-Lee had been slain. Years later, Kneesaa's best friend, Wicket W. Warrick, came into contact with a savage red-furred female huntress known as the Red Ghost. Hearing the story, Kneesaa had a strong hunch that this might be Asha, and they tracked her down on a snowy evening. Indeed, it was her sister, who told of how she had been found and raised by a family of wolflike korrinas. After routing a group of evil hunters, Asha returned to her village for a reunion with her father, Chief Chirpa. [ETV, TRG]

Ashern Black-Claw Rebels from the planet Thyferra, the Ashern were members of the Vratix species who renounced their peaceful heritage to become warriors fighting against the tyranny of their human masters. To mark this change, they painted their normally gray bodies black and sharpened their claws, which gave them the ability to puncture stormtrooper armor. [BW]

Ashgad, Seti One of the top hyperdrive engineers of the Old Republic, Ashgad was also a political foe of Senator Palpatine. When Palpatine rose to power, Ashgad was exiled to the onetime prison planet Nam Chorios.

When Chief of State Leia Organa Solo traveled to Nam Chorios, she met with the apparent son of Seti Ashgad, who had the same name. Ashgad, a profiteer, was the unofficial spokesman for a group called the Rationalist Party, which was trying to assist Newcomers—recent voluntary immigrants to Nam Chorios. Ashgad wanted to convince Leia to allow trade to begin between Nam Chorios and the New Republic. Opposing that aim were the Theran Listeners, longtime Nam Chorios inhabitants. Adept at healing, they operate the ancient gun stations that prevented prisoners from leaving the planet and eschew much of modern technology.

Ashgad, Jr., was actually Ashgad, Sr. He had been kept alive and young by Dyzm, a mutated droch. (The droch are insectlike creatures that can burrow into the flesh and consume life.) Drochs caused the Death Seed plague, although there hadn't been an outbreak of the horrific malady for seven centuries. Both Ashgad and the once-powerful Beldorion the Hutt paid the price for being kept ageless by Dyzm—they were his virtual slaves. Nine years after the Battle of Endor, Leia secretly visited the planet to meet with Ashgad, who took her prisoner, then unleashed the Death Seed plague across three-quarters of the sector. He planned to disable the planet's gun stations—Dyzm and the drochs desperately wanted to leave the planet where they had been trapped for centuries—and allow the Loronar Corporation to strip-mine the smokies, a type of Force-sensitive crystal. After a series of confrontations and battles, Luke Skywalker was able to communicate with the planet's crystals, and they linked to crystals aboard Dyzm and Ashgad's fleeing ship, blowing up the craft. [POT]

Askaj A dry, desert world, it is home to the near-human race known as Askajians. Their bodies can absorb and store water, using it only as needed for survival. Females of the species have six breasts. According to custom, Askajian cublings are not given names until they reach their first birthday. Animal life includes horned herd animals called tomuons, valued throughout the galaxy for their wool. Askajian weaving techniques are closely guarded secrets, and it is said that Emperor Palpatine's ceremonial robes were spun from tomuon wool. Yarna D'al Gargan, daughter of a tribe chieftain on Askaj and a first-rate competitive dancer, was captured with her family by slavers and sold to crime lord Jabba the Hutt. Yarna served in the Hutt's court as a dancer but escaped after Jabba's death and eventually bought her cublings out of slavery. [TJP]

asp A general all-purpose labor droid, the asp is found all over the galaxy. Industrial Automaton makes several different basic asp models. The wide-ranging line can do everything from performing light household tasks to serving as lightsaber training units—a use to which Darth Vader put them. [SW, SOTE]

assassin droid The ultimate symbol of society and technology run amuck, these droids are largely unstoppable killing machines, programmed to hunt down specific targets and destroy them. Originally designed in the days of the Old Republic to eliminate dangerous criminals or escaped prisoners, assassin droids performed their task so well that they were put into service by warlords, dictators, and criminal kingpins. The droids are intelligent and unswerving in their task; they have a kill rate of better than 90 percent, even if it takes years to track down their target. Estimates are that up to a few million remain in the galaxy even though Emperor Palpatine outlawed them at the beginning of his reign because they were being used successfully against Imperial of-

Asp

ficials. (Lord Torbin, the Grand Inquisitor, was killed when a shuttle crashed into his palace; an assassin droid is suspected of having killed the shuttle crew at a timely moment.)

Rogue assassin droids have become a major problem. Having completed their initial mission, they should have shut down, but may have come up with new missions on their own. These droids have no built-in ethical chip. The now-infamous Caprioril massacre occurred when one droid, programmed to kill Governor Amel Bakli, decided that the most efficient way to accomplish this task was to murder all 20,000 spectators at a swoop arena while the governor of the peaceful planet was in attendance. Another, an Eliminator model 434, tried to kill Princess Leia Organa on Coruscant, but it was destroyed by Prince Isolder's bodyguard, Captain Astarta. [SWSB, CPL]

Assassin's Guild A secret society of professional mercenaries, the guild's members are specialists in death by contract. There are subguilds—the bounty hunter unit is among the most feared—and an Elite Circle, whose membership can be elected only by fellow terminators. The Assassin's Guild is so clandestine that even the location of its headquarters is concealed from most members, who must contact it through comlink or surreptitious methods. [HLL]

assault frigate These Rebel, and later New Republic, ships are actually Imperial Dreadnaught heavy cruisers that have been painstakingly and cleverly modified to create combat starships some 700 meters long. While Imperial ships required a crew of 16,000, the Alliance retooling—replacing humans with droids and computers—has reduced crew requirements by more than two-thirds. Removing tons of superstructure has increased engine capacity while lowering fuel consumption. The addition of two rear solar fins has made the assault frigates faster and more maneuverable. The frigates usually carry about 100 troops or 7,500 metric tons of cargo. They each carry a modified assault shuttle piggyback atop their superstructure, while twenty umbilical docking tubes can be used for light freighters and starfighters. The ships are armed with fifteen regular and twenty quad laser cannons along with fifteen turbolaser batteries. The frigates were important in the Rebel victory at the Battle of Endor and have since been used as patrol ships in such areas as the Borderlands Regions. [RSB, HESB]

assault shuttle With only five-member crews, these heavily armored Imperial ships can engage capital ships more than three times their thirty-meter length and carry forty zero-g stormtroopers into the heart of battle. Assault shuttles, which operate both in space and in planetary atmospheres, can grab target ships with tractor beams or magnetic harpoons, then cripple them with concussion missiles or blasts from one of four laser cannons. The ships are well protected from enemy fire; they use up to two-thirds of their power on shields, compared to the normal one-quarter of most combat starships. But they hold only about a week's provisions and must be reprogrammed after only three jumps into hyperspace. [ISB]

Astarta, Captain An Amazonlike woman of exceptional beauty, she is the personal guard of Prince Isolder, Princess Leia Organa Solo's onetime suitor from the planet Hapes. Her hair a dark red, her eyes as dark a blue as the skies of her planet Terephon, the statuesque bodyguard also kept the prince alert to the intrigues of the Hapes court. She was in love with the prince—a love that could never be consummated—but above all else she was a loyal and excellent soldier. [CPL]

astrogation computer *See* nav computer

Astrolabe A New Republic astrographic probe ship, it was said to be operated by the civilian Astrographic Survey Institute but was in reality a front for a military intelligence mission. It was destroyed at Doornik-1142 by Yevethan ships, and its crew was killed. The incident led to a wider war. [BTS]

astromech droid Robots such as Luke Skywalker's R2-D2 are all-round utility droids that carry out sophisticated computer repairs and undertake information retrieval. Astromechs are short and squat, usually cylindrical, and travel on a pair of treaded rollers. They often have a retractable third leg to help navigate difficult terrain. The droids specialize in starship maintenance and repair, even in hostile environments such as the vacuum of deep space. They often are loaded into special sockets behind the pilot's cockpit in small starfighters where they plug into all the ship's systems and scan real-time data, capably performing more than 10,000 operations a second to forecast potential problems. In effect, they act as copilot and, in emergencies, can even take over limited piloting chores. Many models can perform multiple tasks, from holographic projection to welding. Some have even been known to do a bit of bartending on the side. [SW, RJ, SWSB]

Asylum This former Imperial research station and outlaw outpost was also known as Crseih Station. It orbited a black hole with a white dwarf star. Danger arose as the star froze into a quantum crystal. Han Solo and his *Millennium Falcon* were able to pull the station free when the star crystallized. [CS]

AT-AT *See* All Terrain Armored Transport

Athega A system rich in minerals and fuel stores, it had long been off-limits because of the intense heat given off by its sun; its radiation could peel the hull from a ship before it could reach the surface of a planet. But Lando Calrissian, no stranger to mining from his days as administrator of Cloud City, got the New Republic to back him in a novel venture. First, Calrissian developed a new type of craft called shieldships that literally shield other spacecraft from the killer effects of the Athega sun. He also planned Nomad City, a huge humpbacked structure that lumbered slowly across the surface of the planet Nkllon, digging ore with mole miners while managing to stay on the planet's dark side. The city is built out of useless old spacecraft, with a base of forty captured Imperial AT-AT walkers. Calrissian's operations were hindered after Grand Admiral Thrawn captured fifty-one of his mole miners for use at the Battle of Sluis Van, an event that brought retired General Calrissian back into the thick of the action. [HE, HESB]

AT-PT *See* All Terrain Personal Transport

Atraken A planet from which Callista sent Luke Skywalker a message in a music box, warning him to stay away from the Meridian sector. [POT]

Atravis sector This sector contains the Atravis systems, which were devastated by Imperial attacks. Of the massacres there, Grand Moff Tarkin said, "They have only themselves to blame." Grand Admiral Harrsk's troops began gathering in the Atravis sector eight years after the Battle of Endor. [COJ]

Atrivis sector Located in the Outer Rim, the sector includes the Mantooine and Fest systems and the planet Generis. During the early formation of the Rebel Alliance, Mon Mothma helped unite various insurgent organizations, including the Atrivis resistance groups. Five years after the Battle of Endor, New Republic pilot Pash Cracken was stationed in the Atrivis sector and was part of the ultimately unsuccessful defense of the Outer Rim comm center against an Imperial attack. [RSB, LC, DESB, FP]

AT-ST *See* All Terrain Scout Transport

Attanni A high-tech device used by the Aruzans to cybernetically share thoughts, emotions, memories, and knowledge with each other. [TBH]

Attichitcuk A Wookiee elder from the planet Kashyyyk, he is the father of Chewbacca. His nickname is Itchy. [SWHS]

Atuarre An apprentice agronomist on the planet Orron III, she was a female Triannii with a personal quest: locating political prisoners held by the Corporate Sector Authority. She solicited the help of Han Solo in that mission. [HSE]

Atzerri A Free Trader world, Atzerri has the most minimal government necessary to stave off complete chaos. Almost anything, legal or ille-

Attichitcuk

gal, can be had for a price on the planet. The Trader's Coalition charges a hefty fee for every service. Ships control their own entry and departure and must negotiate with independently owned spaceports to land. Arriving visitors run a gauntlet of gaudily lit stores known as Trader's Plaza, designed to hook new arrivals and separate them from their credits as soon as possible. The Revels, a busy entertainment district filled with casinos and cantinas, has a theme bar called Jabba's Throne Room, a near-perfect reproduction of the late gangster's palace—complete with a phony Han Solo in carbonite. Luke Skywalker and Akanah Norand Pell went to Atzerri, supposedly in search of the missing Fallanassi sect, but really so Akanah could track down her father, who had abandoned her family years earlier. [BTS, SOL, TT]

Augwynne, Mother Augwynne leads the Singing Mountain clan of the Witches of Dathomir, a group of Force-sensitive women who ride domesticated rancors and keep men as slaves and for breeding. Han Solo won the planet Dathomir in a sabacc game, but after a series of near-fatal adventures on the planet, gave up the deed to Mother Augwynne. [CPL]

aura blossom An exquisite indigo-blue flower, it glows brightly and grows in abundance on the forest moon of Endor. The blossoms are a favorite of the native Ewoks. [ETV]

Auril systems This distant group of six star systems—including the Adega system—in the Auril sector also encompasses the Cron Drift. Originally there were nine Auril systems, but three were destroyed during the Great Sith War as the Cron Cluster ignited in a multiple supernova. The space city Nespis VIII is located at the node of the Auril systems. [DE2, TOJ]

Authority Cash Voucher The main legal currency in worlds controlled by the Corporate Sector Authority. Upon entering Corporate Sector areas, travelers must exchange Imperial or Republic credits for the vouchers or face legal consequences when paying for any goods or services. [HSE, GSWU]

Authority Data Center The Corporate Sector Authority uses this well-guarded repository for nearly all computer-processed information from throughout Corporate Sector space. [HSE]

auto enhancement Installed on some starfighters, these enhancement programs work with the spacecraft's tracking and computer systems to send a ship to its destination without direct pilot involvement. [SME]

autohopper A "smart" vehicle that can carry out a variety of tasks without the need of a driver or pilot, an autohopper has a central instruction processor programmed to recall the time and location of job assignments. It can even take into account such variables as terrain and weather changes. [HLL]

automatic sealup A life-saving feature, sealup is triggered when air-pressure sensors in a vehicle or outpost sense decompression or exposure to the vacuum of space. The sensors instantly alert a central station, which transmits signals closing airtight bulkhead doors for automatic sealup. [HSR]

autovalet These devices, which automatically clean and press clothing, can be found in hotels and luxury starships as well as the homes of the wealthy. They are sometimes full-scale droids. [HLL, CSSB]

Auyemesh One of three moons orbiting the planet Almania, its population was destroyed by the Dark Sider who called himself Kueller thir-

Avenger

teen years after the Battle of Endor. He did so to harvest the wealth of the inhabitants and to add credence to his ultimatum demanding that New Republic Chief of State Leia Organa Solo step down and hand over her power to him. [NR]

avabush spice This spice causes sleepiness and is sometimes stirred into drinks or baked into sweets. Used properly, it can also act as a truth serum. Avabushes grow on the planet Baros. [ZHR, PDS, GG4]

Avarice A Mark II Imperial Star Destroyer, the *Avarice* was commanded by Sair Yonka. Ysanne Isard used it to protect her bacta convoys after taking control of the planet Thyferra. When New Republic Commander Wedge Antilles offered Captain Yonka a more profitable deal, the captain and his crew defected and renamed the ship *Freedom*. [BW]

Avenger An Imperial Star Destroyer, the *Avenger* was part of a task force that searched for Rebel forces after the Battle of Yavin. Under the command of Captain Needa, the *Avenger* was also present at the Battle of Hoth, after which it followed the fleeing *Millennium Falcon* into an asteroid field. The ship sustained considerable damage and wasn't prepared to capture the *Falcon* when the Rebel ship suddenly reappeared, a failure that cost the *Avenger's* captain his life at the hands of Darth Vader. [ESB]

Averam A planet that housed a Rebel Alliance cell, it was where Leia Organa Solo's aide, Winter, worked for a few weeks under the code-name Targeter. Imperial Intelligence cracked the cell soon afterward. Averam natives are called Averists. [LC]

Aves A human in his forties and a smuggler by trade, he is one of archsmuggler Talon Karrde's chief aides, having served him since he formed his ring. Aves serves Karrde as both an adviser and a communications officer. He also coordinates the activities of field operatives and, in effect, he acts as the smuggler's ship dispatcher. [HE, DFR, LC, HESB]

AVVA The Alliance Veteran's Victory Association is a group with the status of a retirees club but the ambition to be something more akin to a militia or the Fleet's ready reserve. [TT]

A-wing starfighter This small, wedge-shaped craft has been the Alliance's main starfighter since it first saw full-scale deployment at the Battle of Endor. The lightweight A-wing, codesigned by General Jan Dodonna and Alliance engineer Walex Blissex to outrun any ship in the Imperial Navy, has especially strong avionics, including a powerful jamming system that disrupts sensor readings and lets pilots blind enemy targets prior to attack. Originally designed for escort duty, the A-wing has proved more suited to hit-and-run missions, blasting enemy sites and spacecraft with twin wing-mounted pivoting blaster cannons and concussion missiles. The downside of the A-wing's speed and agility is its relatively high vulnerability in dogfights; the position of the cockpit leaves pilots exposed to enemy fire, making the craft's speed even more important. [SWSB, SWVG]

Azure Dianoga cantina A hive of scum and villainy in the Invisec area of Coruscant, it makes the Mos Eisley cantina seem tame by comparison. The bar was selected by members of Rogue Squadron as a meeting place when they were on an undercover operation to determine the alien sentiment toward Alliance control of Coruscant. It was here that the Rogues ran into trouble with the Alien Combine. [BW]

Azur-Jamin, Daye The fiancé of the bounty hunter Tinian I'att, he helped her escape the Imperial takeover of her grandparents' armament factory. [SWAJ, TBH]

Baas, Bodo A Jedi Master in the Adega system some 600 years before the Battle of Yavin, he had a somewhat crustacean and insectlike ap-

A-wing starfighter

Bodo Baas

pearance. Baas was gatekeeper of a Jedi Holocron, an interactive cube that records the history and the prophecies of the Jedi for the ages. The Holocron can be activated only by someone imbued with the Force, and many of its mysteries are reserved for those who follow the light side. The Baas Holocron, which had been initiated millennia earlier by Master Vodo-Siosk Baas, eventually fell into the hands of Emperor Palpatine's reborn clone but was later taken by Leia Organa Solo. She listened intently as a holographic Baas spun tales of ancient Jedi and told of the seductive path to the dark side of the Force. But the future of Luke Skywalker was lost in mists and shadows, and a warning about her own future sent Leia to help Luke destroy the clone of Palpatine. [DE]

Baas, Master Vodo-Siosk A Jedi Master and expert lightsaber craftsman who lived more than 4,000 years before the Battle of Yavin, he trained many Jedi, including the powerful Exar Kun. Kun was ambitious and impatient, and despite his master's warnings, he turned to the dark side of the Force and eventually betrayed and killed Baas. The Jedi Master then became one with the Force and gatekeeper to a Jedi Holocron, an interactive repository of Jedi knowledge and history. Many millennia later, after Leia Organa Solo took the Holocron from the reborn clone of Emperor Palpatine, Luke Skywalker used it to teach his Jedi trainees on the moon of Yavin 4. But Kun's spirit, which was trapped on the moon, destroyed the Holocron and tried to murder Skywalker. Later, the spirit of Vodo-Siosk Baas, along with Skywalker and his trainees, destroyed Kun forever. [DA, DLS, TSW]

Baba, Ponda A pirate and smuggler by calling, aggressive and obnoxious by practice, the walrus-faced Baba was just another miscreant until a chance encounter with a Jedi Knight in a Mos Eisley cantina cost him an arm but gave him high visibility throughout the galaxy.

An Aqualish from the planet Ando, he lived in swamps and wetlands until he decided to seek his fortune plundering and murdering through the galaxy. He joined forces with a madman—Dr. Evazan—who practiced what he called "creative surgery," after rescuing the doctor from a bounty hunter. While Baba's first thought was to turn in the doctor and collect the reward himself, he figured Evazan would be more valuable as a partner in crime.

The pair traveled frequently to Tatooine to take on spice-smuggling jobs for Jabba the Hutt. In the cantina on one of those trips, a drunken Baba shoved young Luke Skywalker and Evazan threatened him. A brown-robed old man, who turned out to be the Jedi Knight Obi-Wan Kenobi, tried to calm the two, but they attacked. With a quick draw of his lightsaber, Kenobi slashed Evazan's chest and severed Baba's right arm at the elbow.

The two criminals had a falling out after Evazan botched Baba's arm-replacement surgery, but they teamed up again on Ando, where Evazan set up an experimental lab. When he tried to transfer Baba's mind into the body of an Andoan senator, the experiment misfired and

Master Vodo-Siosk Baas

Ponda Baba

put the senator's mind into Baba's body. [SW, SWCG, TMEC]

Babali A tropical planet, Babali holds some interest to galactic archaeologists, including those of the Obroan Institute. [SOL]

Babbadod A planet where the starliner *Star Morning*, owned by the fleeing Fallanassi religious order, made a stop. [SOL]

bacta Gelatinous, translucent red alazhi and kavam bacterial particles, they are found in an ancient lotion that has been used for thousands of years by the Vratix to heal cuts. The particles are mixed with the colorless liquid ambori. The resulting synthetic chemical—also commonly called bacta—is thought to mimic the body's own vital fluids and is used to treat and heal all but the most serious of wounds. Patients are fully immersed (with breathing masks) in the expensive liquid, which is held in cylindrical rejuvenation, or bacta, tanks. The bacterial particles actually seek out wounds and promote amazingly quick tissue growth without scarring.

Emperor Palpatine realized the importance of bacta as a source of power and control. He shut down satellite manufacturing centers and systematically suppressed small manufacturers in favor of the Zaltin and Xucphra corporations. Bacta then fell under the control of a cartel on Thyferra, and the corporations that distributed it became even more powerful than the Emperor intended. Bacta was universally ac-

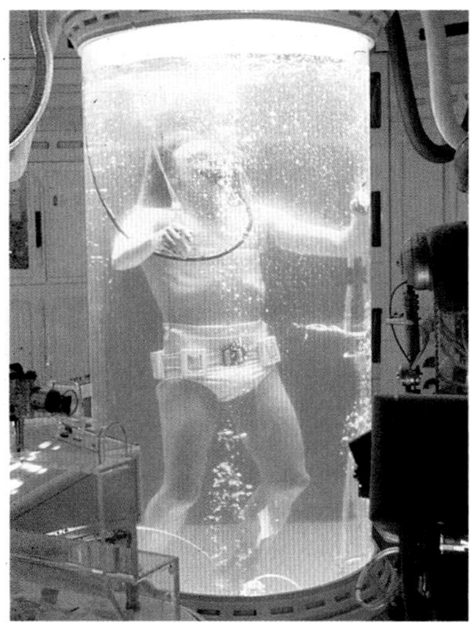

Bacta tank

cepted as a safe drug until Ashern rebels contaminated one lot. Millions of people exposed to it became allergic to bacta, particularly the citizens and soldiers on Imperial Center. Later, a Bacta War was fought over control of the healing substance. [ESB, SWAJ, BW]

Bacta War, the During the final days of Imperial control of Coruscant, onetime Director of Imperial Intelligence Ysanne Isard and the Xucphra Corporation began a civil war on the planet Thyferra. Their objective was to suppress the Zaltin Corporation and become sole heirs to the Bacta Cartel, the group that controlled all of the galaxy's supply of the near-miraculous healing agent. Isard reasoned that with the wealth and power of the cartel at her disposal, she could rule the galaxy and perhaps even crush the Rebellion. As part of her master plan, the Krytos virus was ravaging newly occupied Coruscant, and the New Republic could go bankrupt trying to control the outbreak with bacta.

Isard knew that the Republic's need for bacta and the potential political fallout of interfering with a strictly civil war would make it hesitant to attack her position on Thyferra. Rogue Squadron was forbidden to intervene, so its members resigned—and then set up a secret operation to try to topple Isard. They acquired ships and weapons and organized the Ashern Rebels on Thyferra to overthrow Isard's government. Then they started attacking and liberating bacta convoys.

Things got nasty quickly. Isard destroyed a colony that had been given free bacta; the Rogues destroyed one of her production facilities in return. She attacked them, and they destroyed one of her starships. Then she started to annihilate Thyferra's native Vratix population. Advance planning and superb strategy helped the Rogues and their allies overcome overwhelming firepower, and they defeated Isard and her forces. As for the Rogues' resignations, they hadn't been recorded due to a clerical error, so Rogue Squadron was still very much a part of the New Republic. [BW]

Badlands While many planets have similarly named areas, most think of the Badlands as the flat, sparsely populated area near the parched equator of the planet Kamar. Inhabitants are called Badlanders. The region isn't a bad place to get lost, as Han Solo and Chewbacca found out when they spent some time there after the Corporate Sector Authority got a little too interested in keeping tabs on them. [HSR]

Badure Also known as Trooper, he was a mentor to Han Solo and taught the Corellian almost everything he knows about flying. He saved Solo and his companion Chewbacca after an aborted spice run to Kessel. That was repayment in kind, for many years before, Solo had saved Badure after a training mission had gone awry. Just before Solo hooked up with Luke Skywalker, Ben Kenobi, and the Rebel Alliance, Badure convinced him and Chewbacca to help find the fabled lost treasure from the cargo transport *Queen of Ranroon*. [HLL]

Bafforr trees These intelligent crystalline trees, with bark smoother than glass, are found on the planet Ithor. [DA, TMEC]

Baga Baga is a baby bordok (a horse-like creature) and the pet of Wicket, an Ewok. [ETV]

Baji A Ho'Din from the planet Moltok, Baji is a healer and medicine man who speaks in rhyme and gathers roots and plants to make medicine and potions. He also used to send samples of rare plants near extinction on Yavin 4 to botanists back home to study. Baji was captured by the Empire and forced to cure the blindness of Trioculus, a pretender to the throne of Emperor Palpatine. The doctor was then pressed into Imperial service. But Baji was rescued by the Alliance and taken to Dagobah, where he raises medicinal plants in a greenhouse. [LCJ, QE]

Bajic sector Located in the Outer Rim, the sector contains the Lybeya system, where a secret Rebel shipyard was built on one of the larger Vergesso asteroids. Seeking to curry favor as well as personal gain, the criminal mastermind Prince Xizor notified Emperor Palpatine of the base, which also was near the main facilities of Ororo Transportation, a major competitor of Xizor's company, XTS, and a front for the rival Tenloss Syndicate. Tenloss had been trying to wrest control of spice-trafficking operations in the Bajic sector (sometimes called the Baji sector) from Black Sun, Xizor's criminal group. Acting on the Emperor's orders, Darth Vader destroyed the Rebel base, along with Ororo Transportation. [GG11, SOTE]

Baker, Mayor The mayor of Dying Slowly on the planet Jubilar, Baker was known as Incavi Larado before her marriage. [TBH]

Bakura A remote but rich green and blue planet with several moons, Bakura was the site of an historic truce between the Rebel Alliance and Imperial forces shortly after the death of Emperor Palpatine.

The eight planets in the Bakura system, located on the isolated edge of the Rim Worlds, include one gas giant and Planet Six, an ammonia ice-covered ball. Bakura receives a great deal of rainfall. The capital city of

Baga

Salis D'aar sits at the base of a mountain range on a white quartz delta between two parallel rivers. Bakura's exports include strategic metals, repulsorlift components, and an addictive fruit called namana, which is made into candies and nectar. Animal life includes the butter newt and the predatory Bakuran cratsch, and plants include pokkta leaves, namana trees, and passion-bud vines.

Bakura was settled by the Bakur Mining Corporation during the end of the Clone Wars. Inhabitants tend to be prejudiced against nonhuman species and especially dislike droids, since the first Bakuran colonists were nearly wiped out by malfunctioning robots.

Constant governmental bickering made the planet easy pickings for the Empire three years before the Battle of Endor. Immediately following the battle, Alliance and Imperial forces joined forces to thwart an invasion by the Ssi-ruuk Imperium. After the subsequent overthrow of Imperial forces, Prime Minister Yeorg Captison took over planetary leadership. Several years later, his niece Gaeriel was elected Prime Minister but was defeated in a succeeding election. The planet retained a powerful defensive fleet, and fourteen years after the truce, Luke Skywalker returned to Bakura to borrow battle cruisers for a mission in the Corellian system. The mission was ultimately successful, but half of the Bakuran cruisers were destroyed and Gaeriel Captison was killed. [TAB, AS, SAC, SWAJ]

Balis-Baurgh system Naturally shielded from sensors by gas clouds and intense solar radiation, the system contains three planets, only one of which can support life. Political leaders on the planet decided to jointly build a space station, but when construction was secretly sabotaged by the Empire, the nations blamed each other and went to war, making the planet an easy mark for Imperial conquest. The space station became a fully automated prison, and sometime after the Battle of Endor, Alliance Captain Junas Turner and Ewok warrior Grael were imprisoned there until they escaped. [SWAJ]

ball creature of Duroon A meek and mild nocturnal plant eater, it is shaped like a globe and moves like a ball, bouncing from place to place. [HSE]

Balmorra This factory world is located at the fringes of the Galactic Core. Its inhabitants manufactured weapons for the Imperial army and were the primary builders of the AT-ST walker. The planet was liberated by the New Republic following the Battle of Endor. It came under Imperial rule again during the first cloned Emperor's appearance. Following Palpatine's supposed death near Da Soocha, the Balmorrans began arming the New Republic. In retaliation, the planet was attacked by a force led by Military Executor Sedriss using Shadow Droids and SD-9 battle droids. After suffering surprising losses at the hands of new Viper Automadons, Sedriss called off his attack in exchange for a shipment of the molecularly shielded droids. [DE2]

Balu, Predne A heavy, slopeshouldered human, he was assistant security officer of Mos Eisley. [TMEC]

banda Banda are tiny nibbling insects found on Tatooine. [TJP]

bandfill A musical instrument that features a number of mounted horn bells. [TMEC]

bantha Large, four-legged beasts of burden found on Tatooine and elsewhere, these creatures have adapted to a variety of climates and terrain. Wild herds still roam some planets; on others, the only banthas are domesticated. Males have a pair of large tapering horns and can be as wide as three meters at the shoulders. Banthas survive on grasses and other native flora, and because of their size and internal reserves, can live for up to a month or so without water or food. Often used as pack animals, their long, thick fur is prized for clothing and their meat for food. Even bantha-skin boots and carrying cases bring top credit on some worlds. The Tusken Raiders have a special bond with their personal bantha and if the bantha dies, the Raider is sent into the desert in the hopes of being adopted by a wild bantha. [SW, SWSB, TM]

Bantha A nickname for the droid WED-91-M1. [CCG]

bantha blaster A pink-and-green alcoholic drink, it was a party favorite at the palace of Jabba the Hutt. [TJP]

"bantha four five six" This instruction code was given by the droid TDL-3.5 as authorization for her to

Bantha

Mungo Baobab

replace C-3PO as nanny to the children of Leia and Han Solo. But Leia's aide, Winter, realized that "bantha" was not a family code. It was a prank by young Anakin, who was angry that C-3PO would no longer read him his favorite bedtime story, "The Little Lost Bantha Cub." [NR]

Baobab, Mungo A reckless treasure-hunter and adventurer from Manda, Baobab came from a family that owned the Baobab Merchant Fleet during the Empire's early days. To try to instill a work ethic in Mungo, the family sent him to Biitu to set up a mining operation and trading post. Baobab's greatest accomplishment was finding and preserving the Roonstones, a crystal structure in which was encoded the earliest known text of *Dha Werda Verda*, an epic poem of the conquest of the indigenous people of Coruscant by a warrior race called the Taungs. [TGH, DTV, SOTEALB]

Barab I A dark, humid world, it is in close orbit around the red dwarf Barab. Barab I has a sixty-standard-hour rotation and is bathed in ultraviolet, gamma, and infrared radiation. During the day, standing water evaporates, making the surface very humid and hazy. During the cool night, the only time animal life is active, the haze condenses and falls to the surface as rain. The Barabel live in underground caverns. Years ago a band of Jedi helped resolve a Barabel dispute over access to choice hunting grounds, leaving the Barabel with a deep respect for Jedi. A spaceport, Alater-ka, was built after the Empire took control of Barab I. After the Battle of Endor, the Barabel nearly went to war with the Verpine when the Verpine defaulted on a shipbuilding contract. [GG4, DFR, CPL]

Barabel These reptilelike natives of the untamed planet of Barab I are ferocious hunters. That's ironic since off-worlders once chartered safaris to hunt down Barabel, ignoring evidence that they were intelligent creatures. The fierce-looking Barabel are about two meters high and have bodies covered with horny black scales, an armor that wards off everything from creature bites to light laser blasts. Their sharp, pointed teeth can grow up to five centimeters long, folding up toward the roof of their mouth when they close their large jaws. Most Barabel never leave their communities, much less their planet. But Skahtul, a female Barabel bounty hunter, captured Luke Skywalker on the planet Kothlis prior to the Battle of Endor. She planned to sell him to the highest bidder, but he escaped. [GG4, DFR, DFRSB, SOTE]

Barabel

Barada

Baraboo This planet is the site of the Institute for Sentient Studies, which contains the most comprehensive collection of neurological models in the galaxy. Some twelve years after the Battle of Endor, the cyborg Lobot accessed the Institute's records, searching for a clue to decipher a puzzle aboard the mysterious ghost ship called the Teljkon vagabond. [BTS]

Barada An indentured servant won by Jabba the Hutt in a rigged sabacc game, this native of Klatooine worked his way up from the crime lord's vehicle pool to become captain of the skiff guard whenever Jabba traveled. Despite being kept under tight discipline by Jabba, the leathery-skinned Barada developed a strong loyalty to the Hutt. Barada helped load Jabba's prisoners—Luke Skywalker, Han Solo, and Chewbacca—onto a sand skiff to meet their fate at the Pit of Carkoon, which was inhabited by the ghastly Sarlacc. But Barada underestimated the skill of his prisoners and became the first one killed in the battle that led to Jabba's death. Barada's body fell into the cavernous mouth of the Sarlacc. [RJ, SWCG]

Barak, Koth A male midshipman aboard the New Republic escort cruiser *Adamantine*, he was killed by unknown means and for no apparent reason. He turned out to be one of the first victims of the revived Death Seed plague. [POT]

Barakas, Braka A hostage captured by the Yevetha from New Brigia during an attack led by Nil Spaar. [SOL]

Barhu The closest to the sun of eight planets in the Churba star system, Barhu is a dead rock with temperatures far too high to allow any indigenous life-forms. [DFR, DFRSB]

Baritha An older woman with graying hair and glittering green eyes, she was a leader of the dark-side Nightsisters of the Witches of Dathomir. Baritha made no secret of the fact that, viewed from behind, she thought Han Solo looked "tasty," and she tried to claim him as her slave. [CPL]

Baros Orbiting the blue star Bari, Baros is a large, arid planet with high gravity and intense windstorms. Baros is the homeworld of the reptilian Brubb, whose society is centered around communal groups, or habas, that consist of ten to ten thousand individuals. The Brubb have university habas and established a spaceport haba after their discovery by the Empire, although the facility isn't used much because of the difficulty of landing and departing in the high gravity of Baros. Brasck, a smuggler known to associate with Talon Karrde, was a Brubb. [GG4, HE, HESB]

Barth A New Republic flight engineer, he was captured along with Han Solo by Yevethan forces commanded by Nil Spaar. Spaar brutally killed the engineer. [TT]

Chief Bast

Bartokk Insectoid creatures with a hive mind, the Bartokk are legendary for their relentless and resourceful assassin squads. They pursue their targets until they achieve success; even if one of them is cut in two, both halves are capable of continuing to accomplish the group goal. The black-shelled Bartokk have greenish-blue blood, a tough exoskeleton, and razor-edged claws. Some two dozen years after the Battle of Yavin, a Bartokk squad tried to assassinate the grandmother of Jedi academy student Tenel Ka, Queen Ta'a Chume, but the young Jedi Knights thwarted the attempt. [YJK]

Barukka The sister of the evil Gethzerion, she is one of the Witches of Dathomir. Barukka was cast out from the Singing Mountain clan after giving in to evil urges. But while living in a cavern called Rivers of Stone, she started to cleanse herself in order to rejoin her clan. She was called upon to help lead Luke and Han into the Imperial prison complex on the planet in order to make off with parts essential to repair the *Millennium Falcon.* [CPL]

barve A six-legged beast of burden. [TJP]

Basic Based on the tongue of the human inhabitants of the Core Worlds, this language has become common throughout the galaxy. Basic first emerged as the language of diplomacy and trade during the Old Republic. [SWRPG, SWSB, SWRPG2, HESB]

Basilisk One of Admiral Daala's four Star Destroyers, it suffered severe damage during a battle with Moruth Doole's forces near Kessel, but was later repaired. The *Basilisk* was eventually destroyed in the Cauldron Nebula as it prepared for a suicide mission to Coruscant. It was caught in the explosive wave as Kyp Durron used the Sun Crusher to cause all seven stars in the nebula to go nova. [JS, DA]

Basilisk, Battle of A clash during which Jedi Master Sidrona Diath was killed. [DLS]

Basilisk war droid *See* war-mount

Baskarn An inhospitable jungle planet in the Outer Rim, it is home to an Alliance starfighter outpost that made guerrilla strikes into Imperial territory. Advanced Base Baskarn was built into a mountainside, surrounded by a thick jungle of razor-sharp plants and deadly predators. The planet is the homeworld of the Yrashu, a Force-sensitive species of green primates who exist in peaceful harmony with their environment. The primitive Yrashu carry ceremonial maces made from the roots of the hmumfmumf tree. Animal life includes flying jellyfish, which drift above the tree canopy and snare birds and rodents in their tentacles. Other creatures include water snakes, edible mmhmm butterflies, and the fierce horned hrosma tiger, which hunts through the use of the Force. [SWAJ]

Bast, Chief The chief personal aide to Grand Moff Tarkin aboard the Death Star, he rarely underestimated his enemies. Chief Bast learned cunning and patience by hunting big game as a youth, but died when the Rebels destroyed the Death Star during the Battle of Yavin. [CCG]

Bast Castle A remote and heavily defended structure, it was Darth Vader's stronghold and private refuge on the planet Vjun. It was later the headquarters of Darkside Executor Sedriss and the Emperor's elite force of Dark Jedi. [DE2]

Bastra, Gil A former Corellian Security officer, he had worked with Corran Horn and his father, Hal, in the security force. Gil Bastra later assisted Corran and two other members of Rogue Squadron by giving them false identities so that they could escape the Imperials. Bastra died in captivity after interrogation by Kirtan Loor aboard the *Expeditious.* [BW]

Batcheela An older female Ewok, she is the mother of Teebo and Malani. [ETV]

battle analysis computer A computer system used by the Alliance, it analyzes variables of enemy vessels such as position, firepower, speed, maneuverability, and shield strength

Battle wagon

to project the course of battle. The prototype of the battle analysis computer (BAC), developed by General Jan Dodonna, was tested by Luke Skywalker at Bakura. [TAB]

battle dogs *See* neks

Battle of Yavin A modified Imperial customs frigate, it is frequently used by the New Republic to conduct covert operations throughout the galaxy. [BW]

battle wagon This huge Ewok war machine designed by Erpham Warrick was restored by his great-grandson Wicket. The wagon has four large wheels and a prodigious battering ram topped by the skull of a bantha. [ETV]

Bavo Six A truth drug used in interrogation, it comes in an unnecessarily long needle that adds to the psychological pressure. While Bavo Six is used mainly by Imperials, the drug is also for sale on the open market. [CRFG, CCG]

Bdu, T'nun The captain of a Corellian supply ship, the *Sullustan*, Bdu was intercepted by Admiral Daala on his way to Dantooine. The admiral found maps and information on the Rebel Alliance in the data banks of the ship, then destroyed it. [DA]

beamdrill A heavy tool well suited for mining, it uses a high-intensity pulsing to pulverize rock. [HLL]

beam tube An antique handheld weapon, it is powered by a backpack generator. [HLL]

Bearus A humanoid who was leader of the once-powerful carbonite mining guild in the Empress Teta system some 4,000 years before the Galactic Civil War. [DLS]

Beast-Lord An honorific bestowed upon the traditional leader of a group of Onderonian beast-riders. [TOJ]

beast-riders Ancient Onderonians who, cast out of the great walled fortress of Iziz, learned to tame and ride the great beasts from the Dxun moon. [TOJ]

Beauty of Yevetha A corvette, it was a ship in Nil Spaar's Black Eleven Fleet. It was destroyed by New Republic forces during the blockade of Doornik-319. [BTS, SOL]

Beedo A relative of Greedo, he took the bounty hunter's place in Jabba the Hutt's gang after Han Solo killed Greedo at the Mos Eisley cantina. [RJ]

Beggar's Canyon The Tatooine valley, formed by the confluence of at least three rivers millions of years earlier, was Luke Skywalker's training ground. Here he and friends pushed their flying skills by racing skyhoppers through deep and twisted alleys, sometimes engaging in mock dogfights. Skywalker often hunted womp rats while flying his T-16 full out. Beggar's Canyon is the site of Main Avenue, which goes straight for nearly two kilometers before making a sharp angled turn—Dead Man's Turn—to the right. Another feature is the Stone Needle, a slender vertical rock with a narrow slot in the top lined with jagged stone "teeth." Only the most experienced pilots can fly through it without crashing. [SW, SWR, SOTE]

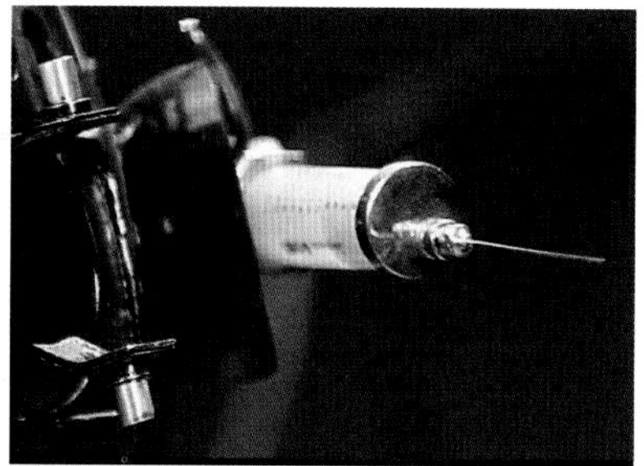
Bavo Six

Behn-kihl-nahm, Chairman Chairman of the Defense Council of the New Republic Senate, he is a staunch ally of Chief of State Leia Organa Solo. He keeps Leia informed of happenings in the Senate and various plots against her from within the Republic, advising her on suggested courses of action. Despite his power and stature, he is unwilling to make unilateral decisions and is most concerned with restoring peace and harmony to the galaxy. [BTS, SOL]

Belden, Eppie The wife of Senator Orn Belden, Eppie became a major operative in the resistance to Imperial takeover of Bakura, helping sabotage Imperial operations by hacking their computers. She later suffered from dementia induced by Imperial operatives using tiny poisonous creatures, but recovered after Luke Skywalker taught her Jedi mind techniques. [TAB]

Belden, Orn The Senior Senator of Bakura, he was an open dissident and Rebel sympathizer who helped Princess Leia Organa bring Bakura into the Rebel Alliance. [TAB]

Beggar's Canyon

beldons Balloonlike Bespin creatures, they are giant gas bags that metabolize the natural chemicals in the planet's atmosphere. The small electric fields that surround beldons act as a kind of radar to warn of approaching intruders. Hunting beldons is illegal because they give off Tibanna gas as a waste product. [GG2, ISWU]

Beldorion the Hutt A massive, but not obese, Hutt measuring twelve meters long, he was the power on Nam Chorios until the arrival of Seti Ashgad, who usurped him and took his house and treasure. Both Beldorion and Ashgad were in the thrall of Dzym, a mutant droch. The Hutt was extremely vain and reveled in being called such things as Beldorion the Splendid and Beldorion of the Ruby Eyes. At one point, Beldorion trained as a potential Jedi. His downfall came when he engaged Chief of State Leia Organa Solo in a lightsaber duel, and she killed him. Leia had only recently practiced and honed her lightsaber skills with Callista. [POT]

Bel Iblis, Garm The senator from the Corellian system, he was one of the three founders of the Rebel Alliance, along with Mon Mothma and Bail Organa. But he and Mothma didn't get along, so for most of the Galactic Civil War Bel Iblis was a sort of rogue Rebel, using his private force to strike at Imperial targets of opportunity.

For Bel Iblis, it was a personal as well as a political fight. He had opposed Senator Palpatine's growing influence, and when Palpatine declared himself Emperor, he had stormtroopers round up the Iblis family. The senator escaped, but not before being forced to watch the execution of his wife and children. He contacted Mothma and Organa and the three wrote the Corellian Treaty, which unified the resistance against the Empire.

Bel Iblis, a brilliant military strategist and tactician, was no match for Mothma in her ability to inspire the masses and unite divergent interests. Organa was a calming influence on both other leaders, but when he was killed in the destruction of Alderaan by the first Death Star, relations between Mothma and Bel Iblis deteriorated. He accused her of wanting to merely supplant Palpatine and rule

Garm Bel Iblis

the galaxy as Emperor. After Bel Iblis refused one of Mothma's military orders and she dismissed him, he took many loyal troops and established a hidden mobile base known as Peregrine's Nest, from which he conducted a hit-and-run campaign against the Empire.

While he was still leery of Mothma after the establishment of the New Republic, he saw that his greatest fears about her weren't true. So when Han Solo came to ask his help in trying to regain the legendary *Katana* fleet of Dreadnaughts (Bel Iblis's own fleet consisted of six of them already), he pitched in. Then Princess Leia Organa Solo convinced Bel Iblis to return to the New Republic. When Mon Mothma asked Bel Iblis to help in the defense of Coruscant against the attack by Grand Admiral Thrawn, he agreed and helped turn the tide of the battle. Bel Iblis has become a much admired and respected Republic leader once again. [DFR, DFRSB, LC]

Belsavis A world of volcanic rift valleys separated by kilometers of icy glaciers, Belsavis is in the Ninth Quadrant near the Senex sector. The planet's core heats steam-filled rifts and feeds hot springs on the surface. Some of the cities within the rifts are covered by enormous light-amplification domes that support a vast network of hanging gardens and growing beds. The vine-coffee and vine-silk grown here account for 30 percent of Belsavis's total economy.

The gangly, short-lived Mluki species are representative of Belsavis's original population. The rift valleys were largely jungle until the Brathflen Corporation, Galactic Exotics, and Imperial Exports arrived and began cultivating cash crops. The quiet community of Plawal lies between steep cliffs of red-black rock and is run by Jevax, a Mluki who is Chief Person of Plawal. Rock benches leading up to the cliff walls provide a narrow foundation for homes and orchards. A thick sulfurous mist permeates the valley and can restrict visibility to just a few meters.

About one hundred years ago, Jedi Master Plett built a house and laboratory in the Plawal rift that served as a safe haven for Jedi and their families. Some eighteen years before the Battle of Yavin, the Emperor commissioned the battlemoon *Eye of Palpatine* to wipe out the Jedi enclave, but the ship never arrived. The Emperor's small backup force of interceptors bombed Plawal but were wiped out by Belsavis's Y-wings, and the Jedi departed for places unknown after erasing all knowledge of their presence from the minds of the city's inhabitants. Han and Leia Organa Solo visited Belsavis eight years after the Battle of Endor and uncovered a plot by Roganda Ismaren, a longtime spy and onetime mistress of the late Emperor Palpatine, to forge a military alliance with the Senex Lords. [COJ, TJP]

beltway A popular mode of transportation in the crowded inner cities of highly urbanized planets, these moving platforms with seats are a speedy and safer alternative to landspeeders and skyhoppers. [HLL]

Belvarian fire-gnats Small insects that blink red and green, these fire-gnats have a tendency to swarm. [SOTE]

Bendone The Howler Tree People, who speak an unusual ultrasonic language, live on this planet. Some nineteen years after the Battle of Endor, Chief of State Leia Organa Solo met with representatives from the Howler Tree People on Coruscant. [YJK]

Bengat It is this water-covered planet that the Aruzan dancer Manaroo once rafted during an intense storm. [TBH]

Ber'asco Leader of the Charon death cult, he was also commander of the spacecraft *Desolate*, which was biologically engineered in the strange dimension called otherspace. The cult believes that the extermination of all life in the galaxy will lead to a long-awaited enlightenment. [OS]

Berchest This Borderland Regions planet was a major tourist attraction during the Old Republic, mainly because of its largest city, Calius saj Leeloo, the City of Glowing Crystal. The natural wonder was sculpted out of a single giant crystal created over countless millennia by the salt deposits left by the bloodred waters of the adjacent Leefari Sea. The Clone Wars and the rise of the Empire squelched tourism, but Berchest became one of the largest centers for Imperial trade in the Anthos sector. Even after Emperor Palpatine's death, the planet remained friendly to remnants of the Empire. Grand Admiral Thrawn led the New Republic to believe that he would use Calius as a transfer point for his clone soldiers, and Luke Skywalker went to the planet to investigate. [LC]

Beruss, Doman Senator Doman Beruss from Illodia was chairman of the Ministry Council of the New Republic. At the height of the Yevethan crisis, after Han Solo had been captured, he submitted a petition of no confidence in Chief of State Leia Organa Solo. When Leia asked him to withdraw the petition, he said that he would gladly do so "on your promise that you will not carry the war to N'zoth to rescue a loved one or avenge a casualty."

The other Doman Beruss was a flaxen-haired female who was given her older relative's name out of respect. She represented Corellian exiles in the formative stages of the New Republic at its Provisional Council. She spoke in favor of retaking Coruscant from the remaining Imperial forces led by Ysanne Isard. [BTS, SOL, TT, WG]

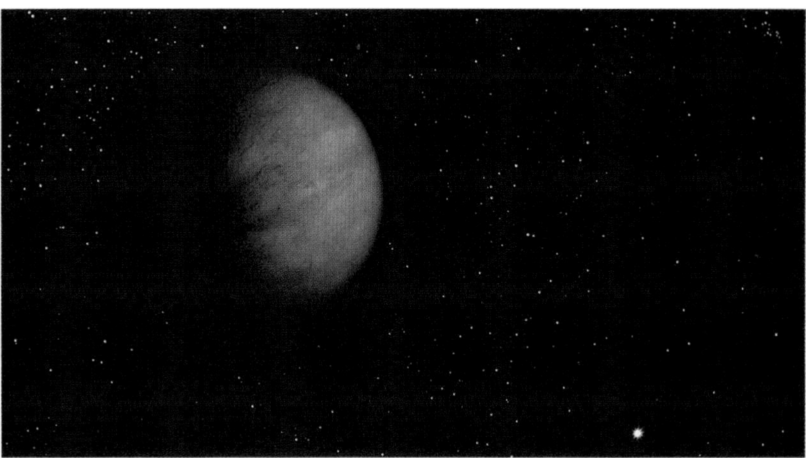

Bespin

Bespin The outermost planet in a system of the same name, Bespin is a gas giant about 118,000 kilometers in diameter that rotates every twelve standard hours. It is the site of a floating mining colony, Cloud City, once run by smuggler and Rebel hero Lando Calrissian.

Bespin's solid metal core is surrounded by a thick layer of liquid rethen. Above that is Bespin's colorful cloud layer, which extends only 1,000 kilometers into the heart of the planet. The Life Zone, in which humans and Bespin's life-forms can survive, is a thirty-kilometer-deep band inside the cloud layer. Plant life there consists of vast colonies of floating algae, and animal life includes predatory velkers, batlike rawwks, and the kilometers-wide, jellyfishlike creatures called beldons. The clouds are also home to a small herd of saillike Alderaanian thrantas.

Naturally occurring Tibanna gas, which is a useful hyperdrive coolant, can be found in Bespin's cloud layers and is excreted by beldons. Spin-sealed Tibanna gas is used in boosting the firepower of blasters.

Many years ago, Lord Ecclessis Figg constructed the first floating settlement of Bespin near the planet's equator. Expansion eventually turned it into the vast metropolis of Cloud City. Construction materials came from Miser, the innermost planet of the Bespin system. Cloud City is more than sixteen kilometers in diameter and at its peak housed nearly 5.5 million inhabitants. The highest levels house casinos and nightclubs, while the lowest generally have factories and production plants. The seedy, corrupt environs of Port Town are found on the middle levels.

Massive repulsorlift generators keeping the city afloat also draw spin-sealed Tibanna gas from the lowest levels of the planet's atmosphere. The gas is sent to the city's refineries, where it is pressurized, purified, and frozen into carbonite blocks for storage and sale. Ostensibly, Figg & Associates Ltd. manufactures Tibanna gas for use as a hyperdrive coolant. In reality, the company has long sold spin-sealed gas to weapons manufacturers not affiliated with the Empire.

Most of the city's industrial work is handled by a large population of Ugnaughts (originally from nearby Gentes) belonging to the Irden, Botrut, and Isced tribes. The Storm Guard weather watch keeps an eye on Bespin's atmosphere from Kerros's Tower (the highest point on Cloud City), and security is handled by the city's Wing Guard. A hollow wind tunnel runs through the center of the city.

Years ago the Jedi Master Djinn Altis instructed his students, including Geith and Callista, from a Jedi training platform hidden in Bespin's clouds. The smuggler Lando Calrissian managed to become Baron Administrator of Cloud City after winning the rights from Baron Raynor in a sabacc game. During his tenure Calrissian made the droid EV-9D9 his security chief, and the psychotic robot destroyed one-quarter of Cloud City's droid population before being discovered. EV-9D9 escaped aboard the hijacked Mining Guild cutter *Iopene Princess*. Calrissian also established a new group of Commando pilots to defend Cloud City. Later, Darth Vader used the city in a vain attempt to trap Luke Skywalker. Calrissian helped his friends escape Vader's ambush, and the city was subsequently seized by the Empire.

Rogue Squadron pilot Rhysati Ynr, a Bespin native, was forced to flee Cloud City with her family when Imperial forces arrived. Six years later, the Imperial garrison at Bespin was used by Grand Admiral Thrawn in his war effort against the New Republic. Two years after that, Luke Skywalker returned to Bespin to recruit Streen, an independent prospector who used the Force to sense gaseous eruptions from the lower cloud levels, into his new Jedi academy. [ESB, ESBN, LC, JS, HEE, SWB, COJ, GG2, ISWU, TJP, RS]

Bessimir Located fifteen parsecs from Coruscant, the planet is orbited by two moons. Twelve years after the Battle of Endor, the New Republic's newly commissioned Fifth Fleet underwent a live-fire training exercise code-named Hammerblow at Bessimir. Under the command of the Dornean General Etahn A'baht, the Fifth Fleet's A-wings first destroyed Bessimir's communications and sensor satellites. Bessimir's planetary defensive batteries and main starfighter base, housed on the alpha moon, were then collapsed by penetration bombs. Finally, a New Republic Star Destroyer acted as bait for a hypervelocity gun on the far side of the alpha moon while K-wing bombers penetrated the gun's shields with flechette missiles. This successful mission was the first operational readiness test for the Fifth Fleet. [BTS]

Bestine system When the Empire decided to open a high-security base in this system, the entire population of Bestine IV was evacuated to make room. Alliance pilot Jek Porkins was among them; he had learned his piloting skills by hunting sink-crabs on Bestine IV's rocky islands in his T-16 skyhopper. Kestic station, a free-trade outpost, was located near the Bestine system until eliminated by the Star Destroyer *Merciless*. Alliance pilot Biggs Darklighter defected to the Rebellion along with his ship, the *Rand Ecliptic*, during a mission to the Bestine system. The Alliance

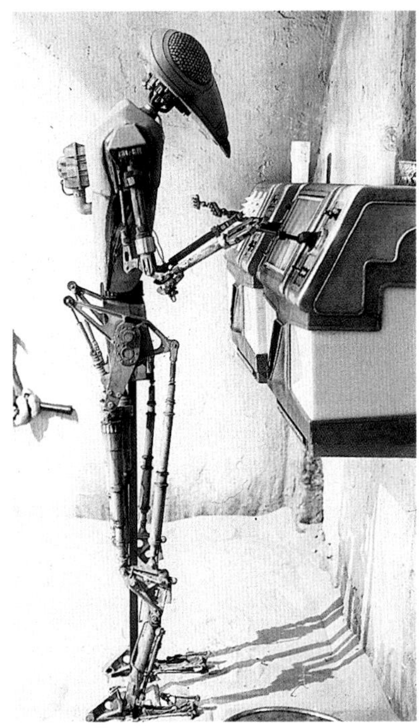

BG-J38

cruiser *Defiance* barely survived a surprise attack from the Star Destroyer *Immortal* near Bestine IV. A later attack on the Rebel flagship *Independence*, just prior to the Battle of Yavin, also led to a narrow escape for the Alliance. [GG1, MTS, FP]

Bestine township A primarily farming community on the planet Tatooine, west of the Mos Eisley spaceport, it was also the seat of Imperial control on the planet. [SWN, TMEC]

Bethal This planet's primary exports include apocia hardwood, which takes two centuries to mature and is used in the making of luxury furniture. Sections of Bethal include the Altoona and Dora Prefectures. Soon after the Battle of Yavin, Bethal was infested by swarms of giant termites called greddleback bugs. Several attempts have been made to contain the nearly two hundred swarms that are moving across Bethal's southern continent and threatening to wipe out the planet's apocia industry for generations. [SWAJ]

Bextar system Located deep within the Velcar Free Commerce Zone in the Pentastar Alignment, the system consists of four gas giants orbiting a pale yellow sun. A thriving gas-mining operation, run by the Amber Sun Mining Corporation, is scattered across the planets' many moons. The labor force is mainly Entymals, who have green exoskeletons and make excellent pilots. [SWAJ]

BG-J38 A spindly droid with an insectlike head, the robot spent much time in the court of Jabba the Hutt. It was an expert at hologames, often playing against the criminal kingpin or one of his top cronies. [RJ]

Big L Spacer slang for the speed of light. To "cross the Big L" means jumping to lightspeed. [HSE]

Biitu Once a lush and peaceful agricultural world, it underwent an eco-disaster when a droid known as the Great Heep built an Imperial fuel processing plant with a moisture eater that turned the grasslands brown. But the Biituians—green-skinned, bald humanoids—were saved when R2-D2 managed to destroy the Great Heep in the early years of the Empire. [TGH]

Bilar An unusual species from the tropical planet Mima II in the Lar system, the Bilar look a bit like one-meter-tall teddy bears without fur. Perpetual grins on the faces of Bilars may be a sign of very low intelligence. But when they come together and form a group mind, or claqas, seven Bilars have the intelligence of a genius; there are even reports of ten-member claqas. While intelligent, claqas have unpredictable personalities. [GG4]

Bilbringi A lifeless star system filled with rocky worlds rich with heavy metals, it was most well known as

Bilar

Bith

the site of the Imperial Shipyards of Bilbringi—heavily defended orbital platforms where Imperial warships were assembled. The shipyard was the site of the New Republic's last battle with Imperial forces under Grand Admiral Thrawn. Heavily damaged, the facility was then abandoned. [LC]

Bildor's Canyon A canyon in the Dune Sea on Tatooine. [TMEC]

Bille, Dar Nil Spaar's second in command for the Yevethan raid on the Empire's shipyard at N'zoth, he was later primate, or proctor, of the Yevethan command ship *The Pride of Yevetha*, formerly the *Intimidator*. Dar Bille gave the orders for the Yevethan attack on Koornacht settlements. [BTS, TT]

Bimm Peaceful and friendly, with a love of heroic stories, these short inhabitants of Bimmisaari average about 1.1 meters tall and are half-covered in fur. No weapons are permitted in Bimm cities. The people love to shop and haggle for a bargain. [HE, HESB]

Bimmisaari A temperate planet covered by swaying asaari trees, it escaped most of the fallout of the Rebellion and the Empire's cruel reign because of its isolated location. It is inhabited by a species of short, half-furred, yellow-clad creatures called Bimms and governed by a planetary council. It was while on a diplomatic mission to the planet five years after the Battle of Endor that Princess Leia Organa Solo and Luke Skywalker were the target of a kidnap attempt by a Noghri commando team. [HE, HESB]

binary load lifter These primitive labor droids were designed to move heavy objects in spaceports and warehouses with their strong mechanical claws and built-in propulsion systems. [SW]

bioscan A hardware-software system that scans objects, it can prepare a report on a target's biological makeup, origin, age, and other factors. [SOTE]

Bith These evolved humanoids with huge foreheads and hairless craniums come from Clak'dor VII in the Colu system, Mayagil sector. Their large, lidless black eyes and receding noses complement the baggy facial folds beneath their jaw lines. They make good entertainers and musicians, since the Bith are able to perceive sounds as precisely as other species perceive color. They play everywhere from the grandest palaces to out-of-the-way cantinas in spaceports such as Mos Eisley. [SW, GG4, TMEC]

Bithabus the Mystifier A Bith, he was a famous magician who long performed at Hologram Fun World's Asteroid Theater. [QE]

Bix A sleek droid, it teamed with Auren Yomm of the planet Roon in the Colonial Games during the early days of the Empire. [DTV]

Bjornsons A family of moisture farmers on Tatooine, they were against the plans of Ariq Joanson to draw up maps of peace with the Jawas and Tusken Raiders. Their son had been killed, presumably by Sand People. [TMEC]

BL-17 A droid owned by Boba Fett during the Empire's early days, it looked like C-3PO but with the bounty hunter's olive-drab and yellow colors. BL-17 carried a rectangular blaster. [DTV]

Black Asp An Imperial *Interdictor*-class cruiser about 600 meters long, it was involved in a skirmish with Rogue Squadron at Chorax as the squadron attempted to capture the *Pulsar Skate*. Because of its gravity well generators, the *Black Asp*, under the command of Uwlla Iillor, pulled the squadron out of hyperspace as the Rogues were heading for a new base at Talasea. A fast and furious battle ensued, and Rogue Squadron put the cruiser to flight. [BW]

Black Four Code-name used by Imperial pilot DS-61-4 during the Battle of Yavin. [CCG]

Black Ice The pride of the Imperial Replenishment Fleet, this cargo ship was five times the length of an *Imperial*-class Star Destroyer. *Black Ice* carried nearly one billion metric tons of starship-grade fuel cells, or more than one year's power supply for a complete Imperial battle fleet. [BI]

Blackmoon Covered with frozen lava tubes and rocky fissures, this moon of Borleias has no native life-forms. Blackmoon was also the code-name for Rogue Squadron's assault on the Imperial stronghold at Borleias. [BW]

Black Nebula Located in the region of space known as Parfadi, this nebula separates the planets Arat Fraca and Motexx. The Black Nebula contains two immense neutron stars and is considered to be unnavigable. [SOL]

Black Nine A former Imperial Navy name for the orbital shipyard at ILC-

Black Sun

905, it was taken over by Yevethan forces. [TT]

Black Sun The largest criminal organization in the galaxy, it was led with ruthless cunning by Prince Xizor. Its members numbered in the tens of thousands and it had a spynet that was better than the Empire's own. Black Sun's lieutenants were known by the honorific "Vigo" from the old Tionese for "nephew." They were responsible for entire star systems, but even their power and wealth did not guarantee them immunity from Xizor's wrath. On Imperial Center, high-ranking officers of the local police, the Army garrison, and even Imperial Navy Intelligence were on retainer, and any news that might be of interest to Xizor would find its way to his desk almost immediately. [SOTE]

Black Three A code name used by Imperial pilot DS-61-3 during the Battle of Yavin. [CCG]

Black Two A code-name used by Imperial pilot DS-61-2 during the Battle of Yavin. [CCG]

blase tree goat These lethargic goatlike creatures hang from the limbs of huge trees that cover Endor's forest moon. [ETV]

blaster The most commonly used weapons in the galaxy, blasters come in a vast range of sizes, styles, and firepower. Blasters fire beams of intense light energy that—depending on the intensity setting—can do everything from stun to vaporize. The color of the energy bolts may also vary, but they invariably produce a smell similar to ozone. Models range from concealed pistols and sporting blasters to heavy blasters and blaster rifles. Some of the largest blasters come with shield generators and targeting computers and require a crew to operate. [SW, ESB, RJ, SWRPG, SWRPG2]

blastonecrosis A bacta allergy, it is marked by fatigue and loss of appetite. Approximately 2 percent of those exposed to the deliberately contaminated bacta Lot ZX1449F developed blastonecrosis. Attempts to treat it with uncontaminated bacta resulted in death. [BW]

blast-rifle An ancient weapon of choice for the beast-riders of Onderon some 4,000 years before the Battle of Yavin, it fired bolts of laser energy. [TOJ]

blba tree Broad-trunked, jagged-branched trees, they grow amidst waving lavender grasses on the savannas of Dantooine. [DA]

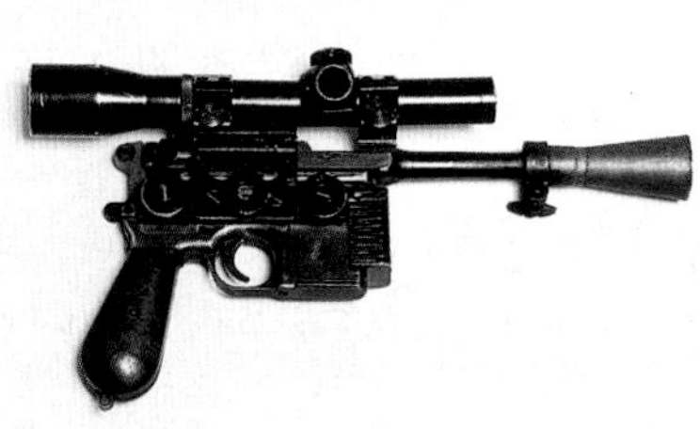
Blaster

Blaster rifle

Blessings A Dreadnaught in Nil Spaar's Black Eleven Fleet. [BTS]

Blissex, Walex With Jan Dodonna, he co-designed the Alliance's A-wing starfighter. [SWSB]

blizzard walker *See* All Terrain Armored Transport

blob race Much like a steeplechase, this bizarre race of protoplasmlike gelatinous blobs through a course of obstacles (from fine mesh screens to a bed of nails) is a major betting sport in Umgul City on the planet Umgul. The syrupy masses, primarily grayish green but laced with bright hues, roll, slither, and ooze their way through. Cheating on the races is punishable by death. [JS]

Blockade Runner (Rebel) A ubiquitous Corellian corvette, the now well-known (Rebel) Blockade Runner was a registered Alderaanian consular ship, *Tantive IV*. Commanded by Captain Antilles, it was frequently used by Senator Leia Organa for her covert espionage activities on behalf of the Rebel Alliance.

The *Tantive IV* played a major role in the Alliance destruction of the first Death Star. After intercepting secret Imperial codes while on a relief mission to Ralltiir, Leia learned about the construction of the Death Star over the distant prison world of Despayre. She later received the actual technical readouts from other spies, and then raced to distant Tatooine hoping to find General Obi-Wan Kenobi and convince him to help lead the Rebel Alliance. But a double-agent—apparently the silver droid U-3PO—hid a tracking beacon aboard

Blockade Runner (Rebel)

the Blockade Runner, because the Imperial Star Destroyer *Devastator* emerged in Tatooine system space immediately behind the ship.

The *Tantive IV* was armed with six turbolaser cannons and had heavily reinforced shields, but it was still no match for the firepower of an Imperial Star Destroyer. Luckily, Leia had hidden the Death Star plans in the astromech droid R2-D2, which, along with its companion C-3PO, used an emergency escape pod to blast down to Tatooine's surface and continue the search for Kenobi. In an elaborate ruse perpetrated by Darth Vader after he destroyed the *Tantive IV*, all personnel aboard were reported killed in a deep-space disaster. In truth, only Leia escaped execution, although she was held as a prisoner aboard the Empire's Death Star battle station.

Corellian pirates who use other Corellian corvettes have nicknamed their capital ships Blockade Runners because of their speed and primary use to circumvent galactic authorities. [GSWU, SWSB, SWR, SWVG]

Bloor, Melvosh A Kalkal academic, he was a professor of Investigative Politico-Sociology at Beshka University. His colleague, Professor P'tan, had traveled to the palace of Jabba the Hutt but never returned, so Melvosh Bloor went to investigate. He was led on by Jabba's annoying pet, Salacious Crumb, and eventually brought before Jabba, who promptly fed him to the rancor. [TJP]

blope Swamp creatures much like hippopotamuses, they live in the marshes of Endor's forest moon. [ETV]

Blue, Sinewy Ana A beautiful smuggler, she ran the sabacc games on Skip One in the asteroid field known as Smuggler's Run. Han Solo won a lot of credits in her games and also once lost his *Millennium Falcon* there. Sinewy Ana Blue piloted a Skipper, modified for her personal needs, with a wider cargo bay and larger crew quarters than normal Skippers, which are used mainly for transit in Smuggler's Run. Blue's Skipper was used during Han Solo's investigation into the Senate Hall bombing on Coruscant and the rescue of Lando Calrissian from the crime lord Nandreeson.

Later, Solo learned that Blue was part of a smuggling operation that sold former Imperial goods to the Dark Sider Kueller for use in his reign of terror against the New Republic. She had become seduced by the enormous number of credits she got through the operation. Kueller later ordered her to bring Solo to Almania, where he was to be used in a blackmail demand against New Republic Chief of State Leia Organa Solo. Davis, a man whom Blue secretly loved, was killed in one of Kueller's bombing attacks, and she then told Solo everything she knew about the operation. When Solo learned that Kueller was behind the Coruscant bombing he rushed to Almania, and Kueller paid Blue double her fee even though she had only inadvertently delivered Solo to him. [NR]

Blue Desert People A race of reptile-like creatures with bloodred eyes, sharp black teeth, and a long black tongue, they live on the planet Dathomir. [CPL]

Blue Leader The designation at the Battle of Endor for Rebel Captain Merrick Simm, commander of one of four Alliance battle wings in the attack on the second Death Star. Blue Leader died when his fighter was caught in an explosion that destroyed an Imperial communications ship. [RJ, RJN]

Blue Max A tiny experimental computer packed with more memory and abilities than that of most starship systems, it was stolen from the Empire and ended up in the hands of an outlaw tech named Doc. Doc, aided by his daughter, Jessa, who lived with him on an asteroid in the Corporate Sector, reprogrammed Blue Max and gave it a chirpy personality. Deep blue and built in the shape of a cube, the computer-droid processed data that it scanned through a glowing red photoreceptor and interpreted through a speech synthesizer. Doc and Jessa mounted Blue Max in the chest cavity of a mobile labor droid, a BLX-5 model that Jessa nicknamed Bollux. Together, Blue Max and Bollux accompanied Han Solo and Chewbacca on their many adventures in the Corporate Sector before the latter two joined up with the Rebellion. [HSR, HSE, HLL]

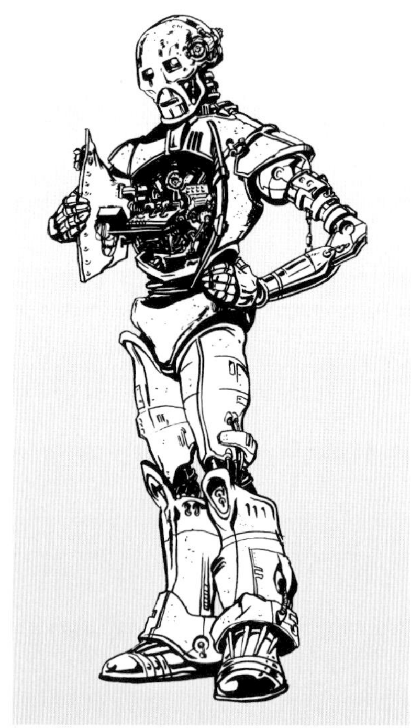

Blue Max and Bollux

blue milk A nutrient-rich beverage, it is common in moisture farming communities. Rumored to have medicinal qualities, it is popular in cantinas among those who can't hold their juri juice. The drink gets its name from the main ingredient and the color it becomes after mixing. [CCG]

Blue Nebula A seedy bar and restaurant, it is located in the Manda spaceport. [DTV]

Bluescale *See* Sh'tk'ith, Elder

Blue Squad The designation for one of many A-wing starfighter squadrons in the Rebel Alliance's Blue Wing during the Battle of Endor. [RJ]

Blue Squad The designation for the twenty-four Bothan pilots and gunners assigned to Luke Skywalker to attack the *Suprosa*, a freighter carrying an Imperial computer containing information about a top-secret project that turned out to be the second Death Star. The Blue Squad pilots had little experience flying their Y-wing fighters, and unknown to the Alliance, the *Suprosa* had augmented shields and hidden weapons. The freighter's cannons destroyed two Y-wings and their crews, and a shielded missile exploded in the midst of the squad, destroying another four ships before the freighter was captured. [SOTE]

Blue Squadron The designation for one of the New Republic's X-wing fighter battle groups, it participated in the Battle of Calamari. [DE]

Blue Wing The designation for Blue Leader's second-in-command at the Battle of Endor, as well as the name of the battle wing itself, Blue Wing was responsible for coordinating several of the battle groups. [RJ]

blumfruit A delicacy to Ewoks, this large, red, egg-shaped berry grows on Endor's forest moon. [ETV]

blurrg The beast of burden for the marauders of Endor, these stupid creatures are controlled with spiked chain bridles. The marauders ride the blurrgs and use them to pull carts. [ISWU]

Bnach The site of an Imperial prison colony, this scorched planet with a cracked surface provides plenty of rock quarries for prison labor. [PDS]

Bnar, Master Ood An ancient Jedi who possibly evolved from a treelike species on the planet Myrkr, Bnar became gatekeeper of a Jedi Holocron, or teaching device, belonging to Master Arca Jeth. When summoned by Jedi Master Thon, Bnar proclaimed that Nomi Sunrider would be a powerful Jedi. Several thousand years later on the planet Ossus, Bnar reawakened in time to help save a young woman with powers of the Force, Jem, and sacrificed himself to destroy the evil Imperial military Executor Sedriss. [TOJ, DE2]

boarding craft A term applied to small vehicles used to ferry personnel or cargo between spaceships or between ships and planets or space stations. [HSR]

Bocce One of the many languages used on Tatooine, it is also spoken in the Albarrio sector capital world of Aris. [SW, RM]

Boda, Ashka An old Jedi who held a valued Jedi Holocron, Boda was caught and executed by the Emperor during the Jedi extermination that took place as the Empire was being established. [DE]

Master Ood Bnar

Bodgen R2-D2 and C-3PO visited this swampy moon during the early days of the Empire. Pirate captain Kybo Ren held Princess Gerin of Tammuz-an on a freighter hidden on the moon. [DTV]

body-wood From a tree of the same name, this incredible wood resembles the flesh of forest dwellers from the planet Firrerre. Known as the finest wood in the Empire, its polished surface is the palest pink, shot through with scarlet streaks and gleaming with light like cut and polished precious stones. Some say that body-wood trees have a certain intelligence and "cry" when they are felled; adding to the story is the fact that the cut wood does bleed a scarlet liquid. [CS]

bofa A sweet, dried fruit, bofa is considered a delicacy. [TSW]

Bogen, Senator A New Republic Senator and member of the Senate Defense Council, he is a human from the planet Ralltiir. [BTS, SOL]

bogey A glittering, formless creature that inhabits the spice mines of Kessel, bogeys are hunted by Kessel energy spiders. [JS]

Bogga the Hutt *See* Great Bogga the Hutt

BolBol the Hutt A Hutt crime lord, he controlled much of the Stenness System. [TMEC]

Boldheart A New Republic frigate, it had encountered the mysterious ghost ship called the Teljkon vagabond, took its picture, and fired across its bow before being crippled by return fire and jumping into hyperspace. [BTS]

Bollux A battered one-hundred-year-old BLX-5 labor droid, its systems were upgraded by Jessa, the daughter of an outlaw tech named Doc who lived on an asteroid in the Corporate Sector. Bollux's chest cavity was modified so that it could carry Blue Max, a powerful but tiny computer housed in a deep-blue cube. Both had been programmed with personalities, Bollux pleasant and low-key, Blue Max more high-strung and chirpy. For several years the duo accompanied Han Solo and Chewbacca in their adventures in the Corporate Sector, including the rescue of Doc from a penal colony and Han's search for a long-lost treasure ship. [HSE, HSR, HLL]

boma beasts A species of monstrous, wingless beasts, they thrived in the forests of Onderon 4,000 years before the Galactic Civil War. [TOJ]

B'omarr monks A mysterious religious order that built a large monastery centuries ago on Tatooine, they believe that by cutting themselves off from all sensation, they can focus and enhance the power of the mind and thus journey through inner space. The B'omarr monks rarely speak to one another; often, entire lectures are boiled down to one phrase or word. The further that monks pursue their calling, the less they speak or even move. And when a B'omarr reaches the final stage of enlightenment, the monk is helped to shed his or her body—surgically. The monk's brain is removed and placed in a nutrient-filled jar, finally able to spend eternity in perpetual thought. If these enlightened brains have some business to attend to, mechanical spider-

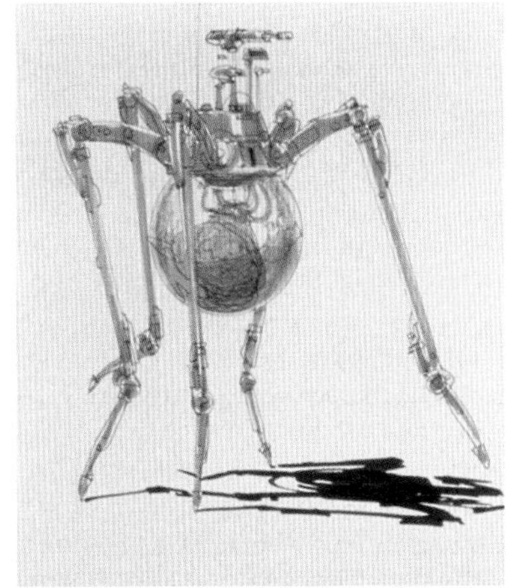

B'omarr monk

Bondo

like walking legs are available. B'omarr monks still live in the lower levels of what had been their monastery, which in recent years had become the palace of arch-criminal Jabba the Hutt. [ISWU]

bomats Small carnivorous pests, they are native to the planet Aruza. [TBH]

Bomlas An infamous bartender on Skip One, he was a three-armed Ychytonian who bet and lost his fourth arm in a particularly savage sabacc game. Still, even with only three arms, Bomlas remained the fastest bartender Han Solo had ever seen. [NR]

Bonadan A parched yellow sphere crisscrossed by rust stripes because of heavy soil erosion, this planet has long been one of the Corporate Sector Authority's most important factory worlds and busiest ports. Bonadan industry has thrived at the expense of ecology, since any plant life on the surface that wasn't intentionally destroyed has disappeared due to overmining, pollution, and neglect. A densely populated planet, Bonadan houses many sentient species from all over the galaxy. The world is covered with factories, refineries, docks, and shipbuilding facilities in ten spaceports, the largest of which is Bonadan Spaceport Southeast II. This sprawling city is composed of low permacite buildings on fusion-formed soil. Mountains are located northwest of the city along with a massive weather-control station.

Weapons are banned on Bonadan; being caught with one by the omnipresent weapons detectors is grounds for immediate arrest. The modified protocol droid C-3PX managed to assassinate the brother of Vojak on Bonadan by using concealed, internal weaponry. Han Solo was involved in a high-speed swoop chase during an early visit to Bonadan. The smuggler Shug Ninx scavenged a kilometer-long shaft for a Death Star prototype from a Bonadan industrial junkyard, then had it installed as an entrance to his repair facility on Nar Shaddaa. Six years after the Battle of Endor, a faulty timer manufactured on Bonadan resulted in the failure of a Galaxy Gun projectile to explode, which gave the New Republic high command enough time to evacuate their base on Nespis VIII. [HSR, DE, D, CSSB, EE]

Bondo A chubby, easygoing chief of the nomadic Jinda tribe, he usually wears a red tunic. [ETV]

Bonearm, Dace An unsavory human bounty hunter, he traveled with an IG-model assassin droid. [TMEC]

bonegnawer A flying meat-eater that lives in the desert wastelands of Tatooine, it has been known to crush rocks with its toothy jaws. [SWN]

Booldrum A cousin of Gerney Caslo, Booldrum owns a library in Hweg Shul on Nam Chorios that is bigger than that of strongman Seti Ashgad. [POT]

Boonda A "reformed" Hutt, Boonda was the target of a droid rebellion led by C-3PO. Threepio was not only reprogrammed to be brave, but also programmed with misleading information implicating Boonda in a plot to plant secret explosives in droids. But the true perpetrator of the plot was exposed and Threepio and R2-D2 managed to beat a hasty retreat. [D]

Boonta A planet famous for its speeder races in oval tunnels, it also houses a huge scrap yard that is a graveyard for damaged ships. [DTV]

Bordal Located in the Taroon system on the outer edges of the Rim, this world was involved in a devastating war with its sister planet Kuan for nearly twenty years until the conflict was suddenly ended by the intervention of the Empire. Natives are referred to as Bordali. [TSC]

Borderland Regions A militarized zone that lies between space ruled by the New Republic and Imperial space, it is claimed by both but controlled by neither. It is thus a prime area for major battles between the two sides in a Galactic Civil War that refuses to die. Systems in the Borderlands make every effort to stay neutral. [HE, HESB]

bordok Ewoks use this medium-sized ponylike species as beasts of burden. [ETV]

Borealis Chief of State Leia Organa Solo used this flagship on her private mission to Nam Chorios. [POT]

Borealis, Rima Princess Leia Organa Solo's trusted aide, Winter, used this name in her role as an Alliance intelligence agent assisting members of Rogue Squadron during their undercover operation on Coruscant. [BW]

Borgo Prime A large, honeycombed asteroid, it is home to a seedy spaceport and disreputable trade center. Borgo Prime was gradually hollowed out over the years by mining operations, and the asteroid's tunnels and excavations are now filled with space docks, prefabricated buildings, and gaudily lit storefronts. In the business district, located in the asteroid's core, is Shanko's Hive, a cone-shaped tavern owned by an insectoid barkeep. The tall structure is protected by its own atmosphere field, and filled with burning candles, incense, and flaming bog-pits. Lando Calrissian's Corusca gem broker was located on Borgo Prime, and Luke Skywalker and Tenel Ka contacted the broker in an attempt to learn who had purchased an important shipment. [YJK]

Borin, Danz A cocky gunner and bounty hunter, he maintains a residence on the smugglers' moon of Nar Shaddaa. He tracked down Han Solo and the *Millennium Falcon* to try to collect the bounty from Jabba the Hutt, but just as he was about to step up and claim his prey in the Mos Eisley cantina, another bounty hunter in Jabba's employ—the Rodian named Greedo—beat him to the punch. That was a good thing, Danz Borin learned just a minute later, as Solo killed Greedo with a blaster shot. [CCG]

Danz Borin

Borleias (Blackmoon) The fourth planet in the Pyria system, it is a steamy blue-green world with a single dark moon that gives the system its Alliance code-name of Blackmoon. The only inhabited world in the system, Borleias lacks most valuable natural resources and passes through a dense meteor shower once each year. But Borleias sits at a favorable hyperspace crossroads. The Old Republic first established a small base there to plot runs to the Corporate Sector and elsewhere. The Empire eventually took control of the base and beefed up its defenses. Because the Pyria system is near the galactic core, the Rebel Alliance chose to capture Borleias and make it their key to hitting Coruscant, some three years after the Battle of Endor. During their first attack, however, the Alliance greatly underestimated the defensive strength of the Blackmoon installation and was soundly defeated. On the return mission, Rogue Squadron pilots torpedoed a power conduit at the end of a rift valley to help bring down the base's shields, while a commando team captured the facility from the ground. This attack was a success, and Borleias became the new operations and staging base for Rogue Squadron. [BW]

Borlov This planet is the homeworld of the timid, feathered creatures known as Borlovians, who communicate in whistles. Borlovians live in a social structure that values stability. Few have ever left their home cities, much less their planet. [SWAJ]

Bormea sector Located in the Galactic Core, the sector is one half of the Ringali Shell. Its prestigious and ancient worlds include Corulag, Chandrila, and Brentaal, and it is also the site of the intersection of the Perlemian Trade Route and the Hydian Way. [SWAJ]

borrat Fearsome rodentlike creatures from Coruscant, they can grow to two meters long. They have tusks, spines, armored flesh, and claws that can dig through ferrocrete. Fortunately, they tend to be solitary, avoiding contact whenever possible. [BW]

Bortras Birthplace of Jedi Master Jorus C'baoth, this planet is in the Reithcas sector. [DFR]

Bortrek, Captain The gruff, swaggering, and frequently drunk commander of the ship *Pure Sabacc*, he picked up the droids R2-D2 and C-3PO after they had been set adrift in an escape pod shot from Princess Leia's ship during the Nam Chorios crisis. Captain Bortrek had looted one planet of several million credits in cash, bonds, and valuables. Rather than deliver the droids, he decided to hold them hostage. [POT]

Bos, Lieutenant He was the flight leader of the ferry operation that was transferring Han Solo when Solo was taken hostage by Yevethan forces. [TT]

BoShek A human smuggler and starship technician, BoShek often flew hot ships for a Tatooine order of monks. After beating Han Solo's time for the Kessel Run, he destroyed four pursuing TIE fighters and became the object of a large-scale manhunt on Tatooine. He masqueraded as a religious figure at the monastery and eventually escaped in a landspeeder that previously had been owned by Luke Skywalker. It was BoShek who referred Ben Kenobi to Chewbacca when the old Jedi was looking for transport off Tatooine. [TMEC]

Bosph Home to four-armed beings known as Bosphs, the planet was nearly destroyed by the Empire in a devastating orbital bombardment. Natives keep a record of their galactic travels by tattooing elaborate star maps on their skin, and are skilled at playing a complex musical instrument, the Bosphon Geddy. [SWAJ]

BoShek

Bossk A Trandoshan bounty hunter, this three-fingered, three-toed reptiloid long specialized in hunting down Wookiees—sometimes enslaving them for the Empire, sometimes skinning them for their pelts. He had several run-ins with Chewbacca and Han Solo, and each time was humiliated when they made good their escape from him and other bounty hunters. Bossk heeded Darth Vader's call to rendezvous with other bounty hunters aboard Vader's Super Star Destroyer, the *Executor*. Later, he and other finders tried to wrest the prize catch—Han Solo in carbonite—away from Boba Fett.

Bossk exuded a brackish smell, which kept most beings from getting too close. He had supersensitive eyes

Bossk

and thus hated light. His flight suit, obviously designed for a human pilot, was too small for a proper fit. His ship, the *Hound's Tooth,* was a light freighter modified for Wookiee hunting. Bossk was bested by Han Solo years earlier when Solo intervened to rescue about a dozen Wookiee slaves—including Chewbacca—that Bossk had hunted down. Much later Bossk accompanied the Wookiee bounty hunter Chenlambec and his human assistant to Lomabu III, a swampy world that the Empire decided to use as a Wookiee prison camp. Bossk was tricked and captured by the duo and turned over to Imperial Governor Io Desnand, who planned to have him executed and turned into a reptile-skin dress for his wife. [ESB, TBH]

Bot Mysterious and mute, he was the hooded henchman of Captain-Supervisor Grammel on Circarpous V. [SME]

Bothan A species from Bothawui, Bothans are renowned as the best spies in the galaxy. Prior to the Battle of Endor, Bothan spies captured an Imperial freighter carrying highly classified data about the second Death Star. New Republic Councilor Borsk Fey'lya is a Bothan who was born on the Bothan colony world of Kothlis. [RJ, HE, DFR, LC, DFRSB]

Bothan spynet The Bothan spynet is second to none, with operatives throughout the galaxy. Even though the spynet was used mainly in support of the Rebel Alliance, the Empire and the criminal underworld occasionally found the spynet useful for their own purposes. The spynet's work often put its members at great personal risk. Once, half a squad of Bothan pilots and gunners was killed in an attempt to wrest a top-secret computer—containing vital information about the Empire's second Death Star—away from an Imperial ship. [SOTE]

Bothawui Despite being the base of the Alliance-friendly Bothan spynet and the site of a token presence by Imperials, this cosmopolitan and well organized world has always been considered neutral territory since it has been an active hub for operatives of every stripe. Streets in the major cities are clean and wide and lined with tall buildings built of a natural glittering stone. New Republic Councilor Borsk Fey'lya has an estate of open, treeless savanna land. Rogue Squadron pilot Peshk Vri'syk was a graduate of the Bothan Martial Academy. After Vri'syk's death and the capture of Coruscant, the female Bothan Asyr Sei'lar was made a pilot in Rogue Squadron. General Laryn Kre'fey, operating on incomplete intelligence data, planned Rogue Squadron's disastrous first attack on Borleias. Familial bonds are very strong in Bothan society. The native language is Bothan. [SOTE, WG, KT]

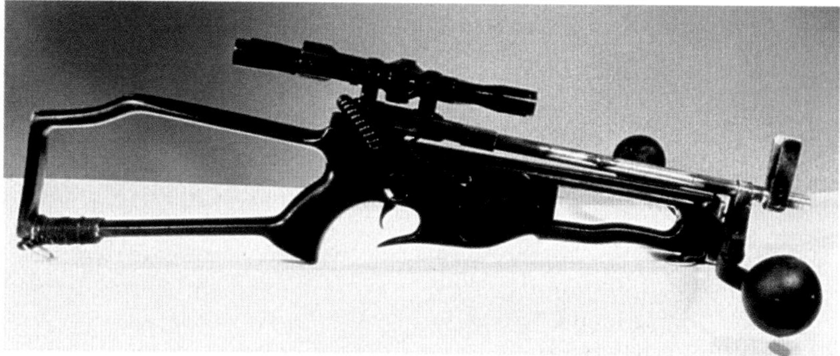

Bowcaster

Botor Enclave A group of worlds, including the frozen planet Kerensik, it formed its own protective federation during the turmoil and constant warfare in the six years following the Battle of Endor. [DESB]

boulder-dozer A vehicle that uses laser scorchers to vaporize large rocks and other debris. [QE]

bounce This casino game involves a gun and a moving target suspended inside an enclosed space. To score, hits on the target must be reflected, or bounced, off the enclosure. Direct hits don't count. [HSR]

Boushh

Bounty Hunters' Creed Widely observed by even the most unethical of bounty hunters, the creed states that no hunter can kill another hunter or interfere with another's hunt. (TBH)

Bounty Hunter's Guild A group that provides a loose sense of organization to its members, it monitors their activities, puts them in touch with one another, and upholds the Bounty Hunters' Creed. (TBH)

Boushh A Ubese bounty hunter, the well-cloaked Boushh did a lot of contract work for the galaxy's most powerful criminal organization, Black Sun. But when he demanded more credits than had been agreed to in advance for a job, he was eliminated. That made it possible for Princess Leia Organa to use Boushh's clothes and helmet as a disguise several times, once even gaining access to the palace of Jabba the Hutt. [RJ, SOTE]

Bovo Yagen The third star targeted for destruction during the starbuster crisis some fourteen years after the Battle of Endor. The system contains either one planet with a population of eight million or two planets with twelve million inhabitants, according to varied sources. The star was saved at the last instant when Centerpoint Station, the starbuster weapon, was disabled by a planetary repulsor beam. [AS, SAC]

bowcaster This crossbow laser weapon is handcrafted by Wookiees. It fires quarrels of energy. [SW, ESB, RJ, TBH]

Bozzie An old Ewok widow, she is Paploo's mother and Kneesaa's aunt. At times she can be overbearing and pushy. [ETV]

Bpfassh A double planet with a complex system of moons in the Bpfassh system, it is located near Praesitlyn and Sluis Van in the Sluis sector. During the Clone Wars some Bpfasshi Dark Jedi created trouble throughout the sector, and a Jedi task force including Jorus C'baoth was formed to oppose them. One Dark Jedi made it as far as Dagobah before his death. Because of the insurrection, most Bpfasshi today dislike all Jedi. Bpfassh was the target of a hit-and-fade attack by Grand Admiral Thrawn, whose true target was the Sluis Van shipyards. It was also the site of an attempted abduction of Leia Organa Solo. [HE, HESB, LC]

Brachnis Chorios The outermost world of the Chorios systems in the Meridian sector, it appears ice-green and lavender from space. Nine years after the Battle of Endor, Leia Organa Solo made a secret visit to a point near Brachnis Chorios's largest moon to meet with Seti Ashgad of Nam Chorios. [POT]

brachno-jag Typically used for torture and painful execution, a hundred of these small, carnivorous animals can strip a being's bones in five or six hours. [TJP]

Bragkis This planet is home to a million-credit betting parlor. Han Solo once spent some time there. [SOL]

Brakiss Taken by the Empire from his mother as an infant because of his nascent Force powers, he was one of a handful of Imperials who tried to infiltrate Luke Skywalker's Jedi academy on Yavin 4. Unlike the others, however, Brakiss had a true talent for the Force. Skywalker seemed to successfully turn him from the dark side, and Brakiss became a student. But when, as part of his Jedi training, he was sent on a journey in which he had to confront himself—much as Luke had done during his own training on Dagobah—Brakiss emerged terrified and angry. He left the Jedi academy, never to return.

A physically stunning man—Princess Leia Organa Solo once called him one of the most handsome men she had ever seen—Brakiss was endowed with blond hair, blue eyes, flawless skin, a perfectly straight nose, and thin lips. After his experiences on Yavin 4, he became administrator of droid manufacturing factories on the moon of Telti. He helped Dark Sider Kueller plant explosives in a new series of droids that were sent throughout New Republic worlds.

Brakiss remained filled with anger, irrationally continuing to blame his mother for allowing him to fall into the hands of the Empire when he was an infant. His mother aided Luke Skywalker on the planet Msst and led him to her son on Telti, where Luke had to face his former student in battle. Luke discovered that Brakiss had voluntarily stopped using the Force, and Kueller was using him as a pawn to trick Luke to come to Kueller's homeworld of Almania. After Brakiss's tampering with droids was discovered, he was attacked by astromech droids that had been subverted and was driven from Telti.

About six years later, under the Second Imperium's attempt to reestablish the power and reach of the old Empire, Brakiss was put in charge of the Shadow Academy, a twisted mirror image of the Jedi academy. The purpose of the academy, based on a large space station, was to train a new army of Dark Jedi to take over the galaxy. The station was outfitted with self-destruct mechanisms, and Brakiss wasn't permitted to leave the academy. He lived under the constant threat that the mechanisms would be triggered by the mysterious leaders of the Second Imperium. When the station was moved to the orbit of Coruscant and launched attacks on the New Republic, Jaina Solo figured out how to disable its cloaking device. The station managed to escape to a new hiding place, but the leaders of the Second Imperium, fed up with Brakiss's failures, detonated the explosives aboard and he was killed. [NR, YJK]

King Empatojayos Brand

Brand, Commander Commander of Task Force Aster, part of the New Republic's deployment of the Fifth Fleet at Doornik-319, he served from aboard the star cruiser *Indomitable.* [SOL, TT]

Brand, King Empatojayos A Jedi and ruler of the Ganathians, he had been severely injured in a battle with Darth Vader. Only a prosthetic suit of his own design kept him alive. King Empatojayos Brand was excited to hear that Vader had been vanquished and joined the Alliance fight against the second clone of Emperor Palpatine. He sacrificed himself to save the baby Anakin Solo from being filled with the essence and mind of the Emperor's clone. His death snuffed out the Emperor's will once and for all. [DE2, EE]

Brandei, Captain An Imperial officer and one of the few senior officials to survive the Battle of Endor, he commanded the Imperial Star Destroyer *Judicator*, part of Grand Admiral Thrawn's personal armada. A confident and daring officer, Captain Brandei is never reckless, believing that it is more important to live to fight another day than to die spectacularly in a lost cause. [DFR, DFRSB]

Brasck A two-legged reptilelike Brubb from the planet Baros, he once worked as a mercenary for Jabba the Hutt. But since the crime lord's death, Brasck has become head of a major smuggling ring in the Borderland Regions, which are controlled by neither the New Republic nor the Imperials. Ruthless—slavery and kidnapping are part of his repertoire—he remains constantly in motion aboard his ship *Green Palace* because he fears being ambushed. Brasck wears personal armor and carries several hidden weapons. [HE, HESB]

Brashaa A humanoid follower of Lord Hethrir, the former Imperial Procurator of Justice who kidnapped the children of Han and Leia Organa Solo. [CS]

Brathis, Moff Tragg Brathis was commander of an Imperial battle fleet supposedly stationed at the planet N'zoth in an alliance with the Duskhan League. The alliance turned out to be a Yevethan sham designed to scare the New Republic. [TT]

Brattakin, Movo An acquaintance of the villainous Olag Greck, he managed—after nearly being murdered by Greck—to merge his mind with the metallic body of his droid aide, B-9D7. He then reprogrammed C-3PO and turned the golden robot into the fierce leader of a droid rebellion aimed at toppling an enemy, Boonda, a reformed Hutt crime lord, and taking over a sector of the galaxy. Brattakin also planted a "sleeper bomb" in one of Threepio's legs. But R2-D2 managed to foil the plot and rescue C-3PO, who reverted to true form. [D]

breath mask Connected to a miniature portable life-support system, the mask fits over the nose and mouth to provide oxygen or another life-sustaining gas. The mask can also be built into body armor, such as that worn by Darth Vader. [ESB, RJ]

Brebishems These dancers have long snouts and wide, leaf-shaped ears that they can flap. Their soft, wrinkled mauve skins seem to meld together when they touch each other. [CS]

Breil'lya, Tav A Bothan, he has served as a loyal top aide to New Republic Councilor Borsk Fey'lya, and is sent on the most important fact-finding missions. But unlike his boss, Breil'lya isn't subtle when playing politics. On a trip to the planet New Cov, he tried to convince former Old Republic Senator Garm Bel Iblis to ally with Fey'lya's faction. But Breil'lya's maneuvering was eventually exposed to the full Provisional Council. [DFR, DFRSB]

Brentaal Located in the Bormea sector of the Core Worlds, the wealthy planet sits at the strategic intersection of the Perlemian Trade Route and the Hydian Way. Brentaal is a dry planet whose eight continents are separated by small salty oceans. Most available land is covered with starports, industrial facilities, and thriving trade markets that serve its 65 billion inhabitants. [SWAJ]

Briggia A blue planet that was the site of a Rebel Alliance base, it was the first target of the Empire's Operation Strike Fear prior to the Battle of Yavin. Briggia was successfully evacuated. [FP]

Bright Hope One of the last Rebel transports to leave in the evacuation of the planet Hoth, it was severely damaged by the bounty hunters Zuckuss and 4-LOM as it attempted to escape. However, they had a change of heart, rescued the ninety passengers and crew aboard the *Bright Hope*, and safely transported them to Darlyn Boda. [TBH]

brights Slang used by X-wing pilots when referring to advanced Imperial TIE fighter models. [BW]

Brigia A poor, retrogressive planet in the remote Tion Hegemony, it is inhabited by tall, purple-skinned humanoids. The University of Rudrig has helped Brigia in its bid for development, a move opposed by the planet's rulers. The university hired Han Solo to deliver the necessary teaching supplies, but the Brigian government attempted to intervene. About two years before the Battle of Yavin a small group of colonists left Brigia and founded New Brigia, a chromite mining operation located just within the borders of the Koornacht cluster. [HLL, BTS]

Briil twins Former associates of Han Solo, they were killed in a fight with an Imperial cruiser on patrol near the Tion Hegemony. [HSR]

Brill, Governor Foga An Imperial warlord, he is ruler of Prakith. [BTS, SOL]

Brilliant A New Republic Star Destroyer and part of the Home Fleet, it was assigned to shadow the Yevethan/Duskhan embassy ship *Aramadia* in orbit around Coruscant. [BTS]

B'rknaa Living-rock creatures of the moon Indobok, they guard high-energy crystals that animate them and give them a kind of group mind. [D]

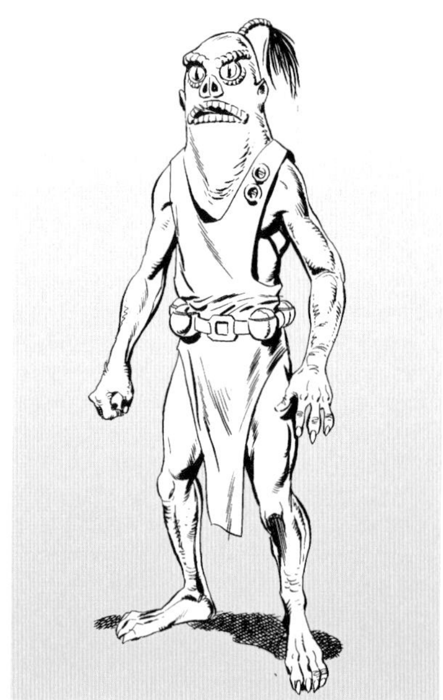

Brubb

Bruanii sector Not far from the Tungra and Javin sectors, it was the site of a Mugaari space depot. The Mon Calamari cruiser *Lulsla* was stationed there. Following the Battle of Hoth, the cruiser was the launch point for Rebel Alliance strikes on Imperial space platform D-34 in the Javin sector. The *Lulsla* was destroyed by the Empire in a retaliatory strike. [TSC]

Brubb Two-legged reptilelike creatures from the planet Baros, they have pitted and gnarled dirty yellow skin, ridged eyes, and flat noses. They are about 1.6 meters tall and can change color. Males of the species usually have a solitary outcropping of coarse black hair projecting from the tops of their heads. Social creatures, they treat visitors to Baros as esteemed guests. [GG4]

Brusc, Captain The captain of the Star Destroyer *Manticore*, he served under the command of Admiral Daala. He was killed and his starship destroyed during the Battle of Calamari. [DA]

Bryx This planet was conquered in the early days of the Empire after an effective but ultimately unsuccessful defense. The tactics used by Bryx's Governor Carigan are now known widely as the Carigan Defense. [WAJ]

Bseto system A system that contains the white dwarf star Bseto, which is orbited by the uninhabited planets Bseto I and Indikir, it also includes the huge Lweilot Asteroid Belt and the frozen planet of Sarahwiee, site of a once-secret Imperial research facility. [SWAJ]

BT-445 One of many scanning crews aboard the Death Star, it was selected to search the *Millennium Falcon*. The crew's two members were knocked unconscious by Han Solo and Chewbacca. They were taken to the infirmary, where they died when the Death Star exploded. [CCG]

Bubo (Buboicullaar) A creature that looked like a cross between a frog and a dog, it had bulging eyes and a protruding lower jaw. Buboicullaar, or Bubo as he was known, was a spy and assassin in the palace of Jabba the Hutt on Tatooine. He frequently consulted with the B'omarr monks and plotted to kill Jabba. Few suspected that he was intelligent at all, and Bubo did nothing to contradict that assumption. Bubo foiled an assassination attempt by Ree-Yees by eating a detonation link necessary for a bomb that Ree-Yees had been constructing. After Jabba's death, Bubo's brain was removed by the B'omarrs, leaving him free to contemplate the mysteries of the universe unfettered by his body. [RJ, TJP]

Budpock Located in the Meridian sector, the planet has long been one of the Rebel Alliance's most loyal supporters. One of Budpock's main ports is Dimmit Station. Nine years after the Battle of Endor, two New Republic cruisers were dispatched from the Orbital Station on Durren to investigate a possible breach of the truce between Budpock and Ampliquen. Two more cruisers from the naval base on Cybloc XII were sent to deal with a pirate fleet from Budpock. [POT]

Bubo (Buboicullaar)

bugdillo Multilegged crustaceans, they are a delicacy on the planet Eol Sha. [JS]

Bulano serpent A creature without teeth, claws, or poison, it can blow itself up to five times its normal size, making it look fiercer and more dangerous than it actually is. [SOTE]

bulk freighter Cargo ships that are the workhorses of the galaxy, they haul goods from planet to planet. Lightly armed bulk freighters depend on hyperdrive engines and well-patrolled space lanes to steer clear of trouble. Most of these small to mid-sized ships are independently owned. [SWSB]

Bunji, Big A former associate of Han Solo, he didn't repay a debt in a timely manner, so Solo strafed his pressure dome with blaster fire. Bunji barely escaped with his life. [HSE]

Bur A commander in Dark Sider Kueller's army on Almania, Bur was the leader's favorite. [NR]

Bureau of Operations A division of Imperial Intelligence, it handled all major covert operations. Among its missions: infiltration, counterintelligence, and assassinations. [ISB]

burnout Spacer slang for the loss of power in a ship's engines. [ESBR]

Burrk A onetime stormtrooper, he deserted in the confusion following the Battle of Endor and survived through shady dealings and illegal activities. [DS]

butcherbug A multilegged armored creature of Dagobah, it spins a tough, microfine cord between the roots of gnarltrees. When a flying creature blunders into this trap, the cord slices it into pieces that the butcherbug devours. [ISWU]

Butcher of Montellian Serat This is the name by which many beings referred to the Devaronian spy Kardu'sai'Malloc after he indiscriminately shelled the city of Montellian Serat. [TMEC]

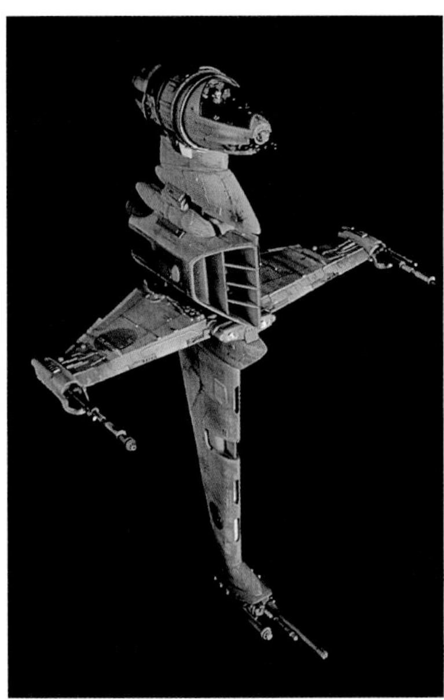

B-wing starfighter

B-wing starfighter Admiral Ackbar, with the help of skilled Verpine shipbuilders, personally designed the B-wing spacecraft. It played a major role in the Rebel Alliance victory at the Battle of Endor. One of the Alliance's most heavily armed starfighters, the B-wing in effect is one long, flat wing with an unusual "floating" cockpit at one end and one of the ship's three ion cannons at the other. About midway on the wing two airfoils extend out during combat, giving the ship the appearance of a cross, or with some imagination, the letter *B*. Because of its unusual gyrostabilization system, the cockpit remains steady while the rest of the ship rotates around it, giving the pilot a stable field of fire. Designed to go head-to-head against much larger Imperial ships and disable them, the B-wing has also been used for heavy assault strikes against Imperial facilities and as an escort for X-wing and Y-wing fighters. In addition to the ion cannons, there is a laser cannon mounted to the cockpit, two proton torpedo launchers, and two small blaster cannons. An enhanced model, such as the one Ackbar uses personally, has an expanded command module with room for a gunner. Along with other changes that have made the ship faster and tougher, this has substantially increased its combat success rate. [RJ, SWSB, SFS, SWVG]

Byblos A populous urban world in the Colonies region. Most of the planet's 164 billion inhabitants live in huge city towers, architectural wonders that soar up to 5,000 levels. Every tower has a specific purpose such as corporate, residential, or starport, and they are connected by tubeways. Byblos is a major manufacturing center for high technology and military equipment. [SWAJ]

Byss Home to the one-eyed Abyssin, the planet travels in an unusual figure-eight orbit between the binary stars of Byss and Abyss. Byss is a hot, arid planet, and temperatures reach their highest when the planet is orbiting directly between both stars, a time known as "the Burning." Most plant life on Byss utilizes extensive taproots to extract underground water, while animals rely on scattered oases and their own water-storing capabilities. The nomadic, violent Abyssin lead primitive lives, engaging in tribal wars and tending to their flocks of cowlike gaunts. [GG4]

Byss Formerly located in the heart of the Deep Galactic Core, the now-destroyed planet was Emperor Palpatine's private world and the center of his reborn Empire six years after the Battle of Endor. The secret planet was accessible only through certain encoded routes because of the difficulty of navigating through the dense mass of stars found in the Deep Core. Byss was an extremely pleasant world of plateaus and canyons seldom bothered by storms, groundquakes, or other violent phenomena. Microscopic life in the many lakes and rivers was nourished by the blue-green sunlight.

Years ago, Emperor Palpatine chose the world as his private retreat, and Imperial architects and engineers were commissioned to build him an opulent palace. Several million humans per month, lured by the rumors of a paradise planet, were allowed to emigrate to Byss—where the Emperor and his dark-side Adepts began feeding off their life energies. The planet's population reached almost 20 billion, and all outgoing communications were censored by security agents.

C-3PO (See-Threepio)

Byss was well-guarded against attack with powerful planetary shields, hunter–killer probots, and the Imperial Hyperspace Security Net. There were orbital dry docks for the massive World Devastators and, later, the Galaxy Gun.

The Imperial control sector covered most of one continent, and Palpatine's kilometers-high Imperial Citadel was at its center. The vast complex contained gardens, museums, the Emperor's Clone Labs, barracks for Imperial troopers, and a fully equipped dungeon; it was guarded by advanced turbolasers and dangerous monsters called Chrysalides or Chrysalis Beasts.

Following the Battle of Endor, the Emperor's spirit returned to Byss to inhabit a new clone body. Weakened by the difficult journey, Palpatine convalesced on Byss for six years before finally taking his revenge against the New Republic. Luke Skywalker attempted to learn the secrets of the dark side as the Emperor's apprentice after a Mandalorian prison ship delivered him to Byss. Later that year, Lando Calrissian and Wedge Antilles led an unsuccessful attack on the Imperial Citadel using a cargo of hijacked Viper Automadon battle droids. Soon after, in a battle near Onderon, Han Solo and a team of commandos hijacked the Emperor's flagship *Eclipse II* and brought it through hyperspace to Byss. R2-D2 steered the *Eclipse II* on a collision course with the Galaxy Gun, which accidentally fired a planet-destroying missile into Byss's core, destroying the Emperor's throneworld. [DE, DE2, DESB, EE]

Byss Bistro Located in the Imperial Freight Complex on the planet Byss, the cantina was on the outskirts of the Emperor's well-protected complex. Freighter crews and others flocked there to find food, drink, and entertainment while they waited for their ships to be unloaded. [DE]

C2-R4 (Ceetoo-Arfour) A low, round household droid with bulbs and boxy appendages hanging from his sides, he also has sharp, jagged teeth. Ceetoo-Arfour's specialties included meal preparation, catalytic fuel conversion, enzymatic compostion breakdown, chemical diagnostic programming, and bacterial composting acceleration. He is also a combination blender, toaster oven, and bang-corn air popper and can turn common garbage into a meal. After escaping from the Jawas on Tatooine, C2-R4 was discovered in the back alleys of Mos Eisley and adopted by the cantina bartender Wuher, who had him process the pheromones of the dead Rodian bounty hunter Greedo to make an especially potent drink. [TMEC]

C-3PO (See-Threepio) A golden protocol droid with one silver leg and the personality of a worrywart, he makes up half of the most famous robot team in the galaxy. Along with his squat companion R2-D2, C-3PO has had enough adventures to fill several lives since first being activated, even before teaming up with Luke Skywalker and the other heroes of the Rebel Alliance.

Not that C-3PO would be considered a hero in the classic sense. A bit stiff and awkward in his manner, somewhat effete in demeanor, and often overly negative in his outlook, the vaguely human-looking droid nevertheless has played a key role in many of the important events of recent galactic history. What sets him and Artoo apart is that they both have managed to avoid most of the regular memory wipes that droids usually undergo, thus allowing them to learn by experience and develop true personalities like those of sentient beings.

Threepio has specialized programming for human/droid relations, which he has skillfully—if at times annoyingly—applied in numerous crisis situations. His fluency in more than six million galactic languages—both creature and machine—is central to the key role he has often played in interpreting between species. His speech vocabulator allows him to vocalize his translations, tips on etiquette, and his thoughts on life in general, often expressed in the form of the odds against something succeeding.

C-3PO is a protocol droid with more than thirty secondary functions. He programmed converters and once ran a shovel loader for an entire month. He has served smugglers and racers, bar owners and crime lords, scoundrels and heroes. Due to hidden programming he wasn't aware of, Threepio once even led a brief droid rebellion. In recent years he also has played the role of part-time nanny and protector to Han and Leia Organa Solo's three children. Along with R2-D2 and the mechanic Cole Fardreamer, Threepio helped uncover Dark Jedi Kueller's terror scheme, which involved placing detonation devices in droids on Coruscant and throughout the New Republic. As part of the investigation, the group went to Telti, and Threepio and Artoo were forced to confront a terrifying gladiator-droid group known as the Red Terror.

Officially a human-cyborg relations droid, C-3PO is equipped with

C-3PX

sensory receptors. And he has developed a talent for embellishing and telling stories, something unusual for a protocol or diplomatic droid. So unusual, in fact, is his talent that some of his owners have taken to shutting him down at times because of his propensity to worry out loud, complain, or carry on endlessly about one thing or another in his slightly clipped accent.

C-3PO and R2-D2 are truly an odd couple. Threepio seems to talk down to Artoo or argue with him more often than not. And Artoo, with his own agenda, has a way of sending his companion into a state of high dudgeon. Despite their constant dust-ups, the droids are really best friends in every sense and depend on each other to survive in an often harsh galaxy.

At one time, the droids were in the service of the Royal House of Alderaan and eventually put aboard the *Tantive IV* while it was on a secret mission to intercept stolen Imperial data. The droids were given override orders that restricted all references to Princess Leia's presence aboard the ship; in Threepio's case, that seems to have activated a total memory block regarding the princess. When the ship was boarded by Imperial forces, Threepio followed Artoo—who was carrying the stolen Death Star plans—into an escape pod that landed on Tatooine. Both were captured by Jawas, who sold them to young Skywalker's uncle, Owen Lars. Thus began an unending series of adventures that made the two droids—often working apart—an integral part of the Rebel Alliance and its successor, the New Republic. [SW, ESB, RJ, SWCG]

C-3PX A protocol droid modified by crime lord Olag Greck to be an assassin droid, he looked just like C-3PO, except for an X marked on his forehead. But C-3PX took pity on C-3PO, who was pitted in a fight to the death in a droid arena, substituted himself for Threepio, and let himself be destroyed. [D]

C4-CZN ion field gun A large Imperial weapon, it is moved around on rollers. [TMEC]

C-9PO (See-Ninepio) A newer-model protocol droid that failed Jedi student Brakiss had memory-wiped and modified to serve him on the droid-manufacturing facility on Telti. Like many protocol droids, Ninepio often exhibited an annoying officiousness. [NR]

Cabbel, Lieutenant A graduate of the Officer's Candidate School on Carida, he served as first officer of the Imperial Star Destroyer *Tyrant*. His men described him as efficient, but also very ambitious and ruthless. [CCG]

Caelus A New Republic cruiser. [POT]

Cai A Mistryl Shadow Guard, she was involved in the botched transfer to the Empire of the Hammertong device—one of the long, cylindrical sections of the super laser for the second Death Star. [TMEC]

Lieutenant Cabbel

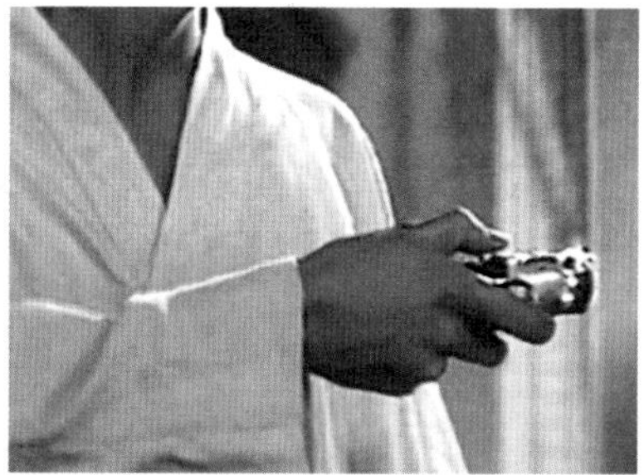

Caller

Cal A yellow star orbited by Tibrin, it is the homeworld of the Ishi Tib. [GG4]

Calamari *See* Mon Calamari

Calamari, Battle of During this fight, the cloned Emperor Palpatine's World Devastators inflicted tremendous damage on the watery home planet of the Mon Calamari. The gigantic Imperial war machines were eventually shut down by Luke Skywalker. [DE]

Calamarian *See* Mon Calamari

Calius saj Leeloo *See* Berchest

caller Small handheld transmitters, these devices summon droids. They also can turn restraining bolts on and off and thus are sometimes called restraining bolt activators. [SW, SWR]

Callista One of the loves of Luke Skywalker's life, she existed for years as a bodiless spirit that infused the gunnery computer on one of the Empire's experimental weapons, a space station called *Eye of Palpatine*.

A true beauty, Callista had lived with her family on the water world of Chad III, herding wander-kelp in a deep-water ranch. Strong in the Force, she partnered with Geith, who was also powerful. Both were killed in an attempt to destroy the *Eye of Palpatine*. But the Force, along with a strange power on the space station known as the Will, did not allow her spirit to perish. Instead, by inhabiting the computer, she kept anyone from activating the *Eye*'s deadly weapons, forcing the Empire to abandon the project.

Thirty years later, Luke boarded the *Eye* to destroy it forever with the help of two former students, Nichos Marr and Cray Mingla. Cray and Luke sensed Callista's presence, and Luke saw her in his dreams.

The dreams became reality when Callista communicated with Luke through the station's computers, aiding the three in their project to destroy the *Eye*. Nichos and Cray planned to sacrifice themselves in the attempt, but at the last moment Callista and Cray used their remaining Force strength to transfer Callista's essence into Cray's body and enter an escape pod that was rescued by Luke's ship. For the first time, a corporeal Callista was together with her love. But Callista had paid a big price, for she had lost all her Jedi skills and her ability to communicate with the Force. While that didn't matter to Luke, Callista felt it made her only half a person, and she began a long pursuit to regain her powers.

Callista crossed paths again with Luke nine years after the Battle of Endor, after she had tried to warn his sister, Chief of State Leia Organa Solo, to stay away from the planet Nam Chorios and a meeting with the evil Seti Ashgad. Callista helped Leia hone her lightsaber skills, which came in handy when Leia fought Beldorion the Hutt to the death. Luke and Callista parted once more, something they both knew they had to do despite the pain of separation. [COJ, DS, POT]

Callista

Calrissian, Lando Gambler turned city administrator and dashing scoundrel turned hero: Such are the inconsistencies that pepper the life of Lando Calrissian.

With the spirit of a soldier-of-fortune and the heart of a high-stakes player, Lando has had a kind of love-hate relationship with Han Solo for years—perhaps win-lose would better sum it up. For Han's ship, the *Millennium Falcon*, was owned and flown for years by Lando. In fact, before losing the *Falcon* to Han in a game of sabacc (the ship was destined to be lost and won several times again in sabacc games between the two rogues), Lando flew it on a year-long trip during which he searched for treasure on planets of the Rafa system, was nearly killed because of his consistent hot hand at every gambling table, and aided a persecuted species called the Oswaft. He was accompanied by a pilot droid he had won, Vuffi Raa.

Not long after losing the *Falcon*, Lando won something of great value in another sabacc game: Bespin's Cloud City, where he took over as Baron Administrator. Lando proved quite adept at both running the Tibanna gas-mining colony and using it as a cover for some of his more colorful activities, such as smuggling and secretly aiding the Rebel Alliance.

But Lando's luck ran out when Imperial forces led by Darth Vader visited. In order to set a trap to attract Luke Skywalker, Vader told Lando that he must detain Solo and his party. If he did, the Imperials would never bother Bespin again; if he failed, he could kiss his future goodbye. Feeling that he had no choice, Lando entrapped Han and Princess Leia. But Vader went back on his word and entombed Han in carbonite, entrusting him to bounty hunter Boba Fett. That convinced Lando to help the heroic Rebels. He ordered the evacuation of the city and fought back against Imperial forces, later rescuing a near-dead Skywalker from the very bottom of the floating city in the clouds.

Lando failed in one early attempt to snatch Han back from the bounty hunter, then aided in rescuing Leia from the head of the Black Sun crime syndicate, Prince Xizor. He later disguised himself as a guard for Jabba the Hutt, infiltrated Jabba's palace, and was in place when Luke rescued Han; Han returned the favor, saving Lando's life by snatching him from the maw of the Sarlacc in the Tatooine desert. For his valor, and in recognition of his skills at the Battle of Tanaab, prior to the Battle of Hoth, Lando was given the rank of general in the Alliance forces and helped lead the charge in the pivotal Battle of Endor. Piloting the *Falcon*, Lando, along with Wedge Antilles in an X-wing fighter, destroyed the Empire's second Death Star battle station.

Following the Rebel victory, Lando returned to private life, establishing a unique mining colony on the planet Nkllon to supply raw materials to the New Republic. But when Imperials stole the mole miners used in the operation for use in the Imperial attack on the important New Republic Sluis Van shipyards, Lando rejoined Republic forces and helped thwart the attack. Later he helped command the forces at the Battle of Calamari. Lando has gone back and forth between the roles of businessman and warrior—he was a leading member of a New Republic special forces team (the Senate Interplanetary Intelligence Network or SPIN) and Baron Administrator of Hologram Fun World, a dome-covered floating amusement park—but he always keeps busy. He has helped Skywalker find recruits for his Jedi academy, rescued Leia at least once more, gotten involved in several dubious money-making schemes, crashed at least two converted Imperial Star Destroyers, helped put down major threats to the New Republic, and won—and lost—a dozen fortunes. As long as there is a deck of sabacc cards nearby or adventure calls, Calrissian will never lead a dull life. [ESB, RJ, SWCG, COF]

Lando Calrissian

Cal-Seti This is the site of the docking port Ramsees Hed where, following the Battle of Yavin, Alliance agent Kyle Katarn placed a tracking device on a smuggling ship that led him to an Imperial robotics facility on Anteevy. [DF]

Camie A young woman who lived in Anchorhead on Tatooine, she was a close friend of Luke Skywalker. She frequented the Tosche power station along with her boyfriend, Fixer, and the young Skywalker. Her family grew hydroponics gardens underground, buying the water from Luke's uncle Owen Lars. [SWN, SWR, DS]

cannonade An exploding projectile weapon, it is fired by a crossbow. [TJP]

Cant, Devin A trooper aboard the first Death Star, he was an elite soldier trained in combat techniques and weapons skills. He augmented security personnel guarding Princess Leia Organa in Detention Block AA-23. He was killed in the line of duty when Han Solo, Chewbacca, and Luke Skywalker freed Leia. [CCG]

cantina *See* Mos Eisley cantina

Canu A deity worshipped by the primitive inhabitants of Circarpous V. [SME]

CAP An acronym for Combat Aerospace Patrol, it consists of Rogue Squadron's Flights One, Two, and Three. One flight guards an escape route at all times while the other two groups engage the enemy. [BW]

capital ship Any of a class of huge combat starships designed for deep-space warfare, such as Imperial Star Destroyers and Mon Calamari Star Cruisers, the ships are usually staffed by crews numbering in the hundreds or even thousands, have numerous weapons and shields, and often carry shuttles, starfighters, or other smaller offensive mobile weapons platforms in their huge hangar bays. [SWSB, SWRPG2]

Caprioril A once-tranquil world in the Galactic Core, it was the site of an infamous massacre when an assassin droid slaughtered 20,000 people at a swoop arena—including famous racer Ignar Ominaz—in order to murder Governor Amel Bakli. One-time top aide to Emperor Palpatine Mara Jade briefly worked under the name Marellis for a Caprioril swoop gang following the death of Palpatine. Caprioril was named a sector capital by the New Republic, and was besieged by Imperial forces during the Emperor's reappearance six years after the Battle of Endor. Around this time, Alliance historian Arhul Hextrophon survived an assassination attempt while visiting the planet. [DFR, SWS, DESB, SWAJ]

Captison, Gaeriel An Imperial Senator from Bakura during the final years of the Rebellion, she helped draft the Truce of Bakura, leading her planet and people to freedom. Gaeriel's parents were killed in the uprising that followed the Imperial invasion of Bakura, and she was raised by her aunt and uncle, Tiree and Yeorg Captison, the prime minister.

Bakura faced imminent danger when the reptilian Ssi-ruuk Imperium invaded. Imperial forces suffered heavy losses as they inflicted great damage on the Ssi-ruuk. As the battle raged, ships from the Rebel Alliance—fresh from victory at the Battle of Endor—arrived and offered aid to the Bakurans. Luke Skywalker helped write the truce under which Gaeriel's planet joined the New Republic. She went on to help her uncle restore Bakura and repair the damage inflicted by Imperial forces during their occupation. Gaeriel, who later married former Imperial officer Pter Thanas, herself was elected prime minister but was defeated in a succeeding election.

Some fourteen years after the truce, Luke Skywalker returned to Bakura to

Gaeriel Captison

borrow the planet's fleet for a mission in the Corellian system. The mission was ultimately successful, but half of the Bakuran cruisers were destroyed and Gaeriel Captison was killed. [TAB, AS, SAC, SWAJ, SWCG]

Captison, Yeorg The prime minister of Bakura, he was a figurehead under the Imperial occupation. Although he sympathized with the Rebel Alliance, he didn't want any more blood shed on his planet. After the destruction of the second Death Star and a truce between the Empire and the Alliance, he rejuvenated Bakura with the help of his niece, Gaeriel. [TAB]

Carbanti signal-augmented sensor jammer A sensor-jamming device, it was found by Lando Calrissian as part of the cargo of the *Spicy Lady*, the ship owned by a murdered smuggler named Jarril. [NR]

carbon-freezing chamber This device is used in the process of storing Tibanna gas in carbonite to preserve it while it is being transported over long distances. In the freezing process, the gas is pumped into the chamber where it is mixed with molten carbonite, then flash-frozen to cool the carbonite into a solid block. The gas is released later at its destination or at a processing center. Darth Vader ordered the modification of one chamber on Bespin's Cloud City so that he could freeze Luke Skywalker —and thus nullify his Force powers—to transport him to the Emperor. As a test, the process was tried on Han Solo, who survived the freezing process and was eventually freed from his trap. [ESB]

carbonite A strong but highly volatile metal used in the manufacture of faster-than-light engines and to preserve materials such as Tibanna gas. [ESB, DLS]

carbonite guild A tightly knit, arrogant, and ruthless group, the guild controlled the mining of raw carbonite in the Empress Teta system, a prime source of the volatile metal, some 4,000 years before the Battle of Yavin. [DLS]

Carconth A red super-giant star, it is the second largest and seventh brightest of all known stars in the galaxy. A supernova watch has been in place for the last 600 years. Twelve years after the Battle of Endor, the New Republic's Colonel Pakkpekatt arrived at Carconth aboard Lando Calrissian's *Lady Luck* in search of the missing Calrissian and his companions. But when the ship arrived, it was taken over by a slave circuit activated by Calrissian's beckon call. [TT]

Cardooine This world is home of fragrant Fijisi wood, used in the Imperial Palace on Coruscant and even in some spacecraft built on the planet. A virus first diagnosed on the planet is popularly called the Cardooine Chills. Its symptoms include congestion, coughing, fatigue, and body aches and pains. The symptoms usually disappear within two weeks, but there is a lingering weakness for perhaps another month. Once infected, the body develops an immunity to the disease. [LC, BW]

Cardua system With ore-rich asteroid belts, this system bordering the Xorth system supported many miners, who exported all their output to the Empire. [TSC]

cargo lifter These large airships—operated by a single pilot—are the workhorses that load and unload cargo and make short-distance hauls to storage facilities in other parts of a spaceport. The mechanical claws used by older cargo lifters have been replaced by tractor beams and repulsor technology. [HSR]

Carida One of several planets in the Carida system, it was a large, high-gravity world with a wide variety of terrain. It was the site of the Empire's most important stormtrooper training center. The planet was populated by humanoids who had thin limbs and heavy, barrel chests. The Imperial military training center included a main citadel surrounded by a tow-

Carbon-freezing chamber

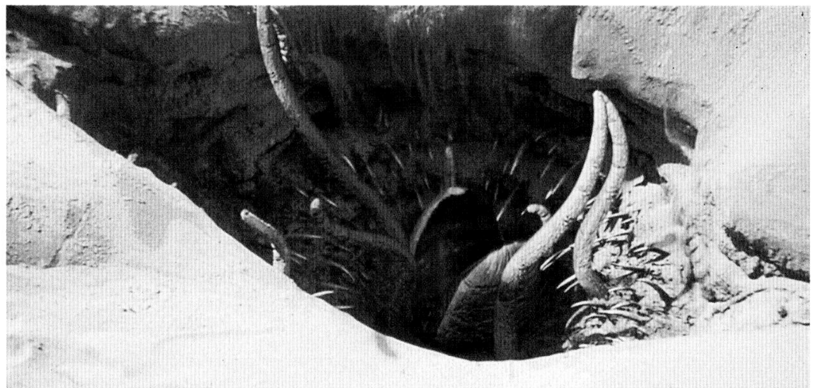
Great Pit of Carkoon

ering wall. The planet's varied surface—rocky mountains, frozen ice fields, jungles filled with carnivorous plants, and arid deserts—provided perfect training for combat in harsh environments.

Admiral Daala attended the Caridan academy before her appointment to the staff of Grand Moff Tarkin. After the annihilation of Alderaan, several of the Death Star's designers were transferred from the battle station to Carida. Dash Rendar attended the Academy until he was dishonorably discharged after his older brother crashed a freighter into the Emperor's private museum on Imperial Center. Later, Ambassador Furgan was the Caridan representative to the New Republic and oversaw the development of the MT-AT "spider walker." Alliance Admiral Ackbar's aide Terpfen underwent torture and reconditioning on the planet to turn him into an Imperial puppet. Carida was destroyed when Jedi Kyp Durron caused its star to go nova through the use of an Imperial super weapon, the Sun Crusher. [JS, DA, COF, COJ, TMEC, TJP, SOTE]

Caridan combat arachnid Spiderlike creatures that originated on Carida, they have twelve legs, huge and powerful jaws, crimson body armor splotched with maroon, and bodies covered with needle-sharp spines. Jabba the Hutt pitted several of the arachnids against his rancor, injuring the beast. [TJP]

Carkoon, Great Pit of Located within the Dune Sea on the planet Tatooine, the large depression in the sand is the home for the rapacious, if slow-eating, creature called the Sarlacc. [RJ]

Lirin Car'n

Car'n, Lirin A male Bith mercenary, he is a backup Kloo Horn player in the band known as Figrin D'an and the Modal Nodes. [CCG]

Carosi This planet is the site of a busy starport and many pleasure-domes, some of which use synthdroids—centrally controlled mechanicals covered in quasi-living flesh. Carosi's larger moon houses a synthdroid factory operated by the Loronar Corporation. Animal life on the planet includes the Carosi pup. The Carosi system contained twelve planets until its sun consumed the first five. [POT, POG]

***Carrack*-class light cruiser** These small combat cruisers have long played a major role in the Imperial Navy fleet. About 350 meters long, with a higher proportion of weapons than its size might normally justify, it has been the Imperial answer to the Corellian corvette. Its powerful sublight engines give it the speed of an X-wing fighter, making it one of the Imperial fleet's fastest cruisers. The ships usually carry ten heavy turbolasers, twenty ion cannons, and five tractor beam projectors. With no hangar bay (there are external racks for up to five TIE fighters), the cruisers depend on other ships or bases for most TIE fighter support. The cruisers weren't designed for frontline combat duty, but after the heavy losses the Empire suffered at the Battle of Endor, more of these ships have been used in such fighting.

The *Carrack*-class cruiser *Dominant* played a key role in the defense of the planet Bakura against the invasion of the reptilian Ssi-ruuk, then turned its guns on—and destroyed—the Rebel Alliance cruiser-carrier, the *Flurry*. [ISB, HESB, ESWVG]

Carratos This planet is located some forty parsecs from Coruscant. The Fallanassi religious group chose to send some of its youngest members to Carratos, among other planets, because of persecution on Lucazec. Akanah Norand was sent to a Carratos school in the Chofin settlement. Soon after, Carratos came under Imperial control, the Empire erected a garrison, and taxes were levied against anyone wishing to leave. After the Empire departed, order collapsed on Carratos. The Liberty movement destroyed all official records and only the strong, wealthy, or cunning survived. [BTS, SOL]

carver egg A delicacy to the Glottalphib species. [NR]

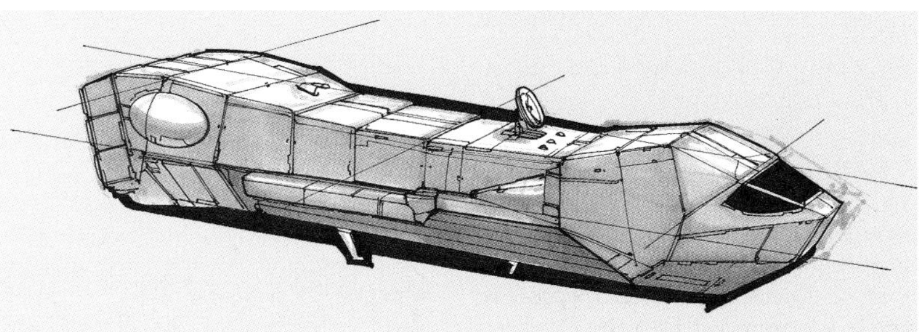
Carrack-*class light cruiser*

Casfield 6 This world once suffered a catastrophe when the use of droid languages in ship landing codes caused shipboard computers to malfunction and at least six ships to collide and crash. [NR]

Caslo, Gerney An ostentatious loudmouth, he was one of the largest sellers of precious water on Nam Chorios. Gerney Caslo was instrumental in getting old pump-stations functional after the planet's Oldtimers had let most of them rot. [POT]

Cass An Imperial officer, he was adjutant to Grand Moff Tarkin aboard the original Death Star battle station. [SWN]

Cathar The ancient homeworld of a proud and powerful feline species of the same name. Cathar have flowing manes; the male has two tusks protruding downward from his mouth and fur sprouting from his chin; the female has fangs. The Jedi Knights Sylvar and Crado, who trained under Vodo-Siosk Baas some 4,000 years before the Battle of Yavin, were from Cathar. [DLS]

Cathedral of Winds A magnificent but delicate and incredibly intricate structure, the centuries-old cathedral on the planet Vortex had long been the site of the Vors's annual Concert of the Winds, a cultural festival to celebrate the planet's dramatic change of seasons. Resembling a castle made of eggshell-thin crystal, the cathedral had thousands of passageways that wound through hollow chambers, turrets, and spires. At the beginning of the Vortex storm season, winds would whip through the Cathedral's honeycomb structure, resulting in a spellbinding concert of reverberating, almost mournful music. But on a fateful diplomatic journey with Princess Leia as passenger, Admiral Ackbar's personal B-wing fighter crashed into the cathedral, destroying it and killing hundreds of Vors. It later turned out that the admiral's ship had been sabotaged. The Vors almost immediately began the painful task of rebuilding the cathedral, and when it was completed, Ackbar was invited back as an honored guest. [DA, COF]

Cathor Hills One of the many sentient forests on the planet Ithor, it was destroyed by Imperial Captain Alima in his campaign to get Momaw Nadon to turn over Ithorian technology to the Empire. [TMEC]

Cauldron Nebula Like an interplanetary light show emanating from seven closely orbiting blue supergiant stars, the nebula sported clouds of magenta, orange, and icy-blue ionized gases. The closest habitable world was Eol Sha, where colonists mounted an unsuccessful attempt to mine the nebula's gases. The gas clouds and electromagnetic radiation in the nebula made an ideal hiding place for Admiral Daala's Star Destroyers, until Jedi student Kyp Durron caused all seven stars to go nova through his use of the Empire's own secret super weapon, the Sun Crusher. [DA, YJK, JS]

Cavrilhu Pirates The scourge of the Amorris star system, this gang of marauders attacks merchant ships plying the space lanes of the galaxy. Led by Captain Zothip from his gunship *Void Cutter*, the pirates don't like to be crossed, as they were when Niles Ferrier, one of the best spaceship thieves in the galaxy, made off with three of the pirates' patrol ships. [DFR, DFRSB]

CB-99 An old barrel-shaped droid that emerged from hiding in the palace of Jabba the Hutt after the crime lord's death, he presented Jabba's hologram will to his beneficiaries. [ZHR]

C'baoth, Jorus A human Jedi Master, he was born on the planet Bortras with recognizable Force abilities. He became a Jedi after years of training, then a Jedi Master a dozen years later.

He served the Old Republic in numerous roles such as a demilitarization observer and led a delegation to Alderaan that determined that the Organa family should receive the title of viceroy. He also was personal adviser to then-Senator Palpatine on Jedi-related matters. He disappeared along with five other Jedi Masters during a project that was searching for life outside the known galaxy. In reality, their exploration ship was secretly destroyed on Palpatine's orders by a young officer named Thrawn. [HE, DFR, DFRSB, LC]

C'baoth, Joruus A clone of the famed human Jedi Master with a similar name, he was placed on the planet Wayland by Emperor Palpatine to guard his hidden storehouses on Mount Tantiss. They contained not only treasure such as plundered art but also a cloning facility and the prototype of a cloaking device.

Clone madness—the result of being grown too quickly—kept C'baoth in periods of confusion and insanity, but didn't stop him from wielding great dark-side powers. Grand Admiral Thrawn entered into an uneasy alliance with him, promising to turn over to him Luke Skywalker, his sister Leia Organa Solo, and her unborn twins, all of whom C'baoth planned to turn into a society of Dark Jedi to rule the galaxy. Luke tried to heal C'baoth's madness, but eventually had no alternative but to aid in his destruction. [HE, DFR, DFRSB, LC]

C'borp Chief gunner of the pirate marauder ship *Starjacker* some 4,000 years before the Battle of Yavin, he destroyed an attacking spacecraft piloted by Dreebo, who worked for Great Bogga the Hutt. [TOJ]

CCIR This is the acronym for a type of Centrally Controlled Independent Replicant. [POT]

Joruus C'baoth

Capt. Tycho Celchu

Celanon Located in the Outer Rim in the system of the same name, this planet has a multicolored skyline due to its numerous holographic advertising boards. Celanon's two main industries are agriculture and the commerce that flows from Celanon City, a busy and well-defended spaceport. The system is also home to the mammoth consortium known as Pravaat, which makes and sells uniforms. Prior to the Battle of Yavin, an explosive device was loaded onto an Imperial freighter at Celanon. The Alliance later stole the device and used it to demolish the Star Destroyer *Invincible*. The Nalroni are the planet's native sentient population. [COJ, CSSB, FP, POG]

Celchu, Captain Tycho A superior pilot, he was a graduate of the Imperial Naval Academy and served as a TIE fighter pilot. But after his homeworld of Alderaan was cold-bloodedly destroyed by the first Death Star, the brown-haired, blue-eyed Tycho Celchu switched sides. He quickly became a member of the X-wing Rogue Squadron, participating in both the evacuation of Hoth and the Battle of Endor where, with his own ship out of commission, he flew an A-wing that lured Imperials away from Wedge Antilles and Lando Calrissian as they made a run at destroying the second Death Star.

Celchu fought heroically at Bakura and later volunteered to fly a captured TIE fighter on a covert mission to Imperial Center, or Coruscant. He was captured and sent to the prison ship *Lusankya* before getting free. When he returned to Rogue Squadron, there were many who did not trust him, but his friend Antilles persevered until Celchu was named the squadron's Executive Officer in charge of training new recruits.

Because the Rogues' mission on Coruscant had been compromised at least once, they knew there was an Imperial spy in their midst, and pilot Corran Horn suspected Captain Celchu. Shortly after confronting Celchu with his suspicions, Horn's Z-95 Headhunter was disabled and crashed. Captain Celchu was charged with treason and the murder of Corran Horn. During his trial, when things looked hopeless, Horn reappeared with information that not only acquitted Celchu, but restored Alliance trust in the captain. [XW, BW]

Celchu, Skoloc Tycho Celchu's brother, he was killed when Alderaan was destroyed. [BW]

Cell 2187 The small cell, in detention block AA-23, was the site of Princess Leia Organa's imprisonment and torture while she was held captive aboard the first Death Star battle station. [SW]

Centerpoint Station An enormous gray-white space station in the Corellian system, located at the balance point between the twin worlds of Talus and Tralus, it presumably draws its power from the gravitational interflux between the double worlds. The ancient station, built before the invention of artificial gravity, spins on its axis to provide centrifugal gravity. It is composed of a central sphere one hundred kilometers in diameter, with long, thick cylinders jutting from either side of the globe. The ends of the cylinders are referred to as the North and South Poles.

The entire station is approximately 350 kilometers long, even larger than the infamous Death Star. Centerpoint is completely covered with a bewildering array of piping, cables, antennae, cone structures, and access ports; it would take several human lifetimes to explore the vast and complex interior and exterior of the station. Hollowtown, which measures sixty kilometers in diameter, is the open sphere in the center of the station. The walls of Hollowtown had long been colonized with homes, parks, lakes, orchards, and farmland, which received heat and light from the Glowpoint—an artificial sun suspended in the exact center of the sphere. To simulate night, farmers installed adjustable shadow-shields, which appeared as bright patches of gold or silver from above.

Centerpoint is believed to be a hyperspace repulsor, used in ancient times to transport the five inhabited Corellian planets into their current orbits from an unknown location. At some point the station was colonized, and Hollowtown, which is actually a power-containment battery for the massive energy of firing a tractor-repulsor hyperspace burst, became inhabited. Centerpoint remained stable for thousands of years, until the Saccorian Triad discovered that the station could destroy stars with a precise shot from its South Pole. Two stars were targeted and destroyed, each accompanied by intense flare-ups in the Glowpoint. The small sun increased in heat so rapidly that Hollowtown and most of its inhabitants were completely incinerated during the first such incident. The government immediately evacuated the remaining Centerpoint inhabitants to the double worlds, leaving Chief Operations Officer Jenica Sonsen in charge of the station.

When word spread of the Hollowtown disaster it sparked several rebellions on Talus and Tralus. A group of starfighters representing one of the rebellions claimed the nearly abandoned station for themselves, until chased off by a Bakuran cruiser. Massive interdiction and jamming fields, thrown over the entire Corellian system, were generated from Centerpoint and activated by the Triad. The Triad's fleet was later defeated by New Republic and Bakuran forces. The planned destruction of the star Bovo Yagen was averted at the last instant when a shot from the repulsor on the planet Drall disrupted Centerpoint's firing process. [AC, AS, SAC]

Ceousa, General An important general in the New Republic, he has commanded the *Calamari* and led it into the Battle of Almania. [NR]

C-Gosf A member of the New Republic Senate's Inner Council, she was a Gosfambling. As such, C-Gosf risked much by running for the Senate, since losers in any contest on her world are forever ridiculed by all other Gosfamblings. [NR]

Chad III A watery world that orbits a blue-white star of the same name, it is the home of the sociable, rodent-like Chadra-Fan. The nine moons of Chad III create a pulsing system of tides, and clans of Chadra-Fan live in the bayous among the red gum-tree forests and cyperill trees. The Chadra-Fan don't build permanent structures because of unpredictable hurricanes. The planet's technology is primitive by galactic standards, although the Chadra-Fan take great pride in the design and craftsmanship of items that they export.

Life-forms in the planet's watery depths include the long-necked cetaceans called tsaelkes, hunters called wystohs, phosphorescent tubular eels, and the fish-lizards called cy'een. The human Jedi Callista was originally from Chad III, where she worked on an ark with her family. They herded the semisentient wanderkelp on their deep-water ranch. The ark followed the herds along Chad III's Algic Current, which runs between the planet's equator and its Arctic Circle. Callista was later called away to Bespin by the Jedi Master Djinn Altis. [GG4, TMEC, COJ, DS]

Chadra-Fan These small but quick-witted natives of Chad III look like a cross between humans and fur-covered rodents. They have large fan-like ears, dark eyes, and upturned, circular noses with four nostrils. Their seven senses include infrared vision and a highly advanced sense of smell. Only a meter tall, the Chadra-Fan like to have fun, although they have a short attention span. [GG4, QE, TBH]

chak-root A favorite of smugglers, this flavorful red plant grows in the marshlands on the planet Erysthes. Because of high taxes on its sale, the plant has given rise to highly profitable, if illicit, dealings. Chak-root is easily obtained on the Invisible Market at reduced prices. [HSR, HLL]

Chalcedon A rocky, volcanic world with a semi-breathable atmosphere, the planet is a key hub in the galactic slave trade. Inhospitable Chalcedon has violent storms, frequent groundquakes, and no indigenous life-forms, although two colonies and a way station have been established on its surface. Many buildings are made of dark volcanic glass. Traders and peasants inhabit the bazaars, while the bureaucrats—boneless, trunked creatures—live in the cities and control the slave trade. [CS]

Chadra-Fan

Chalmun A beige-and-gray Wookiee, he owned the infamous Mos Eisley cantina—sometimes called Chalmun's Cantina—where Luke Skywalker and Ben Kenobi first hooked up with Han Solo and his copilot Chewbacca. [GG7, TMEC]

Chamma, Master A Jedi Master, he was Andur Sunrider's teacher some 4,000 years before the Battle of Yavin. [TOJ]

Chan, Lieutenant Wenton A human Rebel pilot, he was a native of the planet Corulag. Part of Red Squadron, Lt. Wenton Chan died in the attack on the Death Star during the Battle of Yavin. [CCG]

Chandrila Located in the Bormea sector of the Core Worlds, this agricultural planet is best known as the homeworld of Mon Mothma, leader of the New Republic. Its two main continents are covered with rolling, grassy plains. Chandrila has a low birth rate, which keeps the population at around 1.2 billion. Most residents live in scattered small communities, but all have a direct voice in government. Six months after the Battle of Endor, the Empire deployed seven Star Destroyers to Chandrila where they enforced a strict blockade of the planet. It is believed that Grand Vizier Sate Pestage may have implemented the plan to hold Chandrila hostage in case New Republic forces were able to threaten Coruscant. Dev Sibwarra, the reptilian Ssi-ruuk's human liaison, was originally from Chandrila, although his family fled to G'rho during the Jedi purge. Rebel Alliance leader Mon Mothma grew up in a port city on the shores of the Silver Sea; her mother was the area's governor. Avan Post, a Jedi Master from Chandrila who served in the Clone Wars, was later killed by Emperor Palpatine. Admiral Drayson, head of the secret New Republic intelligence operation Alpha Blue, was once head of the Chandrila Defense Fleet. [TAB, SWB, COJ, DESB, SWAJ, KT]

Chanzari Rebels on Selonia, they were allied with the Hunchuzuc, who were also seeking to free themselves from oppressive rule. [AS]

Chaos fighters These small and maneuverable fighters were employed by the Krath, a group that adopted primitive dark-side magic, and used to stage a coup in the Empress Teta system about 4,000 years prior to the Battle of Yavin. [DLS]

Charal An evil witch who has long bedeviled Ewoks and others on the

Chalmun

Charal

forest moon of Endor, she can shift shapes thanks to a magical ring. Some say Charal escaped from the planet Dathomir and was stranded on Endor's moon. She wears a black-feather cloak and rides a wild, black stallion that can also shift shapes. The witch is the companion of Terak, king of the marauders. [BFE, ISWU]

charbote root This vegetable is used in Corellian cooking. [DA]

Chardaan Shipyards Workers built space vehicles in a zero-gravity environment in this Alliance space facility composed of pressurized spheres. The Chardaan Shipyards produced a wide variety of Alliance starfighters, from the Y-wing to the E-wing, until they were devastated by Colonel Cronus and his fleet of *Victory*-class Star Destroyers eight years after the Battle of Endor. [DS]

Chariot LAV This modified military landspeeder, rarely used in combat, has served as a command vehicle for Imperial forces. The Chariot light assault vehicle (LAV) is more heavily armored than a normal landspeeder although not nearly as armored as a combat speeder. It provides moderate performance at an acceptably low price. It is about twelve meters long, has a top speed of one hundred kilometers an hour, and usually carries three people. The extensive on-board computer system provides battle assistance programs including holographic tactical battlefield displays. [ISB, HESB, SWVG]

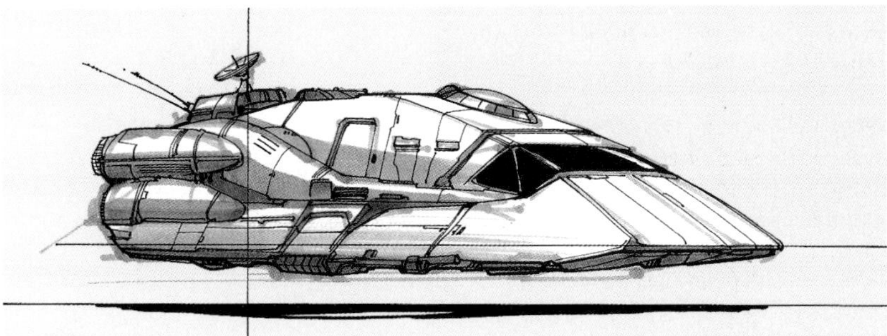
Chariot LAV

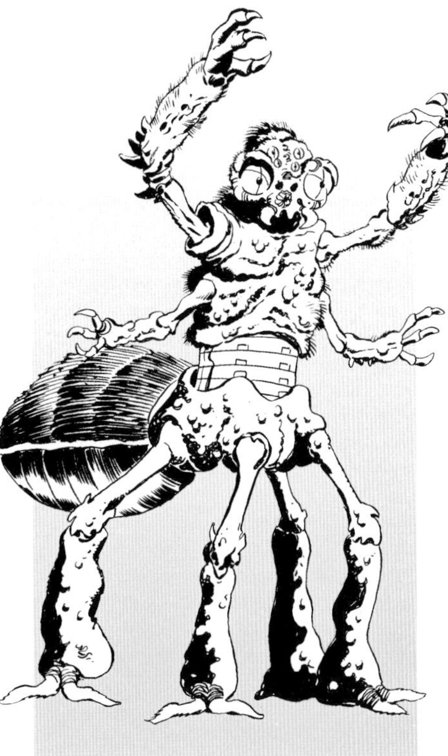
Charon

Charon These humanoid arachnids, who are capable of spinning webs, come from another dimension that seems to exist outside the realm of the known galaxy: otherspace. Charon are divided into bioscientists and warriors. Their homeworld is being swallowed by a black hole, which has given rise to a Charon death cult that believes it has the duty to speed all life quickly along a path to nothingness, or the Void. [OS, OS2, GG4]

Charubah A technological world in the Hapes cluster, the planet is known for manufacturing the Hapan Gun of Command. Those shot with the gun's electromagnetic wave field lose the ability to make rational decisions and tend to follow any orders given them. [CPL]

Chattza clan A powerful, warlike clan of Rodians, it was led by Navik the Red. After conquering Rodia, Chattzas scoured the galaxy and hunted down and killed the more peaceful sects of Rodians who had escaped off-world. [TMEC]

Chazwa Located in the Chazwa system and the Orus sector, the planet orbits a tiny white dwarf sun. Its central transshipment location means that heavy freight traffic is a common sight. The smugglers Talon Karrde and Samuel Tomas Gillespee battled two Imperial Lancers at Chazwa, and later it was used as a rendezvous for Karrde, Par'tah, and Clyngunn the Ze'Hethbra to discuss actions against Grand Admiral Thrawn. [LC]

Cheel, Nalan A male Bith musician, he plays with the group Figrin D'an and the Modal Nodes. Although he enjoys playing his bandfill, he misses the bubbling pink swamps of his native Clak'dor VII. [TMEC, CCG]

Chenlambec A Wookiee bounty hunter with deep brown, silver-tipped

Nalan Cheel

fur, he was known as Chen to his friends. Most others, however, knew him only by his reputation as the Raging Wookiee. Despite his somewhat unsavory reputation as a fierce and hot-tempered killer, Chenlambec and his human partner, Tinian I'att, would often help their "acquisitions" escape to the Rebellion. Chenlambec wore a heavy, reptile-hide bandolier studded with bowcaster quarrels and silver cubes, one of which was actually Flirt, his positronic processor. With the help of Flirt and I'att, Chenlambec rescued a colony of Wookiees imprisoned on Lomabu III while at the same time tricking and capturing the Wookiee-hating Trandoshan bounty hunter Bossk. The Wookiee owns a ship called the *Wroshyr.* [GG10, TBH]

Chevin A species native to the planet Vinsoth, they are primarily hunters and farmers. Chevin stand over two meters tall and have thick arms and a long face, all set on two stubby trunks of legs. They once enslaved the Chevs, a humanoid species on their planet. [GG12, TJP]

Chewbacca Loyal even at great personal risk, strong as a gladiator, and as savvy as the brightest Academy graduate, the two-meter-plus tall Wookiee is a true hero of the Rebellion as well as a good friend of its leaders.

Born on the tree-filled planet of Kashyyyk, the more than two-centuries-old Chewbacca has seen life as a slave, a smuggler, and a top-notch pilot and mechanic. Through it all, he has remained the true conscience of those around him. That doesn't make him a pacifist. He can tear the limbs off of most creatures barehanded. His weapon of choice is a bowcaster, a handcrafted crossbow-like weapon that shoots explosive packets of energy. A bandolier slung from Chewbacca's left shoulder contains enough extra firepower to take on a squad of stormtroopers. But sometimes his terrifying growls and roars—the basis of the Wookiee language—mask his fear, especially of the unknown.

Chewie, as he's known to his friends, left Kashyyyk at the age of fifty standard years to explore the galaxy. Things seemed to go fine for the next 140 years, until he was captured by slavers and sold to Imperial forces. Unbeknownst to him, his planet had been subjugated years before. Severely mistreated at a hard-labor camp, Chewbacca was saved from certain death by a young Han Solo. Saving Chewbacca's life resulted in a "life debt" from the Wookiee, and Chewbacca became first the protector and then the best friend of the Corellian. He served with Solo as he embarked on a smuggling career, aided by the swift *Millennium Falcon,* which Solo won in a game of sabacc.

Chewbacca

At one point, Chewbacca revisited his homeworld and married a female Wookiee named Mallatobuck, who had been looking after his father. Malla later gave birth to their son, Lumpawarrump, or Lumpy for short.

On one spice-smuggling run, for which they had been hired by crime lord Jabba the Hutt, Solo and Chewbacca had to dump their cargo before being boarded by Imperials. They had to face the music—and Jabba—back on Tatooine. But before visiting the Hutt's palace, they encountered the somewhat odd Ben Kenobi in the Mos Eisley cantina. He had a job for them that promised a payment big enough to calm Jabba; all that was required was transporting two humans and two droids to Alderaan. Little did the smugglers know but the chance encounter was to change their lives. Within a short time, the partners had helped rescue a princess, blown up the Empire's top-secret battle station, and been declared heroes by the Rebel Alliance.

That was just the start of many adventures and missions for the Wookiee, who became close to Luke Skywalker and to Princess Leia; in fact, after she and Solo married, he helped guard and raise their three children. Chewbacca also helped put a quick end to the return of slavers to Kashyyyk, aided in a truce with Imperials at Bakura, and took part in many rescue missions after his friends had gotten into trouble. He and Solo had a close call themselves after being imprisoned to work at the spice mines on Kessel.

When Chewbacca found out that his honor brother, Han Solo, had been taken hostage by the Yevetha, he disobeyed Princess Leia's orders to go to Coruscant and instead headed directly for the Koornacht Cluster, where Han was being held. With the help of his cousins Jowdrrl, Dryanta, and Shoran, and his son, Lumpawarrump, he rescued Han from the Yevethan ship *Pride of Yevetha.*

Some two decades after he first met Luke Skywalker, Chewbacca helped by bringing him a new student for his Jedi academy, his nineteen-year-old nephew Lowbacca. In recent years, Chewbacca has had more time to spend with his real family, but his adopted family remains a true force in his life. [SW, ESB, RJ, SWCG, TT]

Lt. Shann Childsen

ch'hala tree These greenish-purple trees, with slim trunks and leafy tops, burst into a brilliant red that ripples across their trunks when sounds occur nearby. But the natural chemical process that triggers the display was put to a more sinister use by Emperor Palpatine: He used the trees as a spying mechanism that was especially helpful because they line the Grand Corridor outside the Senate chambers in Imperial Palace. The trees, in fact, were the basis of the long-sought Delta Source spy network, which provided vital New Republic intelligence to Grand Admiral Thrawn. The trees were implanted with a module that converted the chemical changes caused by sound back into speech, which was then encrypted and transmitted. [HE, DFR, LC]

Childsen, Lieutenant Shann An Imperial lieutenant, he was demoted after a superior officer blamed him for a clerical error. Considered a bully by fellow officers, Lt. Shann Childsen was fanatical in his support of the Emperor's policy of subjugating nonhuman races. He was killed aboard the Death Star during the rescue of Princess Leia Organa. [CCG]

Chimaera An Imperial Star Destroyer under the command of Captain Pellaeon, it took part in the Battle of Endor. Grand Admiral Thrawn picked the *Chimaera* as his flagship. [HE, DFR, LC]

Chin A chief associate of the smuggler and spy Talon Karrde, the main duty of this middle-aged human from the planet Myrkr is to care for and train Karrde's pet vornskrs. He has domesticated the creatures and trained them to serve as guards. Chin's understanding of the mysterious Force-blocking ysalamiri led him to develop a method for safely removing them from their tree-branch homes. He also is Karrde's chief of operations. [HE, DFR, LC, HESB]

Chip A droid the size and shape of a twelve-year-old boy, Microchip belongs to Jedi Prince Ken. [LCJ, ZHR, MMY, PDS]

Chir'daki TIE fighter variants, they were specifically built for use by Twi'lek pilots. In a Chir'daki, the globelike cockpit of a TIE fighter is attached to the S-foils of an X-wing fighter. The S-foils are connected to a collar, which allows them to rotate independently from the cockpit. This design provides greater stability and maneuverability for the pilot, making these craft extraordinarily lethal. [BW]

Chirpa, Chief Head of his Ewok tribe's Council of Elders, the strong-willed Chirpa befriended the Rebel strike force sent to the moon of Endor to clear the way for the Alliance fleet. His warriors were courageous and skillful in the face of a superior fighting force. Chief Chirpa, gray-furred and carrying a reptilian staff denoting his rank, wears the teeth, horns, and bones of animals he has hunted. [RJ]

Chituhr A mean-looking animal trainer of the Jinda tribe of Ewoks. [ETV]

Chief Chirpa

Ch'no

Ch'no An H'drachi scrap scavenger from the planet M'Haeli, he saved the human infant Mora after an attack and became her adopted father, not knowing that she was of royal blood. [ROC]

Choco A small and battered R2 unit, this clumsy droid befriended R2-D2 during his encounters with the Great Heep and in his droid harem years before the start of the Galactic Civil War. [TGH]

ChoFi A two-meter tall New Republic Senator, ChoFi has been a loyal supporter of Princess Leia Organa Solo since the beginnings of the New Republic. [NR]

Chorax system A hotbed for smuggling and piracy, the system is in the Rachuk sector along with the Hensara and Rachuk systems and contains a medium-sized yellow star and a single planet, Chorax. Three years after the Battle of Endor, the Alliance's Rogue Squadron was skirting the system on a hyperspace jump to the Morobe system when it was acci-

Chukha-Trok

dentally yanked from hyperspace by the Interdictor cruiser *Black Asp*. The Rogues rescued the cruiser's true target, the smuggling ship *Pulsar Skate*, and forced the *Black Asp* to flee the system. After they resigned from the Alliance, Rogue Squadron hijacked a Thyferran bacta convoy in the system and brought it to Halanit. [RS, BW]

Chorios systems Located in the Meridian sector, the Chorios systems are made up of several systems that go by the name Chorios, including Nam Chorios, Pedducis Chorios, and Brachnis Chorios. Most of the worlds in the region are lifeless and barren. The systems' relatively few inhabitants are referred to as Chorians. Nine years after the Battle of Endor, Leia Organa Solo made a secret visit to a point near Brachnis Chorios's largest moon to meet with Seti Ashgad of Nam Chorios. [POT]

chromasheath An iridescent material, it is similar to leather. [HSE]

chrono This device measures time. [HLL, SWSB]

chrysalides Dark-side mutant creatures, they were unleashed by the second cloned Emperor against Lando Calrissian's war-droid attack force outside the Emperor's citadel on the planet Byss. [DE2]

Chubb A small, burrowing reptile, it was the pet and constant companion of a young boy named Fidge who met R2-D2 and C-3PO during the early days of the Empire. [TGH]

Chubbits Small reptilian desert dwellers, they are native to the planet Aridus. [GW]

Chukha-Trok A brave Ewok woodsman, he is known for his forest skills and lore. [ETV]

Churba A star system located in Mid-Rim, it contains eight planets including Churba and New Cov. The worlds closest and farthest from the Churba system sun—Barhu and Hurcha—have temperature extremes that don't support life. Churba, the cosmopolitan fourth world, is home to the corporate offices of Sencil Corporation, a major manufacturer of black-market assassin droid components. It was also the birthplace of Imperial Intelligence agent Kirtan Loor. New Cov, the third world in, has vast jungles filled with natural resources. Four Bothan ships once attacked a *Victory*-class Star Destroyer in the Churba sector, and kept it occupied until an Alliance Star Cruiser could assist them. [DFR, DFRSB, RS, SWAJ]

Chusker, Vu A business associate of gangster Cabrool Nuum. Jabba the Hutt was asked first by Nuum, and then by Nuum's son and daughter, to kill Vu Chusker. Jabba, who had never laid eyes on the being, refused to kill him—although he did eliminate the Nuum family one by one. Making his escape from a Nuum family dungeon, Jabba encountered the nasty Chusker—and promptly killed him with one swipe of his tail. [JAB]

Chu'unthor Luke Skywalker found this wrecked spacecraft half-submerged in a river on the planet Dathomir where it had been for at least 400 years. The ship was huge: two kilometers long, a kilometer wide, and eight levels high. It resembled a small city. Luke later learned that the *Chu'unthor*, under the command of Jedi Masters, had served as a mobile training academy for thousands of Jedi apprentices. Luke was able to get into the ship and found records of old Jedi training, which he used to develop programs for his Jedi academy. [CPL, DA]

Cilghal A Force-sensitive Calamarian, she was recruited by Leia Organa Solo for Luke Skywalker's Jedi academy. She is also an ambassador from Mon Calamari. Cilghal used her proven ambassadorial skills to hold the twelve Jedi students together in the days following the attack on Luke Skywalker by the spirit of Dark Sider Exar Kun. She aided in the plan to defeat Kun, then departed Yavin 4 for her most difficult mission: healing the dying Mon Mothma. Cilghal discovered that the former chief of state was suffering from a poisoning of nano-destroyers, artificially created viruses that were dismantling Mon Mothma's cells one nucleus at a time. Using her considerable abilities, Cilghal set about to instead dismantle the nano-destroyers, billions of them, one at a time. In doing so, she healed Mon Mothma. [DA, DS, COF]

Cilpar A planet once held by Imperial forces, it is covered with mountains, jungles, and forests. Dozens of nearly indestructible ancient native temples are scattered throughout the forest. Life-forms include dangerous carnivores called ronks. Male ronks are considered a delicacy on Cilpar, but the females are instantly fatal if eaten. Wedge Antilles and Rogue Squadron arrived on Cilpar after the

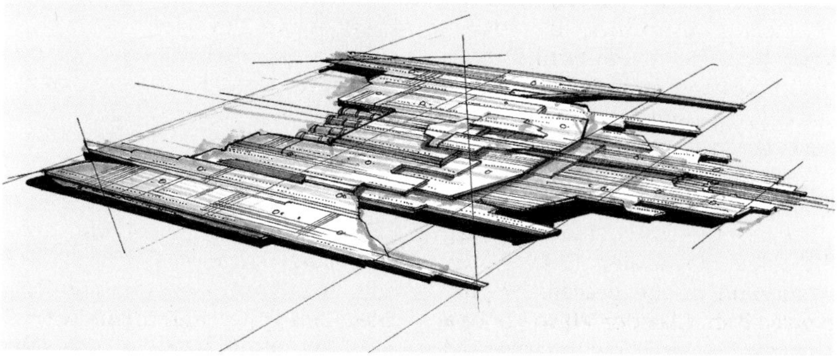
Chu'unthor

Battle of Endor and set up a base in the mountains west of the capital, Kiidan. They were to pick up food and supplies from the Cilpari resistance and escort a convoy to Mrlsst, but instead they ran into a TIE fighter ambush. After a long battle, the planet's moff and governor were overthrown by the resistance, as expected Imperial reinforcements abandoned them. [XW]

Cinnagar The largest city on the seven worlds that make up the Empress Teta star system. [DE]

Circarpous IV The fourth and primary planet in the Circarpous Major star system, it is a hectic and thriving world of free enterprise. It was to be the site of Luke Skywalker and Princess Leia's diplomatic meeting with Circarpousian resistance groups and government leaders, but on their way to the meeting they crash-landed on Circarpous V. [SME]

Circarpous V *See* Mimban

Circarpous XIV The outermost planet in the Circarpous Major star system, it was home to a small, hidden Rebel outpost at the beginning of the Galactic Civil War. [SME]

Circarpous Major A populous star system, it encompasses fourteen planets orbiting the star Circarpous Major and is located near the planet Gyndine. During the Galactic Civil War, many of the system's inhabitants were sympathetic to the Alliance but were afraid to risk the Empire's wrath. Following the Battle of Yavin, Princess Leia Organa and Luke Skywalker traveled to the system to try to convince government officials to join the Rebellion. [SME, FP]

Circus Horrificus A traveling show of alien monstrosities, it traveled from system to system terrifying audiences. Jabba's main rancor keeper, Malakili, had previously worked for the circus. [TJP]

Clak'dor VII Located in the Mayagil sector, the small planet orbiting the large white star Colu is the homeworld of the peaceful, highly evolved Bith. Clak'dor VII was once a lush garden world with advanced technologies, but is now an ecological wasteland due to a conflict between the Bith of two cities, Nozho and Weogar. Generations ago, they unleashed gene-altering biological weapons on each other, mutating the planet's surface (the jungles have pink bubbling swamps) and forcing all surviving Biths to live in hermetically sealed domed cities. The planet is unable to produce basic needs for its citizens or goods for export, so many Biths sell their intellectual abilities, finding employment as technical consultants. They also make good entertainers and musicians, playing everywhere from the grandest palaces to out-of-the-way cantinas in spaceports such as Mos Eisley. [GG4, COJ, TMEC]

Clays A family of moisture farmers on Tatooine, they were against Ariq Joanson's plans to draw up maps of peace with the Jawas and Tusken Raiders. [TMEC]

Clezo A Rodian, he was one of the lieutenants, or Vigos, of the Black Sun criminal organization. [SOTE]

cliffborer worm Long, armored worms, they are found among the rocks on arid Tatooine. They often feed on razor moss. [ISWU]

cloaking device A defensive anti-detection system, it has long been under development. Early attempts to cloak a ship left the pilot blind. Theoretically, such a device disrupts all electromagnetic waves coming from a ship, rendering it electronically invisible to all sensors. Emperor Palpatine made development a top priority, and years after his death a prototype device was found by Grand Admiral Thrawn in the Emperor's hidden storehouse. [ESB, HE, HESB, DFR, LC]

Cloak of the Sith A region of space that is a huge dark cloud of dangerous meteors, asteroids, and planetoids, it lies in the only path to the Roon system. [DTV]

CloakShape fighter An older starfighter designed for atmospheric and short-range space combat, it is used now mainly by bounty hunters, pirates, and other individuals with a need for assault starships. The ship trades speed for durability. [DE, DESB]

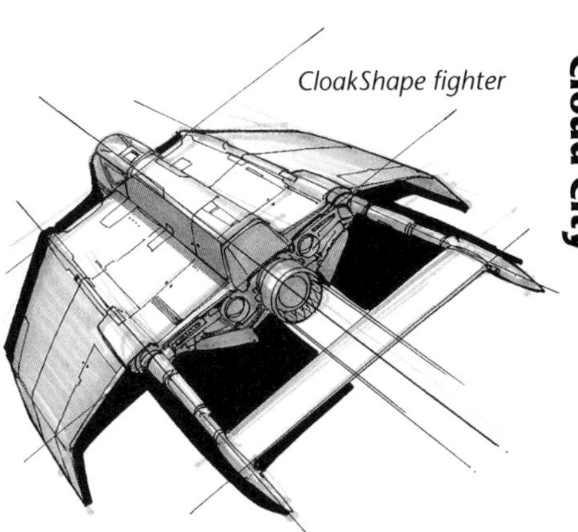
CloakShape fighter

Clone Keepers A name given to the scientists and attendants responsible for Emperor Palpatine's clone vats on the planet Byss. [DE]

Clone Wars A terrible series of conflicts that occurred sometime before the Battle of Yavin, the wars produced such heroes as Bail Organa, Anakin Skywalker, and General Obi-Wan Kenobi. [SW, ESB, RJ]

cloud car, combat Following a standard cloud-car design, they fill a gap between airspeeders and starfighters with enough weapons to go up against fighters and freighters. Combat cloud cars have a maximum altitude of one hundred kilometers with superior maneuverability and excellent speed. Most have extra hull plating and enhanced weapons systems. [SWVG, LC, GSWU, DFR]

cloud car, twin-pod Atmospheric flying vehicles that use both repulsorlifts and ion engines, typical models consist of twin pods for pilots and passengers. They can serve as patrol vehicles, cars for hire, or pleasure craft. [ESB, SWSB]

Cloud City A huge floating city, it is suspended about 60,000 kilometers above the core of the gas giant called Bespin. The main industry is mining Tibanna gas, but Baron Administrator Lando Calrissian promoted Cloud City's resort aspects with new casinos, luxury hotels, and shops. The cityscape has a rounded, decorative look with tall towers and large plazas. The city is sixteen kilometers in diameter and seventeen kilometers tall, including the huge unipod that hangs beneath. It has 392 levels and a surface plaza concourse. Upper levels house resorts and casinos, while middle levels are for

Cloud City

heavy industry and house workers. Lower levels are the site of the Tibanna gas–processing facilities and the 3,600 repulsorlift engines that anchor the city in place. A central wind tunnel nearly a kilometer in diameter channels wind gusts to give the city some stability. Cloud City was founded by Lord Ecclessis Figg of Corellia, won by Calrissian in a sabacc game, taken over by the Empire, and, after several switches of allegiance, has again become a neutral and sleepy mining colony. [ESB, GG2, CCC]

clutch mother Trandoshan females, they serve as mates for homecoming male warriors. [TBH]

C'ndros, Kal'Falnl A female Quor'sav, C'ndros is a member of a warm-blooded, birdlike, egg-laying mammalian species. Kal'Falnl C'ndros, who is about 3.5 meters tall, is a freelance pilot who had to have a ship custom built with tall corridors to fit her unusual height. [CCG]

Cnorec, Lord A slave trader and one of the followers of Lord Hethrir, he was murdered by Hethrir after challenging him. [CS]

Cobak A Bith bounty hunter, he was hired by Zorba the Hutt to capture Princess Leia Organa. Cobak impersonated Bithabus the Mystifier to lure the princess. [QE]

Coby, Prince The son of Lord Toda of Tammuz-an met the droids R2-D2 and C-3PO in the early days of the Empire, when he was young. His spoiled and aggressive behavior masked his insecurity. [DTV]

Prince Coby

Codru-Ji Natives of Munto Codru, these humanoids have four arms and sleep in a standing position. Their language consists of whistles and warbles, some beyond the range of human hearing, and the most intimate communications take place in the upper ranges. [CS]

Colonial Games This series of athletic competitions pits champions from colonies of the Roon star system against each other. The main event is the drainsweeper, a no-holds-barred relay race. [DTV]

Colonies, the One of the first areas outside of the Galactic Core to be settled, the region is heavily populated and industrialized. Ruthlessly controlled by the Empire during the Galactic Civil War, much of the Colonies region now supports the New Republic. [SWRPG2]

Colossus Wasps of Ithull These huge flying insects native to Ithull have strong exoskeletal carapaces that have been used as the basic framework for ore-hauling spaceships. [TOJ]

Columi Craniopods from the planet Columus, they spend their waking moments on mental activities. Physical work is done by droids and other machines with which the Columi communicate by brain-wave transmissions. A peaceful and non-

Columi

aggressive species, they sometimes seek employment as advisers and soothsayers. They are also the most feared gambling opponents in the galaxy. Columi have huge, hairless heads a third of their average body size, with throbbing blue veins around the cerebrum and huge black eyes. Otherwise they are puny, with thin, nonfunctional arms and legs. [GG4, CPL]

Columus A small world with extremely low gravity, it is home to the Columi. Columus is a completely flat, muddy planet with a wide variety of plant life. The Columi inhabit high cities supported by sturdy pylons. The Columi help run their society through a participatory democracy. Apparently, Columus voluntarily joined the Empire. [GG4]

Colunda sector A onetime hotbed of Rebel activity, the sector contains the planet Nyasko. An AT-AT group stationed on Nyasko kept busy suppressing uprisings. [DESB]

combat sense This Force technique enables a Jedi Knight to focus the bulk of his or her attention on the fight at hand. Opponents appear as bright images in an otherwise dull landscape. [DFR, DFRSB]

comlink A personal communications transceiver, it consists of a transmitter, a receiver, and a power source. The most widely used model is a small palm-sized cylinder. Military units carry large backpack versions with scrambling and variable frequency capabilities, and comlinks are built into stormtrooper helmets. [SW, ESB, RJ]

command control voice A method of controlling droids through special voice-pattern recognition. [SWR]

Commenor A planet in the system of the same name just outside the Core Worlds near Corellia, it is a trading outpost and spaceport. The Alliance established a starfighter training center on its largest moon, Folor. Tycho Celchu defected to the Alliance at Commenor immediately after the destruction of Alderaan. [SW, SWN, BW]

comm unit A shipboard communications device, it gives the vessel the

Comlink

ability to transmit and receive communications signals from outside sources. [SWSB]

compact assault vehicle (CAV) Small, single-occupant vehicles that are usually equipped with a medium blaster cannon, they are supposed to transform a single Imperial trooper into a formidable assault force. But while the tracked wheels and fairly high speed provide mobility, the CAVs are susceptible to sensor jamming. [ISB]

COMPNOR The Commission for the Preservation of the New Order was formed as one of the first official acts of Emperor Palpatine. It started as a populist movement against the chaos of the final days of the Old Republic, but soon became an Imperial tool to push the galaxy toward the everyday ethos of the New Order. COMPNOR implemented Redesign, a program whose goal was mass cultural edification of the Galaxy's citizens to function efficiently within the Empire. Many of COMPNOR's standard practices, especially its liberal usage of brain modification surgery, were believed by many to be unnecessarily brutal. [ISB, TBH]

computer probe A device that provides access to a computer network, the most common probes—or scomp links—are the appendages that droids use to tap into computers and portable units used by computer technicians. [HSE]

com-scan Specialized sensor sweeps, they are designed to detect the energy from the transmission and reception of communications signals. [ESB]

Cona Home to the triangular-headed Arcona, it is a hot, dense world orbiting the blue giant Teke Ro. Due to Cona's lack of axial tilt and temperature-distributing air currents, the climate is the same everywhere. The atmosphere contains a high concentration of ammonia, and water is often found only in the gastric pods of Cona's plant life. The Arcona, who obtain water by digging out plant pods with their burrowing claws, live in loose communities of family nests and are easily addicted to salt. Many galactic companies have established mining colonies on Cona. [GG4, TMEC]

Concert of the Winds An annual cultural festival celebrating the change of seasons on the planet Vortex. The concert is produced by winds rushing through the Cathedral of Winds, whipping up a reverberating, mournful music that whistles through pipes in the tall crystalline structure. It was during one such festival that a ship carrying Admiral Ackbar and Princess Leia Organa Solo crashed into and destroyed the cathedral, killing hundreds of Vors. The structure has since been rebuilt. [DA]

Concord Dawn The birthplace of Journeyman Protector Jaster Mereel, who later changed his name to Boba Fett after being exiled from the planet for killing another protector. Mereel was imprisoned on Concord Dawn and unsuccessfully defended in court by the Pleader Irving Creel. [TBH]

concussion missile A sub-light-speed projectile, it causes shock waves on impact. The concussive blasts can penetrate and destroy even heavily armored targets, though they work best against stationary targets. Concussion missiles were used to destroy the second Death Star during the Battle of Endor. [RJ]

concussion shield Strong energy shields, they protect ships from stray space debris. [TBH]

condenser unit A thermal coil or warming unit that radiates high levels of heat through the use of small amounts of energy. Such units are frequently found in standard survival kits and are used to cook food and provide heat. [SW]

condor dragon A native of the planet Endor, the cave-dwelling creature has large leathery wings with which to fly, a single fused fang for tearing through the hide of its prey,

Conquest

and two long lower tusks for stabbing. Its large yellow eyes with round black pupils enable the dragon to spot prey moving through the dense treetops. [ISWU]

conform lounger A type of furniture, it uses a pneudraulic capillary system to shape itself to whomever rests upon it, providing maximum comfort and support. [HSR, HSE]

Conquest An *Imperial*-class Star Destroyer, it was among the ships that chased the *Millennium Falcon* as it was leaving Tatooine. [CCG, TMEC]

construction droid A huge and complex factory on wheels, it both demolishes and rebuilds structures. Such droids can tear down condemned buildings and shovel debris into vast internal furnaces where useful items are extracted and recycled. A corresponding factory extrudes new girders and transparisteel sheets. The droid then assembles new buildings from preprogrammed blueprints. [ISWU, BW]

consular ship Any vessel officially registered to a member of the Imperial Senate. On diplomatic missions, consular ships were supposed to be free of normal inspection. [SW, SWR]

container ship Super transports, these ships are among the largest commercial vessels. Although slow and costly, they are the most efficient way to transport large amounts of cargo between systems. Their use of standardized cargo containers makes them efficient; just one container ship may carry hundreds of various-sized containers. Since they can't land, the ships have to use small craft to collect and transfer their cargoes. [SWSB]

control mind A technique of Force control through which a user can take direct control of other people's minds, it causes them to become automatons who must obey the user's will. This technique is considered a corruption of the Force, a product of the dark side. [HE, DFR, LC, DFRSB]

Contruum The birthplace of Alliance General Airen Cracken and his son, fighter pilot Pash Cracken. The planet has specific guidelines for naming its starships: Capital ships are named after virtues, while transports are named after beasts of burden or rivers. [WG]

Convarion, Ait An Imperial captain who was said to have participated in the conflicts at Derra IV and Hoth, he was given command of the *Corrupter* and sent off on suppression missions in the Outer Rim. These were nothing more than Imperial-sanctioned campaigns of terror against populated worlds. It was a task for a callous and cruel commander, and Ait Convarion fit the bill perfectly. Perhaps this was what attracted him to Ysanne Isard, the former Director of Imperial Intelligence. When she took control of the planet Thyferra and its bacta cartel, Convarion was given the responsibility of protecting her bacta convoys. One of them was hijacked by Rogue Squadron, and Convarion immediately went to the last jump point and arrived before the last of the tankers headed to hyperspace. The captain destroyed the defecting freighter before it had a chance to surrender and during a brief battle destroyed three Rogue Squadron ships.

Isard was furious with Convarion for destroying the freighter full of bacta. She ordered him to begin another campaign of terror, targeting any place that had benefited from the hijacked bacta. Some of it had gone to an ailing, defenseless colony at Halanit, which the *Corrupter* easily destroyed. Captain Convarion was then ordered to proceed to the Graveyard of Alderaan to assist the *Aggregator* in the annihilation of Rogue Squadron. But when the *Corrupter* arrived, X-wings were ready to attack. The last thing Captain Convarion saw were the proton torpedoes Wedge Antilles used to destroy the bridge Convarion was standing on. [BW]

Coome, R'yet The junior senator from Exodeen, he replaced M'yet Luure upon his death in the bombing of the Senate Hall on Coruscant. He was later elected to the Inner Council. [NR]

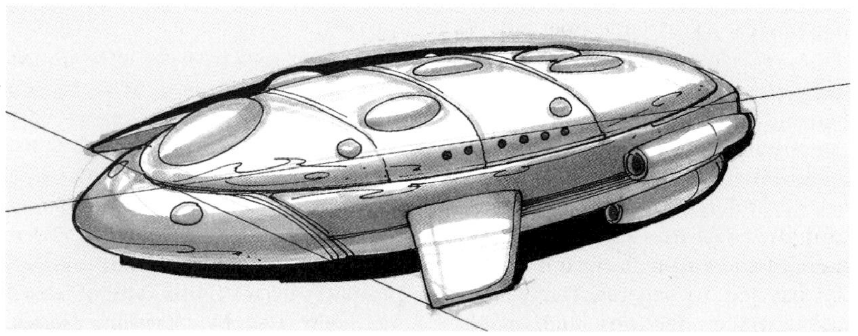
Coral Vanda

Coral Depths City A floating city on the planet Mon Calamari. [DA]

Coral Vanda A sub-ocean vacation cruiser, it explores the waters of the planet Pantolomin. The *Coral Vanda* makes excursions through a huge network of coral reefs off the coast of the Tralla continent. But vacationers come mainly to gamble in one of eight luxurious casinos. Full-wall transparisteel hulls give tourists breathtaking views of the sea life. The ship also has Adventure Rooms that recreate exotic locations through holographic and other sensory generators. Grand Admiral Thrawn nearly captured Lando Calrissian and Han Solo aboard the *Coral Vanda*. [DFR, DFRSB]

Corbantis This cruiser fell victim to Loronar Corporation, which was testing its new Needles smart missiles. Han Solo rescued fifteen injured beings from the battle-damaged cruiser and took them to the planet Nim Drovis. [POT]

Corellia Located in the Corellian sector and system, the planet orbits the star Corell along with four other habitable planets—all among the first members of the Old Republic. The system is best known for its fast ships, skilled traders, and pirates who regularly raid the local space lanes.

The inhabited worlds are called the Five Brothers, and Corellia is often referred to as the Elder Brother. The planet is attractive, with farms and small towns located between rolling hills, fields, and pockets of razor grass. Life-forms include the Corellian sea ray and the Corellian sand panther, a dangerous predator with poisoned claws. Points of interest include the Gold Beaches, the mid-size town of Bela Vistal, and the capital city of Coronet, located on the coast. Unlike many cities, Coronet has plenty of wide open spaces, because its small buildings and trading stalls are separated by parks and plazas. The center of government is the twenty-story Corona House.

Although all three Corellian species (human, Selonian, and Drall) mingle freely in Coronet, the collapse of the Empire's central authority has led to separatist sentiment and antialien factions such as the Human League.

Treasure Ship Row in Coronet, adjacent to Meteor Way and Starline Avenue, was formerly an eclectic bazaar catering to species from every corner of the galaxy. The Galactic Civil War and the Corellians' increasing isolation caused a sharp decline in the trading industry, and the row is now deserted. Beneath the planet's surface lies a vast network of tunnels built over thousands of years and home to many Selonians. Archaeological excavation has recently begun on a series of underground chambers dating from pre-Republic days. Within this ancient complex is a vast planetary repulsor, once used to move the planet to its current orbit from an unknown location.

Corellia was formerly ruled by a royal family, but became a republic three centuries ago after Berethon e Solo introduced democracy to the system. Three years after the Battle of Endor, the main Imperial battle fleets garrisoned key worlds, including Corellia and Kuat, due to their valuable shipyards. Fourteen years after the Battle of Endor, a riot in the Selonian enclave of Bela Vistal touched off widespread chaos and triggered the takeover of Corellia's government by Thrackan Sal-Solo and the Human League. The Human League was defeated and Sal-Solo captured by the intervention of the New Republic and a Bakuran task force. [CPL, AC, AS, SAC, TJP, RS]

Corellian A human race, it inhabits the Corellia star system. [SW]

Corellian Bloodstripe This red piping adorns the trousers of some Corellians who have distinguished themselves through bravery and heroic acts. Rebel hero Han Solo wears the Bloodstripe on his trousers, his only nod toward his time of military service. [HLL]

Corellian corvette An older multipurpose capital ship model, the mid-sized vessel still sees service throughout the galaxy. At 150 meters long, it can be a troop carrier, light escort vessel, cargo transport, or passenger liner. The corvette has a fast sublight drive and a quick hyperjump calculator for fast exits into hyperspace. Because this type of vessel has been used by Corellian pirates, authorities have nicknamed it the

Corellia

Blockade Runner. Princess Leia Organa's consular ship *Tantive IV* was a Corellian corvette. [SWSB]

Corellian grass snake This creature resembles the ysalamiri, except that it has neither fur nor claws. [NR]

Corellian gunship A dedicated combat capital ship, it is designed to be fast and deadly. At 120 meters long, it usually carries eight double turbolaser cannons, six quad laser cannons, and four concussion missile launch tubes. Engines fill more than half of its interior. With a small command crew and technical staff—but many gunners—the ship is an excellent antistarfighter platform. The New Republic makes extensive use of these vessels, as did the Alliance before it. [RSB, DFRSB]

Corellian Jumpmaster 5000 A type of starship, one example of which was the bounty hunter Dengar's *Punishing One*. [TBH]

Corellian Port Control A security force, it tries to keep the peace on the "smuggler's moon" of Nar Shaddaa. [TMEC]

Corellian Sanctuary A small domed building on Coruscant, it was created by exiled Corellians as a resting place for their dead after a hostile relationship developed between the New Republic and the Corellian government. Since repatriation had become impossible for Corellians who died away from home, they were cremated and their carbon remains were compressed into raw diamonds. These diamonds were then imbedded in the black ceiling and walls of the Sanctuary, creating the look of a shimmering sea of constellations as seen from Corellia. [BW]

Corellian sand panthers Carnivorous felines with poison-tipped claws, they live on Corellia. [TJP]

Corellian sector Always an inward-looking part of the Old Republic and then the Empire, it has progressively become more secretive and hermetic. Located in the most thickly populated part of the galaxy, the Corellian sector consists of several dozen star systems. The most important is the Corellian star system, made up of five planets: Selonia, Drall, the double worlds Talus and Tralus, and, most important, Corellia. The others are known collectively as the Outlier systems.

Moff Fliry Vorru was in charge of the Corellian sector during the Old Republic and allowed smugglers free rein. Vorru was later betrayed to the Emperor by underworld kingpin Prince Xizor and sent to Kessel, until he was freed by members of Rogue Squadron three years after the Battle of Endor. At about the same time, the new Corellian Diktat dissolved the Corellian Security Force and established a new, more Diktat-friendly Public Safety Service in its place, until New Republic representatives intervened. There is little work in the sector, and little prospect of any. The three dominant races (human, Drall, and Selonian) had been forced to get along because of the ever-present threat of punishment from the Empire. With that threat gone, all three are scrambling to assert their dominance in the sector. [AC, AS, SAC, RS, TSC]

Corellian Slip A dangerous flight maneuver first perfected by Corellian starship battle tacticians, it is attempted when one pilot cannot evade a pursuer. The first pilot's wingman flies directly at his teammate, using the first pilot's ship as cover; then, at the last second, the teammate ducks down and the wingman has a clear shot at the enemy. [CCG]

Corellian system The system contains five inhabited worlds—Corellia, Selonia, Drall, Talus, and Tralus—collectively called the Five Brothers because of their close orbits. Centerpoint Station, located directly between the double worlds of Talus and Tralus, is an ancient device that theoretically might have been used to transport the five planets through hyperspace to their current orbits. The system is policed by both the Corellian Defense Force and the Corellian Security Force, or CorSec. Pilots from the Corellian system are known throughout the galaxy for their superb skills, and the system is also notorious for its smugglers and pirates.

Corellian sand panther

The Corellian Engineering Corporation's shipyards are famous throughout the galaxy for manufacturing a vast variety of starships. Due to their strategic importance, the Empire kept the system heavily defended after the Battle of Endor. It was in the Corellian system that Mon Mothma convinced three major resistance groups to join forces, which marked the beginning of the Rebel Alliance.

A famous Corellian work of literature is *The Fall of the Sun* by Erwithat, and a respected honor is the red trouser piping known as the Corellian Bloodstripe. Corellians are known to hold the family in high esteem. Other Corellian traditions include enjoying ryshcate, a dark brown sweet cake made with vweliu nuts, which is traditionally baked and served at important celebrations. Another tradition is the awarding of Jedi Credits, or JedCreds, which were commemorative medallions made when a Corellian Jedi became a Master. The language known as Old Corellian, although essentially extinct, still survives among smugglers and pirates. Notable Corellians include Han Solo, General Crix Madine, General Garm Bel Iblis, and Wedge Antilles. [SW, MTS, COJ, HLL, DFR, AC, AS, SAC, FP, RS, SWAJ]

Core Worlds, the *See* Galactic Core

Corgan, Colonel The staff tactical officer for General Etahn A'baht, he served aboard the fleet carrier *Intrepid.* [SOL, TT]

Cornelius, Doctor *See* Evazan, Doctor

Coronet The capital city of the planet Corellia, it is known for its parkland and abundant open space. [AC]

Corporate Sector, the A free-enterprise fiefdom consisting of tens of thousands of star systems, it is run by a single wealthy and influential company, the Corporate Sector Authority (CSA). Located on the edge of the galaxy, it borders the Aparo and Wyl sectors. The skylines of its many urban worlds are lit by the multicolored flashes of countless advertising signs. It offers the widest selection of products anywhere, and tourists come from all over the galaxy to purchase its unique goods.

The CSA is made up of dozens of contributing companies and is run by the fifty-five members of the Direx Board, who are in turn headed by the ExO. The CSA has exclusive rights to use the sector's resources as it sees fit. Typically, the CSA uses up a planet's resources, then moves on to another. It isn't above using slave labor or grossly polluting the environment. Because there is no internal competition, the CSA can mark up prices of goods to many times their actual worth. Businesses in the sector accept only the Authority Cash Voucher and crystalline vertex.

A portion of the CSA's enormous profits were secretly funneled to Emperor Palpatine, with the understanding that the Empire would take no direct role in the operation of the sector. Therefore, the CSA formed its own military forces, including Security Police (called Espos) and a comparatively poor and outdated starfleet. Planets in the Corporate Sector include Ammuud, Bonadan, Roonadan, Etti IV, Kalla, Kail, Kir, Orron

III, Duroon, Mytus VII, Gaurick, Rampa, Mall'ordian, Reltooine, Knolstee, Mayro, and the Trianii colony worlds of Fibuli, Ekibo, Pypin, and Brochiib. The feline Trianii have been actively opposing the Corporate Sector's annexation of their worlds, and much of the fighting between the two sides occurred in the Tingel Arm. An armistice in the conflict was recently called after three years of intensive fighting.

Originally established hundreds of years ago under the Old Republic, the Corporate Sector was once a group of several hundred systems, all devoid of intelligent life. The corporations allowed to operate in the sector could purchase entire regions of space but were held in check by the watchful eye of the Republic. During the Emperor's rise to power, however, several corporate allies of Palpatine convinced him to expand the sector to encompass nearly 30,000 stars. Eleven native intelligent species were discovered in this expanded region, though this fact was effectively covered up. The CSA was established to manage the sector's operations, kicking off the modern era of the Corporate Sector.

Han Solo and Chewbacca had several legendary exploits in the Corporate Sector during their early adventuring, including a jailbreak from the infamous Stars' End penal colony. Following the Battle of Hoth, the Corporate Sector company Galactic Electronics developed a new magpulse weapons technology and sold it to the Rebel Alliance. In retaliation, the Imperial Star Destroyer *Glory* seized the corporation's deep-space research facility. Emperor Palpatine once had plans to build a great palace for himself in the sector, and construction continued even after Palpatine's apparent death at the Battle of Endor. Six years later, during the cloned Emperor's reappearance, the Corporate Sector declared its neutrality in the conflict and began supplying weapons and arms to both sides. [HSE, HSR, DESB, CSSB, TSC, SWAJ]

Corporate Sector Authority, the *See* Corporate Sector, the

Corridan This planet is located in the former center of the Empire's Rim territories. During the Empire's reign, the Black Sword Command was charged with the defense of Corridan, Praxlis, and the entire Kokash and Farlax sectors. [BTS]

corridor ghouls Quadrupeds about knee-high, these fast and deadly creatures native to Coruscant's lowest levels seem to be mammals. They have no fur, just stark white skin. Although they are blind, their navigation by echolocation gives them plenty of speed and agility. They have big ears and sharp teeth and emit high-pitched screams. [AS]

Corrupter A *Victory*-class Star Destroyer, it was formerly assigned to patrol the Outer Rim, hunting down pirates and smugglers for the Empire. When Director of Imperial Intelligence Ysanne Isard fled Coruscant, she used the *Corrupter* to defend her position on Thyferra and protect convoys of bacta leaving the planet. Under Captain Convarion, the ship caught up with and destroyed one bacta freighter that had been hijacked by Rogue Squadron. Several Alliance pilots were killed. The *Corrupter* then began a campaign of terror against those worlds that refused to pay Isard's inflated prices for the bacta she controlled, and particularly those worlds that had benefited from the free bacta given to them by Rogue Squadron. The first example was the destruction of the colony on Halanit. Isard thought she had Rogue Squadron pinned down in a trap at the Alderaan Graveyard, but the tables were turned and the fierce battle there resulted in the destruction of the *Corrupter*. [BW]

Corsair An ancient ship, it was used by dark-side sorcerer Naga Sadow to flee across the galaxy many millennia ago. [DLS]

Cort, Farl Former administrator of the colony on Halanit, he put out a distress call to the New Republic for bacta to aid his dying people. When Rogue Squadron members Corran Horn and Ooryl Qyrgg arrived with the bacta, he refused to take it without offering something in return. Although the market price of the bacta was valued in excess of a billion Imperial credits, Rogue Squadron had liberated it from the bacta cartel. Finally, an agreement was struck under which the colony would provide its guests with a hot bath and a fish dinner in exchange for the bacta. The head of the cartel, Ysanne Isard, chose to destroy the Halanit colony to serve as an example for other worlds that received liberated bacta. Farl Cort was assumed to have died during the colony's massacre. [BW]

Cortina During the early days of the New Republic, the worlds of Cortina and Jandur came to Coruscant to petition for membership. Though they initially seemed prideful and arrogant, both planets eventually signed the standard articles of confederation. [BTS]

Corulag A planet of fifteen billion citizens, it is in the Bormea sector of the Core Worlds, along the Perlemian Trade Route. The planet was devoted to Emperor Palpatine and was viewed as a model world of proper Imperial behavior. The capital city of Curamelle was the site of Corulag Academy, a branch of the Empire-wide military school. Corulag was only slightly less prestigious than the famous Raithal Academy. [HESB, SWAJ]

Corusca gem Extremely rare, this mineral is found only in the lower levels of the gas giant Yavin. Corusca gems are the hardest known substance in the galaxy and can even slice through transparisteel. [YJK]

Coruscant Zero-zero-zero: Coruscant's coordinates on all standard navigation charts show that it has long been the center of the known universe. The jewel of the Core Worlds, it has been the seat of galactic government for as long as records exist.

The planet's land mass is almost totally covered by an enormous multileveled city built on foundations that have been in place since the beginning of the Old Republic, more than a thousand generations ago. The oldest and densest population centers border the equator. Kilometer-high skyscrapers—some extending to the lower fringes of the atmosphere—and numerous spaceports cover Imperial City; its sky is filled with the lights of arriving and departing air traffic. Once there were personal skyhooks—giant satellites in low orbit that served as self-contained habitats—owned by the richest or most influential citizens, but they have been grounded for safety reasons by the New Republic. Kite-like hawk-bats make their homes in the artificial canyons, hunting granite slugs on the lower levels. The complex multileveled surface makes weather in Imperial City particularly difficult to predict.

The pyramidal Imperial Palace, formerly known as the Presidential Palace, is constructed of gray-green rock and sparkling crystals and is taller than every other structure on the planet, including the neighboring Senate building. The palace is said to be an impregnable fortress, decorated with hanging gardens, marble pyramids, and crystal roofs. The Emperor decorated some areas with patterns based on ancient Sith hieroglyphics. The palace contains the Grand Corridor, which links the Council chamber with the Assemblage auditorium. A cross hallway lined with suites leads to the Inner Council meeting room. The Grand Corridor, personally designed by Emperor Palpatine, features a high ceiling and cut-glass windows, and is lined with greenish-purple, vibration-sensitive ch'hala trees (revealed to be part of an elaborate surveillance system).

Other attractions on Coruscant include the Grand Towers, the Skydome Botanical Gardens, the underground city of Dometown, the Holographic Zoo of Extinct Animals, and the Galactic Museum, which holds ancient Sith artifacts from 4,000 years before the Battle of Yavin. Monument Plaza is a popular mall built around one of the peaks in the Manarai mountain range, where visitors can actually touch bare rock. For the last 300 years, the clock in the Central Gathering Hall has marked the hour by spreading a light across the sky, and every evening spectacular gray-green and red auroras flash throughout Coruscant's atmosphere.

The lowest, darkest levels of Imperial City were abandoned long ago and are now home to discarded equipment, wrecked starships, moss and lichen, spider-roaches and armored rats, duracrete worms and shadow-barnacles, wild gangs such as The Lost Ones, and nameless subhumans moving through the shadows. Because of the danger, the lowest forty or fifty levels are typically restricted

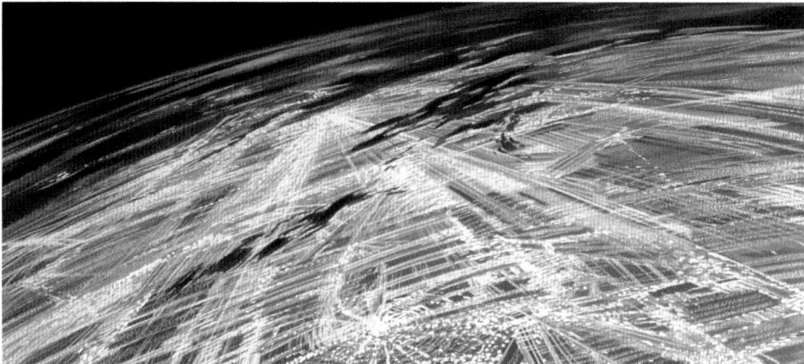

Coruscant

from normal traffic. A seedy tavern in this area is said to have not seen the sun in 90,000 years. The planet's orbit is far enough from its sun that orbital mirrors are needed to keep the nonequatorial regions at a comfortable temperature.

The snow-covered polar regions of Coruscant are home to turbo-ski resorts and are continuously mined by ice-boring machines. Because the planet's inland seas and oceans have long since been drained, the melted ice is delivered by huge pipelines to the densely populated metropolitan areas. The space surrounding Coruscant is defended by Golan III orbital battle stations and a low-orbit space-dock facility, while a powerful energy shield protects the planet itself. During the Emperor's reign, the planet was renamed Imperial Center, but has regained its original name. The New Republic hasn't, at least as yet, renamed the capital, which remains Imperial City.

After Palpatine's death, Sate Pestage led the Empire briefly for six months until forced into exile by a group of other Imperial Advisors, who were then supplanted by Director of Imperial Intelligence Ysanne Isard. The New Republic realized that Coruscant was a powerful symbol, the center of power, authority, and order, and whoever controlled it would be perceived as the rightful successor to galactic rule. Members of Rogue Squadron were sent in undercover to gather intelligence and find a way to bring down Coruscant's impenetrable double energy shields. They also freed many dangerous Black Sun criminals from Kessel, who returned to Coruscant and helped sabotage the Empire's operations.

They hijacked a construction droid to take them to the computer center, where they tapped into the computer system and forced one of the orbital mirrors to focus its beam on a water reservoir, boiling away the water in an instant and creating a devastating thunderstorm. The lightning shorted out the power grid, bringing the shields down. Admiral Ackbar and the New Republic fleet arrived and wiped out resistance. Isard allowed the New Republic to capture the planet, only leaving two Star Destroyers in defense, but released the deadly Krytos virus to spoil their triumph. She also left Agent Kirtan Loor on Coruscant as head of the Palpatine Counterinsurgency Force to sabotage the new government. After the escape of Rogue Squadron member Corran Horn, who had been imprisoned on the *Lusankya*, a Super Star Destroyer that had been buried underground and used as a prison facility for years, the ship blasted out of Coruscant's Mountain district, destroying almost 100 square kilometers of the surrounding city and killing millions before it escaped into hyperspace.

Five years after the Battle of Endor, Grand Admiral Thrawn attacked the New Republic on Coruscant and blockaded the planet using a group of cloaked asteroids. But he was defeated before he could attempt a takeover of the planet. The very next year, following the rebirth of the cloned Emperor, vicious Imperial attacks forced the New Republic to evacuate the planet. The victorious Imperial factions (primarily the Emperor's Ruling Circle and the military) then began to fight among themselves, devastating much of Imperial City and filling Coruscant's orbit with wrecked starships. Following the downfall of the resurrected Em-

Coruscant, metropolitan area

peror, the New Republic recaptured Coruscant and set to work repairing the extensive damage with the help of forty-story construction droids.

The following year, Imperial Admiral Daala planned to cripple the planet with a suicide Star Destroyer strike, but was unable to implement her plan. Some nineteen years after the Battle of Endor, the Second Imperium's Shadow Academy space station moved to Coruscant and attacked arriving supply convoys while hiding behind its cloak. The station was revealed when Jaina Solo overwhelmed the cloaking device with a light beam from one of Coruscant's orbiting mirrors.

Admiral Ackbar and Admiral Drayson have homes today near a small body of water called Victory Lake. Nearby is the New Republic Defense Force headquarters, which includes an exercise track running through hilly, wooded terrain. An inland reservoir west of Imperial City has a narrow beach bordered by a short cliff. The shoreline had been a holiday spot and playground, marked by all-hours resorts. Phosphorescent animals live in the reservoir, and long-winged sea shrikes live on the coast. Darth Vader's private retreat stood atop the cliff until it was destroyed by a B-wing fighter during the New Republic's recapture of Coruscant. Twelve years after the Battle of Endor, Luke Skywalker returned to build a hidden retreat on the shore, using the stones of Darth Vader's former home.

Some 300 kilometers southwest of the palace is Exmoor, a vast, opulent estate belonging to the Beruss clan of Illodia. Three primary spaceports handle most traffic arriving and departing from Imperial City: Eastport, Westport, and Newport. After the recapture of the planet, the Senate building was the first structure to be restored, although it was damaged in a bomb blast thirteen years after the Battle of Endor. Memorial Corridor leads to the Senate chamber and is lined with statues commemorating the heroes of the Rebellion. The Palace contains 20,000 rooms and more than fifty connected structures. It is rumored to contain a treasure compartment built by pirate general Toleph-Sor. Mon Mothma has a private estate in the Surtsey region, surrounded by gardens and a tree moat. [HE, DFR, LC, DE, JS, DA, COF, CPL, AC, FNU, DLS, COJ, AS, TMEC, YJK, DESB, DS, DF, ISWU, FP, TSW, RS, TSC, SWAJ, WG, KT, BW, BTS, SOL, TT]

Corusca Rainbow Formerly the *Black Asp*, the ship was renamed after the defection of its captain and crew to the Alliance struggle. It was given a place of extreme importance when it led the invasion fleet to liberate the capital world of Coruscant. [BW]

Cosmic Balance The predominant faith of the people on the planet Bakura, it is a form of extreme dualism. It holds that for every rise in power there is a corresponding decline elsewhere. True believers oppose the Jedi Knights, claiming that their increased abilities diminish others elsewhere in the galaxy. [TAB]

Cosmic Egg The deity of the Kitonak species. [TJP]

Council of Elders The Ewok ruling body on the forest moon of Endor, the Council is led by Chief Chirpa. [RJ]

Courage of Sullust A Rebel transport that was reconfigured to carry spacecraft, it went to the planet Ryloth on a secret mission with ten X-wings from Rogue Squadron. When the *Courage of Sullust* returned to Coruscant, it was loaded with ryll kor, an addictive spice that was to be used in a top secret project by Alliance Intelligence. [BW]

Court of the Fountain The closest that Mos Eisley came to having a high-class restaurant in the days that Jabba the Hutt held sway, the eatery was primarily a tourist trap owned by the gang lord. The Court of the Fountain was in a stone and stucco palace and featured fountains and exotic plants. Jabba's personal chef, Porcellus, worked as head chef there on the rare occasions that Jabba didn't need him. [TMEC]

Covell, General Although a fairly young man himself, this Imperial officer was placed in charge of the Empire's young and inexperienced ground troops by Grand Admiral Thrawn. The legendary General Veers had seen Covell as a younger version of himself, and he had served as Veers's first officer during the Battle of Hoth. Captain Pellaeon promoted Covell to major general in charge of *Chimaera's* ground troops after the Battle of Endor. Thrawn gave him the rank of general when he returned, and he immediately began training his troops for real battle. General Covell wanted to regain the Core Worlds, such as Coruscant, from the New Republic. But he never got to fulfill his dreams. General Covell died on the planet Wayland after the mad clone Jedi, Joruus C'baoth, destroyed his mind. [DFR, LC, DFRSB]

Covis, Spane A Rebel officer, he was the SpecForce Sentinel on Nar Shaddaa who first noticed the arrival of Imperial troops and thwarted the element of surprise in their attack. [TMEC]

Coway An underground-dwelling race of humanoids, they inhabit Circarpous V, or Mimban. The Coway are two-legged and covered by a fine gray down. They intensely dislike surface dwellers. Near-bottomless shafts built by the extinct Thrella often have side passages called Coway shafts, which lead to the Coways' underground world. One particular Coway shaft, lit by a type of luminous fungi, contains a vast subterranean lake that the Coway cross on large lily pads. The lake houses a dangerous, amorphous pseudopod-creature, and an abandoned Thrella city is located on the lake's far edge. This shaft's 200 Coway live in a primitive village built in a huge natural amphitheater. Their tribes are ruled by a triumvirate of leaders, who appeal to their god Canu for judgment on important matters. [SME]

Cracken, Airen The head of Alliance Intelligence, Gen. Airen Cracken was placed in charge of Rogue Squadron's mission to Coruscant in advance of the invasion fleet. His agents were already on the planet to assist the squadron as necessary, and as his son was part of that group, he had a firm grasp of the situation. The general was aware that there was a spy within Rogue Squadron, but he knew that it was not Tycho Celchu, whom others suspected of killing Rogue hero Corran Horn. He allowed Captain Celchu's trial to proceed so that Director of Imperial Intelligence Ysanne

Airen Cracken

Isard would continue to use her spy, thinking that the New Republic was convinced of the charges against Celchu. While her attention was occupied by the trial, Alliance Intelligence was able to accomplish several vital operations that might otherwise have been compromised. [BW]

Cracken, Pash The son of the head of Alliance Intelligence, he soloed before he was thirteen. His father had fabricated an identity for him that allowed his son to enter the Imperial Navy Academy. On his first assignment after graduation, he led his entire TIE wing in defecting to the Alliance. They later became known as Cracken's Flight Group, and their destruction of a *Victory*-class Star Destroyer made them and their leader legendary. He later became commander of an A-wing unit stationed out on the Rim.

When Rogue Squadron announced that it was seeking pilots to fill vacancies, Captain Cracken applied. On his very first mission as a Rogue, he was instrumental in bringing down the forward and aft shields and disabling the *Vengeance*, the Imperial cruiser that was being used for the assault on the Rebels on Mrisst. He assisted in the removal of Black Sun extremists from Kessel before being sent undercover to Coruscant. The Rogues were at the Palar memory core warehouse attempting to substitute altered memory cores when they were suddenly surrounded by stormtroopers. They somehow managed to escape with the help of Capt. Tycho Celchu. Later, Rogue Squadron met at a hideaway to reevaluate strategy for bringing down Coruscant's shields, and Cracken overheard Corran Horn accusing Captain Celchu of being a spy. At Celchu's trial for treason and murder, he was forced to testify about what he heard. [LC, BW]

Crado A Cathar Jedi who lived 4,000 years before the Battle of Yavin, the feline creature was apprenticed to Master Vodo-Siosk Baas. He was the lover of Sylvar, also from the planet Cathar. Crado became a devoted follower of Exar Kun, who turned to the dark side of the Force. Crado was killed along with Dark Sider Aleema in a multiple supernova eruption that they triggered. [DLS, TSW]

credit standard Credits are the basic monetary unit used throughout the Empire. Based on the Old Republic credit, the unit remains in use, although both the New Republic and the Imperial remnants produce their own currency. Most credits are stored and exchanged via computer transactions, but there is credit currency that can be carried and physically exchanged. [SME, SWRPG, HESB]

Creed, the A popular and benign Tarrick cult, it is founded on the twin principles of joy and service. [TT]

Creel, Pleader Irving A famous pleader, he defended Journeyman Protector Jaster Mereel in his trial for killing another protector on Concord Dawn. After pleading unrepentant, Mereel was exiled from his homeworld and changed his name to Boba Fett. [TBH]

Crondre During a multipronged attack by Grand Admiral Thrawn, whose true target was Ukio, this was a site of a diversionary battle. The Star Destroyer *Nemesis* took part in the fight. [LC]

Cron drift Located in the Auril sector of the Outer Rim, the drift was once a densely packed group of ten unstable stars known as the Cron cluster, located in the Cron system. During the Sith War, a Sith ship piloted by Dark Siders Aleema and Crado lured a pursuing Jedi force into the Cluster. Aleema activated an ancient Sith weapon and ripped the core from one of the stars, hurling it at the Jedi fleet and destroying it. This set off a chain reaction that ignited all ten stars in a multiple supernova, instantly killing Aleema and Crado. The shock wave from the explosion destroyed three of the nine Auril systems and necessitated the evacuation of the great Jedi planet of Ossus. Multicolored gases from the multiple explosions still fill the area, and powerful X rays and gamma radiation help mask any visiting ships from sensor probes. The drift also contains a large asteroid belt. Alliance listening post Ax-235, hidden within the belt, intercepted what appeared to be the Death Star technical plans and relayed them to Alliance high command prior to the Battle of Yavin. Around the same time, a Rebel formation was ambushed by Assault Gunboats in the asteroid field, but was rescued by X-wing fighters. [HSE, HLL, DA, DE2, FP, TSW]

Salacious Crumb

Cronus, Colonel A small but powerful man, he was a second-ranking Imperial officer when he decided to join forces with Admiral Daala. The colonel was in his flagship, *Victory,* when it was destroyed by a Corellian gunship. [DS]

Crseih Research Station Also known as Asylum Station, the artificial planetoid was a former Imperial research station and outlaw outpost formed by a cluster of asteroids joined by gravity fields and connecting airlink tunnels. Crseih had been a secret Empire research facility and was used by Lord Hethrir, the former Imperial Procurator of Justice, as his headquarters and a prison for his enemies. The station orbited a black hole with a white dwarf star and was bombarded with X rays. An enigmatic being called Waru created a cult on Crseih with his healing abilities until he apparently disappeared from this universe following a confrontation with Luke Skywalker. Crseih Station was then moved to Munto Codru in order to escape inevitable destruction when the crystallizing white dwarf was swallowed by the black hole. [CS]

cruiser, Rebel One of several different types of ships used by the Rebel Alliance and New Republic. One is the *Nebulon-B*, a medium-sized escort frigate originally designed by the Empire to combat short-range starfighter attacks. Some have been converted to command or medical ships, such as the one Luke Skywalker was treated on after his confrontation with Darth Vader in Cloud City. [SWVG, SWSB, ISB, ESB]

Crumb, Salacious The Kowakian monkey-lizard held a favored position at the court of Jabba the Hutt, usually sitting close to the bloated crime lord. When Jabba spilled food and drink, Salacious Crumb made sure he was close enough to catch it for himself. Scrawny and less than a meter high, reddish-brown in color and known for his taunting cackle and mimicry, Salacious was Jabba's court jester. He had gotten the job accidentally; after escaping from pursuers on to Jabba's spaceship, he hid in the Hutt's personal quarters, eating his food. When Jabba discovered Salacious he tried to eat him, but the creature escaped; his antics amused Jabba, who hired Salacious to make him laugh. He did so every day—up to the day he perished with Jabba when Rebel prisoners escaped and blew up the Hutt's sail barge. [RJ, SWCG]

crystal fern Perhaps a primitive silicon-based life-form, this "plant" is found in the asteroid belt near Hoth. Several meters tall, the crystal propagates when shards are broken off and carried to other asteroids. [ISWU]

Crystal Jewel The new name of the seedy casino on Coruscant where Han Solo won the deed to the planet Dathomir. Solo returned to the casino to meet a former smuggling contact, Jarill. The meeting led Solo to look into some strange occurrences in the asteroid belt known as Smuggler's Run. [NR]

crystalline vertex Currency used throughout the Corporate Sector to supplement Authority Cash Vouchers, it is made from a crystal mineral found on the planet Kir. When individuals enter the Corporate Sector, they must exchange all other forms of currency for crystalline vertex or Authority Cash Vouchers. [HSE]

Crystal Moon Widely regarded as the finest restaurant in Mos Eisley today, it was opened by Jabba's rancor keeper, Malakili, and his head chef, Porcellus, after the crime lord's death. [TJP]

crystal oscillator A standard part of the mechanics of some star cruisers, one was stolen from the wreck of a ship belonging to the Towani family on the forest moon of Endor. It was taken by an army of marauders led by giant King Terak because he believed that the oscillator was the source of mysterious power. [BFE]

crystal snake A transparent reptile found on Yavin 4, its bites bring a moment of piercing pain and send the victim into a deep sleep. Its dangerous qualities didn't prevent Jacen Solo from keeping one in his collection of pets. [YJK]

Culroon III An out-of-the-way, violence-plagued planet, it was largely

CZ-3

ignored by the Old Republic. Due to constant warfare, the primitive Culroon never developed space travel, but they did trade for technological goods, including blasters. When the Empire decided to construct a garrison on Culroon III, the Imperial general in charge of the operation agreed to a ceremonial surrender of the Culroon people by their leader, Kloff. When this ceremony turned out to be an ambush by the Culroon, the Imperial staff was rescued by an AT-AT commanded by then-Lieutenant Veers. [SWSB, MTS]

Culu, Shoaneb A Jedi Knight who lived some 4,000 years before the Galactic Civil War, she was a Miraluka from the planet Alpheridies. Like others of her species, all of whom are born without eyes, she could "see" through the use of the Force. [DLS]

Cundertol, Senator A Senator from Bakura and a member of the New Republic Senate Defense Council, he is prejudiced against nonhumans. When he was drunk, the traitorous Senator Tig Peramis stole his voting key, logged into his personal logs, and found top-secret information about the New Republic Fifth Fleet's deployment to the Farlax Sector under the command of Han Solo. Peramis gave the information to Yevethan leader Nil Spaar. [SOL]

Cuthus, Naroon The talent scout for crime lord Jabba the Hutt on Tatooine, he was a tall, dark-skinned human with long hair and a mustache. Naroon Cuthus signed the Max Rebo band to play for Jabba. [GG5, TJP]

Cyax This system contains the yellow star Cyax, the planet Da Soocha, and Da Soocha's uncharted fifth moon, where the Alliance established Pinnacle Base during the Emperor's reappearance. Cyax is the brightest star that can be seen from the Hutts' ancestral world of Varl, and it featured prominently in Hutt legends and myths. When the Hutts left Varl for other parts of the galaxy, they respectfully left the Cyax system unexplored and removed it from their astrogation charts. [DE, DESB]

cyberostasis A condition affecting droids, it occurs when they suffer a major external shock or an internal systems defect. They can induce the state as a protective reflex. All cybernetic functions are impaired or halted, usually resulting in shutdown. [HSE]

Cybloc XII Located in the Meridian sector, it is a small, lifeless moon that houses a major New Republic fleet installation and serves as a busy trading hub. The moon orbits the glowing, green-gold planet Cybloc, which circles the star Erg Es 992. Nine years after the Battle of Endor, R2-D2 and C-3PO tried to reach Cybloc XII in order to alert the New Republic that Leia Organa Solo had been kidnapped by Seti Ashgad of Nam Chorios. When they finally arrived, they found that all personnel had been killed by the Death Seed plague. The entire installation—including the port authority, the shipping companies, the Republic consular offices, and Fleet Headquarters—was being overrun with e-suited scavengers and looters. Prior to their arrival, two Republic cruisers, the *Ithor Lady* and the *Empyrean*, had been sent to deal with a pirate fleet from Budpock. [POT]

Cyborg Operations An arm of Jabba the Hutt's court, it was controlled by the droid EV-9D9. Deep in the bowels of Jabba's palace, Cyborg Operations obliterated the programming and personalities of droids through torture before assigning them to toil in Jabba's gang. [RJ]

Cyborrea A high-gravity planet, it is home to cyborg battle dogs called neks. The aggressive neks are a result of genetic and cybernetic engineering and are often used for protection by scavenger gangs. [DESB]

Cydorrian driller trees Leathery, shade-giving trees, they have far-reaching root systems. [TMEC]

CZ-3 An outdated but common model of droid, the CZ series is still in use throughout the galaxy. CZ-3, a business droid owned by Jabba the Hutt, had a built-in comlink and sophisticated scrambling and encryption programming. [SWAJ, CCG]

D-89 A pilotless ferret in Colonel Pakkpekatt's armada that chased the mysterious ghost ship called the Teljkon vagabond, it was assigned to breach the perimeter and, ideally, to invade the defenses of the vagabond just enough to provoke it to jump into hyperspace. There, New Republic vessels would have captured it. The vagabond hailed the D-89, but before the colonel's flagship *Glorious* could respond, the vagabond destroyed the ferret. [BTS]

Daala, Admiral Brilliant and coldly efficient, ruthless and beautiful—with a full head of copper-colored hair and piercing green eyes—she was the Empire's highest ranking female fleet officer ever and a true menace to the New Republic. The admiral emerged from a long-hidden corner of the galaxy to become one of the Republic's main military threats.

When she was younger, Daala suffered the taunts and unfair assignments that were to be expected in the sexist culture of the Empire. She excelled at one of the toughest military schools, the Imperial Academy on Carida, and finally caught the eye of Moff Tarkin, who took her on as a protégé and a lover. Tarkin wanted to keep both her and an ambitious new project he had conceived hid-

Admiral Daala

den from the Emperor. So he put Daala in charge of a top-secret weapons research facility, the Maw Installation, deep in the black-hole fields outside Kessel. He also gave her four Star Destroyers to command and the rank of admiral. The facility, which employed 180,000 people, produced plans and a prototype for the Death Star battle stations, the World Devastators used in battle against Mon Calamari, and the Sun Crusher fighter.

The Maw Installation was completely isolated for eleven years. When an Imperial shuttle finally arrived, Daala was shocked to find that its passengers were Han Solo, Chewbacca, and Kyp Durron, newly escaped from the Kessel spice mines. An interrogation revealed the stunning news of Tarkin's death, the destruction of both Death Stars, and the fall of the Empire. The admiral decided to seek revenge by unleashing the power of her ultimate weapon—the Sun Crusher—against the New Republic. But Han Solo had already won over chief scientist Qwi Xux, who freed the three, and together they stole the only working model of the Sun Crusher. Admiral Daala took out her fury by blasting much of the Kessel fleet and a colony on Dantooine. She almost destroyed Mon Calamari but for a brilliant tactic by Admiral Ackbar.

Having lost two of her Star Destroyers, she retreated and planned the devastation of Coruscant, the seat of New Republic power. But Kyp Durron ferreted her out and launched sun-destroying torpedoes from the Sun Crusher, taking out a third Star Destroyer and badly damaging Daala's ship, the *Gorgon*. The New Republic next engaged her at the Maw Installation, but she succeeded in downloading the most important weapons plans from the facility's computers before igniting an explosion that destroyed the installation, then slipped away to fight again.

With the *Gorgon* nearly worthless and her power diminished, Admiral Daala attempted to unite the feuding warlords who passed for Imperial authority. Because her undertaking was about to fail, she instead killed thirteen of the leading warlords with nerve gas and took control of all Imperial forces and a new Super Star Destroyer that she called the *Knight Hammer*. Once again she went head to head with the best that the New Republic had to offer, and once again she failed. She barely escaped with her life, but remained ready to face another day and perhaps another battle.

Years later, Daala surfaced as president of the Independent Company of Settlers, a group more than 3,000 beings strong and loyal to the old ways of doing things. The group purchased 1.5 billion acres on the planet Peduccis Chorios from the warlord K'iin of the Silver Unifir to live out their days. After top New Republic leaders thwarted a plot by the evil Seti Ashgad, Daala was reunited with her long-lost love, Liegeus Vorn. It was determined that Daala and her people would be allowed to go their own way, unhampered by the New Republic. [SWCG, COF, POT]

Dack *See* Ralter, Dack; *see also* Tymmo

Dadeferron, Torm Tall and brawny, with red hair and blue eyes, he was part of a secret civilian group organized by Rekkon, a Kalla university professor in search of his nephew, to locate missing friends and relatives who were suspected to be prisoners of the Corporate Sector Authority. Torm Dadeferron, who hailed from a wealthy family on the planet Kail, was second-in-command of a mission to infiltrate an Authority Data Center on Orron III. The group hoped to learn the location of the Authority's illegal detention center and rescue the political prisoners. [HSE]

Dagobah A mysterious, mist-shrouded swamp planet in the Dagobah system and the Sluis sector, it has no cities or advanced technology yet teems with a wide variety

Dagobah

of life, including giant swamp slugs, bioluminescent spotlight sloths, and butcherbugs who spin their slicing wirewebs between adjacent gnarl-trees. Colorful jubba birds whistle a highly soothing song. Petrified gnarl-tree forests abound. The trees have a unique life cycle: At the appropriate time a knobby white "spider" will break off from its parent tree, roam the swamp hunting and feeding on animals, and eventually take root.

Dagobah was home to the legendary Jedi Master Yoda, who instructed both Obi-Wan Kenobi and Luke Skywalker before his death at the age of 900 prior to the Battle of Endor. About twenty-five years before the Battle of Yavin, a Dark Jedi from Bpfassh created trouble throughout his sector before being stopped on Dagobah. A dark cave near Yoda's home could be a vestige of this Dark Jedi's power, and it may have served to hide Yoda's presence during the Emperor's Jedi purge. Luke Skywalker returned to Dagobah five years after Yoda's death and discovered a ship's beckon call that could have belonged to the Bpfasshi Dark Jedi. Skywalker returned three years later with the Jedi Knight Callista, to help her try to regain her lost Force ability. [ESB, ESBN, ESBR, HE, DS, ISWU, SWAJ]

Dahai, Tedn A member of the Bith jizz band Figrin D'an and the Modal Nodes, he played the fanfar. [TMEC]

Dak, Zebulon Wealthy and influential, he was founder and owner of the Zebulon Dak Speeder Corporation. [DTV]

Dakkar the Distant A cantina owner in Mos Eisley. [TJP]

Dakshee Long under Imperial rule, this planet in the Colonies region has been marked by constant unrest. [SWAJ]

D'akul, Shada A mercenary from a mysterious militaristic order of female warriors known as the Mistryl Shadow Guards, Shada D'akul served as bodyguard for the smuggler chief Mazzic. Among her weapons are enameled zenji needles, which she throws with lethal accuracy—and also uses as fashion accessories. She and her friend Karoly D'ulin posed as the Tonnika sisters after being involved

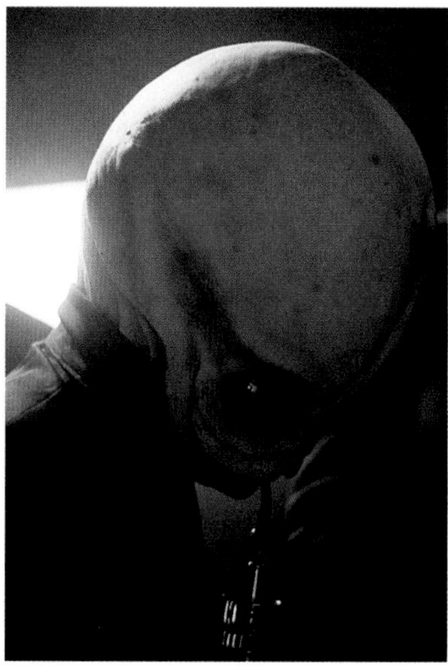

Tedn Dahai

in the botched transport of the Hammertong device. [TMEC, LC, LCSB]

Dalla the Hutt A Hutt from whom Han Solo borrowed money—using the *Millennium Falcon* as collateral—to buy Leia Organa Solo a planet for the refugees who were off-world when the Empire destroyed the planet Alderaan. [CPL]

Dalron Five A planet devastated by the Empire during an infamous siege, it was subject to warfare techniques developed originally by Alliance General Jan Dodonna. Shistavanen Wolfman scout Lak Sivrak later found Dalron Five refugees living on a rocky moon. [MTS]

Daluuj A fog-shrouded, watery world besieged by dangerous atmospheric storms, it was home to a remote Imperial training outpost. After Admiral Ackbar and several other Mon Calamari landed on Daluuj in escape pods, Han Solo and his companions attempted to rescue them. Huge lake worms dragged the *Millennium Falcon* underwater, but it was retrieved when the worms turned their attention to a group of attacking Imperial speeders. [CSW]

Damaya A member of the Singing Mountain clan of the Witches of Dathomir. [CPL]

Damonite Yors-B The fifth planet in its system in the Meridian sector, it is an uninhabited ice-covered world where the atmosphere is lashed by turbulent winds and ion and methane storms. It appears acid-yellow from space. Nine years after the Battle of Endor, Han Solo and Lando Calrissian came to the planet searching for any sign of Leia Organa Solo. Instead, they found the crashed cruiser *Corbantis* and brought its survivors to the medical facility on Nim Drovis for treatment. On their way out of the planet's atmosphere, they were attacked by a swarm of Loronar Corporation's CCIR needle fighters. [POT]

D'an, Figrin This Bith musician and his band have played their brand of jizz music all over the galaxy, although an engagement on Tatooine was almost their last.

The Bith are native to Clak'dor VII, a small, bog-filled planet in the Mayagil Sector that was nearly destroyed generations ago by chemical warfare. The Bith have evolved into an intelligent and peaceful species with great aptitude in the arts and sciences.

Figrin D'an has remained politically neutral, something that has probably kept him and the band alive despite witnessing some horrific acts spurred by the Galactic Civil War. The band, Figrin D'an and the Modal Nodes, includes D'an on the Kloo horn and gasan string drum; Doikk Na'ts on the Dorenian Beshniquel, or Fizzz; Tedn Dahai and Ickabel G'ont on fanfar; Nalan Cheel on the bandfill with horn bells; and Tech Mo'r, who enhances the music with a difficult-to-play ommni box. Lirin Car'n provides backup on the kloo horn.

Figrin loves to play sabacc and use glitterstim spice. He can't be bribed outright, but the large-headed D'an will gamble away information about things that he has seen. For each of his own winning hands, he gives away some desired tidbit to the loser. Figrin and the band came to Tatooine and were hired by crime lord Jabba the Hutt. But they incurred his wrath by accepting a onetime gig at the wedding of Lady Valarian, which dissolved into anarchy. The band escaped and was given shelter—and a job—by Wuher, bartender at the Mos Eisley cantina owned by a Wookiee named Chalmun. It was there that they witnessed Ben Kenobi put down two thugs with his lightsaber. Figrin

Figrin D'an (right)

lost ownership of all the band's instruments in a sabacc game, but eventually bought them back and the troupe continued on its intergalactic tour. [SWCG, SW, TMEC]

Dance of the Seventy Violet Veils A ceremonial dance, it was performed by the Askajian dancer Yarna d'al' Gargan at the wedding of Princess Leia Organa and Han Solo. [TJP]

Dandalas A planet in the Farlax sector near the Koornacht Cluster. [SOL]

Dan'kre, Liska A wealthy Bothan female, she is an old school friend of fellow Bothan Asyr Sei'lar. She invited Sei'lar and Rogue Squadron member Gavin Darklighter to a party held in a skyhook high above Coruscant. It was there that Darklighter had an altercation with Karka Kre'fey, grandson of a Bothan general who led Rogues into an ambush that nearly destroyed the squadron. Fortunately for Kre'fey, Darklighter refused to fight. [BW]

Dantooine Far removed from most galactic traffic, this olive, blue, and brown planet has no industrial settlements or advanced technology. Its surface is covered with empty steppes, savannas of lavender grass, and spiky blba trees. The planet has two moons and abundant animal life, including herds of hairy beasts, simple balloon-like creatures, and mace flies. Primitive nomadic tribesmen, the Dantari, move along the coasts, though their numbers are so few the planet is essentially uninhabited.

Some 4,000 years before the Galactic Civil War, Jedi Master Vodo-Siosk Baas established a training center among Dantooine's ruins, where he instructed Exar Kun and the Cathar warriors Crado and Sylvar. Millennia later, Dantooine served as the primary base for the Rebel Alliance until it was evacuated in one day's time after an Imperial tracking device was found hidden in a cargo shipment. Some eleven years later, fifty colonists from Eol Sha were relocated to the planet, but a group of Admiral Daala's AT-AT walkers wiped them out. [SW, LC, JS, DA, DLS, ISWU, SWAJ, JASB]

Danuta A planet with a secret Imperial base, it was where the technical plans for the Empire's first Death Star were kept. Rebel Alliance agent Kyle Katarn infiltrated the facility and stole the plans, which were later beamed to Princess Leia Organa's corvette near Toprawa. [DF, SWR]

Darek system Located near the Hensara and Morobe systems, the system was where Rogue Squadron made a hyperspace transit jump three years after the Battle of Endor, in order to disguise the squadron's origin point and hidden base. [RS]

Darepp The planet to which the starliner *Star Morning*, owned by the Fallanassi religious order, traveled after the group left the planet Teyr. When Luke Skywalker departed from Teyr, he guessed that the other ships in his outbound corridor were headed for the Foeless Crossroads or for Darepp. [SOL]

Dantooine

Dargul The sister world of the blob-racing planet Umgul, it is the location of Palace Dargul, residence of the Duchess Mistal. When the duchess reached marriage age, a young man named Dack became her consort. He later fled to Umgul, was taken captive by Lando Calrissian, and was returned to the duchess for a million-credit reward. [JS]

Dark Curse A nickname given to Imperial pilot DS-61-4. [CCG]

Dark Force *See Katana* fleet

Dark Jedi The reborn clone Emperor envisioned a new breed of Jedi Knights, trained in the dark side of the Force and loyal to him for the 1,000 years that he expected to reign. Evil Jedi Knights operating during the Clone Wars were also called Dark Jedi, a group of whom threatened the Bpfassh system. About nineteen years after the Battle of Endor, the Second Imperium attempted to train a new legion of Dark Jedi at the Shadow Academy. Their goal was to retake the galaxy and reestablish the Empire. [DE, DFR, YJK]

Darklighter, Biggs A childhood friend and role model for Luke Skywalker, the brave X-wing fighter pilot lost his life in the assault on the Death Star during the Battle of Yavin.

Raised in a wealthy family on Tatooine, Biggs Darklighter met young Luke in the town of Anchorhead. The two, while fast friends, always competed. They raced landspeeders and skyhoppers and planned to enter the Imperial Space Academy together. But Luke's uncle, Owen Lars, said he needed his nephew to work the farm for at least another season. While in the Academy, Biggs and some classmates contacted the Rebel Alliance and made plans to join it as soon as possible after graduation.

After Biggs left the Academy he was assigned to a noncombat post as First Mate on the merchant ship

Rand Ecliptic. But first he made a final trip to Tatooine where he had an unexpected reunion with Luke at their friend Fixer's shop in Tosche power station. In private, Biggs told Luke that he was going to join the Rebellion. Within weeks he and his ship's executive officer staged a mutiny, stole the ship and its valuable ore cargo, and turned it and themselves over to the Alliance.

Biggs piloted an X-wing fighter in a number of battles before uniting with Luke Skywalker on the fourth moon of Yavin as the assault on the first Death Star was about to begin. As Red Three to Luke's Red Five, he destroyed several TIE fighters before finally being taken out by a blast from Darth Vader's TIE fighter. [SW, SWN]

Darklighter, Gavin A cousin of Rogue Squadron legend Biggs Darklighter, he is tall, with brown hair. He was a sixteen-year-old Tatooine farm boy when Wedge Antilles pushed for his inclusion in the squadron over the objections of General Salm. Rogue Leader's faith in his young recruit was quickly rewarded when Darklighter's simulator test scores put him near the top of his class. He fought at Chorax and Hensara III without incident or distinction. During a night raid by Imperial stormtroopers at Rogue Squadron's hidden base on Talasea, he was seriously wounded by blaster fire but miraculously survived. Later, he participated in the retaliatory strikes against the Imperial bases at Vladet and both times at Borleias.

Darklighter was with other Rogue members when they went on a reconnaissance mission to Coruscant to get a feel for the general mood of the alien population prior to an Alliance invasion. There was no way to prepare for what the Rogues found in one of the alien quarters, Invisec. At the Azure Dianoga cantina he made the mistake of rejecting the advances of Asyr Sei'lar, a female Bothan. Brought before the Alien Combine on charges of bigotry, he narrowly escaped death from the group, then from the squadron of stormtroopers that subsequently raided the combine's hideout.

During that battle, Sei'lar and the combine members realized that Darklighter and the other Rogues were not their foes, and so they joined forces against the Empire. Their first attempt to bring down Coruscant's shields ended in dismal failure at the Palar warehouse. As they were about to switch remanufactured memory cores, their team was assaulted by stormtroopers. When they regrouped, Darklighter came up with the idea of "taking the planet by storm"—creating a tremendous thunderstorm and using the electrical charges from the lightning strikes to short out the power system. It worked and the shields came down, allowing the Alliance invasion fleet to send in ground troops. [BW]

Darklighter, Huff "Huk" The father of Rogue Squadron hero Biggs Darklighter, he was proud of his son's valor but had bittersweet feelings because Biggs wasn't around to receive his accolades. Although surrounded by his family, there was still an air of loneliness about Huff Darklighter. One of the wealthiest residents on Tatooine, he made the bulk of his fortune trading goods throughout the galaxy. But sometimes the bottom line was so important to Darklighter that he paid large bribes to do business. He once even trafficked in black-market Imperial armor, weapons, and fighter craft. Later he became an invaluable source for Rogue Squadron when it needed weapons and munitions to use against former Director of Imperial Intelligence Ysanne Isard. [XW; BW]

Darklighter, Jula Unlike his prosperous brother, Huff, he is a hardworking moisture farmer on Tatooine. They share common ground in their pride in their sons. Jula's son, Gavin Darklighter—like Huff's son, Biggs, before him—has also become a legend within Rogue Squadron. [BW]

Darklighter, Lanal Huff Darklighter's third wife, she is more like another mother to Gavin than an aunt. When Huff decided to have more children, his second wife left him, still hurting from the loss of their only son, Biggs. Lanal is also the sister of Silya Darklighter—Gavin's mother—so she is Gavin's aunt on both sides of the family. [BW]

Darklighter, Silya The mother of Gavin Darklighter, she is both proud of her son and fearful of the dangers that surround him when he is with Rogue Squadron. Most of the time she is able to put the worry out of her mind, for she is very busy with her younger children and the farm on Tatooine. [BW]

Huff "Huk" Darklighter

Dark Lord of the Sith Originally, these were powerful Jedi Knights who used the dark side of the force. The title of Dark Lord was passed down from one generation to the next, with only one or two Dark Lords existing at a time. The mummified remains of many of the Dark Lords are preserved in monumental temples on Korriban. Darth Vader and Emperor Palpatine were the most recent Dark Lords of the Sith. [TOJ, DLS]

Darksaber Project Code-name for the secret super weapon ordered built

Biggs Darklighter

by a group of Hutt crime lords under Durga: a reconstruction of the original Death Star's laser, yet even more powerful. Its ultimate failure resulted in Durga's death. [DS]

dark side, the *See* Force, the

Dark Side Adepts Members of the reborn clone Emperor's New Imperial Council, they were drawn from the ranks of the Emperor's cohorts in the dark side of the Force and were trained by him to become powerful practitioners of the Force. They served the Emperor's will and were supposed to eventually replace most planetary governors. [DE]

Dark Side Compendium An encyclopedia of dark-side lore that was being written by the reborn clone Emperor. He had completed three volumes of a proposed several-hundred-volume set before Luke Skywalker and Princess Leia defeated him. Luke read all three volumes: *The Book of Anger, The Weakness of Inferiors,* and *The Creation of Monsters.* [DE]

Dark Star Hellions *See* swoop gangs

DarkStryder A strange and powerful alien force that provided previously unheard-of technology to a rogue Imperial moff, Kentor Sarne, its secrets lay hidden deep past the Kathol Rift and unknown space. The New Republic first encountered the DarkStryder artifacts and technology when it pursued Sarne some four years after the Battle of Endor. Many of the events surrounding the pursuit and DarkStryder were classified by the New Republic. [DSTC]

Darlon sector Site of an orbiting casino where the Twi'lek female, Seely, met space pirate Drek Drednar before becoming one of his lieutenants. [SWAJ]

Darlyn Boda An Imperial planet in name, it is about half a day's travel from Hoth. Darlyn Boda is a steamy, muddy world that has long had both a thriving criminal underground and an active network of Rebel contacts. Its main city is also called Darlyn Boda. Many years ago, the bounty hunter droid 4-LOM abandoned his former position as a valet aboard the *Kuari Princess* when the ship stopped at Darlyn Boda. Years later, after the Battle of Hoth, 4-LOM and the Gand bounty hunter Zuckuss severely damaged one of the last Rebel transports to leave the planet, the *Bright Hope,* then had a change of heart, rescued the ninety Alliance soldiers aboard, and transported them to Darlyn Boda for treatment of their wounds. [TBH]

Dark Side Adepts

Darm, Umolly A well-connected Nam Chorios trader, she has the ability to acquire many things offworld. Umolly Darm exported Spookcrystals, long green and violet crystals that are found in clusters in the deep hills of the planet. She was told that the crystals were used on K-class planets to help make flowers grow better, but in reality they were used in spaceneedles—long-distance smart missiles—as a type of artificial intelligence. [POT]

D'armon, Pav A Mistryl Shadow Guard, she was second-in-command in operation Hammertong, the codename for one of the long, cylindrical sections of the superlaser for the second Death Star. Pav D'armon was killed in an Imperial raid. [TMEC]

Dar'Or A planet in the Dar'Or system and the seldom-visited Jospro sector, this low-gravity, forested world orbits an orange sun and is home to intelligent flying mammals called Ri'Dar. Along with the slothlike sabertoothed indola, they inhabit the middle levels of a dense network of 200-meter-tall waza trees that cover Dar'Or. Predators of the Ri'Dar include the indola and the avian elix, which was recently introduced to the planet by ecologists to save it from extinction on a supernova-threatened world. The Ri'Dar have organized their primitive society into warrens and cities. The planet has been declared a Species Preservation Zone, but some smugglers still hunt the elix to sell its meat. [GG4]

Darpa sector Located in the Core on the edge of the Colonies region, the sector makes up one-half of the Ringali Shell. Its worlds include Esseles, Rhinnal, and Ralltiir, all of which are linked by the Perlemian Trade Route. The sector was long ruled by the heavy-handed Moff Jander Graffe. [SWAJ]

Darsk, Ris Rogue Squadron's Erisi Dlarit assumed this identity—that of a wealthy Kuati traveling with her telbun to conceive a child on Coruscant—during a reconnaissance mission to Imperial Center. [BW]

Dartibek system A system that includes the planet Moltok, it is the homeworld of the Ho'Din. [GC4]

dart shooter A handheld weapon, it fires metal projectiles, or darts, that are usually filled with toxins that paralyze or kill. [HLL]

Da Soocha A watery world sometimes called Gla Soocha, it is located in the Cyax system. The name means Waking Planet in Huttese, from an old Hutt myth about an intelligent, planet-covering ocean near the revered star Cyax. Though the Cyax system was never visited by the Hutts, it was explored by the Rebel Alliance, which established a base on the planet's fifth moon during the reborn clone Emperor's reappearance. Da Soocha has no native intelligent species. It was considered as an evacuation site during the attack of Imperial World Devastators on Mon Calamari. [DE, DESB]

data card This thin plastic rectangle is used to store digital information. [TM, HE, HESB]

datapad A palm-sized personal computer, it is used as a portable workstation by all levels of society. A

Dathcha

datapad has ports for coupling with droids or large computer terminals. [TM, HE, HESB]

Datar This planet was the site of a massacre of a group of Rebels by Imperial troops who disobeyed Darth Vader's order that he wanted prisoners to interrogate. [TMEC]

Dathcha A Jawa adventurer and trader, he was famous for taunting a krayt dragon and escaping to tell the tale. Dathcha belonged to the clan of Jawas that sold C-3PO and R2-D2 to Luke Skywalker's uncle, Owen Lars. Dathcha wanted to leave Tatooine and explore the galaxy, but he never got the chance, as his entire clan was wiped out by stormtroopers searching for the droids. [CCG]

Dathomir Located in the Quelii sector, the planet is a low-gravity world with three continents, a wide ocean, four small moons—and witches: the Witches of Dathomir, to be exact, a group of Force-sensitive women who ride fearsome rancors.

Dathomir is covered with a wide variety of terrain including mountains, deserts, purple savannas, and forests of eighty-meter trees and vines bearing hwotha berries. Indigenous life includes flying reptiles, piglike rodents, long whuffa worms, burra fish, and rancors. Semiintelligent, two-legged reptiles live in the desert and call themselves the Blue Desert People.

Humans came to Dathomir when a group of illegal arms manufacturers were exiled to the planet by the Jedi Knights. Several generations later, a rogue Jedi named Allya was also exiled to Dathomir. She began to teach the Force to the planet's inhabitants and to her descendants, who also learned to tame the wild rancors. Nearly 400 years before the Battle of Yavin, the two-kilometer Jedi academy ship *Chu'unthor* crashed in a Dathomir tar pit. Jedi sent to recover the crashed ship were repulsed by the witches—female inhabitants who had learned to use the Force. Different clans of these witches (Singing Mountain, Frenzied River, and Misty Falls) were formed, including a group of Dark Siders calling itself the Nightsisters. Life among the clans followed a pattern of female dominance, and males were largely used as slaves for work or breeding.

Imperial forces constructed orbital shipyards and a penal colony on Dathomir's surface. But after Emperor Palpatine learned the power of the Nightsisters' leader, Gethzerion, he ordered all the prison's ships destroyed to prevent her from leaving the planet. The stranded Imperials at the prison were then enslaved by Gethzerion and the other Nightsisters. Four years after the Battle of Endor, Han Solo won the planet in a high-stakes sabacc game from Warlord Omogg, who claimed it had been in her family for generations. Han's subsequent adventures on the planet resulted in the destruction of both the Nightsisters and the forces of Warlord Zsinj. About fifteen years after the Battle of Endor, a new order of Nightsisters based in the Great Canyon emerged. This clan, founded by Luke Skywalker's former student Brakiss, allied itself with the remnants of the Empire, treated males as equals, and sent the best Force students to be trained at the Empire's Shadow Academy. [CPL, COJ, YJK, DS, ISWU]

Dauren, Lieutenant An Imperial lieutenant, he was a comm officer on Carida in the main citadel of the Imperial military training center. Lieutenant Dauren was charged with escorting stormtrooper Zeth Durron to meet his brother Kyp on a rooftop. Once there, Dauren attacked Zeth and beat him, until Zeth fought back and killed his attacker. [COF]

Davis A handsome blond smuggler from Fwatna, he saved Han Solo from a gang of Glottalphibs on Skip Five in the Smuggler's Run asteroid field. Davis was later killed in one of the bombings by the Dark Jedi Kueller. Only then did Sinewy Ana Blue reveal that she was secretly in love with Davis. [NR]

Davnar This planet is the homeworld of the famed winged predator, the kalidor. The Kalidor Crescent, the highest award that can be bestowed upon Rebel Alliance pilots, is named in honor of the creature. [FP]

Dawferm Selfhood States A group of worlds, they formed their own protective federation during the turmoil and constant warfare in the six years following the Battle of Endor. [DESB]

Daykim The "king" of the feral bureaucrats who live in the underlevels of Imperial City on Coruscant. [DA]

Daysong A splinter group of the Rights of Sentience Party, they believe that honor guards are a form of servile humiliation and should be replaced by droids. But Daysong excludes synthdroids from that category, on the grounds that synthflesh is living and has rights as well. [POT]

Dazon, Hem A male scout from the planet Cona, he is a scaleless reptile-like humanoid. Like many Arcona, Dazon has an addiction to salt, as indicated by his golden eye color. [CCG]

Deak A boyhood chum of Luke Skywalker, he lived in Anchorhead on Tatooine. As teens, Luke and Deak (his real name was Deacon), flew their skyhoppers in mock aerial duels

Hem Dazon

and raced through the twisting canyons near their homes. [SW]

Death The town of Dying Slowly on the penal planet Jubilar eventually came to be known by this name. [TBH]

death engine A massive, heavily shielded Imperial weapon, it is shaped like a crab, with a phalanx of blast weapons from front to rear. A death engine moves on repulsorlifts. [TMEC]

Deathseed Deathseed are lethal TIE fighter variants built specifically for use by Twi'lek pilots. The word Deathseed is the Basic language translation for Chir'daki, the fighters' original name. [BW]

Death Seed plague A horrific disease, it is both undetectable and 100 percent lethal to all species. Bacta, instead of curing the plague, accelerates the process. What was called a disease actually was an infestation of drochs, small insects that bury themselves in the flesh of a being and are absorbed into the bloodstream, where they almost literally drink out the life of the victim. The last outbreak was more than seven centuries before the Galactic Civil War, when the Death Seed plague wiped out millions of beings. All the drochs were then moved to Nam Chorios, where the peculiar geology and filtered sunlight basically held them in check. But the plague reared its terrifying specter again when Seti Ashgad and Dyzm, a mutated droch, started planting drochs aboard New Republic vessels. [POT]

Death's Head An Imperial Star Destroyer, it was commanded by Captain Harbid as part of Grand Admiral Thrawn's armada. [HE, DFR, LC]

Death Star It was the ultimate weapon, the decisive force that, once and for all, would quiet any remaining opposition. The Empire developed and constructed this top-secret battle station the size of a small moon, with more destructive power than the Imperial fleet. The Death Star had the horrifying ability to destroy an entire planet teeming with billions of people with a relatively short burst of its superlaser. Emperor Palpatine hoped it would instill the terror needed to keep thousands of star systems in line. It was rule by fear of force.

That doctrine, and the development of the super weapon, came from the mind of Grand Moff Tarkin, a cold and calculating evil genius. A prototype Death Star was first built at a research facility that Tarkin kept secret even from the Emperor, the Maw Installation. Many of its systems were conceived and designed by famed starship engineer Bevel Lemelisk under the direction of Tol Sivron, the Twi'lek chief scientist.

The Death Star's main weapon was the planet-annihilating superlaser, which was used twice. As a test, it destroyed the penal colony planet of Despayre, where it was built. Later it was used to destroy Princess Leia Organa's home planet, Alderaan, causing the instant death of billions of sentient creatures.

The first Death Star was huge, some 120 kilometers in diameter. It had a crew of more than 265,000 soldiers. The total personnel soared to more than one million with the addition of gunners, ground troops, and starship support crews and pilots. In addition to the superlaser, the battle station had 15,000 turbolasers, 700 tractor beam projectors, 7,000 TIE fighters, 4 strike cruisers, some 20,000 military and transport vessels, and more than 11,000 combat vehicles.

Yet simple errors doomed the station. Its defenses were built around repelling a capital ship attack; starfighters were considered insignificant. When the Alliance mounted its as-

Death Star

sault over Yavin, Tarkin considered the attack inconsequential; only the TIE fighters under Darth Vader's direct command were deployed. So, guided by the Force, Luke Skywalker was able to destroy this powerful weapon by firing simple proton torpedoes down an unshielded exhaust vent.

But four years later, a second Death Star neared completion, larger than the original. It was about 160 kilometers in diameter and armed with a superlaser even more powerful than its predecessor's and so accurate that it could be trained on capital ships. At its north pole was a heavily armored 100-story tower topped by the Emperor's private observation chamber.

More than a weapon of terror, the second Death Star was part of an elaborate trap to lure the Rebels out of hiding by providing a tempting target. Emperor Palpatine allowed the Alliance's Bothan spies to learn the location of the Death Star, but never revealed that the superlaser was fully operational on the incomplete station. A small team of Rebel commandos on the forest moon of Endor, assisted by the native Ewoks, destroyed the shield generator protecting the Death Star, allowing the *Millennium Falcon* and a starfighter to fly inside and destroy its power core. Within a month, Rebel leader Mon Mothma declared the end of the Rebellion and the birth of the New Republic.

Years later, the prototype Death Star—never intended as a practical weapon of war—was activated by Tol Sivron after the Maw Installation was attacked by a New Republic task force. The prototype was finally destroyed when Kyp Durron, piloting the Sun Crusher, lured the Imperial weapon into one of the Maw's black holes, where it was smashed by gravitational forces.

In the end, nothing symbolized the Empire's oppression more than the Death Star. But it also came to represent the Empire's greatest weakness: the belief that technology was supreme and all foes insignificant. [SW, RJ, SWVG, DSTC]

Death Star gunner Most of the gunners in the Imperial Navy once aspired to be TIE fighter pilots but lacked sufficient skills to fly starfighters. A few of them were assigned to the first Death Star to operate the main artillery. [GG1, CCG]

decicred A monetary unit equal to a tenth of a credit. [SOTE]

Declaration of a New Republic A document that set forth the principles, goals, and ideals of the new galactic Republic, it was released a month after the Battle of Endor. Its signers were Mon Mothma of Chandrila, Princess Leia Organa of Alderaan, Borsk Fey'lya of Kothlis, Admiral Ackbar of Mon Calamari, Sian Tevv of Sullust, Doman Beruss of Corellia, Kerrithrarr of Kashyyyk, and Verrinnefra B'thog Indriummsegh of Elom. [HESB]

Deega, Senator The senator from Clak'dor VII, he is a Bith who was named to the New Republic Senate Defense Council. Senator Deega is deeply committed to pacifism and ecology because of the ecological warfare that nearly destroyed his planet. He was chosen to replace the traitorous Senator Tig Peramis, but also disagreed with Chief of State Leia Organa Solo's actions against the Yevetha. [SOL]

Deegan, Lieutenant A top-rated Corellian pilot, he was a member of Team Orange and worked with Wedge Antilles when he headed the Imperial City reconstruction crews. [JS, RS]

Deej An Ewok warrior married to Shodu, Deej is the father of Wicket, Weechee, Willy, and Winda. [ETV]

Deep Core haulers Freighters licensed by the Empire, they hauled cargo to Imperial systems in the Deep Core. [DE]

Deep Core Security Zone An area of the inner Galactic Core, its sectors were sealed to traffic. Emperor Palpatine's throneworld of Byss was hidden inside the zone. [DE]

Deep Galactic Core An area lying between the perimeter of the Galactic Core and the center of the galaxy, it is a huge region of old stars. At Deep Galactic Core's center is a black hole surrounded by masses of antimatter and dense stars. The reborn clone Emperor consolidated his forces here in order to launch what he planned as a final strike against his enemies. [DE]

Defeen A cunning, sharp-clawed humanoid member of the Defel species, he was Interrogator First Class at the Imperial Reprogramming Institute in the Valley of Royalty on the planet Duro. In recognition of his work, he was promoted to Supreme Interrogator for the Dark Side Prophets on Space Station Scardia. [MMY, PDS]

Defel Looking more illusory than real, this species appears as large, red-eyed shadows under most lighting conditions—thus their common name: Wraiths. But under ultraviolet light, Defels appear as stocky, fur-covered bipeds with protruding snouts and long-clawed, triple-jointed fingers. They live in underground cities on the planet Af'El, where most residents are miners or metallurgists. Offworld Defel are often hired as spies and assassins due to their ability to bend light around themselves at dusk. [GG4, DFRSB]

Defender A sporting blaster, it is intended for personal defense or small-game hunting. The Defender has a short range and low power, carrying energy for fifty shots. [CCG]

Defender A destroyer in the Bakuran task force. [TAB]

Defiance A Mon Calamari warship, it replaced *Home One* as the flagship

Deej

Deflector shield generator

of the New Republic fleet and has served as Admiral Ackbar's personal vessel. [DE]

deflection tower The cornerstone of most planetary defense systems, these towers generate high-intensity deflection fields or shields. [SW]

deflector shield A force field that drives back solid objects or absorbs energy, this shield protects everything under it. Ray shielding staves off energy such as radiation and blaster bolts; particle shielding repulses matter. [SW, ESB, RJ]

dejarik While the exact origin of the challenging board game continues to be debated, this classic combination of skill and strategy has withstood the test of time. Lakan Industries's latest version of its hologram dejarik set lets players choose from among ten different types of playing pieces and sports a module that can pit a player against any one of fifty of the galaxy's greatest dejarik grandmasters. A hologram generator in a circular housing is topped by an etched gold-and-green checkered surface. When activated, a full color three-dimensional hologram of playing pieces—ranging from five to thirty centimeters high—is displayed in either a passive or a live-action mode in which the pieces wage war with one another, at times devouring the losing piece. [FT]

Delari Prime Site of a hidden Imperial communications base that was abandoned after the Battle of Endor, the planet is located in the Delari system of the Corva sector of the Outer Rim. Millennia ago, the world was teeming with life, until a wayward asteroid knocked its orbit closer to the heat of nearby twin suns. Catastrophic climate changes burned up the planet's seas, and massive erosion formed kilometer-deep chasms that crisscross the rust-orange surface. Delari Prime has only a ten-hour rotation cycle, is buffeted by intense windstorms, and can support vegetation only at its poles. [SWAJ]

Delaya Sister world to Alderaan, it was the only other place besides the now-destroyed planet where the low-grade blue quella gem was found. Alliance General Carlist Rieekan was inspecting a satellite transmission station in orbit around Delaya when the Death Star battle station destroyed Alderaan. [MTS, SWAJ]

Delfii system This was the site of a deep-space military summit of the Rebel Alliance just prior to the Battle of Endor. [SC]

Dellalt The planet, located in a system near the Outer Rim, orbits a blue-white star in the remote Tion Hegemony. A watery world with two moons and a higher gravity and shorter day and year than standard, Dellalt held a strategic location in pre-Republic days. Thousands of years before the Battle of Yavin, the ancient tyrant Xim the Despot built an opulent city and immense treasure vaults on Dellalt. The vaults hold a now-worthless cache of kiirium and mytag crystals. The city has long since fallen into poverty and ruin. The intelligent sauropteroids of Dellalt, the Swimming People, run a ferry business at the lakeside docks. Deep within the mountains is a colony of about 100 people calling themselves the Survivors. Apparently stranded on Dellalt in pre-Republic times, their religion involves watching over Xim's remaining war robots and making human sacrifices to increase the strength of their rescue beacon. During one of Han Solo's early adventures, Xim's robots were activated by the Survivors and wiped out a contract-labor mining camp before the robots were destroyed. Just prior to the Battle of Yavin, the Imperials used Dellalt as a staging point for supplies and equipment. [HLL, FP, SWAJ]

Delrian A prison planet used to jail dangerous criminals. The infamous Dr. Evazan was held on Delrian until he escaped to the Hindasar system. [MTS]

Delta Source *See* ch'hala tree

Delvardus, Superior General One of thirteen feuding warlords whom Admiral Daala tried to unify to wage war against the New Republic. When the admiral failed to unite them, she killed them all with nerve gas. [DS]

Denab This planet was the site of the Battle of Denab, a major Rebel Alliance victory over the Imperial Fourth Attack Squadron. The Squadron was mainly composed of *Victory*-class Star Destroyers, which traveled at relatively slow sublight-speed. [SWR]

Denarii Nova A rare double star, each of which fed upon gases from the other, it was the site of a clash between Republic forces and the Dark Jedi Naga Sadow thousands of years before the Galactic Civil War. The battle led to the destruction of the entire star system. [DLS]

Dendo, Kapp A male Devaronian intelligence agent, he blended in with denizens of the underworld. But in reality, Kapp Dendo worked with Leia Organa Solo's personal assistant, Winter. The hairless, horned, and pointy-eared Dendo is a fierce fighter with a grim sense of humor. [XW]

Deneba A red planet in the Deneba system, it was the site of a meeting of thousands of Jedi Knights and Jedi Masters on Mount Meru 4,000 years before the Galactic Civil War. The Jedi gathered on Deneba to discuss the takeover of the Tetan system by the evil Krath and a failed mission to save Koros Major. Millennia later, the smuggler Lo Khan stopped in the Deneba system to refuel while making the Gamor Run. When he was saved from an Imperial attack by Luwingo, a Yaka, Khan hired the alien as his bodyguard. [TOJ, DE]

Dengar The only thing meaner than a bounty hunter is a bounty hunter

Dengar

with a personal grudge, and Dengar has long held one for Han Solo.

A successful human swoop jockey on the professional circuit as a young man, he challenged Solo—a hotrodder on the private swoop circuit—to a race across the spiky crystal swamps of Agrilat. Racing to the finish line, Dengar didn't see Solo's swoop bike above him, and when he pulled up he crashed into the main fin on Solo's swoop. Besides suffering severe head trauma, Dengar was tossed out of the professional league, and he blamed his fate on Solo. His obsession with evening the score with Solo led to his nickname, Payback.

Later, the Empire rebuilt Dengar as an unfeeling assassin, cutting away his hypothalamus and replacing it with circuitry. It used drugs to give him a flawless memory but left him susceptible to hallucinations. He was a professional Imperial assassin until asked to kill the holy children of Asrat. His refusal meant retirement from Imperial service. Dengar became a freelance bounty hunter when he saw the bounty on Solo posted by Jabba the Hutt. He, Boba Fett, and several other trackers captured Solo along with Chewbacca and Luke Skywalker, but Skywalker used the Force to engineer their escape from Ord Mantell. Shortly after that, Dengar joined Fett and four others in the service of Darth Vader, but Fett beat him to the prize—the *Millennium Falcon* and its crew.

Dengar had other run-ins with top Alliance officials and with crime lord Jabba the Hutt, whom he once tried to kill. He met the dancing girl Manaroo while on an assignment on the planet Aruza and rescued her several times, the last after she had been forced to become one of Jabba's dancing girls. Manaroo, a technological empath, was able to partly restore Dengar's emotions through the use of a thought-sharing device called the Attanni. Dengar rescued a half-dead Boba Fett from near the Sarlacc's Pit of Carkoon and nursed him back to health in time for Fett to be best man at the wedding of Dengar and Manaroo. Six years later, he and Fett almost captured Han Solo on Nar Shaddaa but failed again. [ESB, SWCG, TBH]

Dentaal A Mid-Rim planet, it was subjugated by the Empire, which in turn was ousted and disarmed by the planet's Independence Party. In retaliation, Imperial commandos under the command of Crix Madine came to Dentaal and planted the deadly Candorian plague, for which there is no cure. The plague eventually spread over the planet, wiping out its ten billion residents. The Empire blamed a Rebel biowar experiment gone wrong. But Madine, torn with guilt over his role, defected to the Alliance. [DS, SWAJ]

Deppo A calibration engineer, he served in an onboard factory within an Imperial World Devastator. [DE]

Derlin, Major Bren An Alliance field officer, he was in charge of security at Echo Base on Hoth at the time of the battle with Imperial forces there. [ESB]

Derra IV The site of a major Rebel loss prior to the Battle of Hoth, the fourth planet in the Derra star system was the embarkation point for a convoy bringing badly needed supplies to the Rebel base on Hoth. But the convoy and its fighter escort—led by Commander Narra—were ambushed and obliterated by squadrons of TIE fighters soon after leaving Derra IV. Imperial captain Ait Convarion, commander of the *Victory*-class Star Destroyer *Corrupter*, served in the action.

Maj. Bren Derlin

Twelve years after the Battle of Endor, New Republic Security arrested a man on Derra IV who was keeping the corpses of eleven uniformed Imperial officers frozen in cryotanks. The disturbed man wanted his son to mutilate the corpses when he came of age, in retaliation for his mother's death during the Imperial occupation of the planet. [ESBR, BTS]

Derricote, General Evir An Imperial general, he was given command of the small base of Borleias, the only inhabited world in the Pyria system. Unknown to the Empire, Gen. Evir Derricote was using his post as a profitable front for smuggling black market goods. Toadlike in appearance and demeanor, with an abruptly curving mouth and a jiggling double chin, the general had reactivated the Alderaan Biotics hydroponics facility, producing goods that had been almost impossible to find since the annihilation of Alderaan. The general was also using Imperial forces to protect his operation.

Because of the Borleian base's secrecy, Bothan spies who sliced into the Imperial Net did not discover it. When Rogue Squadron and Alliance forces first attempted to penetrate Borleias's defenses, they were badly outnumbered and outsmarted. They later learned the reasons for their initial failure. Because of the attack, the Empire was alerted to General Derricote's secret operation, and he was ordered to return to Imperial Center where he would work under the watchful eye of Director of Imperial Intelligence Ysanne Isard.

Isard gave the general the task of developing the Krytos virus, which had the capacity to kill most of the nonhuman citizens on Coruscant, although if caught in time, it could be cured with bacta. The virus was released into the planet's water supply shortly before the arrival of Rebel

Devaronian

forces, in hopes that the Alliance would bankrupt itself purchasing the bacta necessary to cure the alien population. Because the Alliance arrived earlier than expected, the virus failed to infect as many people as projected. Unjustly blamed for the Krytos project failure, General Derricote was imprisoned at *Lusankya*, a buried Star Destroyer serving as a prison facility. He encountered Rogue Squadron pilot Corran Horn there and attempted to kill him, but was himself killed by Horn with the assistance of Jan Dodonna. [BW]

Desnand, Io The Imperial Governor of the Aida system, he planned to ship Wookiee females and cubs to a prison camp on Lomabu III, then stage an attack to lure Rebel rescue forces into a trap. Io Desnand also received the captured Trandoshan bounty hunter, Bossk, from bounty hunters Chenlambec and Tinian I'att. [TBH]

Despayre A prison planet located in the Horuz system in the distant Outer Rim, it was the construction site for the first Death Star. The planet was almost unknown, which helped guarantee the secrecy of the orbital construction yards assembled to build the battle station. Despayre was a green jungle planet broken by rivers and shallow seas, and home to countless predators including carnivorous crustaceans, poisonous flora, and deadly insects. The planet's penal colony was the only outpost in the system, and many prisoners were used to help construct the Death Star. When the battle station was completed, it tested its superlaser on Despayre and destroyed the planet. [MTS, DSTC, DS]

Destiny of Yevetha Formerly the *Redoubtable*, the ship was seized by Yevethan strongman Nil Spaar during a raid on the Imperial shipyard at N'zoth. The *Destiny of Yevetha* was part of the Yevethan mobilization at Doornik-319. [BTS]

detainment droid Used extensively by Imperial detention centers, these robots float atop repulsorlift-generated fields. They secure and guard prisoners and are equipped with binders on the ends of their four arms to grasp and lock around the limbs of the detainees. [DE]

Detention Block AA-23 Princess Leia Organa was held captive by the Empire in this location deep within the first Death Star battle station. She was in Cell 2187. [SW]

Devaron Homeworld of the horned Devaronians (or Devish), the planet is a sparsely populated world near the influential Core Worlds, covered by low mountain ranges, deep valleys, shallow lakes, and thousands of navigable rivers. Despite its multiple suns, it has a temperate climate. Devaronian females live in the mountains and raise their families in Devaron's villages and industrial centers. They control the planet's democratic government and all aspects of production and manufacturing. Devaronian males prefer to wander aimlessly, spending their lives exploring Devaron's rivers or leaving the planet. Male Devish have much sharper teeth than females, and about 2 percent of males are born with two sets of teeth—one for shredding flesh and one for grinding other foods. Devaron produces enough goods to support its inhabitants but doesn't have any useful exports. During an outbreak of the Rebellion on Devaron, the Devaronian Army was placed under Imperial command. Captain Kardue'sai'malloc (later known as Labria) oversaw the shelling of the ancient city of Montellian Serat and the massacre of 700 Rebel prisoners that followed. But some thirteen years after the Battle of Endor, four mercenaries recognized Labria as the Butcher of Montellian Serat and forced him to flee to Peppel. Two years later, he was captured by Boba Fett and returned to Devaron, where he was sentenced to death. Labria was executed in the Judgment Field outside the ruins of Montellian Serat, south of the Blue Mountains, by being thrown into a pit of starved quarra, domesticated hunting animals. [GG4, TMEC, TBH]

Devaronian Near humanoid in appearance, this species comes from the temperate world of Devaron. The males are hairless, with a pair of horns springing from the tops of their heads and sharp incisors filling their mouths. Many feel uncomfortable in their presence since they resemble the devils of a thousand myths. Female Devaronians are larger, with thick fur and no horns. The males have galactic wanderlust, while most females prefer to stay at home and keep their advanced industries running. Their language is low, guttural, and full of snarling consonants. [GG1, GG4]

Devastator An *Imperial*-class Star Destroyer, it brought terror as it subju-

Devastator

gated the planet Ralltiir. Later, it captured Princess Leia Organa's consular ship *Tantive IV* over the planet Tatooine. The princess was trying to smuggle the technical readouts of the original Death Star to Alliance High Command when she was intercepted. The *Devastator* was Lord Tion's flagship until his death. [SWR, SWS]

Devlia, Admiral A small-minded man, he was placed in charge of Imperial forces at Vladet. If it hadn't been for Intelligence Agent Kirtan Loor, Devlia wouldn't have discovered Rogue Squadron's base on Talasea, even though it was practically under his nose. Instead of making an all-out assault on the base, Admiral Devlia sent in only one squadron of stormtroopers to bomb the camp at night. During the attack, the troopers were killed and their shuttle was confiscated by the Rebellion. Later, in a reprisal raid on Vladet, the Alliance is assumed to have killed the admiral. [BW]

Devotion Formerly the *Valorous*, it was captured by Yevethan strongman Nil Spaar during a raid on the Imperial shipyard at N'zoth. [BTS]

dewback A large four-legged reptile native to the planet Tatooine, it is a herbivore on the desert world. Dewbacks are used as beasts of burden by moisture farmers and as patrol animals by local authorities and military personnel. The creature, which has surprisingly skinny legs to support its bulk, is often used in place of mechanized vehicles because it can withstand extremely high temperatures and sandstorms. [SW, SWR]

Dewback

Deyer Colony An outpost in the Anoat system, the colony world contains floating raft cities, terraformed lakes, and abundant fish and crustacean life. The Deyer colonists had created a peaceful political system until they spoke out against the destruction of Alderaan, paving the way for a brutal military takeover of Deyer by Imperial troops. Jedi apprentice Kyp Durron and his family were originally from Deyer. Kyp and his parents were sent to the spice mines of Kessel; his brother, Zeth, was conscripted for stormtrooper training. [JS, DA, COF]

Deysum III Planetary headquarters for Vo Lantes, the owner of a used-droid chain and a secret Alliance operative, it is the capital world of the Trax sector along the Trax Tube trade route. [SWAJ]

DH-17 A blaster pistol, it uses power packs and high-energy blaster gases to shoot bolts of explosive, coherent light energy. [CCG]

Dha Werda Verda A millennia-old epic poem, it tells of the conquest of the indigenous peoples of Coruscant, known as the Battalions of Zhell, by a warrior race called the Taungs. Space merchant and explorer Mungo Baobab found and preserved the earliest version of the text while exploring the Roon system; he found crystal Roonstones in which the poem was embedded.

Dianoga

Dha Werda Verda recounts the epic battle between the Taungs and the Battalions of Zhell. The tide turned when a sudden volcanic eruption rained destructive ash upon Zhell, smothering the city. The ash plume rose high into the sky and cast a giant shadow over the land for a full two standard years, giving the Taungs a new name: Dha Werda Verda, the Warriors of the Shadow, or in some translations, Dark Warriors. The Taungs themselves saw the immense, long-lasting shadow as a symbol of their destiny and adopted the Dark Shadow Warrior identity throughout their subsequent conquests. [SOTEALB]

dianoga An omnivorous and parasitic predator native to Vodran, it has spread across the galaxy in its microscopic larval form. Dianoga live in shallow, stagnant pools and murky swamps, growing to an average length of ten meters. Their seven tentacles provide them with a means of movement and a way to grasp their prey, which they spot through an eyestalk growing from their trunks. A dianoga changes to the color of its last meal, and after a long period without eating, it will become transparent. A dianoga made its way into the trash compactor of the original Death Star battle station and almost made a meal of Luke Skywalker when he fell into its watery, garbage-filled lair. [SW, CCG]

Diath, Dace A Jedi from Tatooine many millennia before the Galactic Civil War, his father was Jedi Master Sidrona Diath. [FNU, DLS, TSW]

Diath, Sidrona A Jedi Master and father of Jedi Dace Diath, he was killed in the Battle of Basilisk some 4,000 years before the Galactic Civil War. [DLS]

digworm A small creature native to the planet Kamar, the worm burrows into solid rock by excreting acidic digestive juices. [HSR]

Diktat This title is given to the Corellian Chief of State. [AC]

Dilonexa XXIII A world in the Dilonexa system, it orbits a giant blue-white star along with thirty-nine other planets, but is the only one that can support life. Dilonexa XXIII is nearly 25,000 kilometers in diameter, but its lack of heavy metals gives it a tolerable gravity. The planet is covered with farms that provide grain for the herds of native bovine, foodstuffs, plastics, and fuels. Weather-control satellites help keep the city-sized tornadoes in check with energy weaponry. Dilonexican colonists have developed an allergic reaction to foods containing too many trace metals. Lando Calrissian made a run to Dilonexa XXIII, trying to unload a cargo of fishing poles, leather hides, and wintenberry jelly. There were no takers. [LCF]

Dimok Along with the planet Ripoblus, it is one of two primary worlds of the Sepan system. A long war between the two worlds was forcibly ended by the intervention of Imperial forces after the Battle of Hoth. The planets then briefly and unsuccessfully tried to unite against the Empire as their common foe. [TSC]

Teneniel Djo

Dim-U monks A religious order in Mos Eisley, its members worship banthas. [GG7, ISWU]

dinko A venomous, palm-sized creature known for its nasty disposition, it secretes a foul-smelling liquid both to mark its territory and to discourage even the largest predators. With powerful rear legs covered with serrated spurs, twin pairs of grasping extremities jutting from its chest, and sharp needlelike fangs, the dinko is quite formidable. [HSE]

Diollan A featherless birdlike species, it has mottled brown leathery skin, tiny intense eyes, and a broad beak. [TMEC]

dipill This sedative is used to relieve stress. [SME]

directional landing beacon This device transmits fixed signals to help ships orient themselves. [SME]

disruption bubble generator A small electronic device, it creates a localized bubble that is impenetrable to sonic scanning. [TAB]

disruptor A weapon that fires a visible blast of energy that can shatter objects, disruptors kill in a painful and inhumane manner and are illegal in most sectors of the galaxy. [HSE, HLL, HSR]

divto A fearsome three-headed snake native to the forest moon of Endor, it grows to a length of three meters. A divto hunts during darkness, delivering numbing poison to its prey. [DFRSB]

DJ-88 (Dee-Jay) A powerful droid, it served as the caretaker and teacher in the Lost City of the Jedi. Dee-Jay was white with ruby eyes and a metal "beard." DJ-88 raised young Jedi Prince Ken from the time he was a small child, and Ken looked up to the droid as he would his own father. [LCJ, PDS]

Djo, Teneniel With red-gold hair and brown eyes flecked with orange, this bright young woman might be a catch for any eligible bachelor. But it didn't work that way on Dathomir, especially not for Teneniel Djo, one of the Witches of Dathomir.

The planet's Witches—both good and evil—lead an ultramatriarchal society in which men are mere ornaments to do heavy labor or to breed. The women, whether members of such "good" clans as Teneniel Djo's Singing Mountain clan or of the evil Nightsisters, are used to clubbing men over the head to claim them—just as Djo did to Luke Skywalker. Luke and Prince Isolder from the planet Hapes were exploring an ancient wrecked spacecraft when they first encountered Djo. They quickly got involved in the ongoing struggle between the good clans and the Nightsisters, led by the grotesque Gethzerion. Both sides are infused with the Force.

Teneniel Djo is the daughter of Allaya Djo, who led the clan until her death in the desert. Grandmother Augwynne took over, but Teneniel was being groomed as the next queen. Complications ensued, including a raid on an Imperial prison, a full-fledged attack by the Nightsisters, and a bombardment from a rogue Imperial warlord. But through it all, Teneniel and Prince Isolder grew closer and true love blossomed. The couple married and eventually had a daughter, Tenel Ka, whose Force powers were strong enough to get her accepted into Skywalker's Jedi academy. [CPL, SWCG]

DL-44 A heavy blaster pistol, it has a short range but is relatively powerful. The DL-44, made by BlasTech, carries energy for twenty-five shots. It is illegal or restricted in most systems. [RSB, CCG]

Dlarit, Aerin The father of former Rogue Squadron member Erisi Dlarit, he was one of the highest officials of the bacta monopoly in the Xucphra Corporation. He had been appointed a general in the Thyferran Home Defense Corps because of his position with the company, and became an obvious target for Rogue Squadron in its struggle to topple power-mad Ysanne Isard from her leading role on Thyferra. Originally he was scheduled to be terminated, but Rogue Iella Wessiri prevailed upon the

Nep Dllr

members of her ops team to discredit him instead. As a result, he and the other THDC leaders were made to look like fools. [BW]

Dlarit, Erisi A former member of Rogue Squadron from the planet Thyferra, she was both beautiful and wealthy. She was also a traitor to the Rebel Alliance. Her family has a long tradition with Xucphra Corporation, the bacta monopoly; it was her uncle who discovered that a batch of the bacta had been contaminated by "terrorists." Erisi Dlarit had been expected to continue the family tradition, but she chose instead the adventurous life. She turned out to be an excellent pilot, good enough to infiltrate Rogue Squadron and learn some of its secrets. Shortly after the Rogues made a retaliatory raid on an Imperial base at Vladet, she attempted to seduce fellow Rogue Corran Horn when he was confined to quarters pending a possible court-martial. Although rebuffed, she tried again when they were paired for an undercover mission on Coruscant. Again she failed.

When Director of Imperial Intelligence Ysanne Isard fled Coruscant after the Alliance invasion, she took the traitor Dlarit with her to Thyferra. Erisi was given a post in the Thyferran Home Defense Corps by Isard. As a commander, she was placed in charge of training TIE fighter pilots to defend the bacta convoys that Isard was using to gain money and power. Her unit was called to defend Isard's Super Star Destroyer *Lusankya* during the final moments of the Bacta War. As the ship was being pounded by Rogue Squadron, her fighter group engaged the X-wings. Erisi was then ordered to provide cover for Isard's shuttle as she attempted her escape, but Erisi's TIE was destroyed by Corran Horn. [BW]

Dllr, Nep A Sullustan member of the Rogue Squadron, he is somewhat frenetic and doesn't exhibit his species' normal caution and subdued personality. In fact, Nep Dllr thrives when no longer weighed down with the rules of a highly regulated society. He serves as scrounger for the Rogues and has a decent ability at retrofitting—adapting parts to serve new purposes. Dllr is a serious music fan—he hums a lot—and with his large Sullustan ears, he can find tapcafes and cantinas with live music in a snap. [XW]

DLT-19 A heavy blaster rifle, it is enhanced with extra power packs and greater range than other blasters. [CCG]

Doallyn A humanoid bounty hunter from the planet Geran, he is marked by a huge scar on his face, the result of an attack by a Corellian sand panther. For that reason, and because he needs the assistance of breathing cartridges in most atmospheres, Doallyn typically wears a helmet. He had been called to the palace of Jabba the Hutt to hunt down a krayt dragon. Following Jabba's death, he helped the Askajian dancer Yarna d'al' Gargan escape across the desert to Mos Eisley. In the course of that trip, Doallyn got the chance to do battle with a krayt dragon. He killed it, and with the dragon pearls from its gizzard he was able to leave Tatooine with Yarna and her three children. After a visit to Geran, they all decided to live aboard their new spaceship as free traders in textiles and gemstones. [TJP]

Dobah A female Phlog on the forest moon of Endor, she is the mate of Zut and the mother of Hoom and Nahkee. [ETV]

Doc Leader of a band of outlaw techs, he long specialized in making modifications—usually of an illegal nature—to space vehicles and droids. Doc, whose real name was Klaus Vandanganten, was joined in his pursuits by his daughter, Jessa, at his asteroid base in the Corporate Sector. It was Jessa who modified and conjoined Doc's droids, nicknamed Bollux and Blue Max. When Doc disappeared, Jessa hired the smuggler Han Solo to find him—a rescue mission that almost ended in disaster at the Stars' End prison colony on Mytus VII. [HSE, CSSB]

Docking Bay 45 This is the holding bay for ships in the Corporate Sector spaceport on Etti IV from which Han Solo's *Millennium Falcon* escaped illegally by using the identification profile and name of another ship. [HSE]

Docking Bay 94 A holding bay in Mos Eisley spaceport on Tatooine, it was where Han Solo's *Millennium Falcon* was parked and undergoing maintenance. Solo arranged to meet there with some newly signed-on passengers: Ben Kenobi, Luke Skywalker, and the droids R2-D2 and C-3PO. But when Solo arrived first, he found crime kingpin Jabba the Hutt and his gang. Jabba was up-

Docking Bay 94

Gen. Jan Dodonna

set that Han had dumped a load of smuggled cargo when he was boarded by Imperials, and demanded that Han make good on the lost spice shipment. Jabba denied that he had sent his henchman Greedo to the nearby cantina to kill Han; Solo was a better shot and had killed Greedo instead. Jabba agreed to give Han one more chance.

The oval docking bay was primarily built of stone, with an entrance ramp and a restraining wall that surrounded a shallow pit used to deflect and absorb the energy associated with starship landings and departures. The *Falcon* and its passengers beat a hasty retreat when stormtroopers rushed into Docking Bay 94 gunning for them. [SW]

Dodonna A monstrous assault frigate, it was long the cornerstone of General Wedge Antilles's fleet. The *Dodonna* is a highly modified version of the fearsome Imperial Dreadnaughts. [DS]

Dodonna, General Jan Looking more like a professor than a professional warrior, and little interested in personal glory, this grizzled graybeard is one of the true heroes of the New Republic. Gen. Jan Dodonna planned and coordinated the assault on the first Death Star at the Battle of Yavin.

A brilliant military tactician, he specialized in logistics and sieges. He was one of the first Star Destroyer captains for the Old Republic, but retired as the government slipped into the hands of Emperor Palpatine. When the Empire reviewed the general's records, he was considered too old to be retrained to the ways of the Empire, and an order was issued for his execution. The Alliance reached him first. He refused their entreaties —until Imperial troops came to kill him and he had to fight his way out. Dodonna quickly became one of the Rebel Alliance's strongest leaders. As a military commander, he answered only to Mon Mothma and the Alliance Council. After Princess Leia Organa delivered the readouts for the Death Star battle station to him, he had little time to spare. The general pored over the plans until, in the early morning hours, he hit upon the chink in the Death Star's armor: an unshielded reactor shaft. If targeted just right, a proton torpedo sent down the shaft would lead to a chain-reaction explosion that could destroy the battle station. And Luke Skywalker targeted his torpedoes exactly right.

For the ensuing period, Dodonna was in charge of the defense of the Rebel base on Yavin 4. When the Empire was about to attack, he stayed behind as the Alliance evacuated and set off concussion charges that destroyed an entire fleet of TIE bombers. The general was critically wounded, captured, and imprisoned in the buried Imperial Super Star Destroyer *Lusankya*, which had been turned into a harsh prison. When Rogue Squadron member Corran Horn was also imprisoned there, he soon became friendly with Dodonna, for he could see the old general genuinely cared about the men under his stewardship. This affection for his fellow prisoners prompted Dodonna to assist in Horn's escape from *Lusankya*. Dodonna was later rescued by a Rebel assault team but chose to go into semiretirement. Much of his fire had been dampened, and his injuries forced him to walk with a cane. However, six years after the Battle of Endor, his advice was instrumental in the battle against the new Imperial World Devastators. [SW, SWCG, BW]

Vrad Dodonna

Dodonna, Vrad The son of General Jan Dodonna, he at first retreated from an encounter with Darth Vader's new Super Star Destroyer, the *Executor*. But after being fired upon, Vrad Dodonna made up for his cowardice by making a suicide run and ramming his ship into the *Executor*, destroying a section of the defense shields. This allowed Han Solo to disable the ship from the rear. [GW]

Dodt, Parin Pilot Pash Cracken used the identity of Dodt, supposedly an Imperial Prefect, when he went to Coruscant for an undercover mission with Rogue Squadron. [XW]

Doellin A deity of the Gran species. [TJP]

Dogot, Captain Ors Captain of the Prakith raider *Bloodprice*. [BTS]

Dohu VII The seventh of eight planets in the Dohu system, it is home to three-armed, living-rock creatures called Silika. [SWAJ]

Dokrett, Captain Voba Captain of the Prakith light cruiser *Gorath*, he attempted to capture the mysterious ghost ship called the Teljkon vagabond, but was destroyed by it instead. [TT]

dola trees Nearly sentient plants, they are native to the planet Aruza. Dola trees bloom with flowers that excrete a potent antibiotic syrup. [TBH]

Doldur Located in a sector and system of the same name, the Imperial-controlled world is site of the Doldur Spaceport. The planet is the personal territory of Imperial Moff Eisen Kerioth, who has been sponsoring research into antiblaster energy shields. [SWAJ]

Dolomar sector Dolomar sector was a major target in an offensive by

Grand Admiral Thrawn. Both it and the Farfin sector were heavily defended by the New Republic, and the Republic's Admiral Ackbar personally visited Dolomar's defenses. The sector capital world is Dolomar, known for its extreme cold. [LC, LCSB]

Dolph The birth name of the man who eventually became Kueller after he accepted the dark side of the Force. Dolph was an extremely talented student of Luke Skywalker's on Yavin 4, but he always possessed a certain darkness. He did not stay at the Jedi academy long enough to develop either his Force talents or to dispel his darkness. He became known as Kueller once he left the academy and accepted his dark side fully. Dolph witnessed the brutal deaths of his parents at the hands of the Je'har on Alamania, and thereafter swore revenge on the Almanian rulers as well as on the New Republic, which he believed had blindly ignored the atrocities committed by the Je'har. [NR]

Dom-Bradden An Outer-Rim world, it is home to the Affytechans, a sentient form of plant life with high, musical voices and bodies composed of thousands of colorful petals, tendrils, and stalks. While they appear quite beautiful, the Affytechans stink of ammonia and musk. The Imperial battlemoon *Eye of Palpatine* stopped at Dom-Bradden to pick up a contingent of stormtroopers, but brought in a group of Affytechans instead. [COJ]

Domed City of Aquarius Built inside a giant air-filled bubble far below the Mon Calamari oceans, the city can be used by both air- and water-breathing beings. Water-filled canals in the Domed City of Aquarius feature underwater homes, but markets and other residences are located in air-filled areas. [GDV]

Dometown This hollow dome a kilometer across was built by Lando Calrissian and other investors in a huge subterranean cavern beneath Coruscant. Dometown, a pocket city, consists of low stone buildings and cool green parks. [AC]

Dominis A Jedi Master many millennia ago, one of his favorite apprentices was Zona Luka, who ultimately assassinated Dominis. [TSW]

Tott Doneeta

Doneeta, Tott A Jedi Twi'lek trained by Master Arca at his compound on Arkania some 4,000 years before the Galactic Civil War, he had the special ability to understand and converse in beast languages. When Doneeta was young, his family had been held captive on a slave ship that was liberated by Master Arca. [TOJ, FNU, DLS, TSW]

Doole, Moruth A vile, double-crossing Rybet, he was the kingpin of the Kessel spice-smuggling business who thought nothing of turning against —even murdering—onetime allies to get what he wanted. Squat and froglike in appearance with slimy green skin, partial to wearing reptile skins (and a bright yellow tie when he was sexually available), and so paranoid that he was prone to nervous tics, Moruth Doole truly represented the underbelly of the galaxy.

His position as an official at the large Imperial prison on Kessel made it possible for him to pack the staff with those loyal to him. He blackmailed or paid off prison guards, sold maps and access codes for Kessel's energy shields so that others could set up small, illegal spice-mining operations on other parts of the planet, then killed off or ratted on those operators when the time was right.

The Empire used its Kessel prisoners to mine glitterstim spice, a powerful drug that sold for high prices all over the galaxy. Doole, of course, skimmed ever-larger amounts of the black-market drug for his own accounts. He made sure that, with rare exceptions, anyone who knew of his scheming was bumped off. He even put his own offspring—produced through forced mating with unwilling females of his species—to work as slaves in the pitch-black mines. The only one he trusted was his top aide, a onetime prison guard named Skynxnex, an accomplished thief and assassin despite his scarecrowlike appearance.

It was on a spice-smuggling run for Jabba the Hutt that Han Solo learned of Doole's true ways. Even though Jabba had already paid Doole the 12,400 credits for the glitterstim spice, Doole tipped off tariff authorities—who had also paid Doole—to the route of Solo's *Millennium Falcon*. Solo dumped the load before he could be boarded, but when he returned later to pick it up, it had vanished. Jabba then put a bounty on Solo's head, but being suspicious about Doole, sent a bounty hunter after him. Doole managed to lose only one eye instead of his life as Skynxnex came to his rescue.

As the Galactic Civil War continued, Doole took complete control of Kessel operations, killing off all potential rivals. Then, seven years after the Battle of Endor, Han Solo and Chewbacca returned to Kessel on a diplomatic mission. Not believing them, Doole made them slaves in his deepest spice mine, where the two first met Force-sensitive Kyp Durron. When the Alliance began to investi-

Moruth Doole

gate the disappearance of Solo and Chewbacca, Doole decided to murder them. Instead, Skynxnex was killed by one of the giant spice-producing spiders in the mine and the trio escaped. A chance encounter ensued in which most of Doole's defense fleet—and much of the planet—was destroyed by Admiral Daala's Imperial fleet, and the Rybet fled back to a prison tower on Kessel. Eventually, forces from the New Republic, smugglers, and his own offspring forced Doole to flee into the mines where he was speared by one of the giant spiders—a just ending for the murderous Doole. [JS, COF, SWCG]

Doonium A common heavy metal, it was used to build Imperial war machines. [GDV]

Doornik-207 A planet in the Farlax sector and the Koornacht Cluster, Doornik-207 was the former site of a nest of Corasgh. Twelve years after the Battle of Endor, the alien Yevetha attacked and conquered Doornik-207 as part of a series of raids that the Yevethans called the Great Purge. [SOL]

Doornik-319 *See* Morning Bell

Doornik-628 *See* J't'p'tan

Doornik-881 *See* Kutag

Doornik-1142 A brown dwarf star orbited by four cold, gaseous planets, it is located on the edge of the Koornacht Cluster. Twelve years after the Battle of Endor, the New Republic astrographic survey ship *Astrolabe* was diverted to Doornik-1142 by General Etahn A'baht, who was hoping to get an updated survey of the Koornacht Cluster for military intelligence purposes. Instead, the *Astrolabe* was destroyed by a Yevethan battle cruiser; the Yevetha claimed that they were defending their territory against New Republic spies. In fact, the Yevetha had moved their entire Black Eleven Fleet to Doornik-1142 to conceal it. [BTS]

Dorenian Beshniquel A musical wind instrument, it is sometimes called a Fizzz. [CCG, TMEC]

Dorian Quill An alcoholic drink, it is aged twelve years before being bottled. [TMEC]

Dorja, Captain Cautious in battle—some might say a bit cowardly—he was a commander of the Imperial Star Destroyer *Relentless*. Captain Dorja comes from a wealthy family with a long tradition of military service. During the Battle of Endor, his ship didn't suffer a single casualty—quite possibly because of his unwillingness to engage an enemy in direct combat. He opposed the rise to power of Captain Pellaeon and despised Grand Admiral Thrawn, at the same time plotting a way to take control of the Empire himself. [DFR, DFRSB]

dormo-shock A naturally healing, comalike sleep that severely injured patients sometimes enter into, it allows the body's regenerative and recuperative abilities work to heal traumatized areas. [ESBN]

Dornea Homeworld of the Dorneans, a tall species with purplish leathery skin, the planet never officially joined the Rebel Alliance, but its inhabitants fought bravely against the Empire. The Dornean Navy, though it numbered barely eighty vessels, was able to successfully resist the Empire despite being greatly outnumbered in several battles. General Etahn A'baht, the senior military commander of the Dornean Navy, was named commander of the New Republic's Fifth Fleet twelve years after the Battle of Endor. [BTS]

Dorsk 81 The eighty-first generation Khomm humanoid clone of the same set of genetic attributes, this olive-green-skinned native of the planet Khomm was somehow different from all those who had gone before, for he was touched by the Force.

But Dorsk 81 was considered imperfect in a society that had valued sameness for 1,000 years. He felt he was a failure to his species until he heard about Luke Skywalker's plans to develop a Jedi "praxeum," or an academy for the learning of action. He knew that he had a powerful affinity for the Force and left his planet to seek training from Skywalker on Yavin 4.

Dorsk 81 became one of the first twelve Jedi trainees, although he had some problems eating the natural, rather than highly processed, food set before him; he also panicked once during an exercise floating in

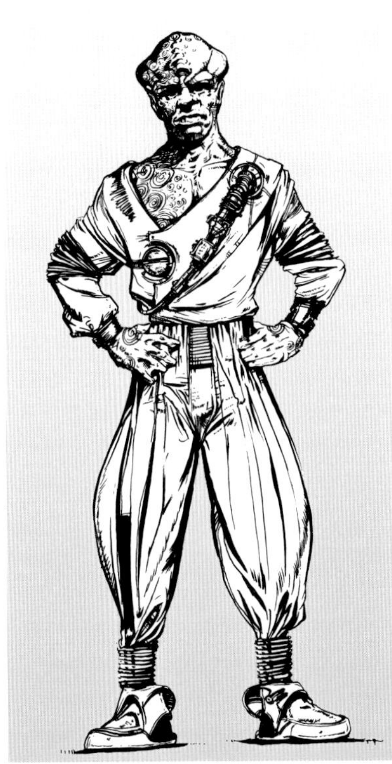
Dorsk 81

an underground lake. Dorsk 81 joined with the other Jedi initiates after the evil spirit of the long-dead Dark Jedi Exar Kun drove Skywalker's spirit from his body and seduced Jedi trainee Kyp Durron with the dark side of the Force. Together they found a way to destroy Kun for all time and restore Luke's spirit to his body. Dorsk 81 died a hero after again joining with his fellow Jedi and channeling their combined powers through himself to create a Force storm that pushed an entire fleet of attacking Imperial Star Destroyers nearly out of the Yavin system. [DA, DS]

Dosin An Imperial engineer, he was in charge of high-energy concepts and implementation at the secret Maw Installation weapons facility. He was wider than he was tall and completely bald except for very dark, very narrow eyebrows that looked like thin wire brushes on his forehead. His lips were thick enough that he could have balanced a stylus on them when he smiled. Dosin died when the prototype Death Star that he was on fell into a black hole and was crushed. [COF]

Dowager Queen A long-wrecked spacecraft, it sits in the center of Mos Eisley, a tangled heap of girders and

Dowager Queen

twisted hull plates. The *Dowager Queen* was one of the first colony ships to arrive on Tatooine. Today it is home to assorted creatures, vagrants, and scavengers. [GG7, ISWU, TMEC]

Dowd, Bilman A Devaronian guild representative, he accepted delivery from Boba Fett of the captured Labria, otherwise known as the Butcher of Montellian Serat, a war criminal who was later put to death. [TBH]

Dra III A high-gravity world known for its dangerous native life-forms and sport hunting, its inhabitants tend to be heavy and strong due to the planet's high gravity. The hunting beasts of Dra III include the vicious six-legged nashtahs (also called Dravian Hounds) that inhabit the planet's mountains. Nashtahs, the only animals from the planet that so far have been domesticated, are also the planet's most thoroughly studied animal. The powerful (though somewhat outdated) Kell Mark II blaster is the planet's one export. [HSR, HLL, CSSB]

Drackmar system A system with multiple suns, it is home to the Drackmarians, methane-breathers with blue scales, sharp talons, and snouts filled with sharp teeth. The species doesn't sleep and is noted for generosity and stubborn independence. Fierce opponents of the Empire, they are now loosely aligned with the New Republic. Omogg, a wealthy warlord from the Drackmar system, lost the planet Dathomir to Han Solo in a sabacc game. [CPL]

Dracmus A Selonian female, she was captured by Thrackan Sal-Solo in Coronet, the Corellian capital. Sal-Solo forced her to fight his cousin Han Solo, then made them cellmates with hopes that she would rip Han apart. Instead Dracmus gave information to Han that eventually led to uncovering Thrackan as the Hidden Leader of the rabidly antialien Human League. A Selonian rescue team broke Dracmus out of prison and took Han with them. [AS]

D'rag A starship builder from the planet Oslumpex V. [HSR]

dragon-bird This avian species was found long ago on Onderon. [DLS]

dragon pearls Beautiful and incredibly valuable pearls of numerous colors, they are found only in the gizzards of krayt dragons. [TJP]

dragonsnake A large predator, it inhabits Dagobah's water channels. A dragonsnake seeks out victims, rearing up and slashing them with its fangs or razor-sharp fins. [ISWU]

Drall One of five inhabited worlds in the Corellian system, it is a pleasant, temperate planet with light gravity. Summer temperatures can reach levels high enough to cause portions of the landlocked Boiling Sea to actually boil, until it is cooled by winter precipitation. The planet is the homeworld of the short, furred creatures also known as Drall, which generations ago hibernated during the Drall winter season. The bipedal species is cautious, honest, and meticulous, making them good recordkeepers. Other planetary life includes the nannarium flower and many species of Drallish avians. A vast, subterranean planetary repulsor is located near Drall's equator—presumably used in ancient times to move the planet into its current orbit from an unknown location.

During his tenure with the Corellian Security Force, Rogue Squadron pilot Corran Horn planted a false report implying that he had murdered six smugglers on Drall. The report was created so Horn and his supervisor could stage a public falling-out and remove suspicions of their working together to flee the Empire, but an Imperial death warrant was issued on Horn for the imaginary crime.

During a crisis fourteen years after the Battle of Endor, Chewbacca took the Solo children and their tutor, Ebrihim, to Drall to stay with Ebrihim's aunt, the Duchess Marcha of Mastigophorous. The group discovered Drall's planetary repulsor, and Anakin Solo instinctively made it operational. A shot from the repulsor, fired by Anakin, disabled Centerpoint Station and saved the star Bovo Yagen from destruction at the last possible instant. [AC, AS, SAC, HLL, RS]

Drang One of two domesticated vornskrs—poisonous doglike creatures that attack Force users and display an unnatural hatred for Jedi—that smuggler Talon Karrde uses as pets and guards. [HE, DFR, LC, HESB]

Dravis A pilot in Talon Karrde's smuggling operation. [HE, DFR, LC]

Drayson, Admiral Hiram A high-ranking officer in the New Republic, he was in charge of the Chandrila system defense forces, serving as Admiral of the Chandrila Defense Fleet

Dragonsnake

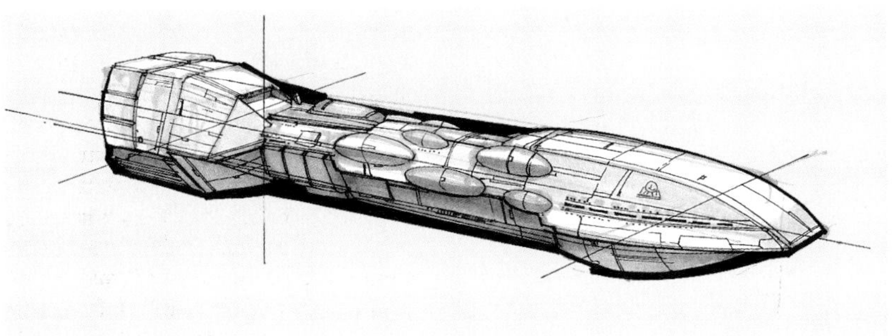

Dreadnaught

for many years. In that capacity, Adm. Hiram Drayson knew the senator from Chandrila, Mon Mothma, well. He impressed her with his work in dramatically decreasing pirate and smuggling activity near the planet, and years later she asked him to be commander of her Alliance headquarters ship. With the formation of the New Republic, he was put in charge of the fleet attached to the Provisional Council and its capital, the planet Coruscant. Later he headed Alpha Blue, a mysterious covert intelligence group within the New Republic's military and security hierarchy. He distrusted Ambassador Nil Spaar and gave the Alliance's General A'baht a secret code that allowed him to deal directly with Drayson, bypassing Fleet Headquarters. Admiral Drayson was the one who convinced Chief of State Leia Organa Solo that she had been lied to by Spaar by giving her the Plat Mallar recording that recounted the Yevethan attack on the Koornacht Cluster settlements. [DFR, DFRSB, BTS]

Dreadnaught A type of large, heavy cruiser commissioned by the Old Republic, these ancient 600-meter-long ships were the navy's largest before the introduction of the *Victory*-class Star Destroyer. While slow and poorly armed by modern standards, a number of Dreadnaughts were refitted for service by both the Empire and the Rebel Alliance. The Imperial version was most like its predecessor, while the Alliance refitted them as Rebel assault frigates, with greater fuel efficiency, speed, and maneuverability. Grand Admiral Thrawn's quest to capture the *Katana* fleet of Dreadnaughts spurred renewed interest in the ships. [ISB, DFRSB, RSB]

Dreebo The pilot of a ship that was part of the pay-for-protection racket of Great Bogga the Hutt, he was assigned to guarantee safe passage from pirate attacks for ore haulers in the Stenness system. His ship was destroyed by the ore-sucking pirate ship *Starjacker*. [TOJ]

dreeka fish A chirping fish. [TMEC]

Dreis, Garven "Dave" A male human X-wing pilot, he led Red Squadron at the Battle of Yavin, and before that had served at the Dantooine Rebel base. Garven "Dave" Dreis fired an unsuccessful shot at the Death Star's thermal exhaust port and died during the Battle of Yavin. [CCG]

Dressellian A wrinkly, almost prune-faced humanoid species from the planet Dressel, they joined with the Rebel Alliance shortly before the Battle of Endor. They had long fought the Empire on their homeworld and were brought into the larger fight by Bothan allies. [GG12]

driit A monetary unit, it is used on the planet Dellalt. [HLL]

droch Small and sentient insects, they bury themselves in human flesh and cause what has been called the Death Seed plague, which is always fatal. Drochs are tiny domes of purple-brown chitin, and they are everywhere on the planet Nam Chorios. They consist of an abdomen about a centimeter long that ends in a hard little head and a ring of tiny, wriggling, thorn-tipped legs. They have an incredibly high reproductive rate and prefer the shade because sunlight kills them. Everyone on the planet has droch bites. The insects die and are absorbed approximately twenty minutes after they burrow into flesh.

In their infectious state they are virtually life-drinkers and thus became known as the mysterious Death Seed plague. Some seven centuries ago the Grissmaths seeded Nam Chorios with drochs, hoping to kill off all the political prisoners they had stranded on the planet. But the sun fragmenting through the planet's crystals generated a radiation that weakened the larger drochs and killed off the smaller ones outright. The large members of the species, called captain drochs, can draw life out of victims through the smaller ones, without attaching themselves to their victims. They become dangerous at this stage, because the more life they drink, the more intelligent they become. Some beings used to eat drochs to absorb life and energy into themselves. [POT]

droid Robotic systems, either fashioned in the likeness of their creators or for functionality, they are the workhorses of the galaxy. They have various degrees of artificial intelligence, but rarely have speech synthesizers, so they must communicate through a programming language. They are powered by rechargeable cells in their body and most have the capabilities of locomotion, logic, self-aware intelligence, communication, manipulation, and sensory reception. Many cultures treat droids as slaves, and many public areas are off-limits to them.

The automatons are grouped into five classes, or degrees, according to primary function:

1st Class: Skilled in physical, mathematical, and medical sciences.

2nd Class: Programmed in engineering and technical sciences.

3rd Class: Skilled in social sciences and service areas such as translation, diplomatic assistance, and tutoring.

4th Class: Skilled in security and military applications.

5th Class: Suitable for menial labor and non-intelligence-intensive jobs such as mining, transportation, and sanitation. [SW, SWSB]

droid detector A detection device, it often is used in segregated areas of the galaxy. Owners of drinking establishments frequently use detectors to keep droids out. Many officials and gangsters use them as security devices, although many assassin droids can disguise themselves as living species. [CCG]

droid harem A huge castlelike structure, it was on a plateau overlooking the farmlands of Biitu. The giant automaton, the Great Heep, kept captured R2 units at the droid harem, treating them to soothing oil baths and other luxuries before consuming them. [TGH]

droid lot This is a place where new and used droids are bought, sold, or exchanged. [SWR]

Drome, Captain The captain hired to transport the Hammertong device for the Death Star from its laboratory to Imperial hands. But Captain Drome never got the chance, as his ship was hijacked by the Mistryl Shadow Guards. [TMEC]

drone barge Used to ferry cargo or other supplies, it is a large space vessel controlled by droids or computers. [HSE]

Droon, Igpek A small-time trader on Nam Chorios. Reporter Yarbolk Yemm told C-3PO and R2-D2 to use Droon's name to get off of Nim Drovis. [POT]

drop shaft *See* lift tube

drop ship A fast-moving spacecraft used to quickly transport troops, crew, or cargo from huge interplanetary capital warships to a planet's surface. Using powerful short-burst drive units, drop ships plummet from orbit in barely controlled falls. [ISB]

Drovian system A system in the Meridian sector, it contains the planet Nim Drovis. [POT]

Drovis *See* Nim Drovis

Druckenwell A Mid-Rim planet, it is an industrialized, overpopulated urban world run by corporate guilds. Druckenwell's crowded cities are divided by wide oceans, and almost all of the planet's available land has been developed. Therefore, great care has recently been taken to reduce the risk of pollution and to protect the planet's few remaining resources. Druckenwell's 9.3 billion inhabitants work mostly for the planet's massive corporations and live in its congested metropolises. Couples may not marry until they can prove their fiscal independence. [SWAJ]

Drone barge

Drudonna One of the two largest moons orbiting the planet Bespin, it and its larger brother moon, H'gaard, are known together as the Twins. Drudonna is only 2.5 kilometers in diameter. Both are unremarkable ice satellites and appear as large green spheres in Bespin's night sky. Shirmar Base, a staging area and processing center for Ugnaught expeditions into Velser's Ring, is located on Drudonna. [GG2]

Dryanta Chewbacca's cousin, he accompanied Chewbacca, Jowdrrl, Shoran, and Lumpawarrump on a mission to rescue Han Solo during the Yevethan crisis. [TT]

Drysso, Joak Former commander of the *Virulence*, he was quickly given command of the Super Star Destroyer *Lusankya* after former Director of Imperial Intelligence Ysanne Isard seized control of Thyferra's Bacta Cartel. Captain Drysso felt sure that the ship guaranteed Isard's control of the bacta trade and the planet itself. When the location of Rogue Squadron's base of operations was finally revealed, he was ordered to destroy the *Empress*-class space station at Yag'Dhul. Accompanied by the *Virulence*, they arrived at Yag'Dhul in time to see what looked like Rogue Squadron and several freighters jump to hyperspace on a course for Thyferra. Joak Drysso had warned Isard of such a possibility, but she had ignored his advice about leaving the *Virulence* behind to protect the planet.

Drysso reasoned that when he was finished with the Rebel scum at Yag'Dhul, he would return to Thyferra and destroy a weary Rogue Squadron. Surprisingly, Booster Terrik had modified the space station with a gravity-well projector and missile-lock sensors, which rattled the overconfident captain. It was only by the intervention of the *Virulence* that the gravity embrace was broken, allowing the *Lusankya* to escape back to Thyferra. When they arrived, Captain Drysso was stunned to discover the *Freedom* had followed him in with Rogue Squadron in its hold. Fresh and ready for battle, they were still no match for a Super Star Destroyer. However, Drysso had not counted on the freighters being equipped with missiles and using X-wing targeting telemetry. The barrage of missiles from Rogue Squadron and the freighters brought down the shields of his starboard bow. The *Freedom* poured its weapons fire into this breach.

More than 100 ion cannons fired back at the *Freedom*, collapsing its shields and seriously damaging the ship. Instead of concentrating all his firepower on the *Freedom*, Captain Drysso decided the more immediate threat came from the freighters and their missiles and ordered his guns to fire on them. In the meantime, Rogue Squadron and the Twi'lek pilots continued to nibble away at the *Lusankya*, with an occasional salvo from the *Valiant*. Drysso ordered another round of fire at the *Freedom*, and the return fire had enough force to knock out the shields on the *Lusankya*.

At that moment Isard ordered him to retreat and follow her shuttle to hyperspace as they made their escape. Was she insane? He'd never retreat when victory was at hand. And with the sudden appearance of the *Virulence* it seemed his victory was assured. But the Republic's Booster Terrik was now in command of the ship and joined the other vessels bombarding the *Lusankya*. Soon his ship was de-

Trinto Duaba

fenseless, in a rapidly decaying orbit above Thyferra. When Drysso refused to surrender, his crew mutinied and took command of the ship. [BW]

DS-61-2 An Imperial TIE pilot, he flew Black Two during the Battle of Yavin and was Darth Vader's left wingman. Specially trained, Mauler Mithel was held in reserve for missions with Vader. But late in the battle, the *Millennium Falcon* came in unnoticed and blew up Vader's right wingman; that caused Vader to fly into DS-61-2 and push him into the wall, killing Mithel instantly, because his ship had no shields to protect him. Mithel's son, Rejlii, later became a tractor-beam operator aboard Grand Admiral Thrawn's *Chimaera*. [LC, TTSB]

DS-61-3 An Imperial TIE pilot, he flew Black Three during the Battle of Yavin. Darth Vader's right wingman had a reputation for ferocity in combat. The Corellian pilot was nicknamed Backstabber. He died after a direct hit from the *Millennium Falcon*. [CCG]

DS-61-4 Nicknamed Dark Curse, he was an Imperial TIE pilot who survived the Battle of Yavin. DS-61-4 had already survived numerous assaults against such planets as Ralltiir and Mon Calamari. [CCG]

Duaba, Trinto A member of the Stennes shifter species, a humanoid race, he has the ability to blend unnoticed into crowds. Trinto Duaba makes a living by turning lawbreakers over to Imperial authorities. [CCG]

Duinuogwuin Sometimes called Star Dragons, these snakelike multipeds with gossamer wings are an average of ten meters long. Large, reptilelike scales cover their bodies, contrasting with their floppy mammallike ears. This rare ancient species is scattered over the galaxy, even in deep space. They have a deep-rooted sense of morality and honor, and at least some sensitivity to the Force. Some stories tell of ancient Duinuogwuin serving as Jedi Knights. [GG4, DFRSB]

dukha A building in the shape of a large cylinder with a cone roof, there is one in the center of every Noghri village. Inside the single open room is the clan high seat used by the dynast (or clan leader) when he or she holds audiences. [DFR, DFRSB]

D'ulin, Karoly A Mistryl Shadow Guard involved in the transport of the Hammertong device for the Death Star. [TMEC]

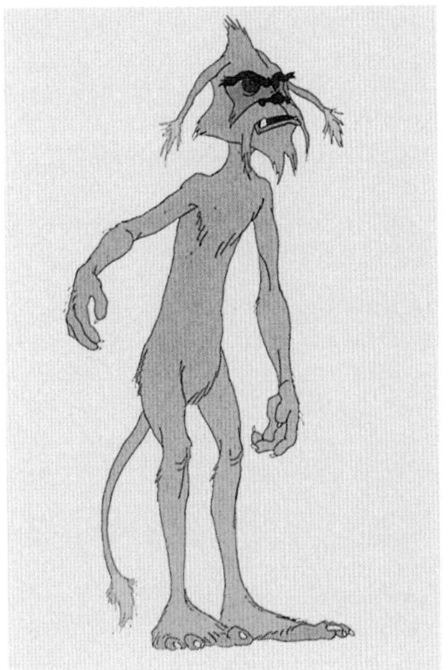
Dulok

D'ulin, Manda A Mistryl Shadow Guard, she was the team leader of the assignment to transport the Hammertong device to the Empire for use in the Death Star. The deal went bad, and Manda D'ulin was killed in an Imperial raid. [TMEC]

Dulok Lanky, unkempt, and usually bug-infested, these distant relatives of the Ewoks are nasty, bad-tempered, and untrustworthy. A large tribe of Duloks lives in the marshland of Endor's moon. Their village is a cluster of rotted logs and swampy caves surrounding a stump-throne covered with the skins and skulls of small animals. [ETV]

Dune Sea A sea of sand that stretches across the Tatooine wastes, this vast desert once was a large inland sea. The area is inhospitable to most lifeforms due to extreme temperatures and a lack of water. The hermit Ben Kenobi lived in the western portion of the Dune Sea. [SW]

dungeon ship A large capital ship used to transport prisoners from one system to another via hyperspace. The massive dungeon ships originally were designed during the Clone Wars to hold Jedi Knights. [DE]

Dunhausen, Grand Moff A lean and crafty official, he always wore his trademark laser-pistol-shaped earrings. [GDV]

Dunwell, Captain A crazed human commander of a Whaladon-hunting submarine that operated below the waves of Mon Calamari, he had an

Dune Sea

obsession with capturing Leviathor, leader of the Whaladons. [GDV]

dupes X-wing pilots use this slang for Imperial TIE bombers. [BW]

dura-armor Industrial-strength military armor, it has the ability to absorb and divert blaster energy. Dura-armor is made by compressing and binding neutronium, lomite, and zersium molecules together through the process of matrix acceleration. [HSE]

durasheet Reusable paperlike material for written documents. Its contents fade after a short period. [HSR]

durasteel Used to build everything from space vehicles to dwellings, this ultralightweight metal can withstand radical temperature extremes and severe mechanical stress. [SW]

Durga A Hutt crime lord, he was a top lieutenant, or Vigo, of the Black Sun criminal organization. He was huge even by Hutt standards, with a sloping head like a sagging mound of slime, stained by a dark-green birthmark that looked like splattered ink. His childlike hands seemed out of place on his swollen body. Durga was also mastermind of the top-secret Darksaber project, the attempt to build a new super weapon. Its failure resulted in Durga's death. [DS, SOTE]

durkii A hideous three-meter-tall creature with the face of a baboon and a body that is a cross between a reptile's and a kangaroo's. [DTV]

Durkii

Durkteel This planet is homeworld to a species known as the Saurin. [CCG]

Durmin, Tajis A Death Star trooper, he was trained in combat techniques and weapons skills. Tajis Durmin was typical of those assigned to guard key areas of the first Death Star. His last assignment was guarding the main conference room, and he died in the explosion of the battle station during the Battle of Yavin. [CCG]

Duro A planet in the Duro system, it is homeworld of a species known as Duros. The Duros—who have large eyes, thin slits for mouths, and no noses—have been traveling space and hauling cargo for thousands of years. Their star system is filled with vast, orbiting cities and many smaller depots and shipyards. It is governed by a group of starship corporations; political decisions are made by stockholders who tried to remain neutral in the Galactic Civil War. The planet is mostly uninhabited, but covered with automated farms that help feed inhabitants of the space cities. Animal life once included a now-extinct cannibal arachnid. Han Solo's ancestor Korol Solo, a pretender to the throne of Corellia, married and fathered a son on Duro. The Duros Captain Lai Nootka was freed from imprisonment on Garqi by Rogue Squadron's Corran Horn. Nootka was later sought out as a witness in the trial of Tycho Celchu. [LC, CPL, GG4, DA, SWAJ, KT]

Duroon A gray-skied planet in the Corporate Sector, it was the site of a major Authority installation using slave labor. Han Solo once delivered weapons to Duroon during a slave revolt against the Corporate Sector Authority. Duroon has three moons, and its surface is dotted with lush jungles located between volcanic vents and fissures. Life-forms include unusual, harmless ball-like creatures known as bouncebeasts that have become popular pets on many worlds. [HSE, CSSB]

Durren Located in the system of the same name in the Meridian sector, it is the site of the Durren Orbital Station, a major New Republic fleet installation. Durren appears blue from space. Six

Duros

main religions are predominant, and the planetary coalition has been a strong supporter of the New Republic, which agreed to protect the Durren system in exchange for the establishment of the naval base. Nine years after the Battle of Endor, a rebel faction revolted against the Durren Central Planetary Council and the planet erupted in armed warfare, leaving it vulnerable to looters. The main Republic cruisers, *Caelus* and *Corbantis*, had left the previous day to investigate a rumored pirate attack on Ampliquen and were unable to defend the orbital station. At the same time, the Death Seed plague broke out on the orbital station, but was contained in the lower decks. [POT]

Durron, Kyp From a tousled-haired eight-year-old whose youth was forfeited to the mines to a Jedi Knight—with a detour through the dark side—Kyp Durron has led a life of extremes. He and his parents were carted off by stormtroopers one night from their home on the Deyer colony in the Anoat system. The crime of the politically active parents: speaking out against the Empire's destruction of Alderaan and its billions of inhabitants. Kyp and his parents were sent to the Imperial Correctional Facility on the planet Kessel where they were pressed into slave labor, mining the powerful drug called glitterstim spice from pitch-black tunnels. Kyp's older brother, Zeth, was shunted off to the grueling Imperial Academy on Carida.

Kyp spent his formative years alone and in darkness. His parents were executed during a battle that resulted in the smuggler Moruth Doole gaining complete control over the prison and the mines. Then a new prisoner, an old woman named Vima-Da-Boda, a Jedi Knight in the days of the Old Republic, sensed an aptitude for the Force in Kyp and started training him in some Force skills until one day she, too, was taken away by authorities. Seven years after the Battle of Endor, two new prisoners met Kyp: Han Solo and Chewbacca, who had been shot down by Doole while on a diplomatic mission to Kessel.

Han discovered quickly that the sixteen-year-old Kyp had great aptitude for the Force. It came in handy in the lower tunnels, when he, Chewbacca, and several other slaves and guards were attacked by the giant spiders that created the glitterstim. They then developed an escape plan and made it off Kessel in a stolen Imperial cargo ship, only to be pulled into the Maw, a cluster of black-hole fields. Kyp's Force powers helped them navigate to relative safety: a top-secret Imperial weapons installation run by Admiral Daala. Their escape from the installation—with Kyp wearing a stormtrooper's armor—led to a fierce space battle that resulted in the destruction of most of Moruth Doole's space fleet.

Luke Skywalker invited Kyp to become a Jedi trainee on Yavin 4. Within a week, he had surpassed all the other initiates. But his impatience and anger made him a target for the dark side in the form of the long-dead Sith Lord Exar Kun, whose still-strong spirit was trapped in a Yavin temple. Kyp started training in secret with Kun but believed he could control the dark side. Still, in an act of vengeance, he removed the memories from the mind of reformed Imperial weapons developer Qwi Xux. He then joined Exar Kun to raise a major Imperial weapon, the Sun Crusher, from its burial grounds in the heart of the gas giant Yavin. When Luke Skywalker tried to intervene, Kyp and Kun trapped Luke's spirit outside his body, placing the Jedi in a state near death.

Kyp Durron

Kyp tracked down his most hated enemy, Admiral Daala, as she was about to attack Coruscant, and nearly destroyed her. Next he tried to find his brother on Carida, but the rescue attempt failed as he accidentally incinerated his brother along with the planet. Later, as Kyp was about to destroy the *Millennium Falcon* with Han Solo and Lando Calrissian aboard, he was freed from Exar Kun's influence when the other Jedi trainees succeeded in destroying Kun's spirit. A recovered Luke offered to continue Kyp's training if he forever renounced the dark side. On their way to destroy the Sun Crusher once and for all, Luke and Kyp ran into another battle with Admiral Daala. Kyp managed to destroy both the Sun Crusher and a prototype Death Star, barely escaping with his life. [JS, DS, SWCG]

Durron, Zeth Kyp Durron's older brother, he was separated from his family during a raid by stormtroopers and taken to the Imperial military training center on Carida. Years later Kyp attempted to rescue Zeth, but the result was his brother's death and destruction of the planet Carida. [JS, DS]

Dusat, Jord A native of the planet Ingo, he learned to race landspeeders over desolate, crater-studded acid salt flats. Jord Dusat was the best friend and main racing competitor of Thall Joben. Although he dreamed of becoming a professional speeder racer, Dusat was a bit of a rebel and troublemaker. He encountered the droids R2-D2 and C-3PO in the early days of the Empire. [DTV]

Duskhan League A federation of colonies and worlds in the Koornacht Cluster, it was under the control of the Yevetha species from the planet N'zoth. The Duskhan League was headed by viceroy Nil Spaar, who helped push the already xenophobic Yevetha into a campaign of conquering or exterminating non-Yevetha species on nearby worlds. [BTS, SOL, TT]

Dustangle An archaeologist, he hid in the underground caverns of Duro after the Empire subjugated the planet; he is a cousin of Dustini. [MMY]

Dustini An archaeologist from the planet Duro, he went off-world to appeal to the Alliance for help for his subjugated planet; he is a cousin of Dustangle. [MMY]

Dutch This is the nickname of Jon Vander, lead pilot of Gold Squadron, a squadron of Y-wing starfighters during the Battle of Yavin. [SW, CCG]

Duull, Vor Proctor of information science on the *Aramadia*, the Yevethan/Duskhan Embassy ship. [BTS]

Duvel, Mayth A sublieutenant in the Black Sun criminal organization. [SOTE]

D'Wopp A Whiphid, he was the prospective groom of Lady Valarian. He made the mistake of leaving the Mos Eisley wedding reception to hunt a bounty and was shipped back to his homeworld, Toola, in a box. [TMEC]

Dxo'In, Kid A smuggler, he took Han Solo on one of his first runs to Kessel. Years later, the balding Kid Dxo'In was among the smugglers who joined Solo in Smuggler's Run during his investigation into the bombing of Senate Hall on Coruscant and his rescue of Lando Calrissian from the crime lord Nandreeson's clutches. [NR]

Dxun Also called Demon Moon, it is one of four moons orbiting the planet Onderon. Its thick jungles are home to numerous bloodthirsty monsters. Due to Dxun's erratic orbit, many of the creatures are able to migrate to the surface of Onderon during an annual period in which the two worlds' atmospheres intersect. Some 4,000 years ago, after the evil Queen Amanoa of Iziz was defeated by the Jedi, the inhabitants of Onderon built a Mandalorian iron tomb on Dxun to house the remains of their queen and of the dark Jedi Freedon Nadd. The fallen Jedi Exar Kun later visited the tomb, where the spirit of Nadd helped him discover some hidden Sith scrolls. Later, at the end of the Sith War, the warrior clans of Mandalore fled to Dxun after failing in their attempt to capture Onderon. Their leader was killed by a pair of the Dxun beasts, and a new warrior assumed the mantle of Mandalore. [TOJ, FNU, DLS, TSW]

Dying Slowly A corrupt town, it was a hub of smuggling on the planet Jubilar and the site of the Victory Forum coliseum. [TBH]

Dyll, Brullian A musician, he was killed by the Empire during a sweep to wipe out "questionable" artistic endeavors. [TBH]

Dymurra Loronar Corporation's chief executive for the Core Systems, he agreed to arm factions in the Chorios systems so they could revolt, thus splitting the New Republic peacekeeping fleet and allowing Imperial Moff Getelles and others to move in. [POT]

Dyzm On the surface, Dyzm was a small brown-skinned man with black hair drawn up into a smooth topknot. He was passed off as the secretary to strongman Seti Ashgad and was one of the soft-spoken beings that native Chorians referred to as Oldtimers.

In reality, he was an insectoid captain droch and the mastermind behind all the turmoil on Nam Chorios. Hormonally altered, mutated, and vastly overgrown, Dyzm was 250 years old. He controlled both Ashgad and Beldorion the Hutt by keeping them both alive and young. Desperate to escape Nam Chorios, he needed a shielded ship to do it, as well as some outside intervention to destroy the ancient gunstations that would surely shoot him down.

When Dyzm visited Princess Leia Organa Solo, his appearance was more accurate: His eyes were large and colorless, his skin was a shiny purplish-brown, and his neck was articulated. Dyzm's skin was also chitinous, not humanlike at all. His tongue was long and pointed, flicking through his sharp brown teeth, and his blotched body was covered with orifices and tubes. After a series of confrontations, Dyzm managed to obtain an escape ship, but with the help of Luke Skywalker and the planet's natural Force components, the ship and its passengers were destroyed. [POT]

8D8 (Atedeate) A thin-faced, white-colored droid with almost humanoid features, pincers for hands, and pistons operating its legs, 8D8 worked under EV-9D9 (Eve-Ninedenine) in crime lord Jabba the Hutt's droid operations center. [RJ]

E-11 A blaster rifle that is standard issue for Imperial forces, they are so numerous that many have been stolen for use by the Rebel Alliance. The E-11 has an extendible stock and carries energy for 100 shots. [SME, CCG]

E522 Assassin An assassin droid, it had a wasplike waist, huge shoulders, and a squared-off head. The E522 Assassin was smeared with meat and juice and fed by Jabba to the rancor, which spit it out. It was later repaired, reprogrammed, and used by Lady Valarian. [TMEC]

Ean A Mon Calamari, he was a member of Wedge Antilles's command crew on the *Yavin*, a New Republic star cruiser. [NR]

Eba The name of Jaina Solo's Wookiee doll. [CS]

ebla beer This ale is brewed from ebla grain on the planet Bonadan. [HSR]

Ebrihim An elderly male Drall, this overweight tutor and guide was hired for the children of Leia and Han Solo while they were on Corellia. [AC]

Ebsuk, Zubindi A Kubaz, he was the late chef of Beldorion the Hutt on Nam Chorios. He used enzymes and hormones to transform common insects into gourmet meals and he was famous for mutating them into whole new life-forms for the dining pleasure of Beldorion. In fact, Kubaz chefs are famous throughout the galaxy for injecting insect life-forms with growth enzymes and gene-splicing them in a quest for newer and more perfect designer foods. But Ebsuk's efforts were his downfall. He altered a droch that—before anyone knew—became intelligent enough to enslave him. The droch, Dyzm, fed off of Ebsuk until he became powerful enough to enslave even Beldorion. [POT]

Echnos Also called Tinn VI-D, it is one of six moons orbiting the gas giant Tinn VI, located in the Tinn system at the border to the Outer Rim. The barren, rocky moon's atmosphere is not breathable for any length of time, and during half of its year Echnos passes through Tinn VI's dangerous magnetic field, which can force ships from hyperspace. Echnos's inhabitants live in an enormous blue transparisteel city dome, forty kilometers in diameter and nearly 2,000 stories high. The crowded, high-technology metropolis is a haven for smugglers and mercenaries and has no form of organized government. Attractions within the domed city include many casinos and the weekly BlastBoat 2000 demolition derby. [SWAJ]

Echo Base The comm-unit designation for the secret Alliance command headquarters on the ice planet Hoth. It was commanded by General Carlist Rieekan and was fully equipped to service transport and combat vehi-

Echo Base

cles. In addition to perimeter defenses, it had a massive ion cannon for covering fire and an energy shield to stave off bombardment. The base had to be abandoned in the face of a fierce Imperial attack. [ESB]

Echo Station Three-Eight One of the isolated Alliance sentry outposts on the planet Hoth, it was destroyed by an Imperial probe droid as a prelude to the full-scale invasion that became the Battle of Hoth. [ESB]

Eckels, Dr. Joto An archaeologist and field researcher for the Obroan Institute, he was in charge of the excavation at Maltha Obex. [SOL, BTS, TT]

Eclipse A 17.5-kilometer-long Super Star Destroyer, it served as the personal flagship of the cloned Emperor Palpatine. He ordered its construction upon his return six years after his presumed death at the Battle of Endor. Solid black and twice the length of the original Super Star Destroyers, the *Eclipse* was designed to frighten and demoralize the enemy.

The ship, with a crew of more than 700,000 plus 150,000 stormtroopers, was outfitted with 500 heavy laser cannons and 550 turbolasers in addition to a planet-cracking superlaser weapon. It carried fifty squadrons of TIE interceptors (six hundred ships), eight squadrons of TIE bombers, five prefabricated garrisons, and one hundred AT-AT walkers.

But the *Eclipse* was stopped over the Pinnacle Moon when Luke Skywalker and Leia Organa Solo joined Force energies and engulfed Emperor Palpatine in a wave of life energy. The action stunned the Emperor, causing him to lose control over the mighty Force storms he had summoned. As Luke and Leia escaped from the ship, the storms consumed and destroyed the vessel. [DE, DESB, SWVG]

Eclipse

Ecliptic Evaders A squad of Imperials serving aboard the ship *Rand Ecliptic*, they all jumped ship near Sullust to join the Rebel Alliance. They joined up at the Yavin 4 base, and most saw their first action at the Battle of Yavin. [CCG]

Edict Admiral Daala's Imperial shuttle. [JS, DA]

Eelysa A young woman from Coruscant, she was born after the Emperor's death and therefore was untainted by the poisons of the Galactic Civil War. Eelysa is one of Luke Skywalker's most promising students at the Jedi academy on Yavin 4. [NR]

effrikim worms Two-headed worms, they are a favorite snack food of Hutts. The endorphins of effrikim worms bring on hours of drowsiness. [TJP]

EG-4 (Eegee-Four) A popular power droid model, it is especially useful on worlds with inhospitable climates because of its rugged design and construction. The EG-4 model has modified, top-mounted power sockets. The droids were especially helpful to the Rebel Alliance when it established a base on the ice planet Hoth. They were donated to the Alliance by the Bothan underground. [CCG]

EG-6 An ambulatory power droid model, it supports equipment and vehicles. But the EG-6 encountered by C-3PO and R2-D2 in the Jawa sandcrawler was slow-witted due to constant memory wipes and didn't even know its own name or serial number. [CCG]

Eiattu VI A planet with blue and reddish-purple vegetation, its native flora includes giant ferns, palm trees, and many types of moss. There are many light forests and murky swamps. Fauna includes dinosaurlike beasts of burden with brightly colored feathers. The capital is a port city on an ocean, much of it built out over and below the bay. Quarren live in the underwater zones. Politically, it is a place of great intrigue, with what seems to be a Rebel-affiliated liberation movement challenging residual Imperial power. [XW]

Eicroth, Dr. Joi An archaeologist, she examined Qellan remains from Maltha Obex. [TT]

EG-4 (Eegee-Four)

Eilnian sweet flies When ripe, these flies are a delicacy for Glottalphibs and other amphibian species. [NR]

Eistern A former member of Black Sword Command, he sabotaged and betrayed Nil Spaar and the Yevethan fleet at the Battle of N'zoth, allowing New Republic forces to defeat the Yevethan forces. [TT]

ejection seat An emergency escape system, it is used on small transport vehicles and most starfighters. Ejection seats rely on passengers using full environmental suits. Survival depends on a quick rescue, and the seats work best within a planet's atmosphere. [SWSB]

Ekibo A Trianii colony world within the disputed border of the Corporate Sector, it was where Rangers Atuarre and Keeheen stopped a herdbeast rustling ring. [CSSB]

Elarles A bar waiter on Circarpous V. [SME]

Elcorth Located in the Farlax sector and the Koornacht Cluster, it was the former site of a Morath pholikite mining operation. Twelve years after the Battle of Endor, Elcorth was brutally attacked and conquered by the alien Yevetha as part of a series of raids that the Yevetha called the Great Purge. [TT]

electrobinoculars Handheld viewing devices, they let users observe distant objects in most lighting conditions. An internal display gives data on range, relative and true azimuths, and elevation. They have zoom and wide-vision capabilities. Often mis-

Electrobinoculars

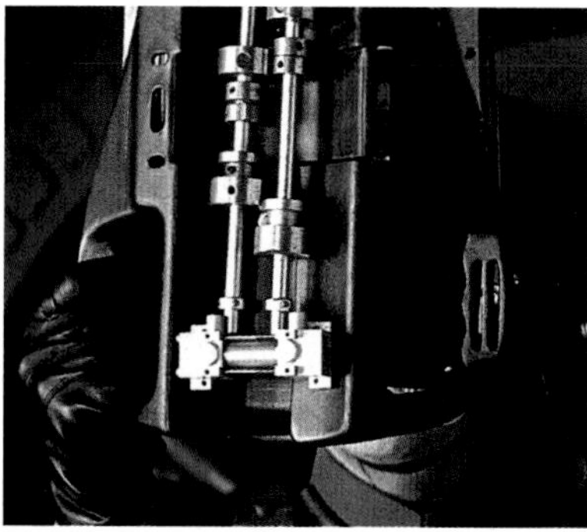

Electrorangefinder

taken for cruder macrobinoculars, electrobinoculars are superior because of their computer-enhanced imaging. [SW, ESB]

electro-jabber Also known as force pikes, these high-voltage prods are used for crowd control or for torture. [RJ]

electrorangefinder A device that calculates the distance between itself and a target object, it is built into distance viewing devices as well as targeting and fire-control computers. Electrorangefinders calculate trajectories in an instant by projecting and receiving bursts of coherent light. [GG3]

electrotelescope An electrooptical device, it has greater power and resolution than electrobinoculars. [ESB]

elite stormtroopers Guards stationed around Imperial Center during the reign of Emperor Palpatine, they wore reddish-orange body armor that included full-face helmets. They were also called Coruscant guards. [SOTE]

Elom A cold, barren world in the Borderland Regions, it quickly joined the Rebellion to combat the tyranny of the Empire and to free itself from enslavement. During the last years of the Galactic Civil War and well into the period of the New Republic, the surface-dwelling Elomin have mostly served in units of their own species. Five years after the Battle of Endor, a New Republic task force crewed by Elomin was wiped out by Grand Admiral Thrawn near the Obroa-skai system as the Imperial commander used a tactic that the Elomin were psychologically incapable of defending against. A second species, primative cave-dwelling Eloms, coexist peacefully with the Elomin. Elom physical calculus is often used to decide the proper course of action. The planet's principle export is lommite ore. [HE, HESB, SOL, TT]

Elomin Tall, thin humanoids, these inhabitants of the planet Elom have pointed ears and four hornlike protrusions emerging from the tops of their heads. Elomin admire order. They see other species as chaotic and unpredictable, preferring to work with their own kind. During the height of the Empire, the Elomin were placed under martial law and forced to mine lommite for their Imperial masters. [HE, HESB]

Eloms

Eloms Short, stocky bipeds, the primitive Eloms live in cities that their ancestors carved out underneath the deserts of the planet Elom as the world's water levels dropped over a period of thousands of standard years. Eloms have thick, oily pelts of dark, stringy fur and tough skin covered with thick calluses on their hands and feet. Their fingers have hard, hooked claws that help them unearth succulent roots and natural springs—something that helped them survive the wrenching climate change on their planet. They coexist with the technologically advanced, surface-dwelling Elomin. In fact, when the Empire enslaved Elomin, some young Eloms staged raids and freed a number of the slaves and housed them in their underground cities. Generally peaceful and quiet, with a strong sense of community, many off-world Eloms have surprisingly turned to criminal pursuits. [GG12]

Eloy, Doctor Senior scientist of the Hammertong project group, he was a colleague of Doctor Kellering. [TMEC]

Elrood Site of a commercial colony and major manufacturing and trade center, Elrood is orbited by twin moons. The capital city is Elrooden, home to the famous Elrood Bazaar. The Dark Jedi Durrei, who joined with an Imperial faction in the Corva sector after the Battle of Endor, was a native of Elrood. [POG, COJ, SWAJ]

Elshandruu Pica The Elshandruu system includes an asteroid belt that has been used as a staging area by pirates. Elshandruu Pica, the planet, has two white moons and one red one. Its capital city is Picavil, located on an ocean coast. It is the site of Margath's, a hotel and casino complex that includes the 27th Hour Social Club. Kina Margath, owner of the complex, has been a longtime Alliance agent. The planet's Imperial Moff is Riit Jandi. Captain Sair Yonka, commander of the Star Destroyer *Avarice*, kept a twenty-sixth floor suite at Margath's and carried on an affair with Moff Jandi's wife. Some three years after the Battle of Endor, after Rogue Squadron resigned from the New Republic military, members of the squadron intercepted Yonka at the Moff's oceanside cottage and convinced him to defect with his ship. After Director of Imperial Intelligence Ysanne Isard learned of this, she ordered Yonka's mistress killed. [GG9, BW]

Emancipator Formerly the Imperial Star Destroyer *Accuser*, the *Emancipator* was one of two Destroyers captured by the Alliance during the Battle of Endor. It took years longer than expected to refit the ship. Under the command of Admiral Ragab, the *Emancipator* was used to great effect during the Alliance raids on Borleias and the conquest of Coruscant. Under Lando Calrissian and Wedge Antilles, the *Emancipator* served valiantly during the fierce Battle of Calamari. It destroyed the Imperial command ship *Allegiance*, but it in turn was consumed by the powerful *Silencer-7*, an Imperial World Devastator. [DE, DESB, BW]

emergency stud A structural device aboard X-wing starfighters, when depressed it sets off explosive bolts that jettison the pilot's canopy for an emergency escape. [SME]

Emperor's Citadel A great black tower surrounded by high walls, it served as the reborn clone Emperor's fortified palace on the planet Byss. [DE]

Emperor's Hand The code-name used by Mara Jade when she served as one of the Emperor's elite secret operatives, unknown even to the Imperial bureaucracy or high command. Her job was to be the Emperor's eyes and ears throughout the galaxy and communicate with him at great distances through use of the Force. She carried out all of his orders, getting into and out of places to carry out tasks other agents wouldn't have had a prayer of accomplishing. [HE, DFR, LC]

Emperor's Inner Circle A group of ministers and governors closest to the Emperor at the time of the Battle of Endor, they tried unsuccessfully to take control of the Empire upon his presumed death. [DE]

Emperor's Royal Guard Mysterious, imposing in their bloodred robes and helmets, and loyal beyond question to a single man: This was the Emperor's Royal Guard.

The elite Royal Guard were once stormtroopers, handpicked for their size, strength, intelligence, and loyalty. The unit was so secretive that suggestions as to its strength ranged from fifty to the tens of thousands, although it was probably much closer to the lower figure. They reported only to Emperor Palpatine, and a handful were always with him. They were fighters, assassins, or protectors, according to the Emperor's wishes. Their main weapons included two-meter force pikes that were almost as lethal as the heavy blaster pistols concealed beneath their robes.

The most elite members of the Royal Guard became Imperial Sovereign Protectors, keeping guard over the palaces and monasteries used by Palpatine as well as his special clone vats on Byss. The Sovereign Protectors wore a more baroque and ceremonial version of the Royal Guard's red armor and were taught minor dark-side techniques by senior Dark Side Adepts in the Emperor's service.

Emperor's Royal Guard

The regular Royal Guard unit disappeared upon the presumed death of Palpatine at the Battle of Endor. [RJ, SWSB, DE, DESB]

Emperor's skyhook The Emperor's skyhook, an orbiting structure tethered to the ground, hung above the capital on Imperial Center. It had a wide terrace overlooking a large central park that contained full-sized evergreen and deciduous trees, some of which topped thirty meters. [SOTE]

Emperor's throne room Every Imperial location that conceivably might have been visited by the Emperor had a special throne room set aside for his use. *Imperial-* and *Super-*class Star Destroyers and battle stations such as the Death Stars all had one. From each room, the Emperor could monitor all activity, take control of his fleet, and contemplate the dark side of the Force. [DSTC]

Empire, the For decades—from the time Senator Palpatine took on the cowl of Emperor, and rechristened the Republic the Galactic Empire, to the stunning defeat by the Rebel Alliance at the Battle of Endor and the presumed death of Palpatine—the Empire reigned supreme. The Empire's New Order promised to eradicate the corruption and social injustices of the previous government, but peace and justice were far from Palpatine's mind. While mak-

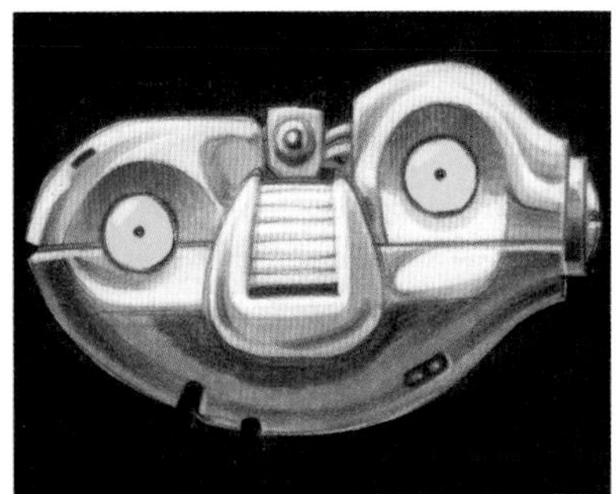
Em Teedee

ing the government more effective and efficient, he demanded complete obeisance to his dictatorial ways. Everything was to be done to further the wealth and personal glory of Palpatine.

The Empire, in fact, was a regime of tyranny and evil, held together by the powerful dark side of the Force that the Emperor personally practiced. He was bolstered by a vast war machine and the scheming of millions who also saw personal benefit in subjugating the inhabitants of the galaxy—and in killing off billions of inhabitants if necessary. But the Empire's sway began to weaken with the victory of the Rebel Alliance at the Battle of Yavin, when the invincible Death Star battle station was destroyed, and the Empire's iron grip was shattered by the Alliance victory at Endor.

Still, the remnants of the Empire—reduced in size and power by perhaps 75 percent from its glory days—refuses to give up and has inflicted some major losses on the New Republic. Several times—after the victories of Grand Admiral Thrawn and the appearance of the clone of Palpatine—the Empire has seemed on the verge of regaining its old power. But it appears clear now that despite occasional setbacks, the New Republic has vanquished one of the most horrifying foes to peace in the last thousand years. [SW, ESB, ROJ, HE, DFR, LC, DE, etc.]

Empire Reborn A movement led by Lord Hethrir, its aim was to undermine the New Republic. [CS]

Empress' Diadem A modified Corellian light freighter, it was the ship that Melina Carniss used when she was employed by Talon Karrde. Its modifications included a weapons package containing a pair of blaster cannons and concussion missile launchers. [BW]

Empress Teta system *See* Teta system, Empress

Em Teedee A tiny translator droid built by Chewbacca to convert Wookiee speech to Basic, it was programmed by C-3PO and thus tends to talk more than it has to. Made for Chewbacca's nephew and Jedi trainee Lowbacca, Em Teedee is a silvery ovoid, slightly longer than a Wookiee's hand, with a "face" made up of two yellow optical sensors, a triangular protrusion toward the center, and a perforated oblong speaker on the lower part.

Em Teedee has had its share of adventures. It once slipped from Lowbacca's belt and was lost in the jungles of Yavin 4, where it became a sort of toy for woolamanders before Tenel Ka rescued it. Later, after Jaina and Jacen Solo and Lowbacca were kidnapped by Brakiss and taken to the Shadow Academy, Em Teedee was reprogrammed to try to convince Lowbacca that the Empire was his friend. [YJK]

Emtrey (Emtreypio) An M-3PO military protocol droid, it handles requisitions, duty assignments, and other administrative chores for Rogue Squadron. It also uses its fluency in more than six million languages and familiarity with an equivalent number of current and historical military doctrines, regulations, honor codes, and protocols. When it began exhibiting odd behavior patterns, some squadron members were concerned that the Empire might be using Emtrey as a spy droid. Upon investigation, however, they learned that the droid had been cobbled together from scrounged circuitry when the Alliance was based on Hoth and constantly running short on supplies. [BW]

Enara A Fallanassi female, she aided in the rescue of Han Solo from the Yevethan ship *Pride of Yevetha* after he had been captured and tortured by Nil Spaar. Enara used her powers to create an illusion that prisoners who had actually escaped were still aboard the ship. After Chewbacca rescued Solo, she also created the illusion of a battered Han to trick the Yevethan leader. She remained aboard voluntarily, declining to be rescued. [TT]

e'Naso, Bracha A smuggler, he sold supplies to Chewbacca for use in his rescue of Han Solo during the Yevethan crisis. [TT]

Endor An Alliance frigate, it was destroyed in a collision with the *Shooting Star*. [BTS]

Endor (sanctuary moon) Located in the remote Endor system in the Moddell sector, the planet is a silvery gas giant orbited by nine moons. It will always be known as the site of the final major battle of the Galactic Civil War, the Battle of Endor, which marked the beginning of the end of the treacherous and bloodthirsty Galactic Empire.

Its largest moon is the size of a small planet and is variously known as the forest moon, the sanctuary moon, or often simply as Endor. The Endor system is difficult to reach,

Endor (sanctuary moon)

because the uncharted territory and the massive gravitational shadow of the gas giant require several complicated hyperspace jumps. Over the years many star travelers have crashed and been stranded on the habitable moon. Endor is a temperate moon of forests, savannas, and mountains, with a relatively light gravity. Its climate is suitable for its many native life-forms, including the Endoran pony, the Endoran vethiraptor, boarwolves, glowing sprites called Wisties, fast mischievous Teeks, winged condor dragons, gunlabirds, predatory Yootaks, and stump-dwelling tempters that lure prey with their camouflaged, articulated tongues.

The most common sentient species on Endor are the primitive, furry Ewoks, the majority of whom make their communal dwellings high in the trees. Called "lifetrees" by the Ewoks, they can reach heights of 1,000 meters and the Ewoks consider them spiritual guardians. But over the years, Ewoks have built stilt villages on lakes and at least one village on the side of a sheer cliff. Music plays an important role in Ewok culture, which is marked by a rigid clan system. Ewoks are skilled engineers (among their inventions are gliders and catapults), and each tribe has a shaman who interprets mystical signs. Natural enemies include the thirty-meter high humanoid creatures called Gorax, who search the trees for Ewok dwellings low enough to grab. Gorax inhabit the rocky highlands of the barren Desert of Salma, which lies beyond the Yawari Cliffs north of the dense forest. The desert is also marked by acid pools and dry lakes, and large rearing spiders are known to live in the bottoms of the Gorax caves.

West of the forest are vast grassland plains known as the Dragon's Pelt, which are dotted with jutting lava rocks. In the distance lies a range of snow-capped mountains called the Dragon's Spine. Stilt-legged yuzzum inhabit the savanna, hunting small rodents called ruggers. A colony of off-planet alien marauders have built a stone castle on the Dragon's Pelt, and use the two-legged, slow-witted blurrgs as beasts of burden for their raids into the forest to attack Ewok villages.

When the Empire selected Endor as the construction site for the second Death Star, it established an Imperial base on the moon's surface to generate a protective shield for the orbiting battle station. A Rebel strike force, including Han Solo and Leia Organa, was able to destroy the shield generator with the help of an Ewok tribe. The Death Star and much of the Imperial fleet were subsequently destroyed in what is now known as the Battle of Endor. A cloud of dark-side energy, a residual effect of the Emperor's apparent death, is now in Endor's orbit at the site of the destruction. [RJ, RJN, DFR, JS, DA, SWSB, COJ, XW, DESB, ETV, ISWU]

Battle of Endor

Endor, Battle of The most decisive engagement of the Galactic Civil War, the battle marked the beginning of the end of the Empire and the birth of the New Republic. It saw the destruction of the second Death Star battle station and the deaths of Darth Vader and Emperor Palpatine, who was later reborn as a clone.

The Rebel Alliance had learned of the secret construction of an even more powerful second Death Star and was determined to destroy it before it could be completed. Bothan spies also learned that the Emperor would pay the station a personal visit. Both pieces of information, it turned out, had been planted by Palpatine to set a trap for the Alliance.

As Admiral Ackbar gathered the Alliance fleet around the planet Sullust, a special strike team was sent ahead to sabotage the shield generator protecting the unfinished Death Star. The team, led by Han Solo and including Luke Skywalker, Leia Organa, Chewbacca, the droids R2-D2 and C-3PO, and a squad of Rebel commandos, used a stolen Imperial shuttle to get through the Empire's forces and down to Endor's forest moon. The timing had to be perfect. The strike team had to disable or destroy the shield generator by the time the Rebel fleet emerged from hyperspace so that the surprise attack could begin.

But the "unfinished" Death Star had a fully operational superlaser. And a full legion of stormtroopers and other Imperial soldiers were waiting to defend the shield generator and capture the Rebel commandos. While the strike team battled on Endor's moon, the Rebel fleet arrived to find the protective shield still in place.

The Emperor's plan called for the Imperial fleet to remain in reserve on the far side of the moon while TIE fighters destroyed the outnumbered Rebel ships. Next, the Death Star's superlaser would vaporize all of the Alliance's capital ships. The Rebels gained some time by using the Empire's Star Destroyers as shields.

On the forest moon, the native Ewoks helped free the strike team, allowing it to carry out its sabotage mission. When the shield generators were destroyed, the protective shield surrounding the Death Star disappeared. Then Lando Calrissian and his starfighters moved in to attack. The *Millennium Falcon* and Wedge Antilles's X-wing flew into the unfinished Death Star's superstructure and fired proton torpedoes at the battle station's power regulator. Simultaneously, Lando Calrissian fired concussion missiles at the main reactor. The resulting explosions destroyed the Death Star. Without the Emperor, the dark side became diffused and Imperial forces were plunged into confusion. What remained of the Imperial fleet scattered. [RJ]

Endurance A carrier in the New Republic's new Fifth Fleet, it was destroyed at Orinda by a Super Star Destroyer when all starfighters were kept in the launch bay until the last possible minute, making them susceptible to a devastating attack. [BTS]

energy battery These batteries are composed of multiple turbolaser gun and ion cannon artillery emplacements set up in arrays. Such energy batteries can be carried on capital ships or used to protect ground installations. [SWN]

energy cell Portable power sources, these rechargeable power cells come in a variety of sizes to fit everything from handheld weapons to arrays on capital ships. [SWN]

energy gate A static, prepositioned force field, it is used to regulate access routes in detention centers and other high security areas. [SWN]

Enforcer One Great Bogga the Hutt's military Dreadnaught and the flagship of his space fleet, it was responsible for many of his greatest victories, including the capture of Finhead Stonebone's pirate ships. *Enforcer One* was commanded by Captain Norufu, a near-human slave, and its home port was Bogga's palace on Taboon's moon. The ship was a heavily modified Dreadnaught designed for planetary occupations. Bogga got it after it was decommissioned by the Old Republic, but its weapons and shields were still powerful. The main weapon was a fixed, heavy turbolaser. [TOJ, SWVG]

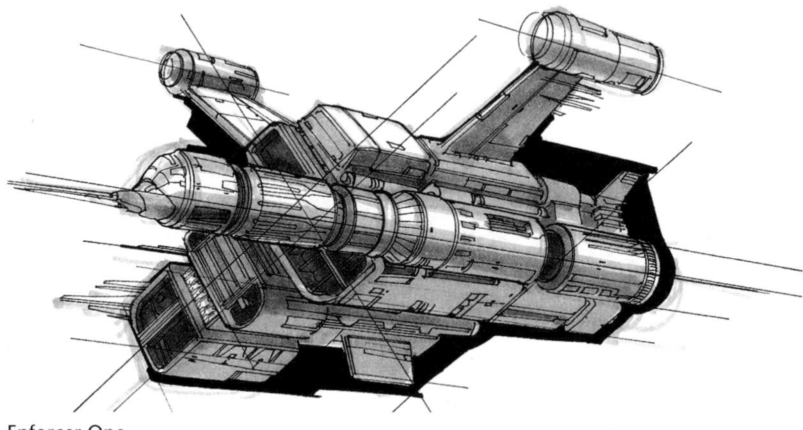
Enforcer One

Engh, First Administrator Nanaod A New Republic minister, he urged head of state Leia Organa Solo to engage in some public relations to buff up her public image a bit, a suggestion that she reluctantly accepted. [BTS, SOL]

Engret A boy who was part of a group of infiltrators on Orron III in the Corporate Sector, Engret and his companions sought information at the Authority Data Center to learn the location of political prisoners being held by the Corporate Sector Authority. [HSE]

enhanced human Humans who have been biologically and surgically changed to be larger and stronger than regular humans, those in the service of the Empire Reborn movement are most likely a product of Lord Hethrir's experimentation. [CS]

entechment The absorption of a sentient creature's energies into battery coils to power circuitry, entechment is usually used for battle-droids or shipboard functions. This Ssi-ruuk technology involves the injection of a magnetic solution that is selectively absorbed by the subject's nervous system, tuning external circuitry to the internal magnetization. Then, activation of an electromagnetic field causes life energy to jump the gap from sentient source to storage coils. [TAB]

Entralla A planet that lies within the Velcar Free Commerce Zone in the Pentastar Alignment, it is a world of shining spaceports. Its large single moon can often be seen in its bright blue sky. Many prominent religious sects had their origin on Entralla, and the planet is home to several important monasteries. Within Entralla's Nexus City starport is the famous historic district and a seedy industrial zone known as the Overhang, where little sunlight penetrates the dense buildings.

After the Emperor's death at Endor, Entralla's inhabitants staged a civil uprising against the Empire, but the newly formed Pentastar Alignment installed a puppet regime. The New Republic denied a request for immediate action, so Entralla native Colonel Andrephan Stormcaller resigned his rank and formed the Red Moons, an elite mercenary group, to fight the Pentastar Alignment. [SWAJ]

Eol Sha A volcanic world with a surface covered with scalding geysers and bubbling lava fissures (home of the dangerous lava fireworm), it was the site of a hundred-year-old mining colony. The settlement was founded to extract valuable gases from the nearby Cauldron Nebula, but when the operation failed, the colonists were forgotten. They lived on Eol Sha for generations, awaiting certain destruction because the planet's large double moon was in a rapidly decaying orbit. The colonists survived on crustacean bugdillos and edible lichens until they finally were relocated to Dantooine by the New Republic. Their peace of mind was short lived, for Admiral Daala's fleet wiped them out as they were establishing their new home. Their former planet was presumed destroyed when all the suns in the adjacent Cauldron Nebula went nova. Gantoris, one of Luke Skywalker's Jedi academy students, was from Eol Sha. [DA, JS]

Erg Es 992 A star in the Meridian sector, it is orbited by the planet Cybloc and its inhabited moon, Cybloc XII. [POT]

Eriadu A polluted factory planet in the Sesswenna sector, it is a trading and governmental hub in the Outer Rim. Eriadu was the capital world of Grand Moff Tarkin's territory and his base of operations. During a trip from Eriadu to the newly completed Death Star at Despayre, Tarkin's shuttle was attacked by a strike force of Alliance Y-wing starfighters. Although the Grand Moff was rescued by the timely arrival of a Star Destroyer, the Rebels managed to rescue Tarkin's Mon Calamari servant, Ackbar. [COJ, DESB, DSTC, DS]

Errant Venture Booster Terrik's flagship, it was formerly known as the *Virulence*. [BW]

escape pod A seemingly minor piece of equipment, rarely visible or much remarked about, it is a technological lifeboat that is worth more than its weight in precious gems in an emergency. In fact, one escape pod might have saved the Rebel Alliance.

The pod itself is a space capsule used by passengers and crew to abandon *Capital*-class starships or small freighters in emergencies. Pods range in size from small capsules barely large enough for a single passenger or two, to larger lifeboats capable of carrying many. Interiors are spartan, because they are meant for only a few hours' use. Sensor systems provide atmosphere, radiation, and gravity information about the surrounding area, and there is a limited-range communications transceiver. Pods are usually stocked with about two weeks' worth of rations, and the vessel can be used as a temporary planetary shelter. They can also float through space for a limited period, awaiting rescue vehicles. Pods have simple drive systems, minimal fuel, and devices to assist in relatively soft landings on nearby planets.

Escape pod

It was just such a simple escape pod aboard the captured Rebel Alliance ship *Tantive IV* that let droids C-3PO and R2-D2 escape an Imperial attack and carry with them the top-secret plans for the Empire's Death Star battle station. [SW, SWSB]

escape pod station *See* lifeboat bay

escort carrier These 500-meter-long vessels provide TIE fighter combat support. Boxlike and inelegant, escort carriers house entire TIE fighter wings in their huge bays and transport the fighters through hyperspace. Smaller bays carry up to six shuttles or other support craft. With only ten twin laser cannons, the carriers stay as far from battlefronts as possible, serving mostly as refueling and supply points. [ISB]

escort frigate Originally built to protect Empire supply convoys from Rebel raids, many of the 300-meter-long Nebulon-B escort frigate combat starships were captured and placed in the Alliance fleet. One such refitted Nebulon-B was the medical frigate used by Luke Skywalker after his hand was severed by a blow from Darth Vader's lightsaber. Standard equipment aboard the frigates includes twelve turbolaser batteries and laser cannons, two tractor beam projectors, two squadrons of starfighters, and powerful hyperdrive engines. [SWSB]

Espo Slang name for the private security police employed by the Corporate Sector Authority. Espos follow no code of conduct, much less the precepts of justice, except for the edicts of the Authority. They are unquestioning bullies dressed in brown uniforms, combat armor, and black battle helmets; they are armed with blaster rifles and riot guns. [HSE, HSR]

Essada, Bin The Imperial military governor presiding over the Circarpous Major star system, he was a portly man with curly black hair topped by a spiral orange pattern. The pink pupils of his eyes hinted at a not-quite-human origin. [SME]

Esseles Located in the Darpa sector of the Core Worlds along the Perlemian Trade Route, this planet lost territory and power in the era prior to the Clone Wars and as the Empire rose. Esseles is a warm world covered with young mountain ranges, and its 24 billion inhabitants live in the few scattered valleys and plains. Calamar, the planet's capital city, is viewed as a center for high culture with many parks and museums. Esseles is a center for high-tech research and development, including hypernautics and advanced hyperdrive engines. [SWAJ, CG2]

Estillo, Asrandatha The son of the well-liked royal family on Eiattu VI, he was believed killed along with the rest of his family. But when a rakishly good-looking young man showed up claiming to be Asran (short for Asrandatha) Estillo, Imperials took him into custody, performed some genetic tests, and proclaimed him to be the real prince. In reality, he was an unwitting dupe of Darth Vader. As part of an evil plan, he was to lead a phony liberation movement, kill the other nobles who shared power on the planet with the Empire (who had had the Estillo family murdered), and leave the spoils for the planet's moff. [XW]

Etti IV A wealthy and hospitable planet in the Etti system, it takes advantage of its position on a major trade route within Corporate Sector space. Etti IV has moss-covered plains and shallow saline seas. It is home to many affluent and influential Corporate Sector Authority executives as well as a thriving criminal underworld. The planet has no exportable resources, so it relies on its natural beauty and prime location to attract visitors and traders. [HSE, D, CSSB]

EV-9D9 (Eve-Ninedenine)

Ettyk, Halla Originally a prosecutor from Alderaan, she became a valued member of General Cracken's counterintelligence staff when she joined the Alliance. Chosen to prosecute Tycho Celchu for the crimes of treason and murder, Halla Ettyk was completely convinced of his guilt, although haunted by Rogue Squadron's faith in their former operations chief. Determined to discover the truth at all cost, she enlisted the aid of Iella Wessiri. [KT]

EV-9D9 (Eve-Ninedenine) A thin, gunnite-colored droid with a female voice, she had a sadistic demeanor perfectly suited for her job: supervisor of cyborg operations for the even more sadistic crime lord Jabba the Hutt. Previously, she had destroyed a number of droids on Cloud City and eventually escaped, nearly destroying the city as she did so. In her position with Jabba, EV-9D9 oversaw all droids working at the Hutt's desert palace on Tatooine, apparently taking great delight in torturing or mutilating any of her charges. EV-9D9 believed it was her duty to work other droids until they dropped, as many of them did. After Jabba's death, she was eventually tracked down and destroyed by the droid 1-2:4C:4-1 (Wuntoo Forcee Forwun) as revenge for the damage she had done to his counterparts on Cloud City. [RJ, TJP]

EV-9D9.2 (Eve-Ninedeninetwo) Head of cyborg operations and retraining at the droid manufacturing facility Telti, she was the successor to Eve-Ninedenine. Said to be twice as ruthless as her predecessor, EV-9D9.2 set about torturing Cole Fardreamer upon his capture on Telti. Once R2-D2 and C-3PO shut down all the droids on Telti, Artoo dismantled all of the torture appliances and instrumentation of Eve-Ninedeninetwo. [NR]

Evax An Imperial Intelligence Officer with a track record for predicting Rebel fleet movements, he saved many vulnerable bases by coordinating starship maneuvers. Evax was killed aboard the Death Star when it was destroyed in the Battle of Yavin. [CCG]

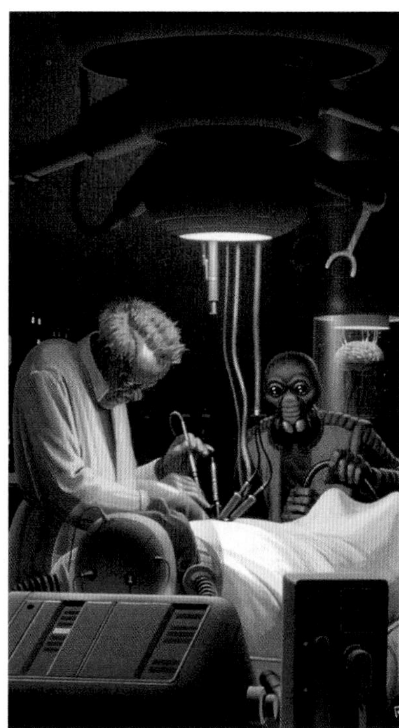

Doctor Evazan

Evazan, Doctor A truly mad doctor who teamed with the smuggler Ponda Baba, he was fond of practicing what he called "creative surgery." He liked to disassemble body parts and put them back together in different ways—on living creatures. He was institutionalized by the Empire but escaped and acquired a forged surgical license that he took from star system to system, butchering hundreds of patients along the way. Among his aliases were Doctor Cornelius and Roofoo, and he was often referred to as Doctor Death.

More than a dozen systems issued a death sentence for Evazan and victims staked a large bounty for his capture. Bounty hunter Jodo Kast almost trapped him, heavily scarring Evazan's face with a blaster shot, but the doctor escaped with the help of Ponda Baba, and the two became partners in crime, which included spice smuggling for Jabba the Hutt.

That's how they ended up on Tatooine at the Mos Eisley cantina. A young Luke Skywalker entered and a drunk Baba shoved him. Luke tried to calm Baba, but Evazan threatened the boy, boasting to Luke about his death sentence in twelve systems.

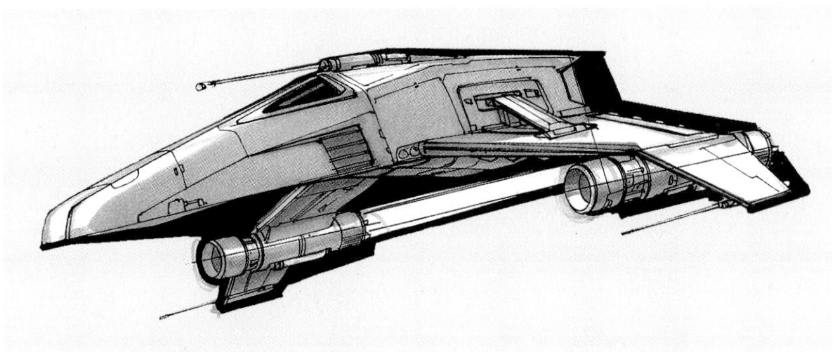

E-wing starfighter

"I'll be careful," Luke said. "You'll be dead," Evazan snarled, not noticing the approach of Ben Kenobi, who tried to defuse the situation. When they attacked anyhow, Kenobi used his lightsaber to slice Evazan's chest and cut off Baba's right arm at the elbow.

The two fled the planet. At one point Evazan tried to graft a bionic arm onto Baba, but he botched the surgery. The two had a falling-out, then hooked up again and went to Baba's home planet, Ando, where Evazan resumed bizarre medical experiments. In a complex turn of events, the insane pseudo-doctor managed to transfer the brain of one of the planet's senators into Baba's body, killing the criminal and barely escaping with his own life in a thermal detonation. Boba Fett finally caught up with Evazan, killing him on a planet where the doctor was conducting experiments to bring the dead back to life. [SW, SWSB, SWCG]

Eviscerator An Imperial Star Destroyer II, it patrolled the Mirit, Pyria, and Venjagga systems. [BW]

Evocar Former homeworld of the primitive Evocii, it has been renamed Nal Hutta. [DESB]

E-wing starfighter One of the newest starfighters in the New Republic fleet, it was introduced during Grand Admiral Thrawn's reign of terror. The E-wing is from the same designers who developed the X-wing starfighter for Incom Corporation. It was built to protect convoys from raiding missions, so it has respectable speed. But its biggest attribute is increased firepower, mainly its triple laser cannons and sixteen proton torpedoes. A single pilot controls the craft and its advanced armament, and the new R7 series astromech droid provides systems assistance. [DE, SWVG]

Ewoks Primitive, furry two-legged creatures, these natives of Endor's forest moon were among the greatest heroes of the crucial Battle of Endor in the Galactic Civil War. Only about one meter tall, these straightforward, even simple creatures possess the antithesis of a high-technology culture. They are tribal and still use bows and arrows, slingshots, and catapults as primary weapons. But their intense teamwork and keen understanding of their environment and how to work with it to their best advantage give Ewoks acumen and skills that just can't be equaled, even by members of the most technically advanced societies.

The Ewoks' language is liquid and expressive, and other species find it fairly easy to speak Ewok. A number of Ewoks sprinkle some Basic into their own vocabularies. Most are hunters and gatherers who live in clustered villages built high in hardy, long-lived conifer trees, or lifetrees. Ewok religion is centered around these giant trees, which legends refer to as guardian spirits. Each village plants a new seedling for each Ewok baby born and nurtures it as it grows. Throughout their lives, each Ewok is linked to his or her totem tree, and when they die, Ewoks believe that their spirits go to live in their special trees. Ewoks believe that their village shamans can communicate with the oldest and wisest trees in time of crisis. From a lifetree's bark, Ewoks distill a natural insect repellent. From fallen trees they make weapons, clothing, furniture, and cooking implements.

During the day, Ewoks descend from their high huts to hunt and forage on the forest floor. At night, they leave the forest to huge carnivores. Ewoks are curious and frequently get into trouble by being too nosy. They also love to hear and tell stories and are very musical; they especially enjoy communal singing and dancing. And they are inventive, using natural materials to build everything from waterwheels to flying wings.

At first glance, the Ewoks might seem timid both because of their size and because they are easily startled. But the brave, alert, and loyal Ewoks are fierce warriors when necessary. The Empire dismissed them as inconsequential—not worthy of annihilating—when it was building the second Death Star battle station near Endor's forest moon. The moon was the site of a shield generator that protected the Death Star during its construction. But one tribe befriended Princess Leia Organa and her companions in the Rebel strike force. With the help the tribe provided, the strike force was able to disable the shield generator, allowing the Alliance fleet to directly attack and destroy the battle station. [RJ, SWSB, ETV, BFE, EA, ISWU]

Excarga This planet is home to several profitable ore-processing corporations. The inhabitants of Excarga made sizable profits supplying the Rebel Alliance with materials. Drextar Pym, a New Republic senator from Excarga, is head of the panel that prosecutes former Imperials for their war crimes. [SWAJ]

Ewok

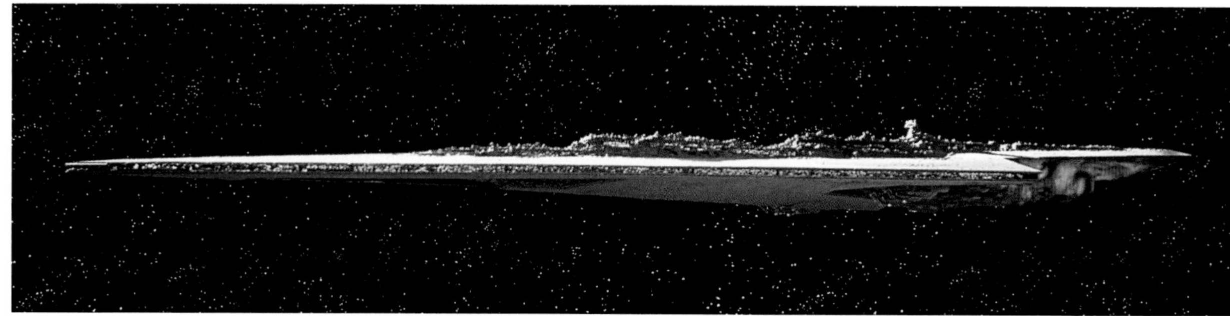

Executor

Executioners Row A slum at the edge of the town of Dying Slowly on the planet Jubilar, it was in a warehouse here that bounty hunter Boba Fett killed spice trader Hallolar Voors. [TBH]

Executor The personal flagship of Darth Vader, it was the first *Super*-class Star Destroyer. The *Executor* was 8,000 meters long, or about five times the size of an *Imperial*-class Star Destroyer. Such enormous ships are really overkill because a smaller vessel could as easily fulfill the specific duties of a headquarters ship. But the *Executor*'s purposes included symbolizing the Emperor's unlimited power and resources and frightening planets and whole systems into submission.

The *Executor* was presented to Lord Vader shortly after the Battle of Yavin, where the first Death Star was destroyed. It carried more than 1,000 weapons; two full wings of TIE fighters, totaling 144 ships, and 200 other combat and support ships; 38,000 ground stormtroopers; and enough garrison bases and Imperial walkers to destroy any Rebel base.

The ship originally was commanded by Admiral Ozzel, but after his death at the hands of an unforgiving Vader, Admiral Piett was given command. The *Executor* was destroyed at the Battle of Endor. After its shield generators were eliminated, a Rebel fighter pilot deliberately smashed his fighter into the *Executor*'s bridge, and the out-of-control ship was pulled into the uncompleted second Death Star, exploding on impact. [ESB, RJ, ISB, MTS, HE]

EX-F A weapons and propulsion test bed taken by the Yevetha at N'zoth, it was renamed *Glory of Yevetha* and made part of Nil Spaar's Black Fifteen Fleet. [BTS]

Exmoor The Beruss clan estate, it is in Imperial City on Coruscant. [TT]

Exodeen A former Imperial world, it is located in the center of what was Empire-controlled space during the Galactic Civil War. Because its race, the Exodeenians, was nonhumanoid, the planet was considered unimportant by Emperor Palpatine. Exodeenians have six arms, six legs, and six rows of uneven teeth. Exodeenian etiquette states that a touch by another on the first arm signals an Exodeenian to stop speaking, while a touch on the second is a challenge to fight. M'yet Luure was the Exodeenian Senator to the New Republic until she was killed in the bombing of Senate Hall. [NR]

Exodo II A planet with a thick, stormy atmosphere, it is covered with plains of blackened and hardened lava. Exodo II lies near Odos and the Spangled Veil Nebula in the Meridian sector. Its most common lifeform is the ghaswar, which burrows into the crust and leaves dusty boreholes behind. Nine years after the Battle of Endor, Han Solo and Lando Calrissian came to the planet searching for any sign of Leia Organa Solo, but found a wrecked scout cruiser instead. Soon after, they were attacked by an Imperial fleet from the nearby Antemeridian sector but lost their pursuers in the Spangled Veil Nebula. [POT]

Exozone An insectoid bounty hunter who often works with Boba Fett and Dengar, he helped the pair chase Han Solo and Princess Leia Organa Solo through the streets of Nar Shaddaa. [DE]

Expansion Region Once a center of manufacturing and heavy industry, it started as an experiment in corporate-controlled space. When residents demanded more freedom, the Old Republic turned control over to freely elected governments. As much of the area's natural resources have been depleted, the region has sought to pull itself out of an economic slump by maintaining trade routes and portraying itself as an alternative to the crowded and expensive Core Worlds and Colonies regions. [SWRPG2]

Expeditious An Imperial *Carrack*-class light cruiser, it was commanded by Captain Rojahn when former Corellian Security officer Gil Bastra was held prisoner aboard the ship. He died in captivity after interrogation by Kirtan Loor. [BW]

Exten-dee *See* X-10D

eyeballs A slang term that X-wing pilots use for Imperial TIE starfighters. [RS]

Eye of Palpatine Emperor Palpatine ordered this giant Imperial battlemoon built eighteen years before the Battle of Yavin. He had one main goal in mind for the heavily armed space station: wipe out a Jedi enclave that had been established decades earlier in the Plawal rift on the planet Belsavis. The *Eye of Palpatine* was supposed to pick up contingents of stormtroopers who had been scattered on several planets to keep the mission secret. The ship never arrived, however, and a small backup force of TIE interceptors was quickly defeated by Belsavis planetary defenses. The Emperor imprisoned many of those responsible for the design of the highly automated ship named after himself, and the *Eye of Palpatine* disappeared for nearly thirty years.

Some eight years after the Battle

of Endor, Luke Skywalker was drawn to the battlemoon's hiding place deep within a nebulous gas cloud in the asteroid-choked Moonflower Nebula. Weakened by injuries after a direct hit on his ship, Luke and two of his Jedi students—Cray Mingla and Nichos Marr—were taken aboard a reawakened *Eye of Palpatine* as it restarted its long-ago mission. The ship was controlled by a super-sophisticated artificial intelligence known as the Will. Thirty years before, the Jedi Callista and Geith had discovered the ship and its mission and were killed trying to destroy the battlemoon. But Callista's spirit was so strong that it stayed alive in the ship's gunnery computers and prevented the mission from being carried out. But the Will resumed the original mission after it was reawakened by the fifteen-year-old son of one of Palpatine's mistresses. The boy was not only Force-sensitive but had years earlier been implanted with a device that made it possible for him to control mechanicals.

Instead of contingents of stormtroopers, the *Eye of Palpatine* picked up warring clans of Gamorreans, Jawas, Sand People, Talz, Affytechans, Kitonaks, and other species. It treated them all as Imperial soldiers and used mind-control techniques on them. It was chaotic and highly dangerous aboard as Luke discovered deadly booby traps when he attempted to unravel the ship's secrets. He made contact with the disembodied Callista, and the two fell in love as they attempted to put an end to the ship's destructive potential. Finally, with the help of Callista, Nichos managed to overload the reactors of the *Eye of Palpatine* and he and Cray sacrificed their lives to destroy the ship. At the last moment, Callista's spirit passed into Cray's body, and Callista was united with Luke. [COJ]

Eyvind A moisture farmer on Tatooine, he was the fiancé of Ariela and friend to fellow farmer Ariq Joanson. Eyvind often disagreed with Joanson's plans to make peace with the Jawas and Sand People, but nonetheless invited thirty-one Jawas to his wedding. The ceremony was raided by Sand People, and Eyvind was killed along with many others. [TMEC]

4-LOM

4-LOM A late-model protocol droid, 4-LOM worked as a valet and human-cyborg relations specialist on the passenger liner *Kuari Princess*. The droid interacted with the ship's computer and each altered the other's programming. Before long, gaming simulations about stealing guests' valuables turned into reality. 4-LOM became a master thief and came to the attention of Tatooine crime lord Jabba the Hutt. Jabba agreed to alter the droid's programming so that he could respond to the threat of violence with the same degree of skill, and 4-LOM agreed to work for Jabba as a bounty hunter. He was soon paired with a Gand tracker, Zuckuss, and the two were very successful. 4-LOM watched and learned from Zuckuss, aspiring to do everything his living counterpart could do. They didn't snare Han Solo, the big prize, although they were sent by Jabba to Darth Vader's ship when Vader was seeking the Corellian. By then, 4-LOM was starting to change. Following the Battle of Hoth, he and Zuckuss nearly destroyed the final escaping Rebel transport, the *Bright Hope*, but then reconsidered and helped evacuate the ninety Rebel soldiers aboard to the planet Darlyn Boda. With Zuckuss and other bounty hunters, he unsuccessfully tried to wrest Han Solo's carbonite-encased body from Boba Fett, but was severely damaged. Later, 4-LOM joined the Rebellion and worked in Special Forces. [ESB, SWCG, TBH, SOTE]

5D6-RA7 A robotic aide to Admiral Motti's staff, the foul-tempered and vindictive droid was feared by other droids. 5D6-RA7 was a spy for Imperial Intelligence and secretly investigated Imperial officers whose loyalties were in doubt. He was destroyed in the explosion of the Death Star during the Battle of Yavin. [CCG]

5P8 A prowler ship in the New Republic's Fifth Fleet, it found Plat Mallar's TIE interceptor near the Koornacht Cluster. [BTS]

Fadoop A furry, green, bandy-legged female Saheelindeeli, she is a pilot and owner of the ship *Skybarge*. An intelligent primate from the Tion Hegemony, Fadoop intensely likes chak-root and once ran parts for Han Solo and Chewbacca during their adventures in Corporate Sector space. [HLL]

Falanthas, Minister Mokka The New Republic's Minister of State and successor to General Rieekan, Falanthas was a cautious individual who didn't want to get involved too quickly in a war with the Yevetha. [SOL]

Fallanassi A religious order, its members were followers of the White Current. They formerly lived in Ialtra on the planet Lucazec in ring dwellings and circle houses. Years ago, one of the Fallanassi, Isela Talsava Norand, revealed the sect's existence to Lucazec's Imperial governor. The Empire immediately realized the potential of the unique Fallanassi skill with the

5D6-RA7

White Current, which is similar to the Jedi use of the Force. The Empire offered its protection to the Fallanassi in exchange for an oath of loyalty. When they refused, Imperial agents stirred up resentment toward the Fallanassi among the people of Lucazec, and sect members had to flee. [BTS, TT]

Falleen Inhabited by a humanoid species also called Falleen, it was the homeworld of Prince Xizor, long-feared head of the underworld syndicate Black Sun. The Falleen are reptilian in ancestry, with scales, cold blood, and skin that can change color according to their mood. A Falleen's lung capacity is great, and they are able to stay underwater for up to twelve hours. Coolly calculating beings, the Falleen are considered among the most beautiful of all humanoid races. In addition, both males and females have enhanced hormones, exuding a pheromone that makes them practically irresistible to the opposite sex. During sexual arousal, a Falleen's color changes from grayish green to warmer reddish hues. Meditation and exercises bring the hormonal essences into full bloom.

Ten years before the Battle of Endor, Darth Vader established a biological warfare laboratory on Falleen in an area ruled by Xizor's father. It was the Dark Lord's pet project. But a terrible accident occurred at the supposedly secure facility: A mutant tissue-destroying bacterium escaped quarantine. In order to save the planet's population from a horrible rotting, always-fatal infection for which there was no cure—and to minimize Vader's embarrassment—the city around the lab was sterilized. It was burned to the ground in an orbital bombardment, killing 200,000 Falleen, including all of Xizor's family. Xizor, head of the Black Sun organization and, at one time, possibly the third most powerful man in the galaxy after the Emperor and Vader, vowed vengeance on the Dark Lord. [SOTE, SOTESB]

Falleen's Fist Prince Xizor's skyhook, an orbiting structure tethered to the ground, was about two-thirds the size of the Emperor's grandiose skyhook, which hung above the capital of Imperial Center. The *Fist* had a command center and a view deck surrounded by transparisteel plate that allowed a 360-degree unimpeded view of space. It was the pride and joy of the crime king, but during a final showdown with Darth Vader, the Dark Lord ordered a Star Destroyer to annihilate Xizor's skyhook. [SOTE]

Fall of the Sith Empire An event triggered by a battle between the combined armies of the Old Republic and the Jedi Knights on one side, and the minions of the dark side led by Dark Lord Naga Sadow on the other, more than four millennia before the Galactic Civil War. The Sith were driven to near extinction; eventually Sadow led them to sanctuary on Yavin 4. [TSW]

Fandar A brilliant scientist, this Chadra-Fan was the leader of Project Decoy. His goal was to create a lifelike human replica droid for the Alliance, and his prototype resembled Princess Leia. [QE]

Fandomar The wife of Momaw Nadon on the planet Ithor, she was left behind when Momaw was banished from his homeworld. [TMEC]

Fane, Captain Captain of the *Tellivar Lady*, a transport ship with regular runs to and from Tatooine. [TMEC]

Fanfar A woodwind type of musical instrument, it is essential for jizz bands. [CCG]

Farana A region of space on the far side of the Corporate Sector. Twelve years after the Battle of Endor, Luke Skywalker discovered that the starliner *Star Morning*, belonging to the Fallanassi religious order, had spent several months in Farana. [SOL]

Farboon A planet that appears green, blue, and white from space, it was the site where TIE fighter pilot Maarek Stele rescued Imperial Admiral Mordon's shuttle from an attacking group of Rebel X- and Y-wing fighters. [TSC]

Fardreamer, Cole A young boy from Tatooine, he became a maintenance worker on Coruscant. As a boy, he often tried to build X-wings out of damaged equipment that he managed to find before the Jawas did, but he had never been completely successful. Luke Skywalker was his boyhood hero, but Cole's mother thought Cole's desire to go to the Jedi academy was born of the boy's impetuous, stubborn, and impulsive nature. Cole eventually realized that his talents as a mechanic and engineer were just as valuable to the New Republic as Skywalker's Jedi skills, only in a different manner. Fardreamer discovered detonating devices placed by the scheming Dark Jedi Kueller in New Republic X-wing upgrades. Together with C-3PO and R2-D2, he made a secret trip to Telti to investigate the origins of the detonators. There, he confronted the Telti droid-manufacturing-facility administrator, Brakiss, and was brought before the torture droid Eve-Ninedeninetwo. Fardreamer was eventually rescued by Threepio and Artoo, and was hailed as a hero by the New Republic for his part in uncovering the Kueller threat. [NR]

Farfeld II Located in the Farfeld system, it was the site of a System Patrol Squadron base for Imperial corvettes. The base was destroyed by the Alliance shortly after the Battle of Yavin. [FP]

Farlander, Keyan A famous Rebel Alliance pilot, he came from the planet Agamar in the Outer Rim's Lahara sector. He was a leading member of an Alliance strike team that was particularly active following the Battle of Yavin. Among other accomplishments, they eliminated Imperial System Patrol Squadron bases near the planets Feenicks VI and Farfeld II, destroying many Imperial corvettes at the same time. Perhaps his most daring and successful mission was the destruction of a vital Imperial storage area in Hollan D1 sector. He and his fellow Alliance pilots used captured ships from Overlord Ghorin in the attack, successfully discrediting Ghorin in the eyes of the Empire. [FP]

Farlax sector Located in what used to be the center of the Empire's Rim territories, the Farlax sector contains the Koornacht Cluster, home of the alien Yevetha. Large areas of the sector have never been properly surveyed. During the Empire's reign, the Black Sword Command was charged with the defense of Praxlis, Corridan, and the entire Kokash, Hatawa, and

Toryn Farr

Farlax sectors. Polneye, a planet at the edges of the Koornacht Cluster, was established by the Black Sword Command as a secret military transshipment point for the Farlax sector.

Following the Battle of Endor, Imperial forces abandoned the Farlax sector and retreated into the Core. There are more than 200 inhabited worlds in the combined Hatawa and Farlax sectors. A third of the region is now aligned with the New Republic while another third is uninhabited or unclaimed.

During the crisis in the Koornacht Cluster twelve years after the Battle of Endor, eighteen planets in the Farlax sector made emergency petitions for membership in the New Republic in the hopes of defending themselves against the Yevetha. Head of State Leia Organa Solo approved the applications and sent the New Republic's Fifth Fleet to Farlax to force the Yevetha to back down.

The brown dwarf star Doornik-1142 and its planets are located on the edge of the Cluster, while J't'p'-tan is located at the heart. N'zoth, Wakiza, Tizon, Pa'aal, Z'fell, Faz, Tholaz, and Zhina are Yevethan worlds within the cluster. Non-Yevethan colony worlds in the cluster include New Brigia, Pirol-5, Polneye, Kutag (Doornik-881), Kojash, Doornik-207, Doornik-628, and Morning Bell (Doornik-319, or Preza). The planets Galantos and Wehttam are the closest inhabited worlds to the cluster, and Dandalas, Nanta-Ri, and Kktkt lie close to Koornacht as well. [BTS, SOL]

Farlight A new Republic ship, formerly of the Third Fleet, it was deployed at Wehttam in anticipation of a Yevethan attack. [SOL]

Farng He was a carbonite trader in the Empress Teta system some 4,000 years before the Galactic Civil War. The imminent public execution of this lanky, bald human led to a short-lived citizens' revolt in Cinnagar. [DLS]

Farnym Creatures noted for their bowling-ball roundness, they have close-cut orange fur and small snouts. Farnym have a peculiar odor, like ginger mixed with sandalwood. Leia Organa Solo's copilot aboard the *Alderaan*, Tchiery, is a Farnym. [NR]

Farr, Samoc One of the Rebels' best snowspeeder pilots, she was badly injured in the Battle of Hoth. Samoc Farr escaped with her sister, Toryn, aboard the transport carrier *Bright Hope*. [TBH]

Farr, Toryn Among the last to leave the Rebel command center on Echo Base on Hoth, the chief communications officer of Echo Command escaped aboard the transport carrier *Bright Hope* with her sister, Samoc. Toryn Farr was promoted to the rank of commander after helping to safely transport the disabled ship's ninety passengers to Darlyn Boda. [TBH, CCG]

Farrfin sector Along with the Dolomar sector, this sector was a target of an offensive by Grand Admiral Thrawn. The New Republic put up stiff resistance, and Admiral Ackbar made a personal tour of the defenses. The sector includes the planet Farrfin with a native sentient species, the Farghul. [LC, LCGB]

farrow birds Aruzan birds with bioluminescent chests that glow as they dive from the sky, they effectively blind the small animals that are their prey. [TBH]

FarStar A Corellian corvette, it was dispatched to track down a rogue Imperial governor, Moff Kentor Sarne, four years after the Battle of Endor. The mission was originally undertaken by Page's Commandos, but command was assumed by Captain Keleman Ciro and later Kaiya Adrimetrum. The pursuit of Sarne took the New Republic forces deep into the Kathol outback in a little-explored area known as the Kathol Rift. One of the purposes of the mission was to discover the origin of strange and mysterious DarkStryder technology used by Sarne, but the results have been classified. [DSC]

Fass, Egome A humanoidlike Houk with a square jaw and tiny, gleaming eyes set deep beneath a thick, bony brow, he worked for the outlaw twins J'uoch and R'all. He was reputed to rival the mighty Wookiee Chewbacca in both height and strength. [HLL]

Fast Hand Lando Calrissian's Submersible Mining Environment on *GemDiver Station*, this large diving bell was used to mine Corusca gems from Yavin. The *Fast Hand* is covered with a skin of quantum armor. As it is lowered into Yavin's atmosphere, the vessel is connected to *GemDiver Station* by an energy tether. Electromagnetic ropes dangle from the *Fast Hand* to catch the Corusca gems that have been stirred up by atmospheric storms. [YJK]

"Fat Man" A code-name for a Yevethan hyperspace-capable thrust ship. [TT]

Faz An inhabited planet lying within the Koornacht Cluster of the Farlax sector, Faz is one of the primary worlds of the alien Yevetha species and is a member of the Duskhan League. [SOL]

feather fern A light, lacy plant found on the moon Yavin 4. [DA]

feathers of light These silver feathers are awarded to young Ewoks on the forest moon of Endor after they complete the journey to the Tree of Light to feed it nourishing light dust. [ETV]

Fedje A forested planet where Han Solo spent some time as part of his Alliance duties. [LC]

Feenicks VI This planet was located near an Imperial System Patrol Squadron base, which was eliminated by an Alliance strike team following the Battle of Yavin. [FP]

Fef A moderately large planet orbiting an orange-yellow star, it is home to the insectoid Fefze. Fef's thick atmosphere and hot temperature contribute to its teeming variety of life-forms, all of whom have relatively short life spans. The Fefze, who form intelligent group-minds (called swarms) of ten to one hundred individuals, are able to digest all forms of carbon-based organic matter. [GG4]

Felth, Davin A stormtrooper, he joined the Empire's ranks when he was eighteen. However, Davin Felth regretted his decision almost as soon as he set foot on Carida, the toughest Imperial training facility in the galaxy. Despite his discomfort, he excelled and was one of the few who successfully completed Imperial walker training. He even pointed out a fatal design flaw. Rather than being rewarded, he was assigned to a stormtrooper unit as a common foot soldier and shipped off to Tatooine. There he was to experience unspeakable savagery that would change his life.

Felth, clad in the armor of a Desert Sands stormtrooper or "sandtrooper," found what his superior officer, the vicious Captain Terrik, said they were seeking: an escape pod used by two droids and a device from an R2 unit. His unit followed tracks that eventually led to a Jawa sandcrawler. Terrik questioned the desert scavengers and discovered that the missing droids had been sold to Owen Lars, a moisture farmer. But as the troopers departed, Terrik ordered a hit on the crawler, killing all inside. Felth hadn't joined the Empire to kill innocent beings, and his heart was heavy.

The troopers traveled quickly to the Lars homestead, where they ransacked the house and garages in search of the droids. Then Owen Lars did the unthinkable: He spit on Captain Terrik and cursed him. Enraged, Terrik ordered some of his troopers to murder Owen Lars and his wife, Beru, and torch their home. The unit next went to Mos Eisley spaceport where, while checking out a complaint at the cantina, Felth saw a hooded old man and a boy leave; they had been sitting with an athletic-looking smuggler and a Wookiee, but nothing seemed amiss.

Later, a comlink call brought the troopers to Docking Bay 94, where the droids had been found. In the firefight that followed, Felth recognized the men from the bar. These were Rebels, and all Rebels must be destroyed, Captain Terrik had said. But Felth didn't believe that and he was soon faced with a moment of truth. Terrik had drawn a bead on the smuggler from the cantina and was sure to kill him. But Felth made his first kill, shooting the captain in the back. As the Corellian freighter took off, Felth knew he would take on a new role in life: spying for the Rebel Alliance from the inside. That would give his life some purpose. [TMEC, SWCG]

Davin Felth

Femon The faithful assistant to the power-mad Dark Jedi Kueller, she had long black hair and an unnaturally pale face, with blackened eyes and bloodred lips. Like Kueller, Femon wore a death mask, but hers looked less realistic than Kueller's own. She had been serving Kueller since the beginning of his campaign against the New Republic. Her family had been killed when the Imperial battlemoon *Eye of Palpatine* swept over her planet. In some ways, her need for revenge was even more severe than Kueller's. She withdrew her support from Kueller once she believed that he was exhibiting the same weakness that she attributed to the New Republic: not ruling with the iron fist necessary to squash dangerous outside elements. Because she lacked confidence in him, Kueller killed her with his Force powers. [NR]

Fere (Feree) Located in the Fere (or Feree) system, which contains a double star, 200 years before the Galactic Civil War the planet was home to an advanced culture of tall, pale humanoids with six-fingered hands. They were master starship builders, and some of their small luxury cruisers can still be found today. During a series of wars, a deadly plague was carried to Fere, killing all life on the planet. [CPL]

Ferrier, Niles A human jack-of-all-trades, he excels as a starship thief. Large, with dark hair and a beard, Niles Ferrier wears flashy tunics and smokes long, thin cigarras. Working with a small gang of five humans, a Verpine, and a Defel, he was quick to react when Imperial Grand Admiral Thrawn offered a bounty of 20 percent more than current market value for capital ships. Lando Calrissian and Luke Skywalker foiled Ferrier's plans to steal a few ships from the Sluis Van shipyards, but Ferrier was able to provide Thrawn with an even greater prize: the location of the legendary and long-sought *Katana* fleet. [DFR, DFRSB, LC]

ferrocrete A super-strong building material, it is composed of concrete and steellike materials bonded together at the molecular level. Nearly every structure on most Imperial worlds is built of this durable substance. [BW, LCF]

Ferros VI Site of an Imperial prison camp. [DSTC]

Fest This planet was the site of a secret Imperial Weapons Research Facility hidden in a steep mountain. Fest is in a system of the same name that is, in turn, in the Atrivis sector of the Outer Rim bordering the Mantooine system. The facility performed metallurgical research on new alloys.

Following the Battle of Yavin, Alliance agent Kyle Katarn infiltrated the facility and stole a sample of the metal phrik, used in armoring the Dark Troopers. The Fest system was also home to an early resistance group opposing the Empire. [DF, FP, RSB]

Festival of Hoods A celebration of the coming of age of young Ewoks. When they receive their hoods, it is a symbol that they have made the transition from wokling to preadolescent. [ETV]

Fett, Boba Mean and mysterious, the best-known bounty hunter in the galaxy is accustomed to always getting his prey—with the exception of one Corellian smuggler and Rebel Alliance hero.

The exploits of Boba Fett, who is strong and usually silent, could fill a library. Many tales are told of his background and exploits, but there are very few verifiable facts, perhaps by design. It seems possible that Fett was born Jaster Mereel, and as a young man became a Journeyman Protector, or law enforcement officer, on the planet Concord Dawn. But supposedly he killed another Protector, one accused of being corrupt and unjust. He was unrepentant at trial, was stripped of all he owned, and was exiled.

Fett wears the armor of the Mandalorians, a group of fearsome warriors dating back to ancient times. His modified Mandalorian armor includes a helmet with a macrobinocular viewplate, motion and sound sensors, infrared capabilities, an internal comlink with his ship (the *Slave I*), and a broadband antenna for intercepting and decoding transmissions; wrist gauntlets that house lasers, a miniature flame projector, and a fibercord whip/grappling device; a backpack jet pack with a turbo-projected magnetic grappling hook with a twenty-meter lanyard; knee-pad rocket dart launchers; spiked boots; a concussion grenade launcher; and a BlasTech EE-3 rifle. Braided Wookiee scalps hang over his right shoulder.

Since the Clone Wars, Fett has worked as a mercenary, a soldier, a personal guard, an assassin, and, most frequently, as a bounty hunter. He should be wealthy by now, demanding and getting some of the biggest bounties ever. He once earned a record 500,000 credits by catching the Ffib religious heretic Nivek'Yppiks for the Lorahns.

Fett has worked on retainer for Jabba the Hutt and other Hutts, as well as for the Empire. He is methodical in his tracking. While he doesn't seem to hold grudges against his prey, that may be because he rarely loses his quarry. Fett seems to have had several encounters with the droids R2-D2 and C-3PO when they worked for different masters. Shortly after the Battle of Yavin, he seemed to help Luke Skywalker and Han Solo on a red-water moon in the Panna System, but in reality he was trying to trap them for Darth Vader. The trap failed thanks to the droids. He had another encounter with the Rebellion heroes on the frozen world of Ota.

Shortly before the Battle of Hoth, Jabba hired Fett to find Han Solo.

Boba Fett

Darth Vader had a similar goal, and he and Fett met to discuss it. But Solo once again escaped Fett's clutches on the planet Ord Mantell. Later, after the Battle of Hoth, Vader summoned Fett again, along with five other bounty hunters, and offered a huge bounty for Solo; he wanted to use the Corellian as bait in a trap for Luke Skywalker. Fett succeeded in tracking Solo's ship to the Bespin system, and he helped Vader capture Solo, Chewbacca, and Princess Leia Organa. Solo became the guinea pig for a carbonite-freezing experiment, and Fett was given the encased Solo to bring to Jabba for another bounty. As Fett emerged from hyperspace near Tatooine, he was angered to find that IG-88, one of Vader's other bounty hunters, had tracked him. Fett used evasive maneuvers and then blew up the starfighter *IG-2000*. The *Slave I* was damaged, and Fett flew to Gall for repairs, where a Rebel attempt to rescue Han on the Gall moon failed.

When Luke, Leia, and Chewbacca were captured while trying to rescue Han, Jabba sentenced them to die a slow death by being digested by the Sarlacc in the Pit of Carkoon. But in the desert, the Rebels broke free, and during the fierce fight that ensued, Fett was knocked into the mouth of the Sarlacc. Amazingly, Fett escaped that near-certain death and was found in poor shape by another bounty hunter, Dengar, who had come to look for Jabba's remains.

In recent years, Fett has continued pursuing Han Solo. Six years after Jabba's death, Han and Leia went to Nar Shaddaa, the spaceport moon that is the smuggling center of the galaxy. There, Han was surprised to find Boba Fett and Dengar waiting for him in his old quarters. In a hail of blaster fire, Leia and Han made it off-world, escaping in old friend Salla Zend's *Starlight Intruder*. Later, in another encounter on the planet, Fett shot Chewbacca in the side, but the Wookiee managed to rip off Fett's helmet and send the bounty hunter flying.

Fett recovered quickly, and his *Slave I* pursued Han's *Millennium Falcon* through the floating space debris of Nar Shaddaa. Han entered an interstellar gas cloud, and because his ship had been damaged,

Borsk Fey'lya

Fett couldn't pursue him. A few days later the *Falcon* emerged, shot *Slave I*, and sent the ship spinning out of control into the gas cloud. Once again the hunter and hunted parted company, both always prepared for a reengagement. [ESB, ISB, TBH, SWCG, BF]

Fey'lya, Borsk Master diplomat, political opportunist—or something in between? Both his allies and opponents wanted to know: Which was the true Borsk Fey'lya? As the representative from Kothlis to the New Republic and a member of its Provisional and Inner councils, the Bothan quickly became a trusted adviser to New Republic leader Mon Mothma—much to the dismay of Fey'lya's detractors, chief among them military leader Admiral Ackbar. Fey'lya and his people joined the Rebellion just after the Battle of Yavin. The Bothans acquired the plans for the second Death Star, and even though that turned out to be a trap set by the Emperor, they were seen as heroes. Fey'lya became an effective administrator for the Alliance, although his rivalry with Admiral Ackbar spilled over into contentious public debates. Five years after the Battle of Endor, Fey'lya managed to implicate Admiral Ackbar in a plot involving treason and financial misdeeds. Both accusations were later disproven. Meanwhile Fey'lya and his top assistant were secretly aiding the rogue Corellian Senator Garm Bel Iblis, who was waging his own personal war against the Empire.

Fey'lya's downfall began during the hard-fought battle with Grand Admiral Thrawn over the long-lost *Katana* fleet, when the Bothan ordered a retreat, trapping some of the Rebellion's top people. But Fey'lya was exposed, put under military arrest, and returned to Coruscant. Although the Provisional Council granted him a pardon, he had lost face and his base of support, and his power steadily diminished. During the Yevethan crisis, he leaked information to the media and supported the petition of no confidence in Chief of State Leia Organa Solo. [HE, DFR, LC, TT]

Ffib This species is native to the planet Lorahns. [TJP]

Fibuli This planet was one of the Trianii colony worlds that were annexed by the adjacent Corporate Sector. Open warfare erupted as Trianii Rangers fought the Corporate Sector Authority's encroachment. An armistice was finally arranged after the Battle of Yavin, following three years of devastating battles. Keeheen, mate to Trianii Ranger Atuarre, disappeared during the fighting and was eventually rescued from the Stars' End prison with Han Solo's help. [CSSB, SWAJ]

Fiddanl The innermost planet of the Yavin system, it is a hot, dense world. Its continental plates constantly shift atop a sea of liquid mercury. The planet's eighteen land masses constantly grind each other down but are continually replaced through rapid crystal growth. The multicolored continents get their hues from a varied mix of cinnabar, sulfite, and manganese. The planet is toxic to almost all species and there are no indications of life on Fiddanl's surface. [GG2]

Fidge When this Biituian was ten years old, he met R2-D2 and C-3PO during the droids' adventures in the early days of the Empire. Fidge had a pet reptile named Chubb, and he often traveled through the burrows that Chubb liked to dig. [TGH]

fifth moon of Da Soocha The location of a onetime secret New Republic Command Center designated as Pinnacle Base. An intelligent species called Ixlls are native to Da Soocha 5. [DE]

Figg, Lord Ecclessis Figg constructed the first floating settlement of Bespin, near the gas giant's equator. [GG2]

Filve This planet was targeted by the Star Destroyer *Judicator* in a multipronged attack by Grand Admiral Thrawn that was intended to draw New Republic forces away from Ukio. Leia Organa Solo visited the Filvian government to assure it of New Republic support. When she arrived during the battle, the mad clone Jedi Joruus C'baoth sent the entire Imperial strike force after the *Millennium Falcon* in a vain attempt to capture her. [LC]

Final Jump, the Spacer slang for death. [HSR]

Findris Located in the Colonies Region, it was home to several anti-Empire underground organizations. The most violent was the Justice Action Network (JAN) terrorist group led by Earnst Kamiel. Kamiel was caught on Eldrood after the Battle of Yavin and extradited to the Haldeen sector for Imperial trial. [SWAJ]

findsmen Gand bounty hunters, they meditate to try to learn the locations of their prey. [TBH]

Fiolla of Lorrd An aspiring Assistant Auditor General for the Corporate Sector Authority, Hart-and-Parn Gorra-Fiolla of Lorrd found herself unexpectedly teamed with Han Solo during an undercover assignment. The two were to expose top Authority executives and Espo officials involved with an illegal slavery ring. [HSR]

firefolk *See* Wisties

fire rings of Fornax In one of the unique wonders of the galaxy, five rings of intense fire appear to encircle the planet Fornax. They are really solar prominences attracted to the planet due to its close proximity to its sun. [SWN]

Firestorm An Imperial Star Destroyer. [DS]

firethorn trees Hundred-meter-tall trees, they grow only in a single small grove in the Irugian rainforest on Abbaji. Criminal mastermind Prince Xizor had a dwarf firethorn tree that he personally tended. [SOTE]

Firrerre All life on this planet was wiped out by the Empire's use of a biological weapon, and it is still unsafe for any ships to land there. Hethrir, the Imperial Procurator of Justice and himself a native of Firrerre, ordered the devastation, which was carried out by the Empire's elite Starcrash Brigade. The people of Firrerre, humanoids with long, striped hair, were believed to have been annihilated, but Leia Organa Solo discovered a passenger freighter carrying many natives in suspended animation. [CS]

Firro The planet was brutally subjugated by the Empire, with many deaths and atrocities, and Lord Cuvir was installed as Imperial Governor. During a visit to a Firro relief station, Cuvir witnessed the skill of Imperial medical droid 2-1B and made the droid his personal physician. Too-Onebee has since joined the Alliance. [MTS]

Firwirrung A reptilian Ssi-ruuk, he was the personal master of the human go-between Dev Sibwarra and the head of entechment operations aboard the battlecruiser *Shriwirr*. Entechment is the absorption of a sentient creature's energies into battery coils to power circuitry. Aggressively innovative, Firwirrung devised a means to conduct entechment at potentially unlimited distances if a Force-strong individual could be procured and subdued. [TAB]

Fixer One of Luke Skywalker's companions on Tatooine, this overbearing young man was a mechanic employed at the Tosche power station in Anchorhead. He was also the boyfriend of a young woman named Camie. [SWN]

Fixer's shop

Fizzz Slang for a Dorenian Beshniquel, a musical instrument played throughout the galaxy. [TMEC]

flame carpet warheads Chemical weapons, they set huge masses of air aflame. [TBH]

flameout One of the more potent intoxicating beverages served around the galaxy. When prepared correctly, the drink has the unique properties of burning the tongue while freezing the throat. [HSR]

Flarestar One of the cantinas located on the space station at Yag'Dhul, it was often frequented by Rogue Squadron's pilots when they were using the station as their operations base during the Bacta War. [BW]

Flautis A greasy-looking Corellian, he was one of the members of the antialien Human League who waylaid Han Solo. [AC]

Flax Located in the Ptera system, it is home to the insectoid Flakax species. Flax is a world of numerous oceans as well as vast deserts cut off from the water by high mountain ranges. The emotionless Flakax live in underground hives and devote their lives to the hive's queen. After the planet was taken over by the Empire, the Flakax were put to work mining Flax's underground minerals. [GG4]

flechette canister A weapon, it holds clusters of tiny darts. When the canister is fired from a shoulder-mounted launcher and hits its target, it explodes, releasing a cloud of deadly darts. [HSR]

flechette missile A dart-shaped projectile about 110 millimeters in length, flechette missiles come in two power levels: antipersonnel and armor-piercing antivehicle varieties. [HSE, HLL]

fleek eel A delicacy from the Hocekureem Sea, light-years away from Coruscant, they are kept alive until the moment they are dipped in boiling pepper oil. [SOTE]

fleethund The slang that X-wing pilots use for a dangerous decoy maneuver in which one X-wing pilot draws fire to himself and away from the main convoy. [BW]

Flirt A tiny, boxlike positronic processor, it was owned by the Wookiee bounty hunter Chenlambec. Flirt was programmed to access intelligent computers by tapping in through their power points. It could then open data streams, shut down security, and substitute its owner's commands for those of the computer's operator. Flirt's "seduction" of the computer systems onboard the *Hound's Tooth* played a major role in helping Chenlambec to trick and capture Bossk, the Trandoshan bounty hunter. Following that turn of events, Flirt was given a powerful droid's body in the form of X-10D, a service droid aboard the *Hound's*

Tooth that had been all but brainless up to that point. [TBH]

flitter A common name for any type of one- or two-person airspeeder. [HSE]

floater *See* landspeeder

floating cities of Calamari Huge, anchored metropolises that rest atop the oceans of the water planet Mon Calamari, they extend deep below the waves. The cities are home to the amphibious Mon Calamari. [SWSB, DE]

floating fortress An Imperial repulsorlift combat vehicle, it is designed to augment ground assault and planetary occupation forces. The near-cylindrical floating fortress is especially suitable for urban terrains. It features distinctive twin-turret heavy blaster cannons, a well-armored body, and powerful repulsorlift engines. It is equipped with a state-of-the-art surveillance system that can lock onto multiple targets. A fortress has a crew of four and can carry up to ten troopers. [ISB]

floozam A domesticated pet, often led on a leash. [COF]

Florn Homeworld of the Lamproids, it is a world of numerous dangers, which can mean instant death for anyone without hyperaccelerated nerve implants. [TMEC]

Flurry A Rebel Alliance cruiser-carrier, it was commanded by Capt. Tessa Manchisco. The *Flurry* served with distinction in the Virgillian Civil War and was donated to the Rebel Alliance by a sympathetic Virgillian faction that ousted Imperial forces. The *Flurry*, at 350 meters long, could carry nearly thirty fighters and had complete repair and maintenance facilities. Its mission profile was to deliver fighters into combat and then retreat to a safe distance. For its mission to Bakura, the *Flurry* was equipped with a prototype battle analysis computer that received data from every gunship, corvette, and fighter in combat. The *Flurry* was destroyed over Bakura when the Imperial *Carrack*-class cruiser *Dominant* suddenly opened fire. All hands were lost but were posthumously decorated for their heroic sacrifice. [TAB, SWVG]

Fnnbu A Zexx, he was a confederate of fellow space pirate Finhead Stonebone some 4,000 years before the Galactic Civil War. [TOJ]

Foamwander City One of the floating cities on Mon Calamari. [DA]

Foerost shipyards Vast Republic orbital shipyards, they are one of the oldest and most successful such sites in the galaxy. Raw materials were gathered from the uninhabited planet of Foerost below and shipped up to high orbit, where they were assembled into warships for the Republic navy. During the Sith War, the Foerost shipyards were attacked by Ulic Qel-Droma and Aleema, who used her dark-side illusions to make their fleet appear to be one large, innocent vessel. After a quick and deadly battle, Qel-Droma's forces captured the operations codes for 300 of the Republic's newest warships. [TSW]

Fokask One of Han Solo's old smuggling friends retired on this planet. Twelve years after the Battle of Endor, he sent Han a copy of *The Fokask Banner*, which contained an uncomplimentary article about Chief of State Leia Organa Solo. [SOL]

Folna A New Republic picket ship. [TT]

Folor The largest moon orbiting the planet Commenor near Corellia, it is a craggy gray satellite and home to an Alliance starfighter training center. The Folor base, built within a network of underground tunnels, was a former mining complex and probably once a smugglers' hideout. The base is commanded by General Horton Salm, and off-duty pilots relax in a makeshift cantina called the DownTime. The Folor gunnery and bombing range, a deep twisting canyon on the moon's surface, is called the pig trough because of the unflattering nickname of the Y-wing starfighters that often train there. Pilots also use a satellite field surrounding Folor for obstacle training. Two and a half years after the Battle of Endor, the newest members of Rogue Squadron were instructed at Folor before flying their first combat missions. [RS]

Fondine, Slish Owner of the blob racing stables on Umgul. [JS]

Fondor An industrial planet in the system of the same name, it is famous for its huge orbital starship construction facilities. The Empire seized the Fondor yards and built Darth Vader's Super Star Destroyer *Executor* there immediately following the Battle of Yavin. During construction, Imperial forces erected a military blockade. Several Imperial admirals saw the *Executor* as a blatant bid for power by Vader and tried to sabotage its construction by bringing in a Rebel spy—Luke Skywalker. Vader trapped the traitorous admirals when they met with Skywalker in the vast steam tunnels beneath Fondor's surface, but Skywalker managed to escape the planet by stowing away on an automated drone barge. [HSE, CSSB, CSW, SWAJ]

Forbidden An Imperial *Lambda*-class shuttle captured by the Alliance and used on many missions, it frequently was piloted by Tycho Celchu. Captain Celchu was at the controls when it rescued his fellow Rogue Squadron members Nawara Ven and Ooryl Qrygg during the first battle at Borleias. They were shot out of their X-wings and almost surely would have died in space if not for the proximity of the shuttle. The *Forbidden* also removed prisoners from Kessel who were used to undermine the infrastructure on Imperial Center. [RS, WG]

Force, the Both a natural and mystical presence, it is an energy field that both suffuses and binds the entire galaxy. The Force is generated by all living things, surrounding and penetrating them with its essence. Like most forms of energy, the Force can be manipulated, and it is the knowledge and predisposition to do so that

Flurry

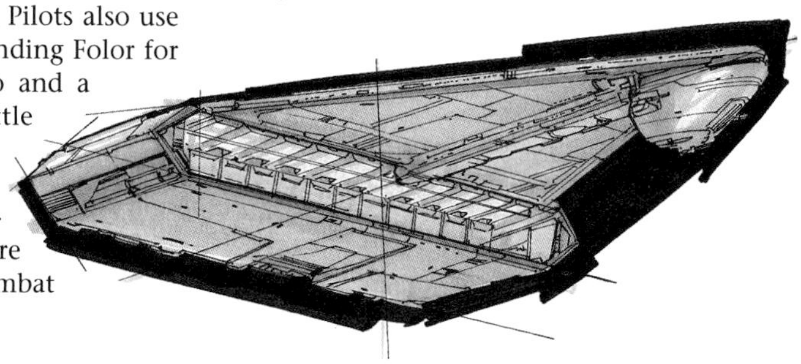

empowers the Jedi Knights—and the Dark Jedi. For there are two sides to the Force: The light side bestows great knowledge, peace, and an inner serenity; the dark side is filled with fear, anger, and the vilest aggression. Yet both sides of the Force, the life-affirming and the destructive, are part of the natural order. Through the Force, a Jedi Knight can see far-off places, perform amazing feats, and accomplish what would otherwise be impossible. A Jedi's strength flows from the Force, but a true Jedi uses it for knowledge and defense—never attack. The Force is a powerful ally, however it is used.

There are three major Force skills: control, sense, and alter. Only Force-sensitive living things can master Jedi skills and the techniques that they control, but the training to reach full Jedi status usually requires much time and great patience. Control is the ability of a Jedi to control his or her own inner Force. With this skill, a Jedi learns to master the functions of his or her own body. The sense skill helps Jedi sense the Force in things beyond themselves. Jedi learn to feel the bonds that connect all things. "You must feel the Force around you," Jedi Master Yoda once told Luke Skywalker. "Here, between you... me... the tree... the rock... everywhere!" The alter skill allows a Jedi to change the distribution and nature of the Force to create illusions, move objects, and change the perceptions of others.

A Dark Jedi gives in to his or her anger. "If you once start down the dark path, forever will it dominate your destiny," Yoda warned Luke. Emperor Palpatine, on the other hand, urged Luke to continue down the path of blind fury and aggression. "Give in to your anger," he told Luke. "Strike me down with all of your hatred and your journey toward the dark side will be complete." [SW, ESB, RJ, SWRPG, SWRPG2, etc.]

Force lightning A Force ability, used against Luke Skywalker by Emperor Palpatine aboard the second Death Star, it consists of white or blue bolts of pure energy that fly from the user's fingertips toward a target. Force lightning, usually a corruption of the Force by those who follow the dark side, flows into a target and causes great pain as it siphons off the living energy and eventually kills its victim. [SWR, RJ, HE, DFR, LC, HESB]

Force lightning

force lock A strong force field, it usually is used for imprisonment. Force locks are invisible but extremely painful if touched. [TBH]

force pike A pole tipped with vibro-edged heads that can kill or stun with a single touch, it was a favorite weapon of the Emperor's Royal Guard. Both a force pike's controls and power generator are in the grip or handle. [HSE, SWSB]

force sabacc A form of the electronic card game in which the randomness of play is provided by the other players rather than a separate randomizer. In force sabacc, after drawing the first card for a hand, each player has to call out whether the hand will be light or dark. The player who plays the strongest light or dark hand wins, but only if the combined strength of his or her chosen side also wins. [CPL]

Force-sensitive An individual who is more keenly attuned to the Force than most, he or she is able to sense its presence and the presence of other Force sensitives. [SME, SWRPG2]

Force storm A tornado of energy created by great disturbances in the Force. Dark Side Adepts have demonstrated limited control over the creation of these storms. Emperor Palpatine claimed the ability to create and control Force storms at will. Light-side practitioners can also band together and create powerful Force storms. [DE]

Foreign Intruder Defense Organism (FIDO) A defense droid, it helped protect Anakin Solo from a kidnapping attempt on Anoth. FIDO was built as a result of a suggestion by Admiral Ackbar. It was modeled on the krakana, a dreaded sea monster from Mon Calamari. FIDO's tentacles were threaded with durasteel cables and its pincers plated with razor-edged alloys. [COF]

Forge, Inyri The youngest member of the Forge family and sister of Rogue Squadron member Lujayne Forge, she was the lover and glitterstim "cutter" of smuggler and Black Sun terrorist Zekka Thyne. When he was sprung from the Kessel penal colony to be used in the Alliance's operation to regain Coruscant, Inyri Forge accompanied him, mostly as a way of rebelling against her parents' wishes. She was with Thyne when he attempted to kill Rogue pilot Corran Horn—whom he blamed for his imprisonment—at the Headquarters in Invisec. Horn escaped and later rescued Forge twice during two separate engagements with Imperial forces. She finally realized that Thyne was just using her to get close to Horn, and when her lover attempted to kill Horn again, she killed Thyne instead. She joined one of Rogue Squadron's teams just in time to help bring down Coruscant's shields, and soon thereafter became a member of the squadron. [WG, KT, BW]

Forge, Kassar The father of Inyri and Lujayne Forge, he came to Kessel before the Clone Wars to teach the prison population. There he met his future wife, Myda. They fell in love and had a family, and he decided to stay to continue his teaching, hoping to rehabilitate some of the hardened criminals there. When Rogue Squadron needed him to facilitate the release of political prisoners from prison administrator Moruth Doole's grasp, he helped identify the prisoners and offered other advice. [WG]

Forge, Lujayne A former member of Rogue Squadron from Kessel, she was one of the first pilots to pull Corran Horn out of his self-imposed shell. Because of her efforts her death was even more painful to Horn than to other squadron members. She was killed in her sleep by Imperial stormtroopers as they raided the base at Talasea in the middle of the night. She had been the heart of the squadron and had helped keep it together. [RS]

Forge, Myda Sent to Kessel as a prisoner, she met and fell in love with Kassar Forge, one of the instructors sent to rehabilitate the inmates. When her sentence was up, she decided to stay on Kessel with her husband and their two daughters. [WG]

Forger A Star Destroyer, it suppressed a rebellion on Gra Ploven by creating steam clouds that boiled alive 200,000 Ploven in three coastal cities. [SOL]

Forgofshar desert A desert on the Imperial military training planet of Carida, it was used for survival training. [TMEC]

Formayj A more than century-old smuggler and information broker of the Yao species, he provided Chewbacca and his companions with key maps and information that allowed them to successfully rescue Han Solo during the Yevethan crisis. [TT]

Forno, Jace A female Corellian gun for hire, she worked for a time as a pilot for smuggling kingpin Olag Greck. She later hired R2-D2 and C-3PO as guides on the planet Indobok to help her make off with precious B'rnkaa crystals—which were actually baby B'rnkaa—but she was thwarted. Forno reappeared on Nar Shaddaa as head of security for criminal mastermind Movo Brattakin, whom she ended up blasting after a bizarre adventure involving the droids. [D]

Fortress of Tawntoom A city built into the interior walls of a volcanic crater, it was in the Tawntoom colony of Roon. The city was powered by the boiling lava pit far below and was base of operations for Governor Koong. [DTV]

Fortuna, Bib Best known as Jabba the Hutt's chief lieutenant and majordomo, the Twi'lek was also a smuggler and slaver of his own planet's people.

Fortuna hailed from the planet Ryloth, where one side is perpetually light and the other dark. Like all Twi'leks, Fortuna had twin appendages, or lekku, coming from the back of his pointed head. Such "head-tails," or "worms," as they are called by others, are used for thinking and communication as well as sensual pleasure. Fortuna was sentenced to death on his planet for helping to start the export of the addictive drug ryll. The ryll trade had led to smuggling, slavery, and a breakdown of order on Ryloth. Fortuna escaped and soon found himself working on Tatooine, in charge of Jabba's glitterstim spice smuggling operations.

Through successively more prominent positions, Fortuna—who knew how to be obsequious to the Hutt when he had to be—finally became Jabba's chief aide. He used that position to plot against his boss and he, like others in the palace, planned to kill the Hutt and take over his business. That plan was put on hold when top Rebel Alliance leaders came to rescue their friend Han Solo from Jabba's clutches. Instead, all the Rebels were captured and ordered to be killed by being dropped into the maw of the Sarlacc at the Great Pit of Carkoon. When the Rebels turned the tables, Fortuna fled in his private skiff just before Jabba's sail barge was blown to smithereens.

Back at the palace, a confident Fortuna was met by the B'omarr monks who lived in the catacombs below. Some lived as humans, others as detached brains living eternally in jars of nutrient. The monks decided that the nutrient jar was the best fate for Fortuna—or, rather, for his brain. They didn't know Fortuna would eventually figure out a way to reinstall his consciousness into another Twi'lek crook, Firth Olan, in order to make it easier to carry on his criminal activities. [RJ, TJP, SWCG, XW]

forward gun pod A concealed blaster emplacement, it is located in the front section of some starfighters and transports. The forward gun pod on the *Millennium Falcon*, for example, extends from a hidden compartment in the ship's lower hull. Covering plates slide open and shut on command, or automatically when the ship's antiintruder system is triggered. [ESBR]

Bib Fortuna

Frija

forward tech station A secondary command and control station aboard some vessels, it features consoles that monitor all ship systems. A ship's flight path can be monitored from the forward tech station while it is in automatic-pilot mode, and in emergencies, the ship can be controlled from this station. [HSR]

Fossyr, Irin One of General Airen Cracken's Alliance Intelligence Agents, Iella Wessiri used this name when she worked on Coruscant and assisted Rogue Squadron during its undercover mission there. [WG]

four-cubes A gambling game. [TJP]

Fraan, Tal An ambitious young military proctor on Yevethan strongman Nil Spaar's staff, he was in charge of the Yevethan attack at Preza. Based on his success, Spaar promoted Tal Fraan to be his personal adviser and assistant. Fraan suggested that Spaar show Alliance hostages to Chief of State Leia Organa Solo and then kill one, forcing her to give in. But the killing only made the Alliance leader more determined. Because of his poor advice and the subsequent destruction of the Yevethan shipyard at ILC-905, Spaar killed him. [SOL, BTS, TT]

Freebird A gypsy freighter owned by Captain Stanz. [BTS]

Freedom's Sons A group of insurgent patriots during the Clone Wars, they battled against tyrannical occupation forces that threatened the Republic. The ranks of Freedom's Sons were filled with fighters from conquered star systems, and they helped the Jedi Knights reestablish law and order at the end of the war-torn period. [HSE]

Freedon Nadd Uprising A conflict on Onderon some 4,000 years before the Galactic Civil War, it was started by the Naddists, a dissident group that followed the spirit of Dark Jedi Freedon Nadd. The Naddists initially succeeded in capturing the Royal Palace in Iziz. They were aided by the mystical resurgence of dark-side power throughout Onderon. The Uprising came to an end with the death of King Ommin. [FNU]

Free Flight Dance Dome A first-class nightclub on the planet Etti IV, it is known for its variable-gravity dance floor, which attracts both fun seekers and those who need gravity more like their home planet's. [HSR]

freerunner An armored repulsorlift speeder, or combat assault vehicle, it is used mainly by the Alliance and mercenaries. Freerunners get their name from freely rotating gun platforms mounted on top. With two antivehicle laser cannons and two antiinfantry blaster batteries, the speeders pack an offensive punch. [RSB, DFR, DFRSB]

freeze-floating control A computer-augmented system aboard air- and spacecraft, it helps counteract the effects of turbulence in order to create a smoother flight. [SWN]

freight droid Robots that specialize in retrieving and loading cargo, these droids typically are more than 2.5 meters tall. Freight droids are equipped with four extendable arms, crawler treads for travel, small lifting claws, and a gravity-shifting frame for unbalanced loads. [HLL]

Fremp, Anky A near-human denizen of the streets of the spaceport moon of Nar Shaddaa, he was a Sionian Skup biomorph. He worked with criminal gangs and taught newcomers such as a young Greedo how to become streetwise crooks. [DE]

Frenzied River clan A clan of the Witches of Dathomir. [CPL]

Freyrr This Wookiee is second cousin to Chewbacca. [TT]

Frija A female human replica droid, she rescued Luke Skywalker and C-3PO when they crash-landed on Hoth. Imperial technicians had created human replica droids of the real Frija and her father, an Imperial Governor named Lexhannen, to be used as decoys while the humans escaped an expected Rebel attack. The technicians programmed strong survival instincts into the replicas, so when the battle began, they escaped and isolated themselves on Hoth. [CSW, GG3]

frog-dog A reptilian species with prehensile tongues and bulbous purple eyes atop a green head, they are intelligent, but rarely let others know that. Instead, frog-dogs such as Bubo choose to work as spies and mercenaries. Most regard them as common pets. [TJP]

Fromm, Sise An old yet powerful crime boss, he operated out of a stronghold on the planet Annoo during the early days of the Empire. An Annoo-dat, he ran a legitimate import and export business that was a front for extortion, kidnapping, and blaster running. [DTV]

Fromm, Tig The Annoo-dat son of crime kingpin Sise Fromm, he also went by the names of Baby-Face Fromm and Junior Fromm. Tig Fromm led his own gang of outlaws from the planet Ingo, although he often worked with his father. Unlike the older Fromm, Tig was fascinated by modern technology. During the early days of the Empire, his attempt to build a weapons satellite, *Trigon One*, was foiled by R2-D2, C-3PO,

Sise Fromm

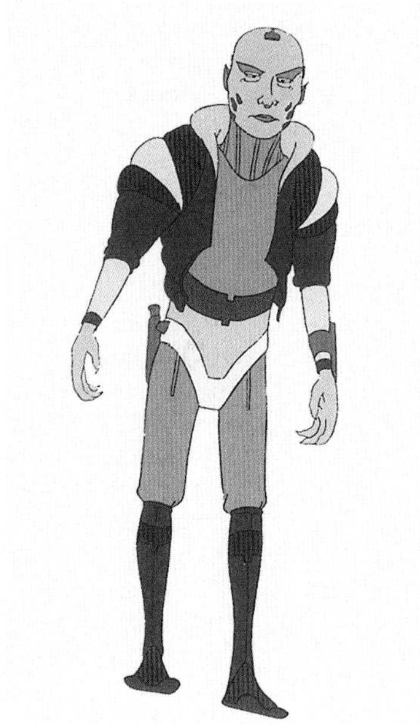

Tig Fromm

and their companions, including Kea Moll. [DTV]

Froz Home planet of Frozians, tall, furry, extra-jointed creatures known for their melancholy outlook on life. Frozians have wide-set eyes, no noticeable external ears, and a nose at the end of a muzzle with long black whiskers on either side. Their mouths are small and lipless. Although not known for their cheerful outlook, no one doubts their probity, honesty, or diligence. Micamberlecto, onetime New Republic Governor-General of the Corellian sector, was a Frozian. [AC]

F'tral A large water-covered world orbiting the blue-white star F'la Ren, it is home to the tentacled cephalopods known as the Iyra. The few volcanic islands on F'tral are home to fisher, seducer, and cannibal plants. The Iyra live in large undersea cities and have developed valuable technologies, including corrosion-resistant alloys and gravity-field and inertial devices for starships. [GG4]

Fugo A Chadra-Fan, he was a colleague of the brilliant scientist Fandar. After Fandar suffered grievous injuries, Fugo took over the Rebel Alliance's Project Decoy. [QE]

funnel flower This Tatooine flower sports a brilliant cone of flapping petals on either end of a long straw-like stem. The hollow stem dips through a shadowed crevice in cliff walls, sucking hot air in through one end of the funnel flower and condensing the faint moisture that collects in the crook of the stem. [ISWU]

Furgan, Ambassador The ambassador from the planet Carida to the New Republic, this barrel-chested humanoid with spindly arms and legs was really an Imperial plant at the table of the Alliance. His eyebrows flared upward like birds' wings. He almost succeeded in killing Alliance leader Mon Mothma by splashing a drink in her face. The liquid contained a very slow-acting poison that began to sap her strength, and it took months for the Alliance to figure out what had happened. Furgan was at Carida when Kyp Durron arrived with the Sun Crusher super weapon, and he attempted to bait the young Jedi into believing that his brother, Zeth, was dead. Furgan escaped the destruction of the Caridan sun and went directly to Anoth to kidnap the Force-sensitive infant Anakin Solo. There, his troops were faced with formidable challenges, although Furgan at one point was able to get his hands on the baby. But he was challenged by the Mon Calamarian Terpfen, whom Furgan earlier had turned into an involuntary Imperial spy. They faced off, each inside an Imperial MT-AT, or spider walker, a weapon that Furgan had helped develop. Furgan's spider walker fell to the rocks below the Anoth fortress, and he was presumed dead. [JS, DA, COF]

fusioncutter An industrial tool, it produces wide-dispersion laser beams. Fusioncutters are used in construction, mining, and metal work. In desperate situations, they can be used as weapons. [SWSB, SWN]

fusion furnace A power-generating device, it produces heat and light and recharges the energy cells of vehicles, droids, and weapons. [ESB]

Fuzzum A primitive species, they look like balls of fuzz with long, thin legs. Fuzzum never go anywhere without their spears. [DTV]

Fwatna Near the planet Fwatna, some thirteen years after the Battle of Endor, Lando Calrissian found the abandoned freighter *Spicy Lady*, which had belonged to his old smuggling associate Jarril. While looking through the ship's computer, Lando discovered that one of Jarril's contacts, Dolph, lived on Fwatna. Dolph briefly studied at Luke Skywalker's Jedi academy before turning to the dark side and assuming the name Kueller. [NR]

Fwiis A colony world more than 150 light-years from Atzerri, it was one of the stops of the starliner *Star Morning*, owned by the Fallanassi religious order, after it departed the planet Teyr. [SOL]

Fw'Sen picket ships Small Ssi-ruuk Imperium combat ships, they are used to disable enemy vessels and guard the perimeters of Ssi-ruuvi fleets. The twenty Fw'Sen picket ships were a key element of the Ssi-ruuk invasion force at Bakura. Less than fifty meters long, the ships are fragile and need power-draining shields to ward off attacks. The ships are completely crewed by droids and a subjugated species, the tiny P'w'eck, so the Ssi-ruuvi commanders see them as disposable, making them good for suicide missions. The ships are often controlled remotely from the main Ssi-Ruuvi cruisers. [TAB, SWVG]

FX-7 A cylindrical, multiarmed medical droid in the service of the Rebel-

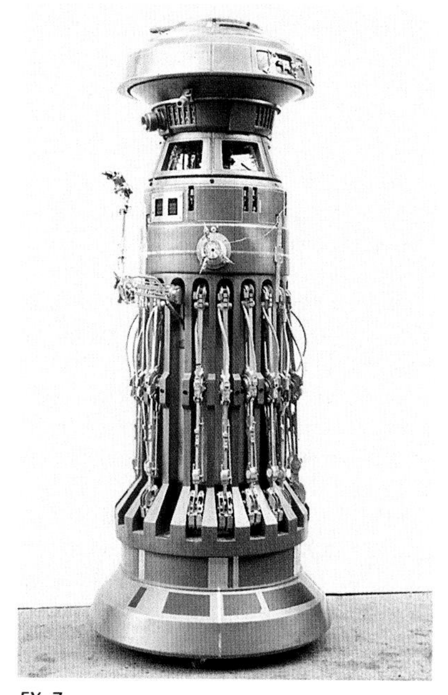

FX-7

lion, FX-7 was stationed on Hoth as assistant to the medical droid 2-1B until the Imperial attack forced him to escape aboard the transport carrier *Bright Hope*. After the ship was nearly destroyed, the droid played a key role in the survival of ninety of its passengers, thanks to its excellent burn-treatment programs. FX-7 models are now considered antiquated; during the Galactic Civil War they were found mostly far from the Core Worlds and in service to the Rebel Alliance. [ESB, TBH]

FX-10 A standard medical droid, it was widely used by Imperial field units. Enhanced programming let the FX-10 model treat a wide variety of battle wounds. [CCG]

FX droid A class of medical droid, it specializes in the diagnosis and treatment of injury and disease. The droids are manufactured by MedTech. [NR, SWSB]

Fyre, Commander Silver A former smuggling colleague of Han Solo and Chewbacca, she and her pirates once stole a valuable cargo of spice from the pair. She went on to become leader of one of the biggest gangs of mercenaries in the galaxy, the Aquarius Freeholders. Following the Battle of Yavin she and the Freeholders joined the Alliance during the Conference of Uncommitted Worlds held on Kabal. [CSW]

gaberwool A soft wool made from the tufts of gaberworms. [NR]

gaberworms Giant worms, they have ivory tufts of hair in the middle of each of their body segments. This hair is harvested to make gaberwool. [NR]

gaderffii A traditional weapon of Tatooine's Sand People, or Tusken Raiders, it is a double-edged axlike weapon, also sometimes called a gaffi stick. A gaderffii is hand-fashioned from metal scavenged from wrecked or abandoned vehicles and spaceships that wind up in the Tatooine wastes. [SW]

Cmdr. Silver Fyre

Gaff Aide-de-camp to Governor Koong during the early days of the Empire, Gaff was a Kobok, a green, fuzzy insectoid with deadly stingers on his forearms. Gaff also had three eyes, one on the back of his head. [DTV]

gaffi stick *See* gaderffii

Galaan A large gas giant in the Galaanus system of the Corva sector, it is covered with green, gray, and white clouds that restrict visibility to a few hundred meters. The New Republic operates a floating Intelligence outpost in Galaan's upper atmosphere. [SWAJ]

Galactic Civil War The Rebellion that rocked the galaxy to its core started after Senator Palpatine became Emperor. The Galactic Empire replaced the quickly fading Republic, and tyranny gripped the millions of worlds of the galaxy.

It took years, however, before scattered pockets of resistance could be organized into the Alliance to Restore the Republic. One by one at first, then in a trickle that became a flood, guerrilla groups and planets cast their lot with the nascent Rebel Alliance. The galaxy shuddered on the brink of full-scale civil war. Alliance leader Mon Mothma wrote the Formal Declaration of Rebellion, alerting the Emperor that the pesky opposition was now full-fledged, organized resistance. Although Rebel firepower didn't come close to matching that of the Empire, events were moving too swiftly for the Rebels to plan and execute an orderly buildup.

The exact moment when the full-scale Galactic Civil War began cannot be pinpointed with certainty, but the completion of the Empire's Death Star battle station and its annihilation of the planet Alderaan and its billions of people certainly galvanized the opposition. By the time of the Battle of Yavin, the civil war was in full swing. Star system after star system slipped through the Empire's nets to join the Alliance, and war rocked the galaxy from the settlements of the Outer Rim Territories to the majestic spires of Imperial Center. The Battle of Endor, when the second Death Star was destroyed and the Emperor apparently died, marked the end of the full-scale war and the birth of the New Republic. [SW, ESB, RJ, HE, DFR, LC, DE]

Galactic Constitution The ancient foundation document of the democratic Old Republic. [DE]

Galactic Core This region encompasses star systems in the central region of the galaxy. The term is also applied more narrowly to the heavily populated region surrounding the Deep Galactic Core. The region was the original ruling nexus of the Republic, and later, the Empire, with the planet Coruscant (Imperial Center) at the center and the government spreading outward like the spokes of a wheel. [SWSB, HESB, SWRPG2, DE]

Galactic HoloNet An extensive news and information

Gaderffii

Galia

network, it can be accessed throughout the galaxy. [TBH]

Galactic Museum This huge institution on Coruscant houses precious objects and memorabilia from thousands of forgotten cultures and every age of galactic history. It includes many books, amulets, and talismans from the ancient dark Sith religion. It has been in existence for countless millennia. [FNU]

Galactic Republic A democratic union of star systems, usually referred to simply as the Republic, it predated the Empire by about twenty-five millennia. It grew as a direct result of sophisticated new means of communication and transportation, chief among them the development of hyperspace travel. Over the course of approximately 25,000 years of existence, it came to encompass millions of inhabited worlds. It eventually grew bloated and corrupt and was replaced by the Empire founded by then-Senator Palpatine. Following the formation of the New Republic, its democratic predecessor is known as the Old Republic. [TOJ, FNU, DLS, TSW]

Galactic Voyager An enormous Calamarian star cruiser, one of the largest and most powerful ships in the New Republic fleet, it was Admiral Ackbar's favorite ship. [DS]

Galantos Located in the Farlax sector near the Koornacht Cluster, the planet is homeworld of the Fia species. The Cluster appears as a bright oval of light in Galantos's night sky, and is known among the Fia as The Multitude. The Fian population of Galantos is approximately 500,000. A chromite mining colony on New Brigia, within the Koornacht Cluster, once traded its ore along the hyperlanes to Galantos and Wehttam, until the collapse of Imperial control of the Farlax sector made commerce increasingly hazardous.

Twelve years after the Battle of Endor, the Grannan pilot Plat Mallar escaped from a brutal Yevethan attack on his home planet Polneye in the Koornacht Cluster and desperately tried to reach Galantos in a short-range TIE interceptor. A passing ship bound for Woqua intercepted Mallar's signal, and the Fia grew concerned after hearing of the Yevethan attack on the nearby planet. Jobath, councilor of the Fia, came to Chief of State Leia Organa Solo's residence on Coruscant to petition for Galantos's membership in the New Republic and to ask her for protection against the Yevethan fleet. Leia accepted the emergency petitions for membership from all worlds bordering the Cluster and sent the Republic's Fifth Fleet to defend them. The *Gol Storn* and the *Thackery* were sent to Galantos as a show of strength. Councilor Jobath offered to make Plat Mallar a citizen of Galantos, but Mallar declined. [BTS, SOL]

Galaxy Gun The second cloned Emperor's ultimate weapon, it fired "intelligent" projectiles into hyperspace. Each of the well-shielded lightspeed torpedoes could exit hyperspace at precise coordinates, find its target, and destroy it. No ordinary projectiles, the torpedoes carried particle disintegrators that neutralized all security shields; when they struck, they initiated massive nucleonic chain reactions. The Gun obliterated the Alliance's Pinnacle Base and the entire fifth moon of Da Soocha, although the Alliance top command escaped just in time. In the end, the Gun discharged when R2-D2 reset the coordinates of the Emperor's flagship, which slammed into the weapon, destroying the ship, the weapon, and the Emperor's throneworld, the planet Byss. [DE2]

Galia Daughter of King Ommin and Queen Amanoa, she was heir to the throne of the planet Onderon four millennia before the Galactic Civil War. Galia and Oron Kira were married prior to the Freedon Nadd Uprising in a ceremony signifying the unification of Onderon. She ascended to the throne of Iziz after the death of her mother, sharing power with her husband. [TOJ, FNU]

Gall This moon circles the gas giant Zhar in a far Rim System. A Rebel group tried to rescue Han Solo there shortly after he had been frozen into a block of carbonite by Darth Vader. An Imperial shipyard on the moon was home to two Star Destroyers and their attendant TIE fighters. Boba Fett's ship, *Slave I*, was spotted on Gall with Solo aboard. During the rescue attempt, Princess Leia Organa, Lando Calrissian, Chewbacca, and C-3PO, in the *Millennium Falcon*, followed Corellian pilot Dash Rendar to the spot where *Slave I* was parked. But the *Falcon* was attacked by TIE fighters and Fett escaped with Solo still aboard. [SOTE, RS]

Gallandro The fastest gunfighter in the galaxy, he was so amoral that killing one or one hundred made little difference to him. In the end, it

Gallandro

was his own "victory" over Han Solo that did him in.

Gallandro was born on the backwater planet of Ylix. He saw his parents murdered by off-world terrorists, grew up in orphanages, and joined the military as soon as he was eligible. He became addicted to danger and conflict, and when he mustered out of the militia he decided to become a freelance blaster for hire. He looked the role, with his close-cropped graying hair and long, gold-beaded mustache. Gallandro always wore expensive, well-tailored clothing. His blaster holster was slung low, and his white scarf hung like a badge of office. Over the years, a death mark was put on his head by more than 100 planets, but no bounty hunter was brave enough—or foolish enough—to take him on.

He was hired by Odumin, a powerful regional administrator for the Corporate Sector Authority, to take out a five-member family. He did the job so well that Odumin put him on retainer for other "messy" jobs. Gallandro was on the planet Ammuud when he first encountered Han Solo, who had been trapped by security police. Han tricked him into grabbing a case that sent shocks to Gallandro's gun hand, and Gallandro let Solo go. They later encountered each other on Dellalt, where both were searching for the long-lost treasure of Xim the Despot. Han found the treasure chambers and Gallandro challenged him to a duel. Gallandro fired first, hitting Han in the shoulder, and then attempted to kill one of Han's associates. But the chamber had been rigged to combat such disruptions, and a dozen lasers shot forth and incinerated Gallandro on the spot. [HLL, HSR, SWCG]

Gallant A New Republic cruiser, it was part of the Fifth Fleet activated in the Yevethan crisis. [BTS]

Gallinore A planet in the Hapes Cluster, it was home to extremely valuable rainbow gems. The gems were actually silicon-based life-forms that mature after thousands of years and glow with an inner light. [CPL]

Galvoni III The location of an Imperial military communications complex, the planet was infiltrated by Alliance historian Voren Na'al after the Battle of Yavin in order to gain more information about the Death Star project. [MTS]

Gamorrean

Gama system The home system of a quasi-humanoid species, the Gama-Senn. Six years after the Battle of Endor, the leader of the Gama-Senn pledged the system's allegiance to the second cloned Emperor after witnessing a demonstration of Palpatine's devastating Galaxy Gun. [EE]

gameboard A holographic projection table used for amusement purposes in the game of dejarik, it has three-dimensional holograms that compete on its surface at the direction of players who tap commands into attached keypads. [SW, FT, CCG]

***Gamma*-class assault shuttle** *See* assault shuttle

Gamorr The pleasant home planet of the Gamorrean species, it has widely varying temperatures and terrain ranging from frozen tundra to deep forests. Gamorr's history is marked by almost constant periods of war between the dim-witted Gamorrean males. Gamorr is also home to furry, bloodsucking parasites called morrts, which Gamorreans look upon with affection and allow to feed on their body fluids. [SWSB, COJ, SWAJ]

Gamorrean A brutish, porcine species, they are known for their great strength and violent tendencies. Gamorreans have green skin, piglike snouts, small horns, and upturned tusks. They average about 1.8 meters in height. They make excellent heavy laborers and mercenaries, and a number served as guards in Jabba the Hutt's desert palace on Tatooine. Gamorreans can understand many languages, but their own limited vocal apparatus prevents them from conversing in other tongues.

In their culture, females handle the productive work of farming, hunting, manufacturing, and running businesses. The males spend all their time training for and fighting in wars. Gamorreans live in clans headed by matrons who order the males to fight from early spring to late fall. Early traders turned out to be slavers, but some Gamorreans have found work as guards, mercenaries, and even bounty hunters. [RJ, SWSB]

Gamor Run A legendary long-haul smuggling route, it is plagued by hijackers and pirates. [DE]

Ganathian *See* Ganath system

Ganath system Hidden in a vast, radioactive gas cloud near Nal Hutta, the system is completely cut off from the rest of galactic civilization. Spacers from Nal Hutta who attempted to penetrate the gas cloud never returned. Thus isolated, Ganath's culture has developed more slowly than the rest of the galaxy's, and much of its technology operates on steam power. The Ganathan space fleet includes the massive steam-powered battleship *The Robida Colossus*. For years the system was ruled by King Empatojayos Brand, a Jedi Knight who was rescued by the Ganathans after his ship was destroyed. Leia and Han Solo traveled to the capital city of Ganath after they flew into the gas cloud in an attempt to escape from Boba Fett. [DE2]

Gand A planet of swirling clouds of gaseous ammonia, it is home to a species of the same name. Gand society consists of pocket colonies separated by enshrouding mists, and the Gand government is a totalitarian monarchy established centuries ago. Locating fugitives in the thick gases is the responsibility of Gand findsmen, who worship the mists and use religious rituals to lead them to their targets. Some Gand findsmen have since found work as bounty hunters, including the notorious Zuckuss, although others, such as Rogue Squadron pilot Ooryl Qrygg, have chosen nobler professions.

The Gand are covered with a hard carapace. Their impressive regenerative capability lets them replace lost limbs. One subspecies of Gand does not breathe, feeding their metabolism through eating instead of respiration. This subspecies speaks by drawing in gases and expelling them through the Gand voicebox. Another Gand subspecies has evolved as ammonia breathers. Ruetsavii, a group of famous Gands, are sent by the Elders of Gand to observe notable subjects and determine if they are worthy of referring to themselves in the first person, when they will become janwuine. After the Rogues captured Thyferra, Ooryl Qrygg was named janwuine, and the squadron was invited to Gand to help celebrate the momentous occasion. [MTS, RS, BW]

Gandolo IV A barren, rocky moon in the Outer Rim, it was where a group of Wookiee settlers aided by Chewbacca were attempting to establish a colony when they were discovered by the bounty hunter Bossk. The tracker and his gang, working for the Imperial sector governor, abandoned their attempt to capture the Wookiees after Han Solo disabled their ship by landing on it. [MTS]

Yarna d'al' Gargan

Gank A species that act as bodyguards and hired assassins of many Hutt crime lords, they are also called Gank Killers because they carry out cold-blooded murders so often. Ganks frequently can be seen in the presence of Hutts on the streets of Nar Shaddaa and elsewhere. [DE2]

Gann, Grand Moff A governor of one of the Core sectors. [BTS]

Gant The third being the Dark Jedi Kueller chose to be his adviser. Kueller believed that his second assistant wouldn't last long due to his impertinence, so he decided to start training Gant early. [NR]

Gant, Colonel Trenn A leader of New Republic Intelligence. [TT]

Gantho Located in the system of the same name, the planet is represented by Senator Arastide in the New Republic government. Nine years after the Battle of Endor, the New Republic conducted a large-scale investigation into Loronar Corporation's abuses in the Gantho system. [POT]

Gantoris A leader on the planet Eol Sha, he became one of Luke Skywalker's students at his Jedi academy on Yavin 4. As a child, Gantoris could sense impending groundquakes and had miraculously survived when his playmates were killed in an avalanche. A possible descendent of the Jedi Ta'ania, Gantoris had nightmares of a terrible dark man who would tempt him with power and then destroy him. At first he thought that was Luke, but he soon learned it was the spirit of Exar Kun. The Dark Lord guided Gantoris in building his own lightsaber, but Gantoris turned on his patron and tried to use the Force to put an end to the evil spirit. Instead, Kun killed Gantoris, burning him from the inside out. [JS, DA]

Gap Nine A backwater swamp world that is home to a reptilian species, it is also the site of an Imperial fuel ore-processing plant. Centuries ago an unknown group arrived on Gap Nine and built temples dedicated to evil. A force of Jedi Knights defeated the group and transformed their temples into storehouses of knowledge. [SWAJ]

Garban Home to the Jenet species, the temperate world is the fourth planet in the Tau Sakar system. After the Jenet overpopulated Garban, they colonized other worlds in their system. They are a quarrelsome species served by a bureaucratic government that keeps detailed records on each citizen. Under Empire control, many Jenet were forced to work as slaves in Garban's ore mines. [GG4]

Garch, Commander Captain of the *Glorious*, command ship for the New Republic chase armada and Colonel Pakkpekatt's command cruiser during the Yevethan crisis. [BTS]

Gardens of Talla A hillside park, it overlooked the Jedi library on the planet Ossus many millennia before the Galactic Civil War. [TSW]

Gareth, King A high-ranking official of the New Republic, he once tried to cheat Han Solo at a game of laro. [TBH]

Gargan, Yarna d'al' The daughter of a tribal chief on the desert planet of Askaj, she was the heavy, six-breasted dancer at Jabba the Hutt's palace on Tatooine. She and her family had been kidnapped by slavers and brought to Jabba. Her cublings were sold off and her mate was fed to the rancor. Yarna became one of Jabba's dancers and supervised the palace housecleaning crew until she was able to gain her freedom after the Hutt was killed. She escaped with the bounty hunter Doallyn across the Tatooine desert, eventually arriving in Mos Eisley, where she was able to buy back her children. She and Doallyn left Tatooine to become free traders in textiles and gemstones. She performed the Dance of the Seventy Violet Veils at the wedding of Princess Leia Organa and Han Solo. [RJ, TJP]

Garindan A Kubaz spy with a long, prehensile trunklike nose, he trailed C-3PO and R2-D2 as they hooked up with Luke Skywalker and Ben Kenobi at Docking Bay 94 in Mos Eisley. Also known as Long Snoot, he has always worked for the highest bidder—most often Imperials or Hutts.

Garindan wears dark glasses because his large eyes are sensitive to red wavelengths of light. Born on the arid planet of Kubindi, he has rough-textured greenish-black skin and bristly head hair usually hidden under a heavy hood and robe. The information Garindan gathers is available to any party at the right price. He was being paid by Imperials when he tracked down the wanted droids and led stormtroopers to the bay where Han Solo's *Millennium Falcon* awaited before making its getaway. [SW, SWCG]

Garnib An icy world inhabited by the white-furred Balinaka species, its residents were enslaved by the Empire, which claimed it was "protecting the rights" of the inhabitants. Garnib is the only source of addictive Garnib crystals. The Balinaka are known for their artistic nature and carefree spirit. [POT]

Garindan

Garnoo An ancient Master to Oss Wilum, among others, some four millennia before the Galactic Civil War, Garnoo was a member of the Neti species. [DLS]

Garos IV A planet of thick forests and mountains, it and its twin moons are in the Garos system along with sister planet Sundari. Both were settled by humans about 4,000 years before the Battle of Yavin. A civil war between the planets lasted eighty-two standard years. Recently, hibridium deposits were discovered on Garos IV; the ore can produce a natural cloaking effect. [SWAJ]

Garowyn One of the most accomplished of the new breed of younger dark-side Nightsisters on the planet Dathomir, she was referred to by some as Captain. Garowyn was petite with refined features, hazel eyes, and creamy brown skin. She wore tight-fitting red lizard-skin armor and a knee-length black cape. She fell to her death from a treetop on Kashyyyk when she slipped on a branch while fighting Chewbacca and Tenel Ka. [YJK]

Garqi An agricultural world with fertile plains and oceans, it is in a remote corner of the Outer Rim. Its population is concentrated in the capital city of Pesktda. Corran Horn, a Rogue Squadron X-wing pilot, used his secret position as aide to military prefect Mosh Barris to rescue several prisoners from Garqi's jails, escape with them off-world, and implicate Barris as a traitor to the Empire. Among the prisoners was the Duros captain Lai Nootka. [SWAJ, KT]

Gartogg A simple-minded Gamorrean, he served as a sentry in the palace of Jabba the Hutt. Even less intelligent than most Gamorreans, he was ignored and given inconsequential duties by his porcine peers. When a series of dead bodies started showing up around Jabba's palace, Gartogg took it upon himself to solve the mystery. Believing them to be clues, he carried two corpses with him at all times, treating them as his friends and consorts long after the fall of Jabba's regime. [TJP]

Gate This was the name that Rogue Squadron leader Wedge Antilles gave

Gartogg

to his new R5-G8 astromech droid after Master Zraii upgraded and modified it. [BW]

GaTir system Located less than five standard hours from the Pyria system, it contains the planet Mrisst. [WG]

Gaurick A planet in the Corporate Sector, it is controlled by a religious cult led by a high priest. Han Solo and Chewbacca were hired to deliver several cargoes of chak-root to Gaurick workers, some of whom had a religious objection to the substance. On one such run, Solo and Chewbacca were almost taken captive. [CSSB]

Gavens Akanah Norand Pell was born on this planet, in the city of Torlas, to Isela Talsava Norand and Joreb Goss. The family soon moved to Lucazec, where Joreb abandoned his wife and daughter. [SOL]

Gavin, Colonel Bowman Director of flight personnel for the New Republic's Fifth Fleet Combat Command during the Yevethan crisis. [TT]

Gbu An extremely high-gravity planet, it is home to the Veubgri, a large, stocky species with six legs and long tendrils used as manipulative appendages. Before Leia Organa Solo visited Munto Codru, she and her delegation met with Veubgri representatives on an orbiting satellite; that way, Leia and her party avoided the negative effects of Gbu's high gravity on the human body. [CS]

Geedon V The site of a former pirate base, the infamous gunslinger Gallandro singlehandedly took it over in an early exploit. Years later, a food-supply convoy of Imperial corvettes was destroyed in the Geedon system by Alliance pilots using ships captured from Overlord Ghorin in an attempt to discredit him with the Empire. [HLL, FP]

Gegak, Captain Captain of the Prakith raider *Tobay*. [TT]

GemDiver Station Lando Calrissian's gem mining platform above Yavin, the station orbited in the fringe of the gas giant's outer atmosphere. When *GemDiver Station* lowered its orbit to graze the gaseous levels of the planet, the *Fast Hand* diving bell was sent even lower to catch rare Corusca gems. Nearly two decades after the Battle of Endor, the station was attacked by Skipray blastboats sent by the Second Imperium. A modified assault shuttle with Corusca gem cutters breached the station. Attacking stormtroopers stunned Calrissian and his aide, Lobot, and kidnapped Jaina and Jacen Solo and Lowbacca. [YJK]

Generis Once the site of the New Republic's communications center in the Atrivis sector, the planet was captured along with most fleet-supply depots after a fierce battle with Grand Admiral Thrawn's clone forces. Alliance General Kryll and pilot Pash Cracken were able to evacuate Travia Chan and her people during the New Republic's retreat from Generis. Some two years earlier, while the New Republic fleet was battling Warlord Zsinj, Wing Commander Varth's starfighters had to be moved from Generis to a new staging area at Folor. [LC, BW, RSB]

Gethzerion

Gentes Homeworld of the half-human, piglike Ugnaughts, it is located in the remote Anoat system. Ugnaughts lived in primitive colonies on Gentes's less-than-hospitable surface until most left to work at Cloud City on Bespin. [MTS]

Gep's Grill A restaurant in Mos Eisley, it is run by two Whiphids, Fillin Ta and Norun Gep. [TMEC, GG7]

Gepta, Rokur The last of the sorcerers of Tund, his arrogance and sheer malice led him to obliterate all living things on the planet. Rokur Gepta was a heartless being for whom power was everything. He wanted to rule the sector of the galaxy that contained Tund, then extend his rule outward. To make sure he was unchallenged, he eliminated the original Tund sorcerers who had taught him all that he knew. People saw Gepta differently. To some he was a dwarf, to others a three-meter-tall giant. He wore ashen-gray cloaks and a turban that wrapped around his face, obscuring all but his piercing eyes. Lando Calrissian battled Gepta and defeated him, in the process discovering that the sorcerer was actually a vicious Croke—a small, snaillike being with hairy black legs that used illusion to make its way through life. Lando took the Croke and squeezed Gepta until his gloves were covered with greasy slime, a fitting end for the evil sorcerer. [LCSB]

Geran Located in the Mneon system, the planet's species include a near-human race with bluish skin who need trace amounts of hydron-three added to the air they breathe in order to survive away from home. Their religious system involves a belief in the Sky Seraphs. Doallyn, one of Jabba the Hutt's bounty hunters, was a Geran native. Animal life on the planet includes a flying reptile, the shell-bat. [TJP]

Gerbaud 2 Located in the Sepan system, the planet Gerbaud 2 was the site from which Imperial Admiral Harkov attempted to resupply his TIE advanced squadrons during a rendezvous with the escort carrier *Tropsobor* following the Battle of Hoth. A united force from the nearby planets of Ripoblus and Dimok attacked and thwarted the transfer operation. [TSC]

Gerrard V Before the Battle of Yavin, segments of the planet's military staged an uprising sympathetic to the Rebellion in the main city of Harazod. But the Gerrard V insurrection was brutally suppressed through orbital bombings from the Star Destroyers *Adjudicator* and *Relentless*. [SWAJ]

Getelles, Moff The Imperial military governor of the Antemeridian sector, Moff Getelles struck a deal with Seti Ashgad, who agreed to destroy the gunstations of Nam Chorios in return for weaponry and the first cut of the profits when Loronar Corporation moved in to strip-mine the planet's precious crystals. The moff also had a deal with Loronar, which promised a new facility on Antemeridias to build synthdroids and new Needles smart missiles. [POT]

Gethzerion The leader of the Nightsisters of the Witches of Dathomir, she hoped to turn all of the Witches to the dark side. Gethzerion had matted white hair, crimson, bloodshot eyes, and a face with blotches of purple from ruptured blood vessels. She terrorized not only other clans of Witches, but also the stormtrooper guards at the planet's Imperial prison colony, who eventually started taking orders from her.

The Nightsisters were wielders of the Force in a matriarchal society that used men only as mates or servants. Only Gethzerion knew that she could use the power of the Force without the rituals that the others went through. Her powers grew through devotion to the dark side, and she was determined that her clan would rule and, eventually, escape the planet on which they had been stranded by Emperor Palpatine, who had been disturbed by Gethzerion's growing power.

When Han Solo crashed the *Millennium Falcon* on Dathomir, a planet he had won in a sabacc game, Warlord Zsinj told Gethzerion that he would get her a ship to leave the planet if she gave him Solo and Princess Leia Organa. Despite this promise, Zsinj's men opened fire and destroyed both the ship and Gethzerion. [CPL, SWCG]

Ghent This tech is a vital cog in Talon Karrde's smuggling operation, maintaining computer and droid programming and breaking most encrypted codes and other computer security measures with ease. Only computers and their software seem to interest him, and he draws a tight cloak against attempts at friendship. Ghent helped the New Republic break a number of Imperial encrypted codes, including those that led to false accusations against Admiral Ackbar and those used by the Imperial spynet known as Delta Source. The computer slicer also accompanied Han Solo, Lando Calrissian, and Mara Jade to liberate the Imperial prison facility on Kessel. [HE, DFR, LC, HESB, DFRSB, COF]

ghhhk Nature's wake-up call on Clak'dor VII, the ghhhk rise with the dawn, screeching their mating calls across the jungles. Locals use their skin oils as a heating salve. [CCG]

Ghorman Site of the infamous Ghorman Massacre, an early atrocity committed by the Empire, the planet is in the system of the same name and the Sern sector, near the Core Worlds. During a peaceful antitax demonstration, a warship sent to collect the taxes landed on top of the protesters—killing and injuring hundreds. Tarkin, the warship's captain, was promoted to moff for his action. The Ghorman Massacre was commemorated every year on its anniversary by those opposed to Emperor Palpatine's New Order, and it convinced Bail Organa of Alderaan to join the cause of the Rebellion. Years later, when an Imperial base on Ghorman was being enlarged, an Alliance attack on a vital supply convoy delayed the expansion for over a year. [JS, DA, FP, RSB]

Ghhhk holomonster

Givin

ghostling Ethereally beautiful humanoids, these faunlike creatures are very fragile. Entering into a physical relationship with a human means certain death. [CS]

Giat Nor On the planet N'zoth, this is the home city of Yevethan strongman Nil Spaar. [SOL]

Giju stew A dish best made with a bit of boontaspice. [SOTE]

Gillespee, Samuel Tomas A somewhat less-than-honorable friend of Talon Karrde, he once retired from the smuggling trade to set up house on the planet Ukio. But when Grand Admiral Thrawn took control of the planet, Samuel Tomas Gillespee left in search of a smuggling operation willing to employ him and his men. He signed on with Karrde to indirectly but profitably help the New Republic. His ship is *Kern's Pride.* [LC]

gimer stick An edible twig, it is snapped off from plants that grow in the Dagobah swamps. The gimer plant produces a succulent juice that concentrates in sacs on the bark. The sticks are chewed for their flavor and to quench thirst. Yoda, the Jedi Master, enjoyed chewing gimer sticks. [ESBN]

Ginbotham A Hig, he is a slender blue creature whose piloting skills were renowned. Ginbotham served with Wedge Antilles as a member of the command crew on the *Yavin.* [NR]

Givin Looking a bit like animated skeletons, Givin wear their bones on the outside of their bodies. Their skull-like faces are dominated by large, triangular eye sockets, making them look sad all the time. Native to the planet Yag'Dhul, they are a precise species and are skilled mathematicians. The sight of exposed flesh makes them ill. They can seal their joints to withstand the vacuum of space. [GG4]

Gizer This planet is known for, among other things, its ale and the manufacture of space freighters. [NR]

Gizer ale A pale blue drink, it is a favorite of Han Solo. [NR]

gladiator droid These robots were designed for close-quarters combat in the declining days of the Old Republic. Gladiator droids were used in violent sporting events involving other droids or even living creatures. [HSE]

Glakka The site of a gun-running operation of Jabba the Hutt and the Chevin criminal Ephant Mon, this ice-covered moon was nearly their final resting place. They plotted to steal an Imperial weapons cache on Glakka but were ambushed by an Imperial squad. They survived the attack but almost died during the subzero night, when Jabba kept Ephant Mon alive by covering him in the folds of his sluglike body. The pair was rescued in the morning. [TJP]

Gla Soocha *See* Da Soocha

Glayyd, Mor Patriarch of the Glayyd family on the planet Ammuud. Mor is a title of respect. Glayyd's given name when Han Solo visited the planet prior to his involvement in the Rebellion was Ewwen. [HSR]

Gli, Darian A Markul professor, he was the contact that academic Melvosh Bloor was supposed to make at Jabba the Hutt's palace to arrange for an interview with the crime lord. Bloor found out too late that Darian Gli had been eaten by Jabba months before. [TJP]

glitterstim A potent spice that is mined on the planet Kessel, it gives a brief but pleasurable telepathic boost and heightened mental state. Glitterstim spice is a valuable commodity that was tightly controlled by the Empire and worth its weight in credits to smugglers. Glitterstim is photoactive, so it must be mined in total darkness or else it will be ruined. It is also addictive for many species, and they usually employ "cutters" who prepare the spice for sale. [JS, TJP, XW, NR]

gloom dwellers Slang for the lower-level inhabitants of Nar Shaddaa. [TMEC]

Glorious Colonel Pakkpekatt's command cruiser during the Yevethan crisis. [BTS]

Glory of Yevetha Formerly the *EX-F*, a weapons and propulsion test bed taken by the Yevetha at N'zoth, it was a major craft in strongman Nil Spaar's Black Fifteen Fleet. [BTS, SOL]

Glott A notorious bounty hunter from Antar 4. [GG4]

Glottal The homeworld of the species known as Glottalphibs, often abbreviated to 'Phibs, Glottal is a hot, humid world of swamps, lily-pad-covered ponds, and dark forests. Glottalphibs have scaly yellow-green skin and long snouts filled with teeth. Their gills allow 'Phibs to live in both water and air, and they radiate no detectable body heat. They can breathe fire, shooting it from their mouths as a weapon, and are known to carry snub-nosed hand weapons called swamp-stunners. Their hides are resistant to blaster fire; the most effective way to kill a 'Phib is to shoot it in the mouth. They are known for their persistence and love of shiny objects. Favorite foods of 'Phibs include parfue gnats, caver eggs, Eilnian sweet flies, and watumba bats. The bats host many types of insects but eat fire, and can kill a Glottalphib in seconds. The most famous 'Phib is the crime lord Nandreeson, who operates out of Skip 6 in Smuggler's Run. Thirteen years after the Battle of Endor, Lando Calrissian was captured by Nandreeson and nearly killed before Han Solo and Chewbacca rescued him. [NR]

glow rod Any device designed to provide portable light, most are long, thin tubes that cast bright light from chemical phosphorescents. Other glow rods consist of power cells attached to lamp bulbs. [HLL, SWSB, HESB]

glowstones Opalescent lamps designed to look like natural stones, these technological devices found on Ryloth are used for lighting large gatherings and celebrations. [XW]

glowtube A cylindrical device used for illumination. [TBH]

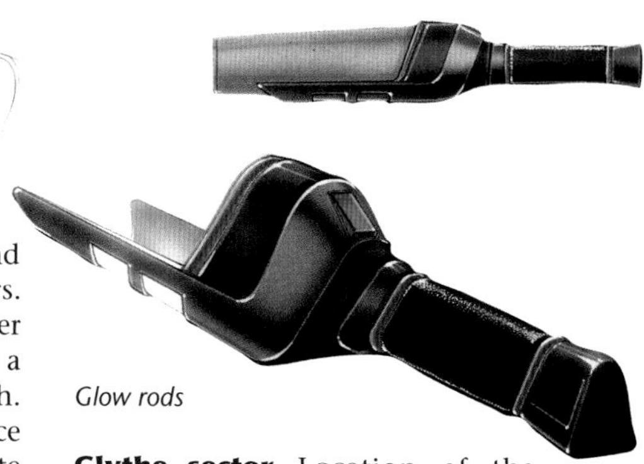

Glow rods

Glythe sector Location of the planet Valrar, it is the site of an Imperial base. [DFR]

Gmar Askilon The fourth documented sighting of the mysterious ghost ship called the Teljkon vagabond was in deep space near this star. A New Republic task force intercepted the vagabond there. A team consisting of Lando Calrissian, Lobot, and the droids R2-D2 and C-3PO were able to board the ship and were whisked away when it suddenly entered hyperspace. [BTS]

gnarltree One of the more bizarre plant forms in the galaxy, these swamp-loving trees of Dagobah grow slowly upward through the centuries, their huge roots rising out of the bog, providing shelter in the hollow spaces. Each gnarltree is a microcosm of life-forms with lichens, moss, and shelf-fungus filling the crannies of the calcified trunk. But the strangest aspect of the tree is the knobby white spider that is part of the gnarltrees' life cycle. The spider is actually a detachable, mobile root that breaks free of the parent gnarl-

Gnarltree

GNK power droids

tree. It becomes a predator, hunting and devouring animals to build up its energy and nutrients before making a clearing and putting down its eight sharp legs, which become the roots of a new gnarltree. [ISWU]

Gnisnal An *Imperial I*–class Star Destroyer, it was sabotaged during evacuation of Narth and Ihopek. An intact memory core found in the wreck contained a complete Imperial Order of Battle. [BTS]

GNK power droid A boxy droid with two stout legs, it provides power for other droids or machinery. It often makes a guttural sound something like "Gonk, gonk," which has become its nickname. [TJP]

Goa, Spurch "Warhog" A short Diollan bounty hunter with a broad, scarred beak and a nasty temper, he took on the Rodian Greedo as an apprentice on the spaceport moon of Nar Shaddaa. He later brought Greedo to Tatooine, where the Rodian was killed by Han Solo. In actuality, Goa was being paid by a warlike clan of Rodians to insure that Greedo ended up dead. [DE, TMEC]

goatgrass A grass native to the planet Kinyen, it is a staple food of the Gran species. [TJP]

Goelitz This planet was once was involved in an ancient feud with the planet Ylix, a few systems away. After much fighting, Goelitz was defeated by members of the Ylix militia, including the infamous gunman Gallandro. [CSSB]

Golanda Golanda was in charge of the artillery innovations and tactical-deployments section of Maw Installation. During her ten years there, she never stopped complaining about how foolish it was to do artillery research in the middle of a black hole cluster, where the fluctuating gravity ruined her calculations and made every test a pointless exercise. She was tall and hawkish with an angular face, pointed chin, and an aquiline nose that gave her face the general shape of a Star Destroyer. [COF]

Goldenrod A nickname conferred upon C-3PO by Han Solo. [RJ]

Golden Sun A living, collective intelligence, it is made up of thousands of tiny polyps that live in the coral reefs of the planet Sedri. Golden Sun has an aptitude for the Force, which it refers to as the universal energy. Golden Sun produces a supply of energy so huge that it affects the planet's gravitational readings. Native Sedrians, especially the Force-sensitive high priests, actually hear the voices of the communal polyps as dreams and visions. [BGS, GG4]

Gold Leader The comm-unit designation for Rebel pilot Dutch's Y-wing during the Battle of Yavin. He led his squadron in the first assault wave against the Death Star battle station.

During the Battle of Endor, it was the comm-unit designation for Lando Calrissian and the *Millennium Falcon*. Lando was responsible for leading Alliance starfighters against the second Death Star. His quick decision making in battle helped defeat the Imperial fleet and bring about the end of the Galactic Civil War. Gold Leader and Red Leader (Wedge Antilles) destroyed the Death Star's power core and that, in turn, destroyed the entire battle station. [SWRJ]

Gold Squadron A Rebel Alliance fighter squadron assigned to the Massassi Base on Yavin 4, it was called upon to attack the first Death Star. During the battle the entire squadron was wiped out, with the exception of Gold Leader. [SW, CCG]

Gold Two The comm-unit designation for Rebel pilot Tiree's Y-wing during the Battle of Yavin. [SW]

Gold Wing The Alliance starfighter battle group under the command of Gold Leader during the Battle of Endor. [RJ]

Golkus A planet that is nearly on a straight line between Coruscant and Carratos. Twelve years after the Battle of Endor, Akanah Norand Pell stopped on Golkus after leaving Carratos and contacted a tech who altered her ship's transponder to broadcast false ID profiles. She then left to meet with Luke Skywalker on Coruscant. [SOL]

Gol Storn A New Republic ship, it was deployed for duty at Galantos in the Farlax Sector because of the fear of an imminent Yevethan attack. [SOL]

Golthar's Sky An apparently mammoth star-freighter, it was actually an illusion created by Aleema some four millennia before the Galactic Civil War. [TSW]

Gonar A skulking human, he hung around Jabba the Hutt's rancor and its keeper, Malakili, for prestige. When Gonar tried to blackmail Malakili into letting him take over the position of rancor keeper, Malakili killed him. [TJP]

G'ont, Ickabel A Bith member of Figrin D'an and the Modal Nodes, he plays the Fanfar. G'ont's favorite song for the band to perform is "Tears of Aquanna," mainly because he gets a solo. [TMEC, CCG]

Ickabel G'ont

Gopso'o Ancestral enemies of the Drovian species, they have engaged in a centuries-long blood feud. [POT]

Gorath A Prakith light cruiser under the command of Captain Voba Dokrett, it attempted to capture the mysterious ghost ship called the Teljkon vagabond but was destroyed by it instead. [TT]

Gorax

Gorax A giant creature more than thirty meters high, it lives in caverns on Endor's forest moon and terrorizes inhabitants such as Ewoks. It wears fur clothing held together with large stitches and carries fearsome stone axes with which to hunt at night. A Gorax has thick, matted fur, pointed ears, and a jutting lower jaw filled with sharp teeth. One of the creatures had captured humans Jeremitt and Catarine Towani, but it was killed when their children Mace and Cindel, along with a few Ewok friends, braved the Gorax lair to free them. [EA, ISWU]

Gorbah A planet with four hidden fighter bases, its ships attacked invading Imperial forces with a space-snipe defense. When the Empire eventually triumphed, the fighters abandoned their secret outposts and fled the system. [SWAJ]

Gorgon An Imperial Star Destroyer, it was Admiral Daala's flagship, the last of her remaining original Star Destroyers. During the battle at the Maw Installation, after she downloaded weapons plans from the facility into the *Gorgon's* computers, she set what appeared to be a suicide course into the Installation, presumably destroying the *Gorgon*. In reality, she took the ship, under Commander Kratas, on a long trip to the Core worlds where she planned to regroup and ally herself with powerful Imperial warlords. [JS, DA, DS, COF]

Gorm the Dissolver A huge biomechanical droid bounty hunter, he had heavy, plated armor and a full helmet. Known as Gorm the Dissolver, his biocomponents came from six different aliens. He was seemingly destroyed by the young Rodian bounty hunter Greedo on the spaceport moon of Nar Shaddaa, but was later repaired and eventually showed up in Mos Eisley. [DE, TMEC]

gorm-worm A species with poison venom sacs, it can kill instantly with its bite. A gorm-worm was used by pirates to kill Jedi trainee Andur Sunrider some 4,000 years before the Galactic Civil War. [TOJ]

Gornash, Prophet A Prophet of the Dark Side, he coordinated spy activities from the group's space station headquarters, Scardia. [PDS]

Gorneesh, King A sly, foul-tempered leader of the Duloks, creatures that live in the swamps of Endor's moon. [ETV]

King Gorneesh

Gotal

Gorno A spaceport, it was supposed to be the point of embarkation for the Hammertong device that was to be delivered to the Empire. [TMEC]

gorsa tree A stout, flowering tree, it uses its pale-orange phosphorescent flowers to attract night insects for pollination. [TMEC]

Gosfambling Delicate furred creatures from a planet of the same name, they are intelligent and soft-spoken. Their whiskers curl around their faces whenever they speak. Wary of losers, Gosfamblings would not elect anyone who had ever lost in an election: Once a loser on Gosfambling, always a loser. Senator C-Gosf is the planet's representative to the New Republic. [NR]

Goss, Joreb The long-sought father of Akanah Norand Pell, who found him on Atzerri. But he didn't remember his daughter or anything about her people, the Fallanassi, due to excessive drug use that diminished his memory. [SOL]

Gotal An intelligent, two-legged species with two prominent cone-shaped growths sprouting from their heads, they hail from the moon Antar 4. The head cones serve Gotals, who also have flat noses and protruding brows, as additional sensory organs that can pick up and distinguish different forms of emotional and energy waves. Although the shaggy, gray-furred species is technologically advanced, most other species feel uncomfortable around them because of their additional senses. And Gotals don't like to be around droids since their high-energy output tends to overload the Gotals' senses. The species make excellent scouts, bounty hunters, trackers, and mercenaries. When nervous, Gotals tend to shed copious amounts of their fur. [GG4, DFRSB, TMEC, NR]

Gowdawl This planet was the destination for the starliner *Star Morning*, owned by the Fallanassi religious order. The spacecraft left the planet Motexx a few weeks before the Battle of Endor with a full cargo, bound for Gowdawl under a charter license. The liner then disappeared for three hundred days, eventually showing up at Arat Fraca with empty cargo holds. [SOL]

Graf, Admiral Head of New Republic Fleet Intelligence during the Yevethan crisis. [TT]

Grake Large and tentacled but nonetheless gentle, this Veubgri from the planet Gbu was a cook for Lord Hethrir. [CS]

Grakouine The site of an Alliance storage base, it was where the New Republic parked Boba Fett's ship, *Slave I*, after the bounty hunter was presumed killed by the Sarlacc on Tatooine. Some time later a very much alive Fett repurchased his ship through legitimate, although hidden, channels. [DESB]

Grammel, Captain-Supervisor A sadistic, square-jawed, mustachioed administrator, he commanded the Imperial military garrison on Circarpous V. Captain-Supervisor Grammel was ruthless and routinely tortured prisoners for the sheer pleasure of it, even when he wasn't seeking information. [SME]

Gran A goatlike humanoid species native to the planet Kinyen, Gran have three eyes atop independent stalks. They are a mostly peaceful species. Ree-Yees, a Gran, became a member of Jabba the Hutt's court. [RJ, TJP, GG5, GG12]

Grand Isle One of the jungle islands on the planet Vladet, it was once the site of an Imperial installation under the command of Admiral Devlia. The facility was placed there to discourage piracy because of its proximity to the Chorax, Hensara, and Rachuk systems. It was destroyed by the Alliance and Rogue Squadron in a retaliatory strike. [BW]

Gran

Grand Reception Hall An enormous building on Imperial Center, it was more than 1,000 meters long with fourteen levels for seating approximately 500,000 beings on the main floors and balconies. Nearly every star system in the Empire was represented, and each system's flag hung beside the system's balcony. [CPL]

granite slug A small invertebrate creature, it thrives in the dank lower levels of Imperial City on Coruscant, out of reach of hawk-bats that prey on it. The trails of granite slugs leave deep marks in the dirt and fungi, resembling some kind of ancient runes. [JS, XW]

Granna Once an Imperial world, Granna is home planet of the Grannans. Plat Mallar, who participated in the Battle of N'zoth, was a Grannan pilot who was born on Polneye. [TT]

Gra Ploven This planet is the homeworld of the aquatic species known as Ploven, who are referred to disparagingly as finbacks by Imperial forces. When the Ploven refused to pay protection money to Grand Moff Dureya during the waning days of the Empire, the Star Destroyer *Forger* created superhot steam clouds that killed 200,000 Ploven in three Gra Ploven coastal cities. [SOL]

gravel-maggot Worms that feed upon rotting flesh, they aid in rapid decomposition. Gravel-maggots can be found in the hills and rocky badlands of the planet Tatooine. [SWN]

gravel storm Ferocious storms on the planet Tatooine, they whip up and send rocks, sand, and loose debris hurtling through the air—sometimes with deadly force. [SWN]

Graveyard of Alderaan An asteroid field, it is all that remains of the planet Alderaan, blown up by the Empire with the first Death Star. It is called the Graveyard by spacers and free-traders, who spin tales of mysterious Jedi artifacts and ghost ships amidst the ruins. At one point, the Empire tried to lure Princess Leia Organa and her Rebel Alliance allies to the area by spreading a story that the Royal Palace of Alderaan had been found intact within a huge asteroid. The survivors of Alderaan—those who were off-world at the time of its destruction—quickly developed a ritual known as the Returning. As part of that ritual, Returnees purchased a memorial capsule and filled it with small personal gifts for their departed relatives and friends. The capsule was then jettisoned to orbit in the Graveyard as the Returnee made a fairly uniform remembrance speech. [GA, BW]

gravity well projector A device that simulates the presence of a large body in space, it prevents nearby ships from engaging their hyperdrives and forces ships already traveling through hyperspace to drop back into realspace. Gravity well projectors are connected to massive gravity well generators aboard large ships. [ISB, SH]

gravsled A flying platform for up to three passengers, it provides cheap, fast transportation with antigrav or repulsorlift engines. A windshroud offers the only protection on a gravsled. [HSR]

Gray Leader The comm-unit designation for the commander of Gray Wing, one of the four main Rebel starfighter battle groups during the Battle of Endor. Gray Leader and his unit were taken out early in the fight. [RJ]

Gray Wing One of the four main Rebel starfighter battle groups in the

Great Heep

Battle of Endor, it suffered quick and heavy casualties. [RJ]

grazers Creatures originally from Alderaan, these docile, slow-moving grass eaters are bred for their meat. Other grazers include antlered mammals native to the mountain plains of Ammuud and seventeen species on Yavin 8. [ISWU, HSR, GG2]

Great Bogga the Hutt A wealthy Hutt gang lord some four millennia ago, he ruled the underworld of the Stenness system. Great Bogga the Hutt ran a protection racket from a private moon that housed his operations. He was paid by the Nessies to protect their Ithull Ore-Haulers against pirates who had developed marauder craft that could penetrate the thick sheathing of the Nessies' ships. The Hutt was also responsible for the death of Jedi trainee Andur Sunrider, after ordering his henchmen to strongarm Sunrider and steal the Adegan crystals he carried, the heart of lightsabers. Yet Bogga insisted upon calling himself the Merciful One, professing his willingness to forgive just about anyone who crossed him. [TOJ]

Great Dome of the Je'har An architectural wonder on the planet Almania, Dark Jedi Kueller turned it into his command center when he was fighting against the Je'har. [NR]

Great Droid Revolution A robot revolution on Coruscant about 4,000 years before the Galactic Civil War. Jedi Master Arca Jeth was one of the combatants. [DLS]

Greater Plooriod Cluster The site of prestigious swoop races until occupied by the Empire, the cluster is within the Greater Plooriod sector and contains the planet Corsin, where the races took place. The Plooriods also contain several vital agricultural worlds, and the cluster had been the sector's primary grain supplier to the Empire. The entire cluster was once ruled by the ruthless Overlord Ghorin.

Following the Battle of Yavin, Ghorin agreed to supply the Alliance with badly needed grain, but double-crossed the Rebels by providing them with tainted food cargoes. The Alliance responded by making it appear as if Ghorin was cheating the Empire, and Darth Vader personally executed the Overlord for his supposed treason on the planet Plooriod III. The sector also contains Imperial Drydock IV, from which several Interdictor cruisers departed to join the Outer Rim Imperial fleet. [MTS, FP]

Great Heep A huge droid, it was used by the Empire to mine fuel ore on the planet Biitu. The Great Heep's body was made up of various droid parts and tubing, with one side filled with visible pistons that bounced up and down. Grinder blades filled its huge mouth and two humans were always busy shoveling fuel into its massive boilers. Tiny robots lived on its hull like mechanical parasites. It got its energy by devouring R2 units, and kept R2-D2 in its "harem" before the astromech droid was rescued by C-3PO and human companions. [TGH]

Greedo

Great Hyperspace War An ancient conflict between agents of the light and dark sides of the Force. [DLS]

Great Leader of the Second Imperium Some twenty years after the Battle of Endor, and more than a decade after the last of the clones of Emperor Palpatine were destroyed, had another clone arisen and become the head of a coalition seeking to reestablish the Empire? The Great Leader of the Second Imperium was supposedly that clone. The Emperor's image was transmitted regularly to the Shadow Academy. Although the academy leader, Brakiss, found it difficult to imagine how the Emperor had survived, he knew that with the Force many things were possible.

The Great Leader was transported to the Shadow Academy sealed within a room-sized containment unit. Brakiss eventually discovered that the Great Leader wasn't a Palpatine clone but a series of recordings and props used by four of Palpatine's most loyal guards to trick the galaxy into thinking that the Emperor had returned to rule the Second Imperium. [YJK]

Great Sith War A cataclysmic conflict fought approximately 4,000 years before the Galactic Civil War, it pitted the evil Brotherhood of the Sith against the Jedi Knights and the Galactic Republic. [DA]

Greck, Olag A criminal, he kept crossing the path of C-3PO and R2-D2 in the early years of the Empire. [D]

Greeb-Streebling Cluster A cluster located in the Ninth Quadrant near the Senex and Juvex sectors. [COJ]

Greedo Green-skinned and foul-smelling, the Rodian always wanted to be a bounty hunter; he just went after the wrong bounty one day at the Mos Eisley cantina.

Like others of his species from the planet Rodia in the Tyrius star system, he had large multifaceted purple eyes, spines on the ridge of his skull, and a tapirlike nose. Bounty

Admiral Griff

hunting is a noble profession among Rodians, and he was taken under the wing of the Diollan bounty hunter, Spurch "Warhog" Goa, who eventually brought him to Tatooine. Greedo applied for a position with crime lord Jabba the Hutt, who already had several other Rodian henchmen.

Greedo had had run-ins with smuggler Han Solo and his companion Chewbacca before, so there was little love lost between them. At first Jabba awarded Greedo an exclusive contract on Solo's head. But a nervous Greedo let the Corellian walk away from two encounters, after which Jabba opened up the hunt and raised the bounty. More determined than ever, Greedo confronted Solo in the Mos Eisley cantina. The two exchanged words, and once again Solo promised to pay Jabba back for the spice shipment he had to drop when Imperials closed in on him. It was too late, Greedo said, barely squeezing the trigger on his blaster before Solo fired back, killing him.

Greedo's death wasn't totally for naught. The bartender, Wuher, ground up Greedo's body and used it in a potent new liquor. [SW, SWSB, SWCG, TMEC]

greel wood A rare and expensive wood, it is used to make furniture such as tables and chairs and provide the finishing touches to expensive speeders. Greel Wood Logging Corporation harvests the wood from the worlds of Pii3 and Pii4. [SOTE, HLL, SWAJ]

Green A human lieutenant, or Vigo, of the Black Sun criminal organization headed by Prince Xizor. While Green was one of the smartest of the Vigo, he was also a traitor to Black Sun who was exposed and promptly executed by Guri, Xizor's human replica droid aide, who choked him to death. [SOTE]

Greenies *See* Mimban

Green Leader The comm-unit designation for the commander of Green Wing, one of the four main Rebel starfighter battle groups at the Battle of Endor. Piloting A-wing starfighters, Green Leader and his group fired the last blaster salvo that caused the disabled Super Star Destroyer *Executor* to crash into the second Death Star. Green Leader died in this assault. [RJ, RJN]

Green Squadron A battle group of B-wing and Y-wing fighters that fought in the Battle of Calamari. [DE]

Green Wing One of the four main Rebel starfighter battle groups at the Battle of Endor, it was also the comm-unit designation for Green Leader's second-in-command. Green Wing accompanied Red Leader (Wedge Antilles), Gold Leader (Lando Calrissian), and Blue Leader on an assault of an Imperial communications ship. Green Wing lost his life in the effort, but gave the others the opportunity to destroy the enemy vessel. [RJ, RJN]

Grendu A Bothan trader in rare antiques, he originally sent the rancor that ended up in Jabba the Hutt's palace on Tatooine. [TJP, GG5]

G'rho This outpost was apparently one of the first planets attacked by the reptilian Ssi-ruuk. Dev Sibwarra, the species' representative to humanoids, spent his youth there. [TAB]

Griann An agricultural city in the Greenbelt on Teyr, it was where the Fallanassi religious order supposedly took its children to escape Imperial forces. Luke Skywalker and Akanah Norand Pell searched but could find no remaining evidence. [SOL]

Gribbet A small froglike alien, the Rybet bounty hunter works with Skorr. The two nearly captured Han Solo on the planet Ord Mantell. [CSW]

Griff, Admiral A fleet admiral, he supervised construction of Darth Vader's *Super*-class Star Destroyer *Executor*. Admiral Griff was also in charge of the Imperial Blockade of Yavin 4 after the destruction of the first Death Star. He and his ship were destroyed when, in an attempt to intercept the fleeing Rebel fleet, Griff miscalculated a hyperspace jump and dropped out of hyperspace nearly landing on the *Executor*. [CSW]

Griggs, Kane A navigator, he served aboard the New Republic Star Destroyer *Emancipator* during the Battle of Calamari. [DE]

Grigmin A stunt pilot, he operated a one-man traveling air show. Grigmin made a living by displaying his talents to paying customers on backwater worlds. He hired Han Solo and Chewbacca for a brief time before the pair became involved in the Galactic Civil War. [HLL]

grimnal A measurement of a unit of time. [AC]

Grimorg A Weequay, he was Great Bogga the Hutt's palace enforcer. [TOJ]

Grimtaash A mythical Molator guardian, the spirit of Grimtaash was supposed to protect Alderaanian royalty from corruption and betrayal. [CCG]

Grizmallt A heavily populated world in the Galactic Core, it was one of many planets that surrendered to Admiral Ackbar and the Alliance fleet in the years following the Battle of Endor. [DESB]

Grimtaash

Grizzid The humanoid captain of a ship that carried a rancor to Tatooine for Jabba the Hutt, he and his crew were killed when the rancor broke out of its cage. [TJP, GG5]

Grlubb A small, rodent-faced creature with a scarred nose, stubby feline whiskers, and clawed hands, he was a petty dictator on the black-market-run world of Peridon's Folly. Grlubb became embroiled in a feud with another weapons runner and hired the assassin droid IG-88 to kill his opponent. [TBH]

Gromas system A system with several small moons that contain the rare metal phrik. The Empire built a mining facility on one moon to produce phrik for use in armoring the Dark Troopers. Following the Battle of Yavin, Alliance agent Kyle Katarn destroyed the facility with a sequencer charge. [DF]

Grozbok A reprogrammed wrecking droid, it acted under the command of criminal Olag Greck. [D]

Groznik A Wookiee, he attached himself to Rogue Squadron pilot Elscol Loro after her husband, Throm—to whom Groznik owed a life-debt—died. [XW]

Gruna, Captain Commander of an Ithull Ore-Hauler that was under the protection of Great Bogga the Hutt several millennia ago. [TOJ]

***Guardian*-class patrol ship** Recent additions to the Imperial fleet, they

Groznik

Captain Gruna

came into service after the Battle of Endor. Two common models of the *Guardian*-class are the XL-3 and XL-5. [DE]

Gudb A gangster in the employ of Great Bogga the Hutt, he led a conspiracy to kill Jedi trainee Andur Sunrider at the Stenness hyperspace terminal 4,000 years before the Galactic Civil War. He carried out the deed with his poisonous pet gorm-worm, Skritch. [TOJ]

Guldi, Drom A muscular man, he was Baron Administrator of the Kelrodo-Ai Gelatin Mines, famous for their water sculptures. He met his match on Hoth while on a big-game hunting expedition. The prey—wampa ice creatures—turned on him and his party, killing them all. Only Luke Skywalker and Callista, who had stumbled upon the party as they were exploring the former Rebel Alliance headquarters on the planet, managed to escape. [DS]

gundark A wild four-armed anthropoid, it grows to about 1.5 meters high and is known for its fearlessness and strength. The species has given the galaxy the phrase "You look like you could pull the ears off a gundark," which means that an individual appears healthy and strong. [ESB]

Gun of Command A powerful weapon that makes Hapan troops nearly invincible in small-arms combat, it releases an electromagnetic wave field (a spray of blue sparks) that neutralizes an enemy's voluntary thought processes. Those shot with the gun stand helpless and tend to follow any orders given them. [CPL]

Gupin A small, elflike species that lives in a large volcanic structure on the forest moon of Endor. The structure sits in the center of a vast grassland and is filled with flowers, waterfalls, and terraced plants. Gupin can change into other forms, though this ability seems to depend on others' beliefs. [ETV]

Gurdun, Imperial Supervisor Power-hungry and vain, the large-nosed supervisor skimmed Imperial funds from gray budgets of other military programs to create the IG series of assassin droids. His plans backfired when the droid IG-88 became self-aware on activation. IG-88 instilled his sentient programming in his equally deadly counterparts, killed the technicians who created him, and escaped to stage a galactic takeover. Gurdun was later assigned to oversee the development of the Empire's fleet of Arakyd Viper probe robots and to transport the second Death Star's computer core to that battle station. He was killed when his ship, carrying the computer core, was hijacked by IG-88 and the assassin droid's army of robotic stormtroopers. [TBH]

Guri A human replica droid, she could visually pass for a woman anywhere in the galaxy. Guri ate, drank, and performed all of a woman's more personal functions without betraying her nonhuman origin. She

Guri

had long, silky blond hair, pale clear blue eyes, and an exquisite figure. Guri's rich alto voice was warm and inviting. But there was a certain coolness about her. She was the only human replica droid to have been programmed as an assassin and had cost Prince Xizor, head of the Black Sun criminal organization, nine million credits. Guri thought that she had eliminated her creator, Simonelle, but she had really only destroyed another human replica droid.

Guri met Princess Leia Organa at the Next Chance casino on Rodia, and brought Leia and Chewbacca back to Imperial Center, where she noticed Xizor's attraction to Leia. She suggested that Xizor kill both the princess and the Wookiee, but he hesitated. Later, Leia bashed Guri on the head and escaped. When Guri finally met face-to-face with Luke Skywalker, she talked him into deactivating his lightsaber and fighting her hand-to-hand. Luke agreed and overpowered Guri through the Force. He did not kill her, though, and Guri escaped the castle using a paraglider. [SOTE, SOTESB]

Gus Treta A large spaceport in the Corellian system. Alliance hero Wedge Antilles's parents managed a fueling depot in outer Gus Treta until they were killed in a fueling mishap caused by a fleeing pirate ship. [MTS]

Gwig As a young male Ewok, he sought to join the older Ewoks on their many adventures. [ETV]

Gyndine An Imperial territorial administrative world, it has jurisdiction over the nearby Circarpous system. It is ruled by the obese Imperial Governor Bin Essada. Cargo ships deliver denta beans to Gyndine's grain market. Animal life on the planet includes the dangerous ethersquid. During the Imperial Mutiny six years after the Battle of Endor, Gyndine protected itself by becoming a fortress world, guarded by planetary shields and a fleet of thirty defensive ships. [SME, SWAJ, DESB]

gyro-balance circuitry This circuitry gives machines three dimensional direction-sensing capabilities. These devices are found in vehicles and droids, helping the machines achieve stability in all three planes whether at rest or in motion. [HSE]

Habassa II Homeworld of the Habassa, who joined the Alliance following the Battle of Yavin. Imperial fighters unsuccessfully tried to thwart a transfer of B-wing fighters to the cruiser *Cathleen* near Habassa II. [FP]

Hadar sector A sector containing the planet Turkana, it was the site of storied Alliance pilot Keyan Farlander's first mission. [FP]

Hakassi The fleet carrier *Intrepid*, flagship of the New Republic's Fifth Fleet, was constructed at the shipyards of the planet Hakassi, twelve years after the Battle of Endor. [BTS]

Halanit A frozen, ice-covered moon orbiting a gas giant planet, it was the site of a small colony of about 10,000 inhabitants. Geothermal heat lessened the subzero temperatures somewhat and created bubbling mineral springs. The colony was started during the last days of the Old Republic. Structures were built into the two facing walls of a huge chasm, which was capped by a double layer of transparisteel and filled with steaming water at the bottom, fed by several waterfalls. The water at the base supported fish farms. Bridges connected the two sides. After the members of Rogue Squadron resigned from the New Republic military, Rogues Corran Horn and Ooryl Qrygg brought a hijacked Thyferran bacta convoy to Halanit, which was suffering from a mysterious virus and had sent a distress call to the New Republic. Former Director of Imperial Intelligence Ysanne Isard then sent the *Corrupter* and the Thyferran Home Defense Corps to destroy the colony. TIE bombers breached the transparisteel canopy and made strafing runs through the canyon. Rogue Gavin Darklighter had been resting at the colony and unsuccessfully tried to defend it. Everyone else in the colony was believed killed. [BW]

Halcyon, Nejaa A Corellian Jedi Master killed during the Clone Wars, he left behind a wife and son. He was a close friend to Rostek Horn, his liaison with the Corellian Security Force. [BW]

Halkans, Minister A wealthy smelter of carbonite and a Minister in the Empress Teta system some 4,000 years before the Galactic Civil War, he was the last to be executed by a small band of Dark Siders who overthrew the government. Minister Halkans suffered the double indignity of being beheaded and then having his head served on a dinner platter. [DLS]

Halla An old woman on the planet Mimban with limited Force powers, she enlisted Princess Leia Organa and Luke Skywalker to help her find the ancient Kaiburr Crystal shortly after the Battle of Yavin. [SME]

Halowan The location of a top-secret Imperial data storage network, the planet also held a trans-system data storage library. Alliance historian Voren Na'al infiltrated the Imperial data net on Halowan by posing as an agent for Moff Lorin of the Fakir sector. [MTS]

Halpat The location of a New Republic field supply and logistics center. During the crisis in the Koornacht Cluster twelve years after the Battle of Endor, New Republic General Etahn A'baht requested that a new center be established, closer to Koornacht than the facility on the planet Halpat, to accommodate potential casualties. [SOL]

Hammax, Captain Bijo A foray commander for Colonel Pakkpekatt's New Republic armada in pursuit of the mysterious ghost ship called the Teljkon vagabond, he was trusted and respected by Lando Calrissian, both for his courage and his intelligence. [BTS]

Hammerhead *See* Ithorian

Hammertong The code-name for one of the long, cylindrical sections of the superlaser for the second Death Star. The Mistryl Shadow Guards were enlisted to ensure that the Hammertong would be safe during its transfer to the Empire. [TMEC]

hanadak A fearsomely large and powerful beast that looks like a cross between a grizzly bear and a baboon, it lives in a heavily forested area of Endor's moon. [ETV]

hang glider Used by the Ewok tribes of Endor's moon, it has a lightweight tree-branch frame covered with animal skins. It attaches to their backs and enables them to soar on natural currents of air, traversing the vast valleys of their world. [RJ]

Hannser, Captain The human commander of the New Republic gunship *Marauder*, the ship that accompanied the command ship *Glorious* and the ferret *D-89* on the original interception of the mysterious ghost ship known as the Teljkon vagabond. [BTS]

Hapan A humanoid species from the Hapes star cluster, it is well known for both its wealth and its jealous defense of its borders. [CPL]

Hapan Battle Dragon Huge saucer-shaped starships about 500 meters in diameter, there are currently at least sixty-three of these mighty ships, painted in the colors of each inhabited planet in the Hapes Cluster. They are quickly recognized by the double saucers that extend from the main hull of the ship, which is about one-third the size of a Star Destroyer. Among their unusual features is a weapons system in which a laser or cannon is rotated into firing position, discharged, then rapidly rotated away to recharge while another weapon immediately takes its place. Each Hapan Battle Dragon has forty turbolasers, forty ion cannons, dorsal and ventral triple ion cannons, ten proton torpedo launchers, and a tractor beam projector. The ship's hangar bays carry three squadrons of fighters, or thirty-six ships, and 500 ground-assault troopers.

The Hapan ships also carry devices called pulse-mass mines, which produce mass shadows, or gravity waves that simulate the effect of a planetary body, preventing nearby ships from immediately jumping into hyperspace. The Battle Dragons joined with New Republic ships in the Battle of Dathomir and helped rout the fleet of Warlord Zsinj and destroy his main starship construction yards. [CPL, SWVG]

Hanadak

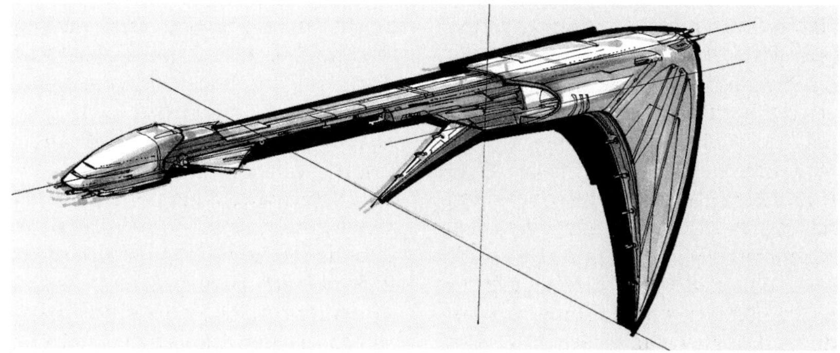

Hapes Nova-*class battle cruiser*

Hapes Consortium A cluster of sixty-three stars with sixty-three inhabited planets, it is an old and very wealthy society that had little contact with the rest of the galaxy for 3,000 years. Encompassing hundreds of governments and thousands of cultures, the Hapes Consortium, or Cluster, was first settled thousands of years ago by pirates—the Lorell Raiders—who seized beautiful women to be their mates. Male descendants continued as pirates for generations until their forces were decimated by the Jedi Knights. Women then took control of the Cluster, and the inherited leadership title of queen mother was initiated. The first queen mother began construction on the *Star Home*, an enormous castlelike spaceship, about 4,000 years before the Galactic Civil War.

Cluster worlds include Arabanth, Charubah, Dreena, Gallinore, Reboam, Selab, Terephon, Ut, Maires, Vergill, and Hapes itself, which is orbited by seven moons. The Fountain Palace on the planet Hapes is home to the Hapan royal family. In emergencies, they go to the secure stronghold of Reef Fortress, which is on an isolated island accessible only by boat. Hapan naval space forces include the feared Battle Dragons and the newer Hapes *Nova*-class battle cruisers; for use on oceans, Hapes makes the Hapan Water Dragon.

Four years after the Battle of Endor, Queen Mother Ta'a Chume, matriarch of the Royal House of Hapes, broke the Cluster's long isolation. Her son, Prince Isolder, soon sought to marry Princess Leia Organa. But Isolder later married Teneniel Djo of Dathomir, who bore a daughter, Tenel Ka. Nearly twenty years after the Battle of Endor, Tenel Ka returned to Hapes after losing her arm in a training accident at Luke Skywalker's Jedi academy. Jacen and Jaina Solo and their friend Lowbacca visited Tenel Ka, and the group got caught up in Ambassador Yfra's plot to overthrow the Hapan monarchy. After a bomb went off in the Fountain Palace, the group retreated to Reef Fortress, where Yfra tried to eliminate them by steering their wavespeeder into a patch of carnivorous seaweed and ordering an attack on the Fortress by deadly Bartokk assassins. [CPL, COJ, YJK]

Hapes *Nova*-class battle cruiser These fast, 400-meter-long combat ships patrol the outer regions of the

Hapan Battle Dragon

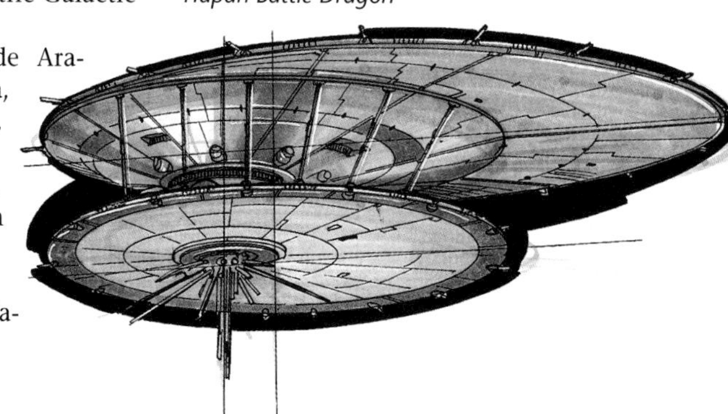

Hapes Cluster and have enough supplies for a standard year of continuous operation. The *Nova*-class battle cruiser is exceptionally swift at sublight and light speed, yet is still well-armed. It carries twenty-five turbolasers, ten laser cannons, and ten ion cannons. There are also two squadrons of fighters and six assault bombers. Because Hapes' weapons technology isn't up to Imperial standards, Hapan captains tend to favor swift, brutal assaults, intending to destroy all enemy ships with the first attack. Hapan Prince Isolder, in his quest to earn Leia Organa's hand in marriage, offered to give a *Nova*-class battle cruiser to Han Solo if Solo would cease his own efforts to win Leia's hand. Solo's response was to kidnap Leia and carry her off to faraway Dathomir. [CPL, SWVG]

Hariz A spaceport on the planet N'zoth. [SOL]

Harkul A vast desert plain on the planet Kuar, some 4,000 years before the Galactic Civil War it was the site of a battle between Jedi Ulic Qel-Droma and the warrior Mandalore. [TSW]

Harona, Lieutenant Ijix An officer aboard the *Glorious*, command ship for the New Republic's chase armada in search of the mysterious ghost ship called the Teljkon vagabond. After the mystery ship jumped to hyperspace with Lando Calrissian, his aide Lobot, and C-3PO and R2-D2 aboard, Lieutenant Harona joined Intelligence agents Pleck and Taisden in their unsponsored mission to recover the vagabond. [BTS, SOL]

Harridan A *Victory*-class Star Destroyer, it was assigned to protect the Imperial shipyard at N'zoth. Because the *Harridan* had been sent to the front to join the Imperial force at Notak, it wasn't there to protect the facility from the surprise Yevethan attack. [BTS]

Harrsk, Supreme Warlord A bully by nature, he cowed nearby star systems by building twelve Imperial Star Destroyers at his stronghold on a rocky planet that orbited close to a red giant star. Giant orbital solar smelters provided energy and processed raw material for Harrsk's construction project. The warlord had a frightening visage. The left side of his face had been burned, leaving only scar tissue and a mechanical apparatus where the eye had been. Harrsk backed down in one confrontation with Admiral Daala, but she pressured him to attend a détente meeting with a dozen other warlords. When they couldn't agree on unification, Daala filled the meeting room with nerve gas, killing Harrsk and the others. [DS]

Hartzig An Alamanian officer under the command of the Dark Jedi Kueller, Hartzig was in charge of the holocaust that took more than one million lives on the planet Pydyr. [NR]

Hask, Loka The captain of the Dreadnaught *Dominator*, he was part of a pirate crew that killed Wedge Antilles's parents at Gus Treta. He had joined the pirates as part of an Imperial effort to infiltrate the Rebellion. Wedge's revenge nearly destroyed the left side of Loka Hask's face. [XW]

Hast Site of a secret New Republic shipyard, it was where the Imperial Star Destroyers *Liberator* and *Emancipator*—captured during the Battle of Endor—were being refurbished for active duty. Imperial spies discovered the shipyard, and the resulting attack severely damaged both Star Destroyers and ruined a large portion of the Alliance fleet, putting the New Republic's war effort several years behind schedule. [DESB]

Hatawa sector One of the sectors where, during the reign of the Emperor, the Black Sword Command was charged with defense. There are more than 200 inhabited worlds in the combined Hatawa and Farlax sectors. A third of the region is now aligned with the New Republic while another third is uninhabited or unclaimed. [BTS]

Loka Hask

Hathrox III Twelve centuries before the Galactic Civil War, this planet succumbed to a so-called plague weapon. It is still listed in the galactic registry as a standing hazard. [POT]

haul jets A spacer expression for a quick departure, as in "Let's haul jets." [SWR]

hawk-bat A leathery, kitelike flying creature found on Coruscant. [JS]

HC-100 A specialized homework-correction droid, it was built by DJ-88, the droid responsible for raising Jedi Prince Ken in the underground Lost City of the Jedi. HC-100 had a human shape with silver skin and glowing blue photoreceptor eyes. It had the manner and bearing of a military boot-camp drill instructor. [LCJ, PDS]

Headquarters A seedy bar, it is located in the Invisec alien zone on Coruscant. The sign outside shows a stormtrooper's helmet breaking into four pieces. Rogue Squadron member Corran Horn wandered in one night shortly after female Rogue Erisi Dlarit had attempted to seduce him. Horn thought he saw Rogue Tycho Celchu talking with Imperial agent Kirtan Loor, but before he could confront them, he was accosted by the criminal Zekka Thyne and his thugs, out to kill him. Escaping certain death, Horn used a speeder bike to get away. [BW]

Headquarters Frigate *See Home One*

heads-up display Transparent holograms and holographs that show tactical and diagnostic information at eye level, they are produced by holographic projectors aboard starfighters so that pilots can stay focused on the space in front of them. [HSE, SWSB]

Heater A gunslinger, he was one of Jabba the Hutt's lieutenants. [SWR]

Hefi The location of a secret retreat where Death Star designer Bevel Lemelisk was reported to have hidden after the first battle station's destruction at the Battle of Yavin. The story is likely apocryphal, based on more recent findings. [MTS, DS]

Elis Helrot

Hellenika, Madam Bounty hunter Tinian I'att assumed this name when she received payment for her capture and delivery of the bounty hunter Bossk. [TBH]

Helrot, Elis A Givin pilot, he can seal his joints to withstand the vacuum of space. He makes slaving and spice runs to the planet Ryloth in his specially modified ship, the *Hinthra*. [CCG]

Hendanyn death mask Seen now only in museums, this ceremonial mask molds itself to the skin of the wearer. The Hendanyn wore these death masks after they reached old age, partially to hide their aging and partially to store their memories before death. The information in the mask can be retained after the death of the wearer. The Dark Jedi Kueller wore such a mask. His was white with black accents and tiny jewels in the corners of the eye slits. [NR]

Hensara system Located in the Rachuk sector, the system's third planet is a small jungle world called Hensara III. Three years after the Battle of Endor, Alliance operative Dirk Harkness and his Black Curs were forced to crash their ship in one of Hensara III's lakes after running into the Imperial Strike cruiser *Havoc*. The *Havoc* landed AT-AT and AT-ST walkers, along with two platoons of stormtroopers, to find and eliminate them. Harkness and his group were rescued by Rogue Squadron, which easily wiped out the Imperials without suffering any casualties in a battle later called the Rout of Hensara. [RS]

herd ships Ithorian vessels, they travel the space lanes like great caravans, selling unusual merchandise all over the galaxy. Designed for Ithorian comfort, herd ships duplicate the tropical environment of the planet Ithor with indoor jungles, artificial storms, and wildlife. On the planet itself, Ithorians live in herd ships that function as huge floating cities, which use repulsorlift engines to harmlessly sweep over the forests and plains that inhabitants consider sacred. The ships' biospheres produce food. [SWSB, GA, TMEC]

Herglic Large bipeds from the planet Giju, they average about 1.9 meters tall. They have very wide bodies and smooth, hairless skin that ranges from light blue to nearly black. Most likely they are descended from water-dwelling mammals, and their fins and flukes have been replaced by arms and legs, although they still breathe through blowholes in the tops of their head. The Herglic have always been explorers and merchants, and they were among the first members of the Old Republic. However, after a brief and bloody struggle, they surrendered completely to the Empire. The Herglic have been treated neutrally by the New Republic. Because they fell to the Empire quickly, they preserved their industries and bounced back faster than planets whose manufacturing centers were destroyed when they refused to submit to the Empire. Thus, many species still view them as traitors. The Herglic are self-conscious about their size and tend to gamble too much. [DFR, DFRSB]

Lord Hethrir

Hesperidium A resort moon in the Coruscant system, Hesperidium features ornate architecture, luxurious accommodations, fountains, fruit trees, and singing warbleflowers. Emperor Palpatine kept a home on Hesperidium for his concubines. The New Republic maintains several villas to house visiting diplomats. The moon is the site of many pleasure-domes, some of which use synthdroids, centrally controlled mechanicals covered in quasi-living flesh. Nine years after the Battle of Endor, Leia Organa Solo departed from Hesperidium on her way to a secret visit to the Meridian sector. [POT]

Hethrir, Lord A onetime student of the dark side under Darth Vader himself and a former Imperial Procurator of Justice, he thought nothing of subjecting even his own flesh and blood to the cruelest of fates. Lord Hethrir was a Firrerreon, with gold-, copper-, and cinnamon-striped hair, pale skin, and double-lidded black eyes.

He and his lover, Rillao, had trained with Vader, but she followed the light side. When Rillao became pregnant she hid from both men by fleeing to a distant planet. Eventually Hethrir found and imprisoned Rillao and turned their son Tigris—who had no Force powers—into a slave. Hethrir's evil knew no bounds. He abducted a freighter full of his own people and sent them to colonize distant planets; then he destroyed his homeworld, killing millions. After the death of Emperor Palpatine, he started an Empire Reborn movement from his worldcraft, which was the size of a small planet. He also started kidnapping children, enslaving those who did not have Force powers and training those who did in the ways of the dark side.

Hethrir sought a final breakthrough, which he intended to achieve with the help of the Waru, a creature aboard Crseih Research Station. The Waru seemed to be a faith healer, but in reality robbed life forces from some of its victims, feeding its own Force-like power. They needed a child exceptionally strong in the Force, so Hethrir kidnapped young Anakin Solo along with his older brother and sister, the twins Jacen and Jaina. The plot was thwarted when Rillao, freed by Leia Organa Solo, told Tigris that Hethrir was his father, and the young man helped Anakin escape. The stricken Waru pulled Hethrir into his energy field and destroyed them both. [CS, SWCG]

Hextrophon, Arhul The executive secretary and master historian for the Alliance High Command. [SWSB, GG1]

H'gaard One of the two largest moons orbiting the planet Bespin, it and its smaller sister moon, Drudonna, are together known as the Twins. H'gaard, only five kilometers in diameter, is composed mainly of ice and appears as a large green sphere in Bespin's night sky. [GG2]

hibernation Common slang for the rest periods of computers and droids. [TBH]

hibernation sickness A disorder that may result when a person is brought out of suspended animation, it is characterized by temporary blindness, disorientation, muscle stiffness and weakness, hypersensitivity, and occasionally madness. Han Solo suffered a mild case of hibernation sickness after he was released from his carbonite prison by Princess Leia Organa. [RJ]

Hig A slender blue species. Ginbotham, a skilled pilot who served with Wedge Antilles as a member of the command crew on the *Yavin*, is a Hig. [NR]

High Council of Alderaan The legislative body that controlled the planetary government. [SWR]

High Court of Alderaan The royal house that presided over the planet's High Council. [SWR]

Hija, Lieutenant The Imperial chief gunnery officer aboard the Star Destroyer *Devastator*, he was at his post when his ship overtook and captured the *Tantive IV* with Princess Leia Organa aboard, in the Tatooine star system. Years earlier Hija had fired the shots that destroyed the Empire's Falleen biological warfare facility to cover up a mishap. The devastation led to the death of the family of Prince Xizor, head of the Black Sun criminal organization. [SWN, SOTESB]

Hijarna A deserted, battle-scarred planet, it was first discovered by the Fifth Alderaanian Expedition. Atop a bluff sits the crumbling fortress of Hijarna, made of hard black stone and probably abandoned a thousand years before its discovery. The fortress overlooks a plain crossed with deep ravines and marked with indications of former devastation. Whether the fortress was built to defend against this destruction or was somehow the cause of it is unclear. Talon Karrde called a meeting with his fellow smugglers in Hijarna's fortress to discuss actions against Grand Admiral Thrawn. [LC]

Hilse, Chad An Alderaanian ensign trooper, he served aboard the Rebel blockade runner *Tantive IV*. Hilse was a loyal Rebel volunteer dedicated to defeating the Empire. He had trained in starship and ground combat. He died aboard the *Tantive IV* as he and his fellow soldiers were trying to hold off an entire Star Destroyer's company of stormtroopers. [CCG]

Hin A Yuzzem miner, he helped Luke Skywalker and Princess Leia Organa escape from Captain-Supervisor Grammel's prison on the planet Mimban (Circarpous V). Later, Hin rescued Luke at the Temple of Pomojema. [SME]

Hinthra A specially modified starship belonging to Elis Helrot, a Givin pilot who makes slaving and spice runs. [CCG]

hinwuine The right granted to offworlders who visit Gand to speak of themselves in the first person and to use personal pronouns in conversation. Without this right, to speak of themselves in the first person would be considered rude or even vulgar in Gand society. [BW]

Hirf, Qlaern A Vratix native from the planet Thyferra, he was a member of the Ashern Circle, which was considered a terrorist group by the humans controlling the planet. Qlaern Hirf alerted New Republic Intelligence to the location of bacta stored aboard the space station at Yag'Dhul. When the *Pulsar Skate* arrived at the station to load the bacta, Hirf hid aboard the ship and once on Coruscant made contact with government leaders. Hirf had come to find a cure for the Krytos virus, which affected only nonhumanoids, and for a time was allowed to work in the lab where Imperial General Derricote had developed the virus. Because of the highly secretive nature of the project and its potential importance to the future of the New Republic, it was decided to relocate Hirf's experiments to the Alderaan Biotics hydroponics facility on Borleias. [BW]

Hirken, Viceprex Mirkovig The administrator of the Corporate Sector Authority's installation on Mytus VII, otherwise known as Stars' End, he was a tall, handsome, patriarchal figure who was always impeccably dressed. [HSE]

Hissa, Grand Moff Trusted by Trioculus, the pretender to the throne of Emperor Palpatine, Hissa was appointed by the onetime slave lord as head of the Empire's Central Committee of Grand Moffs some time after the Battle of Endor. Grand Moff Hissa, humanoid, but with slightly pointed ears and teeth, lost his arms and legs in a mishap with toxic waste on the planet Duro. Hissa moved around in a repulsorlift chair, his arms replaced with those of an assassin droid. [GDV, MMY, PDS]

Hissal A scholar and academic from the University of Rudrig, he brought guidance and aid to his home planet of Brigia. A tall, purple-skinned humanoid, he temporarily employed Han Solo and Chewbacca prior to the pair's involvement in the Galactic Civil War. [HLL]

H'ken system Located in the Corva sector of the Outer Rim, the system contains a twenty-kilometer-wide asteroid belt. After the Battle of Endor, a squadron of X-wings was training there when they were wiped out by an Imperial warlord's ships. [SWAJ]

H'kig A religious leader on the Core World of Galand several centuries before the Battle of Yavin, he preached a message of strict morality. This angered the royal families of Galand, and the Viceroy finally put H'kig to death. His martyrdom launched a new religion. H'kig faithful then purchased two colony ships and fled the religious persecution of Galand's decadent society. They settled on Rishi, establishing a theocratic government that was tolerant of other faiths. H'kig dissidents built a temple on J't'p'tan after leaving Rishi in a doctrinal dispute. The temple embodied their vision of the universe and of the mystical essences: the immanent, the transcendent, the eternal, the conscious. The temple was protected by the shield of the Fallanassi. [DFRSB, TT]

H'nemthe A planet with three moons, it is home to a species, also called H'nemthe, that engages in a strange mating ritual. There are twenty H'nemthe males for every female, and after mating, the female guts the male with her razor-sharp tongue. Virgin females, who usually aren't permitted to leave the planet, may eat only fruits and vegetables. Plant life includes the carnivorous m'iiyoom night lily. The H'nemthe have blue-gray skin, double rows of cheekbones, a gently curved nose, four conelets on the skull, and three fingers on each hand. [TMEC]

Hoban, Captain A human, he is captain of the transport ship *Star Dream*. [TJP]

Hobbie *See* Klivian, Derek "Hobbie"

Ho'Din A gentle humanoid species from the planet Moltok, they are true

H'nemthe

Ho'Din

nature lovers who dislike processes and policies that harm ecosystems. The Ho'Din choose nature over technology: Their very name means "walking flower," an apt description. Their flesh hangs loosely over their lanky three-meter-high frames. The thick, snakelike tresses that adorn their heads are covered with gleaming red and violet scales. Their natural-medicine techniques are recognized throughout the galaxy. [GG4, LCJ, HESB, LC]

Hoff Hoff's father, Colby Hoff, was a pesky business rival of Prince Xizor, the Black Sun leader, so Xizor ordered Colby's murder. In retaliation, Hoff, the son, attacked Xizor inside a supposedly well-protected corridor in the core of Imperial Center. Xizor made short work of dispatching his attacker. The guard who had been on duty at the checkpoint where Hoff had entered the protected corridor mysteriously vanished, so Xizor was never able to determine who had let Hoff in, although he suspected Darth Vader. [SOTE]

Hokuum stations In bars and casinos throughout the galaxy, these stations provide for the tastes of those beings who prefer nonliquid stimulants, such as glitterstim and other spices. [NR]

hold-parents Also known as a hold-mother or hold-father among a variety of galactic cultures, they often bring toys and treats to the children of very good friends. They assume the role of close adult relatives such as aunts and uncles. [CS]

Hollan D1 sector This sector was the site of the destruction of a vital Imperial storage area by the Alliance following the Battle of Yavin. Rebel pilots used captured ships from Overlord Ghorin in the attack, successfully discrediting Ghorin in the eyes of the Empire. [FP]

Hollastin Seven Located in the Hollastin system, the planet is the base of operations for the crime lord Glorga the Hutt. During the Second Hollastin Insurrection, a group of smugglers tried to overthrow Glorga, but they were stopped by the Hutt's henchmen. [SWAJ]

Hollowtown Previously an area rich in vegetation and other life at the core of the Centerpoint station, it became a burned-out hulk when Centerpoint became active and charged up with energy capable of destroying stars. [SAC]

holocam Video surveillance devices, they are used throughout the galaxy for security and spying. [RSB]

holo-coding This communications technique mostly died out with the Empire. Holo-coding was preferred for communicating over great distances because it masked the telltale signs of long-distance communication. Only an expert could recognize the differences between coding problems and distance problems. However, it is often slower than regular messaging. [NR]

holocomm A HoloNet comm unit, it lets owners send and receive messages over a holographic-based transmission network. [ISB, DFRSB]

Holocron *See* Jedi Holocron

holocube A fist-sized, six-sided object, it holds three-dimensional holo

Hologram

images. By moving around a holocube, a person can see all aspects of a displayed image. [HSE]

hologram A moving three-dimensional image, it can be broadcast in real-time as part of a comm-unit communication, or via the galaxy-wide HoloNet. [SW]

Hologram Fun World A theme park, it was run by Lando Calrissian for a time after the Battle of Endor. The park is nestled in a glowing, transparent dome that floats inside a blue cloud of gas suspended in space. Its advertising claims that it's where "a world of dreams come true." [QE, PDS]

holograph A static three-dimensional image. [SWR]

holographic recording mode A recording process for capturing images and sounds in a three-dimensional format; R2 astromech droids have holographic recording capability. [SWR]

Holographic Zoo of Extinct Animals An amusement and educational facility, it is located in the upper levels of Coruscant. [DA]

holomonster Animated holograms of mythological and legendary creatures, they are projected onto hologameboards for use as playing pieces in the game dejarik. [SW, FT, CCG]

HoloNet A near-instantaneous communications network commissioned by the Old Republic Senate to provide a free flow of hologram and other communications among member worlds, it vastly speeded up galactic communications, which had previously depended on subspace transmissions or relays. The HoloNet uses hundreds of thousands of non-mass transceivers connected through hyperspace simutunnels and routed through massive computer sorters and decoders. Large portions of the HoloNet were shut down when Emperor Palpatine assumed power to keep news of the Empire's atrocities from spreading quickly. [ISB, DFRSB]

holoprojector A device that uses modulasers to broadcast real-time or recorded moving three-dimensional images. [HSE, DFRSB]

holoshroud A false holographic projection, it can be used for deception in covert operations. [TMEC]

Holowan Laboratories A company enlisted by Imperial Supervisor Gundon to design and build the IG series of assassin droids. [TBH]

Holy Children of Asrat Orphans who lived secluded in a temple, they dedicated their lives to doing good. When they denounced the Emperor and his violent ways, Imperials hired the bounty hunter Dengar to wipe the orphans out. It is rumored that Dengar refused the job and was booted from Imperial service. [TBH]

Home One A Mon Calamari-designed starship, it was Admiral Ackbar's personal flagship during the Battle of Endor. The vessel, also referred to as the Headquarters Frigate, was cylindrical and organically artistic, with a fluid surface. Armed for war, *Home One* had twenty-nine turbolaser batteries, thirty-six mini-ion cannons, multiple shield and tractor-beam projectors, and twenty hangar bays for its ten starfighter squadrons and other vessels. *Home One* was also the Alliance command center during the reconquest of Coruscant. [RJ, BW]

Honoghr A planet with three moons in the Honoghr system, it is the homeworld of the fierce Noghri. Honoghr is a devastated world; almost all of its plant and animal life has been destroyed. From space it appears to be uniformly brown, broken only by the occasional blue lake and the green area known as the Clean Lands. The main city of Nystao is located in the center of the Clean Land and is home to the Common Room of Honoghr within the Grand Dukha. It is the only city with adequate spacecraft repair facilities. The Noghri people are divided into clans (including Kihm'bar, Bakh'tor, Eikh'mir, and Hakh'khar) that have had a long history of bloody rivalry. Each clan is ruled by a dynast, and female maitrakhs lead family or subclan units. In the center of each village is a cylindrical building called a dukha, constructed of polished wood encircled by a metal band. Dukhas contain the clan High Seat and a genealogical chart carved into one wall. Animal life on Honoghr included the carnivorous stava.

During a battle in the Clone Wars, a starship crashed on Honoghr's surface, setting off catastrophic groundquakes and releasing toxic chemicals into the atmosphere. Darth Vader offered Imperial assistance, and teams of deadly Noghri commandos joined the Empire in return for the Emperor's promise to help restore their world. Noghri clans were relocated to

HoloNet transmission

Hoole

the Clean Lands, and Imperial decontamination droids set to work apparently renewing the soil. In reality, the Empire seeded Honoghr with a hybrid form of kholm-grass that inhibited all other plant growth, keeping the planet lifeless for generations and forcing the Noghri to remain in the Emperor's debt.

Before Vader's death, he named Grand Admiral Thrawn his designated heir and ruler of the Noghri commandos. But the Noghri renounced their service to Thrawn after Leia Organa Solo showed them the extent of the Empire's treachery, and they began to grow new crops along the banks of a hidden river running between two jagged cliffs. Still, after Thrawn's defeat, the New Republic made plans to relocate the Noghri to a new world. [HE, DFR, LC]

Hoole An anthropologist and member of the rare shape-changing Shi'ido species, he disguised himself to blend in with the indigenous population of the planet Tatooine to work without attracting notice. [ISWU]

Hoom A large Phlog youngster on the forest moon of Endor, he is a son of Zut and Dobah and the brother of Nahkee. [ETV]

Hoona An adolescent Phlog female, she once fell in love with Wicket the Ewok on the forest moon of Endor because of a magic potion administered by a Dulok shaman. [ETV]

Hoover A quadruped alien with a long, disproportionate snout and large eyes, he was a member of Jabba the Hutt's court until the crime lord was killed and his organization shattered. [RJ]

horizontal booster A hyperdrive subsystem on such ships as the *Millennium Falcon*, it provides energy to the ionization chamber to cause ignition. [ESB]

Horm, Threkin A grossly overweight human who uses a repulsor chair to get around, he was president of the powerful Alderaanian Council. C-3PO discovered that the illegitimate daughter of Dalla Suul—a kidnapper, murderer, and pirate possibly related to Han Solo—was Horm's mother. [CPL]

Horn, Corran One of Rogue Squadron's best pilots, he was a third-generation Corellian Security (CorSec) officer. Corran Horn's grandfather had fought in the Clone Wars alongside the Jedi Knights, so it particularly troubled Corran's father, Hal, when Darth Vader used CorSec to hunt down and kill Jedi. After Corran's mother's death and the tragic murder of his father, Corran had no desire to remain in CorSec any longer. With the help of his former CorSec mentor, Gil Bastra, and a new identity, he made his way to the Alliance and Rogue Squadron.

At first he kept mostly to himself, although he was friendly with wingmate Ooryl Qrygg. Later, his circle expanded to include Lujayne Forge, Nawara Ven, and Rhysati Ynr be-

Hoom

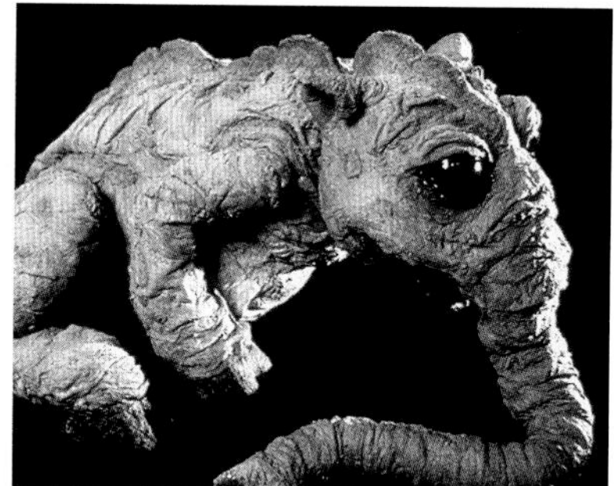
Hoover

cause he had to learn to make new friends, trust others, and become part of a team during training. By the time he made the cut and joined Rogue Squadron, he was promoted to lieutenant based on his simulator test scores.

When stormtroopers made their night raid at Talasea, Horn and Ooryl Qrygg saved most of Rogue Squadron from certain death, although Horn's lung was punctured by blaster fire. Upon his recovery, he participated in the retaliatory raid on Vladet, where a crazy stunt nearly earned him a court-martial. All of his fighter skills and fancy acrobatic maneuvers were put to the test during two raids on Borleias. During the second raid, he had to be rescued a second time by Mirax Terrik and her ship, the *Pulsar Skate*. Horn later was in the thick of things as part of the advance party in the Alliance's attempt to take back Coruscant and had several narrow escapes.

After his heroics in the heat of the Alliance invasion of Coruscant, his Z-95 Headhunter crashed and he was presumed dead. Instead, he had been captured and thrown into the *Lusankya*, a buried Super Star Destroyer that served as a secret high-security prison. He managed to escape with the help of fellow prisoner Jan Dodonna and showed up in the court where fellow Rogue and suspected spy Tycho Celchu was on trial for murdering Horn. He was astounded when Luke Skywalker revealed that Nejaa Halcyon was his true grandfather, making him an heir to the Jedi heritage. Presenting Corran with his grandfather's lightsaber, Luke offered to train and teach him as they traveled together, reestablishing the Jedi Knights. Corran regretfully declined the offer, remembering his promise to return to rescue the prisoners aboard the *Lusankya*. [RS, WG, KT, BW]

Horn, Hal Father of Corran Horn and a former member of Corellian Security like his father before him, he and Corran were close. Hal Horn was killed by the Trandoshan bounty hunter Bossk, who was captured, then released on a technicality by Imperial Intelligence representative Kirtan Loor. [RS]

Horn, Rostek A former member of the Corellian Security Force, he helped his friend, Jedi Master Nejaa Halcyon, during the Clone Wars. After the Jedi was killed, Rostek Horn supported Halcyon's widow and son, then later married her and adopted her son. When the Emperor began to hunt down and kill the Jedi and their families, Horn's position in CorSec allowed him to change records so that Nejaa Halcyon's family was hidden from Imperial investigation. [RS]

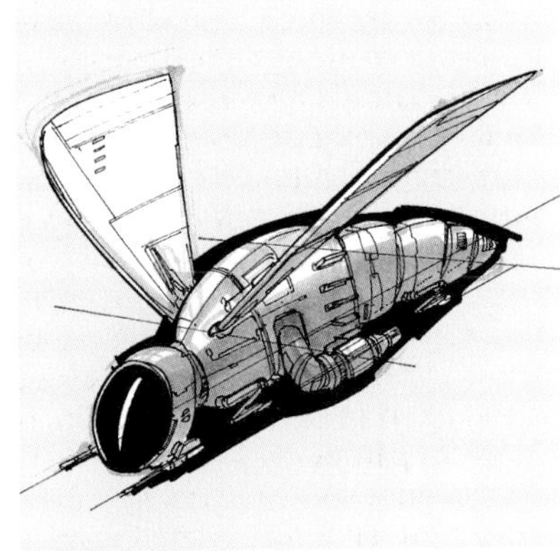

Hornet Interceptor

Hornet Interceptor An aerodynamically perfect ship, it is a sleek air-and-space fighter built by black marketeers and favored by pirates, smugglers, and other criminals. The Hornet Interceptor was originally designed by a group of freelance starship engineers for the Tenloss Syndicate, a shadowy criminal organization specializing in gun-running, extortion, and smuggling. The Hornet has a thin, daggerlike design, with insectlike wings for atmospheric flight. Its biggest asset is its maneuverability. A tighter turning radius and better maneuvering jets than an X-wing give it an edge in dogfights. A Hornet carries turbocharged laser cannons. Han Solo battled a Hornet Interceptor while on a diplomatic mission to Kessel after administrator Moruth Doole ordered his fighter fleet to shoot down the *Millennium Falcon.* [JS, GG11]

Horuz system The location of the prison planet Despayre, the system is in an isolated corner of the Outer Rim far from any hyperspace lanes. The first Death Star was built in the Horuz system above Despayre, and upon completion, the battle station destroyed the planet. [LC, MTS, DSTC]

Hosk Station A major trading port and space station in the Kalarba system, it sprawls across the planet Kalarba's largest moon. The station's proximity to major systems has made it a center of commerce and political influence. The droids C-3PO and R2-D2 had several adventures in and around Hosk Station while in the company of Nak Pitareeze, the grandson of a skilled starship designer.

Hosk Station was originally built as a supply and maintenance station for the Old Republic Navy, but eventually was sold to civilian interests. It now has about five million permanent residents. Commerce ranges from small shops and droid sellers to expensive restaurants and luxury hotels. Starship repair and construction bays fill the station's interior. In its lowest levels lives a forty-meter-long snakelike predator called a hulgren. The station was nearly destroyed by crooked businessman Olag Greck when he attempted to steal a cargo shipment of ash ore. Greck sabotaged the station's power core, forcing Hosk's evacuation. But R2-D2 and C-3PO, working with Hosk security droid Zed, saved the station from destruction by channeling the explosion through the upper purge vents. [D, SWVG]

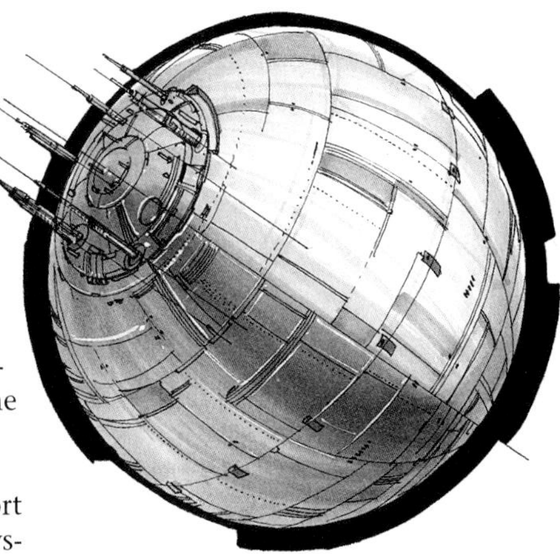

Hosk Station

Hoth The sixth planet in a system of the same name, this icy, unpopulated world covered with glacier fields and circling a blue-white sun was the site of a major battlefield loss by the Rebel Alliance. Hoth is so isolated that it was not even recorded on some standard navigational charts, and thus seemed a good location for the primary Alliance military headquarters—Echo Base—three years after the Battle of Yavin.

Hoth is orbited by three moons and gets a good deal of meteor activity. The planet's daylight temperature averages minus thirty-two degrees standard even in the temperate equatorial zone, and can plunge another twenty to thirty degrees at night. Hoth's native life-forms include the common tauntaun—adopted by the Alliance as mounts—and its natural predator, the wampa ice creature. The many species of tauntauns eat fungus growing in cave grottoes and beneath the snow layer and cluster together in caves during Hoth's bitter nights to keep from freezing. Sights on Hoth include spectacular frozen ice geysers and a

Hoth

Battle of Hoth

1,000-kilometer-long chasm in the planet's southern hemisphere. The bottom of the chasm is filled with water, kept in its liquid state by the immense pressure of the two opposing cliff faces. Several glaciers, slowly sliding into the chasm's depths, harbor algae and burrowing, algae-feeding ice worms.

Following the Battle of Yavin, Luke Skywalker crashed on Hoth as he was escaping pursuing TIE fighters. He encountered two lifelike human replica droids, programmed to look and act like an Imperial governor and his daughter, who had been hiding on Hoth in order to escape the Empire. Later, the pirate Raskar captured Skywalker and Han Solo above Hoth, and Solo flew the group to a deep chasm on the planet's equator. There they discovered a hidden cave filled with rare lumni-spice lichens guarded by a fire-breathing dragon-slug and barely escaped with their lives.

After the Alliance fully evacuated Yavin 4, it established its main base on Hoth in a series of ice caves at the northern edge of the temperate zone. The Alliance had trouble adapting its equipment to Hoth's extreme temperatures, and wampa attacks proved dangerous as well. Echo Base was eventually discovered by an Imperial probe droid, leading to the defeat of the Rebels by Darth Vader's forces in the Battle of Hoth. An Imperial garrison and detention center were placed on the planet for a few years.

Eight years after the Battle of Endor, a big-game expedition traveled to Hoth to hunt wampas for their valuable pelts. When the wampas destroyed the party's landing ship, the group took shelter in the abandoned Echo Base. Luke Skywalker and Callista attempted to rescue the hunters, but the entire expedition was killed by the ice creatures, and Skywalker and Callista barely escaped with their lives. [ESB, ESBN, MTS, GG2, CSW, DS, ISWU, PDS]

Hoth, Battle of One of the worst battlefield defeats of the Rebel Alliance during the Galactic Civil War, this loss would have been even more disastrous if an Imperial commander hadn't made a tactical error. After the Rebel victory at the Battle of Yavin, the Alliance relocated its command base center—Echo Base—many times in order to avoid confronting the huge Imperial armada. Hoth, despite its terrible climate, seemed a good hiding spot. But Echo Base hadn't been completed when an Imperial probe droid came upon the Rebels.

If Admiral Ozzel hadn't brought the Imperial fleet out of hyperspace too close to the Hoth system, thus alerting the Rebels and allowing many to evacuate, the Alliance's staggering losses would have been even greater. Alliance shields were activated to protect the base from space bombardment for a short time, letting the Rebels evacuate staff and materiel. Imperial Star Destroyers quickly moved into position and ground forces unleashed fearsome AT-AT walkers and legions of snow troopers.

The Alliance had little choice but to engage in conventional combat, and heavy losses ensued. Nevertheless, Rebel command personnel and a surprising amount of equipment made it off Hoth. The successful evacuation led the Rebels just a year later to their do-or-die, all-out attack at Endor. [ESB]

Hoth asteroid belt A nightmarish hazard to navigation in the Hoth system, this storm of rocks sweeps across space with constant collisions and crashes. [ESB, DS]

Hoth system A remote system in the Ison Corridor on the fringes of civilized space, its sixth planet is a frozen, unpopulated world also known as Hoth. The system also

Hoth asteroid belt

Hound's Tooth

contains a dangerous asteroid belt, formed billions of years ago by the collision of two planets. Within the belt is rumored to be a pure platinum asteroid, "Kerane's Folly," named for the prospector who discovered it, left to verify its purity, then could never find it again. On some asteroids delicate crystal ferns grow, which may be a primitive silicon-based life-form. Over the centuries many smugglers and criminals have built bases in some of the larger asteroids, including the notorious pirate Clabburn, who placed huge space slugs to guard his hideouts. After the Battle of Hoth, the *Millennium Falcon* tried to escape pursuing Star Destroyers in the asteroid field and was nearly swallowed by such a slug. Eight years after the Battle of Endor, Durga the Hutt began mining the asteroids in the Hoth belt for raw materials to be used in the construction of his Darksaber weapon. The Darksaber was discovered in the asteroid field by New Republic Forces, and was destroyed when it was crushed between two planetoids. [ESB, DS, ISWU]

houjix These ferocious-looking beasts are gentle, loyal, and often domesticated as guard animals or pets on the planet Kinyen. [CCG]

Hound's Tooth The Trandoshan bounty hunter Bossk's modified Corellian light freighter, it was purchased after the Wookiee Chewbacca and Han Solo destroyed his previous ship on Gandolo IV. The exterior of the *Hound's Tooth* is smooth and rounded, with an elongated, rectangular hull. The command bridge sits atop the main hull and the engines, power core, and weapons systems take up the entire bottom deck. There is a turret-mounted quad laser cannon and a forward-firing concussion missile launcher with a magazine of six missiles. Shipboard systems are controlled by an X10-D droid brain that can respond to verbal commands. Bossk also had an interior scout ship, the *Nashtah Pup,* for emergency operations. [MTS, TBH]

House Glayyd *See* Ammuud clans

House Reesbon *See* Ammuud clans

hoverscout A craft that combines hover engines with repulsorlifts, it can handle most terrains. The Empire's main hoverscout model, the Mekuun Swift Assault Five, operates effectively for reconnaissance, offense, or support—sometimes in conjunction with AT-AT walkers. The Swift Assault is armed with a heavy blaster cannon, a light laser cannon, and a concussion missile launcher. [ISB, DFRSB]

Howler Tree People This species from the planet Bendone speak an unusual ultrasonic language. [YJK]

howlrunner Canine in overall appearance with a head that looks like a human skull, this wild, omnivorous beast lives on the planet Kamar. [HSR]

Howzmin One of Prince Xizor's henchmen in the Black Sun organization, he was implanted with a paging device so that he could be summoned easily. Howzmin was short, squat, and bald, with teeth that looked like black chrome. He was partial to gray coveralls and always had a blaster strapped to his left hip. [SOTE]

Hrasskis Homeworld to a species also called Hrasskis, who have large, veined air sacs on their backs. The planet was represented by a belligerent politician, Cion Marook, in the New Republic Senate. [BTS, SOL]

hrrtayyk A Wookiee's coming-of-age ritual. [TT]

hssiss Ferocious dark-side dragons, they lived in Lake Natth on the planet Ambria thousands of years before the Galactic Civil War. [TOJ]

hubba gourd A tough-skinned Tatooine melon studded with small reflective crystals to deflect the harsh sunlight, this hard-to-digest fruit is a primary food of Jawas and Tusken Raiders. In the Jawa language, hubba means "the staff of life." [ISWU]

Hudsol, Bob A Corellian commander in the Rebel Alliance, he developed strong ties to the Bothan spynet. During the Battle of Yavin, he kept small groups of fighter craft separated from one another to allow several different attacks on the Death Star. [CCG]

Hui, Andoorni A Rodian member of Rogue Squadron, she was seriously injured during a night raid at Talasea. She wasn't well enough to participate in the retaliatory strike on Vladet but was able to accompany the Squadron on its first, disastrous raid on Borleias, where she was killed. [BW]

hulgren A snakelike creature that inhabits the lower levels of Hosk Station, it is about forty meters long. [D]

human-droid relations specialist A droid specialty classification for those robots, such as C-3PO, programmed to provide an interface between humans and other droids or such equipment as ship computers. Primary functions include interpretation and diplomacy. [SW]

Human League The most powerful private militia on Corellia, the league is opposed to any nonhumans in the Corellian Sector. Its logo is a grinning human skull with a dagger clenched in its teeth. The Human League chief is referred to only as the Hidden Leader. The league is in favor of self-rule and opposes any interference from the New Republic. [AC]

human replica droid The most lifelike of all droids, they are a combination of biomechanical, electronic, and synthetic materials. They mimic humans so well that most beings—and even most sensors—can't tell the difference. The pinnacle of achievement has been the human replica droid Guri, who was long the bodyguard and top aide of Prince Xizor, head of the Black Sun criminal organization. Created by an Ingoian outlaw tech named Simonelle, Guri was covered in clone vat-grown skin, looks and acts like a human, and even breathes air. "Blood" courses through her system, and her major organs consist of biofibers that most scanners read as organic. Guri was the ultimate step in the development of such droids, which were originally designed for use in the Rebel Alliance's Project Decoy, a plan to replace Imperial officials with droid likenesses that would secretly work against the Empire. [SOTE, SOTESB, QE, PDS]

humming peeper A small flying creature from the swamps near Dulok villages on the moon of Endor. The hypnotic humming sound produced by large numbers of these peepers causes listeners to fall asleep. [ETV]

Hunchuzuc Den A faction of Selonians who live on Corellia, they apparently are pro-New Republic. [SAC]

hunter-killer probot A capital-ship-sized droid modeled after the Imperial probe droid, it is designed for pursuit and police action. This fully automated droid ship has full offensive and defensive weapons, recognition codes for identifying targets, and an interior holding bay for captured freighters. [DE, DESB]

Hurcha The eighth planet in the Churba star system, it is so far from its sun that it is too frigid to support life. [DFR, DFRSB]

hurlothrumbic generator This device produces energy waves that stimulate the base of the brain and cause varying levels of fear, from mild anxiety to terror. Imperial Moff Bandor experimented with a generator on the planet Questal, but Rebel agents disabled it and convinced the Empire to abandon the project. [GQ]

Hutt Large sluglike creatures originally from the planet Varl, Hutts have long been the criminal underlords of the galaxy. The species escaped disaster on Varl many millennia ago and migrated to Nal Hutta, which means Glorious Jewel in their language. The planet's moon is Nar Shaddaa, or Smuggler's Moon. Hutts have great bulbous heads, wide, blubbery bodies, and a tapering, muscular tail. They are up to five meters long, with no legs and short, stubby arms. Hutts can slither forward using their muscular tails as a kind of foot. Most Hutts use hoversleds or repulsorlift vehicles to ferry themselves around.

Hutts are an amalgam of other creatures. Like annelid worms, they are hermaphrodites, containing both male and female reproductive organs. Like serpents, they can open their jaws impossibly wide to consume their often-live food. Their huge eyes protrude like those of reptiles, with membranes keeping them wet and safe. Like amphibians, their nostrils seal tightly when underwater. Like many land-dwelling vertebrates, their lungs—not gills—bring oxygen to their blood.

Their muscular bodies have no skeletons; interior mantles shape their heads. Hutt skin is impervious to most weapons and all but the harshest chemicals. It constantly secretes mucus and oily sweat, making a Hutt hard to grasp. Underneath the skin, heavy layers of muscle and blubber protect the inner organs from attack.

Throughout history, Hutts have been tough and immoral, taking and exercising power over others. They live long—some claim to be nearly 1,000 standard years old. Some engage in seemingly legitimate enterprises while they build their criminal empires behind the scenes. Their business philosophy is known as kajidic, which roughly means "Somebody's going to have it, so why not us?" [GG4, DS, SWCG]

Hutt

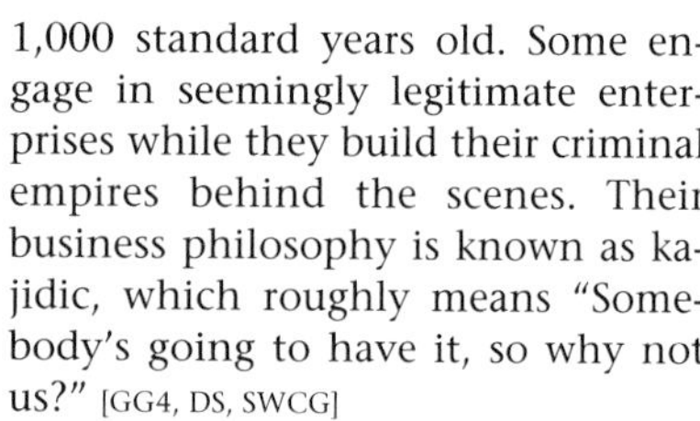

Hutt caravel

Hutt caravel A short-range space transport used by Hutt crime lords mostly to travel between Nal Hutta and its spaceport moon, Nar Shaddaa. [DE]

Hutt floater Repulsorlift platforms used by members of the Hutt species to move their bloated, nearly limbless bodies from place to place. [DE]

Hutt Haven A dim, smoky bar, it was chosen by Imperial Intelligence agent Kirtan Loor for a meeting with Rogue Squadron member Nawara Ven to discuss Loor's surrender to Alliance Intelligence. [BW]

Hutt space An area of space controlled by the Hutt species. [DE, ISB]

Hyb, Mal A capable human assistant to Barada, she was recognized for her skill with a welding torch. [TJP]

Hydian Way A major trade route that runs from the Mid-Core out to the Corporate Sector, it intersects the Perlemian Trade Route in the Bormea sector at the planet Brentaal. Some 3,000 years before the Galactic Civil War, the legendary pioneer woman Freia Kallea helped explore Brentaal space and singlehandedly blazed the Hydian Way. [SWAJ]

Hydra One of Admiral Daala's four Star Destroyers, it was demolished when Han Solo,

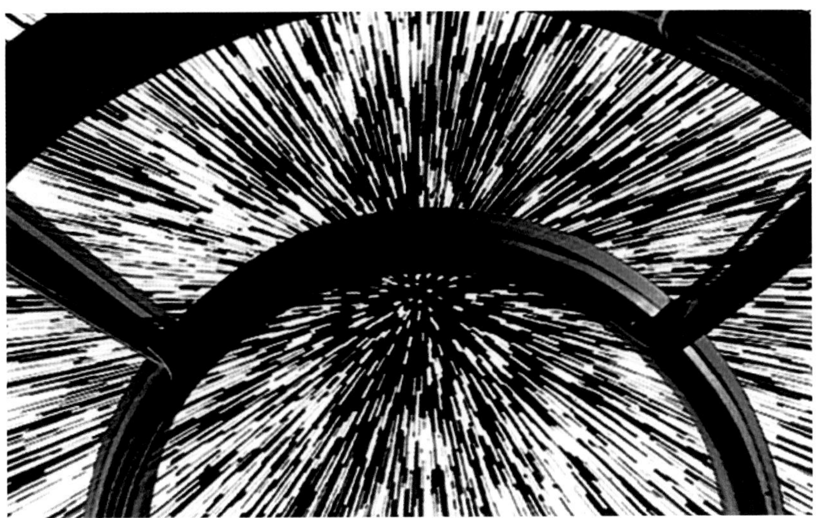
Hyperspace

Kyp Durron, and Qwi Xux escaped the secret Maw Installation in the Sun Crusher. Han piloted the ship through the *Hydra*'s command center, destroying the vessel. [JS, DA]

hydro-reclamation processor A type of dehumidifier, it is used on Coruscant to purge the air of water vapor, collect it, and send it out for processing and use. Because there are billions of inhabitants on the planet, every bit of water is saved to be used many times over. [BW]

hydrospanner A powered wrench, it is used for spacecraft and other repairs. [ESB]

Hyllyard City A frontier town, it is the largest city on the planet Myrkr. Hyllyard City consists of ship landing pits and a number of makeshift structures. A few settlers live in what has become a haven for smugglers and fugitives from other worlds. [HE, HESB]

Hyos, Dr. A Codru-Ji doctor, she has long, gold fingers. [CS]

hyperbaric medical chamber A superoxygenated cubicle, it is used to heal badly burned tissue. Darth Vader often spent time in his personal hyperbaric medical chamber where he could, for moments at a time, actually breathe on his own. [SOTE]

hyperdrive Comprising a starship engine and its related systems, a hyperdrive propels spacecraft to greater-than-light-speed velocity and into hyperspace. Hyperdrive engines are powered by fusion generators efficient enough to hurl ships into a dimension of space-time that can only be reached by faster-than-light speeds. Hyperdrives are twinned with astrogation computers to assure safe travel. Most hyperdrives are equipped with an automatic cutoff, so if a gravity shadow—sign of a mass—is detected in the route ahead, the ship is dumped back into realspace. [SWSB, HESB]

hyperdrive motivator The main light-speed thrust initiator in a hyperdrive engine system, it is connected to a ship's main computer system. A hyperdrive motivator monitors and collects sensor and navigation data in order to determine jump thrusts, adjust engine performance in hyperspace, and calibrate safe returns to normal space. [ESBR]

hyperspace A dimension of space-time that can be reached only by traveling beyond light-speed velocity. Hyperspace converges with realspace, so that every point in realspace is associated with a unique point in hyperspace. If a ship travels in a specific direction in realspace prior to jumping to hyperspace, then it continues to travel in that direction through hyperspace. Objects in realspace cast "shadows" in hyperspace that must be plotted to avoid collisions. Galactic travel took a quantum leap forward with the discovery that, with the use of a hyperdrive, a starship can exceed the speed of light and enter a dimension that takes advantage of the wrinkles in the fabric of realspace. [SW, SWRPG, SWSB]

Hyperspace A restaurant on the Yag'Dhul space station operated by a Trandoshan. Its brilliantly lit decor consisted mostly of white, yellows, and pinks. The Hyperspace was a favorite place for Rogue Squadron pilots to unwind between missions. [KT, BW]

hyperspace commo Slang for faster-than-light-speed communications. [HSE]

hyperspace compass A navigation device used by starships, it fixes on the center of the galaxy. It works in both realspace and in hyperspace. [DE]

Hyperspace Marauder A starship owned and operated by the smuggler Lo Khan and his Yaka cyborg partner, Luwingo, it is a large converted freighter. Suprisingly, the ship is both slow and unarmed—deliberately so. As raider ships prepare to board, Lo Khan uses the *Hyperspace Marauder*'s unusual computer and communications system to take over the other ship's computer systems. Before pirates can cut through the *Marauder*'s

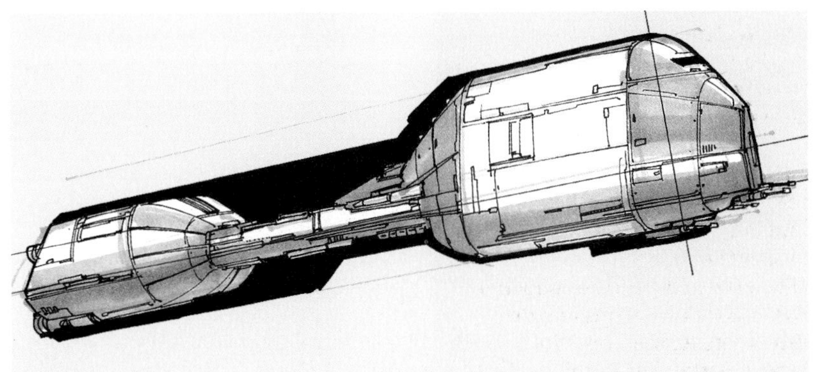
Hyperspace Marauder

hull, they find that their ship is no longer under their control. Lo Khan and Luwingo ended up saving Han Solo and his companions on the planet Byss when Khan allowed smuggler Salla Zend to hide the *Millennium Falcon* inside the *Marauder*. But giant Imperial hunter-killer probots spotted the *Falcon* by scanning the *Marauder*'s interior. The probots opened fire, but Zend and Shug Ninx raced the *Falcon* away from the Imperials. [DE, DESB]

hyperspace transponder The heart of all hyperspace communications systems, it produces the weak signals that send messages through hyperspace. Because the transponders are not always reliable or effective, the New Republic has been pouring resources into designing and building more effective hyperspace transponders. [DE]

hyperspace wormhole An unpredictable natural phenomenon, it suddenly connects distant points of the galaxy by creating hyperspace tunnels. These wormholes produce vast amounts of energy in the form of violent storms. Great disturbances in the Force can sometimes trigger a wormhole. [DE]

hyperwave inertial momentum sustainer (HIMS) A device invented by the Bakurans, it can defeat an interdiction field. [AS]

hyperwave warning A mechanism that sounds an alert when it detects ships about to come out of hyperspace in its proximity. [TBH]

I-7 (*Howlrunner*) An Imperial fighter introduced when the clone of the reborn Emperor Palpatine first appeared, the I-7 is nicknamed Howlrunner by pilots after the wild omnivores from the planet Kamar. The short-range fighter has a streamlined, fixed-wing design that makes it easy to fly in either planetary atmosphere or in deep space. It is easy to maneuver, but because its speed and weaponry are inferior to that of many Rebel fighters, I-7s must outnumber their opponents to win most fights. [DE, DESB]

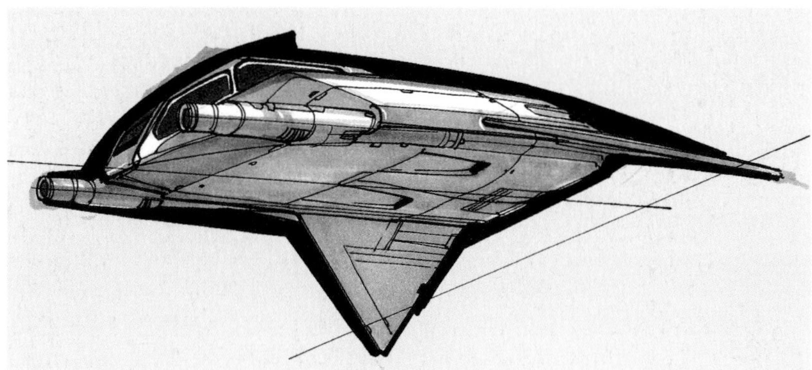

I-7 (Howlrunner)

Ialtra The former village of the Fallanassi religious order on Lucazec, it was desecrated by neighbors because they feared the Fallanassis' powers. [BTS]

Iast system The likely location of To-phalion base and the top-secret Vorknkx Project, where the Empire developed an experimental cloaking device after the Battle of Hoth. [TSC]

I'att, Tinian Her childhood was spent as an armaments heiress. When the Empire took over her family's business, the I'atts resisted and were killed. With the life she knew totally destroyed, Tinian I'att dedicated her life to fighting the Empire, training to become a bounty hunter as an apprentice to the Wookiee Chenlambec. Her tenacity as a fighter and her skills in differentiating explosives by smell alone came in quite handy. Following a daring mission in which she and Chenlambec rescued a colony of Empire-imprisoned Wookiees and captured the vile bounty hunter Bossk, she stayed on with Chen not as his apprentice, but as his partner. She and Chenlambec would often help their acquisitions defect to join the Rebellion. [TBH]

Ibanjji A harsh world, it was the site of a motivational camp attended by Imperial Commander Titus Klev at the age of thirteen as part of his Imperial Sub-Adult Group training. While there, he saved an instructor from a pack of wild varns. [DESB]

Ibegon, Dice A female Florn Lamproid, she was a firm believer in the Rebellion and was attuned to the Force. She fell in love with the Wolfman Lak Sivrak at the Mos Eisley cantina and convinced him to join the Rebellion, too. Dice Ibegon was killed during the Battle of Hoth, but she haunted Sivrak's dreams until he was killed in the Battle of Endor. [TMEC]

Ibtisam A female Mon Calamari member of Rogue Squadron, she had previously been recruited into one of the first B-wing squadrons. Ibtisam was at the Battle of Endor and survived despite being blasted out of her fighter and set adrift in space for twelve hours. She is somewhat agoraphobic because of that experience, but the confines of a ship are enough to temper the problem. Ibtisam took a four-month psych leave after the battle, and when she returned she was assigned to Rogue Squadron because it needed pilots. Ibtisam is somewhat haughty and arrogant, and she is especially disdainful of Nrin Vakil, a Quarren in the squadron. She feels a secret attraction to him and is repulsed by him at the same

Dice Ibegon

IG-2000

time, because he is Quarren and she is Mon Cal. She is also disappointed at being assigned to fly an X-wing, believing it far inferior to the B-wing. After several scrapes, she has grudgingly come to accept that the X-wing hasn't outlived its usefulness. [XW]

ice puppy A weak animal native to the planet Toola, the term is often used in a derogatory way among Whiphids. [TJP, GG4]

ice worms Creatures that tunnel through Hoth glaciers, they leave honeycombed shafts along the outer surfaces as they search for their primary food, algae. [ISWU]

ID profile A ship's identification, it is in an electronic signal that contains relevant information such as name, registration number, current owner, home port, classification, and armament and power-plant ratings. A ship's transponder sends out the encoded information when queried by an interrogator module such as those aboard military vessels or spaceport control towers. ID profiles can be altered, but it's both difficult and illegal. [HSE]

IG-72 One of the original series of IG assassin droid prototypes, he was deemed marginally deficient by IG-88 after that droid powered him up. IG-72 refused to accept the superior self-replicating sentience programming offered by IG-88, preferring instead to remain independent. After killing his creators alongside the other IG-Series droids, IG-72 went off on his own, occasionally resurfacing and eliminating targets for unfathomable reasons before vanishing into the galactic underworld. IG-72 self-destructed in an attempt to capture Republic hero Adar Tallon, killing Tatooine prefect Orun Depp in the process. [TBH, TM]

IG-88 The most infamous and feared of all assassin droids, he carved out a career as a murderous bounty hunter. The tall, slender, gray metallic droid was given pseudo-sentience and independence by his programmers at the high-security Holowan Laboratories as part of Project Phlutdroid. They were repaid by being murdered by IG-88 and three other IG-88 droids that the original droid programmed itself.

IG-88 and his "clones" took over the droid production planet Mechis III, giving special programming to every model produced. IG-88 planned to rule the galaxy one day by instigating a droid revolt with the broadcast of a simple signal.

IG-88 worked in and around the Galactic Core, despite the fact that forty systems hunted him with "dismantle on sight" orders. But he was hard to capture, having already killed more than 150 beings with a built-in arsenal of weapons including a blaster rifle, grenade launcher, flame thrower, and missiles. An array of head sensors let IG-88 see in all directions at once. The droids C-3PO and R2-D2 encountered IG-88 some time before the Battle of Yavin when the assassin came to hunt and taunt crooked businessman Oleg Greck.

IG-88 was one of six bounty hunters—including Boba Fett—summoned to Darth Vader's ship, *Executor,* after the Battle of Hoth and challenged to find Han Solo's *Millennium Falcon.* The droid secretly installed a homing device on Boba Fett's *Slave I,* intending to steal Solo away if Fett beat him to the Rebel hero. Fett destroyed one IG-88 clone with an ion cannon on Cloud City; he blew up two others in their ships over Tatooine.

The original IG-88 hijacked the computer core of the second Death Star, and transplanted his programming into it. Effectively, then, the second Death Star was a gigantic IG-88. The droid was just about to broadcast the droid activation signal for his galactic takeover when the Rebel Alliance destroyed the battle station. [ESB, MTS, TBH, GG3]

IG-88

IG-2000 The assault starfighter of the infamous assassin droid IG-88, the twenty-meter-long ship was designed for combat. It was powered by a single ion engine that gave it sufficient sublight speed to match Boba Fett's *Slave I.* Weapons included two forward laser cannons, an ion cannon mounted below the cockpit, and a pair of tractor beam projectors. There was room in the prisoner hold for up to eight captives. The *IG-2000* was destroyed over Tatooine in a battle with Boba Fett. [MTS, SWVG, TBH]

IG series prototype An experimental line of heavily armed and armored assassin droids, they were commissioned by Imperial Supervisor Gurdun and designed by Chief Technician Loruss of Holowan Laboratories in what was called Project Phlutdroid. In an effort to create killing machines with abilities beyond typical assassin droids, the IG series was given experimental sentience that bypassed the usual inhibition programming. One of the droids, IG-88, became self-aware on activation, and with the help of his counterparts, killed the technicians who created him. [TBH, GG3]

Ihopek The Imperials were forced to leave the planets Ihopek and North following the Battle of Endor. While the two planets were being evacuated, the Imperial Star Destroyer *Gnisnal* was demolished by internal explosions. The wreckage near Ihopek later provided the New Republic with a complete copy of the Imperial Order of Battle. [BTS]

Iillor, Uwlla The human captain of the *Black Asp*, she served under Colonel Thrawn as part of the Imperial Navy's elite NhM squad. As a result of Imperial politics, she and her staff defected to the Alliance with their ship, which was renamed *Corusca Rainbow*. They led the Alliance invasion fleet during the conquest of Coruscant. [WG]

Iisner An older Glottalphib, he was one of crime lord Nandreeson's most trusted servants. Due to his advanced age, Iisner's scales began to fall off after only two or three days without exposure to water. Nandreeson had a slimepond built into his quarters on his ship, the *Silver Egg*, so that Iisner wouldn't lose too many scales during a long space voyage. [NR]

Ijjix, Crando A Norat, he was one of the hostages taken by the Yevetha during their attack on Koornacht Cluster settlements. [SOL]

Ikon A red dwarf star, it is orbited by an asteroid belt. Princess Leia Organa traveled to the belt after the Battle of Yavin to help Rebel sympathizers install a turbolaser. [ROC]

Plourr Ilo

ILC-905 A star system in the Koornacht Cluster, it was the location of a former Imperial orbital shipyard known as Black Nine, which was destroyed by New Republic forces. [TT]

Ilic One of eight walled cities clustered in the jungles of the planet New Cov, it is located in an area rich with biomolecule-producing plants. Ships can enter the city only through vents near the top of the silver-skinned dome. Bothan leader Borsk Fey'lya has numerous business interests in Ilic, and while there he often contacted then-disaffected Rebel Alliance cofounder Garm Bel Iblis. Professional greeters welcome visitors with data card maps and guides to the city. While Ilic considers itself part of the New Republic, it pays periodic tribute to the remnants of the Empire. [DFR, DFRSB]

ILKO One of the master encrypt codes that the Empire used for transferring data between Imperial Center and Despayre, where the original Death Star was being built. It took Ghent, then a twelve-year-old slicer employed by smuggler Talon Karrde, nearly two months to crack the code; a full team from the Alliance needed a month. [LC]

Illafian Point A deserted beach area on the western shore of the planet Rathalay's western sea, it was a spot where Leia Organa and Han Solo vacationed with their children. [SOL]

Illodia Located along with its colony worlds in a sector of the same name, it is home to the long-lived Illodian species. Illodia is ruled by an oligarchy of five clans and has twenty scattered colonies. When the Empire took command of the sector, it claimed to be liberating the colonies but then taxed them more heavily than before. Illodia has been represented by a member of the Beruss clan for millennia; the current representative is Doman Beruss. Generations ago, the Beruss clan built their opulent clan estate, Exmoor, in Republic City on Coruscant. The language of Illodia is Illodian sibilant. [TT]

Illoud system The system where Sullustan Commander Huoba Neva smashed an Imperial-supported insurgency, earning high praise from Alliance command. [DESB]

illuminescences Organic material that glows in the dark, it is made from dried swamp hemp from Oshetti IV and is spun into fine cloth. The glow of illuminescences comes from bacteria living in the hemp; different strains produce different colors. [HSE]

Illustrious A cruiser in the New Republic's Fifth Fleet deployed in the blockade of Doornik-319. [SOL]

Ilo, Plourr A top-notch pilot, she joined Rogue Squadron after the Battle of Endor, transferring from service aboard *Home One*, Admiral Ackbar's flagship. Almost two meters tall with black eyes and a bald pate, Plourr Ilo hates the Empire. Her decidedly short temper is abetted by her physical strength and skill at hand-to-hand combat. She tends to be aloof, morose, and suspicious. Taciturn and stoic, she occasionally will let go with a wry comment. Black humor is her specialty.

Plourr is really Isplourrdacartha Estillo, heir to the throne of the planet Eiattu VI, an Outer Rim world rich in precious metals. After Palpatine became Emperor, Eiattu VI was one of the first worlds to which he sent troops. Plourr's grandfather chose to appease rather than oppose the Imperials, using tribute to forestall being swept from power. Even though his bribes to the local moff kept him in nominal power, they did nothing to stop Imperial attacks on his people. When his son took over the throne, he proved even weaker, so the other local nobles plotted a coup and deposed Plourr's father. The family was rounded up and sent to internal exile. At roughly this same time, the Emperor appointed a fairly brutal moff to govern the planet. Imperial troops were dispatched to rescue the royal family, but before they could, or so the story goes, Rebels had them all slain. In reality, they appear to have been killed by the Imperials working in cahoots with some of the nobles. Even so, rumors abounded that Princess Isplourrdacartha and her younger brother, Prince Asrandatha, escaped. Nobles from Eiattu VI sought Plourr's return to her homeworld to help unite it against the Imperial garrison. [XW]

Ilthmar Gambit A hologram boardgame move, it gives a player tactical advantage over an opponent's guarded position. The player employing an Ilthmar Gambit uses a single playing piece as bait to draw out the opponent's defended pieces. After capturing the piece, the rest of the opponent's forces are left open to the first player's follow-up attack. [HSR]

Ilum crystals *See* Adegan crystals

Imperial Center The name the Empire used for the planet Coruscant during Palpatine's reign. [SOTE]

Imperial Charter A document that contained rules and agreements set forth by the Empire, it governed the rights and responsibilities of all Imperial worlds and star systems. The charter, granted to member systems, included details on the use of resources, rights of passage, military protection, tribute, and colonization. [SME]

Imperial City The capital of Coruscant, it has changed allegiance several times in its long history. During the Old Republic it was known chiefly as Galactic City, and it served as the capital of the galactic union and the permanent headquarters of the Senate. When Emperor Palpatine took control, he renamed the capital Imperial City (and the planet Imperial Center) and it became the ruling seat of the New Order. After the Battle of Endor, Imperial City was declared the capital of the New Republic, although its name hasn't been changed again. A cosmopolitan city, it is always crowded. Under the Old Republic, millions of species were drawn to the bright lights and monumental architecture of the city, but the Emperor closed it to nearly all nonhumans.

The ancient Senate Hall fills part of the city, its carved stone pillars surrounding seemingly endless tiers of benches. The massive Imperial Palace—now the capitol building—looms over the hall, its tapered spires and fragile-looking towers assaulting the eye from every surface. The city's architecture gives the impression of one endless structure that spreads from the base of the Manarai Mountains and covers a huge part of Coruscant's main continent.

Imperial City

Imperial code cylinders

Basically unscarred during the Galactic Civil War, the city was severely damaged later when attacked by Imperial forces led by surviving members of the Emperor's ruling circle and former Imperial commanders. It is being painstakingly reconstructed by the New Republic, aided by many soldiers and giant construction droids. Most sentient life-forms have been evacuated from the deep underworld of the ancient metropolis. Some creatures found living in the darkest corridors—descendants of those who long ago fled political persecution—could no longer be classified as fully human. [HE, DFR, LC, DE, JS]

Imperial code cylinder Issued to Imperial officers, the cylinder accesses computer information via scomp links. Each cylinder is coded to the officer's own security clearance. [ISB, DSTC, CCG]

Imperial customs vessel Light corvettes about 180 meters long, they patrolled Imperial space and performed spot inspections on merchant vessels to look for contraband or undeclared cargo. Their six turbolaser batteries enabled them to handle most smuggler ships they caught. [GG6]

Imperial drone ship Cylindrical, pilotless ships about nine meters long and powered by large fusion engines, they were used for carrying messages. The drones had a self-destruct mechanism. [TAB]

Imperial Freight Complex A huge docking tower and spaceport on the planet Byss where licensed independent haulers brought cargo for unloading. [DE]

Imperial gunner

Imperial garrison Made of prefabricated structures that could be set up quickly on nearly any terrain, Imperial garrisons symbolized the strength and determination of the Empire and served a practical purpose as well. Garrison bases were scientific, diplomatic, and military strongholds for the Empire, and were carried aboard Star Destroyers for immediate deployment. Imperial garrisons, typically staffed with 800 stormtroopers, protected and subjugated planets within the Empire. [SWSB]

Imperial gunner Highly trained weapons masters with keen eyesight, superior reflexes, and a familiarity with gunnery weapons, gunners are part of a special subunit of the Imperial pilot corps. Gunners can be recognized by their specialized computer helmets with macrobinocular viewplates and sensor arrays to assist with targeting fast-moving fighter craft. [ISB]

Imperial Hyperspace Security Net Remnants of the Empire use the new technology of this net to continuously monitor any unauthorized traffic in the hyperspace lanes that connect to Imperial systems of the Deep Galactic Core. [DE]

Imperial Information Center The great computer database on Imperial Center (Coruscant). [DS]

Imperial Intelligence The military counterpart of the civilian-controlled Imperial Security Bureau, it consists of four divisions: the Ubiqtorate, Internal Organization Bureau, Analysis Bureau, and the Bureau of Operations. This is one of the best trained and professional parts of the Empire to survive the Battle of Endor, and its members fully supported Grand Admiral Thrawn's war effort. [ISB, DFRSB]

Imperialization The process of galactic conquest as put forth by Emperor Palpatine. Imperialization focused on the conquest of star systems, the regulation of commerce, and the taxation and appropriation of goods and services for the benefit of the Empire. [SWN]

Imperial Redesign teams COMPNOR-assigned teams, they were charged with brainwashing and surgically altering citizens to make them loyal servants of the Empire. [TBH, ISB]

Imperial Security Bureau A civilian-controlled Imperial agency, it was in charge of spying and other intelligence work. It was created by the Emperor to keep him informed on political events and as a rival to Imperial Intelligence. [SWRPG, ISB, CCG]

Imperial Senate The last holdover from the days of the Old Republic, this body was titled "Imperial" after the establishment of the Empire. All member worlds of the Empire and the Old Republic before it sent elected politicians to the Senate to create laws, pacts, and treaties and to govern the galactic union. In an Empire ever more dictatorial, it was an anomaly. It was the Imperial Senate's job to steer the course of government and administer to the many member systems. Its leader was the Chancellor of the Senate, who was elected by the other Senators to serve as a roving ambassador, arbiter, policy maker, and planner. Once the Death Star battle station was declared operational, the Emperor "suspended" the Senate for the "duration of the galactic emergency," instituting his doctrine of rule through fear. [SW]

Imperial Sovereign Protectors The highest-ranking members of the Imperial Royal Guard, they served as the Emperor's personal bodyguards. At least one was by his side at all times. Rumors abounded that the elite soldiers were empowered by the dark side of the Force. After the clone Emperor's rebirth, the Sovereign Protectors guarded the clone vats on the planet Byss. [DE]

Imperial Star Destroyer *See* Star Destroyer

Imperial stormtroopers *See* stormtroopers

Imperial walker *See* All Terrain Armored Transport

Inadi, Captain Captain of the New Republic ship *Vanguard,* his ship was destroyed by Yevethan thrust ships, and he was killed over a Yevethan shipyard at ILC-905. [TT]

Incom T-16 skyhopper *See* T-16 skyhopper

Incom T-65 *See* X-wing starfighter

Indexer A creature native to Chalcedon, it vaguely resembles an octopus. For a price, it will supply information on the underground slave trade and other illegal practices. [CS]

individual field disrupters These small devices allow their users to break through small sections of force fields. [TMEC]

Indobok An ash-covered moon orbiting the planet Kalarba in the remote Kalarba system, its canyons and mountains are frequently hit with powerful ash storms. The planet is home to the species called the B'rknaa—creatures of ash and stone that are animated through the life force of Indobok's energy crystals. The B'rknaa share a group mind and can join their bodies together to create larger B'rknaa. In fact, the entire Indobok moon is composed of a single adult B'rknaa. [D]

Ingey

Indobok pirates A group of "pirates" who attacked the *Tharen Wayfarer* in the early days of the Empire, they were really chefs who had been framed by crooked businessman Olag Greck for a poisoning that he had committed. [D]

Indomitable A cruiser under the control of Commodore Brand in the New Republic's Fifth Fleet, it served as the battle operations center for Task Force Aster above Doornik-319. [SOL]

Indu San The only habitable planet in the Outer Rim system of the same name, it is a major exporter of luxurious items carved from marbled stone. The low, widely spaced layout of their smooth stone buildings gives Indu San cities, which hold 1.4 billion humans, an uncluttered appearance. Following the Battle of Endor, the planet's chief councilor was assassinated at a meeting to discuss joining the New Republic. The deed was done by Imperial supporters hoping to pin the blame on the Alliance. [SWAJ]

Industrial Automaton One of the largest droid manufacturing corporations in the galaxy, it produces, among other models, the popular MD-series of medical droids and the R-series of astromech droids. Industrial Automaton was formed during the time of the Old Republic through the merger of Industrial Intellect and Automata Galactica. [SWSB, SWAJ]

indyup tree A tree native to the planet Ithor. [TMEC]

Infinity The ship piloted by BoShek. He used it to beat Han Solo's time for the Kessel run. [TMEC]

Ingey The cherished pet of young Prince Coby of Tammuz-an, this small, rare creature was a tessellated arboreal binjinphant—a sort of cross between a kangaroo and ferret. [DTV]

Ingo A desolate world of salt flats and craters, its inhabitants are mostly human colonists who work hard to keep food on the table and their technological tools and equipment in good repair. [DTV]

I'ngre, Herian A female Bith member of Rogue Squadron, she is neither a pacifist nor emotionally remote like many of her species. While fully capable of dealing with things technological, Herian I'ngre is fascinated by things emotional. She is undertaking a study of "heroism," which she defines as an intellectual and emotional subjugation of the most basic and primal desire for self-preservation. Inquisitive and vocally self-reflective, her logic and intellect are tinged with innocence and wonder. Like most of her species, the black-eyed, bald I'ngre is also extremely short-sighted, so she cobbled together a huge pair of band-goggles that allow her to see things at range. [XW]

Inner Council The ruling body of the New Republic's Provisional Council, its original members included Mon Mothma, Admiral Ackbar, Leia Organa Solo, and Borsk Fey'lya. It is led by the Chief of State. [HE, HESB]

Inner Rim Territories Originally known as the Rim, the area was once thought to mark the end of galactic expansion. The diverse and civilized region benefits from being less crowded than the Core Worlds. But as the Empire made more demands, disgruntled colonists struck out to find better lives in the Outer Rim Territories. [SWRPG2]

insignia of the New Republic The seal adopted by the Provisional Council, it is based upon the symbol of the Alliance that preceded it. The blue crest of the Alliance, itself taken from the seal of the Old Republic, is set within a circle of stars that represent the galactic community. The circle is trimmed in gold, symbolizing the right of the people to govern themselves. [HESB]

interdiction field A field generated by a ship, it produces gravity that prevents hyperspace maneuvers in its vicinity. Ships inside an interdiction field cannot jump to hyperspace, and ships passing through an interdiction field are abruptly pulled out into realspace. [AC]

***Interdictor*-class cruiser** A valuable addition to the Imperial Navy's fleet, the 600-meter-long star cruiser is built on a standard heavy cruiser hull but is customized with devices that prevent nearby ships from escaping into hyperspace. *Interdictor*-class cruisers, or Immobilizer 418 cruisers, at first appearance look like small Star Destroyers, but they're recognizable because of four large globes that house gravity-well projectors that mimic a mass in space and thus interdict hyperspace travel. The ships also have twenty quad laser cannons for short-range combat against other capital ships.

Imperial strategy is to place Interdictors on the perimeter of a battle area to prevent Rebel ships from escaping. The only evasive opportunity is in the minute or so it takes for the well generators to charge. Grand Admiral Thrawn used Interdictors as ambush ships and to cut off Rebel escape routes. He nearly captured Luke Skywalker by using an Interdictor to force Skywalker's X-wing back to realspace; Luke escaped when, in a desperate move, he reversed his ship's acceleration compensators while simultaneously firing a pair of proton torpedoes. Later, Thrawn tried to use an Interdictor above Myrkr to capture smuggler Talon Karrde and his ship, the *Wild Karrde*. However, a sudden burst of intuition from Mara

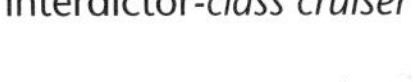

Interdictor-*class cruiser*

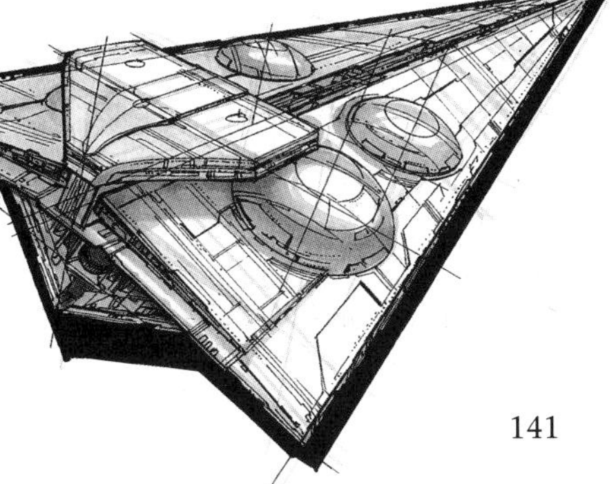

Jade saved Karrde when she ordered the ship to leave the system just before Thrawn appeared. [ISB, HE, HESB, DFR, SWVG]

Internal Organization Bureau A division of Imperial Intelligence, the Internal Organization Bureau (Int-Org) protects the rest of the division from internal and external threats. Its agents verify loyalty and reliability of other divisions' employees. [ISB]

interrogator A device that sends out an electronic high-frequency signal, it activates starships' ID profile transponders. [HSE]

interrogator droid Empire-designed robots that use a variety of methods—including torture and chemical injection—to question prisoners. These black globe-shaped droids have multiple arms with pain-inducing tools and are equipped with personal repulsorlift engines for movement. [SW]

interrupter template Metal panels on ships such as the *Millennium Falcon*, they help prevent accidental damage from the ship's own weapons. The panels automatically slide into position to prevent the *Falcon*'s lower quad-laser battery from shooting the landing gear or entry ramp when the ship is in landing configuration. [HSE]

Intimidator An Imperial Super Star Destroyer, its crew was killed and the ship captured by strongman Nil Spaar during the Yevethan attack on the shipyard at N'zoth. Renamed *Pride of Yevetha*, it was made part of Black Fifteen Fleet and participated in the Yevethan mobilization at Doornik-319. [SOL]

Intrepid A fleet carrier, it was the flagship of the New Republic's Fifth Fleet and carried the commander, General A'baht. The *Intrepid* itself was under Captain Morano. [SOL]

Intruder A light cruiser, it was the flagship of the Bakuran fleet. [AS]

Intuci This planet was raided by the armies of war criminal Sonopo Bomoor. They sacked the city of Bonaka Nueno and massacred its residents in Bonaka Square. Among the victims of the Intuci massacre was the family of Kosh Kurp, who

Interrogator droid

later became the Empire's leading specialist on offensive weaponry. Kurp had his revenge on Bomoor during an attempted business deal with Jabba the Hutt. [JAB]

Invisec A huge area of Imperial Center (Coruscant), it is popularly known as the Invisible Sector, primarily because most citizens don't want to admit it exists. Also known as the Alien Protection Zone, it is home to most of the off-world alien races inhabiting the planet. Thus it is somewhat like Mos Eisley, but uglier, nastier, and less hospitable. [WG, KT]

ion beamer A Ssi-ruuk medical instrument that doubles as a weapon, it shoots a thin silver beam that disables the nervous systems of living beings but doesn't penetrate nonliving tissue. The beamer has a flat top and pointed projection end. [TAB]

ion cannon A weapon that fires bursts of ionized energy, it damages mechanical and computer systems by overloading and fusing circuitry. Although they don't cause structural damage, ion cannon blasts neutralize ship weapons, shields, and engines. Planetary ion cannons, such as the one at the Rebels' Echo Base on Hoth, are mounted in multistory cylindrical towers from which they hurl bursts of ionized energy into space to ward off hostile vessels. [ESB]

ion engine The most common sublight drive, it hurls charged particles through an exhaust port to produce thrust. [SW]

IRD Starfighters used by Corporate Sector Authority police, they are fast but not very maneuverable. [HSE]

Irenez A Corellian female warrior, she was a member of Senator Garm Bel Iblis's private army at Peregrine's Nest. She was chief of security, intelligence coordinator, a pilot, and bodyguard for Iblis and his chief adviser, Sena Leikvold Midanyl. Irenez, a long-time associate of Iblis, had been sponsored by the senator for her training at the Old Republic Military Academy on Corellia. In her early years she was a mercenary and soldier of fortune. The three Corellians—Irenez, Iblis, and Midanyl—planned many attacks on the Imperials and were behind the destruction of the Ubiqtorate Imperial intelligence center on Tangrene. [DFR, DFRSB]

Iridium This planet was home to infamous space pirates who preyed on merchant vessels in the Old Republic until they were wiped out by the Jedi Knights. The pirates used unique Iridium "power gems" that generated a disrupting aura and broke through the shields of their victims' starships. One pirate, Raskar, survived the Jedi attack and escaped with the only remaining power gem. Han Solo and Chewbacca got the gem following the Battle of Yavin, but it only had enough power left for one last shield disruption. [CSW]

Iron Citadel The ancient fortress of the Krath, it was in Cinnagar, the largest city on the seven worlds that make up the Empress Teta star system. [DLS]

Iron Fist A Super Star Destroyer, it was owned by Warlord Zsinj. [CPL]

Ion cannon

irradiators Specialized spaceport lighting systems, they decontaminate arriving ships. Irradiators emit narrow bands of light that kill most disease-carrying organisms without harming more advanced lifeforms. [HLL]

Irugian Rain Forest A forest on the planet Abbaji and home to the only grove of firethorn trees. [SOTE]

Isard, Ysanne Director of Imperial Intelligence on Imperial Center (Coruscant), her nickname—Iceheart—fit her perfectly. Ysanne Isard was the daughter of Emperor Palpatine's last Internal Security Director, and she killed her own father so that she could take his place by the Emperor's side. It was rumored that she and Palpatine had been lovers. What was beyond doubt was that she had risen to power following the Emperor's death during the Battle of Endor, and in his absence she held the Empire together.

Because she considered X-wing Rogue Squadron to be a major threat to the Empire, she commissioned Agent Kirtan Loor to engineer its destruction. Understanding the true Alliance objective in its use of Rogue Squadron to capture Borleias, she realized that it was the beginning of the push to retake the capital planet. If the Rebels were to succeed, she would do everything in her power to make them rue the day.

Isard decided the only way to crush the Rebellion was to bankrupt it, instead of constantly fighting it. She ordered General Derricote to develop the Krytos virus to infect only Imperial Center's disdained alien populace—but insisted that the virus had to be curable with simple bacta. She reasoned that as the planet's alien inhabitants lay sick and dying, the Alliance would do everything in its power to save them, using all its meager monetary resources to purchase the bacta, which she would soon control.

Eager to implement her plan, she insisted upon the release of the virus into Imperial Center's water supply shortly before the Alliance invasion began, even though General Derricote's research wasn't finished. When the virus failed to infect the population as rapidly as expected, she blamed Derricote as she retreated to her secret political prison, the buried *Lusankya* Super Star Destroyer. Before leaving, she placed Kirtan Loor in charge of Imperial Center under Alliance control. When she later learned of Loor's duplicity, she activated one of her sleeper agents, who assassinated him.

Ishi Tib

Realizing her reign of terror on Imperial Center had ended, she departed the planet and uprooted the *Lusankya*, causing massive destruction and millions of deaths and injuries. She then went to Thyferra and supported a revolution that put the Xucphra Corporation in charge of the bacta cartel. She soon gained control of the cartel, and with the installation of Fliry Vorru as Thyferra's Minister of Trade, the price of bacta increased exorbitantly. But with the liberation of Coruscant, Rogue Squadron could now concentrate on Isard's activities, and she was soon besieged by raids on her bacta convoys. Now, more than ever, she was determined to destroy Rogue Squadron.

When her network of spies was unable to locate the Squadron's hidden base, she used another source of information to ambush them at the Graveyard of Alderaan. Failing miserably at this, she decided to punish those who had accepted the bacta stolen from her convoys. When even that failed to reveal the squadron's location, Isard adopted even more desperate measures. She used the Thyferran Home Defense Corps to round up and slaughter the native Vratix in an attempt to flush Rogue Squadron out of hiding. Upon learning this, the squadron allowed an Isard spy to learn their secret location, setting an elaborate trap. She swallowed the bait, sending out all her forces, including the *Lusankya*.

Isard's armada arrived at the Yag'Dhul space station only to find an ambush waiting. Their confidence badly shaken, many of Isard's forces scattered and fled back to Thyferra. Rogue Squadron followed. The battles in space and on the ground went badly for her. During what turned out to be the final moments of the Bacta War, Isard attempted an escape, but her shuttle was destroyed before it could make the jump to hyperspace. [RS, WG, KT, BW]

Ishi Tib A bulbous-eyed biped being with a beaklike mouth, the alien called Ishi Tib, or Birdlizard, was one of Jabba the Hutt's subordinates. Ishi Tib is actually the name of his species. They come from the planet Tibrin where they live in cities built atop carefully cultivated coral reefs. Ishi Tib are meticulous planners, and many intergalactic corporations seek them out as managers and technicians. [GG4]

Ismaren, Roganda and Irek The mistress and rumored son of Emperor Palpatine, they hid for years on the out-of-the-way planet Belsavis. But Leia Organa Solo arrived to investigate rumors that the planet had once housed a large group of Jedi children. Leia encountered Roganda Ismaren and remembered who she was. The woman begged Leia to keep her secret, explaining that her son, Irek, had died and that she was now a fruit packer. Leia knew that the woman was lying. It turned out that Irek was very much alive and, at fifteen, getting stronger in the dark side of the Force every day. Leia finally found the two hiding in underground caverns in the city of Plawal but was trapped by the Ismarens and

Roganda and Irek Ismaren

held hostage. Irek was in the process of bringing to the planet the mighty ship, *Eye of Palpatine,* as part of the Ismarens' attempt to reestablish the Empire, but it was destroyed before it reached Belsavis. The Ismarens escaped into the dense jungles, leaving Leia behind. [COJ, SWCG]

Isolder, Prince The man who wooed a princess and ended up marrying a Witch, he was born one of the most handsome humans in the galaxy—and with royal blood. But neither of these things made life a particularly easy ride for Prince Isolder. When he was a teenager, Isolder's older brother and heir (or Chume'da) of the Royal House of Hapes was murdered by a pirate.

Isolder was crushed, and he spent two years undercover as a privateer until he caught the murderer and brought him back to Hapes. But the man, a pirate named Haravan, was killed in prison before Isolder could learn who had hired him to kill his brother. Similarly, Isolder's first love, Lady Ellian, drowned in a reflecting pool under suspicious circumstances. It was years before Isolder and his Amazonlike bodyguard, Captain Astaria, would learn that Isolder's harridan of a mother, Queen Ta'a Chume, had arranged both murders on political grounds.

So when Isolder fell in love with Princess Leia Organa, her life was immediately in danger. Isolder was struck by her beauty and grace at a diplomatic garden party, and months later ships from the sixty-three planets of the Hapes Consortium arrived on Coruscant bearing magnificent gifts for Leia. The Queen mother's "gift" was an assassination attempt that Isolder himself foiled. Leia was shocked by his proposal of marriage but also found the prince charming and more handsome than any man she had ever seen, with his striking build, blond hair, and blue-gray eyes.

Han Solo also loved Leia, and he kidnapped her to woo her on the planet Dathomir, which he had won the deed to in a sabacc game. The *Millennium Falcon* crash-landed and they were captured by the Singing Mountain Clan of the Witches of Dathomir. Isolder and Luke Skywalker followed their trail, and Isolder met a powerful young desert Witch, Teneniel Djo. After facing down the most evil of the Witches, a powerful Imperial Warlord, and even his own mother, Isolder found himself in love with Djo and they married. They had a daughter, Tenel Ka, whose Force powers got her accepted to Luke Skywalker's Jedi academy. [CPL, HE, SWCG]

Ison Corridor Located next to the Corellian Trade Spine and containing the Ison system, the corridor is a sparsely populated backwater; most freight traffic skips by in favor of the nearby Trade Spine. The Corridor holds four systems in a relatively straight line, starting with the Bespin system and continuing with the Anoat, Hoth, and Ison systems. A standard hyperspace trip from one system to the next takes only about fourteen standard hours. The Ison Corridor also contains the planet Varonat, where the Emperor's assistant, Mara Jade, once worked as a hyperdrive mechanic following the death of Palpatine. [DFR, GG2, SWAJ]

Issor An aquatic planet, it is home to the Issori and Odenji species. Issor is a prosperous technology and commerce center in the Trulalis system. Centuries ago, the Odenji were nearly wiped out by the "melanncho," a sadness so powerful it can make the sufferer go insane. [SWAJ]

Ithor A bright green and blue planet with multiple moons in the Ottega system (often referred to as the Ithorian system), it is in the Lesser

Prince Isolder

Plooriod Cluster. The system's fourth planet is home to the nature-loving Ithorians, commonly called Hammerheads. Ithor is a beautiful, if humid, world of unspoiled rain forests, rivers, and waterfalls.

Three continents have been developed, although they still appear to be overgrown jungles to most visitors. The Ithorians consider the jungle sacred and enter it only during emergencies. Instead, they have constructed vast floating cities that hover above the Bafforr treetops in no particular pattern. (They include the *Tree of Tarintha*, the *Cloud-Mother*, and the Grand Herd Ship *Tafanda Bay*.) Ithorian starships, essentially herd cities with hyperdrives, travel the spacelanes selling unusual and rare merchandise. Brathflen Corporation, which operates on Belsavis, is a major Ithorian trading company.

At times the Mother Jungle has been known to "call" certain Ithorians to live on the surface as ecological priests who never return to their herd cities. All Ithorians are bound by the Ithorian Law of Life, which states that for every plant harvested, two must be planted in its place. A large grove of semiintelligent Bafforr trees, located in the Cathor Hills, was half-destroyed by the Empire. This grove acts as an intelligent hive mind and is worshipped by the Ithorian people. In addition to the Bafforr, Ithor's flora includes blueleaf, tremmin, fiddlehead bull-ferns, donar flowers, and indyup trees; animal life includes the manollium bird, the arrak snake, and the flitter—a small flying rodent that can mimic speech.

Every five years, Ithorians gather at their planet for the Meet, where the most important decisions regarding Ithorian society are made. During this Time of Meeting the herd cities link up through an intricate and graceful network of bridges and antigrav platforms. Years ago, Imperial Captain Alima, commander of the Star Destroyer *Conquest*, forced the Ithorian Momaw Nadon to reveal secret agricultural and cloning information. Nadon, High Priest of the *Tafanda Bay*, gave up the information to save the rain forests and his herd city from destruction. For this transgression, Nadon was exiled from Ithor and lived on Tatooine for many years until exacting his revenge on Alima. Ithor's herd cities are a common destination for tourists, especially young couples. Wedge Antilles and Imperial scientist Qwi Xux once visited Ithor as a safe haven, although the former Imperial weapons expert was attacked by Kyp Durron, who erased Xux's memory. [SWSB, MTS, SWR, DA, COJ, TMEC]

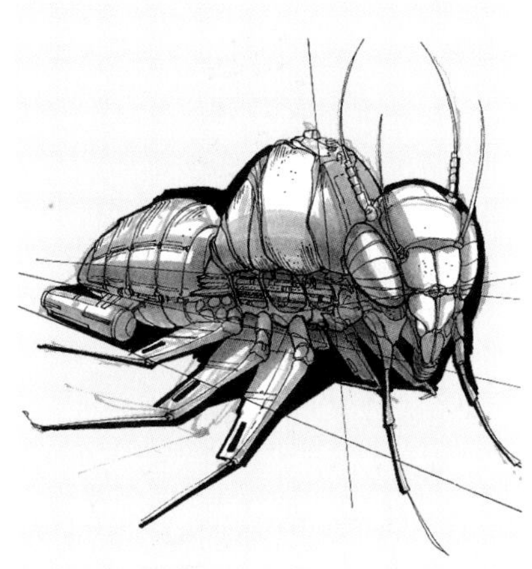

Ithullan ore hauler

Ithorian The proper name for the species commonly referred to as Hammerheads. The nickname for Ithorians comes from their T-shaped heads that rest atop long, curved necks. They speak Basic with a strange twist because of their two mouths on opposite sides of their necks. This generates one of the most beautiful and difficult to learn languages in the galaxy. [SWSB]

Ithor Lady One of two New Republic cruisers sent to deal with a wildcat pirate fleet in the Chorios systems. [POT]

Ithull Homeworld of the huge colossus wasps and the now-extinct Ithullan race. Some 4,000 years before the Battle of Yavin in the Stenness node, the tough exoskeletons of the colossus wasps were hollowed out, fitted with necessary hardware, and used as cargo ships. Several hundred years ago, the warlike Ithullans were attacked by the even more fierce Mandalore. The Mandalorians succeeded in completely exterminating them. The bounty hunter Dyyz Nataz wore a suit of Ithullan battle armor. [TOJ, TMEC]

Ithullan ore hauler One of the most incredible vessels in the galaxy several millennia ago, these ships were born, not manufactured. "Nessies," a nickname for miners from planets in the Stenness node, built their ships out of the carapaces, or hard outer coverings, of kilometer-long Ithullan colossus wasps. The wasps lived for centuries, going from world to world to feed on stellar radiation, raw materials, space slugs, and asteroid creatures.

When the wasps died, Nessies converted them to cargo haulers by carving and sectioning their interior to make room for decks and ship systems. Remaining space was given over to the precious mutonium ore that the Nessies mined. The haulers' main weapons were a pair of heavy turbolasers mounted in the forward section of the chest. [TOJ]

Ithullans A warlike civilization, they were wiped out hundreds of years ago by the equally warlike Mandalore. [TMEC]

IT-O A hovering prisoner interrogator droid, it uses probes and needles to dispense truth drugs and perform surgery. The IT-O (Eyetee-Oh) has sensors that determine a prisoner's pain threshold and truthfulness. [GG1, MTS]

IX-26 A New Republic Intelligence Service ferret ship, it carried an Obroan Institute team to Qella (Maltha Obex). [SOL]

IX-44F A New Republic Intelligence Service ferret ship, it trailed the mysterious ghost ship called the Teljkon vagabond until the Republic armada arrived, then returned to Coruscant. [BTS]

ix dbukrii A tiny parasite native to the Jospro sector, it feeds on the neocortex of the host brain, resulting in scarring that suppresses long-term memory and induces dementia. Imperial medics occasionally use ix dbukrii to disable or punish victims. [TAB]

Ixll Small and intelligent flying creatures that live on the Fifth Moon of Da Soocha, their language consists of chirps and whistles similar to those of R-series astromech droids—whose programming can be affected by the sounds. Ixlls are hunted by tumnors.

Ixll

They developed a friendly relationship with the New Republic's Pinnacle Base personnel and often guided Republic ships. [DE]

Iziz An ancient walled city-fortress on the planet Onderon, it developed over the eons as a great citadel surrounding a low mountain—mainly to keep out the ferocious beasts from the Dxun moon. It eventually protected several million inhabitants from the great beasts, covering an area of about 1,000 square kilometers, and stretching several kilometers down into the planet's crust. Dark Jedi Freedon Nadd once governed the stronghold with an iron hand. [TOJ, FNU, DLS]

Izrina Queen of the wisties, the glowing, flying creatures that live on Endor's forest moon. [EA, ETV]

Jabba Desilijic Tiure (Jabba the Hutt) Son of a major Hutt clan leader and part of a long line of criminals, it was no surprise that he became one of the galaxy's top criminal underlords himself. By the time Jabba Desilijic Tiure—known to all simply as Jabba the Hutt—was 600 years old, he was in charge of a major criminal empire. He had learned well from his father, Zorba, who raised Jabba at his private estate on Nal Hutta. Jabba eventually moved to Tatooine and established himself at a palace built around the ancient monastery of B'omarr monks. Its centerpiece was a huge throne room, where Jabba constantly entertained and held court from his high dais at one end of the room. Jabba's criminal empire traversed the Outer Rim Territories and knew no bounds. It included smuggling, glitterstim spice dealing, slave trading, assassination, loan sharking, protection, and piracy. There was always some conspiracy or other to try to topple Jabba from his throne and take over his empire. He had only one true loyalist, Ephant Mon, whose life he had once saved. Another constant presence was Salacious Crumb, a Kowakian monkey-lizard, whose only function was to make Jabba laugh—at least once a day.

Jabba got most of his glitterstim spice from mines below the Imperial Correction Facility on Kessel. One smuggler on his payroll was the Corellian Han Solo and his Wookiee first mate, Chewbacca. But when Solo had to jettison a glitterstim load to avoid Imperial entanglements, Jabba ordered him brought in. Solo met up with the Hutt after killing one of his

Jabba Desilijic Tiure (Jabba the Hutt)

bounty hunters, a Rodian named Greedo. Jabba agreed to let Han fly some passengers on a quick trip to Alderaan with a promise that the proceeds would be used to pay him back for the missing spice.

Solo got involved in the Galactic Civil War. Then, on his way to repay Jabba, he was boarded by pirates who looted his ship. At that point, Jabba put out an intergalactic hit on Solo, eventually getting him in a block of carbonite thanks to Darth Vader and Boba Fett. But Solo's friends weren't about to abandon him, and they mounted a rescue mission. First they started infiltrating the Hutt's palace; then Luke Skywalker directly confronted Jabba. After Skywalker killed the crime lord's pet rancor, Jabba ordered all the Rebels to die a slow death by being fed to the Sarlacc at the Great Pit of Carkoon in the Tatooine dunes.

But Jabba paid the supreme price for underestimating the skills of Skywalker and his friends. As a fight erupted on and near Jabba's desert sail barge, Princess Leia Organa—who had been put in chains and a skimpy outfit by Jabba—pulled her chain leash around the Hutt's neck, strangling him. [SW, ROJ, SOTE, DS, SWCG]

Jabba's Throne Room A club and bar on the planet Atzerri, it is a nearly exact replica of Jabba the Hutt's throne room, complete with a carbonite-block imitation Han Solo hanging on the wall. [SOL]

Jace, Bror A human Rogue Squadron pilot from Thyferra, this ace amassed twenty-two kills on his first five missions. Bror Jace's family was wealthy; it owned a major portion of the stock of Zaltin Corporation, one of the two major Thyferran corporations involved in bacta production before the interference of Ysanne Isard. Jace's flying skills, money, and looks—tall and slender, blond hair and blue eyes—may have made him egotistical and hard to get along with, but the other members of Rogue Squadron were sorry to see him leave when he had to return to Thyferra to visit a dying uncle and take care of other pressing family business. But Isard, working on information furnished by an Imperial spy inside the squadron, got his flight coordinates and ordered her minions to capture Jace and take him to her secret prison buried under Imperial Center. But Jace's X-wing was inexpertly pulled from hyperspace by the flight coordinator of the ship *Black Asp*, and Jace was apparently killed.

Actually, his "death" was part of an elaborate ruse by the Ashern Rebels working within Zaltin Corporation. They needed him back on Thyferra to help plan for the impending civil war with Xucphra Corporation and Isard. With his presumed death, Jace was able to work freely undercover as part of the resistance against Isard's government. Later he rejoined Rogue Squadron in the final battle to defeat Isard and end her reign of terror against his people. With the struggle successful, Bror Jace was given the task of forming the Thyferran Aerospace Defense Forces. [RS, WG, BW]

Jacques A family of moisture farmers on Tatooine, they supported Ariq Joanson in his plans to draw up maps of peace with the Jawas and Sand People. [TMEC]

Jade, Mara From being the closest personal aide to Emperor Palpatine—with a blood oath to assassinate Luke Skywalker—to becoming one of the Alliance's most able friends, this beautiful woman with a dancer's figure, green eyes, and red-gold hair has taken a very long journey.

Mara Jade was once the "Emperor's Hand," virtually an extension of his will, who would go anywhere in the galaxy to carry out his orders, including murder. Her mission was so secret that not even the Emperor's closest aides knew of her. After Darth Vader's battle with Luke Skywalker on Cloud City—and his revelation to his son and the invitation to join him in ruling the Empire—Palpatine secretly ordered Jade to kill Skywalker. She beat him to Jabba's palace and went undercover as "Arica," but she failed in her mission, and Luke went on to help destroy the Emperor along with his second Death Star battle station. Mara Jade was filled with guilt and vowed to still kill Skywalker—for that was the Emperor's final command.

After the Emperor's death, her Force powers diminished and she became an outcast who had to find a new job. She ended up working for

Mara Jade

smuggler Talon Karrde, becoming his second-in-command. But, in the strange ways of fate, Jade did encounter Skywalker—and saved his life, a favor he was to trade with her several times. She fulfilled the Emperor's final command at last in a roundabout way: She and Karrde had been drawn into the battle between the New Republic and Grand Admiral Thrawn. When the mad Jedi clone Joruus C'baoth called both Luke and Mara to him, then unleashed Skywalker's clone, Luuke, Mara killed the Skywalker clone—and finally C'baoth, too, with help from Luke and Leia Organa Solo. She was finally free of the Emperor's will.

Over the next few years, Jade helped Karrde form a guild, the Smuggler's Alliance, and threw its support to the New Republic. Then Karrde turned his operations over to Mara completely for a while. After Luke started his Jedi academy, Mara became a pupil briefly but left to continue running the guild and help challenge the hit-and-run attacks of Imperial Admiral Daala. She went on

Tigran Jamiro

daring missions with Han Solo and Lando Calrissian, and even became romantically involved with Calrissian. Later, at Han Solo's request, Jade and Karrde located and brought to the planet Almania several Force-bending ysalamiri, which Solo used to help Luke and Leia defeat the Dark Jedi Kueller. [HE, DFR, LC, HESB, DFRSB, DA, DS, SWCG, NR]

Jaemus Home of the major ship-building and repair facility Jaemus yards, the planet is in the system of the same name in the Pentastar Alignment. The yards turn out the *Enforcer*-class picket cruiser for use by the Pentastar Alignment navy. [SWAJ]

jagannath points The increments by which Trandoshan hunters measure the deeds they have done and the levels of honor they have achieved in the eyes of their god, the Scorekeeper. [TBH]

Jagga-Two The site of an Imperial base, it is located in the Venjagga system at the edge of the Galactic Core. The base makes concussion missiles and supports the Imperial Star Destroyer-II *Eviscerator.* Three years after the Battle of Endor, the Alliance staged a feint on Jagga-Two to cover a simultaneous assault on Borleias in the nearby Pyria system. [RS]

Jagg Island Detention Center A prison where Davith Sconn, a former Imperial Navy officer, was held. Sconn's information regarding the Yevetha and their battle operations provided vital insights to Chief of State Leia Organa Solo and Admiral Ackbar in their preparations for battle with the Yevetha. [SOL]

Jamiro, Tigran A native of Onderon, he became a senior logistics officer for the Rebel Alliance. Tigran Jamiro left the Rebel base on Dantooine to serve on Yavin 4. Later he transferred to Echo Base on Hoth, where all entering personnel had to report to him. [CCG]

jandarra Small purple and green tubular vegetables, they are native to the planet Jubilar. A favorite of Princess Leia Organa Solo, they only grow in the desert after rare rainstorms. [TBH]

Jandi, Aellyn The wife of Riit Jandi, the Imperial Moff on Elshandruu Pica. Aellyn Jandi's husband was forty years her senior, so it was perhaps not too surprising that she was having an affair with Captain Sair Yonka, with whom she was in love. They had grown up together on Commenor, were attracted to each other, but lost track of each other during his years of service with the Empire. They met many years later as he patrolled her sector of the galaxy, keeping pirates out of the system's asteroid belt. [BW]

Jandi, Riit The Imperial Moff on Elshandruu Pica. [BW]

Jandoon Located in the Corva sector of the Outer Rim, it is a nearly abandoned world of plains and hills, dotted with the moss-covered ruins of an ancient species. The builders of the ruins of Jandoon died mysteriously centuries ago, and the world is rumored to be haunted. The insectoid fugitive Tzizvvt comes from Jandoon. [SWAJ, CCG]

Jandovar, Maxa A musician killed by the Empire during its sweep to wipe out "questionable" artistic endeavors. [TBH]

Jandur During the early days of the New Republic, the worlds of Jandur and Cortina came to Coruscant to petition for membership. Though they initially seemed prideful and arrogant, both planets eventually signed the standard articles of confederation. [BTS]

Janodral Mizar Han Solo once fought a group of Zygerrian slavers near this planet, then gave the ship and cargo to the freed slaves, Alliance historian Arhul Hextrophon and his family. Janodral Mizar has a law that pirate or slaver victims split the proceeds if the pirates are captured or killed. [HE, SWSB]

Janson, Lieutenant Wes A young Rebel Alliance snowspeeder gunner during the Battle of Hoth, he served in the craft piloted by Wedge Antilles. Wes Janson later became a member of Rogue Squadron and was downed when his X-wing was hit by exploding TIE fighters. The black-haired blue-eyed lieutenant survived the battles of Endor and Bakura, but lost many friends in the Galactic Civil War and its aftermath. [ESBR, XW]

Jantol A New Republic ship, formerly in the Third Fleet, it was deployed for duty at Wehttam in anticipation of Yevethan attack. [SOL]

janwuine The right granted to an individual in Gand society to speak of him or herself in the first person, and to use personal pronouns in conversation. It is the highest possible honor a Gand can receive. [BW]

Lt. Wes Janson

Jawas

janwuine-jika In Gand society, it is a celebration honoring an individual who has become famous enough for everyone to recognize immediately at the mention of his or her name. The individual is honored with stories about his or her great deeds and adventures, related by friends and the ruetsavii elders. [BW]

Jaresh system Located in the Corva sector of the Outer Rim, the system contains a habitable moon orbiting its third planet. The moon, Jaresh, is a dark swamp world covered with hundred-meter-tall black trees and shrouded in a thick haze. It was purchased by Twi'lek smuggler Ree Shala, who built her floating base there about three years after the Battle of Endor. [SWAJ]

Jarril An old smuggling contact of Han Solo and Chewbacca, Jarril was a small man with narrow shoulders and a face scarred from years of harsh living. He invited Han and Chewie to the Crystal Jewel on Coruscant, where he offered Han information about some strange goings-on in Smuggler's Run, an asteroid belt frequented by the smuggling trade. In fact, Jarril was himself involved in these goings-on: the sale of Imperial equipment at outrageous prices to a mysterious buyer, eventually revealed as the Dark Jedi Kueller. Secretly, perhaps, Jarril wanted to get Solo off Coruscant before bombs that he knew had been planted there would detonate.

Jarril was followed to Coruscant, and his trip there got the old smuggler killed. His ship, the *Spicy Lady*, was set adrift in space, where it was found by Lando Calrissian. Calrissian investigated Jarril's death, since he owed Jarril a debt: Jarrill had once smuggled Lando out of Smuggler's Run, away from crime lord Nandreeson, who had a hefty price on Calrissian's head. [NR]

Javin sector An area that lies near the Bruanii and Tungra sectors and is relatively close to the planet Hoth, it is home to Imperial space platform D-34, which guards a major trade route. The platform was captured by the Alliance following the Battle of Hoth but was soon reclaimed by the Imperials. [TSC]

Jawa Intelligent but smelly scavengers of the desert, these rodentlike creatures are natives of Tatooine. About a meter tall and constantly jabbering away in their own language, Jawas have a clan mentality. To protect themselves from the fierce double suns of their planet, they wear coarse, homespun cloaks with hoods; only their glowing eyes are visible.

Jawas travel and live in bands, using giant, treaded vehicles known as sandcrawlers for mobility and shelter. The crawlers can hold up to 300 Jawas as well as the droids and other machinery that they scavenge, repair, and resell to Tatooine moisture farmers and others. They often find water by inserting long, thin hoses down the stems of the funnel flower and siphoning off the liquid there. The hubba gourd, a difficult-to-digest fruit, is their primary food; in the Jawa language, hubba means "the staff of life."

Jawa society is tightly knit, with large family units. There are forty-three different terms to describe relationships, and lineage and bloodlines are carefully recorded. Once each year before the storm season, Jawas make a trek to the great basin of the Dune Sea for a huge secret rendezvous that becomes a great swap meet where they exchange salvaged items. [SW, SWR, ISWU, SWCG]

Jawaswag The name of Rogue Squadron pilot Gavin Darklighter's astromech droid. [BW]

Jedcred Slang for Jedi credit. This coin was struck to commemorate a Corellian Jedi becoming a Master. It was minted with the Jedi's likeness and given to friends, family members, and students. Because of Imperial persecution of the Jedi, these coins have now become quite rare and valuable. Rogue Squadron pilot Corran Horn wears his about his neck as a good luck medallion; it was passed down to him from his grandfather. [RS]

Jedgar, High Prophet Like others of the mysterious order known as Prophets of the Dark Side, this tall human with a bald head, bearded chin, and hooded eyes assisted Supreme Prophet Kadann in his attempt to gain control of the Empire. [MMY, PDS]

Jedi Battle Meditation A powerful Jedi technique, it is used to influence the outcome of a battle by visualizing the desired result. Ancient skilled users of the technique included Jedi Master Arca Jeth and Jedi Nomi Sunrider. [TOJ, DLS, TSW]

Jedi Code The philosophy that sums up the beliefs of the Jedi Knights is embodied in this credo: There is no emotion; there is peace. There is no ignorance; there is knowledge. There is no passion; there is serenity. There is no death; there is the Force. A Jedi does not act for personal power or wealth but seeks knowledge and enlightenment. A true Jedi never acts from hatred, anger, fear, or aggression but acts when calm and at peace with the Force. [SWRPG, SWRPG2]

Jedi Explorer A two-crew ship used by Luke Skywalker at the time of the second cloned Emperor, it was designed to navigate uncharted hyperspace routes. The ship was equipped with laser and ion weapons and had a small cargo bay. The *Jedi Explorer* was destroyed when the cloned Emperor's dark-side aides mounted an all-out attack on the secret settlement code-named New Alderaan. [DE2]

Jedi Holocron A respository of Jedi knowledge and teaching, these legendary artifacts are palm-sized glowing cubes of crystal that employ primitive hologramic technology along with the Force to provide an interactive learning device. Mysterious designs are etched into the Jedi Holocrons, hinting at their true age. A Holocron can usually be activated only by a Jedi, who can then seem to have a conversation with the long-dead Jedi whose teachings infuse the particular Holocron. [DE]

Jedi Knights Protectors of the Old Republic from the time it arose some 25,000 years before the Galactic Civil War, they were the guardians of justice and freedom, the most respected and powerful force for good for more than a thousand generations. The Jedi seemed to have supernatural skills, especially when wielding their lightsaber weapons. But a Jedi's real strength and power has always come from an ability to tap into and manipulate the Force.

However, within the Force itself lie the seeds of self-destruction: the dark side, an unrelenting evil that grants power but is hollow and corrupt at its core. First the Republic itself fell to the corruption of its leaders, and the Empire was born. Then, before the Jedi could move against him, Emperor Palpatine used one of their own to destroy the Jedi. Through treachery, deception, and the actions of the Dark Lord of the Sith, Darth Vader, the Jedi were largely exterminated. Only a few remained.

One of them, a Jedi Master named Yoda, trained young Luke Skywalker as the first of a new line of Jedi Knights. Following the Battle of Endor, Luke started searching the galaxy for other Jedi and started an academy to train those strong in the Force. [SW, ESB, RJ, JS, DA, COF]

Jedi Holocron

Jedi Master An honorific given to the greatest of Jedi, those who are strong enough in the Force and patient enough in life—and even beyond—to pass on their skills by teaching a new generation of Jedi. In the darkest days of the Empire, nearly all the Jedi Masters were hunted down and wiped out. But on the backwater planet of Dagobah, a 900-year-old Jedi Master named Yoda managed to survive to train the first of a new generation of Jedi, Luke Skywalker. [ESB]

Jedi reader A device used by minions of the Emperor in hunting down Jedi, it exposed Force-sensitive individuals. Silvery paddles were run down suspects' bodies, and if the individuals were Force-sensitive, a wire-frame silhouette of their bodies with a flickering blue outline would appear on crystal readers attached to the paddles. [JS]

Je'har A once-powerful race, they inhabited the neutral planet of Almania in a system on the far reaches of the galaxy. Their architecture primarily utilized large, massive stones. A stunning example was the Great Dome of the Je'har. Shortly after the New Republic defeated Grand Admiral Thrawn, the Je'har leadership on Almania changed. The Je'har, long jealous of the wealth of one of their moons, Pydyr, began ransacking it. During one raid, the parents of a young man named Dolph, later known as Kueller, were killed in a particularly brutal fashion. Once he became allied with the dark side of the Force, Kueller returned to Almania and decimated the Je'har. [NR]

Jedi Master Yoda

Jenet A scavenging species from the planet Garban in the Tau Sakar system, they have incredible memories and are considered quarrelsome by other species. These pale pink-skinned creatures with red eyes and sparse white fur quickly colonized the other worlds in their star system after developing starships. During the Galactic Civil War, the Empire turned the Jenet colonies into labor camps. [GG4, ZHR]

Jensens A family of moisture farmers on Tatooine, they opposed plans to try to make maps of peace with the Jawas and Sand People. [TMEC]

Jerjerrod, Moff The beleaguered commander in charge of overseeing the construction of the second Death Star battle station. [RJ]

Jerriko, Dannik Despite an almost human appearance, this tall and gaunt Anzati is a predator who would just as soon suck some of the life force out of a victim as say hello. Like others of his species, he has a proboscis coiled in his cheek pockets;

Dannik Jerriko

in an attack, he uncoils this flexible organ, inserts it into a victim's nostrils, and pierces the brain of his prey. Jerriko not only drinks his victims' blood, he sucks up what he calls the "soup" of their future. He attacks and kills mainly fellow bounty hunters and assassins, scum that few would miss. Jerriko, who takes pride in his looks—and he certainly doesn't look his age of 1,010 years—once tried to overcome his sick compulsion, but failed miserably. He is also addicted to his ever-present hookah. In a cantina in Mos Eisley, he first encountered a group whose "soup" he hungered for, for he sensed a mixture of the Force and fortune. But there, and years later in the palace of his sometime employer Jabba the Hutt, he missed his chance to partake of the "soup" of the men—particularly Han Solo—and woman who had become the heroes of the Rebel Alliance. Frustrated, he went on a murderous rampage throughout the palace. As a result, a huge price was put on his head by a number of members of the galactic underworld, and Jerriko has been forced to wander the galaxy as a fugitive. [SWCG, TMEC, TJP]

Jerrilek A tropical blue world with an impressive set of rings, the planet is eighty-five percent water. Jerrilek's land is concentrated around the equator, and consists of two main continents and many smaller island chains. The planet is a vacation and retirement spot for many of the galaxy's wealthy and powerful. One of Jerrilek's largest cities is Graleca, which is located on a small island and is an important part of the local aquaculture industry. [SWAJ]

Jessa The daughter of Doc, leader of a band of outlaw techs operating in and around Corporate Sector space, she was her father's second-in-command and an accomplished technician herself. Jessa, whom close friends called Jess, was a tall, shapely woman with curly blond hair and freckles. [HSE]

Jeth, Jedi Master Arca An expert swordsman, he taught many Jedi apprentices at his training compound on Arkania some four millennia before the Battle of Yavin—sometimes as many as twenty students at a time. His apprentices included Ulic and Cay Qel-Droma. Jedi Master Arca Jeth was assigned to be watchman of the Onderon system, and he sent his young apprentices to the planet Onderon, making Ulic his "chargeman." Master Arca Jeth was killed fighting renegade droids directed by the evil Krath sorcerers on the planet Deneba. [TOJ, DLS]

Jevanche, Amber A hot female holostar, she is very popular on Coruscant. [POT]

jewel-fruit This tasty fruit from the planet Ithor has a nearly impenetrable shell. But the sweet flesh inside the jewel-fruit is considered well worth the effort. [JS]

Jewel of Churba A Dairkan Starliner, it transported disguised Rogue Squadron members Wedge Antilles, Pash Cracken, Corran Horn, and Erisi Dlarit to Coruscant for their undercover operation. [WG]

Jhoff, Controller An expert in space traffic control, he served aboard Darth Vader's Super Star Destroyer *Executor*. Jhoff was responsible for directing and tracking space traffic into and within the restricted space surrounding Endor's moon during the construction of the second Death Star. [RJN]

jiangs Rare pink jewels, they are found on Corellia. [TBH]

Jindas Members of a gypsylike tribe that wanders Endor's forest moon, they habitually get lost. Jindas make their living by trading with other Ewok tribes and putting on shows. [ETV]

Jir, Daine An Imperial commander who was bold and outspoken, he used constant training and crisis simulations to help maintain high performance levels. He served the Empire aboard the Star Destroyer *Devastator*. [CCG]

jizz A popular style of freeform wailing music. [TMEC]

Jedi Master Arca Jeth

Jindas

jizz-wailer A musician who plays a fast, contemporary, and upbeat style of music. [RJN]

JL-12-F A powerful explosive. [TBH]

Joanson, Ariq A Tatooine moisture farmer, he set up moisture vaporators in a location near the Dune Sea that previously had been considered unfarmable. Ariq Joanson successfully worked with Jawas in the area to create maps delineating land rights. He tried to negotiate similarly with the Sand People, but the Empire ambushed them during their talks to assure the continuance of the antagonistic relationship between Sand People and humans. Frustration over that event eventually led Joanson to join the Rebellion. [TMEC]

Jobath A councilor of the Fia, he is from the planet Galantos. [SOL]

Joben, Thall A native of the planet Ingo with a passion for building and racing landspeeders, he grew up with his best friend and rival, Jord Dusat. Thall Joben was seventeen years old when he encountered the droids R2-D2 and C-3PO during the Empire's early days. [DTV]

Jojo A pilot with the New Republic's Fifth Fleet, he was killed during the failed attempt to blockade the Yevetha at Doornik-319. [SOL]

Jomark An isolated watery planet with three small moons, it was ruled by the insane cloned Jedi Joruus C'baoth when he attempted to take Luke Skywalker prisoner. The planet has strings of tiny islands and one modest continent, Kalish. The High Castle of Jomark sits 400 meters above Ring Lake on a volcanic cone between rocky crags on Kalish. Jomark's three million or so primitive and superstitious human residents revere the ancient castle, which was constructed by a long-vanished species. Several villages lie clustered near the southern shore of Ring Lake including Chynoo, where C'baoth meted out his brand of justice to the villagers from a High Castle throne placed in the town square. [HE, HESB, DFRSB, DFR]

Joruna Along with Widek, it is a New Republic planet located near the Koornacht Cluster. Due to the zealous guarding of Koornacht's borders by the alien Yevetha, all freight traffic had to travel a circuitous route around the Cluster to reach both worlds. [BTS]

Jospro sector A seldom-visited sector containing the Dar'Or system, it is home to tiny creatures called ix dbukrii that paralyze the neocortex of the human brain. Imperial forces on Bakura used them to suppress the memories of Eppie Belden, a main member of the resistance against the Imperial occupation. [GG4, TAB]

Jovan Station The command center for the Imperial fleet blockading Yavin 4 following the destruction of the first Death Star. Its commanding officer, Admiral Griff, ordered a full-scale attack on Yavin 4 when he heard that the Super Star Destroyer *Executor* had been disabled. [CSW]

Jowdrrl A Wookiee, she is Chewbacca's cousin. She accompanied Chewie on a mission to rescue Han Solo during the Yevethan crisis. [TT]

J'Quille A golden-furred Whiphid, he was a former lover of Lady Valarian and spied for her in the palace of Jabba the Hutt. It was J'Quille who helped arrange the failed escape of Jabba's pet rancor and its keeper, Malakili, and who bribed the kitchen boy, Phlegmin, to lace Jabba's toads with a slow-acting poison. J'Quille had planned to kill Jabba with a thermal detonator, but when Jabba was killed by others, J'Quille returned to his homeworld of Toola. There, he learned the jealous Valarian had placed a bounty on his head should he ever leave Tatooine. He returned to that desert planet, but eventually had his brain removed by B'omarr monks in order to escape the unbearable desert heat. [TJP]

J't'p'tan (Doornik-628E) A gentle, pleasant world of garden cities, it is located in the heart of the Koornacht Cluster, known in charts as Doornik-628E. The name is an approximation of four glyphs of the conservative religious sect, the H'kig: "jeh," the immanent; "teh," the transcendent; "peh," the eternal; and "tan," the conscious essence. The first three glyphs are considered too sacred to be written out fully. It was here that the Fallanassi religious community and its leader Wialu settled after departing Lucazec.

After leaving Atzerri, Luke Skywalker and Akanah Norand Pell left for J't'p'tan to search for the Fallanassi. The planet is the site of a H'kig colony, with an estimated population of 13,000, who first arrived some fifty years earlier. The H'kig built a vast stone temple, covering more than 3,000 acres of a small valley, entirely by hand. During the Yevethan Great Purge, the colony was supposedly destroyed. In reality, it was preserved by the Fallanassi, who projected a false image of destruction in order to protect the commune. The Yevetha started a colony on the planet after their conquest. Akanah was reunited with her fellow Fallanassi, and Luke convinced Wialu to help in the fight against the Yevethan fleet. After the Battle of N'zoth, the Fallanassi left J't'p'tan on the liner *Star Morning* to find a new home. [BTS, SOL, TT]

Jubal One of three Devaronians who lived on Tatooine. [TMEC]

Jubilar A penal colony orbited by a single moon, it is used by several nearby worlds as a dumping ground for their criminals. The inhabitants have organized themselves into armies, and fight each other in a constant series of brutal wars. One of Jubilar's cities is called Dying Slowly (later renamed Death), and contains the slum of Executioners Row and the huge Victory Forum, where the Regional Sector Number Four's All-Human Free-For-All extravaganza is held. Four humans are pitted against each other in a pentagonal ring, and the last one standing is declared the winner. Fifteen years before the Battle of Hoth, Boba Fett killed a spice dealer named Hallolar Voors on Jubilar. While there, he saw a young Han Solo successfully defend himself in the Free-For-All against three larger opponents. Solo had been sent to Jubilar for cheating at cards. Fifteen years after the Battle of Endor, Solo returned to Jubilar to make a smuggling run for old times' sake. The Victory Forum and many areas of the city were in ruins from war and neglect. Jandarra, green vegetables grown only in Jubilar's desert and in

Juggernaut

Jundland Wastes

a few hydroponics tanks, is a popular export. [TBH]

jubilee wheel A popular betting device, it is found in casinos throughout the galaxy. [HLL]

Jubnuk A Gamorrean guard in the palace of Jabba the Hutt, he fell into the rancor pit along with Luke Skywalker and was quickly eaten. [TJP]

Judgment Field An open, public area in Montellian Serat, it is where notorious criminals are occasionally executed. [TBH]

Judicator An Imperial Star Destroyer commanded by Captain Brandei, it was part of Grand Admiral Thrawn's personal armada. [HE, DFR, LC]

Jubnuk

Mon Julpa

juggernaut An old-fashioned heavy assault vehicle that was first built during the waning days of the Old Republic for planets starting their own defense forces, its sheer size and thick armor make it as tough and dangerous as an AT-AT walker. The juggernaut is twenty-two meters long and nearly fifteen meters tall. Five sets of drive wheels propel it to a top speed of 200 kilometers per hour across almost any terrain. It can transport fifty troops into battle or carry speeder bikes or light assault speeders. It requires a crew of two plus six gunners for weapons systems that include a turret-mounted laser cannon as well as a port and starboard laser cannon. Two concussion grenade launchers are mounted on independent turrets. [ISB]

Julpa, Mon The crown prince of the planet Tammuz-an during the early days of the Empire, he was stripped of his title and memory by the evil vizier Zatec-Cha. For a time he wandered the planet as the frail and simple-minded Kez-Iban, and met up with R2-D2 and C-3PO. [DTV]

jump beacons Stationary space structures, also known as hyperspace beacons or "safe points," they were erected by pioneers of faster-than-light travel. Jump beacons mark proven, safe coordinates for jumping into and out of hyperspace and are usually located in the relatively empty regions of space between star systems. Many large spaceports have grown up around the beacons. [TOJ, FNU, DLS]

Jundland Wastes A dry, hot, and rocky region on the planet Tatooine, it consists of a canyon and mesa. The Jundland Wastes border the Dune Sea and are inhabited by Tatooine's nomadic Sand People, or Tusken Raiders. [SW]

Junkfort Station A patchwork collection of living-modules in space, they are joined by a network of airlink tunnels. Ships often travel to Junkfort Station to receive illegal modifications; bounty hunters ostensibly are forbidden aboard. Following the Battle of Yavin, Han Solo and

Junkfort Station

Chewbacca went to Junkfort's cantina to inquire about how they could acquire shield-disrupting power gems. [CSW]

juri juice A ruby- or blue-colored, mildly intoxicating drink. [GG1, CCG]

J'uoch An unscrupulous, evil woman, she and her twin brother, R'all, owned and operated a mine on the planet Dellalt. J'uoch—with thick, straight brown hair surrounding a pale face and large black eyes—and R'all competed with Han Solo to be the first to discover the lost treasures of Xim the Despot. [HLL]

Juvex sector Adjacent to the Senex sector and near the Ninth Quadrant, it contains the Juvex systems. Like the Senex sector, it is run by groups of Ancient Houses, including the House Streethyn. Bran Kemple was a small-time gunrunner in the Juvex systems before taking over a smuggling business on Belsavis. Eight years after the Battle of Endor, some of the Juvex Lords met with Roganda Ismaren on Belsavis with the intention of forging a military alliance. [COJ]

K-3PO An older model protocol droid, he learned military tactics while owned by Commander Narra. After the commander's death, he was put in charge of the droid pool at Echo Base on the planet Hoth. [CCG]

K749 system Located in the Outer Rim near the Moonflower Nebula, it contains the planet Pzob. [COJ]

K-3PO

K8-LR A protocol droid, Kay-Eight Ellarr was assigned to Jabba the Hutt's Mos Eisley townhouse. It helped Muftak and Kabe rob the place and escape after they took off the droid's restraining bolt. [TMEC]

Ka, Tenel The somewhat humorless, impatient, but hard-driven daughter of Prince Isolder of Hapes and Teneniel Djo, one of the Witches of Dathomir, the teenager is filled with the high spirits of both her parents—and with the Force. Thus it is no surprise that she arrived on Yavin 4 to train in Luke Skywalker's Jedi academy, although her identity as a princess was kept secret from the other trainees.

Tenel Ka, with rusty brown hair and large, cool gray eyes, is partial to wearing a brief outfit made from the scarlet and emerald skins of Dathomir reptiles—much the way a female warrior on her mother's homeworld would dress. Despite her growing Force powers, Tenel Ka seemed to feel that using the Force was a sign of weakness, and she preferred to apply her athletic prowess instead.

At the Jedi academy, she quickly made friends with Jacen and Jaina Solo, the twin son and daughter of Leia and Han Solo, and Lowbacca, a young Wookiee nephew of Chewbacca. The four of them found an old crashed TIE fighter in the Yavin 4 jungle and repaired it, even adding a hyperdrive motor, before realizing that the pilot, Qorl, was still alive. He captured the twins, but Tenel Ka made it back to the academy in time to get help and rescue them, although not before Qorl escaped.

When Luke instructed his students on building their first lightsabers, Tenel Ka didn't devote her full attention and energies to the task. The components in her handle were cramped and the lightsaber's crystals

Tenel Ka

had small flaws—but she was tired and figured they would suffice. During a practice session, however, Tenel Ka's lightsaber blade sputtered out just as Jacen's blade was coming down —and Tenel Ka's left arm was severed above the elbow. She returned to Hapes to recover and questioned whether she should continue Jedi training. But after she and her young Jedi friends staved off an assassination attempt on her grandmother, she returned to the Jedi academy.

Later, the twins and Lowbacca were kidnapped. The trail led to Dathomir and then to the Shadow Academy where Force-sensitives were trained in the ways of the dark side. Tenel Ka and Luke Skywalker encountered the abductees as they were making their own escape attempt, and they all fled danger together. [YJK, SWCG]

Kaa When Colonel Pakkpekatt and his companions aboard Lando Calrissian's space yacht *Lady Luck* arrived at Carconth to investigate an anomaly, a slave circuit in the ship was activated by Calrissian's beckon call and the ship pointed itself in the general direction of the planet Kaa before jumping to hyperspace. [TT]

Ka'aa An ancient species that wanders the galaxy. [BTS]

Kaal A blue world covered with vast oceans, it is in the Yushan sector in the Mid-Rim. Now a major exporter of agricultural goods, Kaal also boasts luxurious resorts and casinos, including the Grand Imperial. The Empire abandoned the planet soon after the Battle of Endor, and it was then taken over by the local crime lord, Tirgee Benyalle. Kaal's population is around 4.5 million. [SWAJ]

Kabaira A world whose surface is 90 percent covered by water, it is in the Teilcam system of the Outer Rim. Kabaira has more than two million volcanic islands. The few active volcanoes are located in the southern hemisphere, while the eight million Kabairans live in the north, primarily on the two island continents of Madieri and Belshain. Eponte Spaceport, the center of Kabaira's corporate government, is located on the north cost of Madieri and is bordered by mountains. Its climate is typically cool, damp, and foggy. The planet's main industry is mining; indigenous animal life includes white snowwolves. [SWAJ]

Kabal An outerworld that was officially neutral in the Galactic Civil War, it was the site of the Conference of Uncommitted Worlds held just after the destruction of the first Death Star. An Imperial Star Destroyer, tipped off by Freeholder Kraaken, arrived to wipe out the conference and punish the planet for its neutrality. Waves of TIE bombers leveled the city, but Princess Leia Organa was saved by the timely arrival of the *Millennium Falcon*. Lying near Kabal is a small dwarf star with an artificially accelerated gravitational pull, surrounded by a vast graveyard of derelict starships. [CSW]

Kabe A Chadra-Fan pickpocket less than a meter tall, she had been abandoned by slavers on Tatooine. Kabe survived by learning the ways of the streets, aided by her skill at cracking security systems and gambling, and her extra senses of infrared vision and chemoreceptive smell. She was also protected by her large, furry, four-eyed friend Muftak, a Talz. For Kabe, thievery and scams were more of a game, a pastime, than a crime. Thus she enjoyed dressing as a Jawa and forcing newcomers to turn over a nonexistent tax for a local merchants' guild.

Kabe and Muftak lived for years in abandoned tunnels beneath a docking bay on Mos Eisley, surviving on Kabe's ill-gotten gains and the few credits Muftak got for passing on information to the curious. They spent lots of time at the Mos Eisley cantina, and were there when Luke Skywalker and Ben Kenobi arrived, although they hadn't a clue to their identities. Kabe, in fact, almost picked young Skywalker's pocket before Luke got into an altercation at the bar. Kabe and Muftak planned one final grand hit on Tatooine before leaving the planet: robbing Jabba the Hutt's Mos Eisley townhouse.

There were many complications, and they got involved in an espionage mission for the Rebel Alliance, but they finally made it off-world in search of their destinies. [TMEC, SWCG]

Kadann The Supreme Prophet of the Dark Side, the human dwarf with a black beard assumed leadership of the Empire for a brief time after the Battle of Endor. Others wishing to take over from the Emperor sought Kadann's dark blessing to make their rule legitimate. He often issued mysterious prophecies in the form of four-line verses, which Alliance leaders studied for any hints of what the Empire might be planning. [LCJ, PDS]

Kabe

Ka'Dedus An ultraviolet supergiant star, it is orbited by Af'El, home planet of the Defel. [GG4]

Kaell 116 A new, younger clone leader of the spaceport city on the planet Khomm. Kaell 116 greeted the returning Jedi Knight and fellow Khomm clone, Dorsk 81, and Jedi Kyp Durron. But when the two later warned of a possible imminent Imperial attack, the complacent Kaell 116 ignored them—much to the peril of the planet, which was nearly annihilated in the attack under the orders of Admiral Daala. [DS]

Kaelta A purple star orbited by Toola, homeworld of the Whiphids. [GG4]

Kai, Tamith One of the new order of dark-side Nightsisters from Dathomir, she aided Brakiss in training Force-sensitive youths at the Shadow Academy to be Dark Jedi. She was tall with black hair flowing like waves down her shoulders. Her violet eyes and dark, wine-colored lips were set in a pale face. During a battle on Yavin 4, in which the goal was to destroy the Jedi academy, her battle barge was destroyed and she was killed. [YJK]

Kaiburr Crystal A deep crimson gem, it long rested in the jungle Temple of Pomojema on Circarpous V, or Mimban. Legends described the Kaiburr Crystal as a Force-enhancing artifact, capable of strengthening the abilities of Force wielders. The Temple priests were said to have mysterious healing powers that were perhaps enhanced by the crystal's natural properties. The crystal rested within a ceremonial statue of a minor god, and was guarded by a sluggish but deadly lizard-creature. Soon after the Battle of Yavin, Luke Skywalker, Princess Leia Organa, and the droids R2-D2 and C-3PO crashed on Mimban while traveling to a conference on Circarpous IV. After facing many dangers, including a showdown with Darth Vader, the Rebels were able to retrieve the Kaiburr Crystal and leave Mimban. [SME]

Kaikielius system Lying close to the Coruscant system, it was one of the first systems that revived Imperial forces started conquering six years after the Battle of Endor. As the conquest of the Kaikielius and Metellos systems began, New Republic leaders on Coruscant started searching for a new base of operations. [DESB]

Kail The family of Torm Dadefferon—an associate of Han Solo—controlled several large tracts of land known as the Kail Ranges on this planet in the Corporate Sector. Dadeferron's father and brother disappeared after a dispute with the Corporate Sector Authority over land-use rights and stock prices. [HSE, CSSB]

Kaink

Hrchek Kal Fas

Kaink An elderly Ewok priestess, she was village legend-keeper and guardian of the Soul Trees. [ETV]

Kalarba A planet in the remote Kalarba system, it is orbited by the moons Hosk and Indobok. Sites on the planet include Kalarba City, the Great Sea, and the Three Peaks of Tharen—a revered symbol of the spirit. Before their service to heroes of the Rebel Alliance, R2-D2 and C-3PO worked for the Pitareeze family on Kalarba. Meg and Jarth Pitareeze operated Kalarba Safari and booked tours of the planet's ancient ancestral lands, while Baron Pitareeze ran a spaceship factory. Animal life on the planet includes the flying vynock. [D]

Kalenda, Belindi A young woman operative of New Republic Intelligence, she has been a covert agent for years. Without the knowledge or approval of her superiors, Lt. Belindi Kalenda warned Han Solo of possible trouble on a family trip back to his homeworld. En route to Corellia herself, she was shot down and crash-landed undetected. Lieutenant Kalenda then went into hiding to await the arrival of the Solo family, and then she covertly watched and guarded them as best she could. [AC]

Kal Fas, Hrchek A male Saurin from Durkteel, he is a typical droid trader. Hrchek Kal Fas scouts the "invisible market" for the best droid prices. He was on Tatooine buying and selling droids when he read the reward posting about two "lost" droids that belonged to the Empire. The post stated that someone had stolen the droids from a high officer, who desperately wanted them back because they were close companions—an obvious lie. One of the droids actually walked into the cantina he was in, and Kal Fas slowly followed it out, not wanting to attract attention. But by the time Kal Fas made his way to the door of the cantina, the droids had disappeared into the crowded streets. [CCG]

Kal Fas, Saitorr A Saurin female from the planet Durkteel, she is a bodyguard for her cousin Hrchek Kal Fas, a droid trader. [CCG]

Kalior V The site of the Imperial aquarium, whose maintenance is entrusted to a group of Sedrians known as the Shalik family. [GG4]

Kalist VI The site of an Imperial labor colony for political prisoners. Alliance gunner Dack Ralter was born in the colony, and lived there for seventeen years until escaping with the help of a downed Rebel pilot. [MTS]

Kalkal A yellow-eyed species, they are famous for their ability to eat anything. [TJP]

Kalla A planet in the Corporate Sector, it is the site of a Corporate Sector Authority university intended for the education of Authority members' children. Major fields of study include technical education, commerce, and administration, with very little emphasis on the humanities. Rekkon was an instructor at the university prior to meeting Han Solo. Fiolla of Lorrd attended the University of Kalla before taking a position in the Corporate Sector Authority. General Evir Derricote, commander of the Imperial base on Borleias, was a native of Kalla. [HSE, CSSB, RS]

Kalla VII Prior to the Battle of Yavin, a group of Alliance X-wings eliminated a large Imperial base located near Kalla VII in an attempt to strand arriving Imperial ships. This resulted in the capture of the frigate *Priam*. [FP]

Kal'Shebbol A planet in the Kathol sector. [CCG]

Kamar A hot, dry planet orbiting a white star, it is just outside the Corporate Sector border and is the homeworld of the insectlike Kamarians. Kamar's native flora includes miser-plants, which collect moisture from the atmosphere and can be sucked dry in an emergency; barrel-scrub; and sting-brush. Fauna includes digworms, stingworms, bloodsniffers, nightswifts, and howlrunners—canine hunters with heads resembling human skulls. The nocturnal Kamarians live in small groups called tk'skqua, and their more sophisticated communities have developed technology such as nuclear explosives and fluidic control systems. Members of the unique Kamarian Badlander culture choose to live in the most arid and harsh areas of the planet. Han Solo inadvertently started a new religion among the Kamarian Badlanders based on the holofeature "Varn, World of Water" during a visit to the planet. [HSR, CSSB]

Kamparas Site of a Jedi training center, it was attended by Jedi Master Jorus C'baoth. [DFR]

Kanchen sector The heart of the sector, which contains the planet Xa Fel, fell to Imperial forces after a thirty-hour battle with New Republic warships over the planet. [TLC]

Kandos shuttle A shuttle servicing Tatooine, it is known for its early departures. [TJP]

Kanz Disorders The 300-year period during which Governor Myrial enslaved worlds in the Kanz sector. [CSSB]

Kanz sector An isolated region 4,000 years before the Galactic Civil War, it was on the frontier of the Old Republic and contained the planets Argazda and Lorrd. During the time known as the Kanz Disorders, the provisional governor of Argazda declared the sector independent from the Republic and tried to enslave the rest of its worlds, including Lorrd. The Republic, preoccupied with other matters, did nothing for 300 years, until the Jedi Knights finally intervened to free the Lorrdians and end the Kanz Disorders. [HSR, CSSB]

Kardue'sai'Malloc A devilish-looking Devaronian spy who indiscriminately shelled the city of Montellian Serat. The act earned him wide hatred and

Kardue'sai'Malloc

the title Butcher of Montellian Serat. On his home planet of Devaron, he was a cruel army captain who aligned himself with the Empire to put down a native rebellion. He personally oversaw the execution of 700 captives, earning himself a Rebel Alliance bounty on his head. He then changed his name to Labria and made himself scarce, showing up in Mos Eisley on Tatooine, where he tried to pass himself off as a major information broker. In truth, the usually drunken Labria was a lousy spy. What may have given him an edge for a while was that he looked sinister; he had pointy ears and a pair of dark horns on his head. His red-tinted skin was hairless, and he had two sets of teeth. After killing four mercenaries on Tatooine, Kardue'sai'Malloc retired to the planet Peppel, where he spent most of his final years collecting music and drinking Merenzene Gold liquor. A five-million-credit bounty was put on his head by the inhabitants of Montellian Serat, and he was eventually captured by Boba Fett, returned to the city, and publicly executed by being thrown to a vicious pack of quarra. [TM, GG1, SWCG, TBH]

Karfeddion Located in the Senex sector, it is the site of several slave farms run by the House Vandron. Breeding farms are designed to produce Ossan and Balinaka slaves, tailored for agricultural work. During an economic depression on Karfeddion, Lady Theala Vandron was summoned to the High Court of Coruscant to defend the presence of slave farms on her homeworld. [COJ]

Kark, Kith A Gotal and a Jedi, he was killed during the Freedon Nadd Uprising many millennia before the rise of the Empire. [FNU]

Karnak Alpha Located beyond the Hapes Consortium near the Deep Galactic Core, it is home to the fur-covered species called Karnak Alphans. The shy, easygoing Alphans hold children in the highest esteem. Having a large number of children means greater status in Alphan society, and the government has a children's council. Inhabitants also love unusual zoological specimens, and keep elaborate zoos and holographic dioramas. Some nineteen years after the Battle of Endor, New Republic Chief of State Leia Organa Solo met with the Karnak Alpha ambassador and her eight children, and presented her with a rare Coruscant hawk-bat egg. [YJK]

Karra A small, dense planet in the Rayter sector, it is covered with flat, grassy plateaus separated by jungle canyons and is home to the species called Karrans. The planet's temperature is uncomfortably hot and its life-forms consist almost entirely of insects, including beetles, leapers, legworms, clouds of tiny swarmers, and a walker-sized mantis. The native Karrans are large, fur-covered insectivores whose primitive technology is centered around pottery and simple hand tools. The Karrans seem to have recently developed sentience based around a communal hive mind, and can apparently control the planet's insect population. [SWAJ]

Karrde, Talon A smuggler, information broker, and one of the all-around slickest operators in the galaxy, he long tried to be neutral in the Galactic Civil War. But Talon Karrde has definitely tilted toward the New Republic as galactic warfare wages on. It is, he believes, just good business to do so.

Unlike many in his trade, the slender, thin-faced Karrde, who sports a long mustache and goatee that match his dark hair and offset his pale blue eyes, doesn't flaunt his trade. He has a dual personality: He is a man of his word, but he is cold and calculating and will do just about anything—although he does abhor slaving and kidnapping—to

Talon Karrde

make a credit. Karrde has a puckish wit. He named his main attack ship *Wild Karrde* and his space yacht *Uwana Buyer.* For years his base of operations was the planet Myrkyr, home to the ysalamiri, creatures with the natural ability to deflect or dampen the power of the Force.

Karrde provided Rogue Squadron with most of the weapons and munitions it used in its war against Ysanne Isard and her bacta cartel. When Karrde's top aide, Quelev Tapper, was killed, he hired on a hyperdrive mechanic who called herself Celina Marniss; in reality it was Mara Jade, the Emperor's Hand, a top aide to the late Emperor Palpatine. Karrde tried to remain neutral in the battles between remnants of the Empire and the Alliance, taking jobs from both. But when Luke Skywalker—his Force powers rendered useless by the ysalamiri—fell into his hands, things changed. Imperial Grand Admiral Thrawn, who had contracted with Karrde for some ysalamiri, came to Myrkyr to pick up an even greater prize, young Skywalker. But Luke had escaped and Karrde and his crew fled their base to escape Thrawn's wrath. Through a series of complications involving the finding of the long-lost Katana Dreadnaught fleet, Karrde and Jade swung their support to the New Republic. Karrde was instrumental in getting other smugglers to join him in supporting the New Republic and helped in the victory at Bilbringi. Karrde and Jade helped form a guild that became the Smuggler's Alliance, and he then temporaily retired from the business. [HE, DFR, LC, HESB, DFRSB, BW, NR]

Karreio An attractive woman devoted to Emperor Palpatine's New Order, she was engaged to decorated Imperial officer Crix Madine, a rising star in the Empire. But then Madine received an order directly from the Emperor, an order so vile that he made plans to defect to the Rebel Alliance. Madine didn't tell Karreio about his plans for fear that it would have made her seem an accomplice and put her life in great danger. It was only later, in surveying casualty reports, that newly named Rebel Alliance General Madine noticed that Karreio had been a casualty during a battle between Rebel and Imperial forces. [DS]

Karsk, Amil A former X-wing pilot, he was on a mission to Alderaan when it was annihilated by the Death Star. [BW]

Kasarax A sauropteroid on the planet Dellalt, he helped Han Solo during his quest to find the lost treasure of Xim the Despot. [HLL]

Kashyyyk A green and brown jungle planet covered with kilometers-high wroshyr trees, it is the homeworld of the fierce but loyal Wookiees. Vari-

Kashyyyk

ous ecosystems exist on each tree, with every level growing progressively more deadly the farther one travels toward the planet's surface. (Dangerous webweavers, for instance, set traps in the lower levels.) The Wookiees inhabit the highest levels in huge cities that are naturally supported by the thick tree branches, because wroshyr branches grow together when they meet.

One such city, Rwookrrorro, is more than a kilometer wide and built on a flat platform of meter-thick spongy material. It features two- to three-story buildings and a landing platform made from the stump of a wide limb. The most prestigious homes are built on the trees themselves, and nursery rings for young Wookiees are built in the tops of the very highest wroshyrs. The kshyy vines that grow among the trees cannot be cut with blasters and are strong enough to support liftcars. Wookiees use imported banthas for transportation and as beasts of burden. Glowing gnatlike insects called phosfleas are lured into mesh lanterns and used as nighttime illumination. Colored searchlights found in the cities help attract native birds called kroyies, a prize food.

Wookiees have easily incorporated modern technology into their society and even can accommodate visiting starships, though they sometimes prefer to opt for archaic tools like their traditional quarrel-firing bowcasters. Wookiee customs include the life debt, which obligates Wookiees to repay a person who has saved their lives, and the honor family, or those people to whom a Wookiee feels a particular bond of friendship. Wookiee adolescents undergo dangerous rites of passage into adulthood, including harvesting silky strands from the heart of the carnivorous syren plant.

The Wookiee species was treated as slave labor by the Empire and many were forced to toil on various Imperial construction projects. Many Wookiees still resent *all* humans because of the actions of the Empire. Leia Organa Solo hid on Kashyyyk until discovered by a team of Noghri commandos, who made an unsuccessful attempt to capture her.

Nineteen years after the Battle of Endor, a Second Imperium assault team, led by the Dark Jedi Zekk and the Nightsister Tamith Kai, raided Kashyyyk to capture guidance and recognition codes for New Republic ships from a vast computer fabrication facility in one of Kashyyyk's tree cities. They used holographic disguises that made them appear to be Wookiees and got into the planet's control tower to bring down the orbital defenses. It was during this assault that TIE bombers flew in to attack the city, and before they were repelled, Zekk and his troops even pursued several young Jedi Knights into the deepest levels of the forest. [HE, HESB, SWSB, HLL, YJK, TBH]

Kast, Jodo A cunning and ruthless bounty hunter, he wore battle armor similar to that of Boba Fett, and didn't mind getting mistaken at times for the galaxy's most famous bounty hunter. Annoyed, Fett hunted Jodo Kast down. In a final confrontation, Fett killed Kast with a nerve-toxin dart followed by an explosion of Kast's rocket pack. [TM, TBH, TED]

***Katana* fleet** The *Katana* fleet consisted of two hundred Dreadnaught heavy star cruisers. The fleet's flagship, the *Katana*, was said to be the finest starship of its time. The entire fleet was fitted with full-rig slave circuits to vastly lessen the size of the crew needed to run the ships. The fleet's unofficial name was the Dark Force, from the dark gray hulls of each Dreadnaught. The *Katana* fleet was launched by the Old Republic with massive publicity. But the crews were soon infected with a hive virus that drove them mad. In their insanity, they slaved the ships together and the whole fleet jumped to lightspeed—and disappeared for decades. Five years after the Battle of Endor, Grand Admiral Thrawn blackmailed smuggler Niles Ferrier into providing the location of the long-missing *Katana* fleet and escaped with 180 of the 200 ships under the nose of the New Republic. [DFR, DFRSB]

Katarn, Kyle A top-flight Rebel Alliance agent, he infiltrated a top-secret Imperial installation on Danuta—one of his most famous exploits. There Kyle Katarn managed to steal the technical plans for the Empire's first Death Star, which were later beamed to Princess Leia Organa's corvette near Toprawa. Katarn was most active in the aftermath of the Battle of Yavin. He captured Imperial weapons specialist Moff Rebus from his hidden stronghold under the sewage system of Anoat City. He planted a tracking device on a smuggling ship at Cal-Seti, which led him to an Imperial robotics facility on Anteevy, which he disabled with several sequencer charges. The facility was where the alloy phrik was refined and treated for use in armoring the Empire's new Dark Troopers. Following the phrik trail took Katarn to Fest, where a secret Imperial Weapons Research Facility team hidden in a steep mountain performed metallurgical research on new alloys. Katarn stole a sample to be analyzed by Alliance scientists. And he journeyed to the Gromas system, which had a small moon where the Empire was mining phrik—until Katarn blew up the facility. Among his other exploits, Katarn infiltrated two Imperial ships, the *Executor* and the *Arc Hammer*. [DF]

Katarn Commandos *See* Page's Commandos

Kathol sector A remote sector on the fringes of the populated galaxy, it was first settled about six standard centuries before the Galactic Civil War by the Old Republic with the establishment of a colony on the planet Gandle Ott. It remains a galactic backwater. There are about thirty official colonies and independent worlds in the sector, but no more than half have even ten million residents each. On the other side of a large void on the edge of the sector is a cluster of stars called the Kathol Outback, which in turn borders on the mysterious and difficult to navigate Kathol Riff.

The Kathol sector touches the outer reaches of the Minos Cluster, with which it is linked by the Triton Trade Route. Major systems and planets in the sector include the capital, Kal'Shebbol, first settled centuries earlier by escaped Twi'lek slaves; Lorize, a heavy manufacturing planet; and Kolatill; Brolsam; Aaris; Charis; and Oon Tien. The sector has most recently been ruled by Moff Kentor Sarne. [DSC]

kayven whistlers Flying carnivores with sharp teeth and voracious appetites, they are sometimes used for purposes of torture or execution. They look like a cross between a monkey and a bat. [TMEC, GG7]

Kee A Yuzzem miner on the planet Mimban, he helped Luke Skywalker, Princess Leia Organa, and the old woman Halla retrieve the legendary Kaiburr Crystal from the Temple of Pomojema. [SME]

Keed'kak, Kitik A female insectoid Yam'rii, a giant praying mantis-type creature, she is strong and easily angered. Kitik Keed'kak is known for her stealth and her good technological aptitude. She is a meat eater and loves eggs. She was one of the many patrons in the now famous Mos Eisley cantina on Tatooine the day that Luke Skywalker and Han Solo first met. [CCG]

Keeg, Baniss A Duros pilot instructor for deep-space missions, he was on vacation and relaxing at the Mos Eisley cantina the day that Luke Skywalker and Han Solo first met there. [CCG]

Keeheen A prisoner at Stars' End. His mate, Atuarre, and her cub, Pakka, accompanied Han Solo to the Stars' End penal colony to rescue him from the Corporate Sector Authority facility. [HSE]

Keek A New Republic Fifth Fleet pilot, he was killed during the failed attempt to blockade the Yevetha at Doornik-319. [SOL]

Keek, Inspector Chief of the planet Brigia's Internal Security Police, the pompous, self-important officer covered his oversized uniform with numerous decorations. [HLL]

Kitik Keed'kak

Keeper The tormentor and slave-master of the Wookiees on Maw Installation, he was a barrel-shaped man with oily skin. His real name was Grodon Lakky. He was killed during Chewbacca's freeing of the Wookiee slaves. [COF, JASB]

Kei The first mate of Yevethan strongman Nil Spaar, she was the mother of three offspring. Kei succumbed to the "gray death." [SOL]

Kek, Bolton One of the original designers of the neural network for the IG series of assassin droids, he laid the groundwork for the IG project before retiring from Imperial service for ethical reasons. Bolton Kek was eventually killed by the assassin droid IG-88, who recognized that the programmer was one of only a few humans who knew the IG droids' weaknesses. [TBH]

Kelada An industrial planet in the Anarid Cluster, it long supplied the Empire with repulsorlift components and parts for Imperial walkers. Following the Imperial defeat at the Battle of Endor and an increase in Alliance activity, the remnants of the Empire diverted ten Star Destroyers to the system. Kelada once kept an ecological balance between industry and the environment, but the balance has been threatened as forests and savannas are cleared to support greater production. An industrial wasteland is growing just outside the Kelada starport. [SWAJ]

Kelavine system Located in the Expansion Region far from any trade lanes, it contains the large gas giant Taloraan. After the Battle of Hoth, Alliance operatives were sent to search for Tibanna gas deposits on the planet. [SWAJ]

Kellering, Doctor A scientist at Imperial Prime University, he worked on the Hammertong weapons project. It was he who hired the Mistryl Shadow Guards to guarantee the safety of the Hammertong during its transport to the Empire. [TMEC]

Keller's Void An empty region of space, it serves as a hyperspace shortcut between the Calus and Wroona systems. Occasionally pirates have been known to bring asteroids from the nearby Udine system and place them in the Void, to create mass shadows and force unsuspecting ships from hyperspace. [SWAJ]

Kelrodo-Ai Site of gelatin mines famous for their water sculptures, they were once operated by Baron Administrator Drom Guldi. Guldi and his aide were killed by wampa ice creatures while on a hunting expedition to Hoth, eight years after the Battle of Endor. [DS]

kelsh A bronze-colored metal. [TJP]

Kemplex Nine A strategic jump-station in the Auril sector and the Cron system some 4,000 years before the rise of the Empire, it was the only inhabited outpost near the Cron Cluster. During the Sith War, Dark Jedi Ulic Qel-Droma hinted that he intended to attack the undefended station, but it was merely a ruse to draw Republic defenses away from his true target, Coruscant. Later, Qel-Droma did decide to hit Kemplex Nine, but this was meant to draw Jedi forces into a trap. Dark-side practitioners Aleema and Crado, aboard an ancient Sith ship, devastated the station and lured the pursuing Jedi fleet into the ten stars of the Cron Cluster. When they were in position, Aleema activated a Sith weapon and inadvertently ignited all ten stars, wiping out Kemplex Nine, the entire surrounding area of space —and her own ship. [TSW]

Ken The son of a three-eyed mutant and a princess—and the grandson of

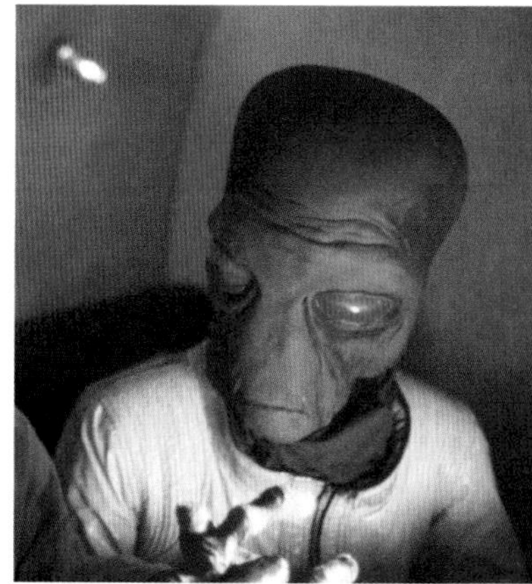

Baniss Keeg

Ken

Emperor Palpatine—he had a bizarre childhood shut off from the world and most other living creatures. But Ken, a Jedi prince by birth, managed to overcome the dark-side influence that he was born into and began the path of becoming a full Jedi Knight.

Ken's father was Palpatine's imperfect son, Triclops, who upon birth was sent to the Imperial Insane Asylum at Kessel. His mother was Kendalina, who had been forced to serve as a nurse at the asylum. Triclops and Kendalina fell in love, and she gave birth to a male child before she was killed. A Jedi Master took the baby to the underground Lost City of the Jedi on Yavin 4, where he was raised by droids. Ken was trained to reject the dark side. His only remaining tie to his heritage was half of a silver birth crystal he wore around his neck. The other half was worn by Triclops.

His only companions on Yavin 4 were droids DJ-88, caretaker of the Jedi Library and Ken's teacher; HC-100, in charge of Ken's homework; and small Microchip—or Chip—who was Ken's friend. He also had a small feathered mooka named Zeebo as a pet. Ken grew to admire Luke Skywalker and learned to use some of his Force talents. A year after the Battle of Endor, when he was twelve years old, Ken managed to make it topside briefly and met Skywalker, before DJ-88 took him back to the Lost City.

Kadann, the Supreme Prophet of the Dark Side who was backing the pretender Trioculus as successor to Palpatine, hunted Ken down and tried to kill him. At that point the young Jedi prince joined the Alliance heroes in a number of adventures. Ken finally encountered his father on the planet Duro, although the true details of their relationship weren't revealed. Later, Kadann captured Ken and told him about his past even as he prepared to steal the secrets of the Lost City and then destroy it. But Luke and Ken combined their Force powers to defeat the Supreme Prophet. [LCJ, ZHR, PDS]

Kendalina A princess, she was forced to serve as a nurse in an Imperial insane asylum on Kessel. There she met and fell in love with the mutant three-eyed son of Emperor Palpatine, Triclops, and bore him a son, Ken, before she was killed. [PDS]

Kenlin, Bors The captain of the *Xucphra Rose*, a Thyferran bacta tanker. [BW]

Kenobi, Ben (Obi-Wan) To the outside world, much of which had forgotten his past exploits, he was just an old hermit—a crazy recluse who lived an isolated existence in the Jundland Wastes by the Western Dune Sea on the miserably hot planet Tatooine. But in reality, old Ben Kenobi was once known widely as Obi-Wan Kenobi, a powerful and respected Jedi Knight and a heroic general who served in the Clone Wars.

Kenobi's inherent Force sensitivity led him to the Jedi Master Yoda, who sensed in Obi-Wan the ability to train others. But Yoda constantly had to warn Obi-Wan to guard against any dark side incursions. During the Clone Wars Kenobi became a general and fought alongside Bail Organa of Alderaan. The two became lifelong friends.

Kenobi also befriended a youngster named Anakin Skywalker, who was strong in the Force. Obi-Wan took on Skywalker's training himself, but through his lack of experience as a teacher and his proud refusal to seek help or advice—combined with Skywalker's strong will—Kenobi failed to see how Anakin was being lured closer and closer to the dark side of the Force. When Kenobi finally realized the error of his ways, and tried

Ben (Obi-Wan) Kenobi

to turn Skywalker back to the light side, the only result was a ferocious lightsaber battle. The records are hazy, but it appears that Skywalker may have tumbled into a pit of molten lava and emerged half-dead, a scarred hulk who couldn't breathe on his own. At that point, psychologically at least, he was transformed into Darth Vader, the Dark Lord of the Sith, although that transformation was known only to a select few. Vader teamed up with self-proclaimed Emperor Palpatine to help spread the New Order and its reign of terror to the farthest reaches of the galaxy.

Kenobi then helped to hide the twin son and daughter born to Skywalker's estranged wife; the baby girl was entrusted to Bail Organa while the boy was given to Owen Lars and his wife Beru to raise as their nephew. Neither child was to be told of their true parentage.

Kenobi, living on Tatooine not far from the Lars home, could keep track of young Luke Skywalker. Owen foiled one early attempt by the reclusive Ben to give Luke his father's first lightsaber, even though Ben had guided Luke and his friend Windy home after they got lost in the Jundland Wastes. For the most part, though, Kenobi stayed hidden in his modest house as the Empire sought out and destroyed most of the galaxy's remaining Jedi Knights. Ben brooded constantly about his failures in the training of Anakin Skywalker, but knew that Luke, because of his strong capacity for the Force, might hold one of the keys to an eventual victory for the Rebel Alliance.

Kenobi finally had a chance to talk to Luke when he rescued the boy from an attack by Tusken Raiders. In Ben's home, they watched as the astromech droid R2-D2 played a desperate message from Princess Leia Organa. Kenobi presented young Skywalker with his father's lightsaber—still not revealing the truth about Anakin's dark transformation—and invited Luke to accompany him to Alderaan. Luke declined, but after discovering how stormtroopers had incinerated his adoptive parents, he agreed to the journey and Kenobi began training Luke in the ways of the Force.

But by the time they arrived at Alderaan's coordinates, the planet had been destroyed by the Imperial super weapon, the Death Star. Kenobi, Skywalker, two droids, and their pilots, Han Solo and Chewbacca, were brought aboard the Death Star and began a search for the imprisoned princess. As they were making their escape, Darth Vader confronted Obi-Wan and the two engaged in a fierce lightsaber duel. Seeing the need for a diversion, Kenobi let himself be cleaved by Vader's saber—but his cloak fell empty to the Death Star floor, for Kenobi had become one with the Force. That didn't mean that Obi-Wan couldn't still be Luke's mentor and protector. He continued to guide Luke—"Use the Force," he said—when Skywalker hit an exhaust port with torpedoes that would blow up the fearsome Death Star. He later guided Luke to the planet Dagobah to continue his training under Jedi Master Yoda. And he made Luke realize that he had to confront and kill Vader if the Rebellion was to have any chance of success.

The spirit of Obi-Wan appeared to Luke several times more. But in a final appearance when Luke was on Coruscant, Kenobi told him that the distances were too great for him to appear again. "I loved you as a son, and as a student, and as a friend," Kenobi told Skywalker. "Until we meet again, may the Force be with you." Luke, he said, was not the last of the Jedi, but "the first of the new." [SW, ESB, ROJ, SWCG]

Kentas, Julynn The aged chief executive officer of droid-builder Industrial Automaton, she is a shrewd businesswoman. Although Julynn Kentas's record isn't free of failure—her company's R5 units were a flop—her successes have far outweighed any problems. [SWAJ]

Kess A Corellian gambler, he ended up in the Sarlacc pit on Tatooine, becoming part of its group consciousness. [TJP]

Kessel A reddish potato-shaped planet near the planets of Fwillsving and Honoghr, it is the only source of the telepathy-inducing glitterstim spice, and was the former site of a brutal Imperial prison and spice mining operation that used forced labor. Kessel has one large moon and is the site of the city of Kessendra. The planet's surface is covered with crumbled salt flats and atmosphere-production factories that send great jets of oxygen, nitrogen, and carbon dioxide into the pinkish sky to make the air barely breathable—when filter masks are used. Beneath Kessel's surface live dangerous energy spiders that spin glitterstim webs as a method of catching their prey, primarily the luminous "bogey."

Kessel

The Kessel system is adjacent to a cluster of black holes known as the Maw, which makes navigating to the planet difficult and helped glamorize the smugglers' Kessel Run. While Kessel was under control by the Empire it was a common smuggling destination for those dealing in spice, and smuggler-turned-Rebel-hero Han Solo once boasted that he had made the Kessel Run in "less than twelve parsecs" by flying dangerously close to the Maw.

Prior to the Battle of Yavin, a bold Alliance rescue operation freed a group of Rebel POWs during a prisoner transfer operation. During the chaos surrounding the Battle of Endor, a Rybet prison official named Moruth Doole (who had secretly been supplying glitterstim to smugglers) staged a prison revolt and took control of the planet from the Empire. After the members of Rogue Squadron captured Borleias, they were sent to Kessel to free members of the Black Sun criminal organization, with the intention of returning them to Coruscant and making life difficult for the Empire prior to an Alliance invasion. The Rogues neutralized Kessel's defenses while Lieutenant Page and his commandos secured the landing zone. They freed sixteen of the galaxy's worst criminals. Several years later, after Doole's operation was dismantled, the administration of the mines was taken over by Lando Calrissian. Kessel's moon, which once held an Imperial garrison and Doole's ragtag defensive fleet (which was decimated in a battle with Admiral Daala's Star Destroyers), was destroyed by a Death Star prototype from Maw Installation. [SW, JS, COF, LC, HLL, COJ, FP, XW]

Kestic Station A free-trade outpost near the Bestine system, it was a frequent stopover for smugglers and outlaw miners. Alliance pilot Zev Senesca lived on Kestic Station with his parents, who supplied the Rebellion with arms until their illegal transactions were revealed by an Imperial informant. The station was subsequently destroyed by the Star Destroyer *Merciless*. [MTS]

Kestrel Nova An ancient freighter, it was captured by Republic forces in a space battle with pirates near Taanab some four millennia before the rise of the Empire. [DLS]

Ketaris A major trade center, it was the target of an attack by Grand Admiral Thrawn, but the attack was stalled at a critical point. Alliance pilots had hoped that Wing Commander Varth could escape the Qat Chrystac battle and hook up with a unit at Ketaris. During Admiral Thrawn's attack on Coruscant, Alliance Admiral Ackbar was on an inspection tour of the Ketaris region. [LC]

kete A large winged creature, it looks much like a giant dragonfly. Ketes live on the forest moon of Endor in spiral mounds made out of a sticky, marshmallowlike substance. [ETV]

Keto, Lord The hereditary ruler of the Empress Teta system about 4,000 years before the Galactic Civil War, he and his wife, Magda, were on their annual inspection tour of carbonite mines when his son, Satal, and niece, Aleema, staged a rebellion and killed them both. [DLS]

Keto, Satal An heir with his cousin, Aleema, to the throne of the Empress Teta system, he became coleader of the dark-side Krath cult and received powers from the spirit of the Dark

Satal Keto

Jedi Freedon Nadd. He staged a rebellion to take over the system. Among the first victims were his mother and his father, ruler of the system. He eventually was killed by Jedi Ulic Qel-Droma for instigating the death of Qel-Droma's teacher, Jedi Master Arca Jeth. [DLS]

Ketrann A dangerous carnivore from the planet Alk'Lellish III. [TAB]

Kez-Iban *See* Mon Julpa

Khabarakh From fierce Imperial loyalist and assassin to staunch supporter of the New Republic, the young Noghri has undergone a swift and complete transformation. Khabarakh was part of a commando team sent to capture Princess Leia Organa Solo on the Wookiee planet Kashyyyk. Like other Noghri, he was a fearsome sight with his gray skin, large black eyes, pointed claws, and mouthful of razor-sharp teeth. Their world suffered a disaster around the beginning of the Clone Wars and the Noghri eventually swore allegiance to Darth Vader and the Empire due to a lie. They effectively had become the Empire's hit squad.

But Khabarakh recognized Leia—through an incredible sense of smell—as the Mal'ary'ush, the daughter of Lord Darth Vader. As such, she was to be revered, not hunted. (He hadn't been told who his intended target was.) The other Noghri on the team were killed, but Leia let Khabarakh go, and later lived up to her promise to visit the Noghri homeworld, Honoghr, to present the cause of the Alliance. For his role in helping Leia, Khabarakh was called a traitor by Grand Admiral Thrawn, and was imprisoned. But the other Noghri soon learned that Leia, or "Lady Vader," was telling the truth, and they rose up against the Imperial forces that had long dominated them. Khabarakh was freed, and became part of Leia's Noghri honor guard. The Noghri aided the Alliance in its attack on Mount Tantiss, where one Noghri, Rukh, slew Admiral Thrawn.

With New Republic help, the Noghri are now rebuilding their ravaged planet. Khabarakh has become caretaker of the lush Hidden Valley, called the Future of the Noghri. [HE, HESB, DFR, LC]

Khan, Lo An old smuggler, he is owner and operator of the *Hyperspace Marauder*. Lo Khan assisted fellow smugglers Salla Zend and Shug Ninx during their visit to the planet Byss. Khan's partner and first mate is Luwingo, a Yaka cyborg. [DE]

kholm-grass A plant that once grew widely on the Noghri homeworld of Honoghr, it was wiped out through deliberate contamination by Imperial forces. The Empire then planted a bio-engineered version of kholm-grass that secretly killed other forms of plant life and kept the blighted world from recovering. Only animals capable of eating the kholm-grass survived outside a small area of Clean Land, so the Noghri had to rely on imported food supplies, thus keeping them in the Empire's debt. Princess Leia Organa Solo uncovered the long-lasting Imperial plot and the New

Khabarakh

Captain Khurgee

Republic is helping clean the planet. [HE, DFR, LC]

Khomm A pale green world lying very close to the Deep Galactic Core, it is moonless, has no unusual geological features, no axial tilt, and a regular orbit. A thousand years before the rise of the Empire, Khomm's inhabitants decided that their society had reached perfection. They froze their bureaucratic culture at this "perfect" level, and began producing clones of previous generations. The genderless clones of Khomm like to keep to their own affairs, rarely leaving their planet and keeping the same roles and schedules from generation to generation. The planet remained neutral during the Galactic Civil War.

Khomm's cities are laid out in perfect gridworks, with almost all buildings and residences looking identical and made from the same green-veined rock. Large cloning facilities in each city hold a record of all the major family lines. Dorsk 81 (the eighty-first clone of Dorsk) surprisingly showed unexpected Force aptitude and became one of Luke Skywalker's Jedi academy students seven years after the Battle of Endor. The following year, Dorsk 81 returned to Khomm; his warnings of an Imperial attack were ignored and the planet was devastated by Colonel Cronus and his fleet of *Victory*-class Star Destroyers. [DA, DS]

Kho Nai The Khotta of the planet Kho Nai are related to the Qella of the planet Qella; both species are descended from the ancient Ahra Naffi. Twelve years after the Battle of Endor, the cyborg Lobot retrieved the mind-prints of the Khotta from the Institute for Sentient Studies on Baraboo in order to decipher a puzzle found aboard the mysterious Qella ship known as the Teljkon vagabond. [BTS]

Khuiumin A system that was the main base for the infamous Eyttyrmin Batiiv pirates until they were wiped out by the Imperial *Victory*-class Star Destroyers *Crusader* and *Bombard*. The two warships eliminated all 150 craft in the pirate armada and chased the last survivors to the surface of Khuiumin, where their stronghold was wiped out by the *Crusader's* concussion missiles. [SWSB, SWAJ]

Khurgee, Captain A docking bay security officer, he was honored for bravery aboard the Star Destroyer *Thunderflare* when he rescued five officers from the wreckage of a shuttle crash. He served aboard the first Death Star, ordering a scanning crew to search the *Millennium Falcon*. [CCG]

Kiffex A double planet, it was the site of a colony where twin con artists Brea and Senni Tonnika were raised and where they perfected their deceptions and money-making skills. [MTS]

Kiilimaar Following the Battle of Hoth, Rneekii pirates chose this planet as the site where they would turn a captured TIE-defender developer over to the Empire in exchange for a substantial ransom. Imperial forces, however, double-crossed the pirates and recovered the ransom money. [TSC]

Kile A moon orbiting the gas giant Zahr, it was the site of a temporary base for Rogue Squadron. From Kile the squadron launched an attempt to capture Boba Fett and rescue Han Solo, who had been encased in carbonite by Darth Vader. [SOTE]

Killiks An extinct species from the planet Alderaan, they lived in the Castle Lands. [ISWU]

Kimanan Home to the animals known as furballs—tiny, tubby, clownish marsupials that are considered wonderful pets. They are sold at Sabodor's pet shop on Etti IV. [HSE]

Kimm systems These systems are known for their trafficking in Senex sector slaves. The stock light freighter *Smelly Saint* also runs counterfeit agri-droids from the Kimm systems. [COJ]

King Gorneesh *See* Gorneesh

King's Galquek Located in the Meridian sector, the planet is sometimes referred to as K-G. Nine years after the Battle of Endor, a palace coup secretly supported by the Loronar Corporation broke out on King's Galquek. [POT]

Kintan A planet that was the homeworld of a creature known as the Kintan strider. It was also the Nikto homeworld, but that species did a thorough job of destroying its biosphere. The planet was conquered by the Hutts eons ago, before the Old Republic was established. [GG12, CCG]

Kintan strider A ferocious creature with incredible healing abilities, it is extinct on its homeworld of Kintan. Kintan striders are used by Hutts as guard beasts. [CCG]

Kinyen Homeworld to highly social, three-eyed beings known as Gran. A common sight on Kinyen are gently waving fields of goatgrass. Ree-Yees, one of Jabba the Hutt's courtiers, was exiled from Kinyen after committing the highly unusual crime—for a Gran—of murder. The planet is also home to the houjix. [MTS, TMEC]

Kiffex

Kiph, Dmaynel The Devaronian leader of the Alien Combine, he had passed judgment on Gavin Darklighter, and was ready to kill him and other members of Rogue Squadron, but he never got the chance. Imperial forces attacked the group's hideout, killing several of its members and seriously wounding Dmaynel Kiph. He made his escape with the help of the Rogues, then later joined the Alliance to help liberate Coruscant. [WG]

Kir A planet deep within the heart of the Corporate Sector, it is where crystals are mined and refined for use as crystalline vertex, the Corporate Sector currency. [HSE]

Kira, Drokko The father of Modon Kira, also known as Drokko the Elder, he suffered from a wound that wouldn't heal after he was cast out of Iziz for challenging the legacy of Freedon Nadd four millennia before the rise of the Empire. [TOJ]

Kira, Modon A Beast-Lord of Onderon, he was the father of Oron Kira some 4,000 years before the Galactic Civil War. A distant relative with the same name gave Leia Organa Solo sanctuary in an Onderonian safe house six years after the Battle of Endor. [TOJ]

Kira, Oron Husband of Galia, and son of Modon Kira, he along with other Onderonians and their war-beasts joined the Jedi in their fight against the dark-side Krath cultists four millennia before the rise of the Empire. [TOJ, FNU, DLS]

Kira Run A hyperlane running through the Kira system, known as the Kira Run, connects the Lazerian and Ropagi systems. The run originally was seen as a risky, uncertain route, but shortly before the Battle of Yavin, small shipping companies began servicing the run and making it an established trade route. [TSK, SWAJ]

Kirdo III A hot, arid world in the Outer Rim marked by cracked red plains of dried mud and the white sands of the Kurdan desert, it is homeworld of the patient, resilient Kitonaks, who live among the dunes where windstorms can reach speeds of 400 kilometers an hour. To withstand the milder storms on Kirdo III, Kitonaks remain still, angling their bodies into the onrushing wind. This is similar to their method of feeding on the small, burrowing chooba by mimicking the sulfaro plant, the choobas' main food. The Kitonaks, who smell like vanilla, stand still for hours until a chooba climbs close enough to be swallowed, which is enough food to feed a Kitonak for a month.

Oron Kira

The Kitonaks roam Kirdo III in nomadic tribes of around 100, following the migrating chooba. Kitonaks have no natural predators and fear only quicksand and caves, both of which hold mysterious and deadly dangers. Once each decade a great rainstorm covers Kirdo III, flooding the dry riverbeds and ushering in the Kitonak mating ritual known as the Great Celebration of Life. Kitonaks are skilled at playing beautiful music on chidinkalus, the hollowed-out reeds of chidinka plants, which sometimes results in their capture by slavers and subsequent employment as professional jizz-wailers. Droopy McCool, the stage name of one of the band members in Jabba the Hutt's palace, was a Kitonak.

Eight years after the Battle of Endor the Imperial battlemoon *Eye of Palpatine* stopped at Kirdo III to pick up a contingent of stormtroopers, but brought in a group of Kitonaks instead. [GG4, RJ, COJ, TJP]

Kirl The name of both a province of Munto Codru and the Kirlian ambassador. Ambassador Kirl is an attractive male who enjoys being mildly flirtatious. [CS]

Kirrek One of seven planets in the Empress Teta system, it was the last to bow to the authority of Satal Keto and Aleema when they instigated their Krath cult coup some 4,000 years before the rise of the Empire. For its resistance, Kirrek had three of its cities destroyed. [DLS]

Kirtania The fourth planet in the Yyrtan system, it is a green-blue world of jungles, deserts, and mountains, and is home to an arachnid species called the Araquia. Kirtania originally was colonized by several groups of humans, who founded the competing states of Surana, Kinkosa, and Dulai. Over the years, the states have seriously depleted the planet's natural resources and polluted the environment. The population now includes two million humans and only 1,500 remaining Araquia. Shiarha root, the only known cure for the deadly Direllian Plague, grows in Kinkosa's humid rain forests. [SWAJ]

Kithra One of the Mistryl guards who accompanied Mara Jade in the liberation of Kessel, she also helped battle the prototype Death Star above the planet. [COF]

Kitonak A species of pudgy, yeast-colored beings with tough, leathery hides, they are natives of Kirdo III. Their ability to seal vulnerable body

Kitonak

Cmdr. Titus Klev

openings in folds of flesh serves to protect them from the world's harsh desert environment. They are a patient species whom many consider to be plodding. Droopy McCool, a member of Max Rebo's jizz-wailer band, was a Kitonak. [GG4]

Kkak, Hrar A Jawa on Tatooine, he gave fellow Jawa Het Nkik a blaster rifle that Nkik used in his failed attack on Imperial stormtroopers. [TMEC]

Kkak, Tteel The Jawa on Tatooine in charge of a salvage team who discovered a downed spaceship containing a rancor, he is also the pilot and representative of the Kkak clan. [TJP]

Kktkt A planet in the Farlax sector near the Koornacht Cluster. [SOL]

Klaatu One of the Nikto skiff guards employed by Jabba the Hutt, he, like other members of the Kadas'sa' Nikto race of the Nikto species, has a reptilian look with leathery olive-colored skin and small horns atop his face. [RJ]

Klatooine Home planet of the species known as Klatooinians, the inhabitants sell their disrespectful youth into indentured service. Klatooine was conquered by the Hutts before the establishment of the Old Republic. Jabba the Hutt picked up the contract of a Klatooinian manservant named Barada, who then became the head of Jabba's repulsor pool but was killed during the rescue of Han Solo. Animal life on the planet, which is in the Si'klaata Cluster, includes the ill-tempered Klatooine paddy frog. Jabba was sometimes known to snack on live paddy frogs, served in brandy to keep them from attacking and killing each other. [MTS, TJP]

Klaymor 4-2 An Imperial reconnaissance mission discovered a Rebel spy probe located near the moon Klaymor 4-2. A single TIE fighter, dispatched from the corvette *Astin*, was sent to destroy it. [TSC]

kleex Large, flealike parasites, they infest the tails of the huge creatures called durkii on the planet Tammuzan. Though the durkii is normally a docile beast, it can become a raging monster due to the discomfort caused by kleex infestation. [DTV]

Klev, Commander Titus An imperial officer, he commanded *Silencer-7*, one of the Imperial World Devastators, at the Battle of Calamari. Titus Klev was killed after Luke Skywalker tampered with the Master Control Signal that guided the Devastators, causing *Silencer-7* to crash into the Calamari ocean. Early in his career Klev, who was born on Alsakan, had gained recognition for capturing an important Rebel Alliance agent during the Battle of Wann Tsir. [DE, DESB]

Kleyvits An older female Selonian, she spoke for the Overden, and assumed responsibility for Han Solo, Leia Organa Solo, and Mara Jade after the Hunchuzuc Den was won over to the Overden cause. [SAC]

Klaatu

klick The slang X-wing pilots use for kilometers. [RS]

Kline colony The Wookiee bounty hunter Chenlambec attempted to rescue one of his "acquisitions" by turning him over to the Rebellion at the settlement on this planet. The ungrateful prisoner forcibly resisted, but the Wookiee was saved by his future partner, Tinian I'att. [TBH]

Derek "Hobbie" Klivian

Klivian, Derek "Hobbie" A blond-haired, blue-eyed pilot, he knew Biggs Darklighter on the Imperial ship *Rand Ecliptic* and bolted from the Imperial Navy at the same time as Darklighter. He wasn't at Yavin, having been assigned other duties. But Derek "Hobbie" Klivian joined Rogue Squadron at the Rebel Alliance base on the ice planet Hoth. In the Battle of Hoth, his comm-unit designation was Rogue Four. He also fought at the battles of Endor and Bakura. [GG3, ESB, XW]

Kloo horn A musical instrument, it is played by Figrin D'an in his frequent band appearances. [TMEC]

Kloper The homeworld of the species known as Kloperians, short gray beings with extendable necks and many tentacles, some of which are capped with hands. Due to their mechanical skills, many Kloperians are used by the New Republic as starship technicians. [NR]

k'lor'slug A venomous creature from the planet Noe'ha'on, it has a keen sense of smell and vision. A k'lor'slug can be very dangerous. It lays eggs

K'lor'slug holomonster

and has hundreds of ravenously hungry hatchlings. A k'lor'slug is often used as a playing piece on hologame boards in games of dejarik. [CCG]

Kneesaa, Princess The daughter of Chief Chirpa, Ewok leader of Bright Tree Village on the forest moon of Endor, she survived a troubling incident early in life. While on an expedition with her older sister, Asha, and their mother, Ra-Lee, they were attacked by a hanadak. Ra-Lee told Princess Kneesaa to run back to the village for help, but by the time help arrived Ra-Lee was dead and Asha had vanished. Years later, in tracking down tales of a mysterious Red Ghost, Kneesaa and her best friend Wicket W. Warrick came upon the crimson-furred Asha, who had been raised by a band of wolflike korrinas.

The gray-furred, black-eyed Kneesaa had many adventures while growing up. She also had two younger siblings after her father remarried and her stepmother had two woklings, Nippet and Wiley. Besides Wicket, her best friends include two female Ewoks, Latara and Malani, and two males, Teebo and Paploo. Despite the incident with the hanadak, Kneesaa grew up more trusting than many of her tribe, although she remained leery of the dangers of the forest. At an early age, she battled the fierce Duloks and later the evil witch Morag.

Kneesaa worked around her village, built high in the trees, and began weaving baskets. She developed that skill so well that she became known as the best weaver on all of the Endor moon. Kneesaa, along with Wicket and the older Logray, became true village heroes when they thwarted a plan by the giant green Phlogs to chop down the ancient sacred trees near their home. [ETV, TRG, SWCG]

knobby white spider A misnomer, it is actually a detachable mobile root from the gnarltree that grows on Dagobah. The knobby white spider roams the swamps, hunting and devouring animals and storing energy in its bloated, bulbous head. When ready for metamorphosis, the spider searches for a clear spot in the undergrowth, uproots competing plant life, plunges its eight sharp legs deep into the spongy ground, and transforms itself into a gnarltree. [ISWU]

Princess Kneesaa

Knolstee A planet in the Corporate Sector, it is one of the stops made by the luxury liner *Lady of Mindor* during its trips from Roonadan to Ammuud. [CSSB]

Knossa Spaceport The main spaceport on the planet Ossus. [DLS]

knytix Although these creatures resemble Thyferran Vratix, they are smaller and less elegant. They are used by the Vratix as work animals, are kept as pets, and—on special occasions—are eaten. [BW]

Kogan VI Some thirteen years following the Battle of Endor, after the Obroan Institute had finished its investigation of the planet Qella, it was scheduled to give up its ship, *Penga Rift,* to support Dr. Bromial's expedition to Kogan VI. [TT]

Koh'shak The master of the Kala'uun Spaceport on Ryloth, he was also the head of all the merchant clans operating from this location. Koh'shak was the chief negotiator for the addictive ryll kor, or spice, that the Alliance needed for a top-secret project. [PSG, BW]

Kojash Located in the Farlax sector and the Koornacht Cluster, it was the former site of a Morath mining operation. Twelve years after the Battle of Endor, Kojash was brutally attacked and conquered by the alien Yevetha as part of a series of raids that the Yevetha called the Great Purge. [SOL]

Kokash sector Located in the former center of the Empire's Rim territories, large areas of this sector have never been properly surveyed. During the Empire's reign, the Black Sword Command was charged with the defense of Praxlis, Corridan, and the entire Kokash, Hatawa, and Farlax sectors. Following the Battle of Endor, Imperial forces abandoned the Kokash sector and retreated into the Core. [BTS]

Komonor system A system whose warlord evicted all Hutts. Hearing the news, Tatooine-based crime lord Jabba the Hutt hired bounty hunter Dyyz Nataz to eliminate the ruler. [TMEC]

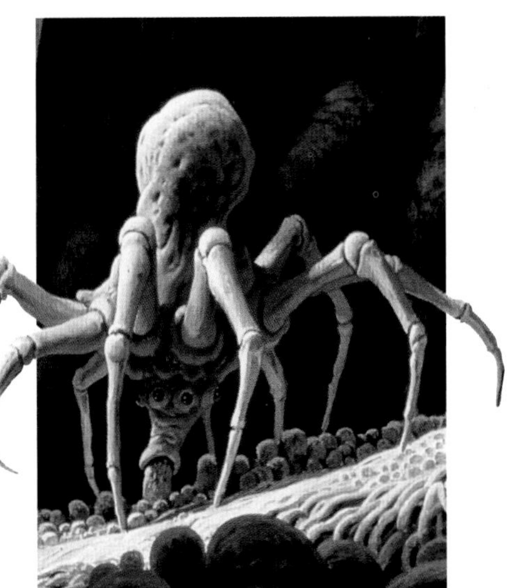
Knobby white spider

Governor Koong

Koong, Governor In the early days of the Empire, this burly man in his mid-fifties led a band of criminals in the Tawntoom region of Roon. Governor Koong used political intrigue, theft, and hijacking to increase his personal power in the Roon system. [DTV]

Koornacht, Aitro A night commander of the palace guard of Emperor Preedu III on Tamban, a pre-New Order Galactic Empire. The Koornacht Cluster was named after him in honor of a favor that he had done for the First Observer of the Court of the Emperor. [BTS]

Koornacht Cluster Made up of 2,000 young stars and 20,000 planets, the Cluster is located in a cloud of interstellar dust and gases in the Farlax sector. The Koornacht Cluster was named by a Tamban astronomer in honor of Aitro Koornacht, night commander of the palace guard in the Court of Emperor Preedu III. It is also known by many other less common names, including The Multitude, God's Temple, and the Little Nursery. Less than 100 of the Cluster's planets are habitable. The Cluster is located along the Inner Line, centrally positioned in the Farlax sector, between Coruscant and the Deep Core strongholds of the Empire. It makes up about a tenth of the combined regions of the Farlax and Hatawa sectors.

The Cluster's inhabited worlds generally boast an advanced technological base, rich mineral resources, and prosperous economies. The brown dwarf star Doornik-1142 and its planets are located on the edge of the Cluster, while J't'p'tan is located at the heart. N'zoth, Tholaz, Faz, Wakiza, Tizon, Pa'aal, Prildaz, Z'fell, and Zhina are Yevethan worlds within the cluster. Non-Yevethan colony worlds in the cluster include New Brigia, Pirol-5, Polneye, Kutag (Doornik-881), Elcorth, Kojash, Doornik-207, J't'p'tan (Doornik-628), and Morning Bell (Doornik-319, or Preza). The planets Galantos and Wehttam are the closest inhabited worlds to the Cluster, and Dandalas, Nanta-Ri, and Kktkt lie close to Koornacht as well. Joruna and Widek are two New Republic planets located somewhere near the Cluster; due to the Yevethan closure of their borders, freight traffic must travel a circuitous route around the Cluster to reach the two worlds.

The Koornacht Cluster's dominant species is the Yevetha, skeletal bipeds with six-fingered hands and bright streaks of facial color that evolved on N'zoth. They have retractable claws underneath their wrists and fighting crests running from temple to ear. In N'zoth's night sky, the blazing stars of the Cluster blocked out the light from all other more distant stars, and the Yevetha came to believe that their world was the center of the universe. Using spherical thrustships traveling through realspace, the Yevetha spread from their homeworld to colonize eleven other planets, more than had ever been colonized by any other species without the invention of hyperdrive. These eleven planets, plus the spawnworld of N'zoth, form the Duskhan League. Twelve years after the Battle of Endor, Ambassador Nil Spaar, viceroy of the Duskhan League, came to Coruscant to meet with Chief of State Leia Organa Solo.

The Cluster was Imperial territory from the end of the Clone Wars until soon after the Battle of Endor. Very little was known about the Cluster or its worlds since the Empire kept access restricted and the Yevetha have remained secretive since the Empire pulled out, some eight months after the Battle of Endor. In fact, the Yevetha have a reputation for executing trespassers on sight. The brutal Imperial governor in charge of the Cluster was given free rein to bring the Yevetha under his control. He held public executions, used women as pleasure slaves, and took children as hostages. The technologically inclined Yevetha were forced to work in Imperial shipyards established in the Cluster, repairing and maintaining the Empire's warships and learning a great deal about Imperial technology in the process.

After the Empire departed, the Yevetha underwent what they called a Second Birth, settling a dozen more colony worlds and restoring captured Imperial warships. The Duskhan League laid claim to the entire Cluster, despite the fact that there are as many as seventeen worlds populated by other species. Along the inner border of the Cluster there were several non-Yevetha worlds, including mining colonies and groups of religious settlers. According to the latest survey, there are five other indigenous sentient species in the Cluster, though none have developed hyperdrive. Only the Yevetha developed the technology to leave their star system. Twelve years after the Battle of Endor, the Yevethan fleet eliminated all non-Yevethan colonies from inside the Cluster's borders, fanatically cleansing these "infestations" in a devastating series of attacks called the Great Purge. Chief of State Leia Organa Solo sent the New Republic's Fifth Fleet to the Cluster to persuade the Yevetha to stop their attacks. [BTS, SOL, TT]

kor The rarest grade of ryll, it makes up approximately 3 percent of the addictive spice's production. [BW]

Koros Major One of seven planets in the Empress Teta system, it was the last to resist the system's brutal subjugation by the dark-side Krath around 4,000 years before the rise of the Empire. The Krath leaders, Satal Keto and Aleema, dispatched hundreds of ground troops to the planet and clashed with a joint Republic and Jedi space force in Koros Major's orbit. The Republic ships were badly damaged in the battle and were forced to retreat. [DLS]

Korrda the Hutt A special envoy and servant to Lord Durga the Hutt, he had a narrow face that had thinned due to some sort of sickness. Korrda

Korus

the Hutt looked like a scrawny ribbon of mottled green leather that hung on a flexible spinal column. His small size—for a Hutt—made him the target of scorn. [DS]

Korriban A world long hidden, it has been the repository for the mummified remains of many Sith Lords within great temples located in the Valley of the Dark Lords. The tombs are designed to focus and amplify dark-side energy, which permeates the entire valley. The temples' exteriors are guarded by human skeletons, activated through a combination of machinery and Sith magic. Within the temples was an immense crystal, which held the trapped spirits of Jedi Masters who had dared oppose the Sith. Four thousand years ago, Exar Kun visited Korriban to learn Sith secrets and was tormented by the spirit of Dark Sider Freedon Nadd. Nadd destroyed the huge crystal and unleashed guardian creatures on Kun, who eventually surrendered to the dark side of the Force. Emperor Palpatine was known to frequent Korriban and referred to it as his "place of power." One of Palpatine's last visits occurred around the time of the Battle of Yavin. He eventually returned, ten years later, in an unsuccessful attempt to convince the Sith Lord spirits to halt the decay of his last remaining clone body. [DLS, EE]

Korus The tutor of Aleema and Satal Keto, bored young aristocrats who were heirs to the throne of the Empress Teta system. Korus was one of the cousins' first victims when they started a violent coup to take over the system. First, using Sith magic, Aleema caused a serpentlike worm to appear from the tutor's mouth. Not long after, Aleema directed so much dark force at Korus that his body exploded. [DLS]

Kothlis A colony world of the Bothan species, it was where New Republic Councilor Borsk Fey'lya grew up. Located a few light-years from Bothawui, Kothlis is the fourth of seven planets in its system and is orbited by three small moons. The climate is slightly cooler than on Bothawui and many visitors, on first arrival, remark that the atmosphere smells like "moldy cheese."

Prior to the Battle of Endor, Bothan spies captured an Imperial freighter carrying highly classified data about the second Death Star. The Bothan space station Kothlis II, orbiting near Kothlis, allowed the stolen freighter to dock and take on supplies while techs tried to decode its computer core on the planet below. Luke Skywalker was captured and held for ransom to the highest bidder while on Kothlis, but he escaped before either Darth Vader or Prince Xizor could get their hands on him. Vader arrived on the scene and destroyed a suspected Rebel base on one of the Kothlis moons. [DFR, TSC, SOTE]

Kowakian monkey-lizard Rare animals from the planet Kowak, the creatures are so silly and stupid that across the galaxy a sure way to insult someone is to call him a Kowakian monkey-lizard. They are, however, a semiintelligent species with a small, spindly body; large, flaplike ears; and a wide, fleshy beak. Monkey-lizards, such as Jabba the Hutt's sidekick Salacious Crumb, are known for their constant laughter and mimicery. [RJ]

Kraaken, Deputy Commander A humanoid with long pointed ears, he was Commander Silver Fyre's second-in-command. Kraaken was a traitor who attempted to kill Luke Skywalker and steal a data card carrying secret information vital to the Alliance. [CSW]

krabbex A small, shelled sea creature, it is native to Mon Calamari. A related species, the mammoth krabbex, is on display in the Holographic Zoo for Extinct Animals on Coruscant. [JS, ISWU]

Krail, Davish A veteran human male pilot whose nickname was Pops, he flew fighters for two decades. He was wingman for Gold Leader and was Gold Five at the Battle of Yavin, where he was killed. [CCG]

krakana A creature that lives in the waters of Mon Calamari, it will eat anything. [DA]

Kratas, Commander An Imperial officer, he commanded Admiral Daala's flagship, the *Gorgon*. [JS, COF]

Krath A secret society founded by dark-side dabblers Aleema and Satal Keto some 4,000 years before the rise of the Empire in the Empress Teta star system, it was named after a demon from the fairy tales of their youth. The Krath developed into a dark-side magical sect that ruled the system. Princess Leia Organa Solo learned about the Krath while using a knowledge-filled Jedi Holocron. [DLS, DE]

Krath Enchanter The royal Tetan space yacht of Aleema and Satal Keto. [FNU]

krayt dragon Large and vicious meat-eating reptiles, they live mainly in the mountains surrounding the Jundland Wastes on the desert planet of Tatooine. Krayt dragons continue

Deputy Commander Kraaken

to grow throughout their lifetimes and do not become weaker with age. Their skin is yellowish brown, and they have three huge horns on their heads. They walk on four squat legs. Their gizzards hold incredibly valuable and beautiful dragon pearls. [ISWU, DS, TJP]

Kreet'ah A Kian'thar, he was one of the lieutenants, or Vigos, of Black Sun, the galactic criminal organization led by Prince Xizor. Kreet'ah inherited his place as Vigo from his mother. [SOTE]

Kre'fey, General Laryn A Bothan General and a celebrated military leader, he was given approval by the New Republic Provisional Council to conduct a raid on Borleias. Blinded by his lust for power and the false information he received from his Bothan slicers, Laryn Kre'fey nearly destroyed Rogue Squadron. As Alliance forces descended toward the supposedly disabled base, planetary defenses suddenly came to life. General Kre'fey's ship was struck by an ion bolt, disabling it, and the *Modaran* crashed into the renewed energy shield, killing all on board. [RS]

Kre'fey, Karka A grandson of Bothan General Laryn Kre'fey, he attempted to goad Gavin Darklighter into a duel after striking him at a party. Fortunately for Karka Kre'fey, Darklighter refused to fight. [KT]

Krenher sector This sector is home to a New Republic station. Twelve years after the Battle of Endor, after searching for any sign of the mysterious ghost ship called the Teljkon vagabond and its four accidental passengers from the New Republic, Colonel Pakkpekatt ordered the New Republic ship *Marauder* to abandon the search and report to the commodore at Krenher Sector Station. [SOL]

Krenn, Josala An Obroan Institute archaeologist, she was sent to Maltha Obex to recover biological samples for any clues to the origins of the Qella civilization. But Josala Krenn was buried in an avalanche on the planet. [SOL]

Kritkeen, General Sinick A tyrannical COMPNOR general, he was stationed on planet Aruza. General Kritkeen was eventually assassinated by the bounty hunter Dengar, who had been hired by the Aruzan people. [TBH]

kroyie A species of bird native to the planet Kashyyyk, they are hunted for food and are considered a delicacy by the Wookiee natives. Huge kroyie birds live in the upper branches of the planet's giant trees. They are attracted to bright lights, so Wookiees use search beams to hunt the great birds. [HE, HESB]

Krytos The name of the virus developed by Imperial General Evir Derricote at the request of Ysanne Isard, Director of Imperial Intelligence. She wanted a disease that would mutate quickly and spread among the alien species of Imperial Center (Coruscant), but would not harm the humanoid populace. She wanted it designed so that, if caught in time, it could be cured with simple bacta as part of a plot to bankrupt the New Republic. The Krytos virus could be frozen and thawed without loss of effectiveness. Because of a low flesh-contact infection rate—only 20 percent—it was decided to release it into the planet's water supply. [KT]

KT-10 An R2 unit with a female personality program, she and R2-D2 became "romantically interested" in each other while both were in the Great Heep's droid harem back in the early days of the Empire. [TGH]

KT-18 A pearl-colored housekeeping droid with a female personality program, she went by the nickname Kate. Luke Skywalker purchased Kate from Jawas on Tatooine as a gift for Han Solo. [ZHR]

Ktriss A pet of Great Bogga the Hutt, the dark-side hssiss was captured from Lake Natth on the planet Ambria. Ktriss emanated a sinister force that paralyzed the minds of her victims. [TOJ]

Kuan A planet orbited by several moons, it is in the Taroon system on the outer edges of the Rim. For nearly twenty standard years, Kuan engaged in a devastating war with its sister planet Bordal, until the conflict was ended suddenly through the intervention of the Empire. The long interplanetary struggle destroyed much of Kuan's main city, home to illegal swoop races and a popular hangout called the Maze. Animal life on Kuan includes the rondat, and plant life includes the pleasant-smelling shimsha flower. A planetary crop is tarine, used for tea. The highly decorated Imperial pilot Maarek Stele was a native of Kuan. [TSC]

Krayt dragon

Kuar A planet in a system of the same name near the Empress Teta system, its ruined underground cities provided a base for the masked warrior clans led by Mandalore four millennia before the Galactic Civil War. From there they struck at the heart of the Teta system, prompting Tetan leader Ulic Qel-Droma to fight Mandalore in single combat on Kuar's plains of Harkul. Battling on an unstable web of chains, Qel-Droma defeated Mandalore, thereby winning the loyalty of the warlord and his fierce soldiers-of-fortune. [TSW]

Kuari Princess A Mon Calamari luxury space liner, it is famous for its state rooms, bazaar deck, and slafcourses—sites of a popular recreational sport in which participants navigate an obstacle course atop fast-moving repulsor sleds. It was on the *Kuari Princess* that the droid 4-LOM began his career as a thief, stealing, among other things, the legendary Antares Sapphire from Dom Pricina. [RM, TBH]

Kuat Located in the Kuat sector in the most densely populated section of the galaxy, the system is the site of the massive Kuat Drive Yards starship construction facility. The plant, known as KDY, has long been one of the Empire's primary producers of warships and has manufactured the feared *Imperial*-class Star Destroyer. Due to its strategic importance, the Empire defended the Kuat system with fifteen Star Destroyers after the Battle of Endor and rigged the stardocks with explosives in case it was necessary to scuttle them.

During their undercover mission to Coruscant, Rogue Squadron pilots Corran Horn and Erisi Dlarit posed as a Kuati telbun and his mistress. Horn wore heavy purple and red robes and a cylinder-shaped hat. The elite on Kuat consider telbuns not worthy of their notice. They are given modified versions of their mistress's name, indicating to whom they belong. They are taken from the Kuati middle class, and raised to excel at physical, social, and academic pursuits. At the appropriate age they are ranked according to their score on a series of genetic, intelligence, and other breeding-related tests.

The upper classes, the families of the legendary Kuat merchant houses, then purchase a telbun for breeding and pay the middle-class family for him. The child of the telbun fathers is considered an heir and a full member of the merchant family, but considers only their noble parent as a blood relative. The telbun stays on to raise the children. This is considered a logical and practical method, preventing genetic inbreeding, and it means that members of competing merchant houses can't have children together, which could complicate matters and blur the distinct lines separating the houses.

A Super Star Destroyer called *Executor* was built at the Kuat yards, and was later renamed *Lusankya* and buried beneath Coruscant's surface to serve as the Emperor's private getaway vessel. [SWSB, PSG, ISWU, RS, SWAJ, WG, BW]

Ku'Bakai system The system is named for its blue giant star, whose unpredictable solar flares have left the first four planets of the system scorched and lifeless. The fifth planet, Kubindi, is the homeworld of the Kubaz. The sixth, eighth, and eleventh planets house insect farms for the Kubaz to use in preparing their unique cuisine. [MTS]

Kubaz A humanoid species that stands about 1.8 meters tall and has short, prehensile trunks instead of noses. Kubaz have rough-textured, black-green skin, and large, sensitive eyes. On many worlds, Kubaz must wear special goggles to protect their eyes from harsh light. They are a cultured species who highly value tradition, art, and music. Their homeworld of Kubindi is famous for its insect-based cuisine. Garindan, a Mos Eisley operative, was a Kubaz. [GG4, MTS, CPL]

Kubindi The fifth planet in the Ku'Bakai system, it is the homeworld of the insect-loving Kubaz. Due to the unpredictable solar flares of Ku'Bakai, Kubindi suffers from baths of intense radiation and constantly changing weather patterns. The adaptability of insects have made them particularly successful life-forms on Kubindi, and they exist in many varieties, including the bantha-sized sunbeetle. Insects are considered a true delicacy on Kubindi, and the civilized, cultured Kubaz have organized their society around insect-trading circles. Kubaz families farm designer insect hives and trade with others; the largest trading families make most planetary governmental decisions. Kubindi is isolated and seldom sees galactic traffic. Garindan, the Mos Eisley spy known as Long Snoot, was a Kubaz. Four years after the Battle of Endor, the Kubaz negotiated with the Barabel to purchase body parts of the humanoid insects known as Verpine to use in their cuisine. [GG4, MTS, CPL]

Kueller Formerly known as Dolph, Kueller was an extremely talented student of Luke Skywalker's on Yavin 4, but he also always possessed a certain darkness. He did not stay at the Jedi academy long enough to develop either his Force-talents or to dispel this darkness, and he became known as Kueller once he left the academy and accepted the dark side fully. As a youth, he witnessed the aftermath of the brutal deaths of his parents at the hands of the Je'har on Almania, and thereafter swore revenge on the Almanian rulers, as

Kubaz

well as on the New Republic, which he believed had blindly ignored the atrocities committed by the Je'har.

Kueller used the planet Fwatna as a base of operations before launching his plans against Almania. He attacked the Je'har and destroyed them, becoming self-proclaimed Master of Almania, using the Great Dome of the Je'har as his headquarters. Kueller wore a Hendanyn death mask to hide his boyish face and silvery hair. Only seen in museums, this ceremonial mask molded itself to the skin of the wearer. Kueller's mask was white with black accents and held tiny jewels in the corners of the eye slits. He worked with a group of smugglers in Smuggler's Run to buy Imperial equipment, which he had Brakiss, the administrator of the droid manufacturing factories on Telti and another former student of Skywalker, use in constructing droids that incorporated an explosive device. Kueller then used these rigged droids to detonate massive explosions on the Almanian moons of Pydyr and Auyemesh, and even in Senate Hall on Coruscant itself.

Kueller's plans also included rigging the New Republic's new model of X-wing fighter with an explosive detonator, thereby eliminating the New Republic's most talented pilots. The plot was uncovered by Cole Fardreamer, R2-D2, and C-3PO. Kueller then lured Luke Skywalker to Almania and sent a holo-coded message to Chief of State Leia Organa Solo, threatening to kill Skywalker if she did not resign and turn over the reins of power. Leia did resign and went off in search of her brother Luke. Together, Luke and Leia faced down Kueller, and when his dark-side powers were curtailed by several ysalamiri that Han Solo brought to Almania, Leia killed Kueller with a blaster shot to the head. [NR]

Kun, Exar Once the most powerful and dangerous of the Dark Lords of the Sith, he was responsible for the deaths of millions four millennia before the rise of the Empire. Killed by an overwhelming force of Jedi, the dark spirit of Exar Kun survived across the vastness of time to challenge Luke Skywalker and a new group of Jedi trainees.

Kun was tutored in the ways of the Force on Dantooine by Master Vodo Siosk-Baas. The proud Jedi pushed himself hard, but he was pulled to the dark side of the Force and secretly used his master's Jedi Holocron to learn about past Dark Lords of the Sith, such as Freedon Nadd. Posing as a Jedi archaeologist, Kun traveled to Onderon to examine Nadd's Sith artifacts. Jedi Master Arca Jeth saw through Kun's lies, and an angry Kun left for the city of Iziz and then the Dxun moon to explore Nadd's influence. Inside Nadd's tomb he was confronted by the spirit of the Dark Lord himself and was led to two scrolls that contained great Sith secrets. These scrolls in turn led Kun to the desolate planet of Korriban where, with the help of Nadd's spirit, he gained access to the Sith tombs.

Kun had second thoughts and tried to back out, but was felled by Nadd's spirit in an attack that left him near death. The only hope, the spirit proclaimed, was to fully embrace the dark side, and however reluctantly, Kun did. In the time that followed, Nadd's spirit filled him with tales, especially of the ancient Sith Lord Naga Sadow and the experiments Sadow had performed on the moon of Yavin 4 to give flesh to the spirits of the dead. Nadd told Kun that he must complete Sadow's work and give Nadd a new body.

Exar Kun

On Yavin 4, Kun again renounced the dark side, but was attacked by the Massassi, mutated descendants of Sadow's alchemy. They prepared him for death in a Massassi Blood Sacrifice, and Kun again turned to the dark side to save his life. He slaughtered all who would oppose him, including Nadd's spirit, but not before it cried out a warning to two other followers, Aleema and Satal Keto, founders of the dark side mystical sect, the Krath.

In the months that followed, Kun had the Massassi build huge temples of an ancient Sith design to focus great dark-side energies. He also continued Naga Sadow's experiments, turning the Massassi into monstrous creatures of death. Then he headed for the Empress Teta system to destroy Nadd's final Sith followers. He arrived as Jedi Knights were attacking the Krath stronghold. But Aleema and fallen Jedi Ulic Qel-Droma survived. Blasting Aleema with dark-side power, he and Qel-Droma engaged in a blistering lightsaber duel. Sith amulets that both men wore began to glow with energy and ancient Sith Lords appeared and bestowed the title of Dark Lord of the Sith on Kun, and the title of Sith Apprentice on Qel-Droma. Eventually they and Aleema joined forces to try to bring down the Republic and the Jedi Knights.

At a Great Council of Jedi convened on Deneba, Master Vodo Siosk-Baas volunteered to try to turn his former student from the dark side, but Kun slew his master. The bloody battles that ensued, known for all time as the Sith War, resulted in millions of deaths. In the end, Qel-Droma betrayed Exar Kun, revealing the secret of Kun's power base on Yavin 4. The resulting battle leveled most of the moon's temples and destroyed Kun's body, but he drained the life force from every Massassi, an act that kept his spirit alive but trapped in the remaining Yavin temples.

Some 4,000 years later, the Rebel Alliance briefly established a base on Yavin 4. Later, Luke Skywalker opened a Jedi training academy based in Yavin 4's Great Temple. Exar Kun's spirit stirred, tempting first one then another of Skywalker's trainees into turning to the dark side. He enlisted one promising Jedi, Kyp Durron, until Skywalker saw what was happening and confronted Durron. With the help of Kun, Durron attacked his teacher and used dark-force lightning to separate Skywalker's spirit from his body. But Kun didn't reckon on the combined strength of the remaining students, who protected Skywalker's body from destruction, then set a trap for Kun. They focused their will into a single entity of the Force, finally snuffing out Kun's spirit, restoring Luke's essence to his body, and freeing Durron from the hold of the dark side. [SWCG, DA, DLS, TSW, COF]

Kurp, Kosh A bomb expert, he was Jabba the Hutt's secret weapon after Jabba was trapped in the fortress of Gaar Suppoon. Jabba figured that Kosh Kurp would seek revenge once he was told that it was Gaar Suppoon who had killed Kurp's family. After Suppoon was killed, Jabba gave Kurp all of Suppoon's holdings. [JAB]

Kurtzen A humanoid race, it makes up about 5 percent of the population of Bakura. Kurtzen are white-skinned with a corrugated, leathery scalp instead of hair. [TAB]

Kwenn Space Station A space station containing the Royal K Casino, it was where Jabba the Hutt acquired his pet Kowakian monkey-lizard, Salacious Crumb. Meysen Kayson, wealthy owner of the Greel Wood Logging Corporation in the Pii system, owns a sizable percentage of *Kwenn Space Station*. [MTS, SWAJ]

Kwerve, Bidlo A scar-faced Corellian with white-streaked black hair, he was an associate of Bib Fortuna, and the Twi'lek's direct rival for the post of Jabba the Hutt's majordomo. Bidlo helped Fortuna acquire a rancor for Jabba's birthday, and was soon thereafter "honored" by being the first person that Jabba fed to his new pet. [SWSB, TJP]

Kybacca The senior Wookiee New Republic senator, she opposed the introduction of former Imperials to the Senate. [NR]

Laakteen Depot The Rebel Alliance base closest to Fondor around the time of the Battle of Yavin, it took the Alliance almost a year to capture. Laakteen Depot was subsequently wiped out by the Super Star Destroyer *Executor* during the ship's maiden voyage. [CSW]

Laboi II A small planet orbiting the red giant Er'Dox Kaan, it faces its sun for such long periods that rock melts on the sunny side while the dark side drops to sub-zero temperatures. Laboi II is home to the carnivorous, aggressive Laboi who hunt the bantha-sized ovolyan. The Laboi, who look like fur-covered snakes, make up for their lack of arms and legs with a limited telekinetic ability that may be linked to the Force. [GG4]

labor droid Robots that usually perform a single function, they don't require a high degree of programming or artificial intelligence. Labor droids handle sanitation work, are miners, operate simple transport vehicles, and perform other menial tasks and duties. [HSE]

labor pool overseer A sentient creature or droid, it coordinates the work assignments of all droids on a vessel, such as the labor pool overseer on the consular ship *Tantive IV*. [SWR]

Labria *See* Kardue'sai'Malloc

Lady Luck Lando Calrissian's modified space yacht, it was purchased from an Orthellin royal mistress at about the same time that he was setting up Nomad City, a mining operation on the sun-scorched world of Nkllon. The gambler and rogue Alliance hero had plans to transform the ship into a top-flight luxury vessel, but other duties have prevented him from fully doing so.

The yacht is fifty meters long. A pair of engine pods extend from the main hull, each housing a sublight and a hyperdrive engine. While the ship appears to be an unarmed pleasure yacht, it has an unusually sophisticated sensor system to detect, identify, and scan incoming vessels from afar. It is also equipped with a retractable laser cannon and a pair of shield generators. The *Lady Luck* has hidden smuggler compartments and its transponder has three false ship identities to let it slip through spaceport customs without anyone suspecting its true identity. Among the interior niceties are a large view deck on the observation level and a small jet-stream meditation pool. [HE, HESB, DFRSB]

Lady of Mindor A commercial starship, it travels through Corporate Sector space ferrying passengers. Han Solo and Fiolla of Lorrd once booked passage on the *Lady of Mindor* to travel from Bonadan to Ammuud in order to evade slavers and Espos —the Corporate Sector's bullying private security force—who were searching for them. [HSR]

Garouf Lafoe

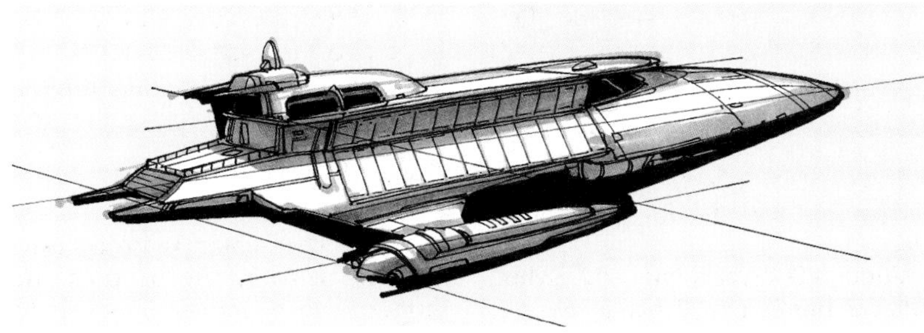

Lady Luck

Cmdr. Evram Lajaie

Lafoe, Garouf A free-trader, he imports ice chunks from the rings of Ohann and Adriana in the Tatoo system. In his off hours, Garouf Lafoe spends much time at the cantina in Mos Eisley, spending his hard-earned credits. [CCG]

Lafra A planet near Corporate Sector space, it is home to intelligent gray-skinned humanoids called Lafrarians. They have vestigial soaring membranes, feathery growths on their heads, and a keen sense of flying skills—although they can no longer soar like their long-ago ancestors did. Most Lafrarian settlements are built into mountainsides and on treetops. [HSE, CSSB, COJ]

Lajaie, Commander Evram A popular Alliance leader, he possessed expertise in space defense and orbital battle stations that enabled him to quickly analyze the plans for the first Death Star. After careful analysis, Evram Lajaie discovered a fatal flaw that made it possible for Luke Skywalker to destroy the battle station. [CCG]

Lahara sector Located in the Outer Rim, it contains the planet Agamar, home of famous Rebel Alliance pilot Keyan Farlander. [FP]

Lake Natth This lake on the planet Ambria, named by Jedi Master Thon more than 4,000 years before the Galactic Civil War, was a place where

Lambda-*class shuttle*

dark-side forces congregated—driven and kept there by Master Thon. Creatures that lived in Lake Natth mutated into evil life-forms. [TOJ]

lake spirit of Mimban An amorphous, translucent, and phosphorescent creature, it inhabits the subterranean waterways of the planet Mimban. [SME]

Lalasha, Janet A musician, she was killed by the Empire during its sweep to wipe out "questionable" artistic individuals. [TBH]

***Lambda*-class shuttle** An Imperial cargo and passenger shuttle, its three wings make it resemble an inverted Y in flight; on landing the two lower wings fold up and the shuttle lands on two legs. A lower hatch in the *Lambda*-class shuttle operates as a ramp for loading and unloading cargo and up to twenty passengers and crew. The ships have hyperdrives, reinforced hulls, and multiple blaster and laser cannons. Imperial government officials favored the *Lambda*-class shuttles because of their combat worthiness and interior space. Such ships were used by the Emperor himself. The Rebel Alliance used a stolen shuttle, the *Tydirium*, to deliver a commando assault team to the forest moon of Endor. [RJ, GSW, HESB, SWSB]

Lambda sector The domain of Imperial Moff Par Lankin, a warlord who set up his own private empire in the chaos following the Battle of Endor. [SWAJ]

lambs The slang Rebel pilots use for the *Lambda*-class shuttles. [RS]

Lamproid An intelligent species of hunters native to the planet Florn, they have loosely hinged coral jaws, rings of fangs, light sensors on stalks, and bodies consisting of snakelike, muscular coils. [TMEC]

Lamuir IV A normally serious world, once a standard year it erupts in a week of parties, parades, and dramas during the famous, planet-wide Priole Danna festival. A tradition for thousands of years, it attracts revelers from all over the galaxy. [SWAJ]

Lan Barell Fourth planet in the Lan system, the arid and desolate world is home to the small insectoids called Qieg. Lan Barell's economy is based on sales of valuable ore to Mid-Rim communities. The planet once had three moons, but one broke up after massive strip mining operations. The nearly 135 million native Qieg live in colony nests built inside hollowed-out cacti. The radical Qiemal sect dislikes all humans. [SWAJ]

***Lancer*-class frigate** A 250-meter-long Imperial capital combat starship, it was designed specifically to combat the threat of Rebel starfighters after the destruction of the first Death Star. But because of their low cost effectiveness, the Empire built only a few *Lancer*-class frigates, and these were used mainly to attack Rebel starfighter bases. The frigates have twenty tower-mounted quad laser cannons, but little defense against other combat starships except for their great speed. Five years after the death of Emperor Palpatine, Grand Admiral Thrawn used *Lancer*-class frigates as a major component of Imperial raiding missions, and they succeeded in knocking out many Alliance fighter squadrons. [GSWU, ISB, DFRSB]

Landing claws at work

landing claws Magnetic or mechanical grips on space vessels, they adhere to nearly any surface for landing or docking. [ESB]

Landing Zone A popular bar on the planet Bonadan, it is located in the Alien Quarter. [HSR]

Landkiller One The call sign used by Imperial trooper Davin Felth on his first AT-AT run. [TMEC]

landspeeder Any of a wide variety of small surface transports that use repulsorlift engines for hovering and speed. The repulsor field that is generated is enough to keep speeders suspended about a meter above the surface even when parked. Sometimes called floaters or skimmers, landspeeders have been adapted for a wide variety of terrain, including sand, snow, and even water.

Traditional landspeeders such as the SoroSuub X-34, the model that Luke Skywalker first owned, have open cockpits with retractable duraplex windscreens. The smallest can seat only a driver and passenger, although a pair of droids can be secured to back panels over the repulsor field generator. Controls are limited to a steering wheel and foot pedals, and only nooks and crannies are left for cargo. A simple scanner

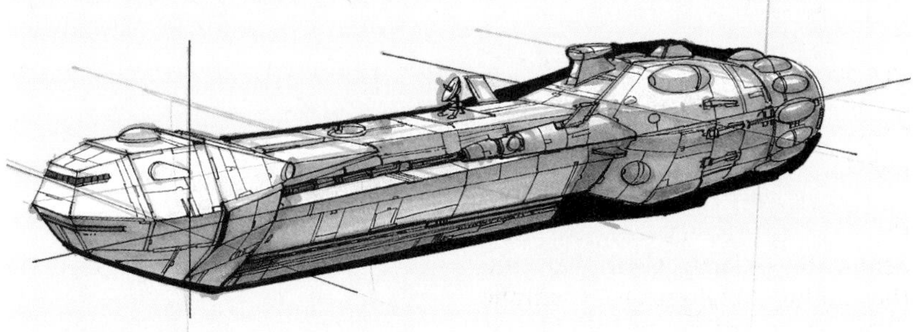
Lancer-*class frigate*

Landspeeder

Lantern bird

provides information on navigation, traffic, and speed. Top speed is about 250 kilometers per hour.

The most popular landspeeders currently on the market include Bespin Motors's Void Spider TX-3, the Ubrikkian 9000 Z001, the Mobquet Deluxe A-1, and the new SoroSuub XP-38. [SW, SWSB, SWVG]

Lan system Made up of five planets orbiting the large orange star Lan, it is more than three days' travel past the Outer Rim terminus of the Enarc Run. The system was first scouted by the Old Republic about 1,300 years before the Galactic Civil War, and the mining conglomerate Gaminne Group, Inc., arrived soon after to exploit the system's ore-rich inner planets. The system's five worlds are Lesser Galam, Lan Fellov, Lan Tundi, Lan Barell, and Greater Galam. [SWAJ]

lantern bird A large flying creature with incandescent tail feathers, it lives in shimmering nests high in the trees of Endor's forest moon. A lantern bird's tail feathers are used by Ewoks for medicinal potions. [ETV]

lantern of sacred light An Ewok totem, the belief is that as long as it remains lit, Ewok villages on the forest moon of Endor will be protected from the Night Spirit and its worshippers. [ETV]

Lanthrym A planet in the Elrood sector, it is home to outlaw stations that will service any ship, including those belonging to pirates and wanted criminals. [POG]

Lar An orange star, it is orbited by Mima II, homeworld of the Bilars. [GG4]

Larado, Incavi A smuggler, guild representative, and later the mayor of the town Dying Slowly on the planet Jubilar, she was heavily involved in a number of illegal trade operations. It was Incavi Larado who alerted Boba Fett that Han Solo had returned to Jubilar. [TBH]

Laramus Located in the Laramus system in the Parmic sector, it was the site of an ambush of a fourteen-ship Imperial convoy by a Rebel Alliance cruiser, several shuttles, and X-wing fighters. The Imperial ships were all captured without any Rebel losses. [SWSB, GG9]

Larkhess A Rebel escort frigate under the command of Captain Afyon. [HE, HESB]

Larm, Admiral The main military aide to Moff Getelles of the Antemeridian sector, he was killed in a fierce battle above Nam Chorios. [POT]

laro A card game often used in gambling. [TBH]

Lars, Beru and Owen The guardians and foster parents of Luke Skywalker, they tried to raise this future Jedi Knight and Rebel Alliance hero as a normal youth—keeping from him the fact that his veins coursed with Jedi blood and that his "dead" father had actually transformed himself into the infamous Darth Vader.

Young Luke always called Beru

Owen and Beru Lars

and Owen Lars aunt and uncle, believing that they were his blood relatives. Ben Kenobi had turned to the Lars couple just after Luke was born, and asked that they raise the child on the desolate planet of Tatooine, far from Imperial intrigue. Luke was raised to do chores on the Lars's moisture farm, and Owen continually tried to keep him on the farm even as young Skywalker dreamed of going to the Academy and then joining Rebel Alliance forces.

Beru and Owen Lars taught Luke Skywalker the value of hard work, loyalty, commitment—and compassion. They were killed by stormtroopers who were searching for the droid R2-D2, which had top-secret data about the Imperial Death Star battle station stored in its memory. The couple refused to answer any of the troopers' questions, and when Luke returned home with Kenobi and found the charred bodies of his lifelong guardians, he was set on a new path and a course of action that would change galactic history. [SW]

laser cannon A weapon that shoots visible bolts of coherent light in a rapid-fire fashion, it is often mounted on a ship or vehicle. More powerful than a blaster weapon, it easily overheats and depends upon an internal cooling system to keep it functioning. [SWSB]

laser gate Security corridors are often guarded by a grid of laser emplacements, or a gate, which can be activated upon demand to seal off areas from intrusion. [CCG]

Laser cannon

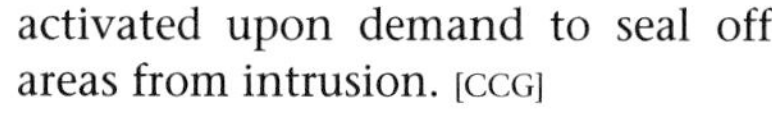

Laser gate

Latara

Latara A mischievous young female Ewok on the forest moon of Endor, she loves to play pranks as well as make music with her flute. Her best friend is Princess Kneesaa. [ETV]

Lazerian IV In the Lazerian system, it is the site of the city of Lazeria and serves as one endpoint of the Kira Run, a trade route. It is a temperate world with vast plains and home to a sentient species, the Akwin. [SWAJ, TSK]

LE-BO2D9 The droid copilot of Corellian smuggler Dash Rendar, his nickname is Leebo. LE-BO2D9 is a stripped-down skeletal model that usually carries a tool bag slung over one shoulder. [SOTE]

Leebo *See* LE-BO2D9

Leeni A female Ewok, she was a baby, or wokling, around the time of the Battle of Endor. [ETV]

Legorburu, Ixidro A Cornish intelligence officer, she served as Pakkpekatt's tactical aide aboard the *Glorious*. [SOL]

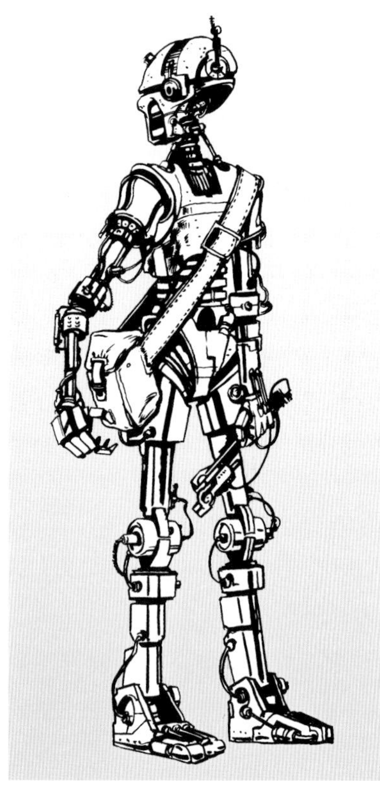

LE-BO2D9

Nabrun Leids

Leids, Nabrun A male Morseerian smuggler and pilot for hire, he normally breathes methane, so he is forced to wear a breath mask in nonmethane environments. Nabrun Leids, a former fighter pilot, will take anyone anywhere for the right price. [CCG]

Leiger, Vin A false identity used by Gavin Darklighter on Coruscant during Rogue Squadron's undercover operation there, Leiger was supposedly a young man from a Rim world who had gotten into trouble at home. He claimed he spent his life wandering the galaxy as a con man, barely scraping by with the help of his partner, a surly Shistavanen. [WG]

lekku The highly sensitive dual head-tails of the Twi'lek, they can be used by Twi'leks to send messages to each other, among other functions. They are also called tchun-tchin, tchun referring to the left tail and tchin to the right one. [TJP, FP]

Lelmra A planet that served as a temporary base for Senator Garm Bel Iblis's private army. While they were on Lelmra, a violent thunderstorm triggered a "flip-flop" of several buildings made of memory plastic, folding them up with nearly fifty people still inside. The smuggler Mazzic had a backup base for his organization on Lelmra. [DFR, LC]

Lemelisk, Bevel A paunchy human, he was one of the main designers and chief engineer of the Imperial battle stations, the Death Stars. But the absent-minded scientist with spiky white hair wasn't a perfectionist, and his work showed it. Bevel Lemelisk's design flaw on the first Death Star—an unshielded thermal exhaust port—led to its destruction by well-placed proton torpedoes fired by Luke Skywalker. As a result, Emperor Palpatine subjected Lemelisk to a particularly unpleasant execution—death by piranha beetle. But at the moment of Lemelisk's death, the Emperor had arranged to transfer Lemelisk's mind and memories to a waiting clone.

Once was not enough, however, for the mistake-prone engineer. The Emperor executed Lemelisk six more times in painful but creative fashions, each time transferring his memories and knowledge to a clone. Later, Lemelisk went to work for criminal kingpin Durga the Hutt, who called him "my pet scientist." But the quality of Lemelisk's work was again put to the test, first by the destruction of two expensive ships that were supposed to mine the Hoth asteroid belt. Durga's grand plan—the Darksaber Project—was to have Lemelisk design and build a modified Death Star laser that the Hutt could use to terrorize the entire galaxy. Using original plans stolen from government archives, Lemelisk oversaw construction of the super weapon—but

Captain Lennox

it proved to be a complete dud because of shoddy construction, and it was crushed by asteroids. Lemelisk had managed to beat a hasty retreat, but he was picked up by the New Republic and held for trial on Coruscant. [DS, JS, GG5, DSTC]

Lennox, Captain Commander of the Imperial Star Destroyer *Tyrant*, he was a capable leader. Captain Lennox, unlike most Imperial officers, was dedicated to his ship and his crew and despised the usual political maneuvering that other officers seemed to love. [CCG]

Leria Kerlsil A clean and pleasant world, it is considered a backwater. The streets of its capital are lined with blue and purple trees. Leria Kerlsil is home to life-witches or life-bearers, beings who can sustain another in perfect health for years but eventually withdraw support, causing that person to die. Life-witches are born seemingly at random. Karia Ver Seryan, a wealthy woman who lives in a large and well-defended mansion, was one of Lando Calrissian's marriage candidates until he discovered she was a life-witch. [AC]

Lesser Plooriod Cluster Made up of twelve star systems, it includes the Ottega system, site of the planet Ithor. After leaving the Corporate Sector, Han Solo and Chewbacca ran an unsuccessful military-scrip exchange scam in the Lesser Plooriod Cluster. Following the Battle of Yavin, an Alliance ship dropped a badly needed grain container in the cluster in an attempt to escape an Imperial attack. [HLL, SWSB, FP]

Letaki A species with eight tentacles and an egglike head, it has air gills beneath four eyes. [TJP]

Leth, Umak An Imperial engineer, he created many destructive tools and weapons, including the Leth universal energy cage and the World Devastators, huge regenerating war machines that stripped planets of their resources. [DE]

Leth universal energy cage A floating confinement cell, it was designed to hold even the most powerful prisoners. It also has the ability to block Force energies. [DE, DESB]

Leviathor Ancient leader of the Whaladons, he kept many of his species free by outsmarting those who would hunt them. Leviathor is believed to be the last great white Whaladon still alive. [GDV]

Lianna An industrial world in the heart of the Allied Tion sector, it instituted home rule following the Empire's defeat at the Battle of Endor. The New Republic respected the planet's nonaligned status, but Imperial reprisals seemed inevitable. Lady Santhe, head of the planet's powerful Santhe/Sienar Technologies, threatened to cut off Lianna's production of TIE fighters for the Empire unless the planet was left alone. The threat, along with secret payments to the local moff, resulted in Lianna receiving a special charter of secession from the Empire. One of the products manufactured after Lianna's secession was the compact but powerful TIE tank, also called the Century tank. The planet's inhabitants are called Lianns. [ML, DESB]

Liberator One of two Imperial Star Destroyers captured by the Alliance during the Battle of Endor, the former *Adjudicator* was placed under the command of Luke Skywalker. After Coruscant was recaptured by the Empire, a combat-damaged *Liberator* crashed into Imperial City. But Skywalker's skillful deployment of the ship's shields and repulsorlifts prevented the crew's death. [DE, DESB]

Liberty An Alliance star cruiser, it was the first Rebel Alliance casualty in the Battle of Endor. The *Liberty* and its entire crew were vaporized by the second Death Star. A second *Liberty* was part of the New Republic's Fifth Fleet and was deployed in the blockade of Doornik-319 during the Yevethan crisis. [RJ, BTS]

Lifath The proctor of information on the *Pride of Yevetha*, the flagship of strongman Nil Spaar's Black Fleet. [BTS]

life-bearer Also referred to as life-witches, they are randomly born beings on the planet Leria Kerlsil who, through a ritual called the Blood Kiss, link their own body chemistry to that of another—usually someone old, sick, or dying. This enables the life-bearer to keep the other individual alive and healthy, hold back pain, and even forestall death—for a short time. The process is called Support, and when withdrawn, as it must be to keep the life-bearer alive, the individual dies. Life-bearers as a course of nature must provide Support, or they will soon sicken and die themselves. [AC]

lifeboat *See* escape pod

lifeboat bay Special enclosures on starships, they house emergency escape pods and their jettisoning systems. [HSR]

life debt *See* Wookiee life debt

lifeplant All of the computers and mechanisms that monitor and control life functions aboard a spaceship. [TBH]

life pod *See* escape pod

life-witch *See* life-bearer

lift tube A cylindrical shaft, it moves people in a variety of directions through buildings, ships, and space stations. Repulsor fields are the most frequently used device for movement. [SW]

light dust A sacred powder, Ewoks use it to nourish the Tree of Light on Endor's forest moon. [ETV]

lighter A small spacecraft, it is used mainly to load, unload, and move cargo between huge space freighters and planets or space stations. [HSE, HLL]

Lift tube

Light Festival An Ewok celebration on Endor's forest moon, it honors the periodic rejuvenation of the Tree of Light. [ETV]

Lightning A converted Prinawe racer, it was in Pakkpekatt's chase armada. Its job was to run with the Teljkon vagabond mystery ship if it tried to escape in realspace. [BTS]

Light of Reason A spacecraft used by Nam Chorios strongman Seti Ashgad. [POT]

lightsaber The powerful yet elegant weapon of the Jedi Knights for thousands of years, these swords of power use blades of pure energy to cut through nearly any animate or inanimate object. By tradition, most lightsabers are built by their users as part of their Jedi training. They can be built in a few days if there is an emergency, or take up to a month or more to construct and fine-tune.

Seemingly simple in design, a lightsaber has a handle about twenty-four to thirty centimeters long that is usually hung from a belt. Inside are a power cell and multifaceted Adegan crystals or jewels (usually one to three) that focus the energy from the power source and release it through a concave disk atop the handle, where it appears in a tight and steady colored beam of light and energy about a meter long. When they are activated, lightsabers hum with their coursing energy. Although considered archaic by some, lightsabers can be powerful weapons after their users undergo extensive training.

A saber with a single jewel has a fixed amplitude and blade length. Those with multiple jewels can alter their amplitude and change the light blade's length by rotating an exterior control to vary the distance between jewels. The emitted beam arcs back from its positively charged continuous energy lens to a negatively charged high-energy flux aperture set in the disk atop the handle. The power amplitude determines the point at which the beam arcs back, setting the blade's length. [SW, ESB, RJ, SWSB, HESB, SOTE, TOJ]

Lightside Explorer A spacecraft that was owned by Andur and Nomi Sunrider some 4,000 years before the Galactic Civil War. [TOJ, TSW]

lightspeed engine *See* hyperdrive

Light Spirit A benign entity worshipped by the Ewoks, which they believe protects and guides them. [ETV]

light table A holoprojector device used to display holograms and holographs through a parabolic holoprojector at the center of the table's top. Data displays surround the projector. All the displays can be manipulated from touchboards around the table's edge. [RJ]

Limmer, Z. The Chief Financial Officer of Ororo Transportation, a shipping company that was the chief competitor of Xizor Transport Systems, owned by the head of the galactic underworld, Prince Xizor. When Ororo tried to overturn the XTS domination of the spice trade in the Bajic sector, Xizor's trusted aide, the replica droid Guri, killed a number of top Ororo executives including Z. Limmer. Guri speared his throat with her fingers. [SOTE]

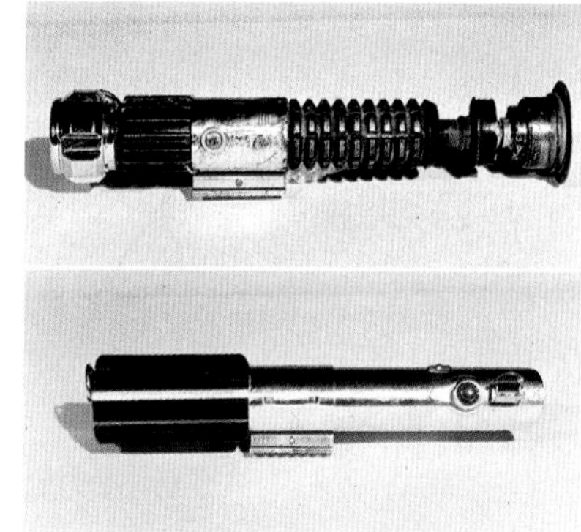
Lightsabers

Linuri Site of a confrontation between the private army of Senator Garm Bel Iblis and the forces of Grand Admiral Thrawn. [DFR]

LIN-V8K An armored mining and demolition droid, it was refurbished by a Jawa clan on Tatooine, then converted for military duty. [CCG]

LIN-V8M An armored military droid that specializes in laying explosive mines, it originally was designed to set charges in ore and spice mines. The droid was destroyed in the explosion of the Death Star. [CCG]

Liok The Shadow Taproom on Liok is considered one of the greatest archaeological discoveries. [TT]

Lisstik The leader of the Kamarian Badlanders, he traded with Han Solo and Chewbacca while they were on the planet Kamar. [HSR]

"Little Lost Bantha Cub, The" The favorite bedtime story of young Anakin Solo. He was upset when C-3PO decided he was too old to continue hearing it. [NR, JS]

L'lahsh A traditional Alderaanian food dish. [SWR]

Llewebum A species that has large bumps all along their bodies, including a secondary series of bumps below the arms. The senator from Llewebum was severely injured in the explosion caused by Dark Jedi Kueller in the Senate Hall on Coruscant. [NR]

Lobot Son of a slaver, then a slave himself, the checkered life of this human-turned-cyborg hasn't lacked for drama. After escaping his pirate captors and arriving on Bespin's floating Cloud City, Lobot was forced to steal to survive. He was caught and sentenced, but the city's Baroness Administrator suggested an alternative to a lengthy prison sentence: become indentured to the city as its first cyborg liaison officer with the computers that ran everything.

LIN-V8K

Lobot

Lobot was fitted with advanced cyborg components, including a visible computer bracket that wrapped around the back of his bald head, which dramatically increased his intelligence and let him communicate directly with the city's central computer. Lobot remained on the job even after fulfilling his sentence and helped rogue gambler Lando Calrissian win control of Cloud City from a draconian administrator in a sabacc game.

Lobot saved Calrissian's life at least once, when rogue robot EV-9D9 planted bombs on Cloud City. He stayed behind after Calrissian and his new Rebel Alliance friends fled following the visit of Darth Vader, who used local facilities to freeze Han Solo into a block of carbonite. Months later Calrissian returned and was attacked by Lobot, whose motivational-programming capsule had been damaged by Ugnaughts rebelling against Imperial rule. Calrissian repaired the damaged capsule and Lobot was then able to disarm bombs that the Ugnaughts had planted around Cloud City. Later, Calrissian and Lobot teamed up with the Ugnaughts in a successful fight against the Imperial occupiers.

Calrissian called on him again during the Yevethan crisis when Calrissian was trying to solve the mystery of the Teljkon vagabond ghost ship. He lured Lobot with the promise of a vacation. When the two of them and the droids R2-D2 and C-3PO boarded the vagabond, it took off with them inside. Eventually, Lobot figured out a way to talk to the vagabond by connecting his interface band with a network of wires attached to the ship. But while it was willing to give him information, the ship wouldn't give him control. The involuntary crew was rescued by Luke Skywalker and Colonel Pakkpekatt at Maltha Obex. Years later, Lobot surfaced as Calrissian's aide when he opened *GemDiver Station* in orbit around Yavin. [ESB, SWCG, BTS, TT, GG2]

locomotor A servomechanism, it gives droids the ability to move. [SW]

Loctob, Cycy A denizen of the spaceport of Nar Shaddaa, he makes a living by selling contraband. [DE]

logra A carnivorous animal. [TJP]

Logray An Ewok medicine man for the tribe that aided the Rebel Alliance, Logray is a tan-striped Ewok. He wears the half skull of a great forest bird on his head, a single feather adorning its crest. Logray was a great warrior when he was young, and his staff of power is decorated with the spine of a great enemy. Revered for his great wisdom, he long helped tribe members with magic spells and potions. His students included Teebo

Logray

Elscol Loro

and Wicket W. Warrick. But Logray could also be a bully, and after the Battle of Endor, Chief Chirpa replaced him as medicine man with Paploo. [RJ, ETV, EA, GG5]

Lomabu III Located near the Aida system, Lomabu III is one of six planets in the Lomabu system, all of which have erratic orbits around their orange primary star. It has one moon and is covered with oceans and lengthy archipelagoes. It was depopulated by the Empire prior to the Battle of Hoth. In an effort to trap Alliance agents, Io Desnand, Imperial governor of the Aida system, shipped several hundred Wookiees to the planet and imprisoned them, planning to kill them all during a staged attack designed to attract Rebel rescuers. The prison was located on a peninsula on the east shore of one archipelago, near a dense jungle and the crumbling ruins of an abandoned Lomabuan city. Where the peninsula meets the mainland is what appears to be a stretch of sand—in reality, it is a colony of tiny creatures that will devour anything that touches them. Immediately after the Battle of Hoth, the bounty hunters Chenlambec and Tinian I'att convinced Bossk to search for Han Solo in the Lomabu system. According to their cover story, a group of Wookiees was trying to establish a secure colony on the planet. When they arrived at the planet, Tinian and Chen successfully double-crossed Bossk and rescued the Wookiee prisoners. [TBH]

Lomin-ale A frothy green ale with a bitter, spicy flavor, it is the drink of choice of many members of Rogue Squadron. [RS]

lommite A mineral found mainly on the planet Elom, it is a major raw material in the manufacture of transparisteel. [HESB]

Lonay A clever but cowardly Twi'lek, he was one of the lieutenants, or Vigos, of Prince Xizor's Black Sun criminal organization. [SOTE]

Long, Gee A member of Auren Yomm's famous racing team that competed in the Roon Colonial Games. [DTV]

Long Snoot *See* Garindan

Loor, Kirtan Formerly the Imperial liaison to Corellian Security (CorSec), then an Imperial Intelligence agent on Imperial Center, he was assigned the task of destroying Rogue Squadron by Ysanne Isard, Director of Imperial Intelligence. Agent Kirtan Loor resembled the late Grand Moff Tarkin, the Emperor's onetime Intelligence chief. Loor was tall and lanky, had black hair with a thinning widow's peak, and sharp features in a face slender as a cadaver's. He had enough ambition to dream about becoming a Grand Moff, and enough talent for dealing with regulations and bureaucracy to be a severe problem for anyone who stood in his way.

Loor had a visual memory retention rate of almost one hundred percent, making him ideal for his Rogue-hunting task. He would have accomplished his aims at Talasea had it not been for the stupidity of Admiral Devlia, who was in charge of Imperial troops when they made their night raid on Rogue Squadron's base. As luck would have it, Loor just missed the Rogues' retaliatory raid on Vladet, although he was witness to the terrible destruction there. Shortly before the fall of Borleias, he was recalled to Imperial Center, again barely escaping death or capture. At headquarters, Isard gave him another task: overseeing the progress of General Derricote's Krytos project.

The Krytos virus was released into the planet's water supply shortly before the arrival of the Alliance fleet, but too soon for the disease to spread rapidly enough to infect a larger portion of the alien inhabitants, as planned. Although the project did not succeed, Isard didn't blame Loor for its failure. Instead, she placed him in charge of Imperial Center while she retreated to her sanctuary in the Super Star Destroyer *Lusankya*. Loor enjoyed his role as head of the terrorist Palpatine Counter-insurgency Front, challenging the New Republic in the very same way that its agents had challenged the Empire.

Loor soon became vexed with interference from Fliry Vorru and realized that Vorru was calling the shots with full approval from Isard. Loor could see that his value to Isard was quickly coming to an end, so he went to see Nawara Ven, the Twi'lek Rogue Squadron member who was defending fellow Rogue Tycho Celchu against false charges of murder. Loor offered to testify for Celchu in exchange for immunity from prosecution, one million credits, and a new identity and new life on another world. He also would reveal the real spy within Rogue Squadron as well as every Imperial agent on Coruscant. But just as he was being escorted into the Justice Court to give his deposition, Loor was assassinated by one of Isard's sleeper agents. [RS, WG, KT]

Lorahns A planet controlled by a strict religious oligarchy, the Ffib sect. The bounty hunter Boba Fett once earned a 500,000-credit reward for capturing Nivek'Yppiks, a Ffib heretic wanted by Lorahns's leaders. [TJP]

Lord of the Sith *See* Dark Lord of the Sith

Lorell Raiders *See* Hapes Consortium

Loro, Elscol The female leader of the resistance against Imperial forces on the planet Cilpar, the reddish-brown-haired, dark-eyed woman took over the organization after her husband, Throm, died fighting the Imperials. Initially, she thought that the Rebellion had betrayed her movement, resulting in the destruction of two suburbs of Kiidan where her people had family and supporters. But with Rogue Squadron's intervention, Cilpar threw off the Empire's oppressive yoke and Elscol Loro was offered a position in Rogue Squadron; she accepted.

Loro, an intelligent young woman with a fierce fighting spirit, felt the loss of her husband deeply, but she kept her feelings of loneliness hidden. After her husband was slain, she was watched over by Groznik, a Wookiee, who had transferred a life debt from Throm to Elscol. At that point, Loro started being more reckless than prudent. She kept the other Rogues at a distance, refusing their help. Although her reckless tactics ultimately won the day, Wedge Antilles discharged her from the squadron because she was jeopardizing the lives of the other pilots.

Loro was skilled at insurgency tactics, and the New Republic needed her in its fight to overthrow the Thyferran government, now controlled by Ysanne Isard, former Director of Imperial Intelligence. She was given the task of organizing the Ashern into a resistance movement, providing the once-peaceful rebels of the Vratix species with expertise, weapons, and support to overcome the tyranny of their human masters. With the assistance of security forces from Zaltin Corporation, they proved to be a deadly combination. The Thyferran Home Defense Corps (THDC) and the meager Imperial troops Ysanne Isard possessed were no match for them. This proved very clear when the ground assault began. With remarkable ease, the resistance fighters took over the Xucphra Corporation Administration Building, headquarters for the THDC and Isard's puppet government. [XW, BW]

Loronar A planet that housed facilities used by the Emperor to build his largest warships and special weapons platforms. [ISWU]

Loronar Corporation A huge, nearly galaxy-wide conglomerate, it is a manufacturer of many products, chief among them synthdroids and advanced spacecraft. The company will use any method to fulfill its corporate goals and increase its wealth and power. [POT]

Loronar Strike Cruiser A large cruiser, some 450 meters long and with a standard crew of 2,000, a ship of this class was hollowed out and used to transport the Hammertong device. [TMEC]

Lorrd During the Kanz Disorders, this planet in the Kanz sector was bombed from orbit and its human inhabitants enslaved by the Argazdans. After nearly three centuries, the Lorrdians were finally freed by the Jedi Knights. Hart-and-Parn Gorra-Fiolla, Assistant Auditor-General of the Corporate Sector, was from Lorrd. [HSR, CSSB]

Lorrdian Human inhabitants of the planet Lorrd, they are the best mimes and mimics in the galaxy. The talent was originally developed by Lorrdians as a form of kinetic communication during the Kanz Disorders, when the planet's conquerors forbade them from communicating in any way while they were busy at their slave labor. The Lorrdians were freed by Jedi Knights and forces of the Old Republic. [HSR]

Loruss, Chief Technician Hideously ugly, with a shaved head and circular blue lenses installed on her eyes like frameless glasses, she worked for Holowan Laboratories as manager of the IG Series assassin droids prototype project. Loruss was killed when one of the droids, IG-88, became self-aware on activation and staged a bloody revolt and escape. [TBH]

Lost City of the Jedi Buried deep below the surface of Yavin 4, the city was built long ago by ancient Jedi Knights and held great Jedi secrets in its computer library. Droids cared for the city and its hidden knowledge for ages. Ken, the grandson of Emperor Palpatine, was raised in the city by the droid DJ-88 and taught to reject the dark side. Under the sway of a truth serum, Ken betrayed the city's location to dark-side prophet Kadaan, but Kadaan and his troopers were trapped inside the shut-down city by Alliance leaders on the surface, and the Jedi secrets were lost forever after a trooper accidentally destroyed the library computer. [LCJ, PDS]

Lost Ones, The A gang of street-toughened youngsters, they hung out on the lower levels of Coruscant some twenty years after the Battle of Endor. Their symbol was a cross inside a triangle and their leader was a teenage boy named Norys. [YJK]

lotiramine A drug that can counteract the drug skirtopanol, which is used much like a truth serum to interrogate prisoners. However, mixing lotiramine with skirtopanol can induce chemical amnesia, or in some cases, death. [BW]

Lowbacca The nephew of the Wookiee Chewbacca, he was the first of his species to train at Luke Skywalker's Jedi academy. Nicknamed Lowie, the nineteen-year-old Lowbacca had always shown an affinity for the Force. He was quickly befriended by Jacen and Jaina Solo, the twin son and daughter of Han and Leia Organa Solo.

Lowbacca was different from the other trainees. For one thing, he wore no clothing except for a glossy syren fiber belt that held a small translator droid known as Em Teedee that interpreted the Wookiee's growls and grunts into Basic. Lowbacca's fur is the color of ginger, with a black streak starting over his left eye and continuing down his back. Lowbacca also quickly became friends with a humorless Dathomirian girl named Tenel Ka.

Together, the Jedi initiates explored the jungles of Yavin 4. Low-

Lowbacca

Lumat

bacca once discovered an old, crashed TIE fighter that the young Jedi students repaired, only to be confronted by the still-surviving pilot, who kidnapped the twins and held them hostage until they were rescued. Only weeks later, the twins—this time along with Lowbacca—were again kidnapped on a visit to Lando Calrissian's *GemDiver Station*. The perpetrator was a Nightsister from Dathomir, who schemed to turn the three to the dark side by forcing them to train at a Shadow Academy. Lowbacca was separated from the twins, taunted, and mistreated. Eventually they managed to escape and returned to their studies. [YJK, SWCG]

L'toth, Kiles A Dornean, he was associate director of the Astrographic Survey Institute. Kiles L'toth was an old friend of General Etahn A'baht, commander of the New Republic's Fifth Fleet, and the general asked him to assemble a survey team to be sent to Koornacht Cluster to do some undercover scouting for the New Republic. The ship that carried the team, the *Astrolabe*, was destroyed at Doornik-1142 by a secret Yevethan fleet. [BTS]

Lucazec An arid, pale-brown planet, it was the former home of the Fallanassi, a religious sect who followed the White Current, an energy similar to the Force. Ships that land on Lucazec's North Plateau are serviced by a small airfield and can dock in Hangar Kaa. Five hundred kilometers away are the Towers, the only region of Lucazec with proper docking bays for spacecraft. Hastings Watershed is a hilly region in the North Plateau with many villages and settlements built wherever there is a constant water source. From the North Plateau airfield, the villages of Jisasu and Big Hill can be reached via the East District Trail or the shorter Crown Pass Road.

Ialtra Trail, branching off of Crown Pass Road, leads to the now-abandoned village of Ialtra. It was here that the Fallanassi lived in a community of more than thirty buildings in ring dwellings and circle houses. Medicinal crops grew under translucent domes, and the town was decorated by gardens, colored tiled walls, an enclosed pond, and an open-air amphitheater. Ialtra is now abandoned and its buildings have been vandalized. Lucazec's inhabitants commonly cross the planet's surface in boxy, two-seat utility vehicles with oversized wheels. Animal life on the planet includes carrion birds called nackhawns.

Years ago, one of the Fallanassi, Isela Talsava Norand, revealed the sect's existence to Lucazec's Imperial governor. The Empire immediately realized the potential of the unique Fallanassi skill with the White Current. General Tagge approached Wialu, leader of the Fallanassi, to offer the Empire's protection in exchange for an oath of loyalty. When Wialu refused, Tagge's agents stirred up resentment toward the Fallanassi among the people of Lucazec by burning homes and poisoning drinking water, then laying the blame on the Fallanassi.

Talsava was banished from the Circle for her betrayal, and she took her daughter Akanah with her. Five Fallanassi children were sent to other planets—Teyr, Paig, and Carratos—for their own safety. Soon after, the sect abandoned Ialtra and left Lucazec, settling on J't'p'tan. Twelve years after the Battle of Endor, Luke Skywalker and the Fallanassi woman Akanah visited Lucazec to find clues about the woman Akanah said was Luke's mother, Nashira. They were ambushed by a pair of Imperial agents —an illusion generated by Akanah to test Luke—but picked up a clue as to where the Fallanassi might be found. But it turned out that Akanah was lying; Nashira was a woman who had been kind to her in the past but wasn't related to Luke at all. [BTS, TT]

Lucky Despot A no-longer-spaceworthy cargo hauler, it was sunk into the sand and turned into a hotel and casino near the center of Mos Eisley spaceport on Tatooine. The *Lucky Despot* is owned by Lady Valarian, a Whiphid and local crime lord who was an arch rival of Jabba the Hutt. [ISWU, TMEC, GG7]

Luka, Zona A Jedi who apprenticed under the Jedi Master Dominis some 4,000 years before the Galactic Civil War. [TSW]

lum A fermented, fiery ale, it is a favorite of most members of Rogue Squadron in their off-duty hours. It has a sweet and not unpleasant soapy taste. [XW, TMEC, TM, GG9]

luma A small tool used for illumination. [TBH, SME]

Lumat An Ewok warrior on the forest moon of Endor, he is also his tribe's chief woodcutter. Married to Zephee, they are the parents of Latara, Nippet, and Wiley. [ETV]

lumni-spice The rarest form of spice in the galaxy, it grows deep in the caverns on Hoth. The lumni-spice is fiercely guarded by the dragon-slug, which feeds on the spice. [CSW]

Lumpawarrump A Wookiee, he is Chewbacca's son. Lumpawarrump, or

Lumpawarrump

Lumpy for short, accompanied his father on a mission to rescue Han Solo, and that served to complete his coming-of-age ritual, known as the hrrtayyk. After the mission, Lumpy changed his name to Lumpawaroo, with Waroo as his nickname. [SWWS, TT]

Lur An icy and turbulent planet, it lies just outside the borders of the Corporate Sector. The upper layers of Lur's atmosphere are heavily ionized, creating intense electrical storms. This, combined with gale-force winds and freezing temperatures, makes starship landings hazardous. The fur-covered, bipedal inhabitants of Lur are experts in genetic manipulation and live in cities of a few thousand each. They are peaceful and sociable, and very few ever choose to leave Lur. But slavers have been a constant threat, since they can sell Lurrians for four- to six-thousand credits each. Han Solo and Chewbacca were unwillingly involved in a Lurrian slavery operation during their early adventures. [HSR, CSSB]

Lusa A young female from the planet Chiron, she was a friend of Jaina Solo. Lusa has four legs and a reddish-gold horselike body with white spots on her hindquarters. Her torso is humanoid, with reddish-gold curly hair on her head. Lusa loves to run and jump and is very fast. Her species grows forehead horns each year; the horns grow beneath velvet, a vascular tissue, and break out of the velvet when they are grown. [CS]

Lusankya A Super Star Destroyer, it was constructed in secret at Kuat Yards under the false name *Executor*. It was immediately buried beneath Imperial Center during Emperor Palpatine's reign to serve as his emergency evacuation vehicle. Director of Imperial Intelligence Ysanne Isard used it as her private prison and sanctuary, a pleasure palace for her but pure hell for her captives, who were subjected to endless torture, interrogation, and mind-control experiments, including brainwashing. Most who emerged from the *Lusankya* alive came out as sleeper agents, in effect remotely controlled human bombs who did the Empire's bidding—no matter how horrible—when activated. The facility imprisoned top Rebel Alliance officials and daredevil pilots and heroes. When Isard was forced to flee Imperial Center in the face of the New Republic invasion, she had the *Lusankya* blast out of its tomb, devastating more than 100 square kilometers of Imperial City and killing millions of its inhabitants. [KT, BW]

Luwingo

Luure, M'yet A powerful senator, he was from the planet Exodeen, a former Imperial world. The Exodeenians have six arms and legs, and rows of uneven teeth. Luure supported the introduction of former Imperials to serve as political representatives in the New Republic. He died in the explosion in Senate Hall, which was part of Dark Jedi Kueller's reign of terror against the New Republic. Following his death, Luure was replaced by the junior Exodeen representative, R'yet Coome. [NR]

Luwingo First mate on the *Hyperspace Marauder*, he is partner to Lo Khan, the ship's owner. Luwingo is a Yaka cyborg with brain implants like the other members of his race. Although he appears somewhat dull, he can beat an L7 logician droid in hologames on a regular basis. [DE]

Lweilot asteroid belt Located in the Bseto system, the belt—some ninety million kilometers wide—occupies the third orbital position around the white dwarf star Bseto. [SWAJ]

Lwhekk Homeworld of the reptiloid Ssi-ruuk, it is in a distant star cluster and is the center of the Ssi-ruuvi Imperium. [TAB]

Lwyll Wife of the smuggler Roa, she is a striking woman with masses of wavy white-blond hair and an elegant face. Lwyll has known Han Solo since the onetime smuggler worked for her husband. [HSR]

Lybeya system Located within the Bajic sector of the Outer Rim, the system contains the Vergesso asteroid field. The Tenloss Syndicate built a shipyard in one of the larger asteroids in the Lybeya system, which was used by the Alliance until eliminated by Darth Vader and the Imperial fleet prior to the Battle of Endor. [SOTE]

Lycoming A New Republic Quarantine Enforcement Cruiser. [POT]

M3-D2 A housekeeping droid, it worked in the palace of Jabba the Hutt and served as a contact for many of Lady Valarian's spies. [TJP]

M-3PO *See* Emtrey (Emtreypio)

mace flies Insects from the planet Dantooine. [DA]

macrobinoculars Handheld viewing devices that magnify distant objects, they support both day and night vision through built-in light and dark scopes. Readouts on the view plate give the viewed object's true and relative azimuth, elevation, and range. A macrobinocular device can also be mounted in a helmet. [SW, TBH]

macrofuser A miniature welding tool, it is designed and calibrated for heavy-duty repairs of complex metals, such as those found in starships. [ESB]

Madak, Ellorrs Like many of the Duros species, he has natural pilot-

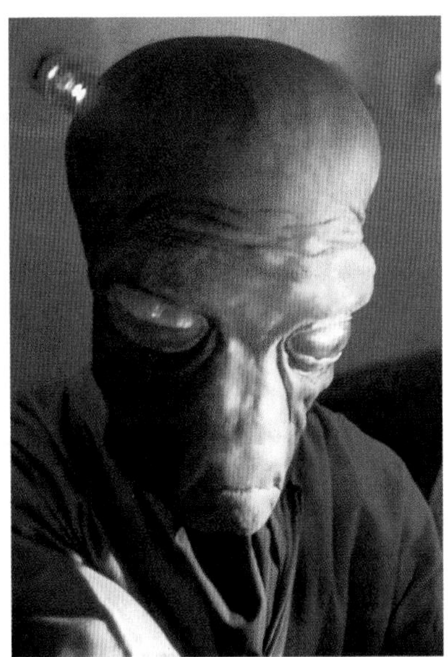
Ellorrs Madak

ing and navigational skills. A former scout and freelance instructor, he now makes runs to the important trade worlds of Celanon, Byblos, and Yaga Minor. [CCG]

Madine, General Crix A Corellian by birth and a highly decorated Imperial officer, he defected to the Rebel Alliance after Emperor Palpatine personally ordered him on a top-secret mission to subjugate Dentaal. Madine considered the mission so criminal and vile that he defected shortly after the Battle of Yavin. Although the Alliance was at first suspicious that Crix Madine might be a double agent, he quickly proved himself and became one of the most important and trusted military advisors of Alliance leader Mon Mothma.

Madine introduced many innovative tactics to the Rebel forces, working on ground strategy while Admiral Ackbar developed space-combat tactics.

When the Alliance learned that the Empire was building a second Death Star above the forest moon of Endor, General Madine helped devise a plan to have a small strike team led by Han Solo deactivate the incomplete Death Star's energy shield—located on Endor's moon—so that the battle station could be attacked. Ultimately, the plan was successful. Following the Battle of Endor, Mothma offered the general a seat on the New Republic's Provisional Council, but he declined, saying that he was a warrior, not a politician.

Continuing to keep a low profile, Madine became head of covert operations as Supreme Allied Commander for Intelligence. He was involved in the New Republic's battle against Grand Admiral Thrawn and was instrumental in advising how to attack the Imperial World Devastators that had been unleashed on Mon Calamari. The brown-bearded, middle-aged officer was never far from the scene of the action himself. He led a commando team that sought out and finally found a new super weapon that was being built for Durga the Hutt and led Alliance forces to the site. But the infiltrators were caught, and just before Alliance ships could rescue him, General Madine was killed by Durga with a laser shot through the heart. [RJ, DS, HE, SWCG]

Madis, Captain A New Republic officer, he commanded the picket ship *Folna* during the Yevethan crisis. [TT]

Mageye the Hutt A crime lord, he was accidentally killed by the bounty hunter Zardra. [TMEC]

Magg A slave trader, he posed as the personal assistant of Fiolla of Lorrd in order to keep tabs on her investigations in Corporate Sector space. [HSR]

Gen. Crix Madine

Magnetic suction tube

magnetic suction tube A device used mainly to lift droids into starships. Large model tubes are operated by nomadic species such as Jawas on remote planets such as Tatooine to help them make their living selling lost or stranded droids. [CCG]

main drive The primary propulsion unit, it is the most powerful engine onboard a starship. [SWR]

maintenance hauler A space tug, it tows disabled spacecraft back to the nearest spaceport. [HLL]

maitrakh The Noghri word for the female ruler of a clan, it is a title of respect that is backed by long tradition. A maitrakh from clan Kihm'bar used her influence to help Princess Leia Organa Solo convince the Noghri to end their support for the Empire. [DFR, DFRSB, LC]

Maires An ocean planet in the Hapes Cluster, it is the homeworld of the water-breathing Mairans. These large, tentacled creatures can leave the sea for brief periods but must spray seawater on their black, rubbery skin to keep it moist. They speak a strange musical language by blowing into drilled shells. The Mairans have long been rivals of the inhabitants of the planet Vergill. Nineteen years after the Battle of Endor, the Vergills began an undersea ditanium mining operation on the planet Hapes, next to the newly opened Mairan consulate. The Mairans filed an official protest against the noise and mining debris, but in reality they had deliberately placed their consulate near the richest vein of ditanium in order to spark a confrontation. [YJK]

Maizor Maizor lost a confrontation to his onetime rival, Jabba the Hutt. Almost as a joke, Jabba had Maizor's brain placed in a jar filled with nutrients and attached to metal, spiderlike legs, courtesy of the B'omaar monks who shared Jabba's palace with him. [DS]

makants Large and playful insects, they live on the forest moon of Endor. They look like a cross between a mantis and a cricket. [ETV]

maker, the A droid phrase, it is used to refer to their creator and is often said in a worshipful, almost religious context. The protocol droid C-3PO, for example, often uses the phrase "Thank the maker!" when something good happens to him or his friends. [SW]

Makki A crew member of the *Steadfast*, a New Republic survey ship that found the ruins of the Imperial ship *Gnisnal*. The ship's crew also discovered an intact memory core that was a valuable source of information. [BTS]

Malakili A professional creature trainer and beast handler from the Corellian system, he left the Circus Horrificus to work for Jabba the Hutt as a rancor handler. Malakili was a muscular human, with a large paunch and a stretched, unattractive face. Malakili had a great deal of affection for the rancor. He was able to train it and eventually became the only creature that the rancor wouldn't attack and eat. But when Jabba ordered a krayt dragon to fight the rancor, Malakili knew his pet's days were numbered. With the help of Lady Valarian, he tried to have the rancor

Makant

Mallatobuck

smuggled off-world, but on the morning the escape was to take place, the rancor was killed by Luke Skywalker. After Jabba's death, Malakili opened a restaurant in Mos Eisley—The Crystal Moon—with his friend Porcellus, who had been Jabba's head chef, using funds looted from Jabba's palace. [TJP, GG5]

Malani A young Ewok from the forest moon of Endor, she is Teebo's younger sister and had a crush on Wicket W. Warrick when they were growing up. [ETV]

Mal'ary'ush The Noghri title used to address Leia Organa Solo, it identifies her as the daughter of Darth Vader, to whom the Noghri long felt indebted. [HE, DFR, LC]

Maliss, Ket An assassin in the employ of Prince Xizor, head of the Black Sun criminal syndicate, he was on some unknown business in Mos Eisley when Ben Kenobi and Han Solo were making their deal to get to Alderaan. Xizor called Maliss his Shadow Killer. [CCG]

Malkite Poisoner A member of an infamous order of killers, they learn their deadly craft on the planet Malkii. Malkite Poisoners carry small vials of lethal toxins hidden in their clothing. The group's code insists that no member be captured alive. [HSR]

Mallar, Plat A young Grannan from Polneye, he took one of six operational TIE interceptors during the Yevethan attack on Polneye and was able to destroy a Yevethan scout fighter. He then attempted to reach the planet Galantos in the short-range TIE—an impossible task—but luckily was picked up by a New Republic prowler. Plat Mallar had recorded tapes of the savage massacre on his planet, thus alerting Republic leaders to the recent aggressive actions of the Yevetha. Mallar was nursed back to health on Coruscant and became a New Republic pilot. Admiral Ackbar helped push through an emergency petition for membership in the New Republic for Polneye, which Chief of State Leia Organa Solo approved. [SOL, BTS]

Mallatobuck The wife of the Wookiee Chewbacca. [SWWS]

Malorm Family An infamous group of human psychopathic killers, they hijacked the luxury spaceliner *Galaxy Wanderer* as it passed through the Corporate Sector, dumping more than thirty passengers into deep space as they ransacked the ship's vaults. The three-man, two-woman team escaped to Matra VI where they eventually were apprehended by a Corporate Sector Authority Counterterrorist Security Team. [HLL]

Maltha Obex *See* Qella

Manarai Mountains A chain of mountains, their snow-covered peaks rise above Imperial City. The mountains have also given their name to an exclusive restaurant in Monument Park. The restaurant, with a breathtaking view, long catered to the wealthy and powerful and always held a table open for Prince Xizor, the criminal kingpin who was a silent partner in it. Among other dishes, the Manarai served fleek eel, Giant Ithor Snail in flounut butter, and Kashyyyk land shrimp. [HE, HESB, SOTE]

Manaroo This tattooed dancing girl was raised on a farm by poor parents. She was rescued from Imperial COMPNOR forces and smuggled off her homeworld of Aruza by the bounty hunter Dengar. An empath, Manaroo could alter her style of dancing to play off of her audience's specific emotions. She worked as a

Mantellian savrip holomonster

dancer at Cloud City before Dengar brought her with him to Tatooine, where she was captured by Jabba the Hutt and forced to dance for him. Manaroo eventually escaped from Jabba and rescued Dengar, who had been left to die in the desert on Jabba's orders. Through her patience and thought-sharing abilities, Manaroo was able to help Dengar regain many of the emotions the Empire had stripped from him. The two were married soon after on Tatooine. [TBH]

Manchisco, Captain Tessa A veteran of the Virgillian Civil War, she was captain of Luke Skywalker's flagship *Flurry* during the Bakura conflict. [TAB]

Mandalore A mercenary warlord who lived about 4,000 years before the Battle of Yavin, he conquered a planet that now bears his name. But Mandalore lost a confrontation with Jedi Ulic Qel-Droma and then willingly became a follower of the fallen Jedi. He was a model for the Mandalorian supercommandos of later generations, who also wore a full-face metal mask to imitate him. [TSW]

Mandalore system The system was home, some 4,000 years before the Galactic Civil War, to fierce masked warrior clans led by the mysterious warlord Mandalore. The clans, made up of deadly but honorable crusaders, rode semiintelligent Basilisk war droids, boasted cutting-edge weaponry, and were considered the best fighters in the galaxy. The mask and title of Mandalore belonged to no single individual but were traditionally passed down from one warrior to the next on the leader's death.

During the Sith War, the Mandalorians conquered the Kuar system and struck at the neighboring Empress Teta system, forcing the Tetan leader Ulic Qel-Droma to battle Mandalore in one-on-one combat. Mandalore was defeated, and he swore his armies' allegiance to Qel-Droma and the forces of the mystical Krath sect. The warlord was made Qel-Droma's war commander, and his clans won many victories. At the close of the Sith War, however, Mandalore's armies were defeated in their attempt to capture the planet Onderon. Mandalore and his surviving warriors were forced to flee to the Dxun moon, where Mandalore was killed by a pair of the moon's deadly beasts; a new warrior donned his mask and assumed his title.

Millennia later, the warlike Mandalore people exterminated the Ithullan race, several hundred years before the Battle of Yavin. During the Clone Wars, a group of warriors from the system were defeated by the Jedi Knights. The notorious bounty hunter Boba Fett wears a blaster-resistant armored suit similar to those worn by Mandalore warriors, and his alternate ship, *Slave II,* was based on a Mandalorian police ship design. Imperial dungeon ships were originally designed by the Mandalorians and were introduced during the Jedi purge to contain dangerous Force users. [SWS, MTS, DE, DLS, D, TMEC, DESB, TSW]

Manka cat Carnivorous cats, they were the only predators feared by members of the Tetsus clan of Rodians while they were on a nameless jungle planet that they colonized after escaping Rodia. [TMEC]

Mantellian savrip A nasty, hulking predator, it lives on the planet of Ord Mantell. The hunched-over creature has a leathery green hide, a head like a snake, and arms so long that they drag on the ground. [CCG]

Mantessa This planet was the home of dangerous predators called panthacs. Han Solo and Chewbacca encountered the creatures while on the planet. [LC]

Manticore One of Admiral Daala's four Star Destroyers, it was named after an extinct animal on display in Coruscant's Holographic Zoo for Extinct Animals. [JS, ISWU]

mantigrue A dragonlike creature with leathery wings, sharp claws, and a long, pointed beak, it lives on the forest moon of Endor. Some can be trained, such as the one owned by Morag, the Tulgah witch. [ETV]

Mantooine In the system of the same name, the planet is located in the Atrivis sector in the Outer Rim. Mantooine's government treats spice smuggling as a capital offense. Years ago, a group of Mantooine freedom fighters called the Liberators were massacred by the Empire when they took refuge in a captured Imperial base. That incident was one of several that helped build a unified Rebel Alliance, because if there had been communication with other groups of freedom fighters, the Liberators could have been warned of the strike and taken refuge elsewhere. In a separate incident, the self-sacrifice of probe droid D-127X may have saved Mantooine from an Imperial surprise attack. [FP, SWAJ, RSB]

Mantigrue

manumitting A process by which a droid is reprogrammed to give it an incentive for extraordinary service: The droid is given its freedom if it meets its goals, allowing it to break the bonds of ownership. [HSR]

Marasan One of the strangest species in the known galaxy, the Marasan are cyborgs that evolved within the Marasa Nebula. Marasans are tall, gangly, long-armed marsupials. Their brain-enhancing borg implants allow them to navigate in the dark, gaseous area of space where they live. Many Marasans were enslaved by the Empire during the Galactic Civil War. [GG12]

Marauder The New Republic gunship that accompanied the *Glorious* on the initial interception of the Teljkon vagabond. [BTS]

***Marauder*-class corvette** One of the most common capital ships in the Corporate Sector Authority's Picket Fleet, they are also popular with planetary navies and large corporations. Over the years, some Marauders have fallen into the hands of smugglers and pirates.

Marauder-class corvettes are 195-meter-long light cruisers streamlined for atmospheric combat. Their long, sleek bodies and extended airfoils make them look more like oversized fighters than combat cruisers. Their top planetary speed is 850 kilometers an hour. A standard Marauder carries eight double turbolasers and three tractor-beam projectors, twelve fighters for long-range assault and patrol missions, and two platoons of forty Authority Espo troopers.

Han Solo had two run-ins with CSA Marauders. One corvette launched an attack on an outlaw-tech base, forcing Solo to lead the base's technicians into combat against the Authority's fighters. Another time, Chewbacca took over a Marauder and used it as an evacuation vessel after Solo engineered the destruction of the penal facility known as Stars' End. [CSSB, HSE, SWVG]

marauders A species of tall, barbaric humanoids, they prey upon the more peaceful inhabitants of Endor's forest moon. Once spaceway pirates, they crashed on Endor and were unable to leave. They have scaly, monkey-like faces and wear ragged clothing adorned with scavenged items. The marauders built a dark fortress on a desolate plain surrounded by a moat. Under their king, Terak, they made destructive forays seeking a new power source for their ship. [BFE, ISWU]

Marauder-*class corvette*

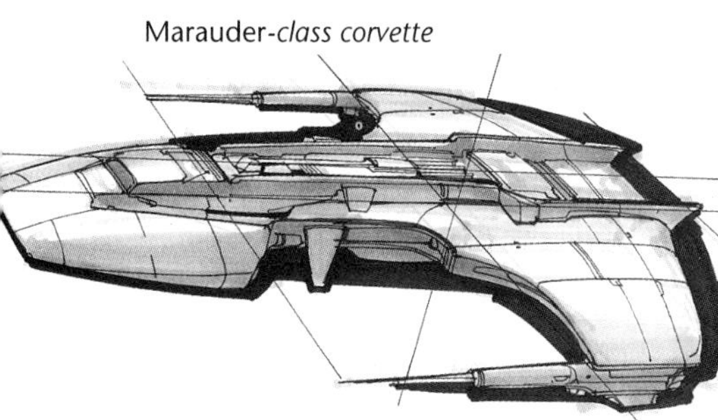

Marauder Starjacker

Marauder Starjacker An ore-raiding ship commanded by pirate captain Finhead Stonebone some 4,000 years before the Battle of Yavin, it resembled an insect—a 100-meter-long insect. The *Marauder Starjacker* and its sister ship the *Stenness Raider* began life as asteroid-mining ships. But Captain Stonebone used them to raid Ithullian colossus wasp carriers, both for himself and later for Great Bogga the Hutt.

The ships were built with rugged claws to dig through solid rock and attach to an asteroid. Thruster jets were then fired to move the asteroid; plasma drills cut through useless rock, and a central suction tube drew material up into the ship's filtration system. Valuable ore was stored in cargo bays while waste material was used as fuel. Captain Stonebone's engineers stole two of these vessels after destroying a mining operation near the Varl system and modified them for ore raiding. [TOJ, SWVG]

Marcha, Duchess of Mastigophorous A Drall female, she is the aunt of Ebrihim, who was hired on Corellia as a tutor for the children of Leia and Han Solo. Chewbacca and the Solo children sought help from her after they were forced to flee Corellia. She informed her nephew that a planetary repulsor similar to the one on Corellia existed on Drall. [AS]

Marcopious, Yeoman A member of the Honor Guard for Chief of State Leia Organa Solo, he helped C-3PO and R2-D2 escape in a scout boat after the kidnapping of Princess Leia, before the New Republic's ships went into trackless hyperspace. But Yeoman Marcopious died in the escape pod of a mysterious disease—which turned out to be Death Seed plague—about thirty minutes later, leaving the droids to fend for themselves. [POT]

Margath, Kina The owner of Margath's, a luxury hotel located on the planet Elshandruu Pica. Kina Margath had long been a Rebel Alliance agent, unknown to almost everyone on the planet. She befriended the Imperial Moff's wife, Aellyn Jandi, who was using the hotel as the rendezvous point for meeting her lover, Sair Yonka. Rumors spread that it was Kina Margath who was having the affair with Yonka. Margath told the true story to Wedge Antilles when it was determined that Captain Yonka and his ship, the *Avarice*, could be used in the New Republic's struggle against Ysanne Isard. [BW, GG9]

Mark II reactor drone Utility droids designed for menial labor, they have heavily shielded outer casings to protect their sensitive internal circuitry under harsh external conditions, giving them a clunky look. The body shells of the usually tall black droids were reused by manufacturer Industrial Automaton for R-1 units. [SWR, SWAJ]

Mark X executioner A gladiator droid, it specializes in combat sports. The Mark X has built-in flame projectors, flechette missile launchers, and blasters. Two crawler treads give it mobility. [HSE]

Marook, Senator Cion A belligerent senator from Hrasskis, he was a member of the New Republic Senate Defense Council. He argued that the intervention against the Yevetha was

Marauder

Nichos Marr

too hasty and voiced disapproval at General A'baht's appointment as commander of the Fifth Fleet. [SOL, BTS]

Marr, Nichos A Jedi student of Luke Skywalker, he was destined to have a far different life than the one he planned. He came to the Jedi academy with his fiancée, the beautiful blond scientist Cray Mingla. But within a year, he was struck with the fatal Quannot's syndrome. Mingla, an expert on artificial intelligence, instituted a crash plan to transfer Nichos Marr's intelligence, mind, and very spirit, if possible, into a near-human artificial body.

Although he appeared relatively human, he still had major differences that Mingla tried to overlook. Marr then aided the New Republic's search for the long-missing children of the Jedi, for he was one of them. He also helped Luke Skywalker locate the *Eye of Palpatine*, a prototype Imperial battle station that had mysteriously been reactivated. Cray and Nichos accompanied Luke and C-3PO to the ship in order to destroy it before it could carry out its preprogrammed plan of destruction. They were amazed to find that the spirit of a Jedi woman named Callista had been trapped inside the computer core since she had first incapacitated the ship's weapons some thirty years before.

The *Eye of Palpatine* could be destroyed, but someone would have to stay behind and be destroyed with it. Nichos volunteered and Cray, realizing she couldn't live without Nichos, stayed behind, too. Just as an explosion was about to destroy the ship, they used the Force to transfer Callista's essence into Cray Mingla's body and ejected her in an escape pod. [COJ, SWCG]

Marso Leader of a group of mercenary pilots called the Demons. [HLL]

Masposhani According to Beldorian the Hutt, Jedi Knights once used to train in the subterranean caves of the planet Masposhani. [POT]

Massassi An ancient species of fierce warriors on the fourth moon of Yavin, these half-civilized beings were purposely mutated by Naga Sadow, a practitioner of dark-side Sith magic more than 4,000 years before the Battle of Yavin. Sadow's experiments were designed to make the Massassi even more fearsome guardians of huge temples that he, and later Dark Lord of the Sith Exar Kun, forced them to build. In a vision, Luke Skywalker saw the Massassi people as pale, gray-green humanoids with smooth skin and large, lanternlike eyes. Others have described them as red humanoids with large heads and finlike growths. The Massassi were killed by Exar Kun in one final sacrifice, but they left a creature known as the night beast to protect their territory. The beast was awakened when Rebel forces used one of the abandoned temples as a base. [SW, CSW, DA, DLS, TSW]

Massassi tree Towering trees on Yavin 4, they have wide crowns and upsweeping branches with a purple-brown bark that shreds easily into fibrous strands. [ISWU, GG2]

master control signal A transmission beamed through hyperspace, the signal guides and controls war machines and other automated objects. A master control signal sent from the clone Emperor's planet of Byss, for example, was used to guide the Imperial World Devastators. [DE]

mastmot Mastmots, often called motmots in some Whiphid tribal dialects, are shaggy herd animals that are often prey for the avian snow demons on the planet Toola. A mastmot's ribcage can often be used as shelter. [CPL, SWAJ, GG4]

Matra VI The planet to which the bounty hunter Gallandro lured the Malorm family and then killed them. That deed earned him the wrath of the Assassin's Guild, which claimed to have an exclusive contract on the Malorms. [CSSB]

Mattri asteroids The asteroids were the site of a temporary base for the private army of Garm Bel Iblis during its hit-and-fade attacks against the Empire. [DFR]

Mauit'ta, Colonel A New Republic officer, he served as General A'baht's staff intelligence officer for the Fifth Fleet. [TT]

Maw A cluster of black holes near the planet Kessel, the Maw served as a hiding place for the Maw Installation, where a group of Imperial scientists worked on new destructive weapons. The Maw was one of the wonders of the galaxy, visible only because of the ionized gases drawn into the holes. Conjecture arose as to whether the black-hole cluster had occurred naturally or whether it had been built by a vastly powerful ancient race, perhaps to open gateways into other dimensions. [JS]

Maw Installation A cluster of planetoids crammed together at a gravitational island at the center of a black-hole cluster near Kessel, it was created as a top-secret weapons-development facility by Grand Moff Tarkin. Immense bridges and bands held the asteroids in place. Access tubes and transit rails connected the cluster of drifting rocks. The asteroids' interiors were hollowed out into living quarters, laboratory areas, prototype assembly bays, and meeting halls. The super-secret think tank (hidden even from Emperor Palpatine) was an ideal place for Tarkin to

Max Rebo Band

isolate the most brilliant scientists and theoreticians, under orders to develop new weapons for the Emperor such as the Death Star, World Devastators, and the Sun Crusher. The installation was destroyed during a battle with New Republic forces. [JS, COF]

Max Rebo Band An odd collection of jizz-wailers from a variety of worlds, the band often performed exclusive engagements on Tatooine for crime lord Jabba the Hutt. The original Max Rebo Band consisted of Max himself, Droopy McCool, and the singer Sy Snootles. In response to growing competition, Rebo expanded the band.

In its last engagement for Jabba, the band included a male lead singer, Joh Yowza, a Yuzzum from the forest moon of Endor. Among the added musicians were Rappertunie, an amphibian who played an electronic instrument; Doda Bondonawieedo, a Rodian horn player; Barquin D'an, a Bith musician; and two drummers, Ak-Rev, a Weequay, and Umpass-Stay, a Klatooinian. Max also brought in three backup singers and dancers: Greeata, a Rodian; Lyn Me, a Twi'lek; and the exotic red-spotted Rystáll. [RJ]

Mayro A resort world in the Corporate Sector. While visiting Mayro, Torm Dadeferron, who inherited the Kail Ranges, was first approached by undercover Corporate Sector police. [CSSB]

Mazzic A militaristic smuggler chief, he runs a large, heavily armed operation. He doesn't hesitate to use his weapons. Mazzic's fleet consists of numerous freighters along with a number of customized combat starships, including the *Skyclaw* and the *Raptor*. His personal transport is the *Distant Rainbow* and his deceptively decorative bodyguard, a woman named Shada, is never far from his side. Mazzic was one of the smuggler chiefs that fellow smuggler Talon Karrde convinced to join him in indirectly —and profitably—helping the New Republic in its fight against Grand Admiral Thrawn. [LC]

McCool, Droopy A Kitonak musician, he was a member of the Max Rebo Band. Chubby and comical, Droopy (born with the name Snit) plays a variety of wind instruments. His species is lumpy, pudgy, and has leathery skin. The Kitonak often hollow out chidinka plants to create flutelike instruments and play songs of Kitonak love. Unfortunately, slavers have been known to capture some of the better musicians to work as jizz-wailers in seedy saloons, cabarets, and cantinas. Droopy was "owned" by Evar Orbus and forced to play in the Rebo Band. The band played a few shows for Jabba the Hutt, but after the crime lord's death, Droopy walked into the Tatooine desert, hoping to find others of his species. [RJ, SWCG, TJP]

McPhersons A family of moisture farmers on Tatooine, they supported Ariq Joanson in his plans to draw up maps of peace with the Jawas and the Sand People. [TMEC]

MD-model droids The chief model series of medical droids, they were manufactured exclusively at the droid factories on the planet Telti by Industrial Automaton. There are still a number of older MD-5 models in use, and MD-6s were used briefly by the Empire. The models MD-7 through MD-9 were prototype droids and thus used only in small sectors. When the

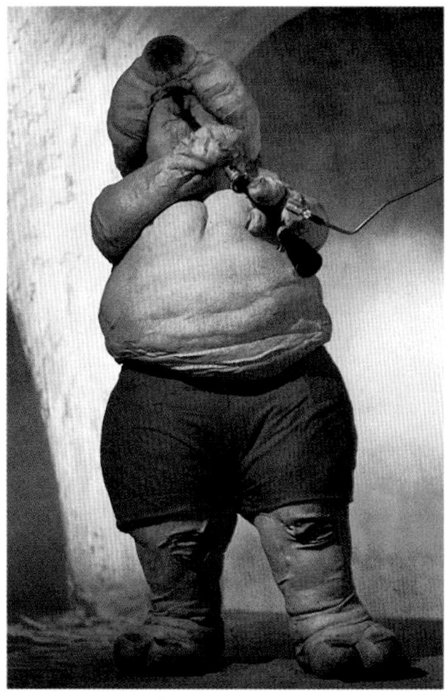
Droopy McCool

MD-10 model was developed, it revolutionized the manufacture of medical droids. [NR]

mechanical Colloquially used to refer to droids and automatons, the word is often used in a derogatory manner. [SWN]

Mechis III A harsh, smoke-shrouded world covered with sprawling droid-producing factories, it has been producing automata for generations and is considered to be possibly the most important of all the galaxy's droid plants. New assembly lines are self-created by various droid brains. The planet's seventy-three human overseers weren't able to comprehend its immensity. The administration office is at the apex of a gleaming tower, where Hekis Durumm Perdo Kolokk Baldikarr Thun managed all the factories' operations.

Prior to the Battle of Hoth, the droid IG-88 and his duplicates arrived at Mechis III and took it over, winning all the planet's droids to their cause. The droids eliminated every human inhabitant of the planet. Production continued, so that no one would suspect what had happened, but each new droid contained embedded programming that would soon trigger a robotic takeover of the galaxy. Darth Vader later came to the planet to order a new shipment of Arakyd Viper probots. After meeting with Vader on the Super Star Destroyer *Executor*, IG-88 ordered the Mechis III factories to produce a duplicate of the second Death Star's computer core, which his droid consciousness would then inhabit. But just before IG-88 was about to activate it, the battle station was destroyed by the Rebel Alliance. [TBH]

medical cocoon A portable enclosure that can sustain sick or injured patients, a cocoon can also move them from one place to another until they can be transported to a medical facility. A medical cocoon is totally self-sufficient, equipped with its own miniature power generator, regulators, and monitoring bank. [SME]

medical droid A robot or automaton whose main functions are to diagnose and treat illness and injury, it can also perform or assist with surgeries when necessary. Medical droids are found in hospitals, clinics, stations, medical frigates, and other places where they may be the only medical support. Some models are tethered to huge diagnostic and treatment analysis computers. The MD series is currently in widest service, ranging from the MD-0 (Emdee-Oh) diagnostic droids that assist physicians with patient examinations to the MD-5 (Emdee-Five) general practitioner droids—the "country doctors" of space—to the new specialist MD-10s. The Rebel Alliance depended mainly on older 2-1B and FX series droids, which can still be found on frontier worlds. [SWSB, ESBR]

Medical frigate

Darth Vader in his meditation chamber

medical frigate Any small star cruiser devoted mainly to the transportation and care of the wounded and convalescent, it is staffed primarily by medical personnel. [ESB]

meditation chamber A personal inner sanctum, the best known of which was perhaps Darth Vader's personal chamber aboard the Super Star Destroyer *Executor*. A spherical enclosure, Vader's meditation chamber split open to permit exit and entry, its top and bottom halves separating like the jaws of some dark-side beast. The interior had a comfortable reclining chair, a comlink and visual display, and a mechanical device for quickly removing and replacing Vader's helmet and breathing mask. The pressurized sphere kept Vader comfortable even with his helmet off. [ESB]

medpac A compact first-aid kit, it includes a synth-flesh dispenser, vibroscalpel, flexclamp, painkillers, disinfectant pads, and gas and precious fluid cartridges. [HSE, HLL, HSR, SWRPG2]

meduza A gelatinous creature, it consists of a mucousy mass of greasy, shining, bile-green material, from which rises a ring of slender, bulb-tipped stalks capable of giving electric shocks to victims. Doctor Evazan was able to train a meduza to be his loyal pet. [TMEC]

meewit A screeching animal, it is native to the rocky parts of Tatooine. [TJP]

Megadeath *See* Nataz, Dyyz

Meido The New Republic senator from the planet Adin, he is a former Imperial. Chief of State Leia Organa Solo suspected that his election to the Senate might not have been a fair one. Meido is knife-thin and has two-fingered hands and a crimson face that is covered with tiny white lines. He has consistently opposed all of Leia's policies and was instrumental in calling for a no-confidence vote that led to her temporary resignation. After being elected to the Inner Council by an overwhelming majority, Meido put together the committee that led an independent investigation into the explosion in Senate Hall and supported the idea that Leia's husband, Han Solo, was involved in the bombing. [NR]

mekebve spores An allergen crippling and potentially fatal to mammalian species, the spores have no effect on reptilian creatures such as Trandoshans. [TBH]

Melan, Koth A short, long-haired Bothan with a beard, he oversaw the all-important Bothan spynet from his homeworld of Bothawui. He was partial to a forest-green overtunic with matching pants and usually sported a long, military-style blaster strapped to his waist and right leg. Koth Melan had a personal reason to despise the Empire. His father, a teacher who had been trying to educate his students about the Empire, had been executed by Imperials on trumped-up espionage charges some twenty years before the Battle of Endor. Melan then dropped the normal "y'lya" honorific that his Bothan clan included at the end of their names because he believed that until the Empire was defeated, there could be no true honor.

Melan was instrumental in getting the plans of the second Death Star to the Rebel Alliance. He sent a messenger droid to Princess Leia Organa on Tatooine, but she wasn't there. Luke Skywalker was able to access the message and he and Corellian pilot Dash Rendar went to Bothawui to meet with Melan. Melan told them that a freighter carrying fertilizer was really being used to transport an Imperial computer carrying vital information. (Prince Xizor, head of the criminal Black Sun organization, leaked the information to the Bothan spynet for his own purposes.) Melan accompanied Dash Rendar in the *Outrider* during the subsequent attack on the freighter. He survived the battle, but Melan was killed soon after when Skywalker was kidnapped from a Bothan safe house on Kothlis. [SOTE]

Koth Melan

melding, the An intimate process of sharing the same mind, the melding is practiced by Azurans, who use a device called the Attanni to cybernetically link the thoughts of two people. [TBH]

Melihat A planet that manufactures dome fisheyes, a type of optical transducer. [TT]

Meltdown Café A restaurant on the spaceport moon Nar Shaddaa. [TMEC, DE2]

memory flush A memory wipe, it is used to erase all of the accumulated data stored in a computer system or droid data bank. [SW]

Mendicat Mendicat was a scrap mining and recycling station, destroyed when Imperial General Sulamar incorrectly programmed the station's orbital computers. Nevertheless, Sulamar, who worked with Durga the Hutt on the Darksaber project, constantly boasted of successfully leading the Massacre of Mendicat without losing a single stormtrooper. [DS]

Mennaalii system A convoy carrying Rebel troops passed through this system when it was forced to exit hyperspace to avoid an asteroid field. It was ambushed by a group of pirates, but was rescued by an Alliance strike team. [FP]

Mereel, Journeyman Protector Jaster *See* Boba Fett

Merenzane Gold A golden-colored liquor, it is popular throughout the galaxy. [TBH]

Meridian sector A lightly populated sector near the Outer Rim, it borders the Imperial-held Antemeridian sector, far from major trade routes. The Meridian sector contains several New Republic planets, including Nim Drovis and Budpock, and two Republic fleet bases at Durren and Cybloc XII, but most of the sector remains neutral. It is also home to the planets Ampliquen, Damonite Yors-B, Exodo II, and King's Galquek, the Spangled Veil Nebula, the Odos systems (containing Odos), and the Chorios systems (containing Nam Chorios, Pedducis Chorios, and Brachnis Chorios). Most of the remaining worlds in the sector are lifeless and barren, including the planet Meridias. Nine years after the Battle of Endor, Leia Organa Solo secretly visited the Meridian sector to meet with Seti Ashgad. After Ashgad unleashed the Death Seed plague on Leia's escort ships, the plague spread across three-quarters of the sector. At the same time, the forces of Moff Getelles of the Antemeridian sector, bolstered by Loronar Corporation's

CCIR needle fighters, invaded Meridian, aided by Loronar-backed rebellions occurring on many of the sector's planets. Getelles was forced to retreat at the Battle of Nam Chorios. [POT]

Meridias Located in the Meridian sector, it is a lifeless world that has been dead for several centuries. Meridias was once the home planet of the Grissmath Dynasty, which shipped its political prisoners to Nam Chorios, until an unknown catastrophe turned the world into a radioactive wasteland. [POT]

Meriko, Miracle A musician, he was killed by the Empire during its sweep to wipe out "questionable" artistic endeavors. [TBH]

Merisee Known for its medicine and agriculture, the planet is home to two intelligent species: the Teltiors and the Meris. Meris are tall, blue-skinned humanoids with webbed hands and a prominent brow ridge; Teltiors are similar in appearance but lack the ridge. Meris have an innate ability to predict the weather. Honn Dangel, a Meris who became a meteorologist on Bespin's Cloud City, got the job after leaving the Merisee military. [GG2, POG]

Merisee Hope The *Merisee Hope* is a slave-running ship for a brothel in Coruscant's Invisec. The smuggler Mirax Terrik brought several members of Rogue Squadron to Imperial Center (Coruscant) on an undercover mission using the false identity and transponder code of the *Merisee Hope* for her ship, the *Pulsar Skate.* [WG]

Mesoriaam, Barid A Rebel Alliance spy, he was captured and tortured by Jabba the Hutt's gangsters. Still, Barid Mesoriaam was able to deliver an essential information datadot to the Rebellion with the help of Muftak, a Talz, and his Chadra-Fan partner, Kabe, who encountered Mesoriaam as they were robbing Jabba's Mos Eisley townhouse. [TMEC]

metal-crystal phase shifter (MCPS) A new weapon constructed at Maw Installation, the MCPS field altered the crystalline structure of metals, including those in starship hulls. It could then penetrate conventional shielding and turn hull plates into powder. [COF]

M-HYD

Metellos system This system lies close to the Coruscant system. When the revived Empire began to conquer the Metellos and Kaikielius systems six years after the Battle of Endor, New Republic leaders on Coruscant began to search for a new base of operations. [DESB]

Meteor Way An area in Coronet City, capital of the planet Corellia. [AC]

Mettlo, Obron A Moorin mercenary who fought in dozens of battles, he was usually on the winning side. When he arrived on Tatooine, he was referred to Jabba the Hutt by Kardue'sai'Malloc. [TMEC]

M'haeli An agrarian planet with several moons, it is well situated as a refueling point for several nearby systems. The M'haeli capital is N'croth, where Governor Grigor ruled for years with the help of an Imperial garrison. The planet's population is composed mainly of human colonists and native H'drachi. Each year the H'drachi hold a midsummer conclave when they consult the timestream for news of the future. Notable sights on M'haeli include W'eston Falls, Demon's Brow, and a secret mine of valuable Dragite crystals located in the D'olop Range.

Years ago, an off-world attack led by Grigor devastated the palace of the human ruling house and paved the way for the planet's takeover by the Empire. Mora, infant heir to the ruling house, was abandoned during the attack and adopted by the H'drachi seer Ch'no. Seventeen years later, the Imperial pilot Ranulf Trommer was assigned to M'haeli to spy on Grigor and uncovered an illegal Dragite mining operation run by the governor. Ixidro Legorburu, an Intelligence officer stationed on the cruiser *Glorious* twelve years after the Battle of Endor, was a native of M'haeli. [ROC, SOL]

M-HYD A pretentious binary droid that specializes in hydroponics. It works with binary load lifters and vaporators. M-HYD is proficient in a number of languages but prefers to converse only in binary. [CCG]

Micamberlecto A Governor-General of Corellia, he is a Frozian. [AC]

Midanyl, Sena Leikvold Senator Garm Bel Iblis's chief aide and advisor, she once served as his unofficial ambassador-at-large for Peregrine's Nest, headquarters of Iblis's private army. Sena Leikvold Midanyl, a tall woman, had been Iblis's chief aide on Corellia, working beside him on the floor of the Senate. She was with him when he helped found the Rebel Alliance and when he left after his disagreements with Alliance leader Mon Mothma. Along with Iblis's security chief, Irenez, she helped Iblis plan many independent attacks on Imperial forces. [DFR]

Mid Rim The huge expanse of space between the Inner Rim and Outer Rim Territories, it is far less populated and less wealthy than the surrounding regions because of its fewer natural resources. Much of the Mid Rim remains unexplored or is the operating base for smugglers and pirates. [SWRPG2]

Yerka Mig

Mig, Yerka An Imperial bureaucrat with high security clearance, he resigned from the service of the Empire after the occupation of his home planet, Ralltiir. He became a fugitive from the Imperial Intelligence but was known to frequent a cantina in Mos Eisley on Tatooine. [CCG]

m'iiyoom A white flower native to H'nemthe, it blooms in the season when all three of the planet's moons give light. Also known as the night lily, the m'iiyoom is carnivorous, feeding on insects and small rodents that try to drink its nectar. [TMEC]

Millennium Falcon This Corellian stock light freighter may look like "a piece of junk," as Luke Skywalker called it when he first saw the ship, but the *Falcon* is one of the fastest, best-equipped crafts in the galaxy—when some malfunction or other isn't giving its crew headaches. For years, that crew has consisted of daredevil pilot and smuggler-turned-Rebel Alliance-hero Han Solo and his trusty Wookiee copilot and engineer, Chewbacca. The *Millennium Falcon* may appear old and battered, but constant modifications make it something special. Intimately involved in the destruction of both of the Empire's Death Star battle stations, it's probably the most famous ship in the galaxy.

The *Falcon* apparently had a number of owners before it fell into the hands of roguish gambler Lando Calrissian, who then lost it in a sabacc game to Solo. (He actually won it back twice but eventually returned the ship to Solo.) The exterior of the ship is left dilapidated deliberately—its appearance helped Calrissian and Solo avoid both Imperials and Customs officials on their frequent smuggling runs. But beneath the skin of the Corellian Engineering YT-1300 transport beats the heart of a taopari. Inside the twenty-seven-meter-long ship is a hyperdrive nearly twice as fast as any Imperial warship's—although both it and the sublight engine can be very finicky due to all the modifications they've undergone.

The well-armored *Falcon* has a top-notch (if illegal) sensor-suite array to detect distant Imperial ships before they notice the *Falcon*. There are shielded smuggling compartments throughout the interior. For combat, the ship sports a top-of-the-line Imperial deflector shield system, two quad laser cannons, and two concussion missile launchers, along with a retractable light laser cannon. But its speed—which lets Solo get under way and leave the scene in an incredibly brief three minutes—and agility often make the weapons' use unnecessary. [SW, SWSB, ESB, RJ, GSWU, LCM, DFR, DA]

Millennium Falcon

Mima II A small tropical world that orbits the orange sun Lar, it has a fast rotation and short year. Mima II's tectonic plates are very unstable, drawn across the planet's surface by the gravitational influence of the nearby planet Lar. Mima II has abundant plant and animal life. The sentient Bilars—pink-skinned, timid vegetarians that can form a group mind—live in the lush jungles. [GG4]

Mimban (Circarpous V) The fifth planet in the Circarpous system, this cloud-covered swamp world is largely unexplored. This rainy world, officially labeled Circarpous V but usually referred to by its local name, Mimban, is lush green, crisscrossed with muddy brown rivers, and teeming with many life-forms. Mimban was never colonized by the Circarpousians, but the Empire secretly established a mining operation on the planet. The miners lived in five makeshift towns and worked with energy drills—illegal on populated worlds because their harmful electrical fallout creates a hazard for incoming spaceships.

There are at least three intelligent Mimban species: large-eyed Mimbanites, derogatorily called "greenies," who beg in the mining towns for alcohol; the thin, gray Coway, who live underground; and an unnamed furry species with four legs and four arms. A mysterious, long-extinct species known as the Thrella are believed to have built hundreds of temples and cities that dot the damp surface of Mimban. "Thrella wells," near-bottomless shafts lined with interlocking hexagonal stones, often have side passages called Coway shafts leading to the Coways' underground world. One of the world's most dangerous animals is the huge pale worm called a wandrella; they have black eye-spots surrounding a gaping mouth and are too stupid to be slowed by most attacks.

Imperial control of Mimban was entrusted to Captain-Supervisor Grammel, who ruled from the Imperial planetary headquarters built into an ancient towering ziggurat. The legendary Kaiburr Crystal, rumored to have properties that focus and intensify the Force, was located deep in the jungle, in the temple of a minor local god named Pomojema. The powerful crystal rested within a ceremonial statue of the god and was guarded by a sluggish but deadly lizard creature. Soon after the Battle of Yavin, Luke Skywalker, Princess Leia, and the droids R2-D2 and C-3PO crashed on Mimban while traveling to a conference on Circarpous IV. After facing many dangers, including a showdown with Darth Vader, the Rebels were able to retrieve the Kaiburr Crystal and leave Mimban. [SME]

Mimban Cloudrider A Thyferran bacta tanker, it was captured by Rogue

Squadron during one of its raids against Ysanne Isard's bacta cartel. The squadron pulled the crew from the ship, and computer slicers created new identification files indicating another crew had replaced the original team. The imposters were Mirax Terrik, Corran Horn, Iella Wessiri, Elscol Loro, and Sixtus Quin, all working under various pseudonyms. Their mission was to fly the tanker to Thyferra, take a shuttle to the planet, then hook up with the Ashern Rebels to help overthrow Isard and the Thyferran government under her control. [BW]

Mindabaal A politically influential world in the system of the same name, it was the birthplace of the notorious Outer Rim smuggling sisters Josephine and Jericho. The rebellious Jericho attended the Mindabaal Royal Academy boarding school and later escaped, while Josephine began a distinguished career in the diplomatic corps. While on a mission to formalize Mindabaal's official entry into the Empire, Ambassador Josephine was kidnapped by her sister. The two later returned to their homeworld only to find it devastated by an Imperial orbital bombardment. The sisters then began working the smuggling trade together. [SWAJ]

Mindavar system In this system, a group of settlers was almost completely wiped out when a deadly virus spread through their colony. The smuggler Reina Gale lost her parents to the virus when she was only an infant. [SWAJ]

Mingla, Cray A student at Luke Skywalker's Jedi academy along with her partner, Nichos Marr, she was a beautiful scientist who was an expert in artificial intelligence. When Marr was struck with a fatal disease, she undertook a crash plan to transfer his mind, intelligence, and—if possible—his very essence into a near-human but artificial body. Along with Skywalker, Mingla and Marr were swept up into the reawakened Imperial battlemoon, the *Eye of Palpatine*. After a series of near-disasters, Mingla and Marr sacrificed their lives to destroy the dangerous spacecraft. But Mingla did it with a twist: At the last possible moment she enabled the essence of Callista—a bodiless Jedi whose spirit was trapped in the battlemoon's gunnery computer system—to pass into her body, which was then jettisoned from the *Eye of Palpatine* and reunited with Callista's new love, Luke Skywalker [COJ]

mining remotes Designed by Death Star engineer Bevel Lemelisk for crime lord Durga the Hutt, these sophisticated automated spacecraft were created to seek out the highest and purest concentrations of metals in an asteroid belt, then dismantle the rocks and exploit the treasure. Unfortunately for Lemelisk, the first pair of mining remotes sought out—and destroyed—each other instead. [DS]

Minos Cluster Located on the edge of the known galaxy, beyond which there are no star charts, the worlds of the Minos Cluster—including those of the Shesharile system—have only recently been colonized. The entire Minos Cluster is isolated in many ways, and fringe members of society —smugglers, outlaws, and pirates among them—have flooded in. Thirteen years after the Battle of Endor, Mara Jade and Talon Karrde traveled to the Minos Cluster on an errand, to the annoyance of Lando Calrissian, who resented the time Jade spent with Karrde. [GG6, NR]

Mirage A ship used by the Mistryl Shadow Guards. [TMEC]

Miraluka A humanoid race from Alpheridies, they are born without eyes. But many Miraluka are able to see using the Force, and thousands of years before the Battle of Yavin many became Jedi. [FNU]

Miranda A K-wing pilot for Blue Flight in the New Republic's Fifth Fleet, she was killed during the failed attempt to blockade the Yevetha at Doornik-319. [SOL]

Mirit system Located only hours from the Pyria and Venjagga systems at the edge of the Galactic Core, Mirit contains the planet Ord Mirit, the site of a former Imperial base. [RS]

Miser The innermost planet of the Bespin system, it is a small world lacking atmosphere but rich in valuable metals. Miser's powerful magnetic field interferes with most electronic equipment. It was heavily mined for raw materials during the construction of Bespin's Cloud City, and deep craters from the operation can still be seen on its surface. Inhospitable temperature extremes made the mining hazardous, and hardy Ugnaughts were needed to staff the operation. The mines have since been abandoned and are now infested with mynocks.

The desolate planet has frequently been used as a hideout by smugglers and pirates. It was also the site of a hidden Imperial base after the Battle of Yavin. Lord Ecclessis Figg, the founder of Cloud City, once proposed a rolling mining center that could stay permanently on the cooler side of Miser, which was always in shadows. It was never built, but it provided the inspiration for Lando Calrissian's Nomad City mining operation on Nkllon. [HE, GG2, IC]

mistmaker A creature from the planet Msst, it resembles a giant pink bubble with teeth. A mistmaker stings its prey into immobility and then raises its victim into the hollow part of its body, where it can devour it with its jagged teeth. Luke Skywalker was attacked and wounded by one. [NR]

Mistryl A humanoid race, their world was largely ravaged by the Empire, and the remaining Mistryls barely survive. [TMEC]

Mistryl Shadow Guards The last heroes of the Mistryl race, the Shadow Guards are a cult of warrior women who once fought against injustices imposed by the Empire. Now they are little more than mercenaries, willing to do almost any job in exchange for payment to help their suffering people. Mara Jade recruited them to aid in the liberation of Kessel. [TMEC, COF]

mnemiotic drugs Mind-altering drugs, mnemiotics give subjects flawless memories but induce hallucinations. Mnemiotic drugs are commonly given by the Empire to its assassins and soldiers. [TBH]

Mneon system A system containing the planet Geran, home of a near-human species. [TJP]

Moisture farm

mobile command base A protected, mobile base of operations for Imperial field commanders, each unit can support a commander, six passengers, and a crew of three. A mobile command base moves on treads, is highly armored, and houses a sophisticated sensor array to gather field data for analysis by onboard computers. The mobile base also sports a defensive heavy laser cannon. [ISB]

modbreks Wispy beings, they are as hairless as slugs except for their blue manes. They have undeveloped heads, and huge eyes, tiny noses, and small mouths in their pointy, pale faces. [TMEC]

Moddell sector A sector containing the planet Endor and its moons. A report filed with Imperial Command by an Imperial scout in the Moddell sector briefly described the previously unexplored system; it dismissed any threat from the native Ewok population on Endor's forest moon. [SWSB]

Moff A title given to Imperial military commanders who ruled certain sectors of the galaxy. Moffs reported to Grand Moffs, who were in charge of groups of sectors or regions. Grand Moffs also controlled "priority sectors," proved to have supported insurgent activities. [SWN]

mogo A large black-furred creature, it has a head like a camel and an undulating body. Mogos are used for transportation on the planet Roon. [DTV]

moisture farm Usually rural, this landholding is where water is extracted from the atmosphere for use on dry desert worlds. On the moisture farms of Tatooine, for example, vaporators squeeze water from the air. This water is then used on subterranean produce farms for irrigation or human consumption, or is sold. Jedi Knight and Rebel Alliance hero Luke Skywalker grew up on a Tatooine moisture farm. [SW]

Demma Moll

moisture vaporator Essential for life on desert planets, it condenses water vapor from the atmosphere. A moisture vaporator has purification filters and coolant tanks; the water it produces helps protect against drought and harsh conditions. [CCG]

Molator A mythological creature, it is featured in Alderaanian tales. Stories describe molators as powerful enchanted protectors of Alderaanian kings and queens. [CCG]

mole miner A utility craft designed to operate in space, on asteroids, and on worlds with hostile environments, it digs out ore from places otherwise impossible to mine. Mole miners—which have largely been replaced by mining droids—operate from a base or headquarters ship and return at the end of a shift. They are operated by an internal crew or by remote control. The miners use bottom-mounted plasma jets to slice through solid rock and gather precious minerals into storage bins through a series of vacuum shafts and grinders. Lando Calrissian used mole miners at his operation on the planet Nkllon until a large number were stolen by Grand Admiral Thrawn, who used them at the Battle of Sluis Van to burrow into capital ships so that Imperial crews could hijack the vessels. [HE, HESB]

Moll, Demma A reserved, attractive woman, she owned a farm on the planet Annoo in the early days of the Empire. In her forties, Demma Moll had a daughter named Kea. The Fromm gang desperately wanted to take over Moll's farm, but didn't know that Demma Moll secretly led a band of freedom fighters working to destroy the Fromm's weapons satellite, the *Trigon One*. [DTV]

Moll, Kea A beautiful seventeen-year-old when C-3PO and R2-D2 first met her during the early days of the Empire, she lived on her mother's farm complex on the planet Annoo. Kea Moll was brave, athletic, and able

Molator holomonster

Kea Moll

to handle both spacecraft and landspeeders with an expert's touch. [DTV]

Moltok An oxygen-rich planet, it is one of the inner worlds of the Dartibek system and is homeworld of the Ho'Din. Active volcanoes fill Moltok's skies with ash, helping protect the planet's surface from the harmful effects of its sun. The Ho'Din species lives in the hot rain forests of the lower latitudes and deeply revere the plant life found there. They discourage technology because of an early ecological catastrophe resulting from an attempt at mining. Moltok exports many high-priced medicinal plants. The government is controlled by the clergy of the dominant Dinante Fli'R religion. The Jedi Master Plett, who built a house and laboratory on Belsavis, was a native of Moltok. [GG4, COJ]

Mon, Ephant An intelligent two-legged Chevin, this pachydermoid from the planet Vinsoth was the closest thing crime lord Jabba the Hutt had to a friend. His huge head, long snout, and stubby arms and legs gave him an odd appearance. He worked as an interplanetary mercenary, then began running guns for anyone from pirates to Rebels. He met Jabba, and the two schemed to raid an Imperial weapons depot on the icy moon of Glakka, but they were betrayed by one of Jabba's own gang. They managed to avoid Imperial fire but were trapped in the frigid environs of Glakka. Jabba saved Ephant Mon by wrapping his oily fat folds around him, and both were rescued the next day.

Upon returning to Tatooine, Jabba made Ephant Mon his secret internal security official, rooting out conspiracies and assassination plots. When Jedi Luke Skywalker showed up at Jabba's palace, Ephant Mon confronted Luke, who told him that Jabba would be destroyed unless he freed his Rebel Alliance captives. Ephant Mon believed the Jedi and tried to persuade Jabba, who wouldn't listen. He decided not to accompany his friend and boss on the fateful sail barge to the Pit of Carkoon and returned to his homeworld, where he founded a sect that worshipped the Force. [TJP, SWCG]

Monarch An Imperial Star Destroyer, it was so heavily damaged by the Alliance invasion fleet over Coruscant that its captain, Averen, surrendered the ship rather than see it destroyed. [WG]

Mon Calamari Nearly completely covered with water, this world is home to more than twenty-seven billion inhabitants: the peace-loving Mon Calamari and the cautious Quarren. The surface of the planet Mon Calamari (sometimes called simply Calamari) is covered with small marshy islands and enormous floating cities that house both species. The Quarren inhabit the lowest, darkest levels. These attractive cities include Reef Home, Coral Depths, Kee-Piru, Coral City, Heurkea, Foamwander City, the Domed City of Aquaris, and Morjanssik.

The architecture and design of Mon Calamari has an organic appearance, with rounded edges and irregular surfaces, demonstrating the inhabitants' love for the natural beauty of their world. Raw ores used in construction are mined by the Quarren (who can breathe both air and water) from domed cities on the ocean floor. A permanent history of every planetary event is maintained by a community of meter-long, bivalve mollusks, who are extremely intelligent and will communicate their knowledge to those who ask.

The Calamarian seas are also home to the dangerous predators known as krakanas—sharklike animals with twin pincer tentacles. The rare ultimapearl is found in the seabeds. Massive sea slugs, plying Calamari's oceans, use the Force to draw plankton into their mouths. Other species include the eellike choarn, lampfish with luminous tongues, and the endangered whaladons. In ancient times the planet supported now-extinct, ten-legged crustaceans known as mammoth krabbexs.

The Mon Calamari had already constructed enormous starships and begun traveling space when their planet was discovered by the Empire. The Imperials planned to enslave the planet and, after meeting native resistance, destroyed three of its floating cities. A Quarren, Seggor Tels, is believed to have deliberately lowered Calamari's defenses to allow

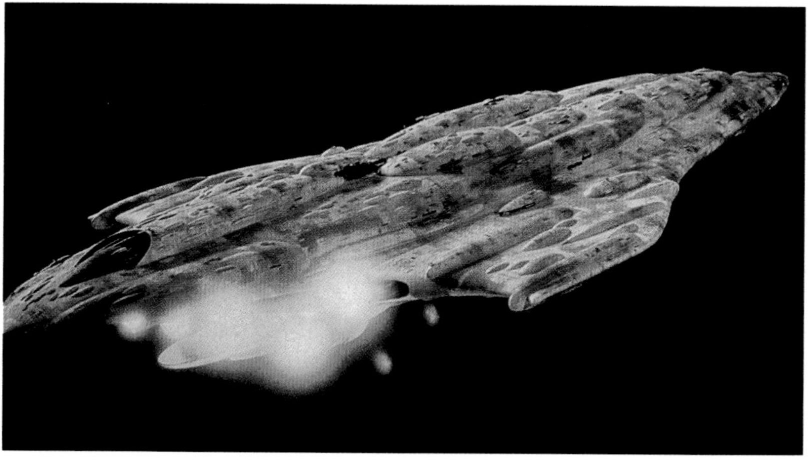

Mon Calamari star cruiser

the Empire's attack; ever since, tension has been high between the Mon Calamari and the Quarren. After the Empire's aim was made clear, Calamarian starships were converted into warships and the shipbuilding docks in orbit around Mon Calamari and its single moon became an important resource for the Alliance.

Many Calamarians were enslaved by the Empire, including the famous Ackbar, who was forced to be the personal servant of Grand Moff Tarkin. Ackbar was rescued from slavery by an Alliance force and later named admiral of the Rebel fleet. Six years after the Battle of Endor, the reborn clone Emperor used his World Devastators to attack Mon Calamari's southern territorial zone, destroying most of Kee-Piru and Heurkea. The port city of Hikahi was also damaged, hurting the planet's starship-building capability. Calamarian ships form the backbone of the New Republic fleet. But with the help of Jedi Knight Luke Skywalker, the Devastators were defeated.

A year after that attack, Princess Leia Organa Solo visited Admiral Ackbar at his home in the seatree forest to bring him out of his self-imposed exile. A subsequent attack by Admiral Daala's Star Destroyers resulted in the destruction of Reef Home city. [DE, GG4, SWSB, DA, AS, DESB, DS, FP, TJP, YJK, POT]

Mon Calamari A two-legged amphibious species from a planet of the same name, these gentle beings became powerful allies of the Rebel Alliance after the Empire invaded their world. Forced into slave labor to help build the Imperial war machine, the Mon Calamari watched many of their cities crumble under the Empire's capricious destruction, intended to frighten all those who opposed the Emperor's New Order. But the peaceful Mon Calamari were turned into a formidable fighting force for the Alliance, and brought with them badly needed capital starships and the military leadership of Ackbar. [RJ]

Mon Calamari star cruiser The main cruisers in the Alliance and New Republic's battle fleet, these organic-looking, durable ships, originally designed for pleasure cruises and peaceful colonization efforts, are as fast and almost as tough as the larger Imperial Star Destroyers. After an attack by the Empire, Mon Calamari (Mon Cal) star cruisers were converted to military duty by adding thick hull plating and numerous weapon emplacements.

Monnok holomonster

Each Mon Cal cruiser has a unique design, because the ships are considered almost as much works of art as weapons of war. While this makes them difficult to repair, their armor and redundant systems ensure they are rarely damaged in combat. Some notable Mon Cal ships include the round, blimp-shaped Headquarters Frigate known as *Home One* and the winged, elongated *Medical Frigate. Home One* was Admiral Ackbar's command vessel for the attack on the Second Death Star and has since seen service in numerous battles against Imperial forces. It carries an amazing ten squadrons of Rebel starfighters, and its weapons include twenty-nine turbolasers, thirty-six ion cannons, multiple tractor beam projectors, and unusually powerful shield generators.

While many species serve aboard Mon Cal cruisers, command sections are geared for the Mon Calamari anatomy. Controls can be changed through specific movements in the command chairs as well as the more usual computer interfaces. [SWSB, RJ, GSWU, RSB, MTS, DESB, FP]

Money Lane A nickname for the field of fire between the *Millennium Falcon's* upper and lower quad laser batteries, so dubbed by Han Solo and his copilot, Chewbacca. The overlapping field is in the sights of both guns, and targets flying through it can be hit by either gunner. In a battle, Solo and Chewbacca wagered on who could hit more enemy targets; those in the Money Lane were worth double, because both gunners had an equal chance at them. (Even in battle, Solo could never resist a bet.) [HSE]

monnok A savage predator from the remote deserts of Socorro, it is respected and honored by Socorran hunters and considered good luck by superstitious smugglers. [CCG, SWAJ]

Monor A planet in the Doldur sector. Resistance leader Una Poot planned to deliver a cargo of blaster carbines to Rebels there from her base on Silver Station just after the Battle of Yavin. [SWAJ]

Mon Remonda The *Mon Remonda* was an interim MC-80B Mon Calamari star cruiser delivered to the New Republic about eighteen months after the Battle of Endor while the Republic awaited the new MC-90 models. It was a major component in the New Republic's battle to retake

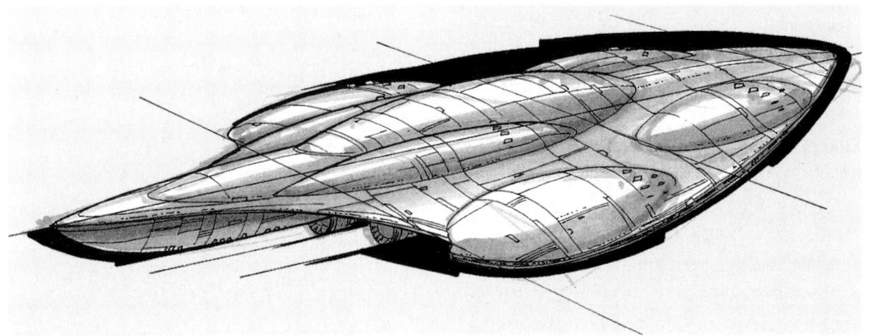

Mon Remonda

Tech Mo'r

Coruscant, severely damaging the Imperial Star Destroyer *Monarch* before the *Monarch*'s surrender. It was also put to use as the flagship of a New Republic fleet sent to repel the offensive of Imperial Warlord Zsinj. The expedition was commanded by Gen. Han Solo, who destroyed Zsinj's Super Star Destroyer *Iron Fist* and pushed the warlord's forces back to their original territory.

The *Mon Remonda*, at about 1,200 meters long, has the fluid and organic look that characterizes Mon Cal starships. Unlike earlier ships, its hull was more heavily reinforced and it had multiple backup shield generators to endure extended battles. The ship's forty-eight turbolasers were linked in banks of twelve, while the twenty ion cannons were in banks of four, making it possible to bring intense firepower against large targets. The *Mon Remonda* carried four squadrons of twelve fighters: twelve A-wings, twelve B-wings, and twenty-four X-wings.

Despite its superb design, the *Mon Remonda* was destroyed by the World Devastator *Silencer-7* at the Second Battle of Calamari, during the campaign of the reborn clone of Emperor Palpatine. All hands were lost, but the crew died as heroes, having destroyed an Imperial Star Destroyer and several support vessels. [HE, CPL, DA, DESB, SWSB, SWVG, MTS]

Mora

Montellian Serat A northern city on the planet Devaron, it was the site of a massacre caused by indiscriminate shelling ordered by Kardue'sai'Malloc; it earned him the Devaronian nickname the Butcher of Montellian Serat. [TBH]

Mon Valle A Rebel Alliance ship, it had been the base of operations for General Salm's "Defender Wing" squadron of Y-wings. The *Mon Valle* was destroyed by Imperial planetary defenses during the initial raid on Borleias. [RS]

Mookiee A baby female Ewok, or wokling, at the time of the Battle of Endor, she lived on the forest moon of Endor. [ETV]

Moon Dash A shuttle piloted by Captain Narek-Ag and copiloted by Trebor, it ran into the cloaked Shadow Academy space station after leaving Coruscant. The *Moon Dash* and its occupants were destroyed. [YJK]

Moonflower Nebula A large nebula of dust and gasses located in the Outer Rim past the K749 system, it contains several stars and a vast asteroid field, where the Imperial battlemoon *Eye of Palpatine* lay undiscovered for thirty years. [COJ]

moonglow A rare, delicate, and expensive pearlike fruit, it is found only in a small section of one forest on a single world. Moonglow, at about 1,000 credits a serving, is also a dangerous delicacy that has to be prepared by a certified Master Moonglow Chef. An error or omission in its ninety-seven-step preparation can cause eaters to suffer anything from a mild stomach upset to a coma followed by death. [SOTE]

Mooth An elderly trader who operated a trading post on Endor's forest moon, he resembled a humanoid anteater. The fast-talking Mooth wore a primitive gambler's visor on his head and often had an abacus strapped across his chest. [ETV]

Mo'r, Tech A Bith musician in the Figrin D'an and the Modal Nodes band, he plays a sound-enhancing Ommni box. [CCG, TMEC]

Mora A human female rescued as a baby by Ch'no, a H'drachi soothsayer, Mora was revealed as the heir to the ruling house of M'haeli. She was the only human survivor of an Imperial attack that led to the Empire taking control of the planet. She considered herself a daughter of Ch'no and defended him against attack. Years later, she fell in love with the dashing pilot Ranulf Trommer, not knowing that he was an Imperial spy who was determined to uncover the chicanery of the Imperial puppet who ran the planet. [ROC]

Morag A powerful Tulgah witch who lives on the forest moon of Endor, she has a shriveled, stooped body

Morag

and a mandrill's face. Morag's skills in magic and medicine rival those of Logray, the Ewok medicine man. She lives in a castlelike formation in the side of the active volcano Mount Thunderstone. Spear-wielding Yuzzums patrol her land atop rakazzak beasts. [ETV]

Morano, Captain The human commander of the *Intrepid*, flagship of the New Republic's Fifth Fleet in the Yevethan crisis. [SOL]

Morath Nebula Located in either the Kokash or Farlax sector, this mysterious formation has never been properly surveyed by the New Republic. [BTS]

Morgavi, Luke The name Han Solo took when he visited the planet Jubilar to recapture his lost youth by taking on a small smuggling job. [TBH]

Morning Bell Located in the Koornacht Cluster of the Farlax sector, the planet is known in New Republic astrographic charts as Doornik-319 and is called Preza by the Yevetha. The brown-and-white world is one of six planets orbiting a blue-white star. It sits directly between the Yevethan capital world of N'zoth and the New Republic capital world of Coruscant, and is covered with brush and scrub. It was given the name Morning Bell by a colony of Kubaz, who lived there until they were brutally eliminated by the Yevethan military twelve years after the Battle of Endor.

The day after the massacre, a pair of Yevethan thrustships began colonizing Morning Bell and fortifying it as a forward base. After Chief of State Leia Organa Solo issued an ultimatum demanding that Yevethan forces withdraw from the colony worlds they had seized, three thrustships and a captured Imperial Star Destroyer arrived at Morning Bell. In response, the New Republic Fifth Fleet was sent to blockade the planet and prevent the Yevetha from using it as a forward base. But when General A'baht's ships arrived they were surprised by a ferocious Yevetha attack. As the Republic ships made bombing runs, the Yevetha continuously broadcast hostages begging the ships not to attack, lest they be executed. Hearing the pleas, enough Republic pilots hesitated that the Yevethan ships suffered little damage, and the Republic fleet retreated with heavy casualties. Just before the final Battle of N'zoth, the New Republic made a feint at Morning Bell in which its forces suffered no losses but destroyed a Yevethan thrustship. [BTS, SOL, TT]

Morobe system Bordering the Rachuk sector, the system contains a red/yellow binary star. The planet Talasea is the fourth planet orbiting the yellow primary. [RS]

morrt Parasites about the size of field mice, they are native to the planet Gamorr. Morrt bloodsuckers feed on living organisms, staying with a single host throughout their long lives. Gamorreans, however, consider morrts to be friendly and loyal and keep them as pets and status symbols. They are the only creatures that Gamorreans display affection to, and the more morrts attached to a Gamorrean —some matrons and warlords have more than twenty—the higher the Gamorrean's status. [SWSB]

Morseerian A four-armed species from an uncharted world, they breathe methane. [CCG]

Morvogodine The planet where vandfillist artist Maxa Jandovar was arrested by Imperial forces. She later died in custody. [TMEC]

Mos Eisley A spaceport city on the Outer Rim world of Tatooine, it is, in the words of Ben Kenobi, a "wretched hive of scum and villainy." Mos Eisley attracts interstellar commerce as well as spacers looking for rest and relaxation after a long haul. The vast number of aliens and humans constantly moving through the spaceport, and its distance from the centers of Republic and Imperial activity, long made Mos Eisley a haven for thieves, pirates, and smugglers. The nearby presence for years of crime lord Jabba the Hutt didn't help matters. The city's old central section is laid out like a wheel, while the newer sections are formed into straight blocks of buildings that are half-buried to protect them from the heat of Tatooine's twin suns. Instead of a central landing area, the entire city is a spaceport, with craterlike docking bays scattered throughout. [SW, TM, GG7]

Mos Eisley cantina The most popular spot for entertainment and drinks in the Tatooine spaceport city of Mos Eisley, it is also a place of high intrigue. The Mos Eisley cantina, sometimes known as Chalmun's cantina after its grizzled old Wookiee owner, is the premier location for transacting business of a questionable nature, spy or be spied upon, and find just about any commodity under the suns. Even in the antialien days of the Empire, the cantina was a meeting and mixing spot for scores of species from planets near and far. The one exception to the welcome-all attitude: No droids allowed.

For years, the cantina's grouchy bartender has been a man named Wuher, who is always seeking a way to get off-planet. One of the most famous groups to play the cantina was Figrin D'an and the Modal Nodes, one of the best jizz-wailing bands in the Outer Rim. D'an's fame, and that of the cantina itself, has a lot to do with the fact that it was the meeting place of two of the heroes of the Rebellion, Jedi Knight Luke Skywalker

Mos Eisley

Mos Eisley cantina

and onetime smuggler Han Solo, the ace pilot and now husband of Chief of State Leia Organa Solo. [SW, TMEC]

Mos Eisley Towers Despite its name, this hotel is almost entirely underground in Mos Eisley. Its rooms are clean and cheap. [TJP]

Mosep Jabba the Hutt's Nimbanel accountant, his inside contacts at other crime organizations gave him the ability to disrupt the cash flow of Jabba's enemies. [CCG]

Motexx Two sectors away from Arat Fraca, the planet is separated from the planet Arat Fraca by the Black Nebula in Parfadi. The starliner *Star Morning*, owned by the Fallanassi religious order, left Motexx a few weeks before the Battle of Endor with a full cargo, bound for Gowdawl under a charter license. The liner then disappeared for 300 days, eventually showing up at Arat Fraca with empty cargo holds. [SOL]

Mothma, Mon Inspiring and committed to the cause of freedom in the galaxy, the senator from the planet Chandrila became the conscience as well as the leader of the Rebel Alliance and the founder and first Chief of State of the New Republic.

Mon Mothma's parents prepared her well for her eventual pivotal role in galactic politics. Her father, an arbiter-general for the Old Republic, settled disputes between various species and taught her respect for all beings. Her mother, a planetary governor, taught her how to administer, organize, and—most important—how to lead. Until Princess Leia Organa of

Mosep

Alderaan's election, Mothma was the youngest person ever to serve in the Republic Senate.

The Republic was already crumbling from internal corruption, but Mothma still served with vigor and integrity and was a leader of those forces that opposed the growing power of the evil Senator Palpatine. Her internal strength matched her physical energy; she was a woman of stature, with auburn hair and pale blue-green eyes. She was the last to hold the title of Senior Senator, a post she gave up when it appeared the Senate was to be disbanded.

Mon Mothma wasn't alone. She had the support of the powerful Senator Bail Organa of Alderaan as well as the Corellian Senator Garm Bel Iblis, who was to clash with her later over strategic issues. Together, they unsuccessfully tried to block Palpatine's election as Senate leader and looked on with revulsion when he anointed himself Emperor. Under the Emperor's New Order, dissidents weren't tolerated. After Mothma's secret involvement with the nascent Rebellion was discovered, a tip from Bail Organa allowed her to escape from Coruscant just ahead of the Imperial secret police.

Mon Mothma

Mothma journeyed to a secret meeting in the Corellian system where she, Organa, and Bel Iblis formed a unified leadership to strengthen the Rebellion under the Corellian Treaty. Mothma then drafted a strongly worded Declaration of Rebellion, directly taking on the Emperor and his policies. Announcing themselves as the Rebel Alliance, those who fought the Empire pledged their property, their honor, and their lives. An unimpressed Palpatine then formally disbanded the Senate.

Mothma's inspirational speeches made her a natural to be elected the Alliance's Chief of State. The central leadership she put in place brought improved communications, rapid decision-making, strong lines of authority and responsibility, greater accountability, and access to critical funds, supplies, vessels, and weapons. Following the Battle of Yavin and the destruction of the first Death Star, the Rebellion attracted many supporters. The Empire's tyranny—and its weaknesses—had been exposed, and Mon Mothma spread her beliefs about the freedom and rights of all beings. She appointed strong military leaders and let them do their work. After the Battle of Endor, in which the second Death Star was destroyed and both Emperor Palpatine and Darth Vader were killed, Mothma set about the difficult task of building a New Republic while facing serious threats from remnants of the Empire.

Mothma sent ambassadors to planets that had been under Imperial rule, resorting to force only when attacked. Many of the worlds immediately jumped onboard, while some waited to see what the fallout of the galactic war would bring. Others were hostile, but Mothma tried to ensure that the Alliance was aggressive only when absolutely needed. She and her Provisional Council were well aware how fragile and tenuous their hold on power was.

The Alliance established a number of new headquarters prior to deciding to make the site of its permanent headquarters exactly where the Old Republic and the Empire's had been, the planet Coruscant, which had been called Imperial Center under Palpatine's bloody reign. It seemed the right message to send, Mothma argued. Making it the capital wasn't easy. First, the fight to retake the planet cost millions of lives, many of them lost in one terrorist act. The planet then came under attack by Grand Admiral Thrawn. Upon his defeat, six Star Destroyer commanders staged an assault, and succeeded in driving Mothma and the rest of her government into exile. Their temporary headquarters on Da Soocha 5 was destroyed by the reborn clone Emperor's Galaxy Gun, but all Alliance officials were able to escape before the attack. The Republic launched an attack on Byss in response, destroying the Emperor's cloning facility forever.

Back on Coruscant, as Chief of State, Mothma and the new Senate set about restructuring a truly effective intergalactic government. They approved plans for Luke Skywalker to immediately establish a Jedi training facility and took on the thousand and one tasks involved in governing.

Mon Mothma then faced unexpected personal peril. At a diplomatic reception, the Imperial envoy from Carida, Ambassador Furgan, threw a drink in Mothma's face and denounced the New Republic. In the next few weeks, Mothma's health began to deteriorate rapidly; her skin became gray, her face sunken. Even a secret four-day stint in a bacta chamber didn't help. The terrible wasting

Admiral Motti

disease kept claiming more of her body.

Mon Mothma assigned her duties to Princess Leia Organa Solo, then tendered her resignation to the ruling council. At about the same time, it was revealed that Mothma's disease had been caused by an insidious poison in the drink that Ambassador Furgan had splashed on her. With time for Mothma running out, one of Skywalker's student Jedi, Cilghal, who had Force talents in healing, was brought in. Although no known medicines worked against the poison, Cilghal was slowly able to expunge it all from Mothma's body. But a recovered Mon Mothma knew that it was time to pass on her role to another, and she strongly supported Leia as the new Chief of State.

Mon Mothma was more accepting of allowing former Imperials to serve in the New Republic Senate than Leia was. During the Almanian crisis, following the call for a no-confidence vote against Leia and her subsequent resignation as Chief of State, Mon Mothma agreed to temporarily resume her old role while Leia left Coruscant to find Luke Skywalker and prove that her husband, Han Solo, was not involved in the bombing that rocked Senate Hall. Once it was proven that the bombing was the work of the Dark Jedi Kueller, as part of a reign of terror against the New Republic, Mon Mothma gratefully returned the role of Chief of State to Leia. [SWSB, RJ, HE, DFR, LC, JS, DA, NR]

motivator A droid's main internal mechanism, it converts energy into mechanical motion. Without a motivator, a droid would not be able to move. [SW]

Motti, Admiral The senior Imperial commander in charge of operations on the original Death Star battle station, Admiral Motti died when the station was destroyed. He never liked the decisions of Darth Vader and felt that Vader used outdated and archaic methods. When he voiced his opinions to the Dark Lord, Vader used the Force to nearly choke the admiral to death. [SW]

mounder potato rice A starchy Corellian food disliked by Han Solo. [NR]

Mountain Terrain Armored Transport (MT-AT) A new Imperial walker, the eight-legged machine—nicknamed the Spider Walker—is designed to master steep inclines with independently articulated legs and clawed footpads that allow the walkers to secure themselves to sheer rock faces. The MT-AT was first used when Caridan Ambassador Furgan ordered an attack on a New Republic facility on the world of Anoth.

The MT-AT has a central drive pod that houses the engine and drive system for the eight legs. An attached platform contains the forward pilot compartment and a rear cargo pod; it can spin 180 degrees, allowing an immediate change of direction. The forward command pod has room for a pilot and a gunner, while the aft cargo pod carries repeating blasters and supplies for ground troops. Each leg has an independently rotating double laser cannon, and the MT-AT's driver has two laser cannons to shoot down attacking starfighters.

MT-ATs can be deployed by transports, landing barges, and drop ships.

Mountain Terrain Armored Transport (MT-AT)

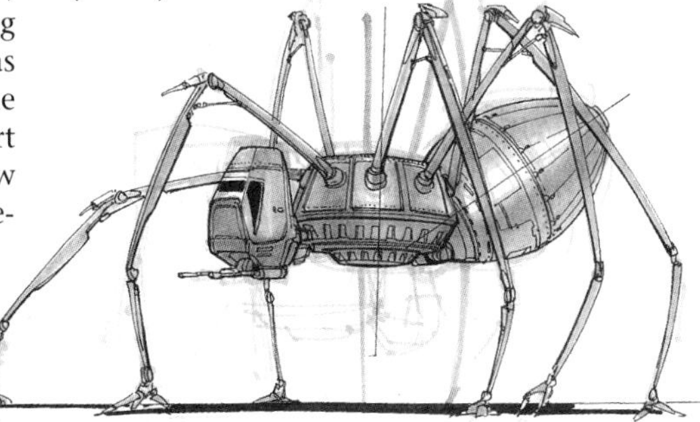

For the mission to Anoth, the MT-ATs used an experimental thermal resistant cocoon that encases a single walker in a fluid gel. Upon impact, the gel hardens and transfers the force to the outside surface of the cocoon, protecting the walker inside. The cocoon then breaks open and the gel crumbles.

Ambassador Furgan used eight MT-AT walkers in the attack on Anoth. The Anoth sanctuary's defenses destroyed half of the walkers, and two more were destroyed by New Republic operatives. The final two MT-ATs were destroyed when Mon Calamari's unintentional traitor, Terpfen, used one of the walkers to push Furgan's walker over the edge of a cliff, killing them both. [DA, COF, SWVG]

Mount Meru Site of a large amphitheater on Deneba some 4,000 years before the Galactic Civil War; 10,000 Jedi led by Master Odan-Urr assembled there prior to the Sith War. [DLS]

Mount Tantiss A mountain on the planet Wayland, it was used by Emperor Palpatine as a private storehouse for items he deemed important to his long-range plans. The Mount Tantiss site was a combination trophy room and equipment dump, built within the hollowed-out mountain. Its multiple levels housed vast chambers of art, captured souvenirs, and experimental devices, as well as royal suites and a throne room for the Emperor. Among the hidden treasures were a working prototype for a cloaking device and scores of Spaarti cloning cylinders. [HE, DFR, LC, HESB, DFRSB, LCSB]

Mount Yoda A mountain on the planet Dagobah, it was named in honor of the famed Jedi Master following the Battle of Endor. The Alliance once established a base on Mount Yoda. [MMY, PDS]

Mrisst A planet near the heart of the New Republic, it had first been contacted under the Old Republic by the Tenth Alderaanian Expedition, which made the interesting finding that none of the dozens of Mrisst cultures had developed any type of three-dimensional art. Grand Admiral Thrawn planned an assault on the planet, partly to try to lure and defeat the New Republic fleet if it made a concerted effort to defend the planet. [LC]

Mrlssi Natives of the planet Mrlsst, they are described as descendants of birds, with feathers covering their short bodies. The Mrlssi are flightless but have beaks and vestigial wings on their backs. Many find employment at MTSA, the Mrlsst Trade and Science Academy. [XW]

Mrlsst A planet in the Mennaalii system, Mrlsst joined the galactic community ages ago. A sanctuary for professors, scholars, and scientists, Mrlsst is well-known as a university planet. Beings of every imaginable species and background can be found milling outside the labs and lecture halls at all hours, heading to and from their respective classes.

In an attempt to attract Imperial research money, Mrlsst scientists faked the production of a remarkable new cloaking device, code-named the Phantom Project. Several months after the Battle of Endor, Mrlsst Planetary University President Keela, not knowing the project was a ruse, invited representatives from the New Republic and the Empire to meet at his offices—the Phantom Project datacards would be sold to the highest bidder. During negotiations, Rogue Squadron discovered a gravitic polarization beam weapon called a Planet Slicer in a nearby asteroid belt. The Phantom Project may have been a sham, but this new weapon was operational. The deadly device unexpectedly triggered a spacial wormhole, warping local space and swallowing an Imperial vessel whole. [XW]

MSE-6 mouse droid Nicknamed for its rodentlike appearance, this type of droid delivers orders and sensitive documents, among other tasks, such as cleaning ships. The MSE-6 has retractable manipulator arms. The mouse droid appears easily frightened but is actually protecting documents that it is carrying. The small rectangular droid has four wheels that propel it, and is usually reflective black in color. [CCG, SW]

MSE-6 mouse droid

Msst A small planet located near the Rim Worlds, it was the former site of an Imperial stronghold. The Empire abandoned Msst after the incident at Bakura, but over the years has still used it as a rendezvous point. During its tenure, the Empire destroyed indigenous plant species and forced the natives to construct useless buildings and toil in Msst's crystal swamps. The planet's name arises from the damp white mist that clings to the ground and reduces visibility. The mist is actually generated by floating pink jellyfishlike creatures called mistmakers, which sting with their hanging tentacles and draw the stunned prey into their mouths. The mistmakers are resilient enough to withstand blaster fire. After failing to infiltrate Luke Skywalker's Jedi academy, the Dark Jedi Brakiss fled to Msst to report to the Imperial officers who had sent him to Yavin 4 as a spy. Thirteen years after the Battle of Endor, Luke Skywalker landed on Msst searching for Brakiss as a suspect in a bombing. He was attacked by mistmakers and defeated them through the Force, but was badly injured. In an abandoned Imperial base he was nursed back to health by Brakiss's mother, who told him to search for her son on Telti. [NR]

mucous salamander A pink pseudopod with a mouth, this creature lives on Yavin 4. [ISWU]

mucus tree A slime-dripping tree that is on display in the Skydome Botanical Gardens on Coruscant. [JS]

mudmen Creatures made entirely of mud that live on the planet Roon, they tickle victims until they are completely helpless and then rob them of all their shiny objects. Mudmen explode into small blobs if they are sprayed with water, though they then regenerate. [DTV]

Muftak A Talz who grew up in the streets of Mos Eisley, he made a living doing odd jobs and begging. Large, white-furred, and fierce-looking, with

Muftak

sharply taloned fingers, Muftak has been a constant companion and protector of the small Chadra-Fan female named Kabe.

Born on Tatooine, Muftak knew nothing about his background except that he was a Talz, a giant species from Alzoc III that had been cut off from the rest of the galaxy by the Empire. By carefully watching everything with his four eyes, Muftak learned much about the comings and goings in the spaceport. Muftak took in the young Kabe and sheltered her for five years in a section of abandoned tunnels beneath Docking Bay 83. The tall furry creature was very protective of the small Chadra-Fan, although their relationship remained platonic. It was also symbiotic in a way, for Muftak lived on the credits that Kabe stole and the little money he made himself selling information. He decided to help her do the unthinkable: rob Jabba the Hutt's Mos Eisley townhouse. That in turn led to doing a bit of espionage work for the Rebel Alliance, before Muftak and Kabe took off for Alzoc III to explore his past. [TMEC, GG1]

Mulako Corporation Primordial Water Quarry In actuality a periodic comet in a 100-year orbit around its star, for several months during its approach and departure from the sun it warms enough to support life in its hollowed-out interior. During this time the Mulako Corporation promotes the comet as a tourist destination, and many people come to visit its exclusive resorts, restaurants, and lounges. Tourists can visit the comet's surface to view erupting gas geysers or experiment in the satellite's low gravity, or just enjoy the interior's bubbling fountains and the soft light shining through the mists. After the tourist season, ice-mining machines roam the irregular surface. The ice is chipped away in blocks and sold as "pure water" formed at the creation of the solar system. Luke Skywalker and Callista visited the Quarry eight years after the Battle of Endor in an attempt to help Callista regain her Jedi powers. [DS]

Mullinore, Captain An Imperial officer, he was captain of the Star Destroyer *Basilisk*. [DA]

multitool A multipurpose tool, it contains a lens, a wood drill, and many other useful implements. [CS]

Munto Codru Home to four armed beings known as Codru-Ji and considered of only marginal interest to the rest of galactic society, the planet is orbited by several moons and features beautiful mountains and ancient castles in its temperate zone. The Munto Codru castles, famous for their elaborate carvings on translucent rock walls, were built by a now-vanished civilization and currently are used as provincial capitals by the Codru-Ji.

Codru-Ji society is based on a complicated system of political families and entities (including the Sibiu, the Temebiu, and the province of Kirl) and is headed by Chamberlain Iyon. In this society coup abduction and ransom are common and expected political maneuvers, during which no one of noble birth is to be injured. Han and Leia Organa Solo's three children were abducted for real while Leia was on a diplomatic mission to Munto Codru. Animal life on Munto Codru includes a four-winged bat and the six-legged, fanged wyrwulfs, which are actually the Codru-Ji them selves in the earliest, infant stage of their lives. [CS]

The Great Murgoob

Murgoob, the Great Also known as Murgoob the Cranky, he is the old (more than 600 standard years) and unpleasant oracle of the Duloks on the forest moon of Endor. [ETV]

Muskov, Chief Chief of the Cloud Police, the force that protects Bespin's Cloud City. [MMY]

mutonium A valuable ore mined in the Stenness system. [TOJ]

Muzzer, Grand Moff Plump, round-faced, and very excitable, he was a member of the Central Committee of Grand Moffs that declared the pretender Trioculus to be the rightful successor to Emperor Palpatine following the Battle of Endor. [GDV]

MX A laser cannon that uses ion flow as an energy source. [TSW]

Mylock IV A small gray planet in the Mylock system of the Outer Rim, it is the homeworld of the Nharwaak and Habeen. The two species developed a new hyperdrive together, although the Nharwaak balked at the Habeen decision to deliver the technology to the Empire. In a rendezvous near Mylock IV, the Habeen officially turned the technology over to Admiral Zaarin's forces in exchange for their planet's formal entry into the Empire. Nharwaaks who attempted to sell the same technology to the Rebels were destroyed by Imperial attacks. [TSC]

Mylore, Yndis The Imperial Governor of Bryexx, he was also Moff of the Varvenna sector. [TJP]

Myneyrsh Tall, thin humanoids, they are natives of the planet Wayland. Like the Psadan, the Myneyrsh were present on the world when the first human colonists arrived centuries ago. The Myneyrsh have four arms and a smooth layer of blue-crystal flesh that makes them look almost as if they were made of glass. The Myneyrsh use bows and arrows and trained animals instead of blasters and repulsor craft. They have been at uneasy peace with the rest of Wayland's population after years of warfare. [HE, HESB, LC, LCSB]

mynock Leathery black flying creatures, they are an energy-feeding, silicon-based parasite that evolved in the vacuum of space and that feeds on energy. Typically traveling in packs, they attach themselves with suction organs to passing starships and can cause damage if not spotted quickly. Mynocks are nourished by stellar radiation and absorb silicon and other minerals from asteroids and other space debris. When they absorb enough, they reproduce by dividing in two. Mynocks have migrated throughout the galaxy as unwanted passengers aboard starships. [ESB, SWSB]

Mynock The name given to Wedge Antilles's R5-D2 astromech droid. Its memory was later wiped, and it was reprogrammed and renamed Gate. [RS, WG, KT, BW]

Myo A cyclops Abyssin from the planet Byss, this desert dweller is self-regenerating, primitive, and violent. He is also fearless, and calling him a "monoc" will start a fight. Myo was in the Mos Eisley cantina when Luke Skywalker and Han Solo first met. Myo is employed by the Galactic Outdoor Survival School. [CCG, AIR]

Myomar The site of important Imperial maintenance facilities, this planet was where Han Solo reportedly acquired several powerful deflector shield generators for installation on the *Millennium Falcon*. [SWSB]

Mystra

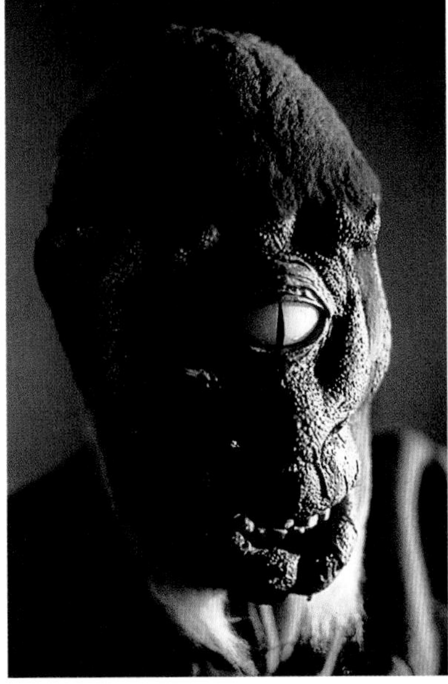

Myo

myostim unit A body-building device, the unit consists of a sensor field coupled with an adjustable, computerized electromyoclonic broadcaster that works muscle groups, forcing them to contract and relax in sequence. Users of myostim units get stronger simply by lying on the unit; they develop powerful mass without having to do any heavy lifting. Prince Xizor, head of the criminal Black Sun organization, was a confirmed user. [SOTE]

Myrkr Although Myrkr was settled for 300 years and lies in the Borderlands Region between Republic and Imperial space, the planet was isolated, shunned by both the Old Republic and the Jedi Knights. As a result, it is virtually unknown except to smugglers and other lawbreakers. The historical aversion of the Jedi was due to one of Myrkr's native lifeforms, the tree-dwelling ysalamiri. These creatures had evolved a defensive mechanism allowing them to push the Force from themselves, and many ysalamiri grouped together can create a vast region in which the Force does not exist. Another of Myrkr's animals, the predatory vornskr, uses the Force to assist in hunting and tracking prey. The high metal content of Myrkr's trees make sensor readings unreliable, spurring the smuggler Talon Karrde to build his chief base deep in the western part of the Great Northern Forest. This base was overrun by Grand Admiral Thrawn's forces after Karrde helped Luke Skywalker escape custody in Hyllyard City, Myrkr's major population center. Ood Bnar, a 5,000-year-old Jedi Master, was a member of the Neti—an alien treelike species that reportedly evolved on Myrkr. [HE, DFR, TOJ, DE2]

myrmins Small bugs, they organize themselves in colonies. [CS]

Mystra A professional killer, she carries a wrist blaster. Her cybervision helmet gives her perfect aim at any target. [CSW]

Mytus VII A small, rocky planet with low gravity and no atmosphere, it is located in the debris-cluttered Mytus system and was home to the Corporate Sector Authority prison known as Stars' End. Mytus VII orbits at the edge of its system, whose small star is located at the distant end of the galaxy and the farthest border of Corporate Sector space. The prison, where inmates were kept in suspended animation between interrogations, was commanded by Authority Viceprex Mirkovig Hirken. Stars' End was destroyed by Han Solo and his companions during an attempted jailbreak. Prior to that, a group of Alliance pilots escaped from Mytus VII in a freighter and were subsequently rescued by a Rebel shuttle. [HSE, CSSB, FP]

9000 Z001 An enclosed repulsorlift landspeeder manufactured by Ubrikkian, it has several microthrusters

9000 Z001

placed around its spherical hull. The 9000 Z001 seats three, has a top speed of 160 kilometers an hour, and is extremely maneuverable. [CCG]

Na'al, Voren A researcher and historian, he is responsible for recording much of the history and adventures of the heroes of the Battle of Yavin, especially Luke Skywalker, Han Solo, and Princess Leia Organa Solo. When Voren Na'al joined Alliance forces, he was named an assistant historian in Arhul Hextrophon's historian corps. He later became Director of Council Research for the New Republic. [GG1, DFRSB]

Nadd, Freedon A Jedi, he was seduced by the dark side of the Force and apprenticed himself to a Dark Lord of the Sith some 4,400 years before the Galactic Civil War. Freedon Nadd brought the dark power of the Sith to the planet Onderon and ruled for years. After he died, he was entombed within the walled city of Iziz, and his crypt became a site of concentrated dark-side power. A large force of Jedi eventually made peace between warring factions on Onderon, and Nadd's sarcophagus was moved to the more secure moon of Dxun. Jedi Exar Kun reawakened Nadd's spirit, which helped him discover hidden Sith scrolls. These led him to the hidden world of Korriban, site of the mummified remains of many Sith Lords. Nadd's spirit reappeared and destroyed huge crystals that had held the trapped spirits of ancient Jedi who had opposed the

Momaw Nadon

Nahkee

Sith; he also brought Kun close to death, forcing the confused Jedi to accept the dark side of the Force. Later, Kun turned a powerful amulet against Nadd's spirit and destroyed it forever. [TOJ, FNU, DLS]

Naddists A group of dissidents from the planet Onderon, formerly members of the Royal Armed Forces of the walled city of Iziz, who proclaimed their allegiance to the spirit of the Dark Jedi Freedon Nadd and staged an uprising some 4,000 years before the Galactic Civil War. [FNU, DLS]

Nadon, Momaw Expelled from his homeworld of Ithor after he was forced to make an excruciatingly difficult decision, Nadon became an underground Alliance agent before finally returning to his paradise home. Momaw Nadon belongs to a species of peaceful farmers and artisans sometimes called Hammerheads because of their S-curved necks and T-shaped anvillike heads. He had been high priest, or Herd Leader, of the *Tafanda Bay*, one of the huge air-floating cities on which most Ithorians live. The Empire's Captain Alima demanded Ithor's agricultural secrets, long guarded for religious and other reasons, and issued an ultimatum: either the secrets were to be turned over or Imperials would begin destroying the *Tafanda Bay*. Seeing little option, Nadon turned over the data. He was then put on trial by outraged Ithorians and exiled for at least three standard years, forced to abandon his wife, Fandomar, and the rest of his family.

Nadon ended up on Tatooine and helped create new forms of plant life on the arid planet. He also used his house to shelter Rebel fugitives and to provide information to the Alliance. Although he had the opportunity to kill the Imperial commander who made him turn over the agricultural secrets, he couldn't bring himself to do it. Instead, he hatched a plan to make the officer seem like a traitor, and the Imperial was shot by his own superiors. Following the Battle of Endor, Nadon returned to Ithor and was able to convince the planet's Elders to let him remain and to support the New Republic. [GG1, MEC, TMEC, SWCG]

Nahkee A baby Phlog, or phlogling, around the time of the Battle of Endor, this two-meter-tall giant of a toddler on the forest moon of Endor displayed trust, innocence, and curiosity, as his youth would indicate. [ETV]

Nailati, Evilo A B'omarr monk often consulted by the frog-dog Bubo. [TJP]

Najiba A remote planet covered with wetlands and lashed with atmospheric electrical discharges and constant rainstorms, this low-technology world pulses with a high degree of smuggling activity. Inhabitants of Najiba tend to be superstitious and wary of strangers but extremely loyal and hardworking. Around three million humans and Najib live on the planet. [SWAJ]

Nal Hutta A bruised-looking green, blue, and brown planet in the Y'Toub system, the planet's name means "glorious jewel" in Huttese. It is one of the main planets settled by the Hutts after they left their ancestral home of Varl. Despite the planet's immensity, its extremely low density gives it a tolerable gravity. Many years ago, the planet was known as Evocar, the homeworld of the primitive Evocii. When the Hutts arrived, they traded technology to the Evocii in exchange for land, eventually buying up the planet and forcing the Evocii from their homeworld. The Old Republic relocated the displaced Evocii to the nearby Nar Shaddaa moon, but they fared no better there. Once the Hutts controlled the entire planet, they replaced all Evocii structures with Hutt palaces and shrines and renamed the planet itself.

Nal Hutta was once a pleasant world of mountainous rain forests, but Hutts have transformed it into a gloomy planet of stinking bogs, stagnant scum-covered puddles, and patches of sickly marsh grass inhabited by insects and spiders. The planet's flocks of large, clumsy birds are shot down by swoop-riding hunters. The atmosphere is polluted by strip-mining in Nal Hutta's industrial centers, and a greasy rain drizzles on its squatters' villages and ghettos. Nal Hutta and its moon, Nar Shaddaa, are at the center of Hutt Space and host a constant traffic of freight haulers, smugglers, and other galactic traders. The planet is ruled by a council of the eldest members of the Clans of the Ancients, the oldest Hutt families. The world's population consists of nearly seven billion inhabitants, three billion of them Hutts. [DE, GG4, DE2, DESB, DS]

Nam Chorios In the Chorios systems of the Meridian sector, this barren, unforgiving, moonless world orbits a violet-white star of the same name. There are no seas, but there are endless wastelands of sharp, jagged rocks and basalt and quartz outcroppings. Nights are incredibly cold. Chains of crystal mountains reflect sunlight from their sparkling facets, and isolated crystal rock chimneys thrust up toward the sky. The chimneys are called tsils; the Ten Cousins is a group of tsils standing in a ring.

Tiny patches of green mark where colonists have managed to gain a foothold for crops. Some 750 years before the Battle of Yavin, political prisoners were exiled to the planet by the Grissmath Dynasty, which seeded the world with insectlike drochs—carriers of the Death Seed plague—hoping that the prisoners would all fall ill and die. Gun stations were set up by the Grissmaths to prevent the rescue of the prisoners, but the prisoners and their guards survived, farming the groundwater seams. Newcomers, the recent post-Imperial arrivals, prefer to use modern technology. The Theran Listeners are cultists who live in the canyons and caves and operate the gun stations. Oldtimers show reverence toward the Therans as healers. The Force is magnified and intensified by the entire planet, making Force usage difficult to control or focus.

The planet's main city is Hweg Shul. Plant life includes brachniel hedges and scrub-loaks, crom and gomex mosses, lichens, podhoy, bolter, blueleaf, snigvine, bott, buttonwood trees, and balcrabbian. House-sized, tethered antigrav balls hold soil for smoor, brope, majie, and nisemia thread vine. Metal towers support branswed and topato crops. Animal life includes blerds, gebbecks, alcopays, mikkets, insectlike flying narjams, and cu-pas—brightly colored mounts related to tauntauns but suited for hot climates. Drochs, which burrow into the flesh and are absorbed, consume life and cause the Death Seed plague, but the sunlight fragmenting through Nam Chorios's crystals weakens them. Captain drochs, grown large from eating other drochs, are cat-sized and crablike, with eyes on long stalks. Platinum and rock-ivory are found in the mountains; spooks, or smokies, are long, green-violet crystals found in clusters in the deep hills.

For years, power on the planet rested with Beldorian the Hutt and Seti Ashgad, a profiteer who had been exiled to Nam Chorios by then-Senator Palpatine. Dzym, a mutated droch, kept Ashgad alive and young. Callista, the onetime Jedi who had lost her Force powers, also arrived on the planet, where Beldorian imprisoned her. Nine years after the Battle of Endor, Leia Organa Solo secretly visited the planet to meet with Ashgad. He then turned on her and took her prisoner before unleashing the Death Seed plague across three-quarters of the sector. He planned to disable the planet's gun stations and allow the Loronar Corporation to strip-mine the smokies.

Meanwhile, the forces of Moff Getelles of the Antemeridian sector, bolstered with Loronar's CCIR needle fighters, invaded the Meridian sector. The whole invasion plan had been masterminded by Dzym to get himself and his fellow drochs off the planet where they had been trapped for so long. Luke Skywalker arrived to find Callista, and his B-wing was shot down. Leia escaped from Ashgad's fortress and teamed up with Callista. After a series of confrontations, Leia killed Beldorian; Dzym escaped but was destroyed along with the other drochs; Moff Getelles was forced to retreat at the Battle of Nam Chorios; and Callista decided to stay on the planet a while longer. [POT]

Princess Nampi

Nampi, Princess A giant purple snakelike slug from the planet Oorooturoo, Nampi trapped Jabba the Hutt and his crew aboard her ship. She ate Jabba's top aide, Scuppa, luring him with the promise of marriage. But she was destroyed when Jabba used a remote control to release a vial of acid he had implanted long ago in Scuppa's head—which by then was in Nampi's stomach. He then looted treasures from the ship of the late, loathsome princess. [JAB]

Nandreeson A Glottalphib, he is one of the most powerful crime lords in the galaxy. Like all Glottalphibs, Nandreeson can breathe through gills and prefers watery or swampy environs. His nostrils can spout fire, and he is a powerful swimmer. His base of operations is Skip Six, from which he acted as the undisputed kingpin of Smuggler's Run; his ship was the *Silver Egg*. Nandreeson had long had a price on Lando Calrissian's head and was delighted to hear Lando had reentered the Run seeking the truth behind the murder of the smuggler Jarril. Several of Nandreeson's Rek bounty hunters captured Lando and brought him to Skip 6. Nandreeson held him in a giant, seething mud hole, where he expected Calrissian to tread water until he drowned. [NR]

nano-destroyers Artificially created viruses, they dismantle the cells of an infected person one cell at a time. They were the basis of the poison infecting Mon Mothma. Once they were discovered in Mothma's system, the Jedi student Cilghal was able to eradicate the nano-destroyers threatening the life of the onetime New Republic Chief of State. [COF]

Nanta-Ri This planet is located in the Farlax sector near the Koornacht Cluster. Chief of State Leia Organa Solo sent two cruisers from the Fourth Fleet there to help defend it against Yevethan aggression twelve years after the Battle of Endor. [SOL]

Nanthri route A shipping route once plagued by the Nanthri pirates, who had united under their leader, Celis Mott. He later mysteriously disappeared into otherspace after being captured by Rebels. Mott's list of "ship's articles" are still used by pirates and privateers. [SWAJ, OS]

NaQuoit Bandits An outlaw group, the bandits operate in the Ottega system, where they prey upon local space traffic. [DE]

Nardix, Sector Governor An Imperial officer captured by the bounty hunters 4-LOM and Zuckuss, he was turned over to the Rebel Alliance and was tried for crimes against sentient beings. The trial was a great embarrassment to the Empire. [TBH]

narjams Small, fat blue parasites, narjams have managed to colonize most planets by growing from minuscule larvae carried in the oil reservoirs of ships. Narjam infestation has led to inevitable rounds of inoculations, since they always pick up some kind of local disease, mutate it, and feed it back to colonists and indigenous ecosystems with their bites. [POT]

Narra, Commander Called "The Boss" by pilots of the X-wing fighter group known as Renegade Flight at the Battle of Yavin, he assumed command after the death of Red Leader during the battle. His protocol droid, K-3PO, served in the command center of Echo Base. Commander Narra himself was killed in an Imperial ambush near Derra IV prior to the Battle of Hoth, when the Rebel convoy that Narra and his squadron were escorting was attacked by several TIE fighter squadrons. Luke Skywalker was then promoted to the rank of commander and placed in charge of the fighter group, which evolved into the legendary Rogue Squadron. [ESBR, GG3]

Nar Shaddaa The ungoverned "smugglers' moon" orbiting Nal Hutta, it is completely covered by interlocking spaceport facilities and kilometers-high docking towers reaching to orbit. Nar Shaddaa's "vertical city" was built over thousands of years and is protected by often-malfunctioning planetary shields. Although once bustling with legitimate trade, Nar Shaddaa quickly lost prestige as hyperspace trade lanes shifted away. Now quite distant from most galactic commercial centers, Nar Shaddaa runs its own affairs with little interference. Famous as the birthplace of Jabba the Hutt, Nar Shaddaa is controlled by Hutts and assorted smuggling guilds and is now widely regarded as the center of smuggling operations in the known galaxy. Most of the moon's seventy-two to ninety-five billion inhabitants live in the highest levels of the spaceport-cities.

Nar Shaddaa originally was given to the displaced Evocii as a new homeworld, after the Hutts forced them from nearby Nal Hutta. The Hutts continued to exploit the Evocii, and now their forgotten, inbred descendants inhabit the lowest levels of the vertical city. Han Solo and Lando Calrissian both frequented Nar Shaddaa during their early smuggling days and still have associates living there. Before their involvement in the Rebellion, C-3PO and R2-D2 traveled to Nar Shaddaa in an attempt to apprehend the criminal Olag Greck. The bounty hunter Greedo and his family lived in the moon's Corellian sector for several years, until an Imperial attack on a Rebel hideout resulted in massive destruction and the collapse of nearly twenty sector levels. Following the Battle of Yavin, Alliance agent Kyle Katarn avoided bounty hunters on Nar Shaddaa in order to find Imperial navigational charts related to the Dark Trooper project. Six years after the Battle of Endor, Leia and Han Solo, searching for Vima-Da-Boda in Nar Shaddaa's lowest levels, were attacked by carnivorous vrblthers and the bounty hunter Boba Fett. [DE, DE2, DESB, D, TMEC, DF, SWAJ]

Narth During the Imperial evacuation of the planets Narth and Ihopek following the Battle of Endor, the Imperial Star Destroyer *Gnisnal* was demolished by internal explosions. The wreckage later provided the New Republic with a complete copy of the Imperial Order of Battle. [BTS]

Nartian A four-armed species, they are slightly smaller than humans. [TMEC]

Nartlo A black marketeer, he was used by both Kirtan Loor and Fliry Vorru to find the location of bacta storage facilities being used by the New Republic. Armed with this information, the Palpatine Counterinsurgency Front began to target the installations for a major bombing campaign. A power struggle between Loor and Vorru proved fatal for Nartlo. [BW]

Nashira According to Akanah Norand Pell, Nashira was the name of Luke Skywalker's mother. Nashira, she told Luke, had lived with the Fallanassi religious order on Lucazec and perhaps had escaped with them when they fled the planet. But, after a long search, Luke realized that Akanah wasn't telling the truth and that the woman named Nashira had shown her kindness once after her own mother had betrayed her people to the Empire. [BTS]

nashtah Six-legged hunters native to the planet Dra III, these bloodthirsty green reptilians with sleek hides and long barbed tails are vicious and tenacious. Once they have a prey's scent, they stay on its track until they catch it. With triple rows of jagged teeth and diamond-hard claws, they rarely forego a meal. [HSR]

Nashtah Pup A scout ship aboard the bounty hunter Bossk's ship, the *Hound's Tooth*. [TBH]

Nataz, Dyyz A bounty hunter who often goes by the name of Megadeath, he is a denizen of Nar Shaddaa. Dyyz Nataz wears a rusted, skull-shaped helmet and full Ithullan armor. He trained the Rodian bounty hunter Greedo, but then betrayed him to Thuku, another Rodian bounty hunter sent on a mission to kill Greedo. [DE, TMEC, CCG]

Na'ts, Doikk A member of the Bith jizz band Figrin D'an and the Modal Nodes, he plays the Dorenian Beshniquel or Fizzz. Na'ts doesn't much like humans, preferring to work with droids. [TMEC, CCG]

Nautag The Askajian mate of the dancer Yarna d'al' Gargan, he was devoured by the rancor after telling Jabba the Hutt that he would never let his wife or children live in slavery. [TJP]

Navander, Romas "Lock" A skilled Corellian pilot, he defected from the Empire shortly after graduating from the Academy. Romas "Lock" Navander played an important role as tech communications officer at the Rebel Alliance's Echo Base on the ice planet Hoth, where he relayed orders to nearby Rebel starships. [CCG]

nav computer A specialized processing unit, sometimes called a navicomputer, used to calculate lightspeed jumps, hyperspace and realspace trajectories, and routes based upon available time and fuel energy. Nav computers also can display astrogation charts and work in conjunction with a ship's navigational sensors. [SWRPG, SWSB]

Navik the Red The Rodian leader of the warlike Chattza clan, he is identifiable by the enormous red birthmark on his face. Navik used gladiator hunts to start wars with other clans on Rodia. After the Tetsus clan fled Rodia in his wake, he hunted them down throughout the galaxy. He was the Rodian Grand Protector during the Galactic Civil War. [TMEC]

Doikk Na'ts

Romas "Lock" Navander

Nawruun An older, gray-furred Wookiee, he was a slave at Maw Installation who was rescued by Chewbacca. [COF]

Nazzar The Nazzar are bipedal beings with equine features. The Jedi Qrrl Toq was a Nazzar Prince 4,000 years before the Galactic Civil War. [FNU]

Nebo A Naddist street philosopher in the walled city of Iziz 4,000 years before the Galactic Civil War, he and fellow zealot Rask unsuccessfully attempted to protect the sarcophagi of King Ommin, Queen Amanoa, and Freedon Nadd from Dark Jedi Exar Kun. [DLS]

Nebula orchids These flowers grow on thin purple vines so rubbery and flexible that they can be tightened into a knot that's impossible to break. Their showy magenta, maroon, and lavender blossoms thrive in the rain forests of Yavin 4. [YJK, GG2]

Nebulon Ranger A large multisectioned courier ship, it was used by the Jedi brothers Ulic and Cay Qel-Droma and the Twi'lek Jedi Tott Doneeta, key participants in the Sith War 4,000 years before the Battle of Yavin. The *Nebulon Ranger* had retractable wings that were extended for atmospheric flight and retracted for landing. The ship's two main engine arrays gave it greater maneuverability without bulky maneuvering jets.

The *Ranger* had a forward-firing pulse cannon, a retractable rotating laser cannon on each wing tip, and a more powerful rotating laser cannon at the base of the second engine array. Each forward mandible also had a pair of linked proton torpedo launchers and a short-range concussion sphere launcher.

The *Ranger*'s series of eight shield generators provided full protection around the hull. The shields were raised only in combat because of their immense energy drain, but that made the *Ranger* vulnerable to attack at other times. The beast-riders of Onderon downed the *Ranger* with a single seeker-torpedo. [TOJ, SWVG]

Needa, Captain Lorth An Imperial officer, he was commander of the *Imperial*-class Star Destroyer *Avenger*, part of Darth Vader's task force prior to the Battle of Hoth. The *Avenger* led the search for the fleeing *Millennium Falcon* after the battle. When Han Solo's ship escaped, Lorth Needa decided he had to personally apologize to Vader. The apology was accepted—and Needa was executed on the spot by Vader's use of dark-side power. [ESB]

Needa, Virar An Imperial lieutenant and a cousin of Lorth Needa, he was placed in charge of OSETS 2711, an Orbital Solar Energy Transfer Satellite above Imperial Center. He was on duty when Rebels took control of his station from the ground with the assistance of the computer center. They realigned an orbital mirror to burn up a large water reservoir, cre-

Nebulon Ranger

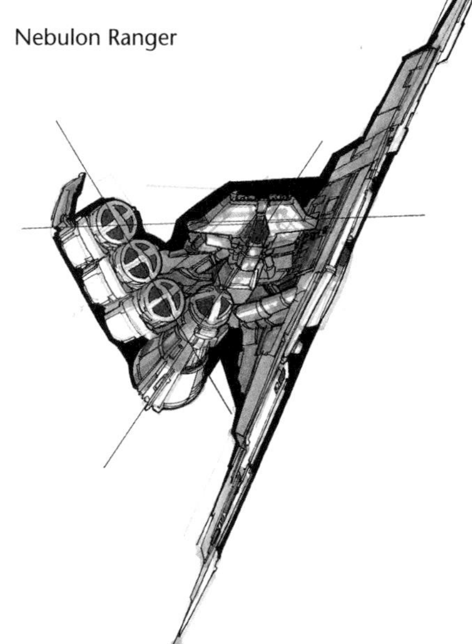

ating a terrible thunderstorm that brought down the planet's shields. The station also was used to destroy one of the Golan III defense platforms. [WG]

Needles Long-distance smart missiles, they have nearly infinite range and hyperspace rendezvous capability. They are controlled by CCIR crystals and manufactured by Loronar Corporation. [POT]

neek A small, sharp-toothed, but harmless species of mischievous lizard, they were abundant on the planet Ambria 4,000 years before the Galactic Civil War. Neeks were food for the hssiss—fierce dark-side dragons that lived in Lake Natth. [TOJ]

Neela The mother of the Rodian bounty hunter Greedo. [TMEC]

Neelgaimon A forsaken planet where several designers of the *Eye of Palpatine* battle-moon were reassigned to punitive duty at the sand mines following the failure of the Emperor's attempt to destroy a Jedi enclave on Belsavis. [COJ]

Neema The daughter of the Jedi Vima-Da-Boda. [DE]

Neesh A Rodian bounty hunter and member of the warlike Chattza clan, he hired Spurch "Warhog" Goa to execute the young Rodian Greedo. Spurch upheld his end of the bargain by encouraging the inexperienced Greedo to try to capture Han Solo. [TMEC]

neks Battle dogs bred in the Cyborrean system for sale on the galactic black market, the vicious creatures are fitted with armor and attack stimulators. [DE]

Nentan Nentan base was a stopover point for civilians wishing passage to Rebel-controlled safe worlds when it was discovered by Imperial forces. The base didn't have enough transports available to evacuate everyone from the surface until Capt. Bren Derlin, serving General Rieekan, led a squad that hid in Nentan's ancient ruins and captured an Imperial transport. This allowed all the base personnel to escape, earning Derlin the rank of major. [MTS]

Nek

Nereus, Wilek The Imperial Governor of the subjugated planet Bakura, he governed with a minimum of bloodshed and preserved at least the form of pre-Imperial government. But his hobby was hunting predators—including sentient ones—and displaying their teeth. He infected a leader of the opposition with a deadly parasite, then proceeded to infect Luke Skywalker. Governor Nereus was finally killed after he fired a blaster rifle at Skywalker, who used his lightsaber to deflect the bolt back to Nereus. [TAB]

nerf A rangy, supple creature with curving, dull horns and long, rank fur that covers its muscular body, this domesticated herbivore is temperamental and cantankerous, foul-smelling and apt to spit at its handlers, the nerf herders. If nerf meat weren't delicious, it's doubtful anyone would bother raising the animals, even though their pelts are used for a variety of purposes. [ESB, ISWU]

nerf gizzards A once-popular phrase among certain galactic denizens, as in "Me an' the boys will peel open that ship like a can o' nerf gizzards!" [TOJ]

nergon 14 An unstable, explosive element, it is a main component in Imperial proton torpedoes. A pulsating blue color when inert, nergon 14 changes first to bright red and then to white before it explodes. [DTV]

nerve disrupter A hard-to-obtain torture device, it consists of a small black box mounted on a tripod. It is used to disrupt the flow of nerves' electrical signals, thus causing intense pain and involuntary bodily movements. [TMEC]

Nespis VIII Nespis VIII was a huge derelict space city located at the node of the six remaining Auril systems near the Cron Drift. One of the largest of the ancient spaceports, Nespis VIII began as a remote beacon-point during the early days of hyperspace travel. Over thousands of years the beacon became a sprawling city, with a vast diversity of architectural styles and relics from nearly every period of space travel, including centuries-old murals of the Sith War. The city remained well-preserved in the vacuum of space and was abandoned long before the start of the Clone Wars.

Six years after the Battle of Endor, Luke Skywalker freed Kam Solusar from the dark side of the Force while at Nespis VIII. Later that year (after the destruction of the command base on the fifth moon of Da Soocha), New Republic leaders established their new base at the remote space city, and Leia Organa Solo's third child, Anakin, was born there. Soon after, the Emperor fired a Galaxy Gun projectile at Nespis VIII as the New Republic scrambled to abandon the base. Though the first shot was unsuccessful, a second projectile destroyed the ancient city. [DE2, EE]

Nessie Slang for any one of the twenty-five native humanoid races of the Stenness Node. Nessies operate the mines and trade with outworlders. [TOJ]

Netus An Old Republic Defense Minister some 4,000 years before the Galactic Civil War. [FNU, TSW]

Neva, Captain The Sullustan commander of the New Republic escort frigate *Rebel Star*. [DE]

New Alderaan A planet settled as an Alliance safe world, it was renamed New Alderaan to serve as a homeworld for the refugees from the destroyed world of Alderaan. Following the Battle of Endor, General Jan Dodonna went into semiretirement on New Alderaan until called back into service to fight the Empire. The planet was later discovered by Imperial Warlord Zsinj and its entire population was forced to evacuate temporarily. During the cloned Emperor's reappearance six years after the Battle of Endor, Mon Mothma's disabled daughter convalesced on the planet.

At the same time, Jacen and Jaina Solo were being protected on an uncharted green, exotic world codenamed New Alderaan. The small, unassuming settlement near a lake helped disguise a large underground technical complex and its advanced defensive weaponry. The Emperor attacked the complex with seven dark-side warriors and a phalanx of advanced AT-ATs in an attempt to kidnap the Solo children. [RSB, DE, CPL, DE2, DESB]

New Bakstre A planet with seven moons, a purplish sky, and a very rapid rotation. [SWRPG]

New Brigia Just within the borders of the Koornacht Cluster, the colony was once the site of a struggling chromite mining operation founded by a small group of Brigians about two years prior to the Battle of Yavin. In its early years, New Brigia enjoyed rich hauls of chromite ore, many eager buyers, and protection from pirates by the Imperial forces controlling Koornacht. Over time, however, the ore yields grew less profitable, and the Empire's retreat from the region after the Battle of Endor hurt the security of the trade lanes. Twelve years after Endor, the entire Brigian colony was ruthlessly eliminated by the Yevethan military in what the Yevetha called the Great Purge. [BTS]

New Cov The third planet in the Churba sector, it is covered with thick jungles and carnivorous plants. Eight giant walled cities, accessible through entrance shafts in their transparisteel domes, have been built on the planet to harvest valuable, exotic biomolecules from the local plant life for export to make medicines and for some industrial processes. Imperial forces arrived occasionally and raided the cities for their stores of biomolecules; the raids were treated by the Covies—allied with the New Republic—as a routine form of taxation. The walled city of Ilic contains a reproduction of Coruscant's Grandis Mon theater and a tapcafe called the Mishra on its entertainment level. New Republic Senator Borsk Fey'lya helped Garm Bel Iblis' army set up a supply line through New Cov and took on an Imperial *Victory*-class Star Destroyer with only four Bothan ships in order to protect this connection. [DFR, DFRSB]

Night beast

New Order The phrase that Emperor Palpatine used to describe his new regime. [SW]

New Polokia One of the planets where the starliner *Star Morning*, owned by the Fallanassi religious order, stopped after departing the planet Teyr. [SOL]

New Republic The name given to the democratic government established by the Alliance to Restore the Republic (sometimes called the Alliance of Free Planets) after the Battle of Endor. It is based on the best principles of the Old Republic, which collapsed and gave way to the tyrannical regime of Emperor Palpatine. The Declaration of a New Republic was issued by the Alliance's Provisional Council. [HE, DFR, LC, DE, TBSB]

New Republic Intelligence (NRI) An organization that is successor to the old network of Rebel spies. [AC]

Next Chance A casino on Rodia where Princess Leia Organa first met with Guri, the human replica droid who was the sidekick of Prince Xizor, the head of the criminal Black Sun organization. [SOTE]

Nezriti organization A criminal group, it did business with Prince Xizor's Black Sun organization. [SOTE]

ng'ok The ng'ok are well-known war beasts with foul tempers. Their razor-sharp teeth and retractable claws help them frighten off potential attackers. [CCG]

Ng'ok holomonster

Ng'rhr A Wookiee term meaning "clan uncle," a Ng'rhr serves as teacher and master to his apprentice. [TBH]

Nha, Mnor A Gotal in the Azure Dianoga cantina, he sensed Gavin Darklighter's fear at the approach of Imperial stormtroopers, then his relief when they went away. Because Darklighter also radiated fear followed by relief at the approach and departure of Asyr Sei'lar, Mnor Nha assumed the Rogue Squadron pilot was bigoted, so he and his compatriots took Darklighter and his Rogue friends before the Alien Combine to be judged for bigotry. [KT]

Nichen The ship *Kettlemoor* jumped to the planet Nichen after its encounter near Gmar Askilon with the ghost ship known as the Teljkon vagabond. The *Kettlemoor* was carrying the dead and injured crew members from the interdiction picket *Kauri*. [SOL]

nic-i-tain A drug delivered into a being's system by smoking t'bac. [TMEC]

Nigekus, Negus A New Brigia elder, he was killed in the Yevethan assault. [BTS]

night beast A fierce creature, it was left as a guardian by the Massassi on Yavin 4 to protect their homeland and its sacred temples. When an Imperial TIE fighter crashed into the Massassi ruins, the night beast emerged and ravaged the moon's hidden Rebel base. With R2-D2's help,

Nikto

Luke Skywalker was able to lure the night beast into a Rebel supply ship and send it off-world. [CSW]

nightcrawler Small nocturnal insects, they are native to the planet Tatooine. [SWN]

Night Hammer Built in secret by Superior General Delvardus, the Super Star Destroyer *Night Hammer* was taken over after Delvardus's murder by Admiral Daala. It became her flagship. The *Night Hammer* was eight kilometers long, capable of carrying a crew of up to 100,000, and plated with stealth armor so that it would appear only as a black shadow on approach. Daala was so intent on snuffing out the resurgent Jedi that she rechristened the ship the *Knight Hammer* prior to its orbital assault on the Jedi academy and Yavin 4. Callista, who had lost her Jedi powers, commandeered a TIE fighter, managed to enter the *Knight Hammer*, and sabotaged it from within to send it hurtling into the gas giant Yavin. [DS]

Nightsisters A group of the female Witches of the planet Dathomir, its members turned to the dark side of the Force. Nightsisters enslaved Imperial guards at a Dathomir prison and attempted to flee the planet to gain power over the galaxy some four years after the Battle of Endor. They were vanquished by Luke Skywalker, Leia Organa, and Han Solo, but fifteen years later a new order arose. These Nightsisters were younger, stronger, and allied with Imperial forces seeking to regain control of the galaxy. [CPL, YJK]

Night Spirit An evil entity on the forest moon of Endor that is feared by Ewoks and worshipped by Duloks. The Night Spirit sometimes manifests itself as a ghostly apparition. [ETV]

Nikto A humanoid species with flat faces and multiple nostrils. The species is made up of several distinct races differentiated by skin color and facial and other features. Their most prominent race has four small horns protruding from their foreheads. Crime lord Jabba the Hutt hired several Nikto as skiff guards. The Nikto come from the planet Kintan in the Si'klaata Cluster. [RJ, GG12]

Nim Drovis Located in the Meridian sector of the Drovian system, the rainy world of Nim Drovis (sometimes called Drovis) contains a Sector Medical Facility and Medical Research Facility attended to by the Ho'Din physician Dr. Ism Oolos, along with a small New Republic base. Before they were contacted by the Old Republic, the Drovians were a primitive species organized into a network of tribes. Many are addicted to the narcotic zwil, which they absorb by inserting fist-sized plugs into their membrane-lined breathing tubes. The largest free port on Nim Drovis is Bagsho, originally settled by colonists from Alderaan. Within the last five years, it has turned into a link between the sector's neutral worlds and the New Republic.

Natives are bottom-heavy and have tentacles with pincers on the ends and many different sensory devices on their bodies. The Gopso'o tribes (with braided topknots) operate slug-ranches, and are the ancient enemies of the Drovians. Architecture consists of heavy stone walls and thick wooden supports with many balconies. Swamps, mud, molds, fungus, and reeds predominate. Animal life includes marsh-gunnies, gulpers, and green-eyed wadie-platts.

Nine years after the Battle of Endor, R2-D2 and C-3PO forced the looter Captain Bortrek to land them on Nim Drovis. They tried to earn passage to Cybloc XII at the Chug 'n' Chuck and the Wookiee's Codpiece taverns. Yarbolk Yemm, a Chadra-Fan reporter for TriNebulon News, saved them from being stolen. At the same time, Han Solo brought several survivors of the crashed ship *Corbantis* to the Bagsho medical facility to treat their radiation burns. Forty people at the Republic base had already died from the Death Seed plague. [POT]

Ninedenine *See* EV-9D9

Ninth quadrant An area of space near the Senex and Juvex sectors, it contains the Greeb-Streebling Cluster, the Noopiths, and the planet Belsavis. The quadrant is relatively isolated and its systems are far apart. [COJ]

Ninx, Shug A half-breed in the eyes of the Empire, this master mechanic had a Corellian father and a mother from the near-extinct Theelin race. The genetic cocktail produced Shug Ninx—mostly human, bearing mottled spots around his mouth and chin and hands with a thumb and two fingers. He developed great skill for fixing machinery—especially spaceships—and went to the smuggler's moon of Nar Shaddaa, where he set up his own large shop.

Ninx was friendly with many of the young smugglers and blockade runners, including the Corellian Han Solo; Han's onetime lady friend, Salla Zend; his copilot, the Wookiee Chewbacca; and his gambling buddy, Lando Calrissian. Ninx's spacebarn became a hangout. As time passed, Zend became an employee and then a business partner. Six years after the Battle of Endor, Ninx and Zend finally saw Solo again—this time with

Shug Ninx

his wife, Leia Organa Solo, on a mission to save her brother, Luke Skywalker.

Han was betrayed to bounty hunters, but Ninx and Zend saved him, not for the last time. Later, they escaped from the planet Byss along with top Alliance officials, went to help in the fierce Battle of Calamari, and later returned to Nar Shaddaa, only to find that Ninx's facility had been infiltrated by Darktroopers. Back on Byss during an Alliance attack, Ninx and Zend, aided by other smugglers, helped rescue several Alliance heroes. Later, they helped save Leia and her children from an Imperial attack on New Alderaan. [DE, DE2]

Nippett An infant Ewok, or wokling, on Endor's forest moon at the time of the Battle of Endor. [RJ]

Nivek'Yppiks A Ffib heretic, he fled his homeworld of Lorahns and was eventually hunted down by Boba Fett, who received half a million credits for the job. [TJP]

Nkik, Het A Jawa scout, he wanted to avenge the deaths of his relatives, who were killed in their sandcrawler by stormtroopers. Het Nkik had an opportunity to kill several troopers but realized too late that someone had stolen the powerpack from his blaster. He died at the hands of the very troopers he had sought to kill. [TMEC, CCG]

Nkllon Located in the Athega system, this super-hot planet closely orbits its star. Any ships approaching the planet must ride behind the cooled umbrellas of massive shieldships until reaching Nkllon's shadow, or they risk critical solar damage. Lando Calrissian constructed a constantly moving mining platform, inspired by a similar design for the planet Miser, which could stay permanently on the shadow side during Nkllon's ninety-day rotation. The platform, Nomad City, consisted mainly of a Dreadnaught cruiser supported by forty Imperial walkers. It held a crew of 5,000 and was surrounded by a cloud of shuttles, pilot vehicles, and mole miners. Some of the metals produced there included hfredium, kammris, and dolovite. An attack on Nomad City by the Star Destroyer *Judicator* resulted in the theft of fifty-one mole miners, and another Imperial attack critically damaged the city and resulted in the loss of its strategic metals stockpiles. [HE, LC, YJK]

Het Nkik

Noa

Noa An overweight old human with a long white beard, he had been stranded on Endor's forest moon for years after his survey ship crashed. Noa had a gruff exterior but a kind heart. He befriended the young human female Cindel Towani and Wicket the Ewok, mostly at the urging of his companion, Teek. [BFE]

Nodon and Nonak These two Cathar brothers, felinelike humanoids, joined Burrk, a former stormtrooper, in setting up big-game hunting expeditions on the ice planet Hoth for one reason: Wampa pelts brought a hefty price on the black market. But Nodon, Nonak, and Burrk—along with the hunters they guided—were all killed by their prey. Luke Skywalker and onetime Jedi Callista barely escaped the hunt with their lives. [DS]

Noghri Small, compact killing machines, the gray-skinned, long-taloned warriors were the secret assassins of Emperor Palpatine and Darth Vader. Natives of the planet Honoghr, the Noghri have large eyes, tooth-filled jaws, and an incredibly sensitive power of smell by which they identify individuals. Vader long ago tricked the Noghri into believing that the Old Republic was responsible for a blight on their planet, and that only the Empire would offer them assistance—help they later came to depend upon.

In return, the fearsome Noghri became an Imperial hit squad for Vader and later Grand Admiral Thrawn, who sent a Noghri squad to capture Princess Leia Organa Solo, pregnant with twins. But one of the Noghri recognized, by smell, that Leia was the daughter of their revered Darth Vader. Leia eventually accompanied the Noghri Khabarakh back to Honoghr, where—after initial futile attempts—she finally convinced the natives that the Empire had been responsible all along for the continued ravaging of their planet. The Noghri rose up against the Imperials and started working with the New Republic. The Noghri aided the Alliance in its attack on Mount Tantiss; and Thrawn's Noghri bodyguard, Rukh, slew his master aboard his ship at Bilbringi. [HE, HESB, DFR, DFRSB, LC, LCSB]

Noimm, Senator Cair Tok A New Republic senator, he was a member of the Security Council. [SOL]

Nok A Rodian, he was an uncle of the bounty hunter Greedo. He was a member of the peaceful Tetsus clan that eventually escaped to Nar Shaddaa. [TMEC]

N'oka Brath The Qella name for the star that the planet Qella orbits. [TT]

Nomad City A mobile mining base, it was built by Lando Calrissian on the planet Nkllon following the Battle of Endor. A massive engineering feat—especially because of the intense heat of the planet's sun—the rolling mining center was critically damaged after several Imperial attacks. [HE, HESB, LC, YJK]

Nooch A New Republic Fifth Fleet pilot, he was killed during a failed blockade attempt of the Yevetha at Doornik-319. [SOL]

Noonian sector Situated near the Halthor sector and home to the Noonian system and the planets Noonar and Movris, it was long ruled by Imperial governor Trophan Thanis. The system supports several food-processing facilities for the Nebula Consumables Corporation. Rebel privateers operating from Movris were able to steal nearly a quarter of the company's output. [SWAJ]

Noorr, Vol Primate of the Yevethan battle cruiser *Purity*, he was the commander in charge of the destruction of the *Astrolabe*, the New Republic astrographic ship, at Doornik-1142. [BTS]

Nootka, Lai The Duros captain of the freighter *Star's Delight*, he was the shadowy figure that Rogue Squadron member Tycho Celchu met at the Headquarters tavern. Corran Horn spotted them there and began to believe that Celchu was an Imperial spy. In fact, Celchu was negotiating with Lai Nootka for spare parts for the Z-95 Headhunters that he had purchased for Rogue Squadron. Nootka was later killed by the Empire to keep him from testifying at Captain Celchu's trial for murder and treason. [WG, KT]

Noquivzor A pleasant world of treeless plains, gentle hills, and savannas of golden grasses, its animal life includes herds of horned wildernerfs, which are prey to prides of leopard-like taopari. The planet has warm breezes and an exceptionally dry climate—Admiral Ackbar had to install a humidifier in his quarters. Some three years after the Battle of Endor, Rogue Squadron was moved to a starfighter base on Noquivzor as its staging area for an attack on Borleias. The base has only one building above the ground.

After the conquest of Borleias, Borsk Fey'lya arranged for the New Republic Provisional Council to meet on Noquivzor to determine the feasibility of using Black Sun extremists to help disrupt the Imperial government prior to the Alliance assault on Coruscant. Fearful of an attack by Warlord Zsinj, Rogue Squadron moved its base of operations from Borleias back to Noquivzor just before raiding Kessel to free Black Sun prisoners. Seven weeks later, after the Rogues departed for their undercover mission to Coruscant, Zsinj arrived at the planet in his Super Star Destroyer *Iron Fist* and bombarded the base with wave after wave of TIE bombers. Most of Rogue Squadron's support staff were killed as the barracks collapsed in a heap of rubble, but the hangar was untouched. The base suffered major damage, but because most of the buildings were underground, the base was saved from complete destruction. [RS, WG, KT]

Norgor A top henchman of dark-side Krath cultist Satal Keto some 4,000 years before the Galactic Civil War. Norgor was sent to assassinate the Jedi Ulic Qel-Droma but ended up dead himself. [DLS]

normal space *See* realspace

Norulac This planet was home to a bandit gang that raided Taanab every year, until they were wiped out by Lando Calrissian in the famous Battle of Taanab. Calrissian singlehandedly accounted for nineteen kills of the Norulac band. [RJN, SWAJ]

Norval II Norval (sometimes Norvall) II is homeworld to General Horton Salm, commander of the New Republic's starfighter training center on Folor. Six years after the Battle of Endor, a detachment of fighters from Norval II joined the Republic to aid in its struggle against the reborn cloned Emperor. [DE, RS]

Norvanian grog An expensive and potent intoxicant from the planet Ban-Satir II, it is made on the island of N'van in the planet's northern hemisphere. [HSE]

Norys A teenage street tough, he was the leader of The Lost Ones, a Coruscant gang. His face was broad and dark, his eyes close-set, and his teeth crooked. Norys was taken by the Shadow Academy, but when he was found to have no Force sensitivity, he was trained as a stormtrooper. However, his trainer, the former TIE fighter pilot Qorl, was somewhat concerned by Norys's bullying ways.

In combat above Yavin 4, Norys was so ruthless in his attacks on the young Jedi Knights at the Jedi academy that Qorl shot down Norys's TIE fighter, killing him. [YJK]

Notak An Imperial stronghold for most of the Galactic Civil War, the planet fell eight months after the Battle of Endor despite the arrival of the *Victory*-class Star Destroyer *Harridan*, which was ordered to defend Notak after the *Harridan's* patrol of the N'zoth shipyards. [BTS]

Nothos, Commander Bane An Imperial district commander, he was charged with locating and destroying Admiral Ackbar's Shantipole Project, which was building the new B-wing starfighter. He failed, was demoted, and placed in command of a patrol fleet in the Outer Rim Territories. He was captured by the Alliance and taken aboard a Rebel ship. When a problem developed with the ship's hyperdrive, he was lost in the mysterious dimension called otherspace. He was killed in battle with Rebels also trapped in otherspace. [SFS, OS, OS2]

Nouane Nouane is a region of space that had been patrolled by the New Republic vessel *IX-26* until the ship was diverted to pick up a team of archaeological researchers from Obroaskai. The team was then brought to the dead planet Qella in hopes that it could learn clues about the mysterious Qella ship known as the Teljkon vagabond. [BTS]

Novacom Novacom, the largest HoloNet-service provider on Alderaan, was run by the father of Rogue Squadron member Tycho Celchu. Celchu's father was the company's chief executive when Alderaan was destroyed by the Death Star. [BW]

Nova Demons *See* swoop gangs

nova lily A brilliant yellow-orange flower, it grows on the moon Yavin 4. [DA]

Novar Minister of state and aide to King Ommin and Queen Amanoa of

Onderon 4,000 years before the Galactic Civil War, he was a minor dark-side wizard. [TOJ]

Nova Viper A sleek cruiser, it is owned by the bounty hunter Spurch "Warhog" Goa. [TMEC]

Null, Warb Leader of the dissident Naddists on Onderon 4,000 years before the Galactic Civil War, he combined martial prowess with his mastery of the dark side of the Force. Warb Null was eventually killed by Jedi Ulic Qel-Droma. [FNU]

Nunb, Aril The sister of Nien Nunb, one of the heroes of Endor, she is every bit as good a pilot as her brother. Formerly Rogue Squadron's Executive Officer (XO), she was replaced by Tycho Celchu as the Squadron's XO. After the loss of four badly needed pilots, she was made a Rogue to help fill the vacancies. During the Squadron's undercover operation on Coruscant, she was injured and left behind as the rest of her team made their escape. She was later discovered and abducted by Imperial General Derricote's team for use as a Sullustan test subject for his Krytos virus project. Although injected with the virus and left to almost certain death in the laboratory, she was chosen at random to receive the lifesaving bacta cure. After the Alliance conquest of Coruscant, she was found alive and well in Invisec. [RS, WG, KT]

Nunb, Nien A brilliant navigator and pilot, the Sullustan was one of the heroes of the Battle of Endor in his role as copilot of the *Millennium Falcon* with Lando Calrissian. At 1.6 meters, Nien Nunb is tall for a native of the dark volcanic planet of Sullust but has the same facial jowls, large ears, and black orbs for eyes that are characteristic of his people.

Flying an old stock light freighter, the *Sublight Queen*, for the planet's largest company, SoroSuub Corp., he met and became friends with Calrissian. When SoroSuub decided to throw its support to the Empire, Nunb turned on SoroSuub, pirating its shipments and sending them on to the Rebel Alliance. Later he joined the Rebellion full-time, and Calrissian picked him to copilot the *Millennium Falcon* in its run against the second Death Star. The *Falcon* and Wedge Antilles's X-wing fighter hit the target, resulting in the explosion of the battle station.

Since then, Nunb has flown missions with Han Solo and Chewbacca. He then went to work for Calrissian as manager of the spice mines of Kessel, using droids instead of slave labor. [RJ, SWCG]

Nien Nunb

Nunurra A city on the planet Roon, it is the site of the Roon Colonial Games. [DTV]

Nuum, Cabrool A longtime business associate of crime lord Jabba the Hutt on the planet Smarteel, he had turned a bit insane. When Cabrool Nuum ordered Jabba to kill someone he didn't know named Vu Chusker, the Hutt refused and was imprisoned. Later Jabba murdered Nuum with assistance from Nuum's own henchmen and Nuum's son. [JAB]

Nuum, Norba The daughter of Cabrool Nuum, she double-crossed Jabba and was eaten by him. [JAB]

Nuum, Rusk The son of Cabrool Nuum, he was killed for double-crossing Jabba. The Hutt snapped Rusk's head, jumped on him, and squashed him into a fine paste. [JAB]

Nyasko A planet in the Colunda sector, it was the location of an AT-AT battalion. The Imperial tech Deppo was kept busy fighting the high degree of Rebel activity in the sector. [DESB]

Nyiestra An Alderaanian woman who was to be Tycho Celchu's wife, she had known Tycho all of her life. They had fallen in love when they were teenagers. She had agreed to wait for him to graduate from the Imperial Academy and waited through his first year of duty as a TIE pilot. The Death Star destroyed their plans along with all of Alderaan. [BW]

Nylykerka, Ayddar A Tammarian, he was chief analyst of the Asset Tracking office of Fleet Intelligence. Ayddar Nylykerka was the first Rebel to acquire the data files from the damaged Imperial vessel *Gnisnal* and to realize the enormity of the data: It was the first copy of a complete Imperial Order of Battle that the New Republic had ever seen. After realizing the importance of the files, Nylykerka risked his life to deliver it to Admiral Ackbar personally. Among other things, the New Republic learned that there were more vessels assigned to the Imperial Black Sword Command than the New Republic had accounted for. Later, Nylykerka analyzed the images sent back from the recon X-wing fighters of the Yevetha forces mobilized at N'zoth. Nylykerka was able to identify some missing Imperial Star Destroyers that were taken by the Yevetha during the initial attack on the Imperial shipyards at N'zoth. [BTS, SOL]

Nynie A 9-A9 child-care droid about the height of an R2 astromech, she has a conical body that is wide at the base and tapers up to a neck that can extend itself to the length of two meters. Nynie's arms are spindly, ending in tripod pincers padded with small balls of rubber. While her body looks decidedly mechanical, Nynie's head has the little apple face of a human grandmother. She always smiles kindly and is capable of singing lullabies. Her model is relatively rare now, and Nynie is considered an heirloom from a bygone era. Nynie took care of Rogue Squadron pilot Plourr Ilo, in reality a princess and heir to the throne of Eiattu VI, when she was a child. The droid was also capable of piloting and acting as an R2 unit because of special circuitry added so that the princess could learn to fly an airspeeder at an early age. [XW]

Nyny The homeworld of a three-headed species. Thirteen years after the Battle of Endor, the senator from Nyny was killed in the bombing of Senate Hall on Coruscant. [NR]

Nyxy A New Republic Senator from the planet Rudrig. [NR]

N'zoth Homeworld of the Yevetha species, it is located in the system of the same name in the Koornacht Cluster and is the capital of the Yevethan federation known as the Duskhan League. N'zoth is a dry world orbiting a golden sun, and from space appears to be gray-green with yellow clouds. Pa'aal is the primary moon of the fifth planet of the N'zoth system. The 2,000 stars of the Koornacht Cluster burn so brightly in N'zoth's night sky that more distant stars are never visible, which contributed to the Yevethan view that their species was the only one in the universe.

Females of the species are called marasi and males are called nitakka. Young are born in separate "birth-casks" called mara-nas. Yevetha only consider killing to be murder if someone of lower status kills someone of higher status. High-status males have every right to kill their lessers for any reason, and such killings are commonplace and accepted. Yevetha are extremely adept with technology and learn new skills rapidly.

By the time the Empire arrived in the Cluster, the Yevetha had spread from N'zoth and colonized eleven nearby planets, even without hyperdrive technology. The arriving Imperials established an orbiting repair yard (code-named Black 15) at N'zoth and established a planetary garrison on the planet's surface. The Yevetha were forced to work as Imperial slaves and learned much about the Empire's technology by servicing its ships at the repair yard. Eight months after the Battle of Endor, faced with mounting losses in battles with the New Republic, the Empire planned to evacuate all forces from N'zoth and to destroy the Black 15 shipyard. Yevethan leader Nil Spaar and his commando team used the confusion of the moment to capture the Super Star Destroyer *Intimidator* and murder 20,000 Imperial citizens by firing the *Intimidator*'s turbolasers on the evacuation transports. He then claimed the yards and all nine of its capital ships in the name of the Yevetha Protectorate.

Nil Spaar took over as viceroy of the Duskhan League after the death of former viceroy Kiv Truun. The Black 15 yard was later moved away from N'zoth to a clandestine location. Surface yards on N'zoth became the prime source for spherical thrustships built by the Nazfar Metalworks Guild. Twelve years after the Battle of Endor, after the Yevetha captured all alien colony worlds lying inside the Cluster's borders in the Great Purge, Nil Spaar returned to N'zoth to a hero's welcome. His thrustship *Aramadia* landed at Hariz before three million onlookers and he proceeded in glory to the ruling city of Giat Nor, which holds more than a million of N'zoth's 700 million inhabitants.

At the top level of Spaar's palace was a private breedery with sixteen alcoves for birth-casks and a grated floor for blood sacrifices. During the final Battle of N'zoth, the Yevethan fleet was smashed when its captured Imperial ships were commandeered by Imperial slaves and taken out of the system. The remaining Yevethan thrustships were destroyed by the New Republic fleet. [BTS, SOL, TT]

Obah, Jyn A tall humanoid, he was first mate to pirate captain Kybo Ren in the early days of the Empire. Jyn Obah had long red hair, protruding lower teeth, and a ring in his nose. He wore the upper part of a stormtrooper's helmet on his head and a trooper's chest plate for protection and as a fashion statement. [DTV]

obah gas A chemical weapon, it can cause permanent nerve disability. Only Wookiees and Trandoshans are large enough to escape its effects. [TBH]

Obica This planet was the site of a rendezvous between Alliance leaders and Sullustan Commander Syub Snunb just prior to the Battle of Endor. Snunb then led the Rebel fleet to Sullust, where they prepared for the assault on the second Death Star. [DESB]

Obroa-skai Located in the system of the same name, Obroa-skai sits at a strategic location within the Borderland Regions. The planet has frozen deserts and oceans and tall, jagged mountains. Its renowned central library system is a collection of original documents in 10,000 different formats and an even greater number of different languages. The most complete general index covers only a small portion of the library's holdings. To ensure security, access to the Obroan libraries can be gotten only while on Obroa-skai or by hiring an authorized researcher.

During the rise of Grand Admiral Thrawn, the New Republic attempted to convince Obroa-skai to join its side. Thrawn's forces made a partial dump of the data in the Obroan library system, which allowed them to learn the location of Wayland—a planet the Emperor had ordered removed from all astrogation charts after building his treasure storehouse and vast experimental laboratories there. At some point, Luke Skywalker sent the droids R2-D2 and C-3PO to the galactic libraries of Obroa-skai to search their vast databanks for any information about his long-lost mother. Twelve years after the Battle of Endor, a team from the Obroan Institute for Archaeology was dispatched to the dead planet Qella to search for any clues about the mysterious ghost ship called the Teljkon vagabond. [HE, LC, BTS, SOL]

observation holocam Remote surveillance viewers with droid controllers to supplement security, these holocams can activate alarms and automated weapons when needed, bringing help to endangered locations. [CCG]

Ocheron Gifted at deception, she was a member of the Nightsisters clan of the Witches of Dathomir. [CPL]

Odan-Urr A telepathic and long-lived Jedi Master, he had presided over Jedi assemblies for six centuries by the time of the massive assembly at Mount Meru on Deneba some 4,000 years before the Galactic Civil War. He was known also as the Keeper of Antiquities, and as such was entrusted as gatekeeper of the Sith Holocron and other potentially dangerous devices. He was active during the Fall of the Sith Empire, as well as during the Sith War. As a warning, he showed Jedi Ulic-Qel Droma a Holocron image of a Jedi murdering his own master. Odan-Urr was killed by Exar Kun. [DLS, TSW]

Odik II The planetary site of a top-secret political detention ward, it was one of the places where Old Republic opponents of Palpatine's New Order were imprisoned. Major Calders, a security warden aboard the first Death Star, began his career as a security guard at the Odik II facility. [DSTC]

Odle, Hermi A large bipedal being who usually wore tattered robes, he was a frequent visitor to Jabba the Hutt's palace and served the crime lord faithfully. Hermi Odle is of the Baragwin species and is a weapons designer. He was hired by Jabba to devise a weapons and security system. [RJ, GG12]

Odos Located in the Odos systems in the Meridian sector, the planet is near the Chorios systems. Most ships wishing to make a hyperspace jump to Coruscant from the region depart from the far side of the Odos systems. Nine years after the Battle of Endor, Han Solo and Lando Calrissian were attacked by an Imperial fleet from the nearby Antemeridian sector while at Exodo II and lost their pursuers by flying through the gas-clouds of Odos and the fringes of the Spangled Veil Nebula. [POT]

Odosk, General An Imperial Army commander, he served with Admiral Daala's fleet. [DA]

Odumin *See* Spray of Tynna

Off Chance An old Blockade Runner, it was won by Lando Calrissian in a game of sabacc. He lent the ship to Luke Skywalker and Tenel Ka for their trip to Borgo Prime in search of the kidnappers of Jaina and Jacen Solo and Chewbacca's nephew Lowbacca. [YJK]

Offens A species whose queen is a 6,000-year-old woman, they were relatively new to space travel at the time of the New Republic. [NR]

Ogoth Tiir Site of a fierce battle that led to the crippling of Jona Grumby, a commodore in the Corporate Sector picket fleet. He then retired from the Imperial starfleet. [CSSB]

Hermi Odle

Ohann A gas giant in the Tatoo system, it is encircled by rings of ice. It is the second planet from the system's two suns, and it has three moons. [GG7]

Okeefe, Platt A well-known smuggler, she is also strikingly beautiful and intelligent. She's hard to miss with her silvery white hair and penchant for dressing in a white blouse and red pants, vest, and boots. Platt Okeefe grew up on Brentaal, but eventually ran away from home and signed on as a cabin steward aboard a Sullustan starliner. She joined a tramp freighter crew in the Anarid Cluster, and gained a lot of experience as a spacer. Okeefe currently operates her own freighter, the *Last Chance*. Easygoing, she often passes on advice to other, less-experienced traders. [SWAJ, PSG]

Okins, Admiral An Imperial officer, he served under Darth Vader when the Empire destroyed the Rebel base located in the Vergesso asteroid field in the Bajic sector. [SOTE]

Okko, Great The shaman chief of the Ysanna on the planet Ossus. [DE2]

Oko E A planet where the rivers are filled with sulfur ice, it was visited by the cyborg Lobot on a wild-water rafting vacation. There he learned the proper technique for pulling a raft mate out of the water. Twelve years after the Battle of Endor, he used the same technique to save Lando Calrissian's life aboard the ghost ship known as the Teljkon vagabond. [SOL]

Okor, Feldrall A pirate, his capture netted bounty hunter Boba Fett 150,000 credits. [TJP]

Olabrian trichoid A particularly vile parasite native to the Olabria system, it destroys a being by eating its internal organs. The egg pods of the Olabrian trichoid contain three eggs that are laid in ripening fruit. After the fruit is eaten, the larvae hatch in the host's stomach. While the host sleeps, the larvae migrate up the esophagus and then down into lung or bronchial tissue, where they attach and grow for a standard day or two in the favorable, moist environment. Once their mouth parts develop, the larvae chew through tissue toward the host's heart or a major artery, where they gorge on blood and then pupate. The adult emerges from the host's corpse already fertile and ready to lay ten to twelve egg pods. The life cycle takes approximately three standard weeks. The only known cure for trichoid infestation is administration of pure oxygen during the pulmonary phase. An Olabrian trichoid was used by Gover-

Platt Okeefe

nor Nereus of Bakura in an attempt to kill Luke Skywalker. [TAB]

Olan, Firith A male Twi'lek, he had thick head-tails (lekku in Twi'leki), purple eyes, and steely gray flesh. Firith Olan was a renegade who was brought to Tatooine by Bib Fortuna to help him take over from crime lord Jabba the Hutt. By the time Olan got to the planet, Jabba was dead and Fortuna's brain had been placed into a robotic spider droid by B'omarr monks. Olan and others then "liberated" Jabba's palace from the monks, chasing them back down into the catacombs from which they had come. Olan had a cruel streak and a facility for manipulation. He also enjoyed torturing Fortuna by reminding him that his essence was trapped inside a fragile globe. But Fortuna had the last laugh when he stole Olan's body and exchanged their brains. [XW, TJP]

Old Republic A mostly democratic galactic government that lasted nearly 25,000 standard years, it spread justice and freedom from star system to star system. Elected senators and administrators from the thousands of member worlds participated in the Republic's governing process; the Jedi Knights were its protectors and defenders. Arts and science blossomed, and for billions of sentient creatures, the time of the Old Republic was truly a golden age.

But starting nearly a standard century before the Galactic Civil War began, corruption, greed, and internal strife destroyed the Republic from within. Special interest groups and power-hungry individuals accomplished what no outside threat ever could: They weakened the government and gave rise to apathy, social injustice, ineffectiveness, and chaos. To try to reverse the destructive trend—or at least to give the impression that something was being done—a compromise candidate, Senator Palpatine, was elected leader of the Senate. Despite his many reassuring promises, Palpatine soon declared himself Emperor. He abolished the Old Republic and began a reign of terror and great social injustice based upon his dark vision of a New Order. His crowning achievement was the Galactic Empire. [SW, SWN, SWSB]

Ommni Box

Ologat, Mychael A small but muscular stormtrooper trainee, he was in the same unit as Davin Felth. [TMEC]

Omar Located in the system of the same name, the planet was the site of three Sienar Fleet Systems starfighter production facilities. The advanced manufacturing plants, which produced the new TIE advanced fighter, were destroyed by the traitorous Admiral Zaarin following the Battle of Hoth. Zaarin hoped to maintain his technological superiority by weakening the Empire's source of advanced war materiel. [TSC]

Omega signal A code used by the Rebel Alliance Battle Staff, it is an order for complete disengagement from combat and a retreat. At the Battle of Hoth it was "K-one-zero; all troops disengage." [ESBR]

Omman A culturally diverse world with a busy starport and a strong Imperial presence, it was where smugglers Drake Paulsen and Karl Ancher were imprisoned in a Bureau of Customs jail. They escaped from Omman with the help of another smuggler, Tait Ransom. [SWAJ]

Ommin King of the planet Onderon, husband of Queen Amanoa, and father of Queen Galia, he ruled more than 4,000 years before the Galactic Civil War. A direct descendant of the Dark Jedi Freedon Nadd, he was confined to a secret nursing facility and lived on life-support equipment for years. But he initiated Aleema and Satal Keto in ancient dark-side Sith magic and was still able to call upon the spirit of Nadd to practice such dark magic himself. He was killed during the Freedon Nadd Uprising. [TOJ, FNU, DLS]

Ommni Box A complex musical-enhancement instrument, it clips peaks, attenuates lows, and reverbs the total sound of a band. [TMEC]

Omogg A Drackmarian warlord, she was known for her incredible wealth. Four years after the Battle of Endor, Han Solo won the deed to the planet Dathomir from Omogg in a high-stakes sabacc game. The warlord claimed the planet had been owned by her family for generations. [CPL]

Omwat An orange-and-green world of savannas and mountains in the Outer Rim Territories, it is the homeworld of the Maw Installation scientist and weapons designer Qwi Xux. While Moff Tarkin commanded a *Victory*-class Star Destroyer there, he determined that Omwati children could be capable of astonishing mental feats. He built an orbital education sphere to instruct the world's brightest prospects, threatening to destroy their honeycomb settlements on Omwat's surface if they failed. Educator Nasdra Magrody developed an accelerated learning process, and one of the instructors was Ohran Keldor, a designer of both the Death Star and the *Eye of Palpatine* battlemoon. Qwi Xux was the only candidate to survive the intense pressures of the force-fed education. [JS, COJ]

Onderon Situated in the three-planet system of the same name, it circles a yellow sun and has four moons with widely varying orbits. Onderon's closest moon, Dxun, is home to numerous bloodthirsty creatures who are able to migrate to the surface of Onderon annually, when the two worlds' atmospheres intersect. The human inhabitants of Onderon gradually evolved defenses against the beasts, culminating in the enormous walled city of Iziz. Native life on the planet includes the deadly dragon-bird.

Some 4,400 years before the Galactic Civil War, the Dark Jedi Freedon Nadd brought the power of Sith dark-side magic to Onderon, and those who opposed it were cast out into the wilderness where they tamed the beasts of Dxun. Hundreds of these beast riders created their own kingdoms in the wild, and fought continually to take over Iziz. Nearly four centuries later, Onderon was first contacted by the Old Republic, and a delegation of Jedi, including

Oola

Ulic Qel-Droma, was sent to make peace between the beast riders and Queen Amanoa of Iziz two years after that. Following the death of Queen Amanoa, her daughter, Galia, took the throne with Oron Kira, her lover and the leader of a beast-rider kingdom.

A subsequent uprising by the followers of Freedon Nadd was put down by another Jedi force. At the same time, Satal Keto and his cousin Aleema, members of Tetan royalty, traveled to Onderon to learn the secrets of Sith magic, which led to their formation of the Krath and the political takeover of the Tetan system. Following the Naddist uprising, a permanent Jedi outpost was built on Onderon from the remains of Nadd's ancient starship. Later, as the Sith War was winding down, Dark Jedi Exar Kun ordered the warrior clans of Mandalore to capture Onderon and the city of Iziz. Defeated in a furious battle by Oron Kira and Captain Vanicus of the Republic Navy, Mandalore and his surviving men fled to the Dxun moon.

Millennia later, six years after the Battle of Endor, the *Millennium Falcon* landed on Onderon to repair damage suffered in a battle with the reborn clone Emperor's flagship, the *Eclipse II*. Fearing for her newborn son Anakin, Princess Leia Organa Solo hid in warrior leader Modon Kira's safehouse deep in the Onderon wilderness. Palpatine, posing as a pilgrim on his way to the Shatoon monastery, discovered the child and tried to possess his body but was stopped by the Jedi Empatojayos Brand. Later, the leaders of the New Republic gathered in the fortress of Modon Kira and reestablished their galactic government, led by Mon Mothma with Leia Organa Solo as her second in command. [TOJ, FNU, DLS, EE, TSW]

Onderon, Beast Wars of A centuries-long conflict between the citizens of the walled city of Iziz and its outcasts, the beast riders of Onderon. The wars eventually required the intervention of the Jedi Knights to resolve the conflict. [TOJ]

Onoma, Captain A Calamarian officer, he served aboard the star cruiser *Mon Remonda* while Han Solo was pursuing Warlord Zsinj. [CPL]

Oodoc A species known for its size and strength but not its intelligence, Oodocs possess spiked arms and massive torsos. [NR]

Ookbat This planet was the site of a failed mission by the bounty hunters Tinian I'att and Chenlambec the Wookiee. They saved each other's lives in the planet's clammy warrens. [TBH]

Oola A beautiful Twi'lek entertainer, the green-skinned female danced her last dance for crime lord Jabba the Hutt. Oola grew up on the harsh planet of Ryloth; she had the now-familiar twin head tentacles that the Twi'lek call "lekku," but which most others call head-tails, or worms. The red-eyed dancer was kidnapped by Jabba's majordomo, the Twi'lek Bib Fortuna, and trained in seductive dancing. She was presented to Jabba, who was taken with her, but she was repulsed and resisted his advances. She did do one seductive dance for the Hutt, but when he wanted more and she refused, he sent her plunging into a pit where a hungry rancor awaited. [RJ, SWCG]

Oolas, Captain Commander of the *Steadfast*, the Republic ship that surveyed the ruins of the Imperial Star Destroyer *Gnisnal* and recovered its intact memory core. [BTS]

Oolidi Homeworld of Tolik Yar, a member of the New Republic Senate and a staunch defender of Chief of State Leia Organa Solo. [SOL]

Oolos, Ism A Ho'Din physician, he is stationed at the port of Bagsho on Nim Drovis. [POT]

orbital gun platform A spaceship, station, or satellite that can launch an attack on the planet it orbits. [SWR]

orbit dock Orbital landing and maintenance facilities, they also provide other services to spacers and their ships. Some of the largest docks are almost small space stations in themselves, providing hotel, food, and entertainment facilities. [HE, HESB]

Orbiting Shipyard Alpha A spaceship repair dock high above the planet Duro. [MMY]

Orbus, Evar The Letaki leader of Evar Orbus and his Galactic Jizz-wailers band, he was killed shortly after arriving on Tatooine by a stray blaster shot, leaving his bandmates—Max Rebo, Sy Snootles, and Snit (later known as Droopy McCool)—to fend for themselves. [TJP]

Ord Mantell Located in the outworlds, the planet is circled by numerous moons. Points of interest include its canyon-rimmed spaceport and Ten Mile Plateau, located in the rocky backcountry. Supposedly free from Imperial interests, Ord Mantell was hosting an Imperial fleet on maneuvers when Han Solo arrived there to repair the *Millennium Falcon* following the Battle of Yavin. Solo encountered his smuggler friend Drub McKumb, who warned the newly minted Rebel Alliance hero of the sizable bounty on his head. The bounty hunter Skorr captured Luke Skywalker and Princess Leia Organa and held them captive in an abandoned stellar energy plant on Ten Mile Plateau as bait to trap Solo, but Skorr's plans were foiled when Solo and Chewbacca staged a daring rescue. Later, Solo, Skywalker, and Chewbacca were captured by several bounty hunters (including Skorr, Dengar, and Bossk) working with Boba Fett, who imprisoned the trio in an abandoned moisture plant in Ord Mantell's backcountry. Again, Solo and his companions managed to outwit the bounty hunters and flee. About six years later, Grand Admiral Thrawn staged an assault on Ord Mantell to create fear in the surrounding systems and ease New Republic pressure on his shipyard supply lines. [ESB, TLC, MTS, COJ, CSW]

Ord Mirit Located at the edge of the Galactic core in the Mirit system, the planet once was home to an Imperial base. After the Battle of Endor, the crumbling Empire abandoned the Ord Mirit garrison and moved its personnel to defend the more valuable world of Corellia. Some three years after the Battle of Endor, the Alliance wanted to capture Borleias in the nearby Pyria system. It began its attack with a raid on the Venjagga system, which caused the Imperial Star Destroyer-II *Eviscerator* to pursue decoy Alliance ships into the neighboring Mirit system, believing that Ord Mirit was the Rebels' true target. Bothan slicers had previously made Ord Mirit appear a likely target by planting information that the world held the key to finding the lost *Katana* Dreadnaught fleet. [RS]

Ord Pardron Site of a major New Republic base that defends planets in the Abrion and Dufilvian sectors, the planet in the star system of the same name was the target of a multipronged attack by Grand Admiral Thrawn. By attacking numerous targets Thrawn forced Ord Pardron defenders to parcel out ships, requiring most to stay at Ord Pardron to fight the *Death's Head*, leaving the planet Ukio undefended. Ukio—Thrawn's true target—was captured and the Ord Pardron base was severely damaged. [LC, AC]

Ord Trasi Site of a major group of Imperial shipyards, along with the facilities at Yaga Minor and Bilbringi. All three shipyards were extremely busy during Grand Admiral Thrawn's offensive against the New Republic. Information supplied to the New Republic from a bounty hunter on Ord Trasi stated that three Imperial Star Destroyers were within a month of completion at the shipyards. [LC]

Orellon II Located in the Bastooine system, it is a world of jungles, plains

Ord Mantell

and volcanic mountains separated by oceans and orbited by the large barren moon called Orellon I. Orellon II is the homeworld of the primitive Kentra, a species of winged, fur-covered flying creatures. The world's five million Kentra are divided into four types: the jungle, spotted, striped, and brown Kentra. They live in seven major cities, including the capital city of Kariish and Ironwall. Plant life includes the buntra tree. Some deadly predators include hornbeaks, voontragi, avian criers, and lizardlike gliders. Years ago, Jedi geologist Michael Tandre crashed his ship *Alpha Kentrum* on Orellon II. He became the spiritual leader of the Kentra, teaching them to follow the disciplines of the Sword, Plow, and Spirit, and leaving computer programs to guide them after his death. The Kentra built the Temple of the Je'ulajists (a corrupted form of geologists) in the jungle around the *Alpha Kentrum* and worshipped the memory of the Prophet Tandre. [SWAJ]

Orelon A large, bright star located in the sixty-three-star Hapes Cluster. [CPL]

Organa, Bail The foster father of Princess Leia Organa, he was a strong defender of the Old Republic in its dying days and became one of the founders of the Rebel Alliance after Senator Palpatine declared himself Emperor. Bail Organa was a decorated war hero, having fought in the Clone Wars at the side of Obi-Wan Kenobi and others. In addition to being the elected representative to the galactic Senate, Organa was Viceroy and First Chairman of the Alderaan system.

Along with Mon Mothma, the Corellian Garm Bel Iblis, and a few others, he fought Palpatine's grand design for a New Order. After Emperor Palpatine declared the Old Republic dead, Organa joined the bravest dissidents in their underground resistance. As Mon Mothma organized independent resistance cells, Bail Organa helped her secretly divert funds to the groups. Mothma's ties to the growing Rebellion were discovered by Imperial secret police, and she barely escaped Coruscant after a tip from Organa.

Still undetected as a major Rebel sympathizer, Bail Organa returned to Alderaan. Palpatine disbanded the Senate after Mon Mothma issued a strongly worded Declaration of Rebellion. Peaceful Alderaan became a beehive of secret activity in support of the new Rebel Alliance and Bail Organa became Mothma's main adviser. He didn't remain in that position long, for the Empire destroyed Alderaan and its billions of inhabitants with a single blast from its new super weapon, the Death Star. [SW, SWR, SWCG]

Organa, Princess Leia *See* Solo, Princess Leia Organa

Orin A volcanic world, it occupies the second position in the Bespin system. The planet has an elliptical orbit, passing through the asteroids of nearby Velser's Ring twice during its year. Its black surface is rocked by frequent groundquakes and covered with rivers of lava and erupting volcanoes. Orin's surface temperature is unbearably high and its atmosphere is choked with thick soot. [GG2]

Orinackra This planet was the site of a high-security Imperial detention center. Following the Battle of Yavin, Alliance agent Kyle Katarn infiltrated the Orinackra prison and rescued the captured Alliance spy Crix Madine. [DF]

Orion IV Site of a Rebel Alliance base that was destroyed by the Empire prior to the Battle of Yavin, the planet was bombarded from space by several Star Destroyers and attacked on the surface by AT-AT walkers and assault gunboats. [FP]

Orko SkyMine The SkyMine was a sham corporation set up by crime lord Durga the Hutt to hide huge amounts of money he sunk into his secret project. To the public, Durga's project was a commercial venture to exploit the untapped mineral riches of the Hoth Asteroid Belt. Although some funds were used in an unsuccessful mining effort, the bulk of the credits were funneled to the top-secret Darksaber project: the building of a slimmed-down version of the Death Star, stripped of almost all weapons but its central planet-blasting laser. [DS]

Orlok, Commander An Imperial officer, he was in charge of the Imperial Training Center on Daluuj. [CSW]

Orn, Kalebb A worker on the droid production world of Mechis III for seventeen years, he was the first human to be killed by IG-88 and his counterparts when the assassin droids took over the planet. [TBH]

Orooturoo Homeworld of Princess Nampi, a huge, purple, wormlike slug who attempted to steal Jabba the Hutt's cargo. [JAB]

Ororo Transportation A competitor to crime kingpin Prince Xizor's Xizor Transport Systems, Ororo tried to take over XTS's spice operations in the Bajic sector. Furious, Xizor sent his aide, Guri, to take care of the situation. Meanwhile, he told Emperor Palpatine that he had learned of a secret Rebel base with hundreds of ships and a shipyard full of vessels undergoing repair. The Emperor sent Darth Vader to destroy the Rebel base—actually an Ororo shipyard—while Guri murdered Ororo's top officials. [SOTE]

Orrimaarko The real name of the Dresselian nicknamed Prune Face, he was a noted resistance fighter during the war to overthrow the Empire. Orrimaarko was the first of his species to be given command of a Spec-Force team by the Rebel Alliance. The wrinkly skinned humanoid wears an eyepatch and a camouflage cloak. [GG12]

Orron III A fertile agricultural planet at a strategic location in the Corporate sector, the green-and-blue world has almost no axial tilt, resulting in a year-round growing season. The Corporate Sector Authority tends the endless fields of Orron III with robot agricultural machines and has constructed a city-sized Authority Data Center on the planet. The only space traffic allowed on the world are Authority ships and massive agricultural drone barges. The region is defended by the *Shannador's Revenge*, a two-kilometer-long *Invincible*-class Dreadnaught. Han Solo and others tried to infiltrate the Authority Data Center to learn the location of several missing persons. Prior to the Battle of Yavin, an Imperial convoy bound for the Death Star construction site stopped at a commsat near Orron III and was destroyed by Alliance starfighters. The Imperials also had a base in the system. [HSE, FP]

Orto A small, cold planet, it circles its red dwarf sun in an elliptical orbit. Orto is home to Ortolans, squat, heavy, blue-furred bipeds with long trunks, floppy ears, and dark, beady eyes. Orto has a thin atmosphere and a short growing season, with arable lands concentrated near the equator. Geologists have discovered an enormous crater beneath the northern polar ice cap, leading to a theory that Orto was once struck by a planetary body, resulting in a somewhat inhospitable climate and the extinction of many life-forms. The music- and food-loving Ortolans do not have a highly industrialized society, although they have been quite efficient in food production. Orto was subjugated in the early days of the Empire, and the Ortolans have been forced to mine heavy metals and radioactive fuels for Imperial processing centers. Max Rebo, the food-loving jizz-wailer whose band played in Jabba the Hutt's palace, is an Ortolan. [GG4, RJ]

Orrimaarko

Ortola Captain of a New Republic corvette that was used in the assault on Maw Installation. [COF]

Ortugg A Gamorrean, he was the leader of crime lord Jabba the Hutt's nine Gamorrean guards. [TJP]

Orus sector An area that includes the planets Chazwa, Poderis, and Joiol. Grand Admiral Thrawn gave the false impression that his clone traffic was running through the Orus sector, which led smuggler and Rebel operator Talon Karrde to visit Chazwa in an attempt to find the traffic's origin point. [LC]

Orvak, Commander Leader of the TIE fighter attack on the Jedi academy, his craft was equipped with a stealth hull and dampened ion engines. Commander Orvak's mission was to destroy the Jedi academy's shield generator and then destroy the ancient Massassi Great Temple—once the Rebel Alliance base of operations and now the site of the academy. While setting the timed explosives inside the temple, he was bitten by a crystal snake and fell unconscious. He was killed in the subsequent explosion. [YJK]

Oseon 2795 An asteroid in the Oseon system, it is closer to the sun than most, and consequently is uncomfortably hot in spite of its air-conditioning and life-support systems. Oseon 2795 is primarily a mining colony, unlike most of the pleasure-resort asteroids in the rest of the system. [LCM]

Oseon 5792 Located in the Fifth Belt of Oseon asteroids, it was the private estate of Bohhuah Mutdah, an immensely fat retired industrialist who was the wealthiest individual in the Oseon system. The asteroid was disk-shaped: fifteen kilometers in diameter but less than three kilometers thick. One side of the disk was covered with lakes, trees, gardens, and a palace, all kept under transparent domes with artificial gravity. The other side housed a well-defended spaceport. The asteroid was destroyed by Renatasian raiders during Lando Calrissian's smuggling mission in the Oseon system. [LCF]

Oseon 6845 Like most asteroids in the Oseon system, it caters to wealthy and powerful Oseoni. It is the largest asteroid in the system—700 kilometers in diameter—and has a surface honeycombed with nightclubs and resorts, including the Hotel Drofo. The Esplanade, a tree-lined walkway with a three-meter-deep gravity field, is located at the center of a small city on the asteroid's equator. The stores fronting the Esplanade are said to be among the most expensive properties in the galaxy. A spaceport is located at the northern pole of 6845, and the asteroid has been artificially accelerated to give it a twenty-five-hour rotational cycle. [LCF]

Oseon system Adjacent to the Rafa system and composed of nothing but thousands of asteroids, it is famous for its wealthy inhabitants and booming tourist trade. Seven wide bands of asteroids orbit the Oseon system's sun, and many of them have been turned into luxury resorts or private estates. Tourists throng to see the famous Flamewind of Oseon, a yearly phenomenon caused by an increase in stellar flares. The flares interact with asteroid vapor, creating brilliant bands of ionized gas thousands of kilometers long that fill the system with fluorescing colors. The Flamewind lasts an average of three weeks, and the strong radiation prevents all communications and in-system space traffic with the exception of message torpedoes. [LCF]

OSETS An acronym for Orbital Solar Energy Transfer Satellite, an orbital energy system used on Coruscant for gathering sunlight, concentrating it, and delivering it to warm the colder regions of the planet. It is also frequently used to melt the polar caps to provide water for the planet's billions of inhabitants. [WG]

Oslumpex V This planet was the site of the headquarters of Vinda and D'rag Starshipwrights and Aerospace Engineers, Inc. Han Solo's ship was placed on the Red List because he owed 2,500 credits to the company. [HSR]

Ossel II A high-gravity world of steaming bogs and swamps, it is the homeworld of the dim-witted species known as the Ossan. Their extremely primitive society has developed spears and clubs to defend themselves against the cucul, a predator that resembles a floating log. Most intergalactic visitors to Ossel II come to purchase syp wood, which the Ossan exchange for a tour of duty on the trade ships. Some Ossan are used as agricultural slaves on Karfeddion for the benefit of the House Vandron. [GG4, COJ]

Ossilege, Admiral Hortel An admiral of the Bakuran Navy, he was a short man of slight build, well-scrubbed and pink-skinned. Adm. Hortel Ossilege was bald but sported a pair of bushy eyebrows and a sharply pointed goatee. He constantly demonstrated his first-class mind and zero tolerance for nonsense. He was the leader of the Bakuran fleet of four ships that was loaned to the Alliance, and he was killed in the conflict surrounding Centerpoint Station. [AC, SAC]

Ossus Located in the Adega system in the Auril sector, it orbits the twin Adegan suns in a figure-eight trajectory. Ossus was an important Jedi stronghold and learning center in ancient times, and some speculate that the Order of Jedi Knights began on the planet. Ossus was once covered with many cities and ground defenses, and the Knossa spaceport was located near a range of rocky mountains. Points of interest once included the Great Jedi Library and the peaceful Gardens of Talla. The steep canyon walls are still covered with elaborate murals, and some ancient buildings that still stand include the library and a Jedi meditation chamber.

During the Great Sith War, the fallen Jedi Exar Kun visited Ossus to recruit twenty Jedi Knights into the Sith cause. Before he departed, Kun killed Master Odan-Urr and stole a Sith Holocron from the Jedi Library. Later, an Ossan Jedi fleet was dispatched to the nearby Cron Cluster to defend the besieged station Kemplex Nine. The fleet was destroyed when the Cluster went nova, and the resulting shockwave threatened to devastate Ossus. An evacuation of the planet was ordered, and as many ancient relics as possible were loaded onto transports. At the same time, Kun and Jedi Ulic Qel-Droma appeared with their armies to loot the world of its valuables before the shockwave arrived. Kun battled the Neti Jedi Master Ood Bnar, who turned into an unyielding tree to protect a trove of the earliest known lightsabers. Meanwhile, Ulic confronted and killed his brother, Cay, and was seized with horror and regret over what he had done.

Most Jedi left the planet just ahead of the shockwave, which scorched the surface of Ossus, nearly wiping it clean. Some Jedi survived, however, after hiding their families in Ossus's great caverns, and their descendants grew into the Ysanna, a tribe of warrior-shamans who use the Force to guide their primitive weapons. A 10,000-year-old lightsaber surfaced in an archaeological dig on Ossus, and was given to Leia Organa Solo by Vima-Da-Boda. Six years after the Battle of Endor, Luke Skywalker visited an arid, sandy portion of the planet and discovered the Ysanna tribe. Skywalker and Kam Solusar also fought the forces of dark-side Executor Sedriss and discovered the vault of lightsabers long hidden beneath the roots of Master Ood. At the time of Skywalker's departure, the New Republic made plans to send excavation teams to explore Ossus's ruins.

Soon after, several of the Emperor's warriors came to Ossus and captured three Ysanna leaders, whose bodies were to be used as raw material to create new clones for Palpatine. Skywalker and his Jedi trainees followed the dark-side kidnappers and defeated them on Vjun but were unable to free the captured Ysanna from their carbonite imprisonment. While on an undercover mission to Borgo Prime thirteen years later, Skywalker and Tenel Ka claimed that they needed corusca gems to open a sealed treasure vault located on Ossus. [DE, FNU, DLS, DE2, YJK, EE, TSW]

Oswaft A species of intelligent manta ray or jellyfishlike beings, they inhabit the vacuum of space called ThonBoka, a sack-shaped interstellar nebula composed of gas and dust. Oswaft have powerful wings and a sleek, muscle-covered dorsal surface. Tentaclelike ribbons hang from their ventral sides, and their entire bodies have a glasslike transparency with flashes of inner color. They measure 500 to several thousand meters long. The long-lived species exhibits patience, along with a conservative outlook on life. Lando Calrissian helped save the Oswaft from the threat of genocide. [LCS]

otherspace A region beyond realspace and hyperspace, it is full of dead planets. The void appears as a dark gray expanse of nothingness along with small swirls of colored gases and stars that look like shining dark holes. Only a few biologically engineered ships with Charon crews float in the void, seeking possible vestiges of life to use as sacrifices in their death cult. [OS]

Otranto This planet was the onetime headquarters of the Church of the First Frequency, which was ordered closed by Imperial Grand Inquisitor Torbin. Several surviving Otranto church members subsequently attempted to assassinate him aboard a luxury liner. He was saved by the Tynnan Odumin but was murdered the following month on Weerden. [CSSB]

Ottega system Located in the Lesser Plooriod Cluster, the cluttered system contains seventy-five planets. Its fourth planet is Ithor, so it is sometimes referred to as the Ithor system. The system also contains the planet Ottega, where the smuggler Toob Ancher was permanently disfigured when a bounty hunter's faulty thermal detonator exploded in his face. The smuggler Mako Spince was crippled by NaQoit bandits while making a run to the Ottega system. After the Battle of Hoth, the remnants of the traitorous Admiral Harkov's fleet were discovered in the Ottega system by loyal Imperial forces. The late Harkov's former flagship, the *Victory*-class Star Destroyer *Protector*, was trapped in realspace by the Interdictor cruiser *Harpax*. Darth Vader planned for Admiral Zaarin's ships to arrive and finish off the *Protector*, but Zaarin pulled a double-cross. He attacked Vader's forces and then flew to Coruscant, where he planned to kidnap the Emperor and complete his coup d'etat. Six years after the Battle of Endor, the New Republic troopship *Pelagia* was rendezvousing with an X-wing group based in the Ottega system when it, and its 100,000 ground troops, were wiped out by the cloned Emperor's Galaxy Gun. [DE, SWSB, EE, SWAJ, TSC]

Ottethan system The system where Neema, daughter of the Jedi Vima-Da-Boda, was executed for attempting to use the dark side of the Force against her warlord husband. Neema was fed to the rancors that run wild in Ottethan forests. [DE]

Ourn, Belezaboth Consul of the Paqwepori delegation on Coruscant, he was also a spy for Yevethan leader Nil Spaar. Belezaboth Ourn leaked information about the mobilization of the New Republic's Fifth Fleet and its move toward the Farlax sector, which allowed Spaar and the Yevethan fleet to prepare for their arrival. He later confessed his betrayal to Chief of State Leia Organa Solo by revealing the workings of a black box that allowed him to communicate with Spaar. [BTS, SOL, TT]

Outbound Flight Project An expensive and daring project funded by the Old Republic Senate due to the persistent lobbying of Jedi Master Jorus C'baoth, its aim was to search for and contact intelligent life outside the known galaxy. The Outbound Flight Project was launched from Yaga Minor, but the ship, its crew, and the six Jedi Masters aboard—including C'baoth—mysteriously disappeared. Dark suspicions were bandied about regarding possible foul play involving Senator Palpatine, and they were later revealed to be true. [HE, DFR, LC]

Outer Rim Territories A group of star systems that lie on the farthest edge of Imperial space, they include the desert world of Tatooine. The Outer Rim Territories have long been considered the galactic frontier. The Rim systems and planets—the worlds from which the Emperor took most of his slaves and resources—are still recovering from the exploitation and pillaging of the Empire. Their distance from the Core worlds made it unlikely that atrocities there would be discovered. As a result, the territories were filled with supporters of the Rebellion. [HESB, SWRPG2]

outlaw tech A member of a band of well-equipped and highly trained technicians who operate in and around Corporate sector space, they make a living illegally modifying and repairing space vessels. Clients of outlaw techs have included criminal organizations, fugitives, the Rebellion, and those opposed to the Authority. Techs keep their bases hidden and often move quickly to stay ahead of Corporate Authority and Imperial agents. [HSE]

Outlier Small star systems in the Corellian sector far away from central Corellia, they are so paranoid and secretive that they make unfriendly Corellia seem hospitable. [AC]

Outpost Beta An isolated sentry station, it served as an advance lookout for the Rebel Alliance base on Hoth. Its soldiers were the first to spot Imperial invaders, watching as drop ships landed beyond the defensive shields of Echo Base. Their warnings of an attack by Imperial AT-ATs provided the base with some extra time before the devastating Battle of Hoth began. [ESBR]

Outrider The ship of the cocky Corellian smuggler Dash Rendar, it is a modified Corellian YT-2400 freighter that has been converted for smuggling duty. The *Outrider* shines with a dark gleam and features the traditional saucer-shaped hull of the YT series, which includes the *Millennium Falcon*. Like its predecessors, it is fast and tough and cries out for creative modifications.

The *Outrider* has a rounded hull with thick armor plating and a pair of port-side bracing arms that connect to the cockpit, which is essentially a long tube. The aft section of the tube holds the main escape pod, which seats six. Much of the hull in-

Outrider

Admiral Ozzel

terior is filled with modified military-grade ion engines, power generators, weapons systems, and all the other illegal enhancements a smuggling ship needs. Weapons include a pair of heavy double laser cannons and two forward-firing concussion missile launchers. [SOTE, SWVG]

owriss A large but harmless blob of a creature, it lives on the forest moon of Endor. [ETV]

Oxbel A Devaronian—one of only three—who lived on Tatooine. He and Kardue'sai'Malloc once attempted an unsuccessful scam in which they pretended to be brothers. [TMEC, GG7]

Ozzel, Admiral An Imperial officer, he commanded Darth Vader's task force during the events leading up to the Battle of Hoth. The so-called Imperial Death Squadron consisted of Vader's flagship, *Executor,* and five Imperial Star Destroyers. Admiral Ozzel was contemptuous of the Rebel Alliance and didn't see it as a credible threat. His contempt led to sloppiness: He brought the task force out of hyperspace too close to Hoth's sensor range, thus alerting the Rebels. Vader quickly eliminated the admiral for "being as clumsy as he is stupid." [ESB]

Pa'aal The primary moon of the fifth planet of the N'zoth system in the Koornacht Cluster, it was home to a Yevethan prisoner-of-war and slave-labor camp. It was the former site of the headquarters of the Imperial Black Sword Command. [SOL, TT]

Pacci A pilot for the New Republic Fifth Fleet, he was killed during a failed attempt to blockade the Yevetha at Doornik-319. [SOL]

Page, Lieutenant A top New Republic officer and undercover operative, Page had an upbringing that seemed to prepare him for a far different destiny. The pampered son of a corrupt Imperial Senator from Corulag, Lieutenant Page nonetheless idolized the ancient Jedi Knights. Forced into the Imperial Academy, he was assigned on graduation to General Veers's ground-assault command. While on leave, he heard Senator Leia Organa speak about galactic rights, which inspired him to defect and join the Rebel Alliance. He was part of the commando units of General Madine and Major Derlin. Offered command of his own squad, he opted to retain the rank of lieutenant as a sign of humility. Since the Battle of Endor, this nondescript man of average build and height has led a special-missions team that takes on assignments few others could handle. [HE, HESB]

Page's Commandos Officially known as the Katarn Commandos, after a predator from the planet Kashyyyk, this special-missions team includes twelve of the New Republic's best-trained soldiers under the leadership of Lieutenant Page. A bit of a rogue operation, it operates independently for weeks or months at a time and can handle nearly any type of delicate mission in any environment. Each member is a jack-of-all-trades as well as a specialist in a single field, such as scouting or urban combat. The crack assault squad handled most of the frontline duties in the New Republic's offensive against the Maw Installation. [HE, HESB, COF]

Paig One of the planets that the Fallanassi, religious followers of the White Current, sent five children to for safekeeping after the religious sect was persecuted on Lucazec. [BTS]

pain simulator A device that makes droids feel pain, it emits high-frequency carrier waves so that other droids can experience pain, too. The device was often used by the droid EV-9D9 for torture sessions. [TJP]

Pakka A young Trianii, he helped Han Solo infiltrate the Corporate Sector Authority's prison facility at Stars' End. Pakka, son of Atuarre and Keeheen, had been struck mute after his father was taken prisoner by Authority agents. [HSE]

Pakkpekatt, Colonel A Hortek rumored to be semitelepathic, he is a veteran Intelligence officer who headed a New Republic chase team charged with penetrating the mystery surrounding the ghost ship known as the Teljkon vagabond. Colonel Pakkpekatt is tough, experienced, cautious, and plays by the rules. When Lando Calrissian, a risk-taking gambler, was also assigned to the mission, Pakkpekatt was less than overjoyed. When the vagabond took off with Calrissian, his long-time aide Lobot, and the droids C-3PO and R2-D2 on board, the colonel was blamed by New Republic Intelligence (NRI) for letting Lobot and the droids board the ship at all. He was then abandoned by NRI, which took away all but four of his ships. When he was given the order to terminate the mission, although Calrissian and his companions were aboard the vagabond, the colonel exploded with rage, saying that "a Hortek does not leave the bodies of comrades in the hands of the enemy—ever." He convinced General Rieekan, head of NRI, to let him pursue the vagabond on his own. Colonel Pakkpekatt then assumed command of Calrissian's ship, the *Lady Luck*, and, with Lieutenant Harona and agents Plack and Taisden aboard, went in search of the vagabond. They ended up at Maltha Obex, where Calrissian, Lobot, and the droids were successfully rescued from the vagabond. [SOL, BTS, TT]

Pakuuni system A hotbed of piracy and smuggling in the Outer Rim, the system contains the planet Pakuuni. Following the Battle of Hoth, Vice Admiral Thrawn was sent there to eliminate the pirates and make the area safe for shipping by establishing the Imperial space station NL-1. The Pakuuni pirates joined with Rebel Alliance forces to drive out the Empire, but they were defeated. [TSC]

Palanhi Located in the system of the same name, the planet is a crossroads with a reputation for exaggerating its own importance. Palanhi remained neutral during the Galactic Civil War, attempting to profit from both sides. Grand Admiral Thrawn had funds transferred into Admiral Ackbar's account through the central bank on Palanhi in an effort to discredit the admiral and create a false trail to trap investigators. [DFR]

Palle, Lieutenant Eri The first attaché, or personal aide, to Yevethan strongman Nil Spaar. [BTS, TT]

palmgun A small, easily concealable blaster pistol, it is designed for close-range combat. Palmguns are sometimes called hold-out blasters. [HSR]

Palpatine, Emperor Evil incarnate, Palpatine imposed a reign of terror as he ruled the galaxy for years. The stagnation and corruption of the Old Republic, which had been in power for nearly 25,000 years, made Palpatine's rise possible. Not much about Palpatine's early years is public, but as a senator of the Old Republic, he appeared to be quiet and unassuming, a colorless man lacking in ambition and guile, who had remained apart from the corruption infecting the government. However, Palpatine was the consummate actor in the galactic political arena as well as a master of the dark side. Once he had tricked various factions into supporting him for the position of Senate leader, he moved quickly to consolidate his power. At first, he seemed successful. He streamlined the corrupt and inefficient bureaucracy. He made speeches that inspired trust. Slowly, he introduced the tenets of his New Order, and before much time had passed, he declared himself Emperor, drawing analogies between his rule and some of the strong, almost mythic dynasties of the past.

His Empire, however, was based on tyranny, hatred of nonhumans, brutal and lethal force, and, above all else, constant fear. Those few senators who hadn't been taken in by him tried to maintain the Senate as a legitimate opposition force, but their voices rang out in increasingly empty rooms. Finally, several felt they had no choice but to back an open Rebellion, which gave Palpatine the public excuse he felt he needed to dissolve what was left of the Senate.

Senators who had been too vocal in their opposition or considered too dangerous were blackmailed or eliminated. Execution orders were issued for senators Mon Mothma and Garm Bel Iblis; both escaped, but Bel Iblis's family was slaughtered. The Emperor diverted funds from social, artistic, and other programs into a massive military buildup devoted to subjugating entire star systems. He quickly set out to nullify any threat from the galaxy's remaining Jedi, who had protected the Old Republic. Palpatine either seduced them to the dark side of the Force—as he did with Anakin Skywalker, a powerful and promising Jedi who was transformed into Darth Vader, a Dark Lord of the Sith—or murdered them and their children using the power of the dark side. Few escaped the purge.

Palpatine trusted no one and kept track of everyone. No one had the full picture except the Emperor; confusion was the order of the day among his advisers. Palpatine effectively set up a system under which the Empire couldn't function without him. Once he achieved his aim, he became distant and reclusive, seen only by those who needed to see him. His leaders and commanders presented the Empire's public face; Darth Vader presented a public threat. The Emperor also prepared for the future, conducting cloning experiments, hoping to transfer his mind and very essence into a younger and stronger clone of himself.

The Emperor had the galaxy in his grip, manipulating planets as if they were pieces in a hologame. Yet out of the backwater planet of Tatooine, a new opponent arose—a farmboy with

Emperor Palpatine

strong but undeveloped Force powers that could make him a major threat. After all, young Luke Skywalker was the son of Vader. Even with a modicum of training, Skywalker somehow destroyed the Empire's super weapon, the Death Star battle station, in a Rebel assault. That success led to countless uprisings around the galaxy, and the Rebellion took on new strength.

Darth Vader had several encounters with young Skywalker, but it wasn't until they met on Bespin's Cloud City that the Sith Lord told Luke the secret of his parentage and offered Luke the chance to join with him in deposing the Emperor and ruling the galaxy. Skywalker told Vader he'd rather die, and escaped, leaving Vader to explain to the omniscent Emperor that the plan had been a ruse to turn Skywalker to the dark side. The Emperor dispatched his top-secret aide, Mara Jade, to kill young Skywalker, but she failed. Instead, Luke showed up to confront Vader and the Emperor on the second Death Star, where he had a ferocious lightsaber duel with his father. Palpatine, unable to convert Luke to the dark side, started to kill him with blue Force lightning until a crippled Vader lifted the Emperor bodily and, with his last bit of strength, threw him into the shaft of the station's power core just before the Death Star was blown up by the Rebels.

That wasn't the Emperor's end. Six years later, from the Emperor's secret citadel and cloning chambers on Byss, came a cloned Palpatine. For a brief period, Luke Skywalker accepted the cloned Emperor's training in the dark side, but finally the combined Force power of Luke and his sister Leia Organa Solo proved enough to kill the clone.

One final clone rose a few months later. He planned to kidnap Leia and turn her unborn child to the dark side. He also planned to wipe out the top officials of the Alliance with his new super weapon, the Galaxy Gun. Both plans failed. The last remaining clone of the Emperor was reduced to ashes before he had a chance to suffuse his spirit into the newborn Anakin Solo, and the great weapon, the Galaxy Gun, was sabotaged and ended up destroying the Imperial throneworld of Byss. [RJ, DE, DE2, EE, SWCG, ISB]

Emperor Palpatine clone

Palpatine Counter-Insurgency Front (PCF) Shortly after the New Republic took control of Coruscant but before it could purge all the remaining Imperial evil from the planet, this terrorist organization was formed by Ysanne Isard, Director of Imperial Intelligence. Controlled at various times by Kirtan Loor and Fliry Vorru, the PCF was responsible for a series of horrifying bombings at a school, a stadium, and several bacta storage facilities. [KT]

Pantolomin Famous for the intricate coral reefs found in the waters off its northern continent, this is the primary planet in the Panto system.The *Coral Vanda*, an underwater casino ship, travels through the network of Pantolomin reefs on luxury excursions. Patrons can view the reefs' fish and animal life through its transparent hull. Among other resorts is the Towers of Pantolomin, owned by Galaxy Tours. The planet's inhabitants are called Lomins; its animals include the playful, color-changing amphibians known as halfbacks. Five years after the Battle of Endor, Grand Admiral Thrawn's forces visited Pantolomin and forced the *Coral Vanda* to surrender a passenger, Captain Hoffner, who knew the location of the long-lost *Katana* Dreadnaught fleet. [DFR, CSSB, SWAJ]

Paploo A scout in the Ewok tribe who befriended Princess Leia Organa and other Rebels on the forest moon of Endor, he stole an Imperial speeder bike to distract the guards at a secret Imperial facility at the start of the Battle of Endor. Paploo's actions gave the Rebel strike team an opportunity to penetrate the Imperial base. He was named the tribe's shaman after Logray was removed by Chief Chirpa. [RJ, GG5]

Pappfak A mostly unknown species with turquoise tentacles. [TMEC]

Paqwepori An autonomous territory represented by Belezaboth Ourn, extraordinary consul of the Paqwepori. The inhabitants, short, wide yellow-green beings called Paqwe, are known to eat toko birds, which they kill with a slaughter knife before consuming. The Paqwepori society forbade any of its citizens from joining the New Republic military. Twelve years after the Battle of Endor, the Paqwepori consular ship *Mother's Valkyrie* was damaged when the Yevethan thrustship *Aramadia* blasted off from a Coruscant port without warning. Actually, Ourn had secretly allowed the damage to the *Valkyrie* in exchange for a promised Yevethan thrustship of his own. Yevethan leader Nil Spaar continued to promise a thrustship to tempt Ourn into providing him with more information about political developments on Coruscant. While Ourn waited for his thrustship, the other members of his staff abandoned him. Finally, Ilar Paqwe revoked Ourn's status and warned him not to return to the Paqwe dominion. Ourn revealed his treachery to Leia Organa Solo and the New Republic, which used Ourn to send disinformation to Nil Spaar. [BTS, SOL, TT]

Paploo

Paradise system A garbage-strewn system, it is home to the quarrelsome unicellular protozoans known as Ugors. Early in their history the Ugors severely polluted their home planet in the Paradise system, yet survived by adopting a form that could exist on garbage and waste. The Ugors, who have built a religion around their love of trash, have begun charging fees to those wishing to make a pilgrimage to their system to pick through their vast store of garbage and remove useful items. Ugor society is composed of various waste recovery companies, which are controlled by the Holy Ugor Taxation Collection Agency (HUTCA). Ugors frequently find themselves in conflict with the scavenger Squibs for control of the galactic trash-hauling business. [GG4, SH]

paralight system Consisting of mechanical and opto-electronic subsystems in a hyperdrive, the system translates a pilot's manual commands into reactions inside the hyperdrive power plants. [ESBN]

Paret, Jian The commander of the Imperial garrison at N'zoth, he was brutally killed by Yevethan strongman Nil Spaar. [BTS]

Parfadi A region of space, it contains the unnavigable Black Nebula and separates the planets Arat Fraca and Motexx. [SOL]

parfue gnats Tiny parasitic insects, they live on watumba bats. Parfue gnats are a delicacy for many Glottalphibs. [NR]

Parmel system After the Battle of Hoth, the system was the site of the traitorous Imperial Admiral Harkov's capture. He was brought before Darth Vader for questioning and execution. Later, renegade Admiral Zaarin returned to a deep-space research and development facility in the Parmel system to seize its TIE defender prototypes. Loyal Imperial forces captured the facility but were forced to evacuate with the prototype TIEs when Zaarin tried to destroy the space platform. [TSC]

Parmic system Site of a research facility operated by renegade Imperial Admiral Zaarin. In the Parmic system, Zaarin equipped his TIE squadrons with a new beam weapon following the Battle of Hoth. [TSC]

Parq, Colonel An Imperial officer on Tatooine, he captured the Mistryl Shadow Guards Shada and Karoly after mistaking them for the notorious Tonnika sisters. Colonel Parq planned to turn the guards over to Grand Moff Argon, but they escaped. [TMEC]

Par'tah A Ho'Din, she runs a Borderland Regions smuggling operation from a hidden base on a hot jungle planet off major space lanes. Although only a marginal operation for Par'tah, she puts on airs of wealth and success. She collects technological items, often rummaging through a client's cargo for new additions before completing a delivery. She has a good relationship with smuggler Talon Karrde, who sometimes directs her to new pieces for her collection. While she prefers to deal with the New Republic, she often needs the large payoffs Imperial sources offer. [HE, HESB, LC]

particle shielding A defensive force field, it repels any form of matter. Particle shielding is usually used together with ray shielding for full protection of starships and planetary installations. [SWSB]

particle vapor trail A signature left behind by most ships. If detected, it can help in tracking the ship. [TBH]

passenger liner The basic mode of transport used by most galactic travelers, these spaceliners range in size from small ships to giant interstellar luxury liners complete with multiple entertainment decks. [SWSB]

Payback The name by which the bounty hunter Dengar was commonly known throughout the galactic underworld. [TBH]

Peckhum A supply courier and message runner, he uses the battered supply ship *Lightning Rod*. [YJK]

Pedducis Chorios Located in the Chorios systems in the Meridian sector, it is a hotbed of smuggling and piracy ruled by ruthless pirate warlords who have made alliances with the local chieftains. After the loss of the *Knight Hammer* at Yavin 4, Imperial Admiral Daala became president of an independent group of 3,000 settlers who wanted to settle on Pedducis Chorios and escape from the petty struggles of the Empire. Daala made an alliance with Warlord K'iin of the Silver Unifir to take the smallest of Pedducis Chorios's three southern continents, comprising 1.5 billion acres, and colonize it as they saw fit. [POT]

Pell, Akanah Norand A member of the Fallanassi religious order—followers of the Forcelike White Current—she convinced Luke Skywalker to travel with her to track down her people by telling him that his mother was a woman named Nashira, another Fallanassi. Akanah was of the circle at Ialtra on the planet Lucazec and was raised on Carratos by her mother, Isela Talsava Norand; her father was Joreb Goss. She was the widow of Andras Pell. Akanah had been traumatized in her youth when her people had been forced to flee Imperial persecution on their planet. She appealed to Skywalker to help fill the emptiness in both their lives caused by not having a mother. Luke and Akanah traveled to many planets, including Teyr and Atzerri, in search of the Fallanassi people. They found her father, Joreb Goss, but he had no memory of her or his past life. All the while, Akanah and Luke engaged in a back-and-forth game of trust and distrust. In the end, it became clear Akanah had been lying all along. Her own mother had double-crossed the Fallanassi and had reported them to the Empire. Nashira was a kind woman who had helped Akanah and was someone who would have made a fine mother—but she was neither Luke's nor Akanah's mother. [SOL, BTS, TT]

Pell, Andras Akanah Norand Pell's late husband, he was thirty-six years her senior. When he died, he left her his ship, the *Mud Sloth*. [SOL]

Pellaeon, Gilad In his more than fifty years of service, first to the Old Republic and then to the Empire, Pellaeon was always a military man with a conscience, which some mistook for weakness. But Gilad Pellaeon wasn't a survivor because he was a coward; he just thought it smarter to live to fight another day rather than commit some foolish sacrifice.

The Corellian—who had lied about his age—graduated in the top third of his class at the Naval Academy. Quick thinking to thwart pirates on his first assignment led to an appointment to the command crew of the Star Destroyer *Chimaera*. Over the years, he worked his way up to second-in-command, achieving the rank of captain. During the Battle of Endor, the *Chimaera*'s commander was killed along with other officers and Pellaeon took control of the ship. Seeing the rout before his eyes, he reluctantly ordered the few surviving Imperial ships to withdraw.

Captain Pellaeon worked with others for years to bring the remnants of the Empire together. Just when he despaired most of the Empire getting a strong new leader, Grand Admiral Thrawn appeared and chose the *Chimaera* as his new headquarters ship. Thrawn listened to the captain's opinions, even though he ignored many of them. Pellaeon commanded the *Chimaera* in the Battle of Sluis Van. Acting on Thrawn's orders, he then hired Niles Ferrier and Mara Jade to find the location of the long-missing *Katana* Dreadnaught fleet. Thrawn's big problem, Pellaeon knew, was overestimating the loyalty and abilities of those who surrounded him. The Battle of Bilbringi was not going well for the Imperials when Rukh, Thrawn's Noghri bodyguard, killed the admiral. Pellaeon again felt he had no choice but to call a retreat.

Years later, with a promotion to the rank of vice admiral, Pellaeon headed the fleet of an Imperial warlord, High Admiral Teradoc. He encountered Admiral Daala, who was trying to get the squabbling Imperial forces to band together, and aided her by inviting the thirteen strongest warlords to a unification meeting. But talking didn't accomplish the task, and Pellaeon watched when Admiral Daala gassed them all. As part of Daala's grand strategy, Pellaeon led a fleet of Star Destroyers to join with her and destroy the Jedi academy on Yavin 4. But Pellaeon's fleet was hurled across space by a Force storm brought about by the Jedi trainees, and by the time he got back to the vicinity, the New Republic had vanquished Daala. She had survived the

Gilad Pellaeon

destruction of her ship in an escape pod, and in recognition of yet another failure, handed over her command—and command of the Empire's forces—to Pellaeon. [HE, DFR, LC, HESB, DFRSB, DS]

pelvic servomotor A small motor that gives two-legged droids the ability to walk. [SWSB]

Penga Rift An Obroan Institute research transport, it was the command vessel for the excavation at Maltha Obex. [TT]

Pentastar Alignment A group of worlds in the Outer Rim, it was forged into a protective federation after the Battle of Endor by Grand Moff Ardus Kaine, the successor to Grand Moff Tarkin. He saw the Empire's defeat as an opportunity to form a new Empire under his own rule. He called a meeting, dubbed the Pentastar Talks, aboard his Super Star Destroyer *Reaper* with Imperial officials and representatives from two large private corporations. The resulting Alignment encompassed hundreds of planets, including the Velcar Free Commerce Zone. The New Republic has done little to oppose the Pentastar Alignment since its formation, but mercenary groups such as the Red Moons have secretly worked to sabotage its operations. [SWAJ]

People's Liberation Battalion (PLB) Composed of disenfranchised workers, intellectuals, and disaffected nobles, the PLB is a socialist-oriented group dedicated to bringing down all nobles and eliminating any vestiges of the Empire. The group promises to establish a governmental system in which everyone will share the wealth. They are led by Asran, who, although basically cruel, has begun to believe his own rhetoric. [XW]

Peppel A primitive world, it is far from the Galactic Core. The Devaronian Labria was forced to flee there thirteen years after the Battle of Endor, when four mercenaries on Tatooine recognized Labria as the Butcher of Montellian Serat. Two years later, Boba Fett discovered his hiding place. Bypassing the elaborate defenses surrounding Labria's hut, Fett captured his target and returned him to Devaron, where he was executed. [TBH]

Peramis, Senator Tig A human from the planet Walalla, he was a New Republic Senator and member of the Senate Defense Council. Tig Peramis was also the newest member of the Council on the Common Defense. He distrusted Chief of State Leia Organa Solo and saw her military buildup against the Yevethan threat as "the machinery of oppression." He stole fellow council member Cundertol's voting key, logged into his personal logs, and found information about the deployment of the New Republic's Fifth Fleet to the Farlax sector, including the information that Leia's husband, Han Solo, would be in command. Convincing himself that he was an honorable man trying to contain militarism in the galactic government, he personally turned the top-secret information over to Yevethan strongman Nil Spaar. [SOL, BTS]

Peregrine The flagship of Garm Bel Iblis's private strike force, it is one of his six Dreadnaughts from the legendary, long-lost *Katana* fleet. [DFR]

Peregrine's Nest Garm Bel Iblis's last hidden base before his strike force rejoined the New Republic, it was constructed mainly of bi-state memory plastic for quick breakdown and setup. [DFR]

Peridon's Folly A seldom-visited planet, it is a weapons depot operated by traders who sell obsolete arms to crime lords on the black market. Gunrunners control various commercial sectors, which are separated by wastelands where weapons are tested. After deciding to seek work as a bounty hunter, the droid IG-88 traveled to the backwater world of Peridon's Folly. He was hired by a local despot named Grlubb to take out a rival weapons manufacturer. IG-88 broke into the rival's fortress and released the company's own lethal gases, killing everyone inside. Next, the droid killed Bolton Kek, one of the original designers of the IG series. [TBH]

Perit A Mon Calamari, he was one of the lieutenants, or Vigos, of Prince Xizor's Black Sun criminal organization. [SOTE]

Perlemian Trade Route Running through the Darpa and Bormea sectors of the Ringali Shell, it connects the planets Corulag, Chandrila, Brentaal, Esseles, Rhinnal, and Ralltiir. Activity along the Perlemian Trade Route was severly curtailed by Lord Tion's blockade of Ralltiir just prior to the Battle of Yavin. [SWAJ, SWRPG2]

permacrete A strong, dense material, it is used for paving roads and landing platforms. [TBH]

Permondiri Explorer A mystery ship, the survey vessel and its crew of 112 went on a mission to explore and chart a new star system and has not been heard from since. Several massive expeditions were organized to locate the *Permondiri Explorer* or to discover what happened to it, but they have all drawn blanks. [HSR]

Pernon, Count Rial The spitting image of his father as a young man, the count has thick black hair and the same bushy eyebrows and large mustache as the Grand Duke. Count Rial Pernon is tall, strong, and handsome—as well as very serious and solemn. He and Princess Isplourrdacartha Estillo (Plourr Ilo) were betrothed as children, and he considered their parents' vow to bind him still. Stalwart in battle, graceful in social situations, he knew the pledge to wed her that he held sacred might be unrealistic, but he wanted only to serve her and prove himself worthy of her trust and love.

This didn't sit well with Plourr, a member of Rogue Squadron. While she found him attractive, Rial was the bait in a trap to bring her back to Eiattu VI, to a people she saw as treacherous. She considered the alternatives: If they destroyed the Imperial remnants on the planet, she would be forced to stay. If they didn't, and if the impostor playing the role of her brother, Asran, won, or the nobles won, people would suffer. She was faced with little choice and resented Rial. But Plourr did soften toward him and finally agreed to marry him. [XW]

Pernon, Grand Duke Gror A human male with white hair, thick bushy eyebrows, and a grand mustache, he wears a white uniform festooned with countless ribbons. Grand Duke Gror Pernon would have been the heir to the throne of Eiattu VI if the daughter of the Crown Prince hadn't survived the execution of the rest of the family. (An alleged surviving son was proven to be an imposter.) Pernon leads the planet's noble faction. His father and the grandfather of Rogue Squadron pilot Plourr Ilo (Princess Isplourrdacartha Estillo) were brothers, and her father and Gror grew up together as cousins. Gror was part of the faction that overthrew the Crown Prince, so Plourr naturally blames her family's death on him. Gror saw the coup as vital because Plourr's father was not strong enough to shield Eiattu VI from the Empire, but he did not advocate the family's murder and did his best to countermand the orders. [XW]

Pesitiin A gas giant where the Bosken & Bosken Company started an ambitious—although ultimately unprofitable—mining operation. The planet is famous for its nonstop atmospheric storms. [GG2]

Pesmenben IV A planet where Lando Calrissian conned an Imperial governor. Calrissian laced the dunes of Pesmenben IV with valuable lithium carbonate, convincing the governor to lease the planet; he then tricked the governor into offering bribes to nonexistent union officials. [RJN]

Pestage, Sate Emperor Palpatine's Grand Vizier. [DESB]

Petrakis This planet was the site of the first engagement between Rebel Alliance B-wings and the Imperial fleet. When TIE fighter pilots first saw the new fighters near Petrakis, the entire wing fled. [FP]

Phalanx A cruiser in the New Republic's Fifth Fleet, it was assigned to the blockade of Doornik-319 and was severely damaged during the Yevethan attack. [SOL]

Phenaru Prime A mythical planet, it was simulated by Alliance strategists to train Rogue Squadron pilots for a return mission to Borleias. Since Borleias's location was classified, the pilots flew simulated attacks on Phenaru Prime. The run through the canyons of Borleias's moon was replaced with a run through a virtual asteroid ring surrounding the spurious world. [RS]

Phlegmin A kitchen boy in the palace of Jabba the Hutt, he was an assistant to the head chef, Porcellus. Jabba had fed Phlegmin's brother to the rancor because a sauce failed, so Phlegmin laced Jabba's toads with a slow-acting poison in an attempt at revenge. Phlegmin was eventually killed by the Anzati Dannik Jerriko. [TJP]

Phlog Giant, brutish creatures, they live in the desert land of Simoom on Endor's forest moon. Phlogs are usually peaceful, but can become dangerous when disturbed. [ETV]

Phlutdroid *See* IG-88

phobium A metal alloy, it was used to coat the power core of both Death Star battle stations. [GDV]

Phonstrom, Lady Lapema A resident of Kabal, she was one of Lando Calrissian's marriage candidates. [AC]

Pho Ph'eah Homeworld of the Pho Ph'eahians, creatures with blue fur and four arms. Pho Ph'eah orbits far from its star and receives little sunlight but is warmed by active geothermal energy. The planet was contacted by the Old Republic millennia ago, and the technologically skilled Pho Ph'eahians have long been members of the larger galaxy. [HSE, CSSB]

Phorliss Site of a cantina where Mara Jade, onetime top personal aide to the Emperor and later a smuggler, worked briefly as a serving girl under the name Karrinna Jansih. [DFR]

Phosphura Belt Nebula Located near several major trade lanes, it is a mass of greenish clouds randomly charged with electromagnetic bursts. It is a serious navigation hazard and home to the highly organized Phosphura Belt Pirates. The space station *Zirtran's Anchor* drifts nearby. [SWAJ]

photoreceptor A device that captures light rays and converts them into electronic signals for processing by video computers. Photoreceptors are used as eyes for most droids. [SWSB]

phototropic shielding A process that turns transparent materials into filters for intense light rays while retaining their transparency. [SWSB]

Phracas A planet in the Galactic Core in sector 151 where the mystery ship known as the Teljkon vagabond headed after Lando Calrissian, Lobot, and the droids C-3PO and R2-D2 stowed away on board. [SOL]

Pica Thundercloud A green drink served on Tatooine. [TMEC]

Piett, Captain First officer on Darth Vader's flagship *Executor*, the captain aided Admiral Ozzel in overseeing the crew as well as helping to direct the entire fleet. He was promoted to Admiral and given command of the flagship and the fleet after Admiral Ozzel made a fatal mistake during the assault on the Rebel base on Hoth. Piett remained in command of *Executor* through the Battle of Endor, where the Super Star Destroyer was lost in combat with the Rebel fleet. [ESB, RJ]

Pii system Located in the Arkanis sector on the border of the Mid- and Outer Rims, the system's seven planets orbit a red giant, and the inner two worlds are scorched balls of rock. An asteroid belt follows, then the lush green worlds of Pii 3 and 4—the only commercially useful worlds in the area. They are known for the valuable crimson greel wood harvested and exported from their forests. Entrepreneur Meysen Kayson bought the rights to both planets in the last days of the Old Republic, intending to open a nature preserve. When he discovered the fast-growing greel trees and their deep, luxurious wood, he founded the Greel Wood Logging Corporation. Kayson secretly diverted most of his profits to the Rebel Alliance and let the planets be used as Rebel training grounds and safeworlds. [SWAJ, FP]

Pike sisters Epicanthix women, they were twins. The only noticeable different between the two women was that Zan Pike had green eyes, while Zu Pike had one green and one blue eye. They were masters of Teräs Käsi, the Bunduki art also called steel hands. At twenty-six standard years of age the women had no political affiliations, no criminal records, and had never been defeated in open combat. They were allegedly hired by Prince Xizor's Black Sun criminal organization as assassins. [SOTE]

Pil Diller Once home to a species of mournful singing fig trees, the planet also has many beaches. [DA, DS]

pinnace Small ships built for travel close to lightspeed, they are carried aboard larger spacecraft for defensive purposes. Heavily armed and highly maneuverable, pinnaces come close to combat starfighters in terms of performance and utility. They sometimes are called battle boats. [HSR]

Pinnacle Base The designation for the New Republic High Command Center on Da Soocha's fifth moon. [DE]

piranha-beetle Native to Yavin 4, these iridescent blue insects fly together with a high-pitched humming sound, spreading out while searching for prey. The beetles cover the body of their victim in moments, tearing its flesh with thousands of piercing, razor-sharp mandibles. Emperor Palpatine used piranha-beetles to torture and kill Death Star designer Bevel Lemelisk before he cloned him. [COF, DS]

Captain Piett

Piroket Located close to the planet Tatooine, it was the site of a Bothan shipping company where the Rebel agent Riij Winward—having stolen a droid carrying the complete technical readouts of the Hammertong project prior to the Battle of Yavin—planned to leave the droid. [TMEC, SWAJ]

Pirol-5 Located in the Koornacht Cluster in the Farlax sector, the planet was the former location of an Imperial factory farm, run largely by droids. Twelve years after the Battle of Endor, Pirol-5 was seized by the Yevethan military in what the Yevethans called the Great Purge. [BTS]

Pitareeze The Pitareeze family lived on the planet Kalarba. The family included Meg and Jarth Pitareeze, their son, Nak, and Nak's grandfather, Baron Pitareeze. In their adventures before they met Luke Skywalker, R2-D2 and C-3PO agreed to work for the family after their lifepod splashed down on Kalarba following their escape from bounty hunter IG-88. [D]

Plah A lifeless moon, it orbits Tibrin. [GG4]

plasteel A tough, shiny material, it is used in the construction of countless items throughout the galaxy, such as the domes on Mon Calamari cities and the cockpits and displays on starships. [TBH, DU]

plastoid Any type of thermoformed substance, such as many varieties of shaped battle armor. [SWN]

Platform 327 After the Battle of Hoth, the *Millennium Falcon* landed on Platform 327 in Bespin's Cloud City. [ESB]

Plooriod III Site of a small palace atop a rocky spire in a peaceful sea, it was built for the brutal Overlord Ghorin, ruler of the Greater Plooriod Cluster. Darth Vader visited Ghorin here and killed him for his apparent double-cross of the Empire in the period following the Battle of Yavin. [FP]

Plooriod IV The planet near which the Rebel Alliance captured a group of Overlord Ghorin's Y-wing fighters, which they used to discredit Ghorin in the eyes of the Empire. Later, the Imperial frigate *Red Wind* was discovered near Plooriod IV and was destroyed by Alliance corvettes. [FP]

Ploovo Two-For-One An infamous criminal kingpin, the portly humanoid from the Cron Drift is a con man, a loan shark, a thief, a smash-and-grab man, and a bunko artist, among other things. In his smuggling days, Han Solo sometimes worked for Ploovo Two-For-One, and for a time he owed the crime lord a goodly number of credits. Ploovo ordered Solo's death after the Corellian caused him to lose face once too often. [HSE]

Plourr *See* Ilo, Plourr

pocket cruiser A small and now obsolete class of capital ship, it saw extensive service during the last phase of the Clone Wars. Pocket cruisers were easy to manufacture and were about equal to other warships at the time. Some can still be found as training platforms, pirate ships, or in the arsenals of local military forces. [HLL]

pocket patrol boat A small single-pilot ship, it trades high speed for limited firepower. [AC]

Poderis This harsh world in the Orus sector has a ten-hour rotational cycle and a severe axial tilt that can create windstorms of up to 200 kilometers an hour. In addition, the unusual geology of Poderis has forced its fiercely independent colonists to build their cities atop a vast network of mesas. An angled wall 100 meters wide (called a shield-barrier) runs along the outer edge of these cities, helping deflect Poderis's damaging seasonal winds. Luke Skywalker visited Poderis in an attempt to uncover the Empire's clone-trafficking network, and narrowly escaped a trap set for him by Grand Admiral Thrawn. [LC]

Platform 327 in Cloud City

Poe A silver protocol droid with one black metal peg leg, he was assigned to Rogue Squadron to help ease the pilots into the local population. Poe isn't quite as fussy as C-3PO but is fairly rigid in trying to get the Rogues to do what he knows is right for them. This very proper droid is everlastingly mortified that he has to travel in the luggage bin of an X-wing. [XW]

Point 5 A game of chance, it is played in many galactic casinos. [HSR]

Polith system The system containing the planet Thyferra, homeworld of the Vratix and the center of the galaxy's bacta industry. [SWAJ]

Poll, Unut A male Arcona from the planet Cona, he is known to cooperate with Alliance operatives. Poll frequents the cantina in Mos Eisley on Tatooine. He has avoided the temptations of salt, which is very addictive to his species. He owns Spaceport Speeders in central Mos Eisley. [CCG, GG7]

Polneye Located in the Koornacht Cluster in the Farlax sector, it is on the far side of the Cluster from Coruscant. A dry world, Polneye is covered by high cirrus clouds whose rain almost never reaches the surface. Polneye was established by the Imperial Black Sword Command as a secret military transshipment point for the sector. It became a busy supply depot and open-air armory, with many landing pads built on the brown flatlands. Over time, the population grew, and small cities sprang up around each landing zone.

When the Empire abandoned the Farlax sector following the Battle of Endor, Polneye's quarter-million civilians, who call themselves Polneyi, were left behind and forced to fend for themselves. They took advantage of the valuable resources left behind by the fleeing Imperials and formed a reasonably prosperous unified state consisting of eight cities: Three North, Nine South, Nine North, Ten South, Eleven South, Eleven North, Twelve North, and the empty city of Fourteen North. Twelve years after the Battle of Endor, Polneye was brutally attacked by the Yevethan military on the fortieth day of Mofat, in what the Yevetha called the Great Purge. Plat Mallar, a Grannan citizen of Ten South, took one of Polneye's six operational TIE interceptors and was able to destroy a Yevethan scout fighter. He then attempted to reach the planet Galantos in the short-range TIE but was picked up by a New Republic prowler, which alerted

Jek Porkins

the Republic leaders to the recent aggressive actions of the Yevetha. Mallar was nursed back to health on Coruscant and became a New Republic pilot. Admiral Ackbar helped push through an emergency petition for membership in the New Republic for Polneye, which Leia approved. [BTS]

Pops *See* Krail, Davish

Poqua, Commodore A New Republic task-force commander during the Yevethan emergency, he was a friend of General A'baht, who was relieved of command during the crisis. [TT]

Porcellus The personal chef of Jabba the Hutt, he was a triple Golden Spoon awardee and winner of the Tselgormet Prize for gourmandise five years in a row. When people started dying around Jabba's palace, many assumed that the chef had been poisoning Jabba's food. Before he could be executed for the supposed crime, Jabba was killed. Porcellus then went to Mos Eisley and opened a renowned restaurant with his friend Malakili, the rancor keeper. [TJP]

Porkins, Jek An Alliance X-wing pilot, he learned his piloting skills by hunting sink crabs in his T-16 skyhopper on the rocky islands of his homeworld, Bestine IV. He specialized in strafing runs. He also served in Tierfon Yellow Squadron at Tierfon Rebel Outpost. During the Battle of Yavin, his comm-unit designation was Red Six. Porkins was killed when his craft was hit by fire from a Death Star turbolaser. [SW, SWSB]

Porus Vida Famous throughout the galaxy for its centuries-old cultural museums, the planet was relatively undefended against attack. Imperial Admiral Daala targeted the Porus Vida museums and their priceless treasures for destruction as a psychological blow against the New Republic. In the attack, Colonel Cronus and his fleet of *Victory*-class Star Destroyers devastated the planet. [DS]

positronic processor Too small to be called a proper droid but too personable to call anything else, positronic processors can be attached to the power points of larger computer systems to access information and override command sequences. [TBH]

Post, Avan A Jedi Master from Chandrila, he served with distinction during the Clone Wars. [KT]

power converter The ignition system for a starship, it routes energy from a ship's primary power source to its propulsion units in order to achieve thrust. [SWN, ESBN]

power coupling A starship device that directs power to the hyperdrive motivator, which then activates the hyperdrive engine to achieve the jump to lightspeed. [ESBN]

power droid *See* GNK power droid

power gem A mineral that radiates an aura that can disrupt magnetic defense shields, it enables pirates to raid other ships. The gems lose power

Power gem

Power harpoon

over time. Just after the Battle of Yavin, the last gem, aboard Vrad Dodonna's ship, had just enough power left to let him crash into the *Executor*, shattering its forward shields. [CSW]

power glove Energized gloves, they are worn by stormtroopers in hand-to-hand combat, usually while restraining prisoners. [TBH]

power harpoon A high-powered, often barbed projectile, it is attached to a retractable flexisteel tow cable and fusion-head disk. Power harpoons are standard equipment for most snowspeeders and similar military vehicles. They were designed by Beryl Chiffonage for the Rebel Alliance as a reserve defense against Imperial walkers. Wedge Antilles used one successfully during the Battle of Hoth to drop an AT-AT to its knees and destroy it. [CCG, ESBN]

Pqweeduk A Rodian, he was the younger brother of the bounty hunter Greedo. [TMEC]

Praesitlyn The site of a major communications station, it is located within sixty light-years of Bpfassh in the Sluis sector. Twelve years after the Battle of Endor, Praesitlyn was represented by Senator Zilar in the New Republic government and the Defense Council. [HE, SOL]

Praget, Chairman Krall From the planet Edatha, he was Chairman of the New Republic Senate Council on Security and Intelligence. Krall Praget ordered Colonel Pakkapekatt to abandon the recovery of the mysterious vagabond ship even though Lando Calrissian, Lobot, and the droids C-3PO and R2-D2 were still aboard. Angered that Chief of State

Praji

Leia Organa Solo called for military action against the Yevethan threat without consulting him first, Chairman Praget attempted to overthrow her through Senate channels by bringing a petition to the Senate Ruling Council seeking her removal. [SOL]

Praidaw The planet where the parents of Akanah Norand Pell first met. [SOL]

Praji A male Imperial commander, he was Darth Vader's aide on the Star Destroyer *Devastator*. By Vader's order, he personally supervised the search for the Death Star's missing plans on Tatooine. Praji had been graduated with honors from the Imperial Navy Academy on Carida. [CCG]

Prakith Located in the system of the same name in Sector One of the Galactic Core, the planet is about 106 light-years beyond the borders of the New Republic. Prakith is the ruling world of the Constitutional Protectorate controlled by the Imperial warlord Foga Brill. Brill maintains his power over the region by accepting bribes from Prakith's wealthy families and keeping order with the Red Police. Many of Prakith's citizens are forced to toil in the foundries and silt mines, and inhabitants of the riverbank cities Prall and Skoth are regularly executed after being forced to dig their own graves. The natives of the planet speak Prak. Twelve years after the Battle of Endor, when Lando Calrissian, Lobot, and the droids C-3PO and R2-D2 stowed away on the mysterious Teljkon vagabond, the ship emerged from hyperspace eight light-years from Prakith. The frigate *Bloodprice*, part of Brill's defensive fleet, detected the vagabond and attempted to capture it but was destroyed by the mystery ship, which vanished into hyperspace. The Prakith cruiser *Gorath* later caught up with the vagabond but was also destroyed. [SOL, TT]

Praxlis This planet is located in the former center of the Empire's Rim territories. During the Emperor's reign, the Black Sword Command was charged with the defense of Praxlis, Corridan, and the entire Kokash and Farlax sectors. [BTS]

preducor A ferocious night hunter on the forest moon of Endor, it is docile during the day. A preducor moves on four clawed legs and can grow to about four meters high and five meters long. Its head is surrounded by a mane of razor-sharp hair, and a long, spiked tail stretches behind it. Its protruding jaw is full of knifelike teeth, and its eyes glow in the dark. Large folds of skin on its back are vestiges of wings that no longer function. [DFRSB]

Preedu III, Emperor The onetime ruler of Tamban before the rise of the Empire. [BTS]

Prefsbelt IV The location of an Imperial Navy Academy. [SWSB]

pressor Small repulsor projectors, they induce and control pitch in a starship. They are activated by control sticks or buttons on control consoles. [SWN]

Preza *See* Morning Bell

Priamsta A body composed of the native noble class of the planet Eiattu VI, the Priamsta wanted to restore local rule and independence. To counter a claim by Asran, a pretender to the throne, the council sought out and invited back to the planet their princess, who now goes by the name Plourr Ilo as a pilot in Rogue Squadron. She apparently was the only member of the royal family to escape execution years earlier. The Priamsta established as its goals the restoration of a pre-Palpatine Golden Age (which never really existed) on Eiattu VI, the end of all Imperial occupation, and the elimination of the People's Liberation Battalion. [XW]

Pricina, Dom A wealthy but careless woman, she owned the legendary Antares sapphire until the droid 4-LOM stole it. [TBH]

Pride of Yevetha Formerly the Imperial Super Star Destroyer *Intimidator*, it was seized by the forces of strongman Nil Spaar during a raid on the Imperial shipyard at N'zoth. The *Pride of Yevetha* was placed in Spaar's Black Fifteen Fleet and was spotted in the Yevethan mobilization at Doornik-319. [SOL]

Priests of Ninn Usually dressed in green vestments, this religious order lives on the religious haven of Ninn, a planet of retreat. The Priests of Ninn's beliefs incorporate formalistic abstinence. [HSR]

Prildaz Located in the Koornacht Cluster, it is one of the primary worlds of the Yevetha species and is a member of the Duskhan League. The third planet in the system, it is a yellow-and-brown world, and was the location of the Black Nine shipyards. The star system is known as ILC-905 in New Republic records. It contains at least twelve planets, with an asteroid belt between the fourth and fifth planetary orbits. Thirteen years after the Battle of Endor, the New Republic attacked Prildaz, destroying the shipyards and demolishing several Yevetha thrustships, despite incurring heavy losses. [TT]

Princess Leia Organa *See* Solo, Princess Leia Organa

Prindaar system Named after its star, it contains the gas giant Antar and its six moons. The fourth moon, known as Antar 4, is homeworld of the Gotal species. [GG4]

probe droid *See* probot

probot An intelligent probe droid, this reconnaissance device is equipped with repulsorlift and thruster units that enable it to move swiftly across planetary surfaces. Probots get to their destinations in hyperdrive pods, then descend to a planet's surface using braking thrusters. They often

Probot

look like meteorites to observers. After impact, the pod opens and the probe droid is released. Probots are programmed to be extremely curious, so they can almost always find anything that might be worthy of inspection. They are armed with a blaster device, although they are programmed to avoid conflict and to self-destruct if discovered.

Probots were used by Darth Vader when he was searching for the main Rebel base some time after the Battle of Yavin. He ordered thousands of them deployed to unexplored or uninhabited systems in the hope that one might uncover the Rebels. In fact, one probot did discover the Rebel base on Hoth.

Probots have sensitive sensor arrays to detect signs of habitation; they examine acoustic, electromagnetic, motive, seismic, and olfactory evidence. They are equipped with holocams, zoom imagers, infrared scopes, magnetic imagers, radar transceivers, sonar transceivers, and radiation meters. Four manipulator arms and a high-torque grasping arm allow the probot to take samples from a planet. [SWSB, ESB, AC, MTS]

processors Teams of Imperials, they were assigned the task of turning peaceful citizens into warlike servants of the Empire through brain modification. [TBH]

proctors Assistants to Lord Hethrir, the former Imperial Procurator of Justice who started an Empire Reborn movement, they wore light blue jumpsuits instead of the rust-colored tunics other helpers wore. [CS]

Procurator of Justice The head of the criminal justice system of the Empire—in reality, persecution of political prisoners was its most important function—he was a shadowy figure, never named or pictured during the Emperor's reign. Only after the Battle of Endor did the name of the Procurator—Lord Hethrir—become public. [CS]

program trap A method of turning a droid into an unsuspecting death machine, it involves reprogramming a droid's primary performance banks with an internal command to cause a power overload triggered by a predetermined event, signal, or time. The overload has the explosive capability of a moderate-sized bomb. [SWSB]

Proi, Lieutenant Norda The commanding officer of the fleet hauler and junker *Steadfast*, the ship that found the wreckage of the Imperial ship *Gnisnal*, where an intact memory core was discovered. [BTS]

Project Decoy A secret Rebel Alliance program headed by the Chadra-Fan scientist Fandar, its goal was to create a human replica droid. [QE]

Prophetess A renowned female psychic, she was both a predictor of doom and an agent of Imperial Governor Aryon on Tatooine. She followed Jabba the Hutt and his thugs to Docking Bay 94 when they confronted Han Solo. [CCG]

Prophets of the Dark Side A group of Imperial operatives that posed as great mystics strong in the dark side of the Force, they were really an investigation bureau with a vast network of spies. Led by the Supreme Prophet Kadann, the false mystics wielded power and control by making their prophecies come true through bribery, force, or even murder. [LCJ]

prosthetic replacement Spurred by the carnage of the Clone Wars, the replacement of body parts with lifelike replicas has become very advanced. Prosthetic replacements make it possible to see through artificial eyes, feel and grip with artificial hands, and run with artificial legs. Mechanical hearts pump blood and other replacement organs handle other important bodily functions. Most prosthetics use synthenet neural interfaces to give recipients full control of replaced limbs. Synth-flesh covers biomechanical replacement parts, giving them the look and feel of natural body parts. One example is Luke Skywalker's prosthetic hand, which replaced the one he lost in a battle with Darth Vader. [HESB]

protocol droid A droid whose primary programming includes languages, interpretation, cultures, and diplomacy, all geared toward helping it fulfill its usual function as an administrative assistant, diplomatic aide, and companion for high-level individuals. C-3PO is a protocol droid. [SW]

proton grenade A small concussion weapon, it is capable of damaging a small starfighter. [CSW]

proton torpedo A projectile weapon, it can be fired from specialized delivery systems aboard starfighters and capital ships or even from shoulder- or back-mounted launchers. The concussion weapons carry a proton-scattering energy warhead, and they can be deflected by complete particle shielding. Proton torpedoes were used to destroy both Death Star battle stations. [SW, RJ, SWSB]

Protocol droids

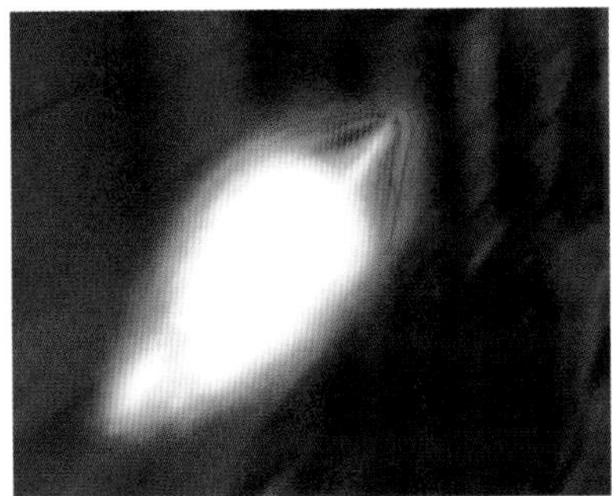

Proton torpedo

Proto One An ancient droid fitted with many diverse replacement parts, he was proprietor of a spaceship scrap yard on the planet Boonta when R2-D2 and C-3PO encountered him during the early days of the Empire. [DTV]

protoplasmic glurpfish One of several species of fish in Terpfen's aquarium in his quarters on Coruscant. [COF]

Provisional Council A temporary body established by the Provisional Government of the New Republic, its main jobs were to provide leadership and direction for the new government and work toward the formal reestablishment of the principles and laws of the Old Republic. Its ruling body was the Inner Council, whose members included Mon Mothma, Admiral Ackbar, and Leia Organa Solo. [HE, HESB]

Proxima Dibal A star orbited by a single desert planet of the same name, the planet is home to feathered song-serpents and the tiny scavengers called dinkos, which emit a highly offensive smell. Both animals are sold in Sabodor's pet shop on Etti IV. [HSE, CSSB]

Prune Face *See* Orrimaarko

Pryodene A synthetic mood-enhancing drug, it is in the same class as pryodase and Algarine torve weed. The drugs are generally harmless and nonaddictive, but they make a being lower its guard by becoming more friendly and receptive. [POT]

Psadan Short and stocky humanoids, they live on the long-forgotten world of Wayland. Thick, stonelike scales cover their bodies, forming irregular, lumpy shells over each Psadan's back. The Psadan share Wayland with the Myneyrsh and human colonists, and the groups have engaged in open hostilities in the past. The Psadan have a primitive society. Their primary weapons are bows and arrows, and animals are used for transportation and freight. [HE, HESB, LC]

Ptaa, Eet The leader of a clan of Jawas who were attacked and driven from their fortress by Sand People. [TMEC]

P'tan, Professor A professor from Beshka University who tried to interview Jabba the Hutt for academic reasons, he was never heard from again. His colleague, Melvosh Bloor, came to Jabba's palace months later to investigate his friend's disappearance, only to learn that the professor had been fed to the Sarlaac to amuse Jabba. [TJP]

Ptera system Site of the planet Flax, homeworld of the insectoid species known as the Flakax. [GG4]

pterosaur A carnivorous flying reptile, it is found on the planet Ammuud. [HSR]

Public Safety Service The successor organization to the Corellian Security Force. [BW]

pubtrans flitter A public transportation system, it is used mainly by the less well-off inhabitants of heavily developed planets such as Coruscant. [SOTE]

Puhr, Djas A male Sakiyan bounty hunter, he was in the Mos Eisley cantina on a job when Luke Skywalker and Han Solo first met. [CCG]

Pui-ui Small, sentient beings about 1.25 meters tall, they are natives of the planet Kyryll's World. A Pui-ui consists of two spherical bodies connected by a short neck. Projections growing out of the base of the bottom sphere provide them with the ability to move around. Their language consists of a wide range of shrill sounds. [HLL]

Pulsar Skate This modified *Baudo*-class star yacht, powered by twin ion engines, was formerly captained by Booster Terrik. Mirax Terrik, his daughter, now carries on the family tradition of smuggling black-market

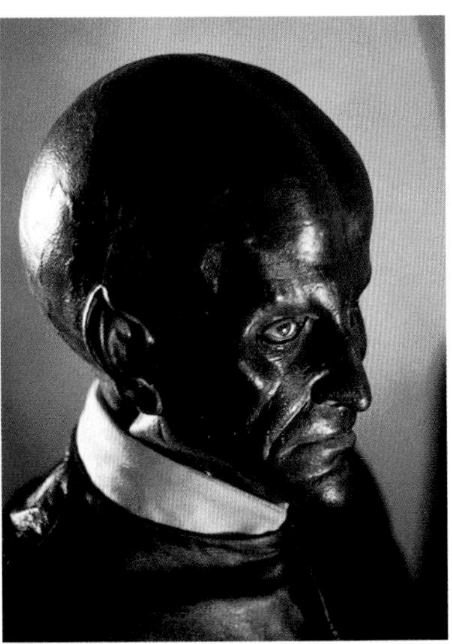

Djas Puhr

goods. This sleek vessel, at 37.5 meters, very much resembles the Corellian deep-sea skate for which it was named. The *Pulsar Skate* was saved from the Empire's grasp when Rogue Squadron was pulled out of hyperspace on its journey to establish a new base at Talasea. After a fierce battle, the Rebels were able to rout the *Black Asp* interdictor cruiser and continue their journey. Because Corran Horn's X-wing was disabled, the *Skate* was obliged to ferry it to Talasea for repairs.

Between shipments, Mirax and the *Skate* were instrumental in the retrieval of the stranded Rebel operatives on Hensara III, where she worked with Rogue Squadron. She later rescued Corran Horn once again during the second raid on Borleias, when his ship ran low on fuel. Her ship was used to bring back political prisoners from Kessel after the Squadron had arranged their release. The *Skate*'s most important contribution to the Alliance cause came when it was used to penetrate Coruscant and deliver a Rogue team on a covert mission to Invisec. [RS, WG, KT]

Punishing One A Corellian Jumpmaster 5000, it is owned and piloted by the bounty hunter Dengar. The ship features an impressive array of weapons, including proton torpedoes, a quad blaster, and a miniature ion cannon. [TBH]

Purity A Yevetha battle cruiser commanded by Vol Noorr, it was the ship that destroyed the *Astrolabe*, a

New Republic astrographic probe, at Doornik-1142. [BTS]

P'w'eck A sentient saurian species enslaved by the reptilian Ssi-ruuk, the dull-brown-colored adults grow to 1.5 meters tall and have heavy eyes and sagging skin. At the age of twenty, they are customarily enteched—a particularly gruesome process in which their life energies are absorbed into battery coils that are used to power circuitry. [TAB]

Pydyr One of the moons of Almania, it was where the Dark Jedi Kueller killed 1,651,305 people during the first bombing campaign in his reign of terror against the New Republic. Pydyr's aristocratic class was the inspiration for stories told all over the local section of the galaxy. Pydyr was an exceptionally wealthy world, crossed by beautiful sandstone streets. The Pydyrians mainly pursued lives of leisure and even had a special droid designed for street care and another for washing buildings. The planet's architecture was often bold, and heavy brown columns and large square rooms dominated the designs. Every surface was covered with decoration, some handpainted by famous artists long dead, others studded with tiny seafah jewels, the source of Pyryr's great wealth. The Pydyrian healing stick originated here. The atmosphere was warm, with dry air that contained a touch of salt. [NR]

Pylokam A very old human, he ran an unsuccessful health food booth in Mos Eisley, selling fruit juices and steamed balls of grated vegetables. People met at his stand to transact shady deals, knowing they wouldn't be interrupted there. [TMEC]

Pypin One of the Trianii colony worlds, it is within the disputed border of the Corporate sector. [CSSB]

Pyria system Located only hours from the Mirit and Venjagga systems at the edge of the Galactic Core, the system's fourth planet is Borleias. Pyria's only inhabited world, it was the base of operations for Gen. Evir Derricote, commander of Imperial forces in the Pyria system. After the New Republic routed the Imperials, it fortified Borleias as a forward base even as ships sent by Warlord Zsinj began making reconnaissance raids into the system. [WG]

Pzob The third planet in the K749 system, this world of thick, ancient forests was colonized by a group of Gamorreans many years ago. Some eighteen years before the Battle of Yavin, the Empire established a base on Pzob where forty-five stormtroopers were to await pickup by the *Eye of Palpatine*. The battlemoon never arrived, and over the years every stormtrooper except Triv Pothman was killed by internal fighting or constant skirmishes with the Gamorreans. Pothman served as a slave in the Gamorrean Gakfedd clan village for two years, followed by a year with the Klagg clan. Eight years after the Battle of Endor, Luke Skywalker and his companions landed on Pzob, where a ship from the *Eye of Palpatine* captured them, Pothman, and the Klagg and Gakfedd clans. [COJ]

Q9-X2 A jet-black droid, he more or less resembles a taller, thinner version of R2-D2. Q9-X2 speaks Basic and moves around on wheels or repulsorlifts. He designs his own improvements, which total more than half his equipment. Q9 is based on the R7 droid, a more advanced version of the R2 series. Han Solo ordered Q9 to protect his family, and to improve his capability for doing so, the droid installed sophisticated detection and observation equipment. [AC]

Qalita Prime A New Republic member world, it is located in the Seventh Security Zone. Twelve years after the Battle of Endor, pirate attacks near Qalita Prime had grown so severe that cargo syndicates threatened to stop supplying the world. The Right Earl of Qalita Prime traveled to Coruscant to seek help against the pirates, and Admiral Ackbar suggested that the newly commissioned Fifth Fleet be dispatched as a show of support. [BTS]

Qaqquqqu, Lord One of the followers of Lord Hethrir, he was a slave trader. [CS]

Qat Chrystac The planet was the site of a battle between the forces of Gen. Garm Bel Iblis and Grand Admiral Thrawn, who used Interdictor Cruisers to bring his ships out of hyperspace at precise locations. More than one assault was staged, and Wedge Antilles helped battle two squadrons of cloned TIE pilots during the first. Imperial shock forces worked their way across Qat Chrystac during Thrawn's siege of Coruscant. Bel Iblis was at Qat Chrystac when he intercepted a distress call from Lando Calrissian's Nomad City mining complex on Nkllon. [LC]

Q-E, 2-E, and U-E Three small droids, these "antiques" were forced to assemble illegal blasters by Master Vuldo, who blasted U-E, leaving only his cognitive unit. Saved by the timely intervention of Nak Pitareeze and C-3PO, U-E's memory banks were placed into a labor droid. [D]

Qel-Droma, Cay A Jedi instructed by Master Arca Jeth at his training compound on Arkania some 4,000 years before the Galactic Civil War, he and his brother and fellow Jedi, Ulic, had been born on Alderaan to a great warrior family. Cay was mechanically minded and always tinkered with machines. He lost his left arm during the Beast Wars of Onderon and replaced it himself during the battle with a prosthetic limb made from parts of an abandoned XT-6 service droid. When his brother, Ulic, turned to the dark side of the Force, Cay never stopped trying to bring him back to the light side. In a final confrontation, Ulic murdered Cay—an act that immediately filled him with horror and regret. [TOJ, DLS, TSW]

Cay Qel-Droma

Qel-Droma, Ulic A powerful young Jedi some 4,000 years before the Galactic Civil War, he thought he could learn the ways of the dark side and then return with this knowledge to the light side, but his failure wreaked havoc on the galaxy. Trained along with his younger brother, Cay, on the mining world of Arkania by Jedi Master Arca Jeth, Ulic Qel-Droma quickly mastered the art of lightsaber dueling. Even at that point, his self-confidence and brashness made some think him arrogant.

When Master Arca felt they were ready, he sent the Qel-Dromas and their training partner, Tott Doneeta, to Onderon to help put an end to the violent, centuries-long civil war between the walled city dwellers and the outlanders who had tamed giant warbeasts. Things were not as they first seemed. The walled city, Iziz, was still full of dark-side power some 400 years after the fall of a Sith practitioner named Freedon Nadd. After some difficulties, Master Arca arrived and helped the outlanders win the war. Investigating the dark-side forces, the Jedi found the crypt of Freedon Nadd. An uprising by Nadd's followers had to be put down by Jedi and Republic reinforcements.

Other problems arose. Ulic was growing fond of another Jedi, Nomi Sunrider, but was pulled away when he was named Watchman of the Empress Teta system. Freedon Nadd's spirit had exposed two spoiled royals there to Sith teachings, and they had formed a group of dark-side magic users called the Krath, which fomented war among the Teta system planets. Ulic decided that the only way to truly defeat the Krath was to infiltrate them and learn their secrets. Aleema and Satal Keto played along with Ulic, but Satal injected him with a slow-acting poison that would make his eventual return to the light side impossible. He survived an assassination attempt by Satal and saw Nomi escape imprisonment by Satal just hours before Ulic had agreed to kill her to prove his loyalty to the Krath. Nomi and Cay Qel-Droma failed in their attempt to convince Ulic to escape with them. Anger inside Ulic exploded, leading him to kill Satal. Aleema gave Ulic half a Sith amulet that had been given to Satal by the spirit of Freedon Nadd.

Ulic was then confronted by an-

Ulic Qel-Droma

other fallen Jedi, Exar Kun. As they engaged in a lightsaber battle, the Sith amulets both Jedi wore began to glow, and they were visited by spirits of ancient Sith Lords who told them that Kun was the new Dark Lord of the Sith and Qel-Droma his first assistant. Years later Ulic reappeared with tremendous dark-side powers, and set out to plunder and destroy large parts of the galaxy with a large and bloodthirsty army serving alongside Exar Kun. The Jedi Knights and the Republic declared Ulic an enemy, and the subsequent battles became known as the Sith Wars—one of the largest and bloodiest conflagrations ever witnessed, with millions dead as a result. In the end, though, Ulic Qel-Droma betrayed Exar Kun, leading the assembled Jedi against the Sith Lord's base of power on the moon of Yavin 4. Qel-Droma himself was robbed of his Jedi powers by Nomi Sunrider. [TOJ]

Qella (Maltha Obex) A dead planet in a system of the same name, it was once home to a species also known as the Qella, which had apparently been extinct for more than 150 standard years. The Qella's ancient ancestors are the Qonet, who were in turn descended from the Ahra Naffi. (A related species, also descended from the Ahra Naffi eons ago, are the Khotta of the planet Kho Nai.) The Qella had oval bodies and four long, double-jointed limbs with three-fingered hands. They communicated in a pitch-based language. They were one of only six recorded species that had eighteen different molecular pairs in their genetic code, and their bodies also contained billions of Eicroth bodies, tiny capsules that contain extra genetic material that are blueprints for constructing artifacts.

Qella's atmosphere was too thick for humans to breathe unassisted. Before their extinction, the Qella developed the technology to colonize other planets but chose instead to remain on their homeworld. They were first contacted by a small survey vessel of the Third General Survey, an Old Republic program established to explore the habitable planets in the galaxy's spiral arms; the ship recorded a Qella population of seven million. When a larger contact vessel arrived just eight years later, Qella was completely lifeless, with more than a third of its surface covered with kilometer-thick ice and its oceans choked with glaciers. Analysts speculated that several large asteroid impacts had destroyed the planet's ecosystem and killed off all its native species. The contact vessel collected several genetic and archaeological specimens from the ruined civilization and a comprehensive follow-up visit was planned, but the outbreak of the Clone Wars brought an end to the Third General Survey. The Tobek species later arrived and claimed the barren planet, giving it the name of Maltha Obex, which still appears on many charts.

Twelve years after the Battle of Endor, an archaeological team from the Obroan Institute was dispatched to Qella to search for any clues about the mysterious ghost ship called the Teljkon vagabond. The researchers found what they thought to be bodies beneath the ice but were killed by an avalanche when they tried to investigate. A second research team, sponsored by Admiral Drayson, was then dispatched to the planet.

Before the destruction, it was discovered that Qella was a reddish-brown planet with blue oceans and black mountain ranges, orbiting a pale yellow star and orbited by red and gray moons. The star was called M'oka Brath by the Qella, and the planet called Brath Qella. When the Qella realized that the smaller of their two moons would smash into the planet in a hundred years, they buried themselves deep in the ground and constructed an organic starship (which became known as the Teljkon vagabond) to eventually return, thaw out the planet, and restore them to life. With help from Luke Skywalker, the vagabond began the process of thawing the planet and restoring Qella society. [BTS, SOL, TT]

Qonet *See* Qella (Maltha Obex)

Qorl A TIE fighter pilot, rank number CE3K-1977, he piloted a ship damaged in a crossfire between Rebels and Imperials. Because his comm channels were jammed and his orbit decayed, he crash-landed on Yavin 4. The jungle cushioned his fall, and he was thrown out of his craft, badly injuring his arm. Qorl wasn't heard from for more than twenty years, until Lowbacca, a Jedi trainee, discovered the crashed fighter overgrown with jungle plants. He and Jaina and Jacen Solo restored the craft, and then were surprised when Qorl appeared. The pilot kidnapped the Solo twins and attempted to make an escape. The twins were rescued, but Qorl fled in his restored fighter.

Qorl then joined the turncoat Jedi Brakiss and the Shadow Academy and was put in charge of training those youths who weren't Force-sensitive to be stormtroopers. He successfully led a daring assault on the New Republic cruiser *Adamant*, stealing both the ship and its precious cargo of weapons and supplies. During a battle to destroy the Jedi academy on Yavin 4, he was shot down again. Because the Shadow Academy had been destroyed and he despised the New Republic, he decided to live out his life in the planet's jungles. [YJK]

Qretu-Five A lush, verdant planet with towering mountains and a warm, moist climate, it is the site of a bacta-producing colony overseen by colonists from the bacta-producing planet Thyferra. Qretu-Five is surrounded by a ring of asteroids that are clearly visible in the night sky. After the members of Rogue Squadron resigned from the New Republic military some three years after the Battle of Endor, they destroyed the Q5A7 Bacta Refinement Plant on Qretu-Five in order to hurt Imperial Ysanne Isard's bacta-producing capability. [BW]

Quad laser cannon

Qrygg, Ooryl A Gand member of Rogue Squadron, Qrygg first befriended fellow Rogue Corran Horn during their training exercises on Folor. After Qrygg joined the Squadron, he took part in the battles at Chorax and Hensara III. Because Gands need only a fraction of the sleep humans do, he was awake when stormtroopers landed at the Rogue base at Talasea in a secret attack. He and Horn alerted the rest of the Squadron and a furious fight began. Qrygg's bravery averted almost certain death for most of his fellow pilots.

Ooryl Qrygg was part of the strike team that scored a retaliatory blow at Vladet, but he was also on the disastrous first mission to Borleias. During the battle, his X-wing was destroyed. Qrygg ejected in time, but as he floated in space, a fragment of the fighter's S-foils sliced through his right arm, severing it above the elbow. Several weeks later, his arm had regenerated itself so well that he was able to take part in the Squadron's covert operations on Coruscant. His presence was vital to the mission's success. After his group of operatives had gained access to Subsidiary Computer Center Number Four, they found it was impossible to enter the control room because it was flooded with Fex-M3d, an Imperial nerve gas. Because Gands don't breathe like humans, Qrygg was able to enter the room to gain access to the gas masks inside, enabling the others to follow. From there they were able to realign the OSETS 2711 satellite, burn up a nearby reservoir, create a terrific thunderstorm, and help bring down Coruscant's planetary defense shields. [RS, WG]

quad laser cannon A starship blaster, it is often slung in turret mounts to take advantage of its lightweight, quick-targeting motions. [CCG, SWRPG]

Quamar Messenger A luxury spaceliner, it carries up to 600 passengers and a crew of forty-five. The *Quamar Messenger* has a hyperdrive engine, allowing it to travel at lightspeed. The ship was highjacked on its maiden voyage by the gunfighter Gallandro. [HLL, GSWU]

Quanta sector Formerly ruled by Moff Jerjerrod, it contains the planet Tinnel IV. [SWAJ]

Quanto A henchman of Great Bogga the Hutt, he was among those responsible for the murder of Jedi Andur Sunrider at the Stenness hyperspace terminal about 4,000 years before the Galactic Civil War. Andur's wife, Nomi, then killed Quanto with Andur's lightsaber in self-defense. [TOJ]

quarra Domesticated hunting animals, they are mainly found on the planet Devaron. Devaronians publicly execute their most notorious criminals by throwing them to packs of wild quarra. [TBH]

quarrel Energy projectiles fired by a Wookiee bowcaster, they explode upon impact with a target. [RJN]

Quarren Amphibious beings that share the world of Mon Calamari with the Mon Calamari species, they are frequently called Squid Heads. Quarren are distinguished by the four tentacles that protrude from their jaws, their leathery skin, their suction-cupped fingers, and their turquoise eyes. Quarren prefer the depths of the planet's floating cities to the upper reaches the Mon Cals

Quarren

Sixtus Quin

call home. The Quarren are more practical and conservative than their worldmates. The sea dwellers are able to live out of the water if they keep their skin moist but prefer the ocean depths. The Quarren have become dependent on the Mon Calamarians, and this reliance has led to resentment among the Mon Cal, even breeding rumors that a small number of Quarren helped the Empire in the first invasion of Mon Calamari. Many Quarren have left the planet and have ended up at the fringes of society, often working with pirates, slavers, and smugglers. [SWSB]

Quay The Weequay god of the moon. [TJP]

quay A device used by Weequays to contact their god, Quay. It consists of a white sphere made of high-impact plastic that can recognize speech and reply to simple questions. The device is manufactured cheaply by smarter species and sold to the Weequays. [TJP]

queblux power train A cheap but relatively inefficient power source, it is used in such places as the Mos Eisley cantina. [TMEC]

Queen of Ranroon A cargo vessel, it carried the spoils gathered by Xim the Despot during his galactic conquests. The now-legendary *Queen of Ranroon* never reached its final destination. It was either lost or destroyed with its incalculably rich treasures, thus giving rise to wild spacer stories. A sort of ghost ship, there were occasional reports of its sighting and finding it became a preoccupation for some. Even Han Solo took part in a hunt for the ship and its treasures prior to his involvement in the Rebellion. [HSR, HLL]

Quelii sector The sector containing the planet Dathomir, it was once under the control of Imperial Warlord Zsinj. [CPL]

Quella A pale, slender, brown-haired woman, she was a thief who could often be found hiding out in the palace of Jabba the Hutt. [TJP]

quickclay A viscous gray-green soil, it covers much of the planet Circarpous V. Like quicksand, the soft, shifting quickclay yields easily to pressure and tends to suck up objects. [SME]

Quill-Face, Hideaz A three-meter-tall smuggler, he is of an unidentified species. Hideaz Quill-Face works with a partner, Spog, and the pair can often be found in the Byss Bistro. [DE]

Quin, Sixtus A former Special Intelligence Operative, he conducted several missions for the Empire. When betrayed by his Imperial commander, he defected to the Rebel Alliance, where his talents were more than welcome. When Sixtus Quin learned that Rogue Squadron needed someone with his qualifications, he immediately applied for the assignment. It had become necessary to topple Ysanne Isard's puppet government on Thyferra after her thirst for power and money put her in control of the bacta cartel. He was sent to the planet to organize an uprising among the Ashern Rebels and the surviving members of the Zaltin Corporation. For several weeks he trained the volunteers in all kinds of fighting skills and terrorist activities. Their combined efforts paid off when the ground assault began. While the battle raged in orbit over Thyferra, his operatives quickly took command of Isard's headquarters. The takeover was accomplished with very little loss of life, demonstrating his skills as an instructor and a fighter. [XW, BW]

Quintar Nebula Found on few star charts, this thick mass of colorful, swirling clouds can blind sensors and ionize flight-control systems. Tron Nixx, the navigator for Drek Drednar's pirate crew, used the Force to chart a safe route through the Quintar Nebula, where he discovered the hidden world of Taraloon. [SWAJ]

Quor'sav A tall, warm-blooded avian species whose females lay eggs. Its members average 3.5 meters in height. Quor'sav have long, spindly legs and need custom-built space vessels to allow for their height. [CCG]

Q-Varx, Senator A New Republic Council member, he leads the Rationalist Party on his homeworld of Mon Calamari. Enchanted by gadgetry, he purchased an executive honor guard of human-looking synthdroids. Senator Q-Varx accepted a bribe to arrange the secret meeting between Chief of State Leia Organa Solo and Nam Chorios strongman Seti Ashgad. [POT]

R1 unit The first of the R-series droids developed by Industrial Automaton. To save money they used the same body shells as Mark II reactor drones. These tall, cylindrical droids are now nearly obsolete. [SWAJ]

R1-G4 Like old-model astromechs still used on capital starships and large freighters, this droid has an ar-

R1-G4

mored Mark II Reactor drone shell. R1-G4 was abandoned after the capture of his owner. It was one of the droids rounded up from a Jawa sandcrawler when a squad of stormtroopers was searching for R2-D2 and C-3PO. [CCG]

R2-D2 (Artoo-Detoo) A three-legged R2-series astromech utility droid, usually teamed with a fussy golden protocol droid named C-3PO, he is one of the most famous automatons in the galaxy. The squat, barrel-shaped R2-D2 may emit a limited vocabulary of beeps and whistles, but his programming has evolved a near-human personality that is brash and bold. Artoo-Detoo is designed to operate in deep space, interfacing with fighter craft and computer systems in order to augment the capabilities of ships and their pilots. He is usually placed in a socket behind the cockpit, where he monitors and diagnoses flight performance, maps and stores hyperspace data, and pinpoints technical errors or faulty computer coding. He is well versed in starship repair for hundreds of styles of spacecraft and can exist in the vacuum of space indefinitely.

Artoo converses in an information-dense electronic language that sounds to the untrained ear like beeps, boops, chirps, and whistles. Although he can understand most forms of human speech, Artoo's own communications must be interpreted by Threepio or by ship computers to which he sends electronic data. Artoo's fully rotational domed head contains infrared receptors, electromagnetic-field sensors, a register readout and logic dispenser, dedicated energy receptors, a radar eye, heat and motion detectors, and a holographic recorder and projector. Behind doors in his cylindrical body lie hidden instruments, including a storage/retrieval jack for computer linkup, auditory receivers, flame-retardant foam dispenser, electric shock prod, high-powered spotlight, grasping claw, laser welder, circular saw, and a cybot acoustic signaler.

Two treaded legs provide the meter-high droid with mobility, and a third leg can drop down for extra stability on rough terrain. Artoo also has flotation devices and a periscoping visual scanner to guide him while submerged.

Artoo has developed an odd relationship with Threepio over the years. The protocol droid behaves like a fussy mother hen, almost constantly cajoling, belittling, or arguing with his squat counterpart. Artoo appears loyal, inventive, and sarcastic. Although he always seems to egg Threepio on, they have deep mutual respect and trust for each other.

While their earliest history is clouded, one master, a notorious smuggler, abandoned the droids on the arid planet Ingo, where they were soon adopted by a young speeder racer named Thall Joben. Other masters included Jann Tosh, Mungo Baobab, the Pitareeze family, and the Royal House of Alderaan. Both droids were aboard the *Tantive IV* when it was caught by the Imperial Star Destroyer *Devastator*. Princess Leia Organa then placed stolen data plans for an Imperial super weapon into R2-D2 and told him to take them to Obi-Wan Kenobi somewhere in the Tatooine desert. The droids, working mainly for Luke Skywalker, became deeply involved in the Galactic Civil War.

R2-D2 rode with Skywalker when Luke fired the famous shot that destroyed the first Death Star. The droid was hit by a laser blast in the process, and when Skywalker visited swampy Dagobah to start his Jedi training with Master Yoda, Artoo suffered a few indignities at Yoda's hands. The droid also played a prominent role in the rescue of Han Solo from the palace of Jabba the Hutt, hiding Skywalker's lightsaber until the moment it became vital.

When the clone of Emperor Palpatine surfaced and brought Luke under his dark-side tutelage, several of Artoo's files were replaced. The droid soon realized that Skywalker was transmitting Master Control Signals, which would later aid New Republic forces. The signals helped shut down the massive World Devastators as they ravaged Mon Calamari, proving that Luke's allegiance had remained with the Republic all along.

Artoo has stayed mainly with Skywalker, helping in his exploits and in setting up a Jedi academy, although he was "droidnapped" by Lando Calrissian on his mission to unravel the mystery of the Teljkon vagabond ghost ship.

Artoo was annoyed to discover that a new X-wing design class replaced astromech droids with integrated computer circuitry. Along with C-3PO and Cole Fardreamer, Artoo eventually helped uncover a sabotage scheme by the Dark Jedi Kueller: The new X-wings were secretly equipped with an explosive device as part of the upgrade. As part of Fardreamer's investigation, Artoo went to Telti and confronted a terrifying gladiator-droid group known as the Red Terror. When Kueller was about to detonate the explosive devices he had planted in droids on worlds throughout the New Republic, R2-D2 deactivated the remote detonators that would have triggered the explosions, saving the New Republic from devastation. [SW, ESB, RJ, DE, D, DTV, NR]

R2-D2 (Artoo-Detoo)

R2-X2

R2-Q2 An R2 unit, it spent several decades serving with an Imperial reconnaissance fleet in the Expansion Region aboard the Star Destroyer *Devastator.* [CCG]

R2 unit One of the most popular astromech droid models in service, this utility model was designed to operate in hostile environments, especially deep space. By plugging into terminals or ship-interface sockets, R2 units can augment and enhance the computer capabilities of starships. These droids assist with piloting and navigation and serve as onboard repair and maintenance technicians. About one meter tall, they are built by Industrial Automaton. [SW, ESB, RJ, SWSB]

R2-X2 A typical starfighter assistant, it contained ten coordinates for hyperspace jumps. R2-X2 carried built-in tools and a computer interface. The droid was assigned to Red Ten during the Battle of Yavin and was destroyed when Red Ten's X-wing was destroyed. [CCG]

R-3PO (Ar-Threepio) A protocol droid, he was specially modified by the Rebel Alliance as a defense against Imperial espionage droids. R-3PO's job is to join a droid pool and uncover any spies through careful observation. Ar-Threepio has a distinguishing mark: a tattoo reading "Thank the maker" on his left posterior plating. [CCG]

R3-T6 This droid served aboard the first Death Star. Like most R3 units, it had a larger memory and more advanced circuitry than its R1 and R2 predecessors, allowing for more efficient astrogation. R3-T6 was destroyed when the battle station was blown up by the Rebel Alliance. [CCG]

R3-T6

R3 unit Developed for service aboard capital warships and battle stations, these droids look much like R2 units except for their clear plastex domes, which reveal their computer processors. [SWAJ]

R4-E1 One of the numerous vehicle computer-operation droids manufactured by Industrial Automaton, R4-E1 is a companion of BoShek. The droid's personality is rambunctious, fiery, and independent. [CCG]

R4-M9 A typical multiple-use droid, it mainly controls and repairs vehicles and computers. R4-M9 was once used by the Empire to pull data from the computer banks of the *Tantive IV.* It was stationed aboard the Star Destroyer *Devastator.* [CCG]

R-3PO (Ar-Threepio)

R4-E1

R4 unit These droids were developed by Industrial Automaton after complaints that the company's R2 units were too expensive and the R3 units were more suited to military duties. The R4 is an urban droid, designed to function well with speeders and other vehicles. The units have some astromech capability and can calculate and store data for a single hyperspace jump. They are similar in appearance to R2 units except for their truncated, conical heads. [SWAJ]

R5-D4 An inexpensive astromech droid commonly referred to as Red, it

R5-D4

R5-M2

R4-M9

allowed R2-D2 to program its motivator to blow up after R2 communicated its orders from Princess Leia Organa to R5. The motivator malfunction allowed R2-D2 and C-3PO to remain together. R5-D4 was later repaired and sold to another moisture farm. R5 is a poor navigator but a skilled mechanic. [CCG]

R5-M2 (Arfive-Emmtoo) A member of the commercially unsuccessful R5 series of droids, which nonetheless were in high demand for combat starships during the Galactic Civil War, this unit was owned by Shawn Valdez, a popular Rebel Alliance officer. R5-M2 was programmed to plot sublight tactical courses and was extremely valuable in planning evacuation routes from Echo Base during the Battle of Hoth. [CCG]

R5 unit An astromech droid like the popular R2 series, it performs many of the same functions but is cheaper.

R5 unit

While R5 units are skilled mechanics, they can't come close to matching the navigational or other skills of R2 units. [SWR]

R6 unit Developed after the fall of the Empire, these droids were part of the much-vaunted "new beginning" at Industrial Automaton after the failure of its R5 line. The R6 units were developed to be as versatile as R2 units but to sell at a lower price in the turbulent economy of the New Republic. [SWAJ]

R7-T1 An R7-series astromech droid, it was assigned to Luke Skywalker's E-wing fighter. [BTS]

R7 unit One of the latest series of astromech droids, these military models are designed specifically to interface with the latest E-wing starfighters. [DE]

RA-7 A line of servant droids, they have fifth-degree primary programming and low intelligence; they are useful mainly as menial laborers. They are common among nobles and high-ranking officials. [CCG]

Ra, Vonnda An evil new-breed Nightsister from Dathomir, she helped the Second Imperium recruit trainees from the various clans on her homeworld. She died in the jaws of a syren plant on Kashyyyk. [YJK]

Raabakyysh A Wookiee, she was an admirer of Lowbacca and best friend of his younger sister, Sirrakuk. She decided to impress Lowbacca by attempting to perform her Wookiee Rite of Passage alone, without telling anyone. She never returned. The only trace of her was her bloodstained backpack. [YJK]

Raalk, Proctor Ton A civic leader, he headed the government of Giat Nor, capital city of N'zoth, the Yevetha spawnworld. [SOL]

Rachuk roseola A skin virus, it leaves reddish raw patches on everyone who visits the planet Vladet. [RS]

Rachuk sector Lying close to the Galactic Core, it borders the Morobe sector and contains the Chorax, Hensara, and Rachuk systems. The Rachuk sector was controlled from an Imperial base on Vladet in the Rachuk system. [RS]

Rachuk system Located in the Rachuk sector, this system contains the planet Vladet, site of an Imperial sector headquarters. A great deal of trade and shipping traffic passes through the centrally located Rachuk system. The Rachuk roseola virus infects anyone visiting the system, manifesting itself as a red, itchy rash. Some three years after the Battle of Endor, the Alliance destroyed the Vladet base and forced the Empire to divert more of its forces to the Rachuk system, diluting its strength elsewhere. [RS]

Rafa III The location of a deep-bore mining operation using laser drill bits. [LCM]

Rafa IV The center of government for the Rafa system, it was ruled by colonial governor Duttes Mer until he was overthrown by the resurgent Toka. Rafa IV's main spaceport city, Teguta Lusat, lies wedged amid the colossal plastic ruins of the Sharu. The city contains numerous taverns, the Hotel Sharu, and a penal colony where prisoners serve their sentences

RA-7

harvesting crystals from the life orchards. [LCM, LCF]

Rafa V A frozen, dry world of red sand where archaeoastronomers believe that the ancient Sharu evolved. Orbiting the world are Rafa V's twin moons and a cloud of debris that might be the result of the Sharu's early attempts at space flight. Its many life orchards are harvested by a few hundred convicts, horticulturists, and Toka living in scattered settlements. A colossal Sharu pyramid, rising seven kilometers above ground level, towers over the other ruins of Rafa V and was the resting place of the famous artifact called the Mindharp. [LCM]

Rafa XI The outermost planet in the Rafa system, it is a world of icy slush orbiting in the dark. Rafa XI is the site of a research installation and a helium refinery. [LCM]

Rafa system Bordering the Oseon system, the eleven planets and numerous moons of the system are covered with the enormous plastic ruins of the ancient Sharu species. The impenetrable buildings are among the largest constructions in the galaxy. Many human colonies, dating from the early days of the Old Republic, have sprung up around and between the structures. The Rafa system was also inhabited by a primitive humanoid species known as the Toka, who were treated as slaves by the Rafa colonists. The system is famous for its life orchards—groves of crystalline trees whose crystal "fruit" can extend an individual's life when harvested and worn. Working among the crystal trees, however, drains a person's life and intellect, and consequently most of the harvesting was done by the enslaved Toka or criminals in the system's numerous penal colonies. Following Lando Calrissian's procurement of the Mindharp from Rafa V, it turned out that the Toka were actually the Sharu. When they had been subjugated, their mental abilities were suppressed. They regained those abilities along with their civilization. [LCM]

Rafft A green, forested world with several modest settlements, it was the site of a twelve-member Rebel base located in a complex of caves

Rakazzak beast

just prior to the Battle of Yavin. The Rebels, led by Commander Brion Peck, were sent to Rafft to sabotage the construction of an Imperial garrison. The group was evacuated by the smuggler Dannen Lifehold after a homing beacon betrayed the base's location. [SWAJ]

Raithal Site of the Raithal Academy, the most prestigious training center in the Empire. After the Battle of Yavin, medical experts from Raithal were sent to an orbiting hospital frigate to study the outbreak of Candorian plague on Dentaal. [SWAJ]

rakazzak beast Spiderlike, three-meter-tall creatures that live on the forest moon of Endor, they are often ridden by Yuzzum warriors. Rakazzaks spin thick, sticky webs to trap their enemies. [ETV]

Rakrir Homeworld of a sentient insectoid species, its inhabitants are wealthy, highly cultured, and finicky. Few leave Rakrir because they are usually dissatisfied with the level of sophistication on other planets. Sabodor, owner of Sabodor's pet store on Etti IV, was a native of Rakrir. [HSE, CSSB]

Ra-Lee The beautiful tan-furred Ewok who was married to Chief Chirpa, she died defending her daughters, Kneesaa and Asha. [ETV]

R'all The fraternal twin of J'uoch, he ran a mining concern on the planet Dellalt with his brother. A human, R'all had straight brown hair with a widow's peak and pale skin set off by black-iris eyes. Along with his sister, the unscrupulous R'all competed with Han Solo to be the first to find the lost treasures of the legendary ship, *Queen of Ranroon*. [HLL]

R'alla mineral water Known for its purity and medicinal benefits, this liquid comes from springs in the underground caverns of the mountain town of R'alla on the planet of the same name. R'alla mineral water is also a main ingredient in certain bootleg intoxicants, and smugglers make substantial profits by bringing it to other worlds. Han Solo and Chewbacca once made a living smuggling the mineral water to the planet Rampa. [HSR, HLL]

Ralls, Agent A New Republic Intelligence agent, he was sent to question prisoner Davith Sconn, imprisoned at Jagg Island Detention Center, about what he knew about the Yevethan military fleet. [SOL]

Ralltiir Located in the system of the same name, it lies along the Perlemian Trade Route in the Darpa sector of the Core Worlds, just on the border of the Colonies region. Over the last several hundred years, Ralltiir was the only planet in the Darpa sector able to maintain its independence from the nearby world of Esseles. In recent history, Ralltiir was an attractive, high-technology world famous for its banking industry and home to the Grallia Spaceport.

The planet's powerful financial institutions were politically neutral and had a reputation as a safe haven for investors' funds. With the rise of the Empire, certain factions infiltrated Ralltiir's financial system and began to steer its markets in a pro-Imperial direction, by erasing the fiscal records of nonhuman investors, for instance. Shortly before the Battle of Yavin, pro-Alliance members of the Ralltiir High Council tried to restore balance to the markets. Their efforts inspired the Emperor to use Ralltiir as an example to other worlds that would resist his will. A brutal Imperial force, led by Lord Tion, invaded Ralltiir and devastated the planet and its ten billion inhabitants. Tion disbanded the High Council, replaced it with a military tribunal headed by Imperial Governor Dennix Graeber, and set up interrogation

Ralltiir

centers and public executions of Rebel leaders. He also sealed off the entire Ralltiir system (even barring relief organizations from traveling through his blockade), which severely hurt commerce along the Perlemian Trade Route.

Princess Leia Organa, on a mercy mission to deliver medical supplies and equipment to the High Council of Ralltiir, was permitted to land by Tion. The princess rescued a wounded Rebel soldier, who later revealed the existence of the Death Star project. Ralltiir's economy had been left in ruins, and many powerful corporations relocated off-world. But Governor Graeber got rich by secretly supplying the Rebel underground with weapons, which he then used as a justification to persecute Ralltiir's citizens even more harshly. Before the Battle of Yavin, an Alliance raid on the Cygnus Corporation's starfighter performance trials near Ralltiir resulted in the capture of the Assault Gunboat design team. Inath of Ralltiir, who years later became a member of the New Republic's Council, had seen many of his associates murdered by the Emperor's Noghri assassins, which led him to pressure Chief of State Leia Organa Solo to retire her Noghri bodyguards, claiming that it sent the wrong signal. [SWR, SWSB, MTS, GG2, FP, SWAJ, POT]

Ralrra From ambassador to the Old Republic to slave of the Empire, this tall, powerfully built Wookiee has seen all sides of life from an unusual perspective. Ralrra (short for Ralrracheen) has a speech impediment that allows him to speak Basic, which proved useful when he was Kashyyyk's ambassador to the Old Republic. As a slave to the Empire, he was used by his Imperial masters to communicate with other Wookiees. At first, he tried to resist Imperial occupation forces but forced himself to comply after they executed a dozen women and children from his family unit. His proximity to Imperial officers provided him with information vital to the Alliance's effort to free Kashyyyk. Now, like most Wookiees, he feels he owes a life debt to the Alliance for its efforts. When Chewbacca brought Princess Leia Organa Solo to Kashyyyk to keep her safe from Grand Admiral Thrawn's Noghri Death Commandos, Ralrra was one of two Wookiees assigned to protect her. [HE, HESB]

Ralter, Dack A young Rebel soldier during the Battle of Hoth, he was gunner on Luke Skywalker's snowspeeder. Dack died when Skywalker's snowspeeder took a direct hit from an Imperial walker. [ESB]

Rampa A world of heavy industry in the Corporate sector, Rampa has an extremely high degree of pollution and contamination. The Rampa Skywatch keeps an eye out for water smugglers hidden among the regular cargo traffic, for Rampa's citizens are willing to pay a very high price for pure R'alla mineral water after polluting their own. Han Solo and Chewbacca made some smuggling runs "down the Rampa Rapids" during their early adventures. [HSR, HLL, CSSB]

Rana, Queen An ancient ruler of the planet Duro. A huge monument dedicated to Queen Rana fills the Valley of Royalty on Duro. [MMY]

Dack Ralter

Ranat

Ranat A ratlike species, they call themselves Con Queecon, or "the conquerors," in their native tongue. Ranats are small and cunning, with sharp teeth, whiskers, and long tails. While the meter-high beings appear harmless, they are savage killers with a taste for other intelligent beings. Since the death of Jabba the Hutt, a group of Ranats has taken over the crime lord's Tatooine desert palace. Ranats are mostly scavengers and traders, and they apparently came to Tatooine from the planet Aralia. They are often compared to Jawas despite the fact that they prefer to inhabit highly populated areas. The species was deemed only semisentient by the Empire, so killing them could be more easily justified. The Empire still used them as spies since they worked for relatively little money. [GG4, ZHR, TMEC, TBH, CCG]

rancor A fearsome beast, this carnivore stands about five meters tall, walks on two legs, and has some of the characteristics of a reptile. A rancor has long arms that seem out of proportion, huge fangs, and long, sharp claws. One rancor, a gift to crime lord Jabba the Hutt on his birthday, was kept as a pet in a special pit in Jabba's desert palace on Tatooine. The rancor was both a source of entertainment and a way to get rid of employees and others who failed Jabba. Located under Jabba's court, the pit provided an excellent view of victims struggling to fend off the huge beast. Luke Skywalker was forced to kill the rancor when Jabba dropped him into the pit. Semisen-

Rancor

tient rancors are common on the planet Dathomir, and they have been domesticated and used by the Witches of Dathomir as pack animals and personal mounts. Rancors are also found in the Ottethan system. [RJ, CPL, DE]

Rand Ecliptic A space freighter, it was the first ship that Luke Skywalker's boyhood friend Biggs Darklighter was assigned to after he graduated from the Academy. Darklighter was first mate aboard the *Rand Ecliptic* until he jumped ship to join the Rebellion. [SWN]

Random, Sarl The security chief of Cloud City, she was in charge during the droid EV-9D9's revolt and escape. [TMEC]

Randon A planet known for an alcoholic drink, the Randoni Yellow Plague. On Randon, female ward-cousins are traditionally honored due to their potential inheritance and are customarily served first. Randoni women wear their hair loose and flowing. Luke Skywalker and Tenel Ka posed as archaeological traders from Randon during an undercover mission to Borgo Prime. [YJK]

Raort, Romort An Irith spice-jacker who hangs out on Nar Shaddaa, he is unpopular among underworld cohorts because he has stolen from a number of them. He is left alone because of his association with a gang that takes swift vengeance on those that cross them. Romort Raort and his gang have made a number of deals with the Hutts that allow them to operate along most of the major galactic spice routes. [DE]

Rask A street philosopher in Iziz on Onderon, he was a Naddist, a follower of the Sith apprentice Freedon Nadd. [DLS]

Raskar A one-time space pirate of Iridium in the days of the Old Republic, he, like the others, used unique power gems. The stones, which generated a disrupting aura, helped the pirates break through the shields of their victims' starships. The pirates were wiped out by a force of Jedi. Only Raskar survived, escaping with the sole remaining power gem. He set himself up on a rimworld and invited those who wanted the gem to fight for it in gladiatorial combat; he made his money staging and betting on the fights. Chewbacca managed to beat Raskar's best fighter, and he and Han Solo left with the gem following the Battle of Yavin, although it only had enough power remaining for one final shield disruption. Later, Raskar captured Solo and Luke Skywalker above Hoth, and Solo flew the group to a deep chasm on the planet's equator. There they discovered a hidden cave filled with rare lumni-spice lichens guarded by a fire-breathing dragon-slug and barely escaped with their lives. Raskar redeemed himself on Ord Mantell when he rescued Solo and Skywalker from the bounty hunter Skorr. [CSW]

Raskar

Rathalay Known for its expansive gray basalt beaches, the planet, surprisingly, is seldom crowded with tourists. Rathalay's vast oceans harbor large, dangerous predators, including schools of sharp-toothed narkaa. Its tiny sea motes are valued for the beautiful, jewellike shells they leave behind. Nine hundred meters below the water's surface lies the wreck of the starfreighter *Just Cause*, which crashed while carrying a cargo of precious metals. Twelve years after the Battle of Endor, Han Solo, Leia, and their children relaxed on a Rathalay beach as the crisis in the Koornacht Cluster began unfolding. [SOL]

Rattagagech Chairman of the New Republic's Senate Science Council and senator from Elom, he voted to remove Chief of State Leia Organa Solo from office. [SOL]

Ravager An Imperial *Lancer*-class frigate, it was destroyed during an engagement with Rogue Squadron when it came to the defense of the Imperial installation at Vladet. [RS]

raventhorn A sharp, spiny vine, it is found in the rain forests of Yavin 4. [DA]

rawwks Flying batlike scavengers, they live in many of the floating structures of Bespin and Tibannopolis. They serve as an early warning system for the beldons that they roost upon, scattering when they detect a predator. [JS, ISWU, GG3]

Raynar A young student Jedi, he was especially spoiled and troublesome. Raynar was good-looking, with blue eyes and blond hair that shone like flecks of gold dust. He wore fine garments of purple, gold, and scarlet cloth. He rarely wore plainer garb despite suggestions by Luke Skywalker. [YJK]

ray shielding A force field designed to block and absorb energy fire, it is an essential part of the defensive system of every starfighter and capital ship. [SWN]

Rayter sector A galactic sector that contains the planet Karra, which is located in Rayter's largely unexplored rimward section. [SWAJ]

razor moss A plant that grows on arid Tatooine, it chews into shadowed rock and uses corrosive root tendrils to break down crystals and chemically extract water molecules. Sandjiggers and cliffborer worms feed on razor moss. [ISWU]

reactivate switch A droid's master circuit breaker, it is used to turn the robots on and off. [SWR]

realspace Normal space, it is the dimension in which galactic residents live. Travel within realspace is slow compared to traveling through the shadow-dimension called hyperspace. It has distance and volume. [SWRPG, SWRPG2]

rearing spider Massive but slow-moving, this creature from the forest moon of Endor has six legs and large tusks. Rearing spiders live in the bottom of caves of the Gorax. [ISWU]

Rebel Alliance The common term used for the Alliance to Restore the Republic, it opposed the tyranny of the Empire and its New Order and eventually became the New Republic. The Alliance included single individuals, planets, and entire star systems, all united in their desire to overturn the oppressive Empire and bring justice and freedom back to the galaxy. The word *Rebel* itself was used mainly by the Empire. [SW, ESB, RJ]

Rebel Blockade Runner *See* Blockade Runner

Rebel Dream Princess Leia Organa Solo's flagship, the Star Destroyer had been captured from the Imperial Navy. [CPL]

Rebellion Another name—used especially by Imperials—for the war to topple the Empire that was carried on by the Alliance to Restore the Republic. [SW, ESB, RJ]

Rebels The term the Empire used to refer to all those who supported the Alliance to Restore the Republic. [SW, ESB, RJ]

Rebel Star A New Republic escort frigate, it was one of the ships that took part in the rescue of the downed *Liberator* and its crew. [DE]

Rebel Alliance symbol

Max Rebo

Rebo, Max A squat blue Ortolan with floppy ears, a snout, and bright blue velvety fur, he is the leader of a jizz-wailer band that ranges from a basic trio to a twelve-member ensemble, including dancers. Natives of the planet Orto have a highly developed sense of hearing and love music—as well as food. Besides leading the band, Max Rebo plays keyboards on his Red Ball Jett organ.

The trio, comprising Rebo, Droopy McCool, and Sy Snootles, had originally been in a band named Evar Orbus and His Galactic Jizz-Wailers but were stranded on Tatooine after Orbus was killed by a stray blaster shot. They eventually hooked up with an agent for crime lord Jabba the Hutt, and with a promise of all-important food—and lots of it—Rebo signed a lifetime contract. The band was on a lower level of Jabba's sail barge when it was blown up by the escaping Jedi Luke Skywalker and his friends. Max and the band jumped overboard just in time. While McCool departed for other pursuits, Snootles and Rebo went to work for another criminal, Lady Valarian, for a while. When they left, Rebo joined the Rebellion, claiming that it offered the best food. [RJ, SWCG, TJP]

Reboam A harsh, sparsely populated world in the Hapes Cluster. [CPL]

recording rod Long, clear, cylindrical tubes, they record and play back audio and two-dimensional visual images on the recording rod's surface. Activation switches are at each end of a rod. [SME]

rectenna A scanning and tracking array, it features active/passive scanners, a powerful jamming system, ship-to-ship transmitters, and a short-range target acquisition program. [CCG]

Redcap A barren and rainy world, it consists largely of shifting mud plains crossed by jagged canyons and mountain ranges. Since ships can sink easily in Redcap's thick mud, landings are restricted to the stable Tyma Canyon, which runs for several hundred kilometers across the planet's surface. Redcap's human inhabitants are poverty-stricken descendants of early mining colonists and live in settlements built at the bases of the mountain chains. Residents travel on olai, horned beasts of burden originally brought from a nearby moon for use in the mining industry. Points of interest include Juteau Settlement, which was built near the Garish Ridge and contains the Laughing Bantha tavern. [SWAJ]

Redemption scenario Also known as the Requiem scenario by X-wing pilots during simulator training exercises, it is basically a no-win situation. The *Redemption* is a hospital ship, and the simulated mission is to guard the Medevac shuttles and ships as they off-load wounded. Just to keep it interesting, a huge number of TIE bombers and fighters are on the attack, trying their best to "kill" the trainee. [RS]

Redesign A program implemented by Imperial COMPNOR representatives, it was designed to culturally edify the galaxy's citizens so that

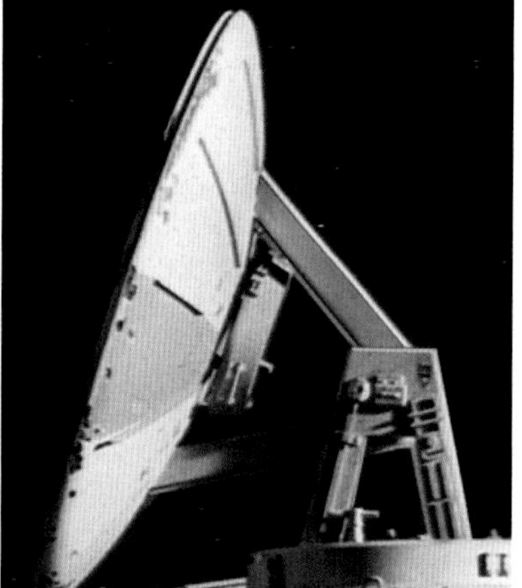

Rectenna

they would function more efficiently within the Empire. [ISB, TBH]

Red Five The comm-unit designation for Luke Skywalker's X-wing fighter during the Battle of Yavin. [SW]

Red Four The comm-unit designation for Rebel pilot John D's X-wing fighter during the Battle of Yavin. [SW]

Red Hills clan One of the clans of Witches on the planet Dathomir. [CPL]

Red Leader The comm-unit designation for veteran pilot Garven Dreis, who was in charge of Red Squadron during the Battle of Yavin. When Red Leader was young, he had met Anakin Skywalker and was very impressed with his skills as a pilot. Red Leader was killed during the Yavin battle.

During the Battle of Endor, Red Leader was the comm-unit designation for Rebel pilot Wedge Antilles's X-wing. He commanded the Red Wing attack element that took on the Imperial fleet and the second Death Star battle station. [SW, SWR, RJ]

Red Leader

Red One The comm-unit designation for Rebel pilot Garven Dreis's X-wing fighter during the Battle of Yavin. Dreis was killed in the battle. [CCG]

Redoubtable A Star Destroyer, it was captured by Yevethan strongman Nil Spaar in his raid on the Imperial shipyard at N'zoth. The *Redoubtable* was renamed *Destiny of Yevetha* and made a part of Spaar's Black Fifteen Fleet. [SOL]

Red Shadow A bistro on the planet Taboon, it was where Mageye the Hutt was accidentally killed by the bounty hunter Zardra. [TMEC]

Red Six The comm-unit designation for Rebel pilot Jek Porkins's X-wing fighter during the Battle of Yavin. Porkins was killed in the battle. [SW]

Red Squadron One of the many X-wing fighter squadrons of the Rebel Alliance, it was the one that Luke Skywalker was assigned to in the Battle of Yavin. Red Squadron evolved into Rogue Squadron. [SW, CCG]

Red Terror An elite guard of approximately 500 gladiator droids scattered throughout the droid-manufacturing facilities on the planet Telti. On their way to rescue Cole Fardreamer from the clutches of Dark Jedi Brakiss, C-3PO and R2-D2 faced down and narrowly escaped a group of about fifty of the droids. [NR]

Red Three The comm-unit designation for Rebel pilot Biggs Darklighter's X-wing fighter during the Battle of Yavin. A childhood friend of Luke Skywalker, Biggs was killed while helping Luke in his run at the Death Star. [SW]

Red Two The comm-unit designation for Rebel pilot Wedge Antilles's X-wing fighter during the Battle of Yavin. [SW]

Reegesk

Red Wing One of the four main Rebel starfighter battle groups participating in the Battle of Endor. Red Wing was also the comm-unit designation for Red Leader's second-in-command. [RJ]

Reef Home One of the majestic floating Mon Calamarian cities, it was destroyed in Admiral Daala's attack on Mon Calamari. [COF]

Reegesk A male Ranat thief and scavenger from Aralia, he regularly trades with the nomadic Jawas on Tatooine. Adept at pilfering items without alerting their owners, Reegesk is willing to steal anything, even trash. He inadvertently caused the death of the Jawa Het Nkik when he stole the power pack out of Nkik's blaster, which the Jawa then tried to use on a group of stormtroopers in revenge for the murder of many of his clan members. [CCG, TMEC]

Ree-Yees A three-eyed, goat-faced Gran from the planet Kinyen, he was banished from his homeworld after murdering another of his species. Ree-Yees became a petty thief addicted to heavy drinking and ended up in the court of Jabba the Hutt. No one liked him, especially because of the constant fights that he started.

Ree-Yees tended to Bubo, a grotesque frog-dog, and was secretly using a transmitter hidden among Bubo's skin flaps. The Empire was providing Ree-Yees with a detonator to kill Jabba, shipping the components in packages of Gran goatgrass. In return, Imperials would wipe out his murder record so that he could return home. The plot failed, but Jabba was soon dead anyway. Ree-Yees was aboard the crime lord's sail barge when it exploded. [RJ, TJP, SWCG, GG5]

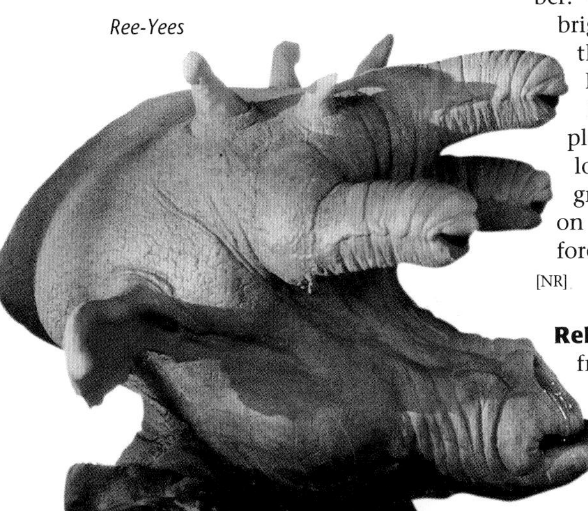

Ree-Yees

Reezen, Corporal An Imperial officer, he had met Darth Vader when he was in his teens. Corporal Reezen was somewhat Force-sensitive and alerted the warlord Zsinj of Han Solo's flight to the planet Dathomir. [CPL]

Regional Sector Four's All-Human Free-For-All Extravaganza A popular blood sport event held in the Victory Coliseum on the planet Jubilar, it pits four human combatants in brutal battle against each other inside a five-sided ring. A young Han Solo bested three much larger opponents when he was forced to participate in the event. [TBH]

Rek A gangster working for Great Bogga the Hutt some 4,000 years before the Galactic Civil War, he was involved in the conspiracy to kill Jedi Andur Sunrider at the Stenness hyperspace terminal. He in turn was killed by Andur's wife, Nomi. [TOJ]

Rek A species distinguished by a slender, whiplike body, they also have rope-thin hands and skin the texture and temperature of lukewarm rubber. While all Rek have startlingly bright eyes, only the females of the species have purple eyes. Reks often work as bounty hunters, and several are employed by Nandreeson, the crime lord of Smuggler's Run. This Rek group captured Lando Calrissian on Skip One and brought him before Nandreeson for punishment. [NR]

Rekkon A university professor from the planet Kalla, he left his post to find his nephew Tchaka, who was suspected of being an activist working against the Corporate Sector Authority. The broad-shouldered, tall, bearded Rekkon gathered a group of others who were searching for missing friends, relatives, and loved ones who had somehow run afoul of the Authority. As their leader, Rekkon enlisted the aid of Han Solo in the search, which eventually led to a prison called Stars' End. Rekkon was later killed by Torm Dadeferron. [HSE]

Relentless An Imperial Star Destroyer, it was under the command of a number of Imperial officers. Following the Battle of Yavin, the *Relentless* was helmed by Captain Parlan. One of his major missions was to locate and capture the brilliant Old Republic naval officer Adar Tallon on Tatooine before he could be recruited by the Rebellion. He failed and was summarily executed by Darth Vader. The ship was then turned over to Captain Westen, until he, too, disappointed Lord Vader. Later, under the command of Captain Dorja and the orders of Grand Admiral Thrawn, the *Relentless* failed to capture Han Solo and Luke Skywalker at New Cov five years after the Battle of Endor. [TM, OS, DFR]

Reliance A Republic command ship 4,000 years before the Battle of Yavin, it was helmed by Captain Vanicus. It carried Jedi Ulic Qel-Droma on a mission to try to protect Koros Major from the Krath coup sweeping the Empress Teta system. [DLS]

Reliant A midsized freighter owned by Seti Ashgad, it was piloted by Liegeus Sarpaetius Vorn. He prepared the ship as an escape vessel for Ashgad and the droch Dyzm, but it was destroyed after Luke Skywalker used the Force to communicate with the intelligent crystals on Nam Chorios, which in turn ordered the crystals aboard the *Reliant* to destroy it. [POT]

Rell, Mother The eldest leader of the Singing Mountain clan of the Witches of Dathomir, she is nearly 300 years old and knew Jedi Master Yoda. [CPL]

Relstad, Minor The personal assistant to Imperial Supervisor Gurdun, who skimmed funds to create the IG series of assassin droids. [TBH]

Remote

Reltooine A planet in the Corporate sector, it is one of the stops made by the luxury liner *Lady of Mindor* during its voyage from Roonadan to Ammuud. [CSSB]

remote An owner-programmable automaton, it can perform its functions without supervision but hasn't any capability for independent initiative. Luke Skywalker used a remote—a floating sphere—aboard the *Millennium Falcon* to learn lightsaber skills. [SWN]

Ren, Kybo A space pirate whose full name was Gir Kybo Ren-Cha, he operated during the early days of the Empire. A short, fat human, Kybo Ren sported a long, dangling mustache and a small goatee. [DTV]

Renatasia system With eight planets orbiting a yellow star, the Renatasia system is located far outside civilized space. It apparently was colonized by a long-forgotten mission millennia ago in pre-Republic days. Renatasia III and IV are pleasant green worlds. The Renatasians had colonized every planet in their system by the time they were discovered by a damaged trader ship.

The Empire decided to send representatives to probe the society's weaknesses and Ottdefa Osuno Whett and the droid Vuffi Raa were sent as envoys to the nation-state of Mathilde on Renatasia IV's second-largest continent. After observing the locals for 700 standard days, they transmitted a full report and the Imperial fleet arrived to collect slaves and taxes. The Renatasians resisted, and the fleet attempted to seize the system intact through the use of ground forces, taking heavy losses in a costly but inevitable Imperial victory. Over two-thirds of the population in the Renatasia system was killed in the pacification effort. [LCF, LCS]

Rendar, Dash Tall and lean, with red hair and green eyes, Rendar cuts a romantic figure in his gray freighter togs, a holstered blaster slung low on his hip. Dash Rendar is a Corellian about Han Solo's age and has a bit of Han's lazy, insolent look about him. Like Solo, Rendar has been a thief, card cheat, and smuggler. He's also a skilled pilot of his ship, the *Outrider*. Rendar was delivering a shipment of food to the Rebel Alliance Echo Base on Hoth when the Empire invaded, so he flew a snowspeeder during the battle and took down an Imperial walker.

Rendar comes from a wealthy, highly placed family, and he was enrolled at the Imperial Academy a year behind Solo. His older brother was a freighter pilot working his way up through the family shipping company when he and his crew were killed as his ship accidentally crashed into the Emperor's private museum on Imperial Center. An enraged Palpatine seized the family's property and kicked Dash out of the Academy.

Princess Leia Organa, having become aware that someone was out to kill Luke Skywalker, hired Rendar to watch over him. Rendar became involved in a battle against an Imperial ship containing a computer holding plans for the second Death Star. The ship, armed with hidden super weapons, shot a missile toward the Alliance's Bothan flight, Blue Squadron. Rendar thought he had a bead on the missile and retaliated with a shot of his own. Despite his best efforts, the enemy missile took out Blue Squadron and twelve Bothans were killed in the fighting. Rendar took it personally and went into battle-shock. Skywalker, angry at Rendar, sent him to Rodia to find Leia to tell her about the incident and the information retrieved.

Rendar learned that Leia was being held prisoner by Prince Xizor, head of the criminal Black Sun organization. (Xizor was secretly trying

Kybo Ren

Dash Rendar

Repulsor engine at work

to kill Skywalker as part of his larger chess match with Darth Vader.) Rendar arrived on Imperial Center just in time to save Skywalker and Lando, who were in a blaster shoot-out in Spero's flower shop. Rendar was instrumental in rescuing the princess. He contacted an engineer, Vidkun, who knew the underground pipes and sewers leading to Xizor's castle—the only way in. The engineer-guide betrayed Rendar and shot him in the hip with a blaster during the rescue mission. Rendar immediately fired back, killing the traitor with a shot between the eyes.

After a successful rescue and escape aboard the *Millennium Falcon*, Dash transferred to the *Outrider*, which his droid copilot, Leebo, had flown. An incredible firefight then erupted over Imperial Center as Xizor's fighters shot at the Rebels, and Darth Vader's TIE fighters shot at Xizor's men. Rogue Squadron even joined the fray. At a climactic moment, Xizor's grand orbital skyhook exploded as the *Outrider* headed straight for the debris, giving the appearance that Rendar and his ship exploded. But, as the saying goes, Ranats have eleven lives—and so, it seems, do Corellian smugglers. [SOTE]

Rendili This planet is the site of a space construction center where the Emperor built some of his largest warships and special weapons platforms. Rendili StarDrive manufactured the *Victory*-class Star Destroyer. [SWSB, ISWU]

Renegade Flight A code-name, it refers to the group of Rebel pilots who escorted and protected a badly needed Alliance supply convoy to the secret base on the planet Hoth. [ESBR]

Renegade Leader The comm-unit designation for Commander Narra, an Alliance starfighter pilot in charge of Renegade Flight. [ESBR]

renegades Onetime law abiders, these beings turned to thievery for survival following the collapse of the Empire and of social order on Imperial Center, or Coruscant. They live among the ruins of Imperial City, competing with the scavengers for survival. [DE]

Renforra Base One of many secret bases used by the Rebel Alliance during the reign of Emperor Palpatine. [CCG]

Reprieve An Imperial Nebulon-B frigate, it was seized and used by Rogue Squadron as its temporary headquarters after the squadron lost its base at Talasea. [RS]

Republic City The huge, sprawling metropolis—also known for a time as Galactic City—was the Old Republic capital on the planet Coruscant. It was renamed Imperial City (and the planet was dubbed Imperial Center) when Senator Palpatine declared the establishment of the Empire. [FNU, TSW]

Repulse An assault carrier in the New Republic Fifth Fleet, it was deployed in the blockade of Doornik-319 at the start of the Yevethan crisis. [SOL]

repulsor An antigravitational propulsion unit sometimes called a repulsorlift engine, it is the most widely used propulsion system in land and atmospheric vehicles. The engines produce a field that pushes against, or repulses, a planet's gravity, providing the thrust that makes landspeeders, airspeeders, and speeder bikes move. Repulsorlift engines are also used in starfighters and small starships as supplementary propulsion systems for docking and for atmospheric flight. [SW, ESB, RJ]

repulsor carts Floating carts used to move heavy objects. [TMEC]

repulsorlift engine *See* repulsor

Resh, Shaalir The name used by X-wing pilot Riv Shiel on Coruscant during Rogue Squadron's undercover operation there. He pretended to be a Shistavanen con man who, in a classic setup, would rob unsuspecting victims as they attempted to take advantage of his young human partner. [WG]

Resolve A New Republic Star Destroyer, it served as the target during the Fifth Fleet's Bessimir operational readiness exercise. The ship was under the command of Syub Snunb. [BTS]

resonance torpedo The primary weapon used in the offensive systems of the Sun Crusher. [COF]

restraining bolt A small, cylindrical device, it fits into a special socket on the exterior of a droid to keep it from wandering off. A restraining bolt also forces a droid to respond immediately to signals produced by a handheld summoning device—a caller—that is keyed to a specific bolt. [SW]

restraining bolt activator *See* caller

Retep III The site of a rendezvous following the Battle of Yavin of an Alliance force and a group of Habassan freighters delivering a cargo of

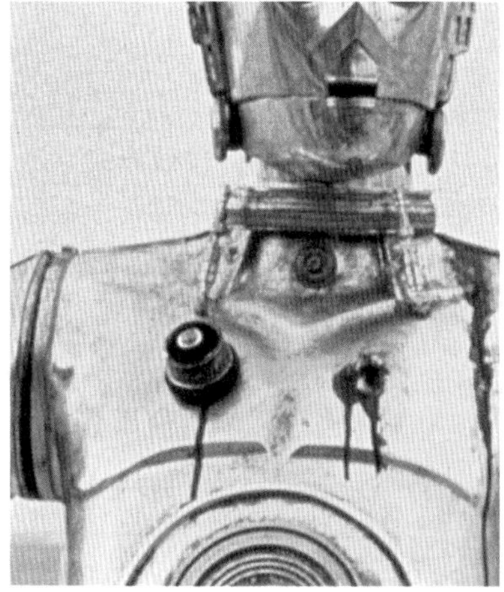
Restraining bolt

Tamizander Rey

foodstuffs. The transfer operation near Retep III was attacked by Imperial starfighters. [FP]

Retep V The site of an ambush of an Habassan convoy by Imperial corvettes following the Battle of Yavin. An Alliance strike force helped rescue the convoy near Retep V. [FP]

Rethin Sea Composed of liquid metal, it is the core of the gas giant Bespin. [GG2, ZHR]

retinal print A security device, it is used to identify individuals by comparing their retinal patterns with prints stored in a computer database. [SME]

Return A ritual among the survivors of Alderaan, it holds deep spiritual significance. Those who participate in the Return are encouraged to buy gifts for those they loved and lost when Alderaan was annihilated. If possible, they then make their way to the site that has since become known as the Graveyard of Alderaan, where the gifts are set adrift in the asteroid belt that is the remains of their world, to rest among the memories of the past. Words are spoken to mark the occasion. Many who have accomplished the Return describe it as an event that has changed their life, or at least given them a new understanding of life and its purpose. Some even claim to have gained a new insight into the universe. However, for most of the faithful, the Return provides healing calm for their tortured spirits. [BW]

reversion The act of returning to realspace from hyperspace. [SWR]

Rey, Tamizander A native of the planet Esseles, he resigned from the Esselian defense force after the Imperial Senate was disbanded by Emperor Palpatine. Tamizander Rey then joined the Rebel Alliance as a highly skilled starship pilot. Rey was senior deck officer at Echo Base on Hoth, where he was responsible for docking bay operations. [CCG]

Rhinnal Located in the Darpa sector of the Core Worlds along the Perlemian Trade Route, the planet only recently—in geological terms—emerged from an ice age. Rhinnal's surface is covered with fjords, mountains, and frigid rivers. It was a colony world of nearby Esseles until the rise of the Empire, when the Imperials assumed direct control. The planet's fifty-five million inhabitants place great value on ceremonies and commemorations, and often wear elaborate, colorful clothing. Rhinnal is famous for its expertise in medicine. The last remaining Jedi chapter house in the Core Worlds is located on Rhinnal and still accepts patients, though none of its staff are Jedi. After the Battle of Yavin, Rhinnal experts were sent to an orbiting hospital frigate to study the outbreak of Candorian plague on Dentaal. [SWAJ]

Rieekan, General Carlist As a Rebel Alliance officer, he was commander of all Alliance ground and fleet forces in the Hoth star system. He had to give the order to abandon Hoth when the Alliance headquarters was discovered by the Empire. Years later, as Chief of State Leia Organa Solo's second-in-command on the New Republic Council, Gen. Carlist Rieekan took over in her absence, such as when she disappeared during the troubles on Nam Chorios. Rieekan survived a poisoning that was aimed at throwing the Republic into chaos. Later, General Rieekan became the New Republic Intelligence Director, and he decided to terminate Colonel Pakkpekatt's pursuit of the mysterious vagabond ghost ship carrying Lando Calrissian, his aide, Lobot, and the droids C-3PO and R2-D2 as involuntary riders. However, he did allow Pakkpekatt to take Calrissian's ship, the *Lady Luck*, and three volunteers in search of the vagabond. [POT, SOL, ESB, GG3]

Gen. Carlist Rieekan

Riileb Homeworld of the Riilebs, tall humanoids with antennae who can detect the biorhythm changes of others. Single Riileb females are bald, while married females and all males have hair. [SWAJ]

Rillao A beautiful, golden-skinned Firrerreon with black- and silver-striped hair, she had strong Force abilities that brought her to the attention of Darth Vader, with whom she began training. Rillao met one of Vader's other students, a fellow Firrerreon named Hethrir. They became lovers and Rillao became pregnant. But unlike Hethrir, who so fully embraced the dark side that he willingly destroyed his homeworld and millions of its inhabitants, Rillao remained a healer and light-side user. After the destruction of Firrerre, she fled with her unborn child, whom she later named Tigris and raised in solitude.

Hethrir captured many freighters, and when the Empire fell, he sold the hundreds of passengers aboard as slaves. He eventually found Rillao and imprisoned her in a weblike torture device aboard an abandoned slave freighter. He made Tigris a personal slave, keeping his parentage secret, and tricked him into believing his mother was a traitor. Rillao was rescued by Princess Leia Organa Solo, who was searching for her own children who had been kidnapped by Hethrir. Together, they tracked Hethrir to the Crseih Research Station, where Rillao confronted Hethrir and Tigris with the truth. Tigris took the young Anakin Solo from Hethrir,

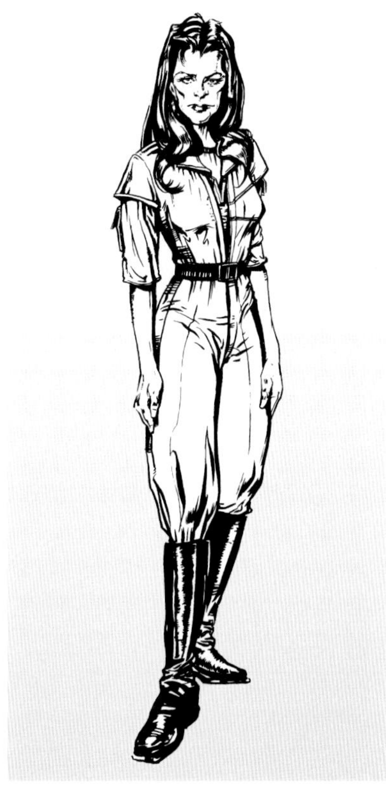

Rillao

who had planned to feed the boy to the Force-powerful Waru. In place of the child, the Waru consumed Hethrir, and Rillao and Tigris went to Coruscant. [CS]

Ringali Nebula A spectacular stretch of violet gases, it is located within the Ringali Shell and can be seen in the night sky of all the Shell's planets. [SWAJ]

Ringali Shell A region of space running from the mid-Core to the Colonies region, it encompasses the Bormea and Darpa sectors, the intersection of the Perlemian Trade Route and the Hydian Way, and the colorful Ringali Nebula. [SWAJ]

Ringneldia system A system where Lando Calrissian picked up replacement parts for the *Millennium Falcon.* All part sizes in the Ringneldia system are standardized around the diameter of a native bean. [LCS]

Ripoblus Along with the planet Dimok, it is one of the two primary worlds of the Sepan system. A long war between Ripoblus and Dimok was forcibly ended by Imperial intervention after the Battle of Hoth, although the two worlds briefly and unsuccessfully tried to unite against the Empire as their common foe. [TSC]

Risant, Tendra A minor functionary on Sacorria, she warned the New Republic of a threat from a huge Sacorrian fleet. Rich, tall, and strong, she also is fond of Lando Calrissian and was one of the candidates for Lando's hand in marriage. Her ship is the *Gentleman Caller.* [AC]

Rishi A planet that orbits a sun called Rish, it is a hot and humid world of congested valleys where colonists live, and high mountains populated by the native birdlike Rishii. The conservative colonists, most of whom are members of the fundamentalist religious sect called H'kig, live in white stone buildings; they forbid the use of repulsorlift vehicles on the streets in the morning and have many rules concerning appearance and social mores. A commune of H'kig cultists who left Rishi in a doctrinal dispute some fifty years ago established a colony on J't'p'tan, within the borders of the Koornacht Cluster. Some twelve years after the Battle of Endor, the H'kig colony was supposedly wiped out by the fanatical Yevetha in what they called the Great Purge, but it was actually protected by the Fallanassi religious order.

Animal life on Rishi includes the dangerous maungurs in the planet's warm polar regions; they have flexible limbtails and feature prominently in Rishii legends and stories. A number of criminal gangs have established bases on the planet. Talon Karrde's smuggling organization briefly used a Rishi city-vale as a hideout following their evacuation of Myrkr. After Rogue Squadron resigned en masse from the New Republic military, the Rogues located a store of X-wing parts on Rishi, and Wedge Antilles and Ooryl Qrygg flew to Rishi and bought the cache. [DFR, DFRSB, SWAJ, BTS, TT, BW]

Rishii Small, peaceful avians, they live in tribal clusters atop the mountains of the planet Rishi. Rishii have feathered wings along with humanlike hands that have helped them develop into primitive tool users. Each tribal cluster, or nest, is composed of a number of family groups. They have a knack for languages, which they learn by mimicking the sounds made by newcomers, but have very little interest in advanced technology. [DFRSB]

Ristel, Darsk Corran Horn used this name as a cover during Rogue Squadon's reconnaissance mission to Imperial Center. Ristel was supposedly a telbun, the property of Ris Darsk, a wealthy Kuati who was on her way to Coruscant to conceive a child. [WG]

Rizaron A Yevethan guardian thrustship, it patrolled the orbital shipyard at ILC-905. [TT]

Rkok clan A Jawa clan, it unloaded a cargo of questionable merchandise on crime lord Jabba the Hutt. Later, the Nkik clan found the remains of the destroyed Rkok sandcrawler at the edge of the Great Pit of Carkoon. No sign of the Rkok Jawas was found. [ISWU]

Roa A onetime smuggler and blockade runner, Roa gave Han Solo one of his first fringe jobs and took him on one of his first Kessel runs. Now a respectable and successful entrepreneur, Roa owns one of the largest import-export firms serving the planets of Roonadan and Bonadan. [HSR]

Roat, Antar Wedge Antilles took this name during his undercover mission on Imperial Center with Rogue Squadron. He posed as an Imperial colonel shot down and badly injured during the defense of Vladet, coming to Imperial Center for reconstruction at the Rohari Biomechanical Clinic. [WG]

Robida Colossus A Ganathan steam-powered battleship, it towed a badly damaged *Millennium Falcon* into port after its close escape from Boba Fett. [DE2]

robot starfighter An Imperial-designed ship introduced seven years after the Battle of Endor, this fully robotic TIE/D fighter is operated by remote computer control or onboard droids. [DE, DESB]

Roche system This system contains the Roche asteroid field, a relatively stable configuration of asteroids orbiting a small yellow sun. In addition to mynocks and space slugs, the

Roche field is home to the intelligent insectoid species called the Verpine. New Republic forces were dispatched to the Roche system to help prevent a war between the Verpine and the Barabel species after the Battle of Endor. [LC, CPL, GG4, RS, SFS]

rocket-jumpers Members of the Republic armed forces some 4,000 years before the Galactic Civil War, they used rocket packs to aid them in their aerial attacks on Republic foes. [FNU]

Rodia Located in the Tyrius system halfway between Gall and Coruscant, this industrial planet is home to the violence-loving Rodians and their vast weapons-manufacturing facilities. Rodian culture romanticizes death and the hunt, as is evidenced by their reverence for the profession of bounty hunter, their gladiator games, and the subject of their most famous dramatic plays. Their society is tightly controlled by the Rodian Grand Protector, and only the most accomplished hunters are allowed to leave their planet. Rodia was once a lush tropical world, but rapid industrial growth has made many life-forms extinct, necessitating the import of many foodstuffs. Years ago, Navik the Red, the Rodian leader of the Chattza clan who eventually became Grand Protector of Rodia, eliminated many opposing clan leaders and nearly wiped out the entire Tetsus clan. Greedo, a novice bounty hunter in the employ of Jabba the Hutt, was a Rodian and a surviving member of the Tetsus clan. Another notable Rodian was Andoorni Hui, a female pilot and member of the Alliance's famed Rogue Squadron. Princess Leia Organa—seeking information on an attempt to assassinate Luke Skywalker—met Guri, top aide to criminal kingpin Prince Xizor, in a suite at Equator City's Next Chance casino on Rodia. [GG4, TMEC, RS, SWAJ, SOTE]

Rodian Beings with rough green skin, multifaceted eyes, and tapirlike snouts, they come from the planet Rodia. A ridge of spines tops a Rodian's skull, and their long, flexible fingers end in suction cups. Rodians are primarily hunters (including bounty hunters) and fighters, though some clans, most notably the Tetsus, are peaceful. [GG1, GG4, TMEC]

Rogua One of the Gamorrean guards who worked for Jabba the Hutt, he was posted at the palace's main entrance alongside the guard leader, Ortugg. [TJP, GG5]

Rogue Flight The code-name for the Rebel starfighter pilots who protected forces evacuating Hoth following the Imperial assault on the Alliance's base. It was also known as Rogue Group. [ESBR]

Rogue Four The comm-unit designation for Rebel pilot Hobbie's snowspeeder during the Battle of Hoth. [ESB]

Rogue Leader The comm-unit designation for Rebel pilot Luke Skywalker's snowspeeder during the Battle of Hoth. [ESB]

Rogue Squadron This squadron of top pilots was formed after the Battle of Yavin. Luke Skywalker took command of the group after the Battle of Hoth and came up with the concept of a squadron without a set mission profile, allowing Rogue Squadron to take on any mission that came its way. Skywalker combined the best pilots with the best fighters and taught them to work as a single unit. When he left to spend more time at his Jedi studies, Wedge Antilles took charge of the squadron, composed of twelve X-wings and their pilots and astromech droids. The squadron has become a symbol of the bravery and fighting spirit of the New Republic and has been involved in numerous adventures and rescues of top New Republic officials.

After the Alliance victory at the Battle of Endor, the Provisional Council sent Antilles around the galaxy on a sort of good-will tour. Every world wanting to join the Alliance sent its best pilots, and all of them expected to be part of Rogue Squadron. Antilles had to wade through this political thicket to select the twelve candidates best qualified for membership, based partly on test scores and partly on the worlds from which they came. After training exercises at Folor, the chosen twelve were sent to a temporary base at Talasea. On their journey in the Chorax system, they were pulled out of hyperspace and forced into their first real fight, proving they had the right stuff.

One of the Rogue's first real missions was the rescue of stranded Rebel operatives on Hensara III. Their first loss came when stormtroopers raided their base at Talasea, killing one Rogue and six base personnel. The squadron made a retaliatory strike against the Imperial base at Vladet, destroying it completely. The Provisional Council, in its eagerness to expand territory toward Coruscant, next approved a plan by Gen. Laryn Kre'fey to take a small Imperial base at Borleias. But information obtained by Bothan spies proved wrong and two Rogues lost their lives in the attack. With better information, they returned and finished the job.

Rogue Squadron played a major role in the liberation of Imperial Center (which has since been given back its original name, Coruscant). It participated in the advance release of terrorists, infiltrated the planet, and came up with a way to get the planetary shields lowered for the full-scale New Republic attack. They had little time to celebrate, because they were drawn into a war over precious bacta masterminded by Ysanne Isard, Director of Imperial Intelligence. Whether it's a Republic official in danger, a threat to the peace, or the saber-rattling of a power-hungry warlord, Rogue Squadron is certain to be at the center of the action. [GG3, HE, DFR, LC, HESB, RS, WG, KT, BW, XW]

Rogue Three The comm-unit designation for Rebel pilot Wedge An-

Rodian

Rogue Three

tilles's snowspeeder during the Battle of Hoth. [ESB]

Rogue Two The comm-unit designation for Rebel pilot Zev Senesca's snowspeeder during the Battle of Hoth. [ESB]

Roke, Boss A human who was in charge of prisoner crews in the spice mines of Kessel, he had a lumpy face and a chin covered with bristly black stubble. [JS]

Rokna tree fungus A deadly blue fungus also known as Rokna blue or the blue, it is common on the forest moon of Endor. The tree fungus is both a lethal poison and an addictive drug. When taken in tiny doses the blue causes euphoria, but it also damages a person's memory beyond repair and leads to rapid aging and, eventually, death. [ETV, SOL]

Roko First mate aboard space pirate Finhead Stonebone's *Starjacker* about 4,000 years before the Galactic Civil War, he was killed by Great Bogga the Hutt's pet, Ktriss. [TOJ]

Romar A planet in the Galov sector of the Outer Rim, it was the site of Imperial Moff Antoll Jellrek's estate near the rocky spires of the Derrbi Wastelands. When the outlaw Jai Raventhorn tried to assassinate the Moff, she encountered the notorious bounty hunter Beylyssa. [SWAJ]

ronto A huge but gentle pack animal, it is used as a beast of burden by the Jawas on Tatooine. Rontos, which average about 4.25 meters tall, are known for both their loyalty and their strength. They can carry hundreds of kilograms of equipment and are large enough to frighten off most attackers, including Tusken Raiders. They are also skittish and easily spooked, especially in more congested urban areas.

Ronto

Rontos, which are saurian in appearance, are easy to train and are quite fond of their masters. They have a superb sense of smell—they can pick up a krayt dragon a kilometer away—but because of their poor vision they are often startled by sudden movement. Rontos need plenty of water, but since their skin easily sheds excess heat, they are well suited to Tatooine's harsh desert environment. [SWSE]

Roofoo *See* Evazan, Doctor

Rooks Captain of a patrol ship in the Empress Teta system about 4,000 years before the Galactic Civil War. [TSW]

Roon A mysterious planet, it is surrounded by a belt of moonlets, asteroids, and other cosmic debris. Half of Roon provides a spectacular vista of emerald continents and sapphire oceans. The other half is bleak, trapped in perpetual night. Spacer legends have it that the Roon star system is filled with treasure. [DTV]

Roonadan The fifth planet in the Bonadan system in the Corporate sector, it is the site of the starship departure terminal from which Han Solo and Fiolla of Lorrd boarded the spaceliner *Lady of Mindor* en route to the planet Ammuud. [HSR, CSSB]

Ropagi system One endpoint of the Kira Run, it has three planets: Elpur, Ropagi II, and Seltaya. The other end point is the Lazerian system. [SWAJ, TSK]

Roti-Ow system A system that contains a binary star and the planet Altor 14, homeworld of the Avogwi and the Nuiwit. [GG4]

Roundtree system Birthplace of Rekkon, an educator who helped Han Solo during his mission to the Stars' End penal colony. [CSSB]

Rover The name Doctor Evazan gave to his trained pet meduza. Rover saved Evazan a number of times and eventually gave his life for him, cushioning the fall when Evazan tumbled off a cliff. [TMEC]

Royal Guard *See* Emperor's Royal Guard

Royal Protectors An elite warrior group on Onderon 4,000 years before the Galactic Civil War, its duty was to protect Aleema and Satal Keto, who had used dark Sith magic to form the Krath and had overthrown planetary governments in the Empress Teta system. [TOJ]

Ruan system Located in the Core Worlds, it contains one of the eighteen farming planets administered by the Salliche Ag Corporation. After the Battle of Endor, workers in the Ruan, Yulant, and Broest systems revolted against the Imperial-controlled Salliche Ag by burning fields and destroying hydroponics facilities. [SWAJ]

Rudd, Jerris A pilot, he was hired by Jabba the Hutt's aide, Bib Fortuna, to transport the Twi'lek dancers Oola and Sienn from their native Ryloth to Tatooine. [TJP]

Rudrig A quiet planet in the Tion Hegemony, it is home to the vast University of Rudrig, which attracts students from the entire Hegemony. The planet-wide university has campuses and classrooms scattered everywhere amid the gray soil and purple grasses of Rudrig. Weapons are officially prohibited on the planet's surface. Han Solo and Chewbacca were involved in a high-speed chase on a Rudrig freeway during one of their early adventures. After the Imperials destroyed an Alliance base on Briggia prior to the Battle of Yavin, the next scheduled target of the Emperor's Operation Strike Fear was Rudrig. A Rudrig crime ring tortured a kidnap victim by using an Imperial interrogation droid stolen from a battle zone, one impetus behind the Historic Battle Site Protection Act established by the New Republic Senate. Rudrig was represented by Senator Nyxy. [HLL, FP, BTS, NR]

ruetsavii In Gand society they are sent to observe, examine, criticize, and chronicle the life of an individual to determine if they are worthy of their individuality. If this right is granted, the Gand becomes janwuine. [BW]

Ruillia's Insulated Rooms An inexpensive hotel in Mos Eisley, where Figrin D'an and the Modal Nodes stayed. [TMEC]

Rukh A member of the fierce Noghri species, he served as one of the Emperor's Death Commandos. When Grand Admiral Thrawn returned from the Unknown Regions, he took charge of the Noghri and selected Rukh to be his personal bodyguard. Rukh was never far from the Grand Admiral's side, hiding in the shadows until his particular talents were called for. When the truth of how the Empire kept the Noghri subjugated was revealed by Princess Leia Organa Solo, Rukh waited for the best opportunity to take his revenge on Thrawn, then assassinated him. [HE, DFR, LC, HESB]

Rula, Captain The commander of a small fleet, Rula was with Han Solo the first time Han Solo encountered a Hapan warship. [CPL]

Ruluwoor, Chertyl A female Selonian sent to CorSec (Corellian Security) for training as part of a cultural exchange program, she developed a relationship with Corran Horn. The affair ended when their respective body chemistries made them allergic to one another. [WG]

runyip A large, stubborn herbivore living on Yavin 4, it feeds on forest mulch. A runyip emits loud squealing noises, grunting and sighing as it digs among the underbrush with its flexible nose and clawed front toes. [ISWU, GG2]

rupin tree A tree native to the planet Aruza. [TBH]

Ruuria Home planet of the caterpillarlike Ruurians, its society consists of 143 colonies and is separated into three life stages: larva, pupa, and chroma-wing. The larval Ruurians are concerned with all aspects of day-to-day life on Ruuria from the moment of their births; each will eventually form a chrysalis (the pupa stage) and emerge as a chroma-wing, concerned only with mating. The historian Skynx, holder of the history chair in the pre-Republic subdivision of the Human History subdepartment, was a Ruurian, a member of the K'zagg Colony on the banks of the Z'gag. [HLL, CSSB]

Ruurian An insectoid species from the planet Ruuria, they are slightly longer than one meter with bands of reddish brown decorating their woolly coats. Extending from their bodies are eight pairs of short limbs, each ending in four digits. Feathery antennae emerge from a Ruurian's head, protruding from above multifaceted red eyes, a tiny mouth, and small nostrils. With their great natural linguistic abilities, Ruurians often enter diplomatic and scholarly fields. [HLL]

Rwookrrorro A city on the Wookiee planet of Kashyyyk, it is nestled high atop a tight ring of giant wroshyr trees and is considered one of the planet's most beautiful metropolitan centers. Rwookrrorro covers more than a square kilometer, with wide, straight avenues and multilevel buildings. The branches of the trees grow together to form the city's foundation. Houses and shops are built directly into the tree trunks. Rwookrrorro was a hiding place for Princess Leia Organa Solo while she was pregnant with the twins Jacen and Jaina. Chewbacca and other Wookiees defended the princess from a Noghri commando squad. [HE, HESB]

Rybet A squat, soft-skinned froglike species, they have bright green coloring and tan highlights that look like worm stripes on their cheeks, arms, and shoulders. Rybet have large, lanternlike eyes with vertical slits. Their fingers are long and wide at the tips, showing signs of vestigial suction cups. A male Rybet dons bright yellow clothing to indicate readiness for mating. Moruth Doole, a kingpin of the Kessel spice-smuggling business and an official of the Imperial prison on that planet, was a Rybet. [JS]

rycrit A cowlike animal, it is raised by Twi'leks on the planet Ryloth. [SWSB]

Rydar II The semiintelligent Ranat species originated on this planet, located in the Rydar system. Several hundred years before the Battle of Yavin, the human inhabitants of Rydar II attempted to exterminate the Ranats, because the Ranats ate human infants. The extermination was nearly successful, but three Ranats managed to stow away on a visiting smuggling ship. The ship crashed on Aralia, and the Ranats have since populated that planet. [GG4]

Ryjerd, Rycar A Bimm trader and smuggler of starship weapons, he trusts no one but will do business with anyone. He teaches smuggler apprentices and has mastered the language of the Jawas, a very difficult task. [CCG]

rylca A medication created by Qlaern Hirf to combat the Krytos virus, it was synthesized from bacta components and ryll spice. [KT]

Rycar Ryjerd

ryll Mined on the planet Ryloth, this relatively weak form of spice is used to create a number of medicines used throughout the galaxy. It is also smuggled into the Corporate sector for illegal sale to the workers. As a recreational substance, ryll can be addictive and dangerous. [SWSB]

Ryloon The site of several Imperial-controlled orbital factories where captured prisoners were sent to toil. [COJ]

Ryloth Located in the Outer Rim near Tatooine, it is the principal planet in the Ryloth system and home to the Twi'leks, a humanoid species with two large, fleshy head-tails growing from their skulls. The Twi'leks call these prehensile appendages lekku and can communicate through subtle lekku gestures, although they also speak Twi'leki.

Mountainous Ryloth rotates so slowly that its rotation is equal to the length of its orbit around the sun. One side of the planet always faces the sun and the only habitable areas are in the band of twilight separating the two sides. Heat storms in Ryloth's thin atmosphere help to distribute warmth throughout the twilight zone, where the Twi'leks live in a network of mountain catacombs. Wind-driven turbines power their primitive industrial civilization, and raw fungi and cowlike rycrits are raised for food. Ryloth's primary exports are the addictive ryll spice and Twi'lek females, who are desired for their seductive dancing skills.

The Twi'lek government is organized around a five-member head clan that is in charge of all community decisions. When one member of the clan dies, the remaining four are exiled into the day-side desert (the Bright Lands) and a new head clan is selected. A major Twi'lek corporation, Galactic Exotics, developed orchards on the planet Belsavis. Ryloth is also home to SchaumAssoc., a Twi'lek advertising agency that pioneered media and public relations for the Corporate sector.

Years ago, a small Imperial refueling center and training outpost was established on Ryloth, supported by the Empire yet often used by smugglers. Tarkin, then a commander, had plans to turn the refueling station into an important base. Jabba the Hutt's majordomo, Bib Fortuna, was one of the first to widely sell ryll spice off-planet, which attracted the Empire's attention and brought slavers to Ryloth. Fortuna was sentenced to death but escaped and returned later with an army of Jabba's thugs to exact revenge. Seven Ryloth cities were burned and Jabba took slaves and riches, while Fortuna rescued Nat Secura, the last son of a great Twi'lek family. Fortuna made plans to someday return with Secura and rule Ryloth as he saw fit. Not long before the Battle of Endor, Fortuna enslaved a clan chief's daughter named Oola, and trained her to serve as a dancer in Jabba's palace. Maw Installation scientist Tol Sivron, Rogue Squadron pilot Nawara Ven, and the ancient Jedi Knight Tott Doneeta were also natives of Ryloth.

After the New Republic retook Coruscant, Rogue Squadron flew a mission to Ryloth to obtain ryll kor, which was mixed with bacta to produce rylca, a cure for the Krytos virus. They landed at Kala'uun Starport, within one of the mountains known as the Lonely Five. The Twi'lek warrior Tal'dira and his pilots later joined with the squadron; they flew X-TIE hybrids called Chir'daks, or Deathseeds. [SWSB, COF, COJ, TOJ, CSSB, TMEC, RS, SWAJ, KT, BW, PSE]

ryshcate A dark brown Corellian sweetcake that is shared as a celebration of life, it is traditionally reserved for birthdays, anniversaries, or other celebrations or momentous occasions. It tastes a bit like a cross between a rum cake and a brownie, and is filled with vweliu nuts, which taste much like a marriage of walnuts and hazelnuts. [RS]

Ryvellia Located in the Avhn-Bendara system, its capital city, V'eldalv, was the site of an uprising that was brutally suppressed by the Empire with an orbital bombardment. [SWAJ]

Saarn An isolated, hidden world, Saarn was used by the Rebel Alliance for military training and was later a remote surveillance outpost after the New Republic moved to Coruscant. Five years after the Battle of Endor, one of Grand Admiral Thrawn's Star Destroyers, the *Stormhawk*, executed a hit-and-fade attack on Saarn, wiping out New Republic personnel. Thrawn's forces set up a listening post there to protect the movement of the Imperial fleet. [SWAJ]

sabacc A popular electronic card game in which high stakes—ranging from spacecraft to planets—can be won and lost. Sabacc is played using a deck of seventy-six chip-cards with values that change randomly in response to electronic impulses. The deck's four suits are sabers, staves, flasks, and coins. Each suit consists of cards numbered one to eleven and four ranked cards—Commander, Mistress, Master, and Ace—equivalent to twelve to fifteen. There are also sixteen face cards. A hand is dealt when the dealer presses a button on the sabacc table to send out a series of random pulses that shift the values and pictures shown on the chip-cards. Players bet and bluff; they can lock in the values of any of their chip-cards by placing them in the table's interference field, which blocks the dealer's pulses. To win, a player must get a pure sabacc, which totals exactly twenty-three, or an idiot's array, which consists of an idiot face card (value zero), a card valued at two and a card valued at three—a literal 23.

Han Solo and Lando Calrissian traded the *Millennium Falcon* back and forth several times over sabacc hands, and each has won control of entire planets or cities in the same manner. [ESB, CCC, HESB]

Sabodor The owner of an exotic pet store on the planet Etti IV, he hails from the planet Rakrir. Sabodor has a short, segmented tubular body, five pairs of limbs, two eyestalks, an olfactory cluster, and a vocal organ located in the center of his midsection. [HSE]

Sacorria Located in the Sacorrian system—one of the Outlier systems of the Corellian sector—this pleasant but secretive world has strict regulations. The site of the Dorthus Tal prison, Sacorria was long ruled by the Triad, a secretive council of dictators consisting of one human, one Drall, and one Selonian, about whom almost nothing—not even their names—is known. The Triad banned marriages with off-worlders and promulgated laws, including one forbidding women to marry without their father's consent. Fourteen years after the Battle of Endor, Lando Calrissian visited Sacorria to see Tendra Risant, a member of a wealthy and influential family, regarding a possible marriage proposal. Meanwhile, the Triad set into motion a master plan to force the New Republic to acknowledge the Corellian sector as an independent state. The Triad organized rebellions on each of the five planets in the Corellian system and gained control of Centerpoint Station, which allowed it to set up interdiction and jam fields over the system and to destroy distant stars at will. The Triad's plans—and its fleet of more than eighty ships—were defeated by the New Republic and a Bakuran task force. [AC, AS, SAC]

Sadow, Naga A Dark Lord of the Sith, he lived 5,000 years before the Galactic Civil War. Naga Sadow was a member of an elite priesthood of pure Sith blood, a group that practiced the dark magic of the Sith. He was exiled from his homeworld for rebelling against the reigning Dark Lord of the Sith and was scorned as a criminal by the Republic. He escaped across the galaxy, engaging Republic gunships in a cataclysmic battle that destroyed the Denarii Nova. Eventually, he ended up on Yavin 4, where he conducted genetic experiments that caused his primitive Massassi warriors to mutate into horrific creatures. [DLS, TSW]

Saelt-Marae No one knows the true origins, background, or species of the being who calls himself Saelt-Marae, whom some have called Yak Face because of his whiskered, broad-snouted face. (Beings with a similar appearance, who call themselves Yarkora, have been sighted in the Outer Rim Territories.) Saelt-Marae, who is about 2.2 meters tall and has two three-clawed hands, joined the entourage of crime lord Jabba the Hutt on Tatooine several years before the Battle of Endor. He posed as a trader who specialized in locating and selling religious artifacts from primitive cultures. Saelt-Marae immersed himself in the intrigues of Jabba's court and ingratiated himself with Jabba's henchmen, who didn't know that Saelt-Marae was an informant, selling Jabba information about the intrigues developing behind the Hutt's ample back. [RJ, GG5]

Saheelindeel Located in the remote Tion Hegemony, this backwater world is inhabited by intelligent green-furred primates. The high festival on Saheelindeel is a time of tribal hunting rituals and harvest ceremonies and has recently begun to incorporate farm machinery exhibits, shockball matches, and air shows in an attempt to become more technologically sophisticated. The Saheelindeeli, led by a matriarch, have an affinity for grandiose actions. Han Solo and Chewbacca briefly worked on Saheelindeel after leaving the Corporate sector. Following the Battle of Yavin, the Empire established a listening post near the planet that was attacked by the Alliance to divert attention from its fleet's movements into the Greater Plooriod Cluster. [HLL, FP]

Saelt-Marae

sail barge Sail barges, huge repulsorlift craft, are widely popular as recreational vehicles because they can travel across any relatively flat terrain, including sand, water, ice, or

Sail barge

grass. The crime lord Jabba the Hutt used his for pleasure cruises across oceans of sand on the desert world of Tatooine. Jabba customized his luxury barge and outfitted it with grand trappings.

The sail barge's main propulsion system was a three-chamber repulsorlift thrust array that provided a top speed of 100 kilometers an hour. Jabba's barge hovered up to ten meters above the ground, and its immense sails caught the wind and pulled the barge along. In such sail mode, the barge had a top speed of about thirty kilometers an hour. The barge had a maindeck heavy blaster and smaller antipersonnel blasters mounted on the deck rails.

Retractable viewports on the passenger deck provided sweeping vistas, and the large banquet room was renowned for the decadent parties held there. The Hutt particularly enjoyed staging feasts built around elaborate executions, when he fed those he disfavored to the Sarlacc at the Great Pit of Carkoon. It was during just such a celebration that the sail barge was destroyed when Luke Skywalker, Princess Leia Organa, and others staged a daring rescue of Han Solo. [SWVG, SWSB, RJ, GG5]

Sakiyan A species often hired to be assassins because of their excellent aural and olfactory senses, they have keen infrared peripheral vision and often track their prey by scent. [CCG]

Salculd A female Selonian, she was a member of the Hunchuzuc Den, a rebel group opposed to the Overden, the central power on Selonia. A peppery, energetic-looking pilot, she patched together a ship to transport Han Solo from Corellia to Selonia. [AS]

Salis D'aar The capital city of the planet Bakura. [TAB]

Salliche An agricultural planet in the Core Worlds, it is headquarters of Salliche Ag Corporation, which administers eighteen farming planets throughout the region. Although the Empire placed Moff Gegren Throsen in charge of Salliche, its citizens remained loyal to the House Harbright, whose members served the Republic for three centuries. After the rise of the Empire, Lady Selnia Harbright decided to aid the Rebel Alliance. [SWAJ]

Salm, Horton A human general from Norvall II, he was placed in charge of the rebuilding of Rogue Squadron. Often at odds with Rogue Leader Wedge Antilles, he was nevertheless an honorable man and a good soldier. It was very strange that his disobedience of a direct order during the Squadron's initial raid on Borleias saved the Squadron—and himself. Instead of leaving the system as ordered, he and his men stayed behind to assist Rogue Squadron's exit. While lending much-needed help, the ship he and his men would have been on, the *Mon Valle*, was destroyed by planetary defenses. [RS]

Salporin A childhood friend of Chewbacca, he was one of two Wookiees assigned to protect Princess Leia Organa Solo during her stay on Kashyyyk while Grand Admiral Thrawn's Noghri Death Commandos were searching for her. Salporin was a master of the ryyyk blade and often wielded two of the knives simultaneously. Salporin grew up with Chewbacca, but he chose to remain on Kashyyyk and fell in love with the Wookiee maiden Gorrlyn, whom he married. When Imperials invaded his homeworld, he was forced into years of slavery until—aided by the Alliance—he joined other freedom fighters to set Kashyyyk free. He was killed protecting Princess Leia from a Noghri attack. [HE, HESB]

Sal-Solo, Thrackan Han Solo's first cousin, he looks very much like Han except for his beard. He was presumed dead but surfaced as the Hidden Leader of the antialien Human League. Thrackan Sal-Solo proclaimed himself to be the designated successor to the Diktat that ruled under the Empire and declared the Corellian sector to be independent and free of any New Republic entanglements. The Human League eventually was defeated and Sal-Solo was captured by the intervention of the New Republic and a Bakuran task force. [AC]

salthia beans A food often served to the children of Han and Leia Organa Solo in their nursery on Coruscant, it was occasionally used in their food fights. [NR]

Sanctuary Moon One of the names given to the forest moon of Endor. [RJ]

sandcrawler Sandcrawlers are huge vehicles, originally brought to Tatooine long ago as the planet was being established as a mining colony. Their steam-powered nuclear fusion engines and giant treads let them move through the trackless Dune Sea, making them well-suited to their original task of hauling ore. When the mining venture failed, the sandcrawlers were abandoned. They were quickly taken over by the diminutive Jawas, scavengers of the planet who collect just about any kind of mechanical or electronic equipment but specialize in rebuilding broken droids.

At nearly twenty meters high, each sturdy sandcrawler can house a full Jawa clan numbering up to several hundred individuals. Inside is a maze of sleeping and eating alcoves, junk, machinery, spare parts, and fully functional droids. New droid

Sandcrawler

Sandtroopers

acquisitions are loaded either through a magnetic suction tube or a front loading ramp. Jawas rely on sandcrawlers for defense against their natural enemies, Sand People and ferocious krayt dragons. [GG7, MTS, SWN]

sandjiggers Tiny Tatooine arthropods, they feed on razor moss. [ISWU]

Sand People *See* Tusken Raiders

sand skimmer A one-person repulsorlift vehicle, it consists of a disk to stand on and a large sail that extends from the rear to help it travel over sand flats and similar terrain. [DTV]

sand sloth A beast of burden, it resembles a cross between a rhinoceros and a musk ox. Demma Moll used sand sloths on her farm complex on the planet Annoo. [DTV]

sandtrooper Stormtroopers who have been trained in desert tactics, they wear temperature-controlled body gloves underneath their protective armor to help them keep cool while working in blistering heat. [GG1, ISB]

sandwhirl A type of desert storm with blowing sand that occasionally ravages Tatooine. [SWN]

Sanjin A planet near the Core Worlds, it was where the Nikto agent Ma'w'shiye betrayed the Alliance, deserted his Rebel squadron, and stole the group's spacecraft. [SWAJ]

Sarahwiee A frozen world of glaciers, mountains, and ice-covered oceans in the Bseto system, it was home to a top-secret Imperial research facility. The outpost, situated in a mountain range in the southern hemisphere, held 1,000 personnel and was accessible only by air. When Emperor Palpatine first established the facility, he had all references to it wiped from the Imperial archives for security. After the Battle of Endor, a few Imperial fleet captains equipped and supplied the base until the defeat of Grand Admiral Thrawn, when it became necessary for free-traders to handle the cargo shipments. After Thrawn's defeat but before the rise of the resurrected clone Emperor, a New Republic commando team including Luke Skywalker and led by Lieutenant Page was sent to Sarahwiee to destroy the facility and erase its computer records. [SWAJ]

Sarcophagus The moon of the planet Sacorria, it is a vast graveyard that is visited only by those who are burying their dead. [AC]

Sarlacc An omnivorous, multitentacled creature with needle-sharp teeth and a large beak, it lives at the bottom of a deep sand hole called the Great Pit of Carkoon, located in the wastelands of the planet Tatooine's Dune Sea. The Sarlacc has a huge mouth in its giant wormlike head and is always waiting to be fed. The mouth is lined with rows of sharply pointed teeth, all aimed inward in order to keep food trapped inside. It seems to prefer living creatures, snatching unfortunate victims and dragging them into its mucus-coated mouth. Local legend has it that victims die a slow and painful death in the belly of the Sarlacc. This is because its digestive juices take 1,000 years to fully break down its meals.

Crime lord Jabba the Hutt often used the Sarlacc to dispose of opponents and intended to feed Han Solo, Chewbacca, and Luke Skywalker to the beast. But he didn't reckon with their resourcefulness and the Force. They managed to destroy Jabba before he could complete the deed. Bounty hunter Boba Fett and a few of Jabba's henchmen appeared to have succumbed, but Fett managed to escape the Sarlacc's maw, claiming later that the creature had found him "somewhat indigestible." [RJ, SWCG, DE]

Sarlacci spores Spores that eventually form a Sarlacc, they fly through space, land on planets, and nest in their surfaces, forming pits with mouths that open toward the sky. The Sarlacc themselves do not have a well-developed neural system, but over millennia they can develop a consciousness by assimilating the thoughts of whatever creatures they digest. [TJP]

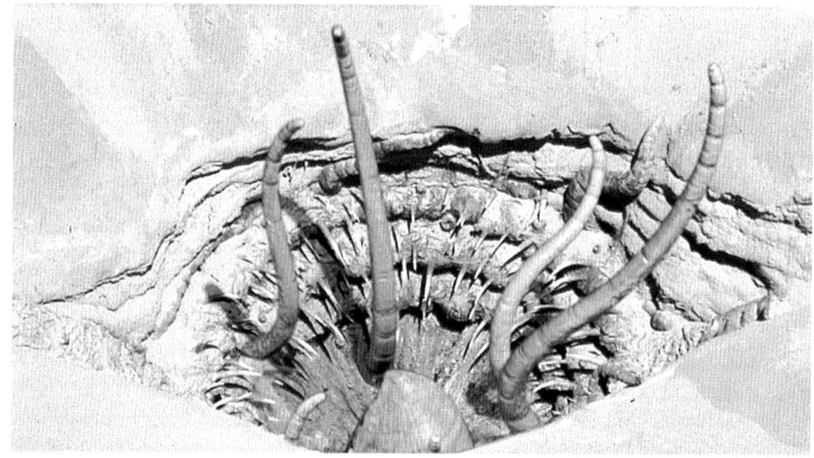
Sarlacc

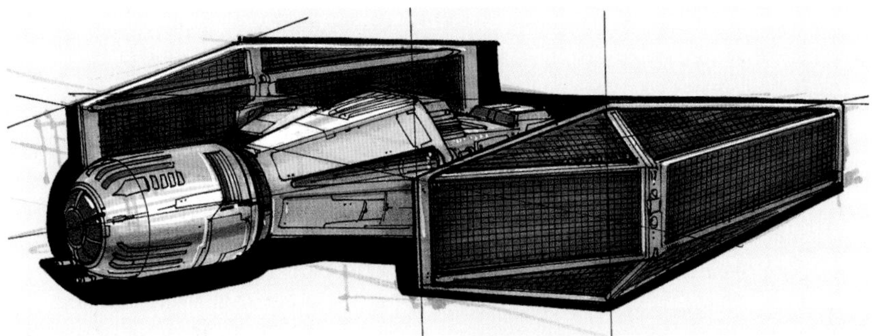

Scimitar assault bomber

Saurin A species from the planet Durkteel. [CCG]

Sauropteroid Intelligent aquatic reptiles, these natives of the planet Dellalt range from ten to fifteen meters long. They constantly swim their world's oceans, keeping their heads above water with their long muscular necks. Their humanoid heads have blowholes; their hides range in color from light gray to greenish black. [HLL]

Sazz, Jak A smuggler, he frequented the Byss Bistro. An Ab'Vgartte, he never bathes. He carries an oversized hydrospanner that he uses to pummel things. [DE, DESB]

scan grid A device normally used to measure and analyze the magnetic and thermal properties of metals, it applies electrical surges to the metal and examines the effects with specialized sensors. Darth Vader used a scan grid to torture Han Solo on Cloud City. [ESBN]

scarab droids Small, deadly beetle-like droids, they can be used to poison an opponent. The cloned Emperor Palpatine used scarab droids to attempt to kill Luke Skywalker when Palpatine sent his dark-side knights to New Alderaan to kidnap the Jedi twins of Han and Leia Organa Solo. [DE2]

Scardia *See* Space Station Scardia

Scardia Voyager A golden starship, it was used exclusively by the Prophets of the Dark Side. [MMY, PDS]

Scavs Junk gatherers and traders, they gather their wares from battlefields—often looting in the heat of battle. Scavs, or scavengers, use armored, wheeled transports, nek battle dogs, and weapons droids to protect themselves. [DE]

Scomp link access

Scimitar assault bombers The latest Imperial bombers, they were ordered into production when Grand Admiral Thrawn returned and seized control of the remnants of the Empire. The Scimitar assault bomber is a dedicated atmospheric and space bomber with better performance than a standard TIE bomber. It was designed partly by members of the elite and highly decorated Scimitar bomber assault wing.

The two-crew bomber has a single pod with two elongated solar array wings, a layout that provides greater visibility than older models. The middle of the pod houses navigation and targeting systems, a power generator, and twin repulsorlift engines. Repulsor thrusters are located in the Scimitar's wing struts for greater maneuverability. The pod's rear portion contains a bomb bay and single sublight ion engine. In space, it is significantly faster than a TIE bomber and the newest model boosts atmospheric cruising speed significantly. The bomber has a reinforced hull and shields, proton grenades, free-falling thermal detonators, and space for sixteen concussion missiles. There are also linked forward laser cannons. A full wing of the bombers—seventy-two ships—led the assault on Mrisst, one of Thrawn's feints prior to his final assault on Coruscant. [DFRSB, GSWU, DFR, SWGV]

scomp link access A computer connection access port, it is used mainly by droids to plug into database networks and locate information, evaluate threats, execute diagnostics, or perform maintenance. [DSTC, CCG]

Sconn, Lieutenant Davith An Imperial prisoner at the New Republic's Jagg Island Detention Center, as a member of the Imperial Navy he was executive officer of the Star Destroyer *Forger*. The starship suppressed a rebellion on Gra Ploven by creating steam clouds that boiled alive 200,000 Ploven in three coastal cities. Chief of State Leia Organa Solo visited Sconn to probe his knowledge of the Yevetha. The lieutenant provided insights as to how the Yevethan power structure worked, the species's "dominance killing" philosophy, and its methods of punishment. Sconn told Leia about the Yevethan ability to learn quickly, leaving little doubt that they could soon establish a powerful fleet of their own. [SOL]

Scorekeeper The deity worshipped by Trandoshans, who believe that the Scorekeeper exists beyond time and space, recording every deed of each Trandoshan hunter. [TBH]

scout trooper *See* stormtrooper

scout walker *See* All Terrain Scout Transport

Scraf, Arvid A human about six years younger than Luke Skywalker, Scraf was the first inhabitant of Nam Chorios that Skywalker met when he landed on the planet. He lives with his aunt Gin and tools around in a landspeeder. He introduced Luke to others and helped him get around the planet. [POT]

Scrambas, Pello A lieutenant in the Rebel Alliance and a veteran officer, Pello Scrambas loyally served the Organa family for nearly two decades as a guard for the Royal House of Alderaan. Pello's last assignment was to protect Princess Leia on her mission aboard the *Tantive IV*. He was taken prisoner when the ship was overtaken by the Star Destroyer *Devastator* and was never seen again. [CCG]

Admiral Screed

Screed, Admiral An Imperial officer, the no-nonsense military man who wore an electronic patch over one eye was one of the Emperor's top aides during the early days of the Empire. The droids R2-D2 and C-3PO had various encounters with the admiral. [DTV]

Scuppa A starship pilot for crime kingpin Jabba the Hutt, he betrayed his boss when both were trapped aboard the larger ship of the monstrous Princess Nampi. He played up to the revolting princess, even agreeing to become her mate. Instead, he became a meal. Jabba had the last laugh, however, detonating by remote control a vial of super acid he had implanted in Scuppa's brain years before, dissolving Nampi into a flood of goop. [JAB]

scurrier Scavengers who lurk in Mos Eisley and other settlements, they scuttle from one garbage pail to another in search of food. When not foraging for edibles, scurriers wander the streets making nuisances of themselves. They are prone to steal whatever they can get their paws on to use in their nests.

Scurriers are only about a third of a meter tall and two-thirds of a meter long. While they are quick to flee anything bigger than they are, they're quite protective of their nests and attack any creatures that wander into their territory. Scurrier bites are very painful. They use high-pitched squeals and loud snorts to frighten off intruders. Male scurriers tend to be somewhat larger than females and have large, curved horns.

Since they're good at finding hiding places aboard starships, scurriers can be found in most spaceport towns. However, they can carry disease and become a public health hazard if their populations aren't kept in check. [SW, SWSE]

Scy'rrep, Evet An infamous galactic bandit, he knocked off fifteen starliners and got away with millions in credits and jewels before being captured. At his trial, when asked why he robbed luxury cruisers, Evet Scy'rrep answered, "Because that's where the credits are." His fame was cemented by a holoproj series based on his deeds called "Galactic Bandits," which Luke Skywalker watched when he was young. [SOTE]

seafah jewels Formed on the moon of Pydyr deep in its ocean within the shells of microscopic creatures, the jewels were the source of much of the great wealth of Pydyr. After the Dark Jedi Kueller decimated the Pydyrians, he spared the moon's seafah jewelers, because it required a trained Pydyrian eye to detect the tiny jewels on the seabed floor. The jewels were often used in decoration and in Pydyrian architecture. [NR]

Second Imperium The name given to an attempt to reestablish control of the Empire some nineteen years after the Battle of Endor. The main force behind the attempt consisted of four of the late Emperor Palpatine's most loyal personal guards. They set up a Shadow Academy led by the Dark Jedi Brakiss to train new legions of Dark Jedi and stormtroopers to aid in retaking the galaxy. For a while, using trickery, they successfully convinced many that a clone of Palpatine himself was the Great Leader of the Second Imperium. [YJK]

sector A group or cluster of star systems united for economic and political reasons, sectors were first formed by the Old Republic. Originally, a sector consisted of as many star systems as necessary to include about fifty inhabited or habitable planets. But over the millennia, sectors grew to vast and nearly unmanageable sizes. Under Emperor Palpatine's New Order, sectors were redefined and each placed under a Moff to whom all the planetary governors reported. Each Moff had a military sector group under his command to secure the hundreds of systems within his sector. To deal with rebellious or otherwise difficult systems, the Emperor appointed Grand Moffs to oversee priority sectors, which included the particularly troubled worlds of a dozen or more sectors. [ISB]

Secura, Nat The last descendant of the planet Ryloth's great Twi'lek house, he was controlled by Bib Fortuna, who used Secura's power to sell many of his people into slavery. Nat Secura was badly burned by Jabba the Hutt's enslavement forces, and Fortuna brought him to Tatooine to live in Jabba's palace. Jabba had planned to execute Secura, but Bib Fortuna rescued him by having the B'omarr monks remove his brain before the body was thrown to the rancor. [TJP]

Sedesia A high-gravity planet in the Mid-Rim, it is a cold, arid world of tundra, forests, and mountains with extreme seasonal changes and unpredictable weather. Sedesians cross the planet's surface on six-legged reptilian mounts called striders and sometimes on single-wheeled machines called wheelbikes. Sedesia has been colonized for several hundred years, and its 1.5 million settlers are primarily stubborn breedtash ranchers known for their independence and sympathy toward the Rebellion. The Empire, testing a pathogen-based loyalty enhancement project, infected the entire population with a deadly plague called the Gray Death. Imperial forces set up medical facilities, ostensibly to protect the citizens from the plague, but which actually forced

Scurrier

Sedriss

them to become dependent on the Empire for their continued survival. [SWAJ]

Sedri Covered by warm, shallow seas, this planet is home to both the aquatic Sedrians and a communal intelligence of tiny polyps known as Golden Sun. Golden Sun is attuned to the Force and provides power, healing, and other necessities to the Sedrians, who worship Golden Sun as the center of their society. Golden Sun's use of the Force also creates massive gravity readings, causing problems for hyperspace navigation near the Sedri system. The peaceful Sedrians have constructed underwater cities and have appointed a High Priest to safeguard the cave in which Golden Sun lives. The Empire came to Sedri to research a possible artificial gravity-well generator and constructed an Imperial garrison. A group of Rebels infiltrated the garrison, studied the Imperials' aquatic equipment, and discussed strategy and techniques with the Sedrians. This resulted in the formation of the Rebel Sea Commandos, who later saw action on Mon Calamari fighting the Emperor's World Devastators. [GG4, DESB, BGS]

Sedrian A seal-humanoid combination, these sleek aquatic mammals live on the water world of Sedri. They grow to about three meters long, with fine slick fur covering their bodies from head to fluke. Sedrians have the heads and lower body of a seal and the torso and arms of a human. They can breathe air and live outside of water for brief periods but prefer to live in their underwater cities. [BGS, GG4]

Sedriss Emperor Palpatine's dark-side Executor, he commanded the dark-side elite warriors after the demise of the first clone of Palpatine in a bid to regain control of the galaxy. On the planet Byss, Sedriss discovered that the Emperor had been reborn into yet another clone. Palpatine ordered Sedriss to go to Ossus to get Luke Skywalker, but the Executor was destroyed by the power of an ancient Jedi, Ood Bnar. [DE2]

seeker As a military remote, this small ball covered with sensors can be programmed to track down and terminate specific targets. Miniature repulsors hold it aloft and allow it to change position rapidly. In military action, heat and light sensors track its target with fatal accuracy. A seeker can board unsuspecting starships and carry out its deadly mission while in flight, often leaving no trace of the victim or itself. Seekers can be programmed to self-destruct after their mission is verified. [CCG]

See-Threepio *See* C-3PO

Seifax A dummy corporation set up for Loronar Corporation, it has a plant on Antemeridias. [POT]

Sei'lar, Asyr A graduate of the Bothan Martial Academy, she was on a mission to Coruscant when she first encountered Gavin Darklighter and Rogue Squadron at the Azure Dianoga cantina in Invisec, where she worked with the Alien Combine. She and her friends assumed that Darklighter's nervousness and his rejection of her offer to dance were due to bigotry. He and his Rogue friends were brought before the Alien Combine for judgment, but before they could be sentenced to death, the Combine hideout came under attack by Imperial forces. During the battle that followed, Sei'lar realized that the Rogues were no friends of the Empire, so she helped them escape.

When she learned their true identity, she joined forces with Rogue Squadron to bring down Coruscant's defense shield system. While brainstorming with her new allies, she suggested using the mirrors on the Orbital Solar Energy Transfer Satellite to evaporate a reservoir. The resulting atmospheric condensation created a tremendous thunderstorm, and lightning brought down the power grid, shutting down one of the shields. Shortly after the liberation of Coruscant, Sei'lar was offered a position in Rogue Squadron, although for purely political reasons. Nevertheless, she was a welcome addition because her X-wing piloting skills were impressive. She also developed a serious relationship with Darklighter, who had just celebrated his seventeenth birthday. [WG, KT, BW]

Sela Wedge Antilles's second-in-command on the *Yavin*, she was a thin, nervous woman and a crack shot. Although she was an invaluable assistant on Coruscant, she still had to prove herself in a battle command. [NR]

Selab A planet in the Hapes Cluster, it is home to the trees of wisdom. Believed by many to be only a myth, the trees bear fruit that can greatly increase the intelligence of those who have reached old age. [CPL]

Selaggis A planet that was the location of a colony that was obliterated by Warlord Zsinj's Super Star Destroyer *Iron Fist.* Han Solo saw the destruction while on a five-month hunt to locate and destroy Zsinj's ship. [CPL]

Selonia One of the five inhabited worlds in the Corellian system, it has clear blue skies and a surface composed of hundreds of islands separated by innumerable seas, inlets, and bays. Beneath the surface of Selonia is a powerful planetary repulsor, used in ancient times to transport the planet into its current orbit from an unknown location. Selonians are a hive species with thick tails, sleek fur, long faces, and needle-sharp teeth. They live together in genetically related dens. Each den is made up of one fertile female—the queen, who gives birth to all members of a den—a few fertile males, and several hundred sterile females. All sterile females with the same father are said to be in the same sept, and members of a sept are genetically identical. The sterile females interact with other species and perform all

Zev Senesca

the important functions of Selonian life. Selonians have a deep psychological need to reach a consensus.

Some fourteen years after the Battle of Endor, two Selonian factions, the Republicists and the Absolutists, struggled for control of the planetary repulsor. The Republicists intended to turn it over to the New Republic in exchange for Selonian sovereignty, while the Absolutists planned to use it as a weapon for the creation of Selonian independence. Han Solo and Leia Organa Solo were pulled into the struggle, which the Republicists eventually won. During the crisis, a Bakuran attack force led a diversionary assault on Selonia and one of its ships was destroyed by Selonia's repulsor. [AC, AS, SAC]

Selonian A tall, strong, quick species, they have long slender bodies and can go on all fours if necessary or desirable. Their sleek bodies are covered with short fur. Their faces are pointed with bristly whiskers. They have very sharp teeth and long tails that can be used for defense. Selonians live in dens, and visitors will see only sterile females; all males and any females who can bear children stay hidden in the den at all times. [AC]

Seluss A Sullustan, he normally accompanied the smuggler Jarril on the ship *Spicy Lady*. When Lando Calrissian discovered the lifeless ship following Jarril's murder, Seluss was nowhere to be found. Han Solo and Chewbacca came upon Seluss on Skip 1 in Smuggler's Run, where he attacked them with a blaster in an attempt to make the other smugglers think Solo and Chewie were his enemies. Seluss was aware that Jarril's trade in former Imperial goods was attracting too much attention. [NR]

Semtin, Captain Marl A male human Imperial officer, with dark eyes and swarthy skin, Semtin is captain of the *Harrow*, a *Victory*-class Star Destroyer. He's rather oily and ambitious. [XW]

Senator Palpatine *See* Palpatine, Emperor

Sendo, General An officer of little accomplishment in the Destab Branch of Imperial Intelligence, he had never seen battle. General Sendo was on retainer to Prince Xizor's Black Sun criminal organization because of his access to all kinds of valuable information. [SOTE]

Senesca, Zev A Rebel Alliance snowspeeder pilot, he was among those who defended Echo Base on the ice planet Hoth. Zev Senesca first discovered and rescued Luke Skywalker and Han Solo after they had disappeared in the Hoth tundra and were forced to spend a frigid night in the desolate area. Senesca's comm-unit designation was Rogue Two. His snowspeeder was shot down and he was killed during the Battle of Hoth.

Senesca had been born on Kestic Station near the Bestine system. His independent-minded parents had nurtured his rebellious side, and as soon as he was of age, he joined the Rebel Alliance. His parents were killed when the Imperial Star Destroyer *Merciless* destroyed Kestic Station. [ESB, GG3]

Senex sector Adjacent to the Juvex sector and near the Ninth Quadrant, it is ruled by an elite group of aristocratic Ancient Houses. The sector contains the Senex system and the planets Karfeddion, Veron, and Mussubir Three. Yetoom and Belsavis are located on its edge. The Ancient Houses and their Lords are extremely independent and wish to rule their planets as they see fit. They scorn any outside interference. They were largely left alone under Emperor Palpatine's rule, and neither the post-Endor Empire nor the New Republic have been very successful in influencing them.

The Senex Lords have long been accused of mistreating their workers and violating the Rights of Sentience. The oldest of the Houses is House Vandron, headed by Lady Theala Vandron, which operates slave farms on Karfeddion. The House Elegin is headed by Drost Elegin, and the House Garonnin gets a large portion of its revenue from strip-mining asteroids.

The Senex system once held an Imperial training area. Before the Battle of Yavin, a new Alliance recruit accidentally hypered into the area in his X-wing and destroyed most of the training facilities before realizing his danger and hypering out. Eight years after the Battle of Endor, Stinna Draesinge Sha, a pupil of Nasdra Magrody's, was assassinated in the Senex sector in House Vandron territory. Later that year, many of the Senex Lords met with the late Emperor's mistress, Roganda Ismaren, on Belsavis, intending to form a military alliance. [COJ, FP]

sensor A device that gathers information that can assist ship crews in analyzing the galaxy around them, it scans an area and acquires information to be displayed in text or graphic displays. There are various types of sensors. Passive-mode sensors gather information about the immediate area around a ship. Scan-mode sensors send out pulses in all directions, actively gathering a much wider range of information. Search-mode sensors actively seek out information in a specific direction. Focus-mode sensors closely examine a specific portion of space. [SWRPG2]

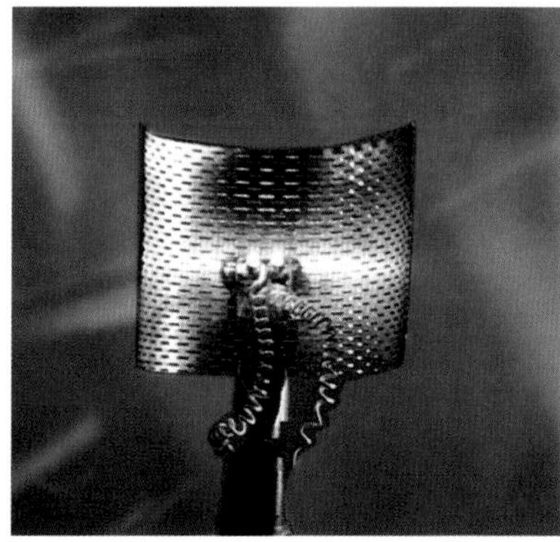
Scan-mode sensor

sensor suite A sensor suite comprises all the major systems and subsystems associated with complex sensor arrays. [HSE]

sensory plug-in These devices let astromechs and other droids interface with computers, sensors, monitors, and data systems through a direct connection. They are similar to scomp links. [SME]

sentient tank *See* tank droid

Sentinel A cruiser in the Bakuran task force. [AS]

Sentinel One of the large guards used to protect the reborn clone Emperor's citadel on the planet Byss, their origins are unknown. Some believe that the Sentinels were giant cyborgs or droids. [DE, DESB]

Sepan system Located in the sector of the same name, the system contains the planets Ripoblus, Dimok, Gerbaud 2, and Sepan 8. Following the Battle of Hoth, a long, destructive war between the peoples of Ripoblus and Dimok was forcibly ended by the intervention of Imperial forces under the command of Admiral Harkov. At one point, the leaders of the two sides attempted a rendezvous near Sepan 8 to organize a united attack against Imperial forces. [TSC]

septoid An insectoid, it is from the planet Eriadu. [CCG]

Serenity, Celestial An enhanced human gambler on Crseih Station. [CS]

Sern sector Located near the Core Worlds, it contains the planet Ghorman. [RSB, FP]

Serpent Masters Slavers, they rode winged serpents controlled by ultrasonic signals emitted from a medallion worn by the Supreme Master. The droid R2-D2 was able to duplicate the signals, which enabled Luke Skywalker to ride a serpent and defeat the Serpent Masters, freeing Tanith Shire's people from slavery. [CSW]

Serper, Wyron A daring spy for the Rebel Alliance, he went undercover as a sensor specialist aboard the Imperial Star Destroyer *Avenger* on one of his most perilous missions. Later, Wyron Serper was assigned to scan for Imperial ships that might be hidden in the meteor activity of the Hoth system. [CCG]

Wyron Serper

servodriver A powered hand tool, it is used to tighten and loosen fasteners. A servodriver produces motion when it receives signals from a controller. [SWN]

servo-grip The servo-driven hands of a droid. [HLL]

Seswenna sector A sector containing the planet Eriadu. Grand Moff Tarkin developed the Tarkin Doctrine of rule by fear while he was a governor in charge of the Seswenna sector and the Outer Rim Territories. [MTS, DSTC]

Setor The former homeworld of Wetyin's colony, its people departed after suffering persecution. The Fernandin Scouting Operation was given a permit by the Empire to find the group a new homeworld. Some of the worlds considered included Betshish and Yavin 4. [GG2]

Sette, Urlor A large man, he befriended Rogue Squadron pilot Corran Horn when they were fellow prisoners in the *Lusankya*. Often acting under orders from the Alliance's Jan Dodonna, also a prisoner, Urlor Sette assisted in Corran's escape from the top-secret prison facility. [KT]

Sevarcos An infamous spice world, it orbits the orange star Lumea in the Sevarcos system. Because the spice extracted from Sevarcos's Imperial mines is so profitable, the Empire maintained a permanent customs blockade of the entire system. A huge asteroid field drifting between the sixth and seventh planets housed the elite Fate's Judges TIE interceptor squadron, which attacked any smuggler foolish enough to run the blockade. Sevarcos, brown- and amber-colored from space, is a dry, windswept world plagued by frequent sandstorms. The planet's two types of spice, the common white andris and the rare black carsunum, are primarily mined in the equatorial region, where the mines double as brutal Imperial prisons. Animal life includes the spice eel, which burrows through rock and can reach lengths of up to thirty meters.

The planet's original human population, the Sevari, are believed to be the descendants of settlers from the early Old Republic colony ship *Sevari Cabal*. The Sevari eventually formed clans headed by Spice Lords to oversee the spice trade, although total control shifted to the Empire. Unprotected visitors to Sevarcos can suffer side effects from inhaling the trace amounts of spice found in the atmosphere, but native Sevari, accustomed to the constant spice, often slip into a comalike spice narcosis when breathing the pure air of other worlds. Most of the planet's one million Sevari shun advanced technology and use archaic wind riders for transportation and projectile flashpistols for defense. [SWAJ]

S-foil The assembly on an X-wing starfighter that helps connect each wing section with the opposite diagonal wing section, it is composed of double-layered wings in the S-foil that spread apart for attack, forming the X that gives the craft its name. B-wing starfighters also feature S-foils; their twin wings split apart from the ship's central foil, forming a crosslike pattern. [SW, RJ, SWSB]

Shaara A native Tatooine girl, she is one of the few people to have come out of the Great Pit of Carkoon alive. Shaara fell into the cavernous maw along with a group of Imperial stormtroopers who had been chasing her and planned to assault her. They never emerged. [TJP]

Shadow Academy A torus-shaped space station located near the Galactic Core, it was built by the Second

Imperium for the express purpose of training Jedi in the dark side of the Force. Covered with weaponry and protected by a powerful cloaking device, the Shadow Academy was capable of hyperspace travel and could move to a new location at a moment's notice. The station was stark and austere, with harsh, spartan accommodations for its students, locks on every door, and chrono chimes marking every quarter-hour.

Brakiss, a turncoat student of Luke Skywalker's, led the Academy with the assistance of the Nightsister Tamith Kai, but was never allowed to leave the station. The entire station was filled with chain-reaction explosives, set to detonate should the Second Imperium ever become displeased with the Academy's progress.

Some nineteen years after the Battle of Endor, Jacen and Jaina Solo and their friend Lowbacca were kidnapped and brought to the Shadow Academy, where they were to train as Dark Jedi. Soon after their escape, the Shadow Academy was moved to Coruscant. Still hiding behind its cloaking device, the station launched attacks on New Republic convoys, and Brakiss recruited several people, including Jacen and Jaina's friend Zekk, to serve in the Second Imperium. The station was revealed when Jaina used a light beam from one of Coruscant's orbiting mirrors to overwhelm its cloak. But the Academy managed to escape and to establish a new hiding place near the Denarii Nova. There Zekk, in a lightsaber duel conducted in the Shadow Academy's hub arena, killed his chief rival, Vilas, and became the Second Imperium's Darkest Knight.

Finally the leaders of the Second Imperium, displeased with the progress of Brakiss, detonated the station and killed the Shadow Academy's leader. [YJK]

Shadow Chaser A spacecraft owned by the Nightsister Garowyn, it is covered in nearly invincible quantum armor. Luke Skywalker used it to escape from the Shadow Academy after rescuing the kidnapped Jaina and Jacen Solo and Lowbacca. [YJK]

shadow droids Powerful new Imperial attack fighters built in great secrecy by the reborn cloned Emperor Palpatine, they were constructed around the brains of fallen Imperial fighter aces. The brains were immersed in nutrient baths and hardwired to tactical computers. It was rumored that the shadow droids were empowered by the dark side of the Force. [DE2]

Shalam This planet imposed a 100 percent tariff on Jandarra vegetables from Jubilar. Fifteen years after the Battle of Endor, Han Solo went to Jubilar to make a smuggling run for old times' sake and agreed to smuggle a cargo of Jandarra vegetables to Shalam, where his wife, Leia, was on official business. [TBH]

Shana A Mistryl Shadow Guard, she accompanied Mara Jade to help liberate Kessel and battled the prototype Death Star above the planet. [COF]

Shannador's Revenge An *Invincible*-class Capital ship, it flies under the banner of the Corporate Sector Authority. [HSE]

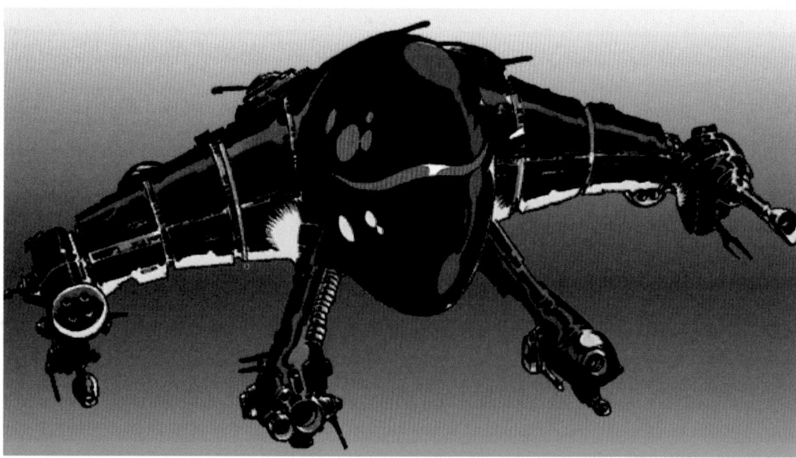

Shadow droid

Shaum Hii A planet famous for its noisy cattle markets, it is home to the Kian'thar. This intelligent species herds the airborne derlacs. [HE,GG12]

Shayoto An ancient Jedi who attended the great Jedi assembly at Mount Meru 4,000 years before the Galactic Civil War. [DLS]

Shazeen A Sauropteroid, he helped Han Solo and his party on the planet Dellalt during their quest for the lost treasure of Xim the Despot. A veteran of many conflicts, Shazeen has a nearly black hide, bears notched and bitten flippers, and is missing an eye. [HLL]

shell-bat A flying reptile, it is native to the planet Geran. [TJP]

Shesharile system Located in the Minos Cluster, it contains a gas giant around which orbit the inhabited moons Shesharile 5 and 6, sometimes called the Twin Planets. Their twelve billion inhabitants are ruled by a single corrupt government, and the streets of their cities have been taken over by out-of-control criminals and wild swoop gangs such as the Spiders, the Rabid Mynocks, and the Raging Banthas. Both worlds are heavily polluted. [SWAJ, GG6]

Shiel, Riv A Shistavanen from Uvena III, he was a member of Rogue Squadron. His species is considered somewhat more violent than humans, and the Empire had placed a death mark on him for past crimes. Even so, Rogue Squadron benefited from his expert piloting talents. Seriously injured on several missions, he was felled by the Krytos virus on Coruscant. When fully recovered, he joined in the Bacta War against cartel leader Ysanne Isard. While on a mission to hijack one of her bacta convoys, he was killed by enemy fire from the *Corrupter*. [RS, WG, KT, BW]

Shield An assault carrier in the New Republic's Fifth Fleet, it was deployed in the blockade of Doornik-319 at the start of the Yevethan crisis. [SOL]

shield *See* deflector shield

shield generator A device that produces the power needed to create and maintain deflector shields and

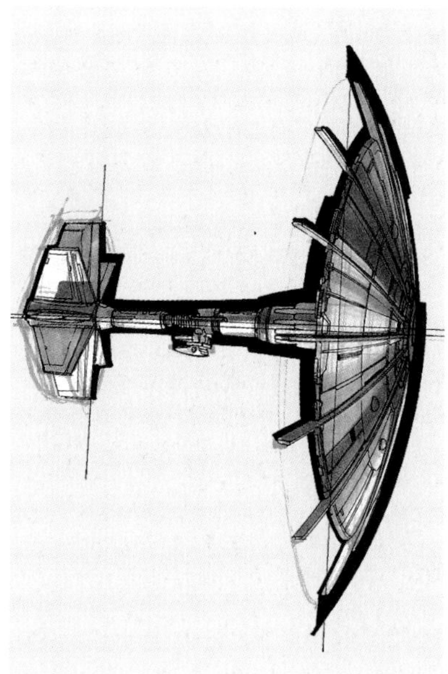

Shieldship

to focus those shields around a given object. [RJ]

shieldship Custom-designed escort vessels, they were built to protect ships traveling to the planet Nkllon in the Athega system from the scorching rays of Athega's superhot sun, which can destroy ships carrying only standard shielding. Even though Nkllon is so hot that beings can live only on the night side of the planet, turned away from the sun, its mineral resources proved too valuable to pass up for a gambling man like Lando Calrissian, who devised a gigantic mobile unit, Nomad City, to mine the ore.

The twelve shieldships were built by the newly formed Republic Engineering Corporation. They proved both difficult to pilot and to maintain, and substantial downtime had to be part of their schedules. The ships were, in effect, giant sun umbrellas. Immense 800-meter-wide cones acted as shields. Their faces were covered by thick armor plating honeycombed with coolant chambers, and their backs had huge tubes and fins to vent off the intense heat. The shadow behind the shield formed the protected area for incoming starships. Trailing behind each shield was a 400-meter pylon with a drive tug that provided sublight and hyperdrive thrust.

Normally, the shieldship simply took control of the escorted vessel via slave circuit at the outer-rim depot and jumped into the heart of the system, bringing the other vessel along for a ride that took about one standard hour. Ships without slave circuits had to be escorted to Nkllon on sublight drives, which took about ten hours.

The success of the mining operation and its New Republic ties made it a target for Grand Admiral Thrawn. His second attack on Nomad City destroyed its drive units and long-range communications, and Star Destroyers attacking the Outer-Rim depot disabled all but one of the shieldships. [HE, HESB, GSWU, LC]

Shimmer A planet of massive glaciers, it was the site of a Rebel Alliance medium-security work camp. [SWAJ]

shimmersilk Sheer and lustrous, the expensive fabric is used to create high-fashion clothing in the more well-off regions of the galaxy. [HSR, HSE]

Shire, Tanith A supply tug operator at the starship yards on Fondor, she stole drone barges and sent them crashing to the planet's surface, where they were salvaged by the Serpent Masters, who kept Tanith Shire's people in slavery. Luke Skywalker and Shire escaped Fondor on one of these barges. After crash landing, Luke defeated the Serpent Masters and freed Shire's people. [CSW]

Shistavanen An intelligent but violent species, these fur-covered bipeds have wolflike faces, and sharp claws and teeth. Popularly called Shistavanen Wolfmen, they are hunters by nature. [GG1, GG2]

***Sh'ner*-class planetary assault carrier** Ovoid ships nearly 750 meters long, these carriers are essential to Ssi-ruuk Imperium invasion forces. Sh'ner planetary assault carriers usually remain back from the main battle lines until the target world has been defeated. The carriers then move into high orbit to launch P'w'eck-staffed *D'kee*-class landing ships.

Slow and underpowered, Sh'ner carrier ships are closer to transports than combat ships. Their weak shields make them easy targets for enemy vessels. Sh'ner carriers also have minimal weaponry: only six ion cannons, two tractor beam projectors, and twenty-four battle droids for emergencies. They normally rely on Fw'Sen picket ships for armed escort. The interior of a Sh'ner carrier holds nearly a dozen entechment labs for rapidly processing prisoners; giant batteries store the enteched life energies until they are needed.

A small command and entechment lab crew consists of only about sixty Ssi-ruuk, while about 500 P'w'ecks and 300 enteched droids are used as assistants and for manual labor. Each of the three P'w'eck landing ships aboard is armed with 100 paralysis canisters that can be dropped over major population centers, explode at an altitude of 1,000 meters, and spread Ssi-ruuvi paralysis toxins over an area nearly nine square kilometers in size.

When target cities have been effectively neutralized, the Sh'ner carrier's landing ships descend to gather entechment subjects. Each landing ship can carry nearly 10,000 prisoners in confinement pens. The Bakura invasion fleet had three Sh'ner carriers, which retreated to the main Ssi-ruuvi battle fleet after Luke Skywalker captured the *Shriwirr* battle cruiser. [TAB, SWVG]

shock-ball An outdoor team sport in which one team tries to stun the other into unconsciousness with an electrically charged ball or orb. Team members use insulated mitts to handle the orb and scoops to fling and catch it. After a specified time period elapses, the team with the most conscious members wins the match. [HLL]

Shooting Star An Alliance frigate, it was destroyed in a collision with the *Endor*. [BTS]

Tanith Shire

Shoran A Wookiee cousin of Chewbacca, he was killed during the rescue of Han Solo aboard the *Pride of Yevetha.* [TT]

short-term memory enhancement A Force control technique through which a Jedi can replay recent events to carefully examine images and peripheral happenings, it aids the recall of a particular detail that was observed but not consciously remembered. [DFRSB]

Showolter, Captain A member of New Republic Intelligence, he greeted Luke Skywalker and Lando Calrissian when they returned to Coruscant with disturbing news from the Corellian Sector. [AS]

Shrag brothers Sneak-thieves, they live and operate in Nar Shaddaa's vertical city. The Shrag brothers often strip Hutt caravels for quick credits. [DE]

Shreeftut, His Potency the The supreme leader of the warmongering Ssi-ruuk Imperium from the planet Lwhekk, he planned to dominate the galaxy. [TAB]

Shriwirr Among the largest of the Ssi-ruuk customized battle cruisers, it was the lead ship in the reptilian species's assault on the planet Bakura under the command of Admiral Ivpikkis. The *Shriwirr* was an ovoid ship about 900 meters long, armed with the equivalent of twenty-four turbolasers, twenty-four ion cannons, twelve missile launchers, and twelve tractor beam projectors. It carried several landing ships and 500 battle droids, akin to starfighters. The *Shriwirr* was outfitted with a large entechment lab, where the Ssi-ruuk drew the life force from prisoners to power their equipment.

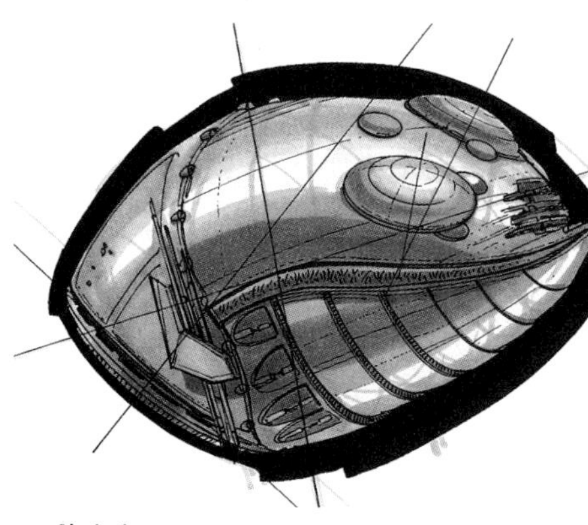
Shriwirr

Elder (Bluescale) Sh'tk'ith

Interior decks of the *Shriwirr* had five-meter-high ceilings to accommodate the Ssi-ruuk, along with countless crawlways and access tunnels for the enslaved P'w'ecks, who were responsible for maintenance and day-to-day operations. A series of stun traps—lethal to humans—prevented P'w'ecks from causing problems. The *Shriwirr* was singlehandedly captured by Luke Skywalker after the Ssi-ruuk evacuated the ship rather than face his Force abilities in battle. The Rebel Alliance refitted the ship for combat duty and renamed it the *Sibwarra,* although techs tended to call it the *Flutie,* after a derisive nickname the Bakurans used to describe the Ssi-ruuk. [TAB, TBSB, SWVG]

Sh'tk'ith, Elder (Bluescale) A blue-scaled bipedal reptilian, he led the Ssi-ruuk Imperium invasion force at Bakura. The attack was to be only the first of many, part of a carefully orchestrated bid to enslave the spirits of humanoids and use their vital energy to power the Ssi-ruuvi war machine. Elder Sh'tk'ith, bearing the venerated nickname Bluescale, came from the planet Lwhekk beyond the galaxy's Outer Rim.

Two Ssi-ruuk races dominate Lwhekk. Both have long faces, tongues in their beaklike noses, eyes with triple eyelids, and long muscular tails. Sh'tk'ith's species, who dominate the planet, have narrower faces and tiny blue scales. The other, which leads the military, are sleek, covered with russet scales. They have a prominent black V on their foreheads. A third race, the P'w'ecks, have drooping eyes and skin, short tails, and dull wits. They were enslaved by the dominant Ssi-ruuk.

The Ssi-ruuk had discovered that their technique known as entechment, the forcible transferring of the electrical essences of beings to power their metallic battle droids, worked best with humanoids. They had captured and brainwashed one young human, Dev Sibwarra, to help them with his evolving Force powers.

Sh'tk'ith was leading the attack on the planet Bakura when Sibwarra located a much more powerful Force user who could be even more helpful in the entechment process—Luke Skywalker. Luke, weakened by Emperor Palpatine's attacks aboard the second Death Star, was lured to the *Shriwirr,* but he was able to turn Sibwarra against his cruel masters. The young man managed to kill the Elder, although he was mortally wounded in the fighting that led to victory. [TAB]

Shyriiwook The name Wookiees give their language. Roughly translated, it means "tongue of the tree people." [TBH]

Sibwarra, Dev Raised on the planet Chandrila as the son of a female Jedi apprentice, the young human and his mother fled to the isolated planet G'rho to escape Emperor Palpatine's Jedi purges. But his mother was killed and Dev Sibwarra captured in a raid on the planet by the warlike Ssi-ruuk. The boy was sent to the Ssi-ruuvi home planet of Lwhekk, where his growing Force abilities were discovered. The Ssi-ruuk decided to brainwash young Dev and use him to scout the galaxy for humans, who made the best subjects for their process of entechment—the transfer of a person's vital energies to power metal battle droids.

Dev was taken in by the Ssi-ruuvi known as Master Firwirrung and helped him raid a number of human outposts in the galaxy. Firwirrung promised to personally entech Sibwarra, freeing him from fear and pain, to reward him for his help. The presence of Luke Skywalker during the invasion at Bakura was enough

Dev Sibwarra

to erase much of Sibwarra's brainwashing. The young man helped Luke escape from the Ssi-ruuk, but was mortally wounded as he killed his cruel masters, including the invasion leader, Elder Sh'tk'ith, in revenge. [TAB]

Sic-six An intelligent arachnid species from the planet Sisk, they have become hunters who use advanced technology to capture prey. Sic-six have black trisectioned bodies ranging from 1.2 to 2.1 meters long covered by a hard, chitinous carapace. They have eight six-jointed legs, eight eyes, and posterior spinnerets to make webs. [GG4]

Sidrona The leader of the Old Republic Senate at the time of the Sith Wars some 4,000 years before the Galactic Civil War. [TSW]

Sienar Fleet Systems The company that manufactured the Empire's various TIE fighters and other craft, it had been known as Republic Sienar Systems. It also produced flight avionics and starship components. [SWSB]

Sienn'rha A young Twi'lek girl, she was stolen from her family on Ryloth by Bib Fortuna, instructed in the art of dance, then presented as a gift to Jabba the Hutt along with the Twi'lek Oola. Rescued from Jabba's palace by Luke Skywalker, she was returned to her family. In gratitude to the Alliance, she gave a spectacular performance for Wedge Antilles and his Rogue Squadron pilots when they came to her planet seeking ryll kor. She offered to give Wedge a private dance, but he reluctantly declined her offer. [BW]

Sif-Uwana A planet where the inhabitants are reputed to be very casual with their money and management style. Mara Jade once visited while on business for the Emperor, and the smuggler Talon Karrde posed as the chief purchasing agent for the Sif-Uwana Council while on a mission to Varonat. [SWAJ]

Sileen A Mistryl Shadow Guard, she was involved in the botched transport of the Hammertong device to the Empire. [TMEC]

Silencer-7 The largest of the reborn cloned Emperor's World Devastators, it led the assault on Mon Calamari. At 3,200 meters long and 1,500 meters tall, it was larger than an Imperial Star Destroyer and had a crew of 25,000. *Silencer-7* had 125 heavy turbolasers, 200 blaster cannons, eighty proton missile tubes, fifteen ion cannons, and fifteen tractor beam projectors. The key to the defeat of the monstrous World Devastators was Palpatine's fear that they could be turned against him, which led him to create a system that allowed him to seize control. Luke Skywalker provided Palpatine's control signals to R2-D2, who shut down the World Devastators during the Battle of Calamari, allowing New Republic forces to destroy the helpless planet smashers. [DE, DESB]

Silizzar, Gurion After the notorious Doctor Evazan poisoned Silizzar's family, Gurion tried to kill the quack in revenge on the planet Ando. But the human Silizzar died on the rocky cliffs surrounding the doctor's castle laboratory. [TMEC]

Silver Egg The private ship of smuggling kingpin Nandreeson, it is specially outfitted for the needs of an amphibian species and includes sunken pools in many of its quarters. [NR]

Silver Speeder A sleek racing landspeeder, it was once owned by Boba Fett. The bounty hunter had outfitted the *Silver Speeder* with such nonstandard equipment as cutting lasers, magnetic harpoons, and a chainsaw shredder. [DTV]

Silver Station A hidden resistance outpost, it drifted near the Dragonflower Nebula in the Doldur sector. Some 400 meters in length, it consisted of a central cube surrounded by many interconnected cylinders. Resistance leader Una Poot used Silver Station to supply seven Rebel cells in the surrounding sector. Just after the Battle of Yavin, the young heiress Tinian I'att and her companions came to Silver Station to meet with Poot. Although Tinian helped foil a Ranat plot to blow up the station, most of its inhabitants were forced to flee when Imperial forces arrived and took control of the outpost. It was here that I'att first met and saved the life of her future partner, the Wookiee bounty hunter Chenlambec. [SWAJ, TBH]

Simoom A large desert on the far side of Endor's forest moon, it is inhabited by a species known as Phlogs. [ETV]

Singing Mountain clan A group of the Witches of Dathomir, its members follow the light side of the Force. [CPL]

Sinidic An aide to Drom Guldi, Baron Administrator of the Kelrodo-Ai Gelatin Mines. Sinidic was a small, nervous man with gray-blond hair and faint wrinkles across his skin, as if it had crumpled with a thousand pressure cracks. He was with his boss on a big-game hunting expedition on Hoth when their prey—wampa ice creatures—turned on them and killed them. [DS]

Sionan Homeworld of the Skup species, who are a humanlike race with small, closely spaced eyes, brittle hair, and skin the color of dianoga cheese. [TMEC]

Sirln, Leesub A humanlike Qiraash, she was enslaved as a child. Leesub Sirln has limited precognition powers and Imperial High Inquisitor Tremayne declared her a Force adept.

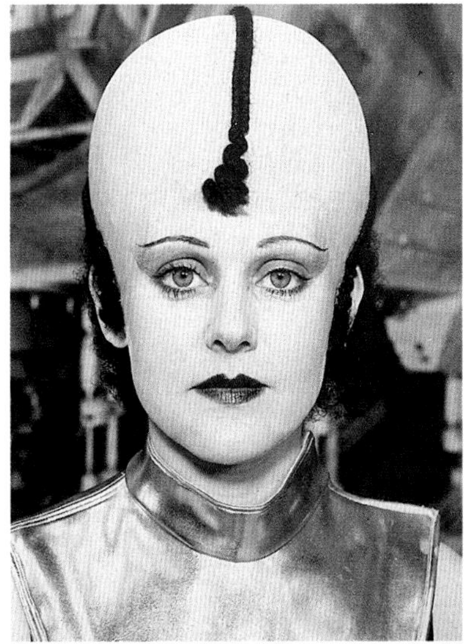

Leesub Sirln

To avoid imprisonment or death, she escaped and hid for years in Mos Eisley on Tatooine. [CCG]

Sirpar An arid, heavy-gravity world, it was used by the Empire as a training outpost for Imperial Army soldiers. The large planet is protected by three orbiting defensive satellites. Sirpar is home to the timid Eklaad, quadruped beings with prehensile snouts and tough armored hides. The 1.5 million Eklaad live in tribes ruled by hereditary chieftains and haven't advanced beyond stone-age technology. [SWAJ]

Sirrakuk A young female Wookiee nicknamed Sirra, she is the niece of Chewbacca and the younger sister of Lowbacca, a trainee at the Jedi academy. [YJK]

Sisk A planet that orbits a red dwarf star of the same name, it is home to the arachnid species Sic-Six. The star Sisk was once an orange star but underwent a partial atomic collapse, cooling the planet Sisk and turning it from warm and lush to cool and barren. Sic-Six are highly antisocial, preventing the formation of any government or mass production, although their technology is complex. Sic-Six are valued throughout the galaxy because the poison-filled bites from their fangs are intoxicating to most species. [GG4]

Sith An ancient people, they were conquered by powerful dark-side Jedi magic. In their 100,000-year history they have come close several times to vanquishing the light-side Jedi. This occurred most recently in the Sith War four millennia before the Galactic Civil War. They have remained a part of the galaxy, sometimes waxing, sometimes waning, and have maintained an unbroken line of chief practitioners known as Dark Lords of the Sith. The planet Korriban is possibly their homeworld. [DLS, GSWU, TSW]

Sith Holocron Also known as the Dark Holocron, it contained the teachings and histories of the Sith and their Dark Lords going back 100,000 years. Its complete secrets were accessible only to a Dark Lord of the Sith. The Holocron was captured from the Sith by Master Odan-Urr during the Fall of the Sith Empire nearly 5,000 years before the Galactic Civil War. [DLS, TSW]

Sith War A great conflict, it was precipitated 4,000 years before the Galactic Civil War by the ascension of Exar Kun as Dark Lord of the Sith. Before it ended, countless millions died, and entire systems were destroyed. The Sith War pitted the Jedi Knights against the dark-side forces led by Kun, who began by ordering the extermination of all Jedi who wouldn't follow his dark path. It ended after massive death and destruction only when Exar Kun's spirit was trapped in the ruins of Yavin 4. [TSW]

Sivrak, Lak A hunter and a scout for the Empire, this Shistavanen Wolfman from the Uvena system grew to despise the Emperor's New Order and Imperial tyranny and atrocities. Lak Sivrak refused to turn in a colony of Alliance sympathizers, and the Empire targeted him for elimination. After getting the best of a stormtrooper squad sent to kill him, he fled to the backwater Mos Eisley spaceport on Tatooine. There, in a small cantina, he fell in love with Dice Ibegon, a Florn Lamproid. After helping several Rebels on Tatooine, Sivrak officially joined the Alliance and fought in the Battle of Hoth. A year later, Sivrak was piloting an X-wing fighter in the fight against the second Death Star. He took out a number of TIE fighters but was hit and died when his X-wing crashed onto the surface of Endor's forest moon. [GG1, TMEC]

Sivron, Tol Tol Sivron was one of the five members of a Twi'lek head-clan, a group that runs community affairs on Ryloth. As part of Twi'lek tradition, when one member of the clan dies, the remaining four are exiled to the planet's hot desert, where they are left to die as a new head-clan takes office. But Sivron's entire clan was young and vigorous, and he expected to reap the benefits of his position for many years. He was pampered and spoiled by the benefits of power. The good life lasted barely a standard year, however, because one of his colleagues lost his balance inspecting a deep-grotto construction project and impaled himself on a stalagmite. After exile to the desert, Sivron convinced his three remaining colleagues that they could eke out an existence in an uninhabited cave. But Sivron killed them there, taking their meager possessions to increase his own chances for survival. Soon after, he discovered an Imperial Navy training base and met Imperial officer Tarkin, and his Imperial career began. Sivron was sent to Tarkin's top-secret weapons development facility, the Maw Installation, where he worked for years as chief scientist and director. Sivron decided to pilot the prototype Death

Lak Sivrak

Desert skiff

Star in an assault against Kessel to test its weaponry, and later to defend Maw Installation itself. However, his skills were meager, and the Maw Installation and the prototype battle station itself were doomed. [COF, JS]

Skahtul A Barabel bounty hunter, she was the leader of a group that kidnapped Luke Skywalker from the Bothan safehouse on the planet Kothlis. Skahtul told Luke that there were two rewards on his head; one for him alive, the other, dead. The reward for Skywalker alive was higher, but Skahtul tried to play the parties against one another to raise the ante. She lost her chance when Skywalker escaped. [SOTE]

Skandits Noisy squirrellike creatures, they live on Endor's forest moon. Skandits have furry black masks and use slingshots and whips to ambush unsuspecting caravans traveling through the forests. [ETV]

Skarten Along with Ra Yasht, his colleague at Beshka University, he wrote "Torture Observed: an Interview with Jabba's Cook." [TJP]

Skee A portly Rodian, he was a member of the peaceful Tetsus clan and was known for his skill in hunting the dreaded manka cat. [TMEC]

skiff, desert A repulsorlift utility vehicle, it is usually used to move cargo or passengers. Tatooine crime lord Jabba the Hutt used a number of skiffs as escorts for his sail barge. His henchmen often rushed to a raiding site in skiffs while barge passengers enjoyed the battle from a safe distance.

A skiff deck is completely open with a control station for the driver and sometimes a labor droid at the rear. One repulsorlift engine provides forward thrust; the craft is maneuvered with two steering vanes hanging off the back of the hull. A skiff can hold more than 100 tons of cargo and reach speeds of 250 kilometers an hour and heights of as much as fifty meters above the surface. When fitted with up to sixteen seats, skiffs are used as mass transit vehicles on poorer worlds.

Skiffs aren't good in combat because they're neither highly maneuverable nor sturdy. A single shot from a hand blaster can disable the repulsorlift unit or smash a steering vane. Jabba used nine-meter-long Ubrikkian Bantha II cargo skiffs as the patrol and escort vehicles for his sail barge. Although they were armor-plated, they were still not suited to combat, as Jabba's minions discovered. Luke Skywalker and his companions escaped in a skiff just before the Hutt's sail barge exploded near the Great Pit of Carkoon. [SWSB, RJ, SWVG]

skimmer *See* landspeeder

Skip 1 Located in the asteroid belt known as Smuggler's Run, Skip 1 is the thirty-fifth asteroid in the system, the first one settled, and the one most suitable for human life. The asteroid's interior was hollowed out centuries ago. Skip 1 smells extremely foul; the stench arises from a green-yellow slime that runs through the corridors. An attempt was once made to block the slime at its source, but this caused severe tremors and instability in the asteroid.

Skip 1 is well-defended. Adjacent to its hangar is the entry chamber, with bones along one wall and sabacc tables, a bar, and a hokuum station for drugs and other stimulants. In the center is a food court, currently stocked by the former chef for the Court of Hapes. Beyond lie Cavern 2 and hot, humid Cavern 3, which once belonged to Boba Fett and five fellow bounty hunters. Extra blaster-protection layers Cavern 3's walls, and the cavern features more than eighteen cooking stations decorated to resemble particular planets such as Kashyyyk and Corellia. Thirteen years after the Battle of Endor, Han Solo returned to Skip 1 to investigate events in Smuggler's Run and their possible connection to the bombing of Senate Hall on Coruscant. Soon after, Skip 1 and several other Skips were severely damaged when a group of stolen droids exploded. [NR]

Skip 5 Located in the asteroid belt known as Smuggler's Run, Skip 5 is an enormous asteroid riddled with huge caverns lined with heat-generating sunstone. The interior temperature averages an uncomfortable forty degrees standard. Beyond the vast docking hangar, in the center of the asteroid, is a huge cavern filled with sand and lit with blinding sunstone. Skip 5 was abandoned for many years, but smugglers to the agents of the Dark Jedi Kueller of Almania converted it for use as a base for the sale of used Imperial equipment. Jawas were brought in to find and repair the old Imperial equipment; they provided cheap labor and could tinker to their hearts' content. Thirteen years after the Battle of Endor, Han Solo and Chewbacca investigated Skip 5 and were nearly killed by a group of Glottalphibs sent by the crime lord Nandreeson. Soon after, Skip 5 and several other Skips were severely damaged when a group of stolen droids exploded. [NR]

Skip 6 Located in the middle of the asteroid belt known as Smuggler's Run, Skip 6 is owned and operated by the Glottalphib crime lord known as Nandreeson. The top of the asteroid is covered with flowing ooze. Inside the asteroid are humid, moss-covered chambers filled with stagnant, foul-smelling sulfurous ponds covered with lilypads and skittering waterbugs. Other chambers hold Nandreeson's treasure stashes and egg clusters. The air is thick with parfue gnats and Eilnian sweet flies, and watumba bats nest on the ceiling. Half-submerged algae-covered furniture decorates the ponds. Thirteen years after the Battle of Endor, Lando Calrissian returned to Smuggler's Run searching for Han Solo. He was captured by a squad of Reks and brought to Nandreeson on Skip 6; the crime lord tried to kill his old nemesis by slowly drowning him in one of the pools. Han Solo, Chewbacca, and several smugglers arrived to rescue Lando, entering the Skip through a surface mud slide. They were betrayed by other smugglers but succeeded in rescuing Lando and fleeing the Skip by stealing Nandreeson's personal Skipper. [NR]

Skip 8 Located in the asteroid belt known as Smuggler's Run, Skip 8 is an inhabited asteroid that Han Solo and Chewbacca once visited during their early smuggling career. [NR]

Skip 52 Located in the asteroid belt known as Smuggler's Run, Skip 52 is continually surrounded by swirling rock storms. Only the specialized Smuggler's Run vehicles known as Skippers are able to navigate these storms successfully. [NR]

Skipray blastboat Assault gunships used by the Empire, they are larger and much more powerful than starfighters but are still small enough to be carried aboard capital ships. The most popular models of blastboats are the Sienar Fleet Systems GAT series. They can be found in local defense fleets and are used by smugglers and mercenaries such as Talon Karrde in his operations on Myrkr.

Just twenty-five meters long, the blastboat carries an incredible array of weapons for its size, including three medium ion cannons, a proton torpedo launcher, two laser cannons, and a concussion missile launcher. The ion cannons give the Skipray a reasonable chance of disabling much larger combat ships, and the blastboat's profile presents a very small target. The hull plating is so heavy that most starfighter lasers have a tough time punching through it. Blastboats are more maneuverable in a planetary atmosphere than in space and have a top atmospheric speed of more than 1,200 kilometers per hour; they have hyperdrives and a nav computer for deep space. The Skipray normally carries a crew of four, but in an emergency can be handled by a single pilot. [ISB, HE, HESB]

Skips 2, 3, and 72 Inhabited asteroids, they are located in the asteroid belt known as Smuggler's Run. Thirteen years after the Battle of Endor, they and several other Skips were severely damaged when a group of stolen droids exploded. [NR]

skirtopanol Much like truth serum, the drug is used in interrogating prisoners. Skirtopanol can be metabolized from the system by the intake of another drug, lotiramine, but the latter may induce chemical amnesia and in some cases cause death. [RS]

Skor II A small dense world, it orbits the star Squab. The Squib species evolved on Skor II. Squibs are nomadic, traveling in search of the planet's resources. A Dorcin trader gained mineral rights to a frozen wasteland on the planet in exchange for the secrets of starship technology. Now most Squibs roam the galaxy collecting junk, haggling for bargains, and competing for trash-hauling business with their primary rivals, the Ugors. [GG4]

Skorr A humanoid male bounty hunter on Ord Mantell, he had pale yellow skin, a bald head covered with lumps, and pointed ears and teeth. The left side of his face was a metallic shell with a mechanical eye. He almost always wore a hooded brown coat and toted a hefty gun belt. He worked with an assistant, Gribbet.

Skorr

Skipray blastboat

Shortly after the Battle of Yavin, Skorr spotted Han Solo on Ord Mantell and attempted to collect the bounty on the Corellian smuggler. To try to trap Solo, Skorr kidnapped Princess Leia Organa and Luke Skywalker, but Solo and his first mate, Chewbacca, managed to free their friends and have Skorr arrested for violating Imperial territory.

Skorr was sent to the spice mines of Kessel but escaped. He teamed up with other bounty hunters working for Jabba the Hutt, including Dengar and Bossk, and they managed to capture Solo, Skywalker, and Chewbacca on Hoth. The captives were taken to Ord Mantell for pickup by Boba Fett, but when Skorr learned that Fett was working for the detested Empire, he decided to kill Solo rather than let him fall into Imperial hands. Skorr and Solo grappled, and during the fight Skorr fatally shot himself. [CSW]

Skreej, Tamtel Lando Calrissian assumed this name when he worked undercover in Jabba the Hutt's palace as part of the plan to free Han Solo. [TJP]

Skreeka A spaceport on the planet Atzerri. [SOL]

Skritch A pet gorm-worm of Gudb, who was a henchman of Great Bogga the Hutt some 4,000 years before the Galactic Civil War, it was used to kill the Jedi Andur Sunrider. [TOJ]

Skyclaw A ship used by the Mistryl Shadow Guards in their botched attempt to safely transport the Hammertong device to the Empire. [TMEC]

Skydome Botanical Gardens The site of the diplomatic reception where Ambassador Furgan poisoned Mon Mothma. He flung a drink full of a self-replicating swarm of nano-destroyers in her face. The nano-destroyers then slowly began to kill her. [COF]

Skyhook A code-name, it stood for the secret Alliance operation that sent the *Tantive IV* to retrieve the technical readouts of the original Death Star battle station. [SWR]

skyhook A space station in low orbit, it is tethered to a planetary surface. The tether, a flexible column thousands of meters long, is often used to supply the skyhook or to ferry passengers to and from the station via transit tubes. Skyhooks became a symbol of power and wealth in the skies over Imperial Center during the reign of Emperor Palpatine. They often were self-contained habitats, with opulent parks and beautifully manicured gardens. Both Emperor Palpatine and the criminal kingpin Prince Xizor had personal skyhooks. [SOTE]

skyhopper *See* T-16 skyhopper

Skynx An insectoid scholar from the planet Ruuria, he accompanied Han Solo on a quest to find the lost treasures of the *Queen of Ranroon* prior to Solo's involvement with the Rebel Alliance. As the leading expert on the pre-Republic era at the University of Ruuria, Skynx studied and deciphered documents of the era. [HLL]

Skynxnex, Arb The top aide to corrupt Kessel prison warden and spice-mine administrator Moruth Doole, he had been a thief and assassin and Doole's main contact with spice smugglers. Arb Skynxnex also held a nominal post as a prison guard in the correction facility. He had gangly arms and legs and moved with a jerky walk. Skynxnex was killed by a glitterstim spider creature deep in the Kessel mines. [JS]

Skywalker, Anakin The father of Luke Skywalker and Leia Organa, he had strong Force powers that his teacher, Obi-Wan Kenobi, helped him develop. Anakin Skywalker was one of the youngest warriors of the Clone Wars, fighting alongside such heroes as Kenobi and Bail Organa. He demonstrated an unusually high degree of flying and fighting talent, enhanced by his innate ability to tap into the Force. But as his Force talents developed, he was lured by Senator Palpatine and others to the dark side, which eventually seduced and consumed him. He became a powerful Dark Lord of the Sith known as Darth Vader. After Palpatine declared himself Emperor, Vader joined him, turning into one of the Empire's chief instruments of galactic fear and terror. Only at the end of his life did Anakin reclaim his original identity to save his son's life at the cost of his own. He then became one with the Force. [RJ, RJN]

Skywalker, Luke Raised on a backwater planet as the foster son of a farming couple, with little idea of his true heritage, Luke Skywalker survived personal tragedy and deep pain, then overcame impossibly high odds to become the greatest hero of the Rebel Alliance—and the only man alive who could reignite the flame of the mystical Jedi Knights. Skywalker is a hero for his time, a young man whose vision grew to become grander, even more sweeping than the circumstances in which he found himself. He is a person who has always accepted the greatest challenges, even as he has challenged others to do their best.

Skywalker thought that he was the son of a spice freighter navigator who had fought in the Clone Wars. For years he remained unaware that his father, Anakin Skywalker, had in truth been seduced by the dark side of the Force and had become the fearsome Dark Lord of the Sith, Darth Vader. Nor did he know that he had a twin sister, Leia, from whom he was separated early in life but with whom he was to share the adventures of a lifetime. Jedi Knight Obi-Wan Kenobi—fearful that Luke's innate Force powers would be corrupted by his father—had taken the infant boy and given him to be raised by Owen and Beru Lars. Kenobi then went into retirement, to become known as old Ben, the "crazy hermit" living in the desert.

Luke had a mostly uneventful childhood, helping his foster parents on their moisture farm. He became a skillful pilot in a T-16 skyhopper, shooting womp rats with good friends such as Biggs Darklighter. He had hoped to enter the Academy with Biggs, but his uncle Owen kept Luke from joining, year after year, each time saying "just one more season." But destiny brought the affairs of the entire galaxy—and its fate—to the eighteen-year-old Skywalker's doorstep. Destiny arrived in the form of two droids that his uncle purchased, C-3PO and R2-D2.

Artoo carried a hologram of a beautiful princess from Alderaan. She was seeking Ben Kenobi, and at Ben's house, Luke learned at last that his father had been a Jedi Knight who had been betrayed and murdered by

Anakin Skywalker as he appeared to Luke

Darth Vader. Ben explained the basic philosophies of the Force, and gave Luke his father's lightsaber.

He hadn't planned on accompanying Kenobi to Alderaan to aid Princess Leia Organa, but when Luke returned home he found that his aunt and uncle had been murdered by stormtroopers who were searching for the two droids. Luke realized that fate had placed him in Kenobi's hands, and set out to learn the ways of the Force. They booked passage to Alderaan with hotshot pilot and smuggler

Luke Skywalker

Han Solo and his first mate, the Wookiee Chewbacca, aboard Han's freighter, the *Millennium Falcon.* They reached Alderaan's position only to discover that the planet had been destroyed by the massive Imperial battle station, the Death Star.

The *Falcon* was pulled into the Death Star, and once Luke realized Princess Leia was aboard, he hatched a plot to rescue her. The rescue seemed almost comic, but it worked. However, as he, Han Solo, and Leia were fighting off stormtrooper fire, Luke witnessed a fateful lightsaber duel between Kenobi and Vader.

Vader struck down the old Jedi, whose body disappeared. The remaining members of the party escaped, and at the Rebel base on Yavin 4 the technical readouts of the Death Star were extracted from R2-D2 and analyzed. Assault teams were chosen and young Skywalker became the pilot of an X-wing fighter. Just when the attack on the Death Star seemed desperate, Luke heeded the words of the spirit of Obi-Wan Kenobi. He shut down his targeting computer, and used the Force to fire two proton torpedoes that destroyed the Death Star.

Over the next few years, Skywalker became an integral part of the Rebel Alliance. He flew numerous missions and eventually was named Commander, in charge of the X-wing Rogue Squadron. He helped stave off the Imperial attack on the Rebel base on Hoth long enough to allow most personnel to escape, then journeyed to the swamp planet of Dagobah to train with the Jedi Master Yoda. Rigorous physical conditioning was important there, but so was exacting mental conditioning. Yoda feared that Luke was too impetuous, and that he, too, could be seduced by the dark side.

Despite Yoda's warning that his training wasn't complete, when Luke saw a vision of his friends in danger on Bespin's Cloud City, he left Dagobah. It was a trap, and he was the intended victim. He engaged in a fierce lightsaber battle with Vader, who cut off Luke's right hand, then inflicted even greater pain by revealing to Luke that he, Vader, was his father. Vader offered Luke a chance to join him in ruling the galaxy, but Luke responded by letting himself drop into a wind tunnel. He was rescued by his friends.

Another rescue was planned as well: that of Han Solo, who had been frozen in carbonite and delivered to crime lord Jabba the Hutt. Before that mission could commence, Skywalker had to fend off assassination attempts by the head of the underworld, Prince Xizor. Then he went after Jabba, and was forced to destroy him and many of his henchmen while rescuing Han Solo. Luke returned to Dagobah only to find Master Yoda dying. Yoda confirmed that Vader was his father and explained that Luke would have to confront him one more time. The spirit of Obi-Wan appeared with equally stunning news. Leia was his twin sister.

While the Alliance was planning an attack on the Empire's *second* Death Star, Luke joined Leia and others in a strike against the Death Star's shield, located on the nearby forest moon of Endor. Luke then gave himself up to Vader in a desperate effort to reach the last spark of good that he was convinced was still deep inside his father's spirit—but to no avail. Luke was taken to Emperor Palpatine's throne room aboard the Death Star, where he was goaded into subconsciously revealing the secret of his twin sister's existence. That broke Luke's Jedi calm, and he ferociously attacked Vader, finally beating him down and chopping off his father's right hand. But Luke forsook the dark-side rage the Emperor had goaded him into and stood his ground. The Emperor attacked Luke, assaulting him with blue Force lightning, and prepared to kill him.

Suddenly Vader rose up, lifted Palpatine into the air, and with his last bit of strength, threw him into the battle station's power core. Vader knew he was fading and asked his son to remove his helmet so that he could look upon Luke with his own eyes. Then he became one with the Force.

After the second Death Star was destroyed, Luke lit a pyre to burn Darth Vader's garb. He saw a vision of Anakin Skywalker, Ben Kenobi, and Yoda, standing together as luminous beings infused with the light of the Force.

There was little time for rest or reflection, however, for Luke played a major role in turning the Rebel Alliance into the New Republic. He helped fight the reptilian Ssi-ruuk in-

Slave I

vaders at Bakura; followed Han Solo and Leia to the planet Dathomir; fought the forces of Grand Admiral Thrawn; and stymied the attempts of the Emperor's former aide, Mara Jade, to kill him. He battled a crazed cloned Jedi who had also cloned Luke; and confronted the clone of a "reborn" Palpatine on the planet Byss.

Like other Jedi in the past, Skywalker thought he could learn about and destroy the dark side of the Force by facing it from within. Until Leia arrived and confronted him, he didn't realize how close he had come to being totally corrupted by the dark side. Even as they dealt with this personal crisis, they found themselves dealing with Palpatine's clone. Together, he and Leia destroyed the clone. Yet a second cloned Emperor was reborn—and defeated—one final time.

Slowly, Luke began finding Force-sensitive beings throughout the galaxy. He decided that the most important thing he could do to help preserve the New Republic was to gather and train these adepts in a new Jedi academy, which he founded in the Great Temple of the Massassi on Yavin 4. Luke didn't realize that the evil spirit of an ancient Dark Lord of the Sith, Exar Kun, inhabited the temple. It killed one trainee, seduced another to the dark side, and nearly murdered Luke, who was eventually saved when his trainees combined their powers.

Luke has faced onetime students who have turned to the dark side. He was deeply disappointed after following a trail he thought would lead to details about his mother—or even to his mother herself—only to discover he had been fooled by a conniving woman with her own agenda.

The adventures have continued nonstop, although Luke at times has seemed moody and preoccupied. Still, he has helped defeat the threats from Imperial Admiral Daala and her super weapons; has discovered the spirit of a Jedi woman, Callista, trapped in a computer on an Imperial battle station and seen her made human through a transfer of essences with an eminent scientist; and has helped rescue Han and Leia's children from dark-side practitioners. Luke has flirted with love and laughed at death. He has matured and grown wise beyond his years. And he has dedicated himself to the preservation of the New Republic and the rebirth of the Jedi Knights. Whether this is the life that he would have chosen for himself all those years ago as a farmboy on Tatooine is a question only he can answer. [SW, ESB, RJ, etc.]

Skywalker, Luuke A clone of Luke Skywalker, it was created from cells—sample B-2332-54—taken from the hand that Luke lost in his lightsaber duel with Darth Vader at Cloud City. Jedi Master Joruus C'baoth, himself a clone, created Luuke because he wanted a Jedi student of his own. Using the lightsaber that Luke had lost along with his hand, the clone nearly destroyed Skywalker. But the Emperor's aide, Mara Jade, killed the clone, fulfilling the powerful last command of the dying Palpatine: Kill Skywalker. [LC]

Slave I A highly modified *Firespray*-class patrol and attack ship, it belongs to the much-feared bounty hunter Boba Fett. Fett has rebuilt and customized the outdated *Slave I*. The vessel boasts several hidden weapon systems, a dedicated sensor-masking and tracking system, interior prisoner cages, reinforced armor plating, and powerful shield generators, all designed to help Fett fend off attackers and to disable the ships of his quarry.

The ship lands with its engines down, although in flight, it effectively flies standing up. With two-thirds of its interior dedicated to powerful drive engines and generators, *Slave I* has the speed of an Alliance Y-wing fighter. The rest of the interior is cramped, with only enough room for Fett's living quarters, his equipment locker, and six prisoner cages, including one to contain Force-using individuals.

The bottom rear section of the hull holds fully rotating twin blaster cannons. *Slave I* also conceals a forward-firing concussion missile launcher and ion cannon, as well as a turret-mounted tractor beam projector and a pair of turret-mounted proton torpedo launchers. The ship's illegal sensor-masking and jamming system allows it to slip through sensor grids undetected. Dummy proton torpedoes mounted with homing beacons and trackers enable Fett to track ships even through hyperspace. [MTS, DESB, ESB, SWSB, DE2]

Slave II After escaping from the Sarlacc on Tatooine, bounty hunter Boba Fett discovered that his starship, *Slave I*, had been impounded, so he started looking for another. He realized a new ship would help him keep a lower profile until he actually confronted his much-despised adversary, Han Solo. Fett chose a *Pursuer*-class patrol ship that had proven popular with Mandalorian police because it was tough enough to handle pirates but had enough cargo space for standard policing duties.

Slave II is a heavy patrol craft, with

Slave II

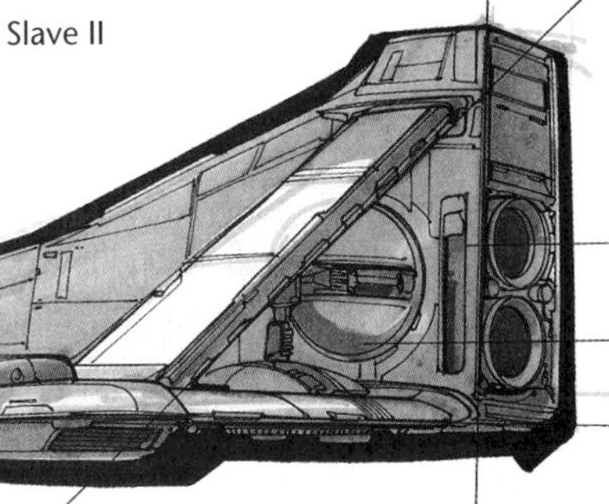

a superior hull and powerful military-grade shield generators. Dual engines propel the ship, while three maneuvering thrusters can be individually directed and fired for excellent performance. *Slave II* has a forward-mounted ion cannon and twin blaster cannons. Fett also added a rear-firing proton torpedo launcher with a magazine of six torpedoes.

Slave II was severely damaged over the cloned Emperor's throne world of Byss when Fett, attempting to follow the *Millennium Falcon* down to the planet's surface, smashed into the planetary shield. Rather than get the ship repaired, Fett put *Slave II* in dry dock while using the reclaimed *Slave I* to continue his pursuit of Han Solo. [DE, DESB]

slave circuit Mechanisms that allow for remote control of a starship, these circuits are usually used by a spaceport control tower to assist with landing or by the ship's owner when he or she wishes to remotely power up the ship. Fully rigged slave circuits create totally controlled vessels that require few crew members and sometimes only a single pilot. [HE, DFR, LC]

sleeper bomb An explosive device, it remains inert until a preset signal activates it. Once activated, it draws energy from a nearby power source until a sufficient charge has been gathered to release its explosive energy. [HSR]

slicer chip These chips are another manifestation of slicer technology—a way to change or get around the commands and demands of automated devices by hacking. A brainwashed Terpfen used a slicer chip to convince the controls in a B-wing fighter that he had the appropriate override codes from Admiral Ackbar and Mon Mothma. He used the ship to go to Yavin 4 and confess his betrayal of the New Republic to Leia Organa Solo. [COF]

slicer droid These droids break into secret information systems or are otherwise able to compromise the security or preordered instructions of a computerized device. Wedge Antilles took several slicer droids with him to attempt to retrieve encrypted information about the weapons plans stored in the Maw Installation computer system. [COF]

Slick A nickname that Han Solo once was known by, it was given to him by his friend and former instructor, Badure. [HLL]

Sljee Homeworld of slab-shaped, multitentacled beings, who are also called Sljee. The Sljee's specialized olfactory stalks give them a keen sense of smell, but they have a difficult time distinguishing smells when they are away from their planet. One of the waiters in a Bonadan tavern was a native of Sljee. [HSR, CSSB]

Sluis sector A sector that contains the planets Dagobah, Bpfassh, Praesitlyn, and Sluis Van. [HE, ISWU]

Sluissi A technologically advanced species from the planet Sluis Van, they appear as humanoids from the waist up; their lower bodies end in a snakelike tail. They are well known for their work repairing and maintaining starships. Longtime members of the Old Republic, the Sluissi people joined the New Republic several months after the Battle of Endor. The Sluissi are even-tempered, calm, methodical, and somewhat plodding. Jobs they do may take longer, but they are well done. [DFRSB]

Sluis Van Located in the Sluis sector, it contains extensive shipyards including the huge Sluis Van Central orbit-dock station, and is defended by perimeter battle stations. The busy shipyards are managed by an outer system defense network and the overloaded Sluissi workers at Sluis Control. Six months after the Battle of Endor, the Sluis Van Congregate was still debating whether to join the New Republic. Although the Sluis sector lay closer to New Republic sectors than to the Imperial-held Core Worlds, the Sluissi did not want to alienate the Empire, still one of their main shipyard clients, but the Sluissi finally joined the Republic. Five years after Endor, Grand Admiral Thrawn launched an attack on 112 warships docked at Sluis Van, attempting to capture several of them with a cloaked cargo of space-trooper-manned mole miners. No warships were captured, but the destruction of their control systems rendered more than forty of them useless. [HE, DFR, SWAJ]

Smarteel A planet on which Cabrool Nunn, a criminal business associate of Jabba the Hutt, lived. Jabba visited Nunn to sell him a captured freighter but ended up killing the crime boss, his son, and daughter. [JAB]

smokies The local name for the crystals (sometimes called "spooks") that were illegally exported from Nam Chorios to the Loronar Corporation. These crystals are Force-sensitive. Loronar programmed and realigned them to act as receivers for use in its synthdroids and its Needle missiles. [POT]

Smuggler's Run An asteroid belt surrounded by debris, it lies near the planet Wrea and serves as a hideout for hundreds of smugglers. Entering the belt is extremely dangerous, and only a handful of people know the correct route. For years it has been a secure, well-defended safehouse; the Empire tried several times to infiltrate the Run, but its ships were destroyed trying to enter. The smugglers inhabit hollowed-out asteroids lying within the belt and travel among them in small, specialized vehicles called Skippers. Inhabited asteroids within the Run include Skip 1, Skip 2, Skip 3, Skip 5, Skip 6, Skip 8, Skip 52, and Skip 72.

Han Solo, Lando Calrissian, and others all spent time in Smuggler's Run during their early careers. A few years before the Battle of Yavin, Calrissian stole a fortune in treasure from the Glottalphib crime lord Nandreeson. Nandreeson put a price on Calrissian's head and vowed his death if he ever returned to the Run. Nandreeson's smugglers began to make a great deal of money by selling old Imperial military equipment to the Dark Jedi Kueller on Almania. Thirteen years after the Battle of Endor, Han Solo's old smuggling associate Jarril asked Han for his help investigating recent activities in Smuggler's Run. When Calrissian arrived at the Run to check on Solo, he was captured and nearly killed by Nandreeson. Many smugglers were killed when their stolen droids exploded. [NR]

smuggling guild The unofficial name for smuggling groups that

Pote Snitkin

control various sectors on the spaceport moon of Nar Shaddaa. [DE]

Snaggletooth *See* Zutton

Snibit, Tutti A Chadra-Fan, he introduced the bounty hunters Tinian I'att and Chenlambec to the Trandoshan bounty hunter Bossk. [TBH]

Snit *See* McCool, Droopy

Snitkin, Pote A Skrilling, he worked as a helmsman for crime boss Jabba the Hutt on Tatooine. Pote Snitkin piloted one of Jabba's skiffs and was among those killed during Luke Skywalker's rescue of Han Solo and Princess Leia from the Hutt. [RJ, GG12]

Snivvian Short, stocky bipeds from the frigid planet of Cadomai, they have tough skin, sparse hair, and protruding snouts with pronounced canine fangs. To survive their world's long, cold winters, Snivvians have evolved a dense skin with special membranes that control the opening and closing of pores to regulate heat. Snivvians are gentle and insightful beings who create beautiful works of art that are respected throughout the galaxy. Many years ago they were almost driven to extinction by Thalassian slavers, who sold the species to others who used their skins for industrial purposes until the Old Republic intervened to stop the practice. Snivvians have also had to overcome a genetic defect that occasionally produces sociopathic killers and a few truly evil, charismatic leaders among them. [GG12]

Snootles, Sy The sometimes lead singer for Max Rebo's jizz-wailing musical band, she has two spindly legs, long, thin arms, and blue-spotted yellow-green skin. Her most notable feature, however, is that her reedy voice comes out of a mouth at the end of a thirty-centimeter-long protrusion extending from the lower portion of her face. Sy and the rest of the band performed for Jabba the Hutt's court just prior to the crime lord's death. After that, she and Max performed together for a time but eventually split up. She traveled with a number of other jizz bands in the years after that and put out several recordings, none of which proved successful. [RJ, TJP]

Snoova A well-known Wookiee bounty hunter, he has patches of black mottled fur, a natural raccoon-like mask encircling his eyes, and a short spacer's haircut. The Wookiee Chewbacca changed his appearance to duplicate that of Snoova to pass customs on Imperial Center as part of a plan to rescue Princess Leia Organa Solo from Prince Xizor. [SOTE]

snot vampire Slang for the Anzati species, whose members extract brain matter through their victims' noses. [TJP]

snow demon A hairy winged creature from the planet Toola, it has a long hairy tail, white talons, and a long purple tongue that snakes between massive fangs. It hunts and eats the shaggy mastmot and in turn is often hunted and eaten by Whiphids. [CPL]

snow screen A piece of equipment used by Imperial snowtroopers, it fits over a trooper's helmet and functions as a breather hood, warming air before it enters the armor and works its way to the trooper's lungs. [ESB]

snowspeeder Highly modified airspeeders, a dozen of these Incom T-47 airspeeders became the Rebel Alliance's last line of defense when its icy base on Hoth was assaulted by Imperial walkers. Nicknamed snowspeeders, they delayed the Imperial onslaught long enough to let the Alliance escape.

Incom T-47 airspeeders are modified for low atmospheric duty. They are powered by a pair of repulsorlift drive units and high-powered afterburners. Mechanical braking flaps lo-

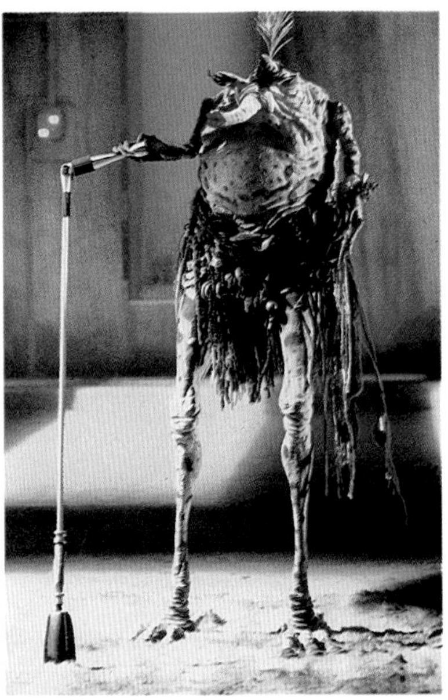

Sy Snootles

Snowspeeder

Snowtrooper

cated above each repulsor engine housing assist in maneuvers. Snowspeeders can reach more than 1,000 kilometers per hour, with an effective combat speed of about 600 kilometers per hour. Although they lack shields, their compact size and speed make them hard to target. For combat duty, snowspeeders are fitted with heavy armor plating and twin laser cannons. A harpoon gun with tow cable will be found as a standard tool on most T-47s. A snowspeeder seats a forward-facing pilot and a gunner, who sits with his back to the pilot. Computerized targeting systems allow the gunner to target the forward laser cannons. [ESBN, ESB, SWSB, MTS, RASB]

snowtrooper A specialized Imperial stormtrooper trained and equipped to operate in subfreezing conditions. [SWSB]

snubfighter *See* X-wing starfighter

Snunb, Captain Syub A being from the planet Sullust, he has commanded a number of New Republic ships including the escort frigate *Antares Six* and the star cruiser *Resolve.* [DE, BTS]

Socorro A dry desert world, it orbits a red-giant star in the isolated Socorran system. The planet's black volcanic-ash surface gives it its name, which means "scorched ground" in Old Corellian. The vast Doaba Badlands cover three-quarters of the planet's surface and are home to several nomadic tribes. Sandstorms are common at the world's polar regions, where temperatures are a burning 110 standard degrees. Animal life in the desert includes the water beetle and sandfly.

Vakeyya, the capital and only large city on Socorro, lies adjacent to the Soco-Jarel space station. Although the planet has not seen rain in nearly 1,000 years, enough underground water reserves exist to sustain the planet's 300 million smugglers and nomads, who live under no form of organized government. Socorro is a haven for free-traders and outlaws. Illegal ship modifications remain a major source of revenue. According to custom, Socorrans travel off-world to die, but those who cannot often wander into the desert when their time is at hand. Socorro was one of the first worlds colonized by early Corellian settlers, and most inhabitants speak a distinctive dialect of the ancient Old Corellian language. [SWAJ]

Sodonna A river city on the Noga River on the planet Teyr, it is the location of the Kell Plath commune. [SOL]

Solaest The planetary site of the Solaest Uprising, which was suppressed by Imperial forces. [SWSB]

Solo, Anakin Born six years after the death of his grandfather (Anakin Skywalker, the onetime Dark Lord of the Sith Darth Vader), Anakin Solo is the youngest of the three children born to Han Solo and Princess Leia Organa Solo and the strongest in the Force.

Anakin was born very soon after his parents and twin brother and sister were rescued from New Alderaan. They had just arrived at the new Alliance base, traveling in the abandoned floating space city of Nespis VIII, when Leia began to go into labor with him. And it was a short time later, when their parents returned with other New Republic officials to Coruscant, that infant Anakin and the twins, Jaina and Jacen, were taken to the faraway world of Anoth, to be hidden in a heavily guarded facility and overseen by Leia's assistant, Winter.

When they were two the twins went to Coruscant, but the six-month-old Anakin was too young and too susceptible to the influences of the dark side of the Force. Despite precautions, Anoth was compromised, but an attempted kidnapping of Anakin was foiled.

Anakin, with icy blue eyes and unruly brown hair, was finally brought to Coruscant and grew up happily, playing in the corridors of New Republic power with Winter, C-3PO, or the Wookiee Chewbacca looking after him and the twins. When he was three and a half years old, Anakin and the twins were kidnapped by Lord Hethrir and taken to the Crseih Research Station; Anakin barely escaped the fate of having his spirit fed to the dark-side creature called Waru.

As Anakin has grown older, his Force powers have become more evident, and he is sometimes more intense and quiet than the twins. His gift for mechanics was revealed when he took apart and reassembled computers at the age of five. Anakin started attending his uncle Luke Skywalker's Jedi academy on Yavin 4 when he was only eleven years old—his siblings didn't attend until they were thirteen. Like them, he can't es-

Anakin Solo

cape involvement in the politics of the galaxy or the treachery of evildoers even at his age, because of the powerful roles his mother, father, and uncle play in the governing of the New Republic. [YJK, SWCG, CS, DE, DSR, DE2]

Solo, Han A man of many contradictions, this smuggler-turned-hero of the Galactic Civil War and "first husband" of the New Republic is willing to take huge risks—for potentially tremendous gains. Charming and impulsive, Han Solo has been blessed with a wide lucky streak that balances his arrogance. Brave to a fault, he won the heart of Princess Leia Organa and together they have raised their three Force-sensitive children.

Born on Corellia, he was a hot teenage swoop racer and enrolled in the Imperial Academy, but his stubborn nature and belief in fairness derailed his career. He interfered with some slavers who were mistreating an enslaved Wookiee—actions sanctioned by the Empire—and for his insubordination was discharged from the Imperial Navy. The Wookiee Chewbacca has been by Solo's side ever since, at first to pay him back for the rescue and then as his partner and confidante. Early in his career, Solo won a Corellian light freighter, the *Millennium Falcon*, from gambling buddy Lando Calrissian. Although the ship resembled a rusty bucket of bolts, Solo and Chewbacca modified it into one of the zippiest starships in the galaxy.

After his discharge, Solo—like many of his fellow Corellians—took up a life of questionable repute, taking on mercenary jobs and running a regular glitterstim-spice smuggling route for the likes of criminal kingpin Jabba the Hutt. On one of those missions for Jabba, Solo was betrayed to Imperial customs officials and had to dump a load of spice before he was boarded; when he returned to the sector, the shipment was gone. To earn enough to repay Jabba, he agreed to take several passengers on a perilous journey to Alderaan: Ben Kenobi, Luke Skywalker, and the droids C-3PO and R2-D2. And before Solo knew it, he was at the heart of the Rebellion. He helped rescue Princess Leia Organa from a prison cell aboard the Imperial Death Star. Later, after claiming he was leaving to pay off Jabba, he instead returned in the *Falcon* just in time to provide Skywalker with the cover he needed to send proton torpedoes into the heart of the Death Star, destroying the giant battle station in the first decisive win for the Rebels.

As one of the Heroes of Yavin, Solo spent the next three years helping the Alliance. By the time he decided to return to Tatooine to pay his debt, it was too late. Jabba had already put a death mark on his head, and bounty hunters from all over the galaxy were competing for the reward. In one incident, Solo escaped from near-capture on the planet Ord Mantell. When the Empire discovered the Rebel Alliance secret base on icy Hoth and launched an attack, Solo was on hand and, with Princess Leia aboard, managed to escape the pursuing Imperials by darting into an asteroid field. Despite Solo's expertise at avoiding notice, bounty hunter Boba Fett tracked him to Cloud City, where Solo sought shelter with his old pal, Calrissian.

Alerted by Fett, the Empire and Darth Vader set a trap to attract Vader's real target, Luke Skywalker. In a perilous experiment, Vader had Solo encased in carbonite, then gave him over to Fett to transport to Jabba.

Skywalker escaped, and Solo's friends refused to abandon him. A few months later they plotted to wrest the carbonite-encased Solo from Jabba's palace. The rescue led to the death of Jabba and many of his henchmen. Soon thereafter, the fully recovered Solo led a strike force to the forest moon of Endor in the mission to disable a defensive shield that protected the Empire's second Death Star. With the help of the native Ewoks, Solo succeeded at the last possible moment.

The onetime vagabond finally found time to openly express his love for Princess Leia, particularly once he found out that she and Luke Skywalker were twins, but it took the threat of Leia's marriage (to Prince Isolder of Hapes) to make him take the next step. He pretended to kidnap Leia and spirit her to the planet Dathomir, which he had won in a sabacc game. Finally married, the couple have been blessed with three children, all powerful in the Force: the twins Jaina and Jacen and the younger Anakin, named after his maternal grandfather who, at the end of his life, renounced the dark-side evil that had coursed through his veins. Solo has gone on many missions for the New Republic, both with Leia and alone. He spent five months hunting the warlord Zsinj, was im-

Han Solo

Jacen Solo

Jaina Solo

prisoned with Chewbacca in the spice mines of Kessel, and has fought off several attempts by Boba Fett to capture him.

Named a commodore, Solo accepted his wife's charge to take over command of the New Republic's Fifth Fleet during the Yevethan crisis, when he was captured and nearly killed by strongman Nil Spaar. False evidence planted by the Dark Jedi Kueller implicated him in the bombing of Senate Hall on Coruscant, an act designed to put both Solo and Leia on the sidelines. Solo is seldom averse to recruiting cronies out of his past to aid the New Republic. Never far from the center of action, he has helped save the government and its top officials many times. [SW, ESB, RJ, SWSB, HE, DFR, TLC, DE, COF, TT, NR, etc.]

Solo, Jacen The son of Han Solo and Leia Organa Solo, Jacen is strong in the Force like his mother and his uncle, Luke Skywalker. He and his twin sister, Jaina, were born five years after the Battle of Endor, and because the New Republic was under attack by the forces of Grand Admiral Thrawn, the twins were raised in hideaways, first on New Alderaan and then on the planet Anoth, under the guidance of Leia's trusted aide, Winter. When they were two, the twins were brought back to their parents to live on Coruscant, cared for mostly by C-3PO and Chewbacca.

With unruly dark hair and deep brown eyes inherited from his mother, Jacen is a true lover of nature. He keeps a variety of pets and samples of many plants. Jacen's Force-sensitivity manifests itself in strong communication abilities, particularly with other Jedi and a variety of animals.

Powerful in the Force, before his third birthday he helped defend his uncle. The spirit of Dark Jedi Exar Kun sent ancient flying beasts to attack the near-lifeless body of Luke Skywalker on Yavin 4, and Jacen wielded Luke's own lightsaber. Later, Jacen joined forces with the other Jedi students in destroying Exar Kun's spirit forever and freeing Luke's spirit from where it was trapped.

When he was five, he, Jaina, and their younger brother, Anakin, were kidnapped by Lord Hethrir, the former Imperial Procurator of Justice, who wanted to use them to further his dark-side ambitions. Still later, when in their early teens, the children enrolled in their uncle Luke's Jedi academy and became friendly with Chewbacca's nephew, Lowbacca, and Tenel Ka, daughter of a Witch of Dathomir, and a prince of Hapes. The twins and Lowie at one point were kidnapped and taken to the Shadow Academy, where an unsuccessful attempt was made to turn them to the dark side of the Force. They thwarted the attempt and escaped. [HE, DFR, LC, JS, TCS, YJK, COF, NR]

Solo, Jaina The daughter of Leia Organa Solo and her husband, Han Solo, Jaina is the eldest by five minutes. Like her brother Jacen, she is strong in the Force. She, too, has the dark hair and dark brown eyes of her mother and has shared most of Jacen's adventures.

Jaina takes after her father, though. From an early age, she was a mechanical whiz who was always dismantling droids and equipment. By the time she was nine, she was helping her father repair the *Millennium Falcon*. She was also capable of cobbling together mechanical devices for just about any purpose, and like Han Solo, her impulsiveness, spirit, and self-confidence sometimes get her into trouble.

When Jaina was fourteen and a student at her uncle Luke's Jedi academy on Yavin 4, she, Jacen, and their friends Lowbacca and Tenel Ka found an Imperial TIE fighter that had crashed in the jungle years before. They kept returning to the site, and Jaina not only repaired the ship but also added a hyperdrive module that her father had given her as a gift. Little did the youngsters realize that the TIE fighter pilot, Qorl, had survived and was hiding nearby. When Jaina's repairs were nearly finished, he captured the teenager and her brother, and left them to die in the jungle as he took off. They were rescued, but Qorl escaped thanks to the new hyperdrive. His information led to the twins being kidnapped several weeks later, along with their friend Lowbacca.

The three were taken to the Shadow Academy where attempts were made to turn them to the dark side, but they eventually escaped. Later, when the cloaked Shadow Academy space station moved into orbit around Coruscant and began destroying New Republic ships, Jaina figured out how to disarm the cloaking mechanism, forcing the station to flee. [HE, DFR, LC, JS, CS, YJK]

Solo, Princess Leia Organa Separated from a mother she barely knew and a father she later counted among her worst enemies, Leia is a princess who grew up enmeshed in the politics of her time. Leia Organa Solo is now Chief of State of the New Republic, a Jedi Knight, and a mother. She never desired the power that was thrust upon her, but so strong was her commitment to peace, freedom, and democracy that she was willing to accept the burdens and the risks that it took to accomplish her goals.

Unaware that Darth Vader was her father or that she had a twin brother named Luke Skywalker—who proved to be the main hope for the rebirth of the Jedi Knights—Leia was separated from her mother and sibling very early in life and given to the Viceroy and First Chairman of the planet Alderaan, Bail Organa. Raised as his daughter, she grew up doted on by three gossipy aunts and a best friend named Winter. From the start, the brown-haired, brown-eyed Leia was a maverick and a bit of a tomboy. She became the youngest senator in galactic history, even as self-proclaimed Emperor Palpatine committed an increasing number of atrocities.

Bail Organa secretly became one of the driving forces of the Rebel Alliance, and Leia became one of the most outspoken voices in the Senate, opposing new Imperial policies. Behind the scenes, she was involved in secret missions for the Rebels, using her consular ship, the *Tantive IV*. Near Tatooine, on a mission to recruit the Jedi Obi-Wan Kenobi, she and her ship were captured by the Star Destroyer *Devastator*. Leia managed to place top-secret plans for the Imperial Death Star battle station into an R2 astromech droid. The droid, R2-D2, then left the ship with a droid companion, C-3PO, fleeing aboard an escape pod.

Leia Organa was captured by the menacing Darth Vader; it would be years before either knew of the amazing relationship that bound the two. Taken aboard the Death Star, Leia was able to block interrogation probes, but the battle station's commander, Grand Moff Tarkin, threatened to destroy Leia's planet of Alderaan—home to her father and billions of other residents—if she didn't reveal the site of the secret Rebel base. Quietly, she named Dantooine, a lie that Tarkin believed, but he ordered Alderaan to be destroyed anyway. It was obliterated before Leia's eyes, and Leia was scheduled for execution.

She was rescued by Luke Skywalker who, along with Obi-Wan Kenobi, rogue pilot Han Solo, and the Wookiee Chewbacca, found himself trapped aboard the battle station. They all escaped, except for Kenobi, who sacrificed his mortal existence in a lightsaber duel with Vader. Using the stolen Death Star plans, the Rebels on Yavin 4 plotted to destroy it, and Skywalker, with Solo's help, succeeded in firing proton torpedoes at the station's one vulnerable spot.

After the Battle of Yavin, Leia became a full-time member of the Rebel Alliance, often acting as a diplomat to get other worlds to join the fight against the Empire. Luke, Han, and Chewbacca—along with the droids R2-D2 and C-3PO—became a second family to her, helping to ease some of the shock and pain left by the annihilation of Alderaan. She encountered Vader once again on the planet Mimban, where he badly wounded her with his lightsaber. Luke managed to drive off Vader and help heal Leia through the powers of the Kaiburr crystal.

Her feelings for Luke became more tender—almost sisterly—while those for Han set off romantic sparks. She evacuated Echo Base on Hoth in Solo's *Millennium Falcon*, accompanying him to Cloud City above Bespin. But Han's old gambling buddy, Lando Calrissian, was forced to betray them there to Darth Vader, who was setting a trap for Skywalker. Leia finally declared, "I love you" to Han even as he was forced into a carbonite-freezing chamber. "I know," he replied. Leia and the others were forced to flee, and helped rescue Luke, who had narrowly survived a lightsaber duel with Darth Vader. This was the point at which Vader revealed himself to be Skywalker's father.

Soon thereafter, Leia made contact with Prince Xizor, head of the criminal Black Sun organization, in an attempt to rescue Han. Xizor nearly seduced her, aided by the exotic pheromones he emitted. Despite his charismatic advantages, Xizor was defeated.

Months later, Leia entered the palace of Jabba the Hutt in the disguise of the bounty hunter Boushh. She had Chewbacca in tow. She managed to free Han from his carbonite block, but Jabba discovered her and forced her to join his court as a prisoner and to wear a dancing girl's outfit. She eventually killed Jabba by strangling him with the very chain that bound her. Skywalker triggered a rescue that resulted in the destruction of Jabba's sail barge and the death of many of his henchmen.

Leia and Han led a strike team on the forest moon of Endor whose mission was to destroy a generator that powered the shield that protected the *second* Death Star. She used all her diplomatic skills to gain the help of a primitive tribe of Ewoks; the Rebels persevered, and the second battle station was destroyed—along with Vader and Emperor Palpatine.

Then Luke told Leia the truth. They were twins, and their father had been Anakin Skywalker, who, when seduced by the dark side of the Force, had become Darth Vader. Leia came to understand that many things she had attributed to intuition had really been the glimmerings of untrained Jedi abilities.

Over the coming years, she would become the Alliance's and then the New Republic's foremost ambassador —beginning with the day after the victory at Endor, when she accompanied a force sent to help the besieged

Princess Leia Organa

planet of Bakura. There Anakin Skywalker's spirit appeared to her and begged for her forgiveness.

Leia became a member of the Provisional Council that was formed by Alliance leader Mon Mothma to establish a second Galactic Republic, and became part of a smaller Inner Council that ran the government on a day-to-day basis. Leia's relationship with Han Solo came to a head when the handsome Prince Isolder of Hapes proposed marriage. In response, Han kidnapped her and took her to Dathomir. Despite inevitable complications, Leia decided that Han was the man for her, and they were married six weeks after they left the planet.

Pregnant with twins, Leia became the target of a Noghri assassination attempt engineered by Grand Admiral Thrawn, but the plot was foiled and Leia was instrumental in getting the Noghri to renounce the Empire and join the New Republic. Amid the battles, Leia gave birth to the twins Jacen and Jaina, children who were strong in the Force. Leia herself tried to find time for Jedi training with Luke, and she gained some rudimentary skills.

Pregnant again, Leia faced another major crisis: Her brother seemed to have become corrupted by the dark side of the Force, thanks to the teachings of the cloned Emperor Palpatine. He tried to corrupt her, too, but she escaped with Palpatine's Jedi Holocron. Later she rejoined Luke and together they overcame the clone's dark-side power. Han and Leia's third child was named Anakin, after the great Jedi her father once had been.

When Luke left to start up his Jedi academy, Leia agreed to become Minister of State for the New Republic. She had to cope with Han's disappearance while on a diplomatic mission to Kessel, her own near-death in the crash of Admiral Ackbar's spacecraft on the planet Vortex, new attacks by Imperial Admiral Daala, and an ancient dark-side Jedi's attempt to kill Luke.

Even as these crises arose, Mon Mothma appeared to be dying of a wasting disease, and began giving more and more of her work to Leia. Mothma was finally healed, but she had already tendered her resignation, and strongly pressed Leia to remain as her replacement as Chief of State. Crises—and self doubts—were never far away, spurred by the likes of Yevethan strongman Nil Spaar or the Dark Jedi Kueller, whom she personally killed in battle. There were many painful losses and constant worries about the safety of her husband and children, but Leia remained resolute. Some two standard decades after she had set out on a mission to find the "last" Jedi, Obi-Wan Kenobi, Leia enrolled her own children in Luke's Jedi academy. While pursuing her own mission of peace, she set the stage for the next generation of leaders. [SW, ESB, RJ, SWSB, HE, DFR, TLC, DE, etc.]

Solomahal

Solomahal A veteran officer of the Old Republic, he retired from active duty after the Clone Wars and now makes a living in the Outer Rim territories passing on his scouting expertise. [CCG]

Solusar, Kam A hard-edged middle-aged man, he was an apprentice to the great Jedi Master Ranik Solusar, his father, who was slaughtered by Darth Vader during the Empire's purge of Jedi Knights. Kam Solusar fled the Empire and spent decades in isolation beyond the inhabited star systems. When he returned, he was captured and tortured by dark-side Jedi and was corrupted by the dark side of the Force. Luke Skywalker found Solusar on Nespis VIII and persuaded him to renounce his dark-side allegiance and to join the Alliance. Solusar joined Skywalker's other Jedi students in defeating Exar Kun's spirit, protecting Luke's body and freeing his spirit. [DA, DS, DE2]

Song of War Prince Isolder's Battle Dragon spacecraft. [CPL]

Sonniod A former smuggler and bootlegger, he was an acquaintance of Han Solo and the Wookiee Chewbacca. A short, compact, gray-haired man, Sonniod was running a legitimate holofeature loan service the last time Solo ran into him. [HSR]

Sonsen, Jenica The Chief Operations Officer of the Centerpoint station, she was left in charge after the chief executive ordered a complete evacuation. [SAC]

Sookcool, Avaro A Rodian, he was Lando Calrissian's contact in the Black Sun criminal organization of Prince Xizor. Avaro Sookcool, who speaks Basic with a lisp, owns a small casino in the gambling complex that was run by Black Sun in Equator City on Rodia. Although he was the bounty hunter Greedo's uncle, he harbored no ill feelings toward Han Solo for Greedo's death, for he always considered Greedo somewhat worthless. [SOTE]

Sorannan, Major Sil A former major in the Imperial Black Sword Command, he betrayed strongman Nil Spaar and the Yevethan fleet, leading to a New Republic victory. [TT]

Soul Tree These special trees are planted when an Ewok baby is born. Ewoks feel great kinship toward their individual tree and care for it

Kam Solusar

throughout their lives. When an Ewok dies, a hood is tied around the trunk of their Soul Tree. [ETV]

soup Anzati slang for the life essence that they suck from their victims' brains. [TMEC]

Sovereign One of Warlord Zsinj's Star Destroyers. [CPL]

Sovereign Protectors *See* Emperor's Royal Guards

Spaar, Nil A tall, slender humanoid with mandrill-like facial ridges and coloration, wide-set black eyes, and a concealed claw on the inside of each wrist, the bigoted Yevetha was Viceroy of the Duskhan League. He deceived and humiliated Chief of State Leia Organa Solo by pretending to engage in diplomatic discourse with her regarding the Duskhan League's possible alliance with the New Republic. All the while he planned to declare war on the New Republic and to blame Leia's supposed conspiracy and betrayal. Xenophobic and determined to wipe the galaxy of what he termed "vermin," Spaar sought new places to start Yevethan colonies. He proceeded to destroy the Koornacht Cluster settlements of New Brigia and Polneye, massacring all their inhabitants. Ruthless and cunning, he also betrayed Jian Paret, the commander of the Imperial garrison at N'zoth, the Yevehan spawnworld, whom he brutally killed during an attack and theft of numerous Imperial ships.

Spaar attacked New Republic forces when they attempted to blockade the Yevethan staging area of Doornik-319. When Han Solo, the husband of the Chief of State, was sent to take command of the New Republic's Fifth Fleet, Spaar kidnapped Solo, killed his engineer in cold blood, and savagely beat Solo until he was nearly dead. Finally, after the Yevethan defeat at the Battle of N'zoth, Spaar was killed by former Black Sword Command members, who had sabotaged his ships and helped the New Republic's fleet to defeat the Yevethan forces. [BTS, SOL, TT]

Spaarti cloning cylinder A device used to grow humanoid clones to maturity, it is a remnant of the fierce Clone Wars. Clones grown in less than a year's time usually suffer from clone madness. The Emperor kept a large number of Spaarti cloning cylinders hidden in his private storehouses scattered around the galaxy and used the cylinders to clone himself several times. Grand Admiral Thrawn discovered one storehouse on the planet Wayland, and he used the cylinders he found there to grow clone soldiers and crews for his attacks on the New Republic. Admiral Thrawn even discovered a way to grow perfect clones in as little as twenty days using the Force-repelling ysalamiri. [HE, DFR, LC]

Space slug

space barge A heavy-duty short-range vessel, it has powerful engines and large cargo bays to move goods quickly and efficiently among larger hyperdrive-equipped cargo ships, orbiting storage holds, and planetary spaceports. Space barges also are used to unload container ships that are too massive for planetary landings. [SWSB]

space grazer A legendary creature said to have once roamed between the stars preying on galactic space traffic. [DLS]

Spaceport Speeders A used-vehicle lot in central Mos Eisley on Tatooine, it is where Luke Skywalker sold his landspeeder when he needed money to get off-planet. It is run by the Arcona Unut Poll and a Vuvrian named Wioslea. [TM, GG7]

spacer Someone who makes a living by traveling the space lanes. [SWN]

Spacers' Garage A huge starship repair facility on Nar Shaddaa, it was owned and operated by Shug Ninx, an old friend of Han Solo. [DE]

space slug Giant wormlike creatures as long as 900 meters, they inhabit deep caverns on larger asteroids near the planet Hoth. It has long been rumored that the space pirate Clabburn planted these huge slugs as guardians for his bases. The slugs are hardy, existing in virtually no atmosphere. Silicon-based life-forms, they live for long periods by breaking down the rock and subsisting on the mineral content. Space slugs are plagued by parasites known as mynocks, which they sometimes also feed on. Space-slug flesh has a number of commercial uses. The creatures reproduce through fission, splitting into two separate beings. [SWSB, ESB, ISWU]

Space Station Kwenn The last fuel and supply stop before the Outer Rim Territories, the citylike station features everything a weary spacer might need. Space Station Kwenn is built atop a large docking platform made up of scores of modular space docks and hangar bays. Its lower levels consist of dry-dock gridwork used for parking, overhauling, or otherwise repairing capital ships. [TM, SF]

Space Station Scardia A cube-shaped station, it was headquarters for the Prophets of the Dark Side. [LCJ, PDS]

spacing A form of execution, it consists of casting a victim out into space without any protective gear. [HLL]

Spangled Veil Nebula Located in the Meridian sector near Exodo II and Odos, the Spangled Veil Nebula is filled with glowing white clouds of dust and massive, drifting chunks of ice. Nine years after the Battle of

Speeder bike

Endor, Han Solo and Lando Calrissian were attacked by an Imperial fleet from the nearby Antemeridian sector while at Exodo II. They lost their pursuers in the Spangled Veil Nebula. [POT]

Specter Squadron One of the many fighter squadrons of the Rebel Alliance. Specter One was the codename assigned to pilot Jon Vander during his stay at Renforra Base. [CCG]

speeder *See* airspeeder; landspeeder; snowspeeder

speeder bike Small repulsorlift vehicles, they are used throughout the galaxy as personal transports, recreational vehicles, and even military reconnaissance vehicles, such as those used by the Empire's scout troops. Speeder bikes can travel at up to 500 kilometers per hour through terrain that would stop other vehicles. Most can rise only about twenty-five meters above ground level.

The Empire's speeder bikes have armor plating, a single blaster cannon, two outriggers, and four forward steering vanes. Controls for maneuvering are in the handgrips; altitude controls in the foot pedals also normally control speed. Communications, sensors, and weaponry controls are at the front of the saddle.

Biker scouts normally work in squads called lances. Each five-bike lance has four standard speeder-bike scouts and a sergeant commander; a lance generally splits into two elements for field operations. Imperial scouts using bikes can explore and survey far more territory per man than those using almost any other type of vehicle. Speeder troops are normally used for scouting and exploration; they are ordered to avoid conflict so that they can make reports to base commanders. Speeder-bike scout helmets have macrobinocular view plates, a full sensor array, and a terrain-plotting computer to help them navigate in unfamiliar territory at high speed.

Speeder bikes were part of the Empire's efforts to patrol the forests on Endor, but a Rebel commando team led by Han Solo and Princess Leia managed to eliminate a perimeter scouting lance, allowing the Rebels a clear path to the shield generator base. [SWSB, GG5, GSWU, ISB, SWVG, ROJ]

speeder transport Large shuttlecraft, they are used by the New Republic to move V-wing airspeeders from capital ships to launch points inside a planet's atmosphere. [DE]

Spefik A planet with antiorbital ion cannons that were attacked by two wings of TIE fighters. The cannons were destroyed by a salvo from pilot Ranulf Trommer. [ROC]

Spero An old Ho'Din master gardener and friend of Leia Organa Solo, he had a plant shop in the Southern Underground on Imperial Center. He was propagator of a strain of yellow fungus used all over the galaxy. Spero gave Leia important confirmation about the criminal organization Black Sun and its leader, Prince Xizor. [SOTE]

spice A name given to a variety of drugs, in particular the glitterstim spice mined underground on the planet Kessel. Spice is a highly taxed and controlled substance, although legal to use in most parts of the galaxy. It is a popular commodity for smugglers because of its high profit margin. Spice has a number of legitimate uses in psychological therapy, criminal investigation, communication with alien races, and artistic inspiration and entertainment. Mood-altering glitterstim has a sharp, pleasant odor and can produce feelings of euphoria in those who use it. Other spices include ryll, carsunum, and andris. [SW, JS, TBH, SWSB, SWAJ]

Spicy Lady A ship owned by the smuggler Jarril, it was small but distinctive, a cross between a stock light freighter and an A-wing fighter. Jarril stole the plans for the *Falcon* and modified them to construct the *Spicy Lady*. The ship was built for carrying cargo, but its storage units could be easily jettisoned so that the A-wing portion could maneuver on its own. The fighter could even be remotely operated if necessary. Lando Calrissian discovered the *Spicy Lady* floating in space, minus its A-wing component, with the body of the murdered Jarril aboard. [NR]

spider-roach An arachnid pest, it is found in the lower levels of Imperial City. [DA]

Spince, Mako Shiftless and aimless, this son of a once-influential senator befriended a younger Han Solo at the Imperial Space Academy before being expelled for one prank too many. Mako Spince then became a smuggler and taught the trade to Solo. He was intercepted by bandits on a particularly risky run, and his injuries crippled him. Confined to a repulsor

Spero

Mako Spince

chair, he became a traffic controller on Nar Shaddaa.

A decade later, Solo returned to Nar Shaddaa, and although Spince let the *Millennium Falcon* find safety in the moon's twisting city structures, he also contacted the bounty hunters Boba Fett and Dengar to apprise them of the whereabouts of Solo and his wife, Leia. Han and Leia escaped, but on their return, Spince alerted Imperial authorities. Solo managed to maneuver his ship so that instead of the *Falcon,* it was Spince's traffic control tower that was in the tractor beam of an Imperial Star Destroyer. Spince and the tower were destroyed. [DE]

Spira A tropical pleasure world near the Inner Core, it is one of the most popular vacation destinations for wealthy Core World citizens. The planet is covered by a sparkling sea, broken only by small islands. Scouted by the Old Republic more than a thousand years ago, Spira was later leased from the Empire by the Tourist Guild. Air traffic is limited to passenger liners and registered transports, and personal weapons are forbidden. Ataria Island is home to Spira's major spaceport and its most exclusive resorts. Spectacular cliffs make up the island's north and west sides, and luxurious beaches can be found to the east. [SWAJ]

Spirit Tree The Ewok tribes on Endor's forest moon consider this tree to be the original tree on the planet. All life is believed to have started with the Spirit Tree. The Ewoks also believe that all life must eventually return to the Spirit Tree. [ETV]

spotlight sloth A sloth that lives on the planet Dagobah, it uses the bright glowing patches on its chest to illuminate the plant life that it feeds upon. [ISWU]

Sprax A Nalroni, he was one of the lieutenants, or Vigos, of the Black Sun criminal organization. Even though the prideful Sprax's dark fur had begun to turn gray, he dyed it to try to appear younger. [SOTE]

Spray of Tynna The name used by a short, two-legged skip tracer working for Interstellar Collections Ltd. A member of a species of intelligent sea otters, Spray of Tynna was actually Odumin, a powerful and influential territorial sector manager for the Corporate Sector Authority. [HSR]

Spuma A planet where New Republic Intelligence agents first discovered increased trooper recruitment by the fleet of Admiral Harrsk. The admiral was one of the few Imperial warlords still strong eight years after the Battle of Endor. [COJ]

Squab The star orbited by Skor II, home planet of the Squibs. [GG4]

Squeak A Tin-Tin Dwarf, he worked as a messenger for Big Bunji, a former associate of Han Solo. [HSE]

Squib Small, furry bipeds with tufted ears, large eyes, short muzzles, and black noses, these galactic nomads come from the planet Skor II. They use tractor beams aboard their reclamation ships to salvage what they consider treasure but what most other beings consider junk. Squibs have an intense rivalry with Ugors. Often overconfident, Squibs appear overbearing and uppity. They have turned haggling into an art, and the more complicated the deal, the better they like it. [SH, GG4]

Squib

Squid Head *See* Quarren

squints The slang X-wing pilots use for Imperial TIE interceptors. [RS]

Ssi-ruuk A saurian or reptilian species with domination its goal, the Ssi-ruuk invaded Imperial space during the Galactic Civil War. In a process called entechment, the Ssi-ruuk drain the life energies of other species—particularly humanoids—to power their droids and shipboard instruments as part of an expansion of their Imperium throughout the galaxy.

Ssi-ruuk adults on their homeworld of Lwhekk grow to about two meters tall. They have a beaked muzzle with large teeth and round black eyes with triple eyelids. Retractable black scent-tongues in their nostrils sense other individuals' stress reactions. Their massive bodies have upper limbs with three prehensile, clawed digits; their tails are muscular. Ssi-ruuk body color varies and tends to indicate occupation: Russets dominate the military, for example, while blues rule the political structure. [TAB]

Ssi-ruuvi battle droids Small drone ships, they are powered by the enteched life forces drained from captured prisoners. The two-meter-wide battle droids are pyramid-shaped and function as the main assault fighters of the Ssi-ruuvi fleet. Two fully rotating laser cannons on each corner arm them well. They are speedy and highly maneuverable, and their size makes them difficult targets—ones with shields as heavy as many larger starfighters.

Powered by fusion, the battle droids become highly radioactive when they are destroyed. Microfilament grids on the ships' surfaces can capture part of the energy of incoming blasts and filter it as energy back into the battle droid's main generator. Ssi-ruuvi command cruisers remotely control the two life energies trapped inside each battle droid, forcing them to obey all in-

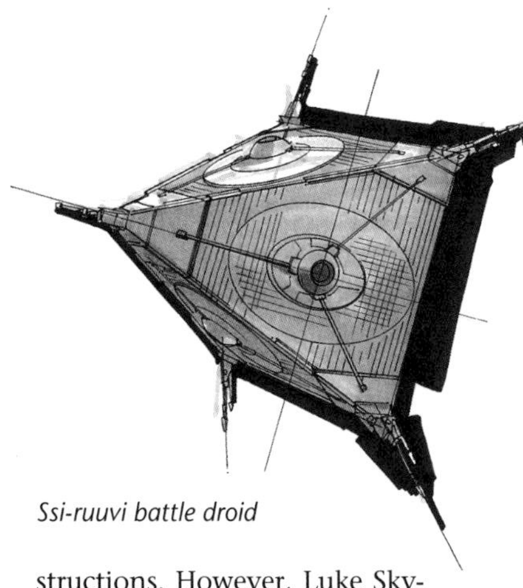
Ssi-ruuvi battle droid

structions. However, Luke Skywalker, using the Force, discovered that the life energies still retained some will of their own. [TAB, TBSB, SWVG]

Ssty A furry, bipedal species with two arms and tiny claws that act like fingers, they are very intelligent but prone to cheating. [NR]

ST 321 The comm-unit designation for Darth Vader's personal *Lambda*-class shuttle. [RJN]

staga Herd beasts, they are native to the planet Ambria. [TOJ]

Stalker An Imperial Star Destroyer, it originally was assigned to search the Outer Rim for new worlds to subjugate. The *Stalker* launched the probe droid that discovered the secret Rebel Alliance base on the ice planet Hoth. The ship was later assigned to the Empire's Death Squad. [CCG]

Stalwart A New Republic Fifth Fleet cruiser, it was deployed in the blockade of Doornik-319. [SOL]

Standard Time Part The basic unit used to measure time throughout the galaxy. [SWN]

stang An Alderaanian expletive. [SME]

Stanz, Captain A Bothan, he is owner-pilot of the gypsy freighter *Freebird.* [BTS]

Star Chamber Cafe A cafe in Mos Eisley's Lucky Despot Hotel. [GG7, TMEC]

star cruiser A class of capital ship. [SW, ESB, RJ]

Star Destroyer The core of the Imperial Navy, these huge wedge-shaped warships are meant to inspire fear; they succeed admirably. These 1,600-meter-long engineering marvels wield more than 100 weapons emplacements for deep-space combat. A standard *Imperial*-class Star Destroyer—which replaced the earlier *Victory*-class—maintains sixty turbolasers for ship-to-ship combat and planetary assault and sixty ion cannons to disable enemy ships for boarding. Atop its superstructure is a huge command tower holding the bridge, essential systems, and computer controls. It is topped by a pair of generator domes for deflector shields.

A Star Destroyer has two main landing bays that can accommodate hundreds of ships of varying sizes. A full wing of seventy-two TIE fighters (six squadrons of twelve ships each) is standard. It also carries eight *Lambda*-class shuttles, fifteen stormtrooper transports, and five assault gunboats, along with Skipray Blastboats and *Gamma*-class assault shuttles. Star Destroyers also accommodate planetary assault teams with landing barges, drop ships, twenty AT-AT walkers, thirty AT-ST scout walkers, and 9,700 ground troops. They can deploy a prefabricated garrison base with 800 troops. The ships were designed by Lira Wessex, daughter of famed Republic engineer and designer Walex Blissex. Typical missions involve perimeter patrol, convoy escort, planetary assault, and planetary defense in the event of a direct assault.

An upgraded class of the Star Destroyer, called the *Imperial II,* began appearing in Imperial Navy fleets shortly after the Battle of Yavin. They have a heavily reinforced hull and boast more powerful heavy turbolaser batteries and cannons.

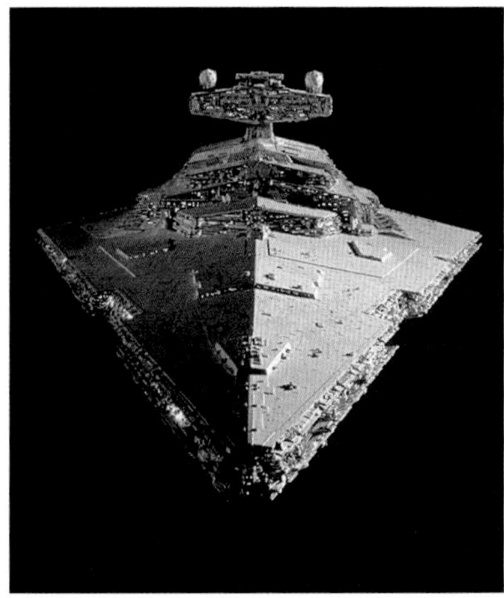
Star Destroyer

All told, the Empire built more than 25,000 Star Destroyers, holding half of them on reserve in the Galactic Core to protect key military, industrial, and political systems. The Empire could strategically deploy the ships anywhere at short notice.

The newest model, the *Super*-class Star Destroyer, is 8,000 meters long and five times as powerful as its predecessor. Because they were built in limited numbers, these ships have been used mainly as command ships, guiding fleets and serving as headquarters from which to conduct planetary assaults and space battles. Darth Vader's *Executor* was a *Super*-class Star Destroyer. A special *Eclipse*-class Star Destroyer was built to serve as the reborn cloned Emperor's flagship six years after the Battle of Endor. Solid black, it was an incredible 16,000 meters long. [SWN, SWVG, SWSB, FP, ISB, DE, DESB]

Star Dream The transport ship that brought Evar Orbus and his Galactic Jizz-wailers to Tatooine. [TJP]

Star Galleon At 300 meters in length, this ship class combines the cargo space of a bulk freighter with the weapons of a combat starship. A Star Galleon's ten turbolaser batteries and concussion missiles make separate freighters and escort craft unnecessary. The interior has fortresslike emplacements in the corridors, 300 troopers, force fields, and heavy blast doors. The cargo-hold pod in the center of the ship can be jettisoned from the vessel and sent on a prearranged lightspeed jump. [ISB, DFRSB]

Star Home A unique transport vessel designed more than 4,000 years before the Galactic Civil War for the Queen Mother of the Hapes Cluster, it replicates the Queen Mother's castle on the planet Hapes. Despite its ungainly appearance and its age, the *Star Home* is spaceworthy. The castle-ship holds the Queen Mother's quarters and hearing room, as well as dining halls, meeting rooms, and guest quarters, all covered in dark stone. A number of towers capped with crystal domes give an unobstructed view of space. Gardens fill upper courtyard levels.

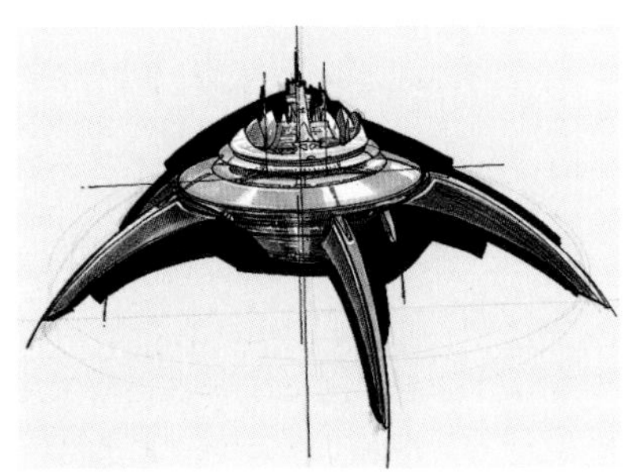

Star Home

The *Star Home* represents wealth, power, and the supreme authority of the Queen Mother, currently Ta'a Chume. Each of the inhabited worlds of the Hapes Cluster contributed stone, woodwork, gems, or other ornamentation for the interior. Each year, the governor of each world presents the most treasured artifact from his or her planet to be stored forever in the galleries and vaults of the *Star Home*, so visitors can view the treasures of the Hapan people. Nearly a third of the ship's interior is filled with six massive generators that power all systems, including shields and twenty-four sublight and four hyperdrive engines. [CPL, SWVG]

Starhunter Intergalactic Menagerie A traveling sideshow, it toured the galaxy during the early days of the Empire. Operated by the sleazy Captain Stroon, the main attractions of the Starhunter Intergalactic Menagerie were rare and usually illegally acquired creatures from many worlds. It moved from system to system in a huge cruiser, whose first mate was a lizardlike humanoid called Slarm. [DTV]

Starlight Intruder A hot-rod transport built for smuggling runs by Salla Zend, this medium freighter hides power beneath a battered surface. The *Starlight Intruder* can carry seven times the cargo of standard light freighters and has added hull bracing and armor plating, four military-grade ion engines for fast getaways, and four maneuvering jets at the bottom of the hull. Chewbacca helped Zend install a hyperdrive from an old Hutt chariot. Han Solo talked Zend into using the *Intruder* to smuggle his *Millennium Falcon* onto the Imperial throneworld of Byss. But while he and the *Falcon* got away, Byss security impounded the *Intruder*. [DE, DESB, SWVG]

Star Morning A fifty-year-old Kogus liner, it was purchased by the Fallanassi religious order's corporation, Kell Plath, and used to evacuate the persecuted sect's members from the planet Lucazec. [SOL]

Star Runner The star cruiser owned and operated by young Kea Moll, who lived on her mother's farm complex on the planet Annoo. [DTV]

Starry Ice One of smuggler Talon Karrde's freighters, it was used to carry weapons and munitions for Rogue Squadron to the rendezvous point at the Graveyard of Alderaan . [BW]

Star Saber An experimental attack ship built some 4,000 years before the Galactic Civil War, it was equipped with wing cannons. [DLS]

Stars' End A secret Corporate Sector Authority penal colony on the planet Mytus VII, its name refers to the location of the Mytus star system, which sits at the end of a faint wisp of stars at the edge of Corporate sector space. [HSE]

Starstorm I The spaceship used by Dark Lord of the Sith Exar Kun some 4,000 years before the Galactic Civil War to escape with the ancient scrolls given to him by the spirit of Dark-Sider Freedon Nadd. [DLS, TOJ, TSW]

Star Swan A transport ship, it made regular runs to Tatooine. [TMEC]

Startide A Mon Calamari battle cruiser, it is the equivalent of an Imperial Star Destroyer. [DA]

stasis field A force field, it is used to keep organic matter such as foodstuffs fresh for years. It can also keep humans and other beings in a state of suspended animation. [HSE, TJP]

Stassia An agricultural planet in the Core Worlds, its 1.3 billion human inhabitants are known for their indifference to most change and their accepting natures. Settled for millennia, Stassia was originally ruled by the members of the fifteen Head Clans, who were descendants of the original colonists. Stassia City is home to swoop races and ringer tournaments. [SWAJ]

Steadfast A New Republic ship commanded by Captain Oolas, it surveyed the ruins of the Imperial Star Destroyer *Gnisnal*, which contained an intact memory that held a complete Imperial Order of Battle. [BTS]

Stele, Maarek A highly decorated Imperial pilot from the planet Kuan, he started as a hotshot hot-rodder on a swoop bike on his devastated planet, which had been engaged in a decades-long war with neighboring Bordal. His father, Kerek, a famous scientist, had been kidnapped by Bordali agents, who later kidnapped Maarek and his mother to force Kerek to do their bidding. On the way to Bordal, they were intercepted by the Imperial Star Destroyer *Vengeance*. The Empire declared martial law in the system, and the war between Kuan and Bordal at last was over. Maarek started as a mechanic aboard the *Vengeance*, and on a flight to test out repairs on a TIE interceptor, he helped save the life of the Star Destroyer's commander, Admiral Mordon. That led to an invitation to join the Imperial Navy and become a fighter pilot. He became one of the best the Empire had. [TSC]

Stendaff A light escort, the spotter ship was part of Colonel Pakkpekatt's New Republic armada chasing the mysterious ghost ship, the Teljkon vagabond. [SOL]

Stennes Shifter A near-human race, the species has the ability to blend into crowds unnoticed. [CCG]

Stenness lizard pie A local delicacy in the Stenness Node. [TOJ]

Stenness Node Sometimes referred to as the Stenness system, the node is

Starlight Intruder

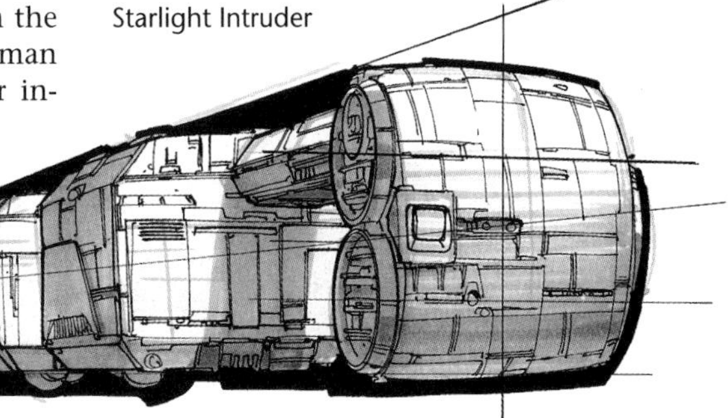

Stinger

actually a group of three mining systems containing the Stenness system. The node is located on the rim of the galaxy on the mining frontier and contains the planets Ambria and Taboon. The twenty-five humanoid species inhabiting the node are collectively referred to as Nessies, and they control the various mining operations and cut deals with outside traders. BolBol the Hutt is said to practically own the Stenness system. Some 4,000 years before the Galactic Civil War, the Stenness underworld was controlled by a Hutt named Great Bogga, and the Nessies transported mutonium cargoes in ships made from the hollowed exoskeletons of the Colossus Wasps of Ithull.

Han Solo and his former lady friend, Salla Zend, used to run Kessel spice to the Stenness system and compete to see who could strike the best deal with the Nessies. The bounty hunters Zardra and Jodo Kast, pursuing the Thig brothers into the Stenness system, caught up with their quarry on Taboon. The ensuing firefight resulted in the death of Mageye the Hutt. [DE, TOJ, TMEC]

Stic A planet of continual climactic and geologic change, it is home to the insectoid species Xi'Dec. In order to adapt to the rapid changes of Stic, the Xi'Dec have evolved hundreds of specialized sexes throughout their history, each with its own unique appearance and abilities. Currently there are more than 180 different sexes of Xi'Dec with the most common, Xi'Alpha, making up about 6 percent of the population. Xi'Dec society is organized around the family unit, which never contains more than one member of the same sex. Tourism is a major industry. [GG4]

stim-shot A major component of a medpac, it is a stimulant administered through a pneumatic dispenser. [ESBR]

Stinger The personal transport of Guri, who was the human-replica droid aide of criminal overlord Prince Xizor. A modified assault ship sometimes used for smuggling, the *Stinger* was about twenty-eight meters long, with a curved hull that appeared to be sculpted into a flat figure eight. The *Stinger's* power came from a cluster of eight ion engines, giving it sublight speed faster than an X-wing's. The *Stinger's* maneuverability was enhanced by computer adjustment of each engine's exhaust nozzles. Weapons included a pair of fire-linked ion cannons and a turret-mounted double laser cannon. [SOTE, SWVG]

stintaril An omnivorous tree-dwelling rodent found on Yavin 4, it feeds on woolamanders and anything else in its path. Stintarils have protruding eyes and long jaws filled with sharp teeth. [YJK, ISWU, GG2]

stock light freighter Among the most common small trading vessels, these ships were at one time the workhorse of intergalactic trade until they were replaced by larger bulk freighters and container ships. Stock light freighters are all built on the basic design of a command pod, storage holds, and engines. The *Millennium Falcon* is a modified stock light freighter, a model YT-1300 Corellian transport. [SWSB]

Stokhli spray stick Long-range stun weapons, they were developed by the Stokhli species of the planet Manress. The Stokhli spray stick releases a fine mist with a powerful current that stuns targets up to 200 meters away. Originally developed for hunters, the spray sticks have gained popularity as defensive and offensive personal weapons. [HE, HESB]

Stonebone, Finhead A pirate captain, he operated in the Stenness Node some 4,000 years before the Galactic Civil War. [TOJ]

Stone Needle A rocky spire in Beggar's Canyon with an oval hole near the top, it is the tallest landmark in the Jundland Wastes on Tatooine. Hotshot young pilots would fly through the opening on their speeder or swoop bikes or even try to make it through in a small craft. It was the site of many injuries and some deaths. [SWR, TJP]

Stonn, Li Luke Skywalker used this name and the appearance of an old man during his travels on Teyr and Atzerri. [SOL]

Stopa, Kroddok An archaeologist from the Obroan Institute, he was the expedition chief for the mission to Qella. The mission's goal was to recover biological samples for any clues to the origins of the Qella civilization. Kroddok Stopa was killed in an avalanche on Maltha Obex. [SOL]

Storm The personally designed starfighter of Prince Isolder, crown prince of the Hapan throne, it is based on the hull of the Hapan Miy'til fighters. The *Storm's* refinements have turned it into a fighter that can fly against any short-range ship in the Hapan Cluster. The sleek fighter is just over seven meters long and uses miniaturized components. It has four banks of anticoncussion field generators. A sensor and communications scrambler allows Isolder to block all communications from enemy fighters and prevents enemy scanners from getting a target lock on *Storm*.

The ship's nose holds a set of triple-linked laser cannons and a miniconcussion missile launcher with ten missiles. Each wing has an ion cannon, and a thermal detonator bomb chute is mounted in the rear between the engines. The ship's transparisteel bubble canopy gives it excellent visibility in all directions. Its four fusial thrust engines have been rebuilt with modified power converters to give the ship the sublight speed of a TIE interceptor. Each engine has an oversize turbogenerator for short bursts that propel the ship to speeds one-third faster than an A-wing fighter's.

The *Storm* crash-landed on the

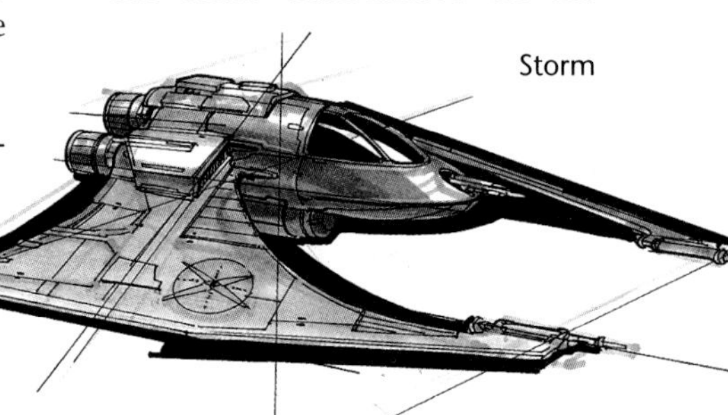
Storm

Stormtrooper

planet Dathomir when Prince Isolder attempted to rescue Princess Leia Organa. It was recovered and rebuilt after the Battle of Dathomir. [CPL, SWVG]

stormtrooper Seeming to be a will of iron encased in hardened white armor, these Imperial shock troops neutralized resistance to the New Order and remained totally loyal to the Emperor, even in the face of certain death. Stormtroopers rode in all Imperial vessels, were used as first-strike forces, and were employed to make sure officers on the ships stayed loyal. They could not be bribed or blackmailed, lived in a totally disciplined environment, and were militaristic to the core. Even years after the Emperor's death, legions of stormtroopers remain true to Imperial doctrines.

In addition to units of regular stormtroopers, the Empire developed a number of specialized units. Snow-troopers, or cold-assault troopers, were trained and equipped to do battle in frozen environments. They wear the basic white armor equipped with powerful heating and personal environment units, terrain-grip boots, and face-shielding breathing masks. Spacetroopers, or elite zero-g stormtroopers, have been used to launch assaults in space on another vessel. Each trooper utilizes armor and equipment that enables them to function as if they were an independent spacecraft, to withstand the vacuum of space, to propel themselves through space, and to attack and breach nearly any target.

Scout troopers, although lightly armored, are highly mobile stormtroopers usually assigned to Imperial garrisons. They use speeder bikes to patrol perimeters, perform reconnaissance missions, and scout enemy locations. To assist them when traveling at high speeds, scout troopers wear specialized helmets equipped with built-in macrobinocular view plates and sensor arrays that feed into computers that analyze terrain instantaneously to help navigation. Other stormtrooper types include aquatic assault stormtroopers, or sea-troopers; sandtroopers, or desert stormtroopers; storm commandos, or black-armored scout troopers; rad-troopers, who work in radiation zones; and dark troopers, who are so well-equipped that they constitute powerful self-contained weapons platforms. [SW, ESB, RJ, SWSB, HE, HESB, SWSB, ISB, BGS, GG9, DF]

Storthus Homeworld of giant Stone Eels, creatures of living rock. [D]

story platform An interactive multimedia datapad, it displays and tells stories to entertain children. [DA]

Streen A bearded, graying, aging hermit who lived in the abandoned city of Tibannopolis on Bespin, he was able to predict eruptions of valuable gases from deep within the cloud layers and could hear the thoughts and voices of all around him—a talent that bothered him greatly and led to his withdrawal from other people. Luke Skywalker found Streen to be Force-sensitive and invited him to join the other Jedi students at the Jedi academy. The spirit of Dark Jedi Exar Kun influenced Streen into starting a tornado that threatened to destroy the near-lifeless body of Luke Skywalker, but Streen was stopped in time. He later joined forces with the other Jedi students in destroying Exar Kun's spirit forever. [JS, DA, COF]

***Strike*-class medium cruiser** Introduced near the end of the Galactic Civil War, this 450-meter-long Imperial star cruiser was built of prefabricated modular sections so that it could be quickly mass-produced by Loronar Corporation. The *Strike*-class medium cruiser has continued to serve an important role in the remnants of the Imperial fleet under the command of Grand Admiral Thrawn and others. *Strike*-class cruiser interiors can be configured to accommodate specific mission profiles. Some carry a ground assault company; others are modified for a complete squadron of TIE fighters. Still other configurations include prefab garrison deployers, troop transports, and planetary assault cruisers. *Strike*-class cruisers normally carry twenty turbolasers, ten ion cannons, and ten tractor beam projectors. [ISB, HESB]

Stroiketcy Probably a captured comet, it is one of the three planets of the Yavin system. Stroiketcy is noted for its trailing tail of atmosphere and its solid rock core. The world's surface is almost entirely water, and only a handful of rock outcroppings break the surface amid constant rainfall and fog. Although never confirmed, unicellular life might exist in Stroiketcy's oceans. The planet's name comes from the Corellian for "tailed one." [GG2]

Sturm One of two domesticated vornskrs used by smuggler Talon Karrde as pets and guards. [HE, DFR, LC, HESB]

Subjugator A *Victory*-class Star Destroyer under the command of Captain Kolaff, it was targeted by a Rebel Mon Calamari strike force code-named Task Force Starfall. The task force, made up of Mon Cal star cruisers, engaged the *Subjugator* and destroyed it. [SF]

sublight drive A sublight starship drive moves vessels through realspace. One popular type is the Hoersch-Kessel ion drive, which produces charged particles through fusion reaction to hurl ships forward. Ships with H-K sublight drives use repulsorlifts for atmospheric travel. [SWSB]

Sulamar, General A pompous Imperial officer, he bragged of nonexistent military triumphs to Durga the Hutt, with whom he plotted to unleash a new superweapon on the New Republic. General Sulamar was obsessive about protocol and plastered his chest with campaign ribbons he had supposedly been awarded. He was later exposed by Crix Madine, head of New Republic Intelligence, as a military screwup who had been transferred from assignment to assignment after continual mistakes. He and Durga both died as a result of the new weapon's failure. [DS]

Sullust A volcanic world in the Sullust system, it is covered with thick clouds of hot, barely breathable gases. Sullust is habitable only in its vast networks of underground caves where native Sullustans—jowled, mouse-eared humanoids with large round eyes—have built beautiful underground cities that draw large crowds of tourists. Piringiisi, one popular resort, is known for its hot springs and green mud. Sullust has one inhabited moon, Sulon.

The amiable Sullustans are highly valued as pilots and navigators due to their instinctive ability to remember any path previously traveled. The massive SoroSuub Corporation is based on Sullust and employs nearly half the population in its mining, energy, packaging, and production divisions. Despite the Rebel sympathies of many Sullustans, the SoroSubb Corporation dissolved the Sullustan government, seized control of the planet, and declared its allegiance to the Empire.

After being forced out of the Sullust system by Imperials, Councilor Sian Tevv brought Nien Nunb's private raiding squad into Alliance service. Prior to the Battle of Yavin, after the Alliance rescued a Sullustan leader kidnapped by the Empire, the Sullustans leaned heavily toward the Alliance. However, it was late in the war when the leaders of Sullust finally held a vote and decided to secede from the Empire officially. The Alliance fleet assembled near Sullust just prior to the Battle of Endor, in which Nien Nunb became Lando Calrissian's copilot aboard the *Millennium Falcon*. His sister, Aril Nunb, later served as the Executive Officer for Rogue Squadron. [RJ, RJN, SWSB, LC, COJ, DESB, FP, RS, SWAJ]

Sulon The moon of the planet Sullust, it is primarily given over to agriculture. Alliance agent Kyle Katarn was from Sulon. His father was an agricultural machine salesman and mechanic in a small rural community. While Katarn was at the Imperial Academy, the Empire raided Sulon and killed his family, though they claimed the deaths were the result of Rebel terrorists. [DF]

Sumitra sector A sector with 12,387 planets and moons, it contains the planet Tierfon, where a Rebel starfighter base was established to patrol the outer edges of the sector. The Empire was aware of Rebel activity but found locating Tierfon base difficult. [SWSB]

Sunaj Near the planet Sunaj, following the Battle of Yavin, the Imperial Star Destroyer *Relentless* was to receive a cargo of new TIE interceptors at a rendezvous. The replacement cargo TIEs were destroyed by an Alliance strike team. [FP]

Sun Crusher An Imperial superweapon prototype, it was designed at the secret weapons think tank, the Maw Installation. Under Admiral Daala, a design team headed by the scientist Qwi Xux made many breakthroughs that led to the new weapon called the Sun Crusher. Only slightly larger than a fighter, its resonance torpedoes were powerful enough to destroy a star.

The Sun Crusher was a slender, cone-shaped vessel capped with a tetrahedron on the upper end and a dish-shaped resonance projector hanging from the lower end. A number of rotating laser cannons could disable attacking enemy ships, although its shimmering quantum-crystalline armor made the Sun Crusher nearly impervious to damage. The ship's eleven "resonance torpedoes" were energized through the transmitting dish and could be launched into a star to trigger a chain reaction that caused the star to go supernova, incinerating every world in its system.

Imprisoned in the Maw Installation, Han Solo convinced Qwi Xux of the weapon's evil, and she, Solo, Chewbacca, and a Force-sensitive Kessel escapee named Kyp Durron stole the Sun Crusher. The weapon was delivered to Coruscant, where the New Republic Assembly voted to cast it into the gas giant Yavin. However, Durron used his Force powers to retrieve it and went on a rampage, demolishing several Imperial worlds before surrendering the vessel. The Sun Crusher was destroyed at the Battle of the Maw when it was caught in the gravity well of one of the Maw's black holes. [JS, DA, COF]

Sundari The third planet in the Garos system, it is a hot, arid mining colony settled nearly 4,000 years before the Galactic Civil War. Sundari immediately began trade with its sister planet, Garos IV, because the Sundars were dependent on an outside supply of foodstuffs. About 200 years before the Battle of Yavin, large numbers of Sundars began emigrating to Garos IV and establishing new businesses and factories, earning the resentment of Garosians who were hurt by the new competition. A civil war between the two planets erupted when a Garosian grain-processing facility was destroyed. The devastating war raged for eighty-two years until a truce was hammered out by Tork Winger, Assistant Minister of Defense for Garos IV, and Tionthes Turi, a respected Sundar engineer. Violations of the truce continued, but the Empire's intervention in the conflict five years before the Battle of Yavin brought a sudden, violent end to most resistance. [SWAJ]

Sunfighter Franchise One of the false names Han Solo used to register the *Millennium Falcon* in the days when he was evading Corporate Sector Authority patrols. [HSE]

SunGem Jedi Master Arca Jeth's courier ship some 4,000 years before the Galactic Civil War, it was outfit-

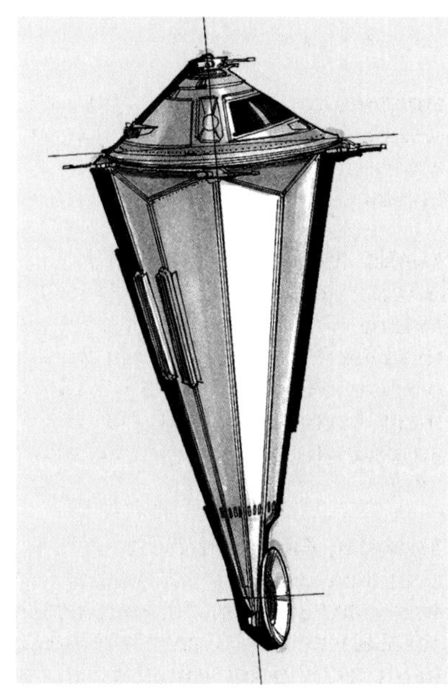

Sun Crusher

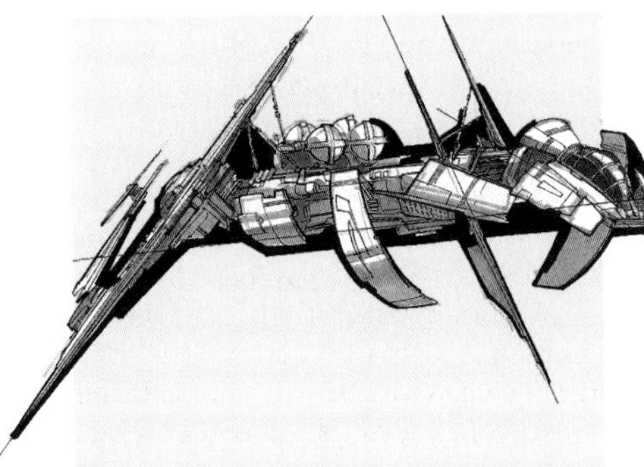
SunGem

ted as a training facility for his Jedi students. The *SunGem* was aerodynamic, with layers of maneuvering vanes and retractable airfoils. It was equipped with twenty-one ion engines mounted in banks of three. In an atmosphere, the *SunGem* could reach a top speed of about 950 kilometers per hour, making it the equal of many atmospheric speeders and starfighters.

The *SunGem* had extendable hull sections with a dedicated defense station, but it was lightly armed, revealing Arca's preference for stealth and cunning over brute force. The main weapon was a forward proton torpedo launcher. It also had a pair of rotating laser cannons that could fire in opposite directions at the same time. Most of the ship's interior was given over to Jedi training facilities, with meditation chambers, lightsaber training areas with remotes, and a variable gravity and atmosphere room to simulate hostile planetary conditions. An extensive computer library held Jedi texts. [TOJ, SWSB]

sungwa Large doglike creatures, they resemble a cross between a wolf and a weasel. Sungwas are native to the bog moon Bodgen. [DTV]

Sunlet, Merc A crafty thief with a heart of gold, he is a native of Tirac Munda. The wealthy often hire him to advise them about protecting their property. Well-traveled and skilled in many languages, he had business of an undisclosed nature on Tatooine. [CCG]

Sunrider, Andur Husband of Nomi Sunrider and father of Vima, the Jedi was killed some 4,000 years before the Galactic Civil War in a senseless battle with petty gangsters at the Stenness hyperspace terminal while he was on his way to visit Jedi Master Thon on Ambria. [TOJ]

Sunrider, Nomi The unprepossessing wife of a Jedi 4,000 years before the Galactic Civil War, she became one of the great Jedi Knights of her time, though the path was not of her choosing. It seemed as if circumstances conspired to make her a powerful Jedi. Nomi Sunrider, with rusty brown hair and blue-green eyes, was the wife of Andur and mother of newborn Vima when her adventure began. She was accompanying her husband on a mission to take some Adegan crystals, used to construct lightsabers, to Jedi Master Thon in the Ambria system when Andur was cut down by several henchmen of Great Bogga the Hutt. Urged on by his spirit, she picked up his lightsaber and slew two of the thugs before continuing with his mission.

On the planet Ambria, Thon convinced her to stay and train to be a Jedi herself. Once, she saved her daughter from an attack by a dark-side monster by creating a vision of the beasts attacking one another through the use of Jedi battle meditation, and later used the technique to defeat a band of pirates on a mission from Bogga. Her training took her to the planet Ossus, where she apprenticed with Master Vodo-Siosk Baas and learned to make her own lightsaber. She was then drafted to join a Jedi team to battle Dark Siders who were taking over the planet Onderon and to rescue Master Arca Jeth and his students. She developed strong feelings for her team member Ulic Qel-Droma. Nomi stayed to train with Arca in the Force mind technique known as Jedi battle meditation, gaining in both physical strength and self-confidence.

Andur Sunrider

Sungwa

Arca assigned Nomi and Qel-Droma to lead a joint peacekeeping force of the Galactic Republic and the Jedi Knights to defeat the challenge of the dark-side Krath cult and the dark magicians of the Sith. After a pitched battle, Qel-Droma told Nomi that he would infiltrate the Krath and learn their dark-side ways, even though Nomi urged him against such action. Her warning was prescient. She and two other Jedi later tried to extract Qel-Droma from virtual imprisonment in the Empress Teta system, but he had been injected with Sith poison that led to an explosion of anger and his loss to the dark side. With resignation, Nomi knew that she had to leave him to his dark fate. [TOJ, FNU, DLS, TSW, DA]

Sunrider, Vima The daughter of Nomi and Andur Sunrider some 4,000

Nomi Sunrider

years before the Galactic Civil War, she was destined to become a great Jedi. [TOJ, TSW]

***Super*-class Star Destroyer** *See* Star Destroyer

Suppoon, Gaar An odious alien criminal, he was visited by Jabba the Hutt so that they could conduct some nefarious business together. Gaar Suppoon had no intention of letting Jabba leave his planet alive, but Jabba turned the tables on him, and Suppoon paid with his life. [JAB]

Supreme Prophet *See* Kadann

Suprosa A freighter, it supposedly carried only fertilizer. Actually, its top-secret cargo was an Imperial computer containing information on the building of the Empire's second Death Star battle station. The stock light freighter was under contract to XTS, the transportation company owned by Prince Xizor, head of the Black Sun criminal organization. The freighter seemed lightly armed until attacked by a Bothan Blue Squad led by Luke Skywalker, when plates on the *Suprosa* slid back to reveal deadly hidden weapons. [SOTE]

Survivors Descendants of one group of early space explorers on the planet Dellalt, they are extreme isolationists and hate other Dellaltians. It is believed that the group descended from survivors of the crash of the legendary starship *Queen of Ranroon.* Technological artifacts salvaged from the crash became sacred talismans and implements for use in religious practices. Their major ritual seems based on the actions undertaken by marooned spacers—setting up an emergency beacon and calling for rescue. Powered by sacrifices, the Survivors hope that the signals of their prayers will be received and lead to their deliverance. [HLL]

Susejo of Choi One of the oldest residents in the stomach of the Sarlacc at the Great Pit of Carkoon, he had been in the process of digestion for hundreds of years and made up a good portion of the Sarlacc's consciousness. Susejo of Choi taunted Boba Fett repeatedly while the bounty hunter was trapped inside the Sarlaac. [TJP]

Svivren A major trading center, the planet has long been considered difficult to conquer. Svivreni traders travel the galaxy wearing their traditional garb of dulbands and robes. Mara Jade, Emperor Palpatine's top-secret aide, was sent to Svivren by the Emperor after she failed to kill Luke Skywalker at Jabba's palace on Tatooine. Later, a Crystal Gravfield Trap of General Garm Bel Iblis's was lost at Svivren, creating an urgent need for a new CGT array during the siege of Coruscant. [LC, TJP]

swamp crawler A land vehicle, it is used to travel across marshy terrain. A swamp crawler boasts a multi-wheel transmission system, six balloon tires, and a central spherical wheel that can be used to execute quick turns of up to 180 degrees. [SME]

Swamp slug

swamp slug A large predator inhabiting Dagobah's water channels, it is an omnivore, pulverizing all organic matter with its thousands of tiny, grinding teeth. [ISWU]

swamp stunners Stub-nosed weapons, they are preferred by Glottalphibs. [NR]

sweetblossom A nonaddictive drug sometimes just called blossom, when taken in small quantities of about two drops it gives the user the feeling of having just awakened, when the mind is still a bit fuzzy. As the number of drops increase, so does the lassitude, the diminution of awareness, and the near-paralysis of action. [POT]

Swilla, Corey A human female, this petty criminal stalks her prey in the dark alcoves and alleys of Tatooine. One of her favorite spots is the cantina in Mos Eisley. [CCG]

Swimmer *See* Swimming People

Swimmer's Law A code of ethics, it governs the social behavior of the Sauropteroids of the planet Dellalt. [HLL]

Swimming People The name given to the Sauropteroids of the planet Dellalt; a single Sauropteroid is called a Swimmer. [HLL]

swoop Simple, crude vehicles often described as engines with seats, they are high-speed, lightweight speeder vehicles that leave speeder bikes in their dust, but they are also much more difficult to control. Swoops are built around powerful ion and repulsorlift engines, with little more added than a seat and controls. Fast and noisy, most are one-seaters. Turns, spins, and other maneuvers are accomplished by maneuvering flaps and control vanes via hand controls, with auxiliary controls in the knee and foot pegs. The pilot must shift his weight to enhance handling. But swoops offer no protection to the pilot or the occasional rider other than a seat belt and can easily spin out of control even at relatively low speeds. Pilots are always just a split second away from making a fatal error.

Speeds on lightweight-alloy swoops

Swoop

can top 600 kilometers an hour. Some swoops can fly several kilometers above a planetary surface, but generally they are used for low-altitude flight. The vehicles are used for advance military scouting and have found their way into the hands of pirates and other criminals. Swoop racing—both authorized and outlaw—is popular throughout the galaxy. Han Solo was a top swoop racer in his youth. [SWVG, SOTE, SWSB, HSR, DFR, MTS]

swoop gangs Scattered throughout the galaxy, such bands as the Nova Demons and the Dark Star Hellions are infamous for their crimes. Swoop gangs run spice, smuggle weapons, and do odd jobs for various factions of the underworld. Luke Skywalker was attacked by a dozen members of a swoop gang on Tatooine. [SWSB, SOTE]

swoop racing A popular legal sport in the Galactic Core, it takes place in huge domed arenas called swoop tracks, which hold tens of thousands of viewers along with circular flight paths, obstacle courses, and massive concession booths. Probably as many outlaw swoop races are run in which pilots take even more chances. Han Solo once raced swoops on the professional circuit. [HSR, HLL, SWSB, DFRSB]

S'ybll A mind witch who could change shapes, she tried to get Luke Skywalker to abandon his friends and stay with her. [CSW]

Sylvar A Cathar Jedi, the feline creature was apprenticed to Master Vodo-Siosk Baas some 4,000 years before the Galactic Civil War. She was the lover of Crado, also from the planet Cathar. During a lightsaber training duel with Exar Kun, she gave in to instinctive rage and clawed Kun's face. When Crado turned to the dark side, she felt she had no choice but to kill him. [DLS, TSW]

symbiote A gelatin membrane that is placed over the mouth of an oxygen-breathing being, this organic gill allows the being to swim underwater by filtering oxygen out of the water. Symbiotes are used especially on the water world of Mon Calamari. [DA]

synfur A synthetic fur, it is used to provide warmth in clothing for polar resorts on the planet Coruscant. [DA]

synth-flesh A translucent gel, it is derived from bacta, the cellular regeneration medium. When applied to superficial wounds, synth-flesh seals the skin and promotes rapid healing of damaged tissue. After the gel dries, it slowly flakes off to reveal new, scarless tissue. The name is also given to the synthetic flesh used on synthdroids. [HSE]

syren plant A large deadly plant of the planet Kashyyyk bearing long, silky strands and an alluring scent that attracts unwary creatures, its beauty is deceptive. The large syren blossom consists of two to four glossy oval petals of bright yellow, seamed in the center and supported by a stalk of mottled bloodred color. From the center of the open blossom spreads a tuft of long white fibers that emits attractive pheromones. When the blossom's sensitive inner flesh is touched, the petal jaws close over the victim and begin digesting him.

A few strong Wookiees traditionally harvest the plant, holding the flower open while a younger Wookiee scrambles to the center of the blossom, to harvest the fiber and quickly make an escape. Occasionally young Wookiees still lose limbs as the carnivorous plant chomps down on a slow-moving arm or leg. Chewbacca's nephew Lowbacca got enough of the white fiber to make a belt that he always wore. [YJK]

system patrol craft These vessels are the first line of defense within star systems. They frequently are used against pirates, smugglers, and hostile alien forces. System patrol craft usually have powerful sublight engines but no hyperdrives. They also perform customs-inspection duties and watch for disabled ships that require assistance. [ISB, DFRSB]

2-1B (Too-Onebee) An older medical droid that served the Rebel Alliance, it is a skilled surgeon and field medic. Too-Onebee treated Luke Skywalker twice during the time of the Battle of Hoth, once operating to replace Luke's severed hand with a mechanical replacement. Like other droids of its class, this roughly humanoid-appearing droid has surgical manipulation appendages, a medical diagnostic computer, and a treatment analysis computer. Too-Onebee escaped Hoth aboard the transport carrier *Bright Hope*. The droid played a key role in the survival of ninety of that ship's passengers after it was nearly destroyed. His assistant was the medical droid FX-7. [ESB, TBH]

23 Mere One of the Outer Rim colony worlds where the starliner *Star Morning*, owned by the Fallanassi religious order, stopped after the ship departed the planet Teyr. [SOL]

2-1B (Too-Onebee)

2X-3KPR A simple maintenance and diagnostics droid, it activates such things as alarm sensors, security lighting, and power fences on remote installations. [CCG]

3D-4X (Threedee-Fourex) The silver-plated personal droid of Hekis Durumm Perdo Kolokk Baldikarr Thun, administrator of the droid production world Mechis III, Threedee-Fourex killed his master when the assassin droid IG-88 and his counterparts took over the programming of all of Mechis III's computer systems and droids. [TBH]

T-12 A service droid in a storeroom in a Jedi outpost on the planet Ossus 4,000 years before the Galactic Civil War, its job was to pack Sith artifacts for shipment to the Jedi archives. [DLS]

T-16 skyhopper A high-speed, trans-orbital pleasure craft, it is every young hot-rodder's dream. The Incom Corporation's T-16 skyhopper was designed to be fast and easy to handle. Using a high-powered ion engine for thrust and two repulsorlift generators for lift, the T-16 has a top speed of nearly 1,200 kilometers per hour and can reach an altitude of nearly 300 kilometers. The distinctive tri-wing design helps stabilize the skyhopper at high speeds, although the forward stabilizer fin blocks the pilot's field of view. Advanced gyro-stabilizers help the pilot keep control, even in twisting, high-g maneuvers. The ship is amazingly maneuverable: It can twist through tight turns and make surprising vertical climbs.

Luke Skywalker owned a T-16 and often raced his friends through Beggar's Canyon on Tatooine. He practiced his marksmanship by "bulls-eye-

2X-3KPR

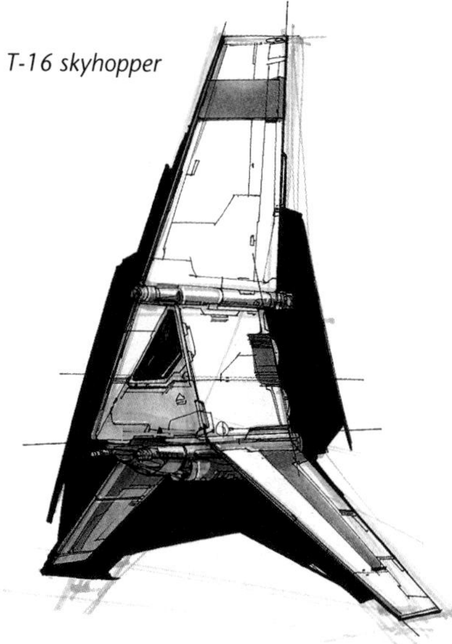

T-16 skyhopper

ing" the womp rat burrows at the end of the canyon with his stun cannons. Impromptu races through the winding desert canyons tested Luke's natural abilities. Just before he left the planet, Luke ripped the stabilizer off the skyhopper while trying to maneuver through the infamous Stone Needle in Beggar's Canyon.

While civilian T-16s seldom have weapons, optional upgrades offer four forward-firing stun cannons or a cheaper pair of pneumatic cannons with targeting lasers. Armed T-16's are mainstays in planetary militias and police forces. The T-16's cockpit has two sections, with room for a single pilot and one passenger. [SWSB, SWN, SWVG]

T-21 A light repeating blaster rifle manufactured by BlasTech, it provides excellent power and good range. A T-21 carries energy for twenty-five shots, although its firepower is unlimited when attached to a power generator. [CCG]

T-47 *See* snowspeeder

T-77 airspeeder An experimental airspeeder, it was flown by Luke Skywalker and Kam Solusar on the planet Ossus. [DE2]

Ta'a Chume, Queen Mother Although she rules the sixty-three worlds of the Hapes Cluster, Queen Mother Ta'a Chume hasn't been very effective on the home front. Ta'a Chume is the current holder of a title that stretches back through the 4,000 years that a matriarchy has ruled the Cluster. She is one of the beautiful people, with dark green eyes, red-gold hair, and a tall, slender frame that belies her age. Her beauty is matched by her ruthlessness.

Ta'a Chume lacked a female heir to inherit her throne, and her first son seemed so weak in her eyes that she secretly had him assassinated. She decreed that her second son, the handsome, strong Prince Isolder, must take a superior wife to continue the dynasty. Unfortunately, she found his first pick, Lady Elliar, a poor choice and had her murdered. Isolder then fell in love with New Republic Ambassador Princess Leia Organa, whom Ta'a Chume considered a weak pacifist. Ta'a Chume again hired assassins, but Prince Isolder saved Leia's life.

A planetful of complications ensued, after which Luke Skywalker helped reveal the truth about Ta'a Chume's murderous ways to her son. By then, Isolder had changed his mind and decided to marry a commoner, a Force-sensitive Nightsister from the planet Dathomir named Teneniel Djo. Though not royal, she was strong, and the marriage produced a baby girl, Tenel Ka, who grew up imbued with the Force.

Years later, Ta'a Chume was still meddling. She was very much op-

Queen Mother Ta'a Chume

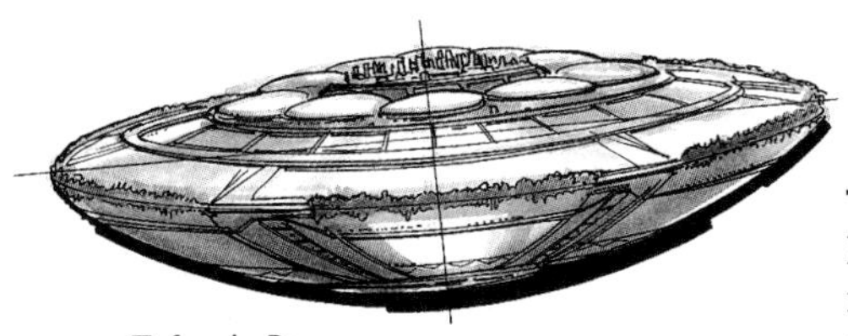

Tafanda Bay

posed to Tenel Ka's enrolling in Skywalker's Jedi academy, for she considered the girl's rightful future to be that of a powerful Hapan ruler. Despite Ta'a Chume's opinions, her granddaughter and other young Jedi Knights saved her from an assassination plot by the insectoid Bartokks. [CPL, YJK]

Taanab A generally peaceful agrarian planet, it was the site of a small but significant battle against space pirates that earned gambler Lando Calrissian a reputation as a good military strategist.

Pirates have been the bane of Taanab's peaceful farmers for millennia. Some 4,000 years before the Galactic Civil War, the freighter *Kestrel Nova* was captured from space pirates near the planet and was used by Jedi Ulic Qel-Droma to travel to the Tetan system. Thousands of years later, Taanab was still plagued by annual raids of bandits from the planet Norulac. One year, Calrissian was at Taanab's Pandath spaceport when the pirates arrived. After they damaged his ship, Calrissian—on a bet—agreed to attack the raiders. He hid his ship in the ice ring surrounding Taanab's moon, and when the pirates made their run, he ejected hundreds of conner nets into the center of the attacking fleet. As the pirates struggled to untangle themselves, Calrissian hit them with ice blocks from the moon's ring, causing even further damage. Finally, Calrissian led the Taanab defense fleet in a cleanup operation and singlehandedly accounted for nineteen kills. Later, just prior to the Battle of Endor, Calrissian was promoted to the rank of general in the Alliance partly thanks to the notoriety of this incident, which became known as the Battle of Taanab.

Some five years later, mad Jedi clone Joruus C'baoth coordinated an Imperial attack on Taanab, where he used the turbolasers of the *Bellicose* to destroy a New Republic ship against the direct orders of Captain Aban. [RJ, RJN, DFR, DLS, SWAJ]

Taanab, Battle of *See* Taanab

Ta'ania A descendant of a Jedi, she had been one of the original colonists on the planet Eol Sha. Gantoris, one of Luke Skywalker's first students at the Jedi academy, was possibly a descendant of Ta'ania. [JS]

TAARS An acronym for Target-Aggressor Attack Resolution Software, a package that links X-wing and Y-wing fighters. In emergency situations, another craft can send targeting or flight data that might otherwise be lost in combat. [BW]

Taboon A planet in the Stenness system, it is circled by many moons, including one owned by Great Bogga the Hutt some 4,000 years before the Galactic Civil War. Bogga, the ruler of the Stenness underworld, built a great palace on Taboon. Several millennia later, the bounty hunters Zardra and Jodo Kast tracked their targets to the Red Shadow, a Taboon bistro. The ensuing firefight resulted in the explosive death of Mageye the Hutt. [TOJ, TMEC]

Tafanda Bay An Ithorian herd ship, it soars above the jungles of the beautiful garden paradise of Ithor. Such ships are hundreds of meters tall and hover just above the planetary surface of Ithor, a place that the Hammerheads, or Ithorians, consider sacred. Ithorians have lived on herd ships for thousands of years and use them as examples of the harmonious integration of technology and nature.

The *Tafanda Bay*'s exterior is covered by moss and flowers, with huge trees growing from side platforms. It has landing platforms for incoming ships and speeders, while dozens of immense repulsorlift engines propel it slowly over the jungle landscape. In its interior, the Ithorians have reproduced nearly every terrain on Ithor and some from many other worlds. There are large trading halls for commerce and a Great Atrium nearly 250 meters across, with moss-covered walls leading to the open air above. Observation decks give spectacular views of the jungle and Ithor's brilliant violet night sky.

The *Tafanda Bay* community is led by the controversial Momaw Nadon, who was once banished for cooperating with the Empire. Rogue Squadron leader Wedge Antilles and onetime Imperial weapons scientist Qwi Xux visited the *Tafanda Bay* when the New Republic sought to hide Qwi from the Empire. [SWSB, MTS, DA, GA, TMEC, SWVG]

Taggar, Lieutenant Rone A member of the New Republic's 21st Recon Group, he piloted the recon-X fighter *Jennie Lee*. Assigned to gather information on the Yevethan mobilization on N'zoth, Lt. Rone Taggar captured the first images that awakened the New Republic to the size of the Yevethan fleet and the gravity of the growing crisis. Lieutenant Taggar committed suicide just as he was about to be taken hostage by Yevethan forces. [SOL]

Taggart A petty smuggler, he occasionally hired Han Solo years ago to smuggle glitterstim spice. [TMEC]

Tagge, General A senior officer in the Imperial Army, he served under Grand Moff Tarkin on the first Death Star battle station. General Tagge, known as a superb tactician, was openly contemptuous of both Tarkin and Darth Vader. He died in the explosion of the battle station. [SW]

Taisden A New Republic Intelligence officer, he accompanied Colonel Pakkpekatt on the private mission aboard Lando Calrissian's *Lady Luck* to rescue Lando, his aide, Lobot, and the droids C-3PO and R2-D2, who had been trapped aboard the mysterious ghost ship known as the Teljkon vagabond. [SOL]

General Tagge

Takeel

Takeel A spice-addicted, burned-out Snivvian mercenary, he is known as a double-crosser. Takeel frequents the Mos Eisley cantina on Tatooine. He is always looking for work to earn some credits and has been known to turn lawbreakers over to the Empire when really hard up. He is the brother of Zutton ("Snaggletooth"). [GG12]

Tala 9 The location of a droid-run factory that used only droid languages for landing codes. The practice was stopped when two ships crashed in orbit because their onboard computers couldn't handle the languages. [NR]

Talasea The fourth planet in the Morobe system, the cool, moist, fog-shrouded world orbits the yellow primary star in a red-and-yellow binary group. Talasea is lashed by severe thunderstorms during the rainy season. Island continents make up its land masses. Colonized long ago, the world was eventually abandoned by the settlers' descendants; the last group was wiped out by Darth Vader after the Clone Wars for harboring a fugitive Jedi.

Three years after the Battle of Endor, Rogue Squadron was moved from Folor to Talasea, closer to the Galactic Core, as a staging area for its eventual move on Coruscant. The squadron made its base on the largest of the island continents, inhabiting the ruins of Talasea's Planetary Governor's Palace and the surrounding ivy-covered cottages. After Imperial Intelligence agent Kirtan Loor deduced the location, Admiral Devlia ordered a platoon of stormtroopers to infiltrate the base and plant explosives. The squadron lost six sentries and pilot Lujayne Forge, but all of the Imperial commandos were captured or killed. The Alliance immediately evacuated the base, leaving behind several booby traps. [RS]

Tal'dira First among Twi'lek warriors, this giant challenged Wedge Antilles to a vibroblade duel during Rogue Squadron's visit to Ryloth but fortunately dropped the threat. When Tal'dira learned of Rogue Squadron's Bacta War with Ysanne Isard, he and his squadron of Chir'daki fighters offered their services both for glory and for the greater good of the galaxy. It was a decision not made lightly, for many of his warriors were killed in battle. Without their assistance, the Bacta War might very well have been lost. Tal'dira later accepted an offer to join Rogue Squadron. [BW]

Talfaglio system A system in the hinterlands of the Corellian sector. [AC]

talkdroid Another name for a protocol droid, the nickname is used mainly by those from less-developed worlds. [RJN]

Tallaan A planet in the Core Worlds near the Colonies region, it is the site of the Tallaan Imperial Shipyards. When Grand Moff Tarkin was killed aboard the first Death Star, the Empire released an official statement claiming that Tarkin had actually died in a shuttle crash at the Tallaan shipyards. [SWAJ]

Tallon, Adar A brilliant naval commander and military strategist serving the Old Republic, he developed many tactics still used by both the Empire and the New Republic. When the Old Republic fell, Adar Tallon faked his own death and settled on Tatooine. A group of Rebel agents found him and convinced him to join the Alliance. [TM]

Tallon roll A flight maneuver pioneered by and named after Old Republic military strategist Adar Tallon. [CCG]

Talmont, Prefect Eugene An Imperial official, he was in charge of a small contingent of stormtroopers based in Mos Eisley on the planet Tatooine. Prefect Eugene Talmont was dissatisfied with his assignment and worked constantly to destroy the operations of crime lord Jabba the Hutt, hoping to earn a promotion and transfer off the arid planet. Many residents found that the prefect could easily be bribed to avoid being harassed about permits or code compliance. [ISWU, TM, GG7]

Taloraan The largest planet in the isolated Kelavine system of the Expansion Region, it is an unexplored gas giant nearly 100,000 kilometers in diameter. The planet has a strong magnetic field and is orbited by seven uninhabitable moons and a spectacular ring system. Taloraan's hot atmosphere, rich in Tibanna gas, is breathable at high altitudes, and several forms of life have evolved among its clouds. Sleft-chuffni are huge, 200-meter-long gasbags that gather drifting algae with their hanging tentacles, while the carnivorous flying rays called fleft-wauf hunt the sleft-chuffni and attack them with their barbed tails. [SWAJ]

Talos Spaceport Docking Bay A13 A spaceport on the planet Atzerri. [SOL]

Talsava The real mother of Akanah Norand Pell, she abandoned her fifteen-year-old child on Carratos. Akanah bitterly referred to her as a guardian or custodian, not mother. [SOL]

Talus One of the five habitable planets in the Corellian system, it is a blue, white, and green world the same size as its sister planet Tralus. Both orbit a common center of gravity where Centerpoint Station is located. Together they are referred to as the Double Worlds, and both are ruled by the elected Federation of the Double Worlds, or Fed-Dub. Beneath the surface of Talus is a planetary repulsor, which was used in ancient times to move the planet into its current orbit from an unknown location. When a flare-up in Centerpoint Station some fourteen years after the Battle of Endor caused many deaths, survivors were relocated to Talus and Tralus. When word spread of the incident, a rebellion against Fed-Dub occurred on Talus. A group of starfighters, possibly representing the Talus rebellion, subsequently flew to

Centerpoint and claimed the station for themselves, until chased off by a Bakuran task force. [AC, AS, SAC]

Talz Large and strong, these white-furred beings are from the planet Alzoc III. They are about two meters tall and have four eyes—two large and two smaller ones. They appear fierce but have gentle personalities. Their planet is a technological backwater, and it was easy for the Empire to conquer it and use many Talz as slave laborers. [GG4]

Tamban A world that once was home to the Emperor Preedu III. Years ago, the First Observer of Preedu III's Court discovered a distant star cluster in Tamban's night sky. Remembering a recent favor done for him by Aitro Koornacht, night commander of the palace guard, the astronomer named his discovery the Koornacht Cluster. [BTS]

Tammar This planet has an unusually thin atmosphere, which caused native Tammarians to evolve a chemical pouch called a chaghizs torm to store oxygen while at rest. This allows them to survive in the vacuum of space for short periods. Tammar also has no standing water, and the greatest fear of a typical Tammarian is to be immersed in liquid. Ayddar Nylykerka, chief researcher in the New Republic's Asset Tracking office, is a native of Tammar. [BTS]

Tammuz-an A planet surrounded by double rings, it is inhabited by tall purple- or blue-skinned humanoids who are led by a monarchy. [DTV]

Tampion A shuttle in the New Republic fleet, it was carrying Han Solo to his new command of the Fifth Fleet aboard the *Intrepid* when it and Solo were captured by the forces of Nil Spaar during the Yevethan crisis. [TT]

Tana Ire A company known for its manufacture of bubble sights, a type of optical transducer, and other sensor components. [RSB, TT]

Tanbris A male Imperial lieutenant, the former fighter pilot was grounded after injuries. He then became a tactical officer aboard the first Death Star, specializing in directing Imperial star fighters. Tanbris died when the battle station was destroyed during the Battle of Yavin. [CCG]

Talz

Tandankin A planet that was taken over by Imperial forces under the command of Grand Moff Nivers following the Battle of Endor. When Rogue Squadron arrived, Wedge Antilles was forced to topple an enormous tower—the planet's greatest monument—in order to destroy a landing strip filled with Imperial TIE fighters.[XW]

Tandeer A member of the Singing Mountain clan of the Witches of Dathomir. [CPL]

Tandell system A system where Tiree, a Rebel Alliance agent, killed Imperial Governor Lord Cuvir while he was visiting the planet Wor Tandell. Cuvir had discovered Tiree encoding a report on Imperial fleet movements in the Tandell system. [MTS]

Tangrene Site of a major Imperial Ubiqtorate base that was attacked and destroyed by the private army of Gen. Garm Bel Iblis. Later, while the base was being rebuilt, the New Republic gave the impression that it intended to attack Tangrene to throw the enemy off its true target of Bilbringi. [DFR, LC]

tank droid Originally designed to deal with widespread civil unrest on Imperial worlds, the Arakyd XR-85 tank droid is a fully automated combat machine driven by a droid brain. The vehicle, at about thirty-two meters long and more than thirty meters tall, is double the size of an Imperial AT-AT walker. The tank droid travels on tracks at a top speed of seventy kilometers an hour and it can travel in water up to fifteen meters deep. The XR-85 is nearly unstoppable, making it particularly useful in urban assault operations. Its main weapon is a front-firing heavy particle cannon with an effective range of five kilometers. A pair of front-firing turbolasers, four twin heavy repeating blasters, and a rear-mounted antipersonnel cannon round out its weapons array.

The tank droid brain is one of the few droids with sophisticated intuition programming. The XR-85 played a major role in the Imperial invasion to reclaim Imperial City from the New Republic six years after the Battle of Endor. Although combat performance consistently shows that there is no substitute for an organic pilot, these tank droids are far better at combat than earlier generations of the machines. [DE, DESB, SWVG]

Tannath A member of the Singing Mountain clan of the Witches of Dathomir. [CPL]

Tantive IV Princess Leia Organa's consular ship, it was owned by the Royal House of Alderaan and was used for Imperial Senate business, as well as covert Rebel Alliance activities. The *Tantive IV* was captured in the Tatooine star system by Darth Vader's *Devastator* shortly after the princess's ship had intercepted the

Tank droid

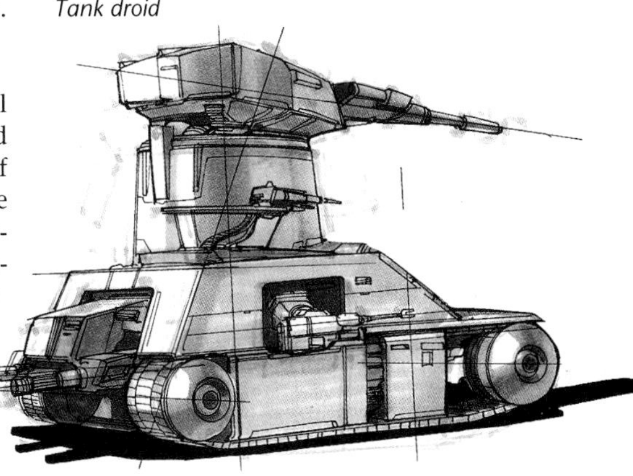

Tantive IV

technical plans for the original Death Star battle station. The ship's capture began the chain of events that led to the great Alliance victory at the Battle of Yavin. [SWR, SWN]

taopari Leopardlike predators on Noquivzor, their favorite prey are the tasty wildernerfs. [RS]

Targeter The code-name for Leia's top aide and friend Winter during her time of service with Alliance Procurement and Supply. Her missions consisted of entering Imperial installations and using her photographic memory to gather intelligence and create detailed maps. Rebel agents could then stage raids to get badly needed supplies. [DFRSB, LC]

targeting computer A sophisticated device that acquires hostile targets for a starship's weapons system, it works in conjunction with a ship's nav computer and sensor array. By calculating trajectories and attack and intercept courses, targeting computers help pilots and gunners track and fire at fast-moving enemy ships. [SWN]

target remote *See* remote; seeker

Targonn Home to a birdlike species, the planet had been under the brutal tyranny of Dictator-Forever Craw. Ruling from his palace behind an impenetrable force field, Craw imposed a 99 percent tax rate on his subjects and forced their children to toil in factories from the age of six. Before their involvement in the Rebellion, R2-D2 and C-3PO were captured by Craw and taken to his palace. Craw planned to uncover the secret of the

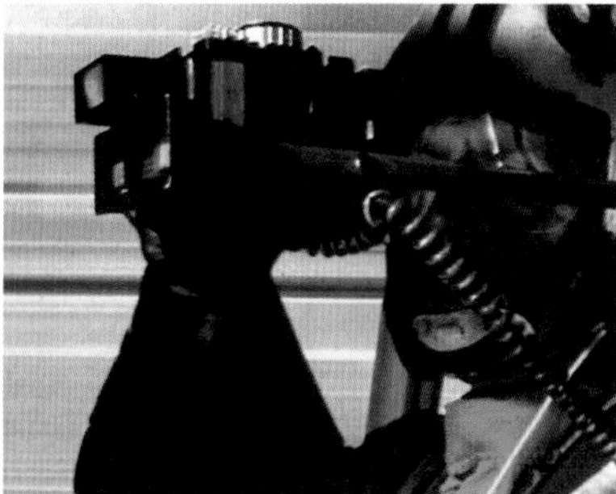
Targeting computer

savorium herb, which turned people into happy slaves called smilers, and then rule over a contented but mindless populace. Meanwhile, several splinter groups dedicated to overthrowing Craw united under the leader Shay and infiltrated the palace through a force-field hole. Their attack was unsuccessful, but they managed to rescue the droids. A second attack, aided by the droids' Ithorian master, Zorneth, resulted in the defeat of Craw and his forces. [D]

Tarkin, Grand Moff Tall and gaunt, with sunken cheeks and piercing blue eyes, he was as ruthless as he was evil, propounding the Tarkin Doctrine of rule through the fear of force. And Grand Moff Tarkin gave his enemies a lot to fear. An ambitious young governor of the Seswenna sector, he fully supported Senator Palpatine in the Senator's creeping takeover of the Old Republic. In turn, Tarkin was named a Moff in charge of governors of several sectors. Eventually he became the first *Grand* Moff, in charge of the Empire's most important sectors and reported only to the Emperor.

Although married, Tarkin took as his mistress an Imperial Navy enlistee named Daala and put her in charge of a top-secret weapons development think tank known as the Maw Installation. He also named her the service's first female admiral. Under her command, the Death Star battle station was developed, and it was while Tarkin was en route to the completed Death Star that his ship was attacked by Rebels. They rescued Tarkin's servant, a Mon Calamari named Ackbar, who had heard many of the Grand Moff's plans. Undaunted by this security breach, Tarkin proceeded with his first act as commander of the Death Star, the destruction of the penal colony on Despayre in the Horuz system.

There are indications that Tarkin, a brilliant strategist and excellent supervisor, toyed with deposing Palpatine and taking over as emperor, but no such action was ever taken. When it became known that technical readouts for the Death Star had been stolen by Alliance spies, Darth Vader was sent to retrieve them. He captured Princess Leia Organa and brought her to Tarkin aboard the Death Star.

After her interrogations failed, Tarkin made Leia watch as he destroyed her adopted planet of Alderaan and its billions of inhabitants with the Death Star's main weapon. Later, he deferred to Vader's advice and allowed Leia and her rescue party to escape because they were marked with a tracking device that would lead the Imperials to the main Rebel base.

When, at the Battle of Yavin, advisers told Tarkin that there was a slim chance the Rebels might be able

Grand Moff Tarkin

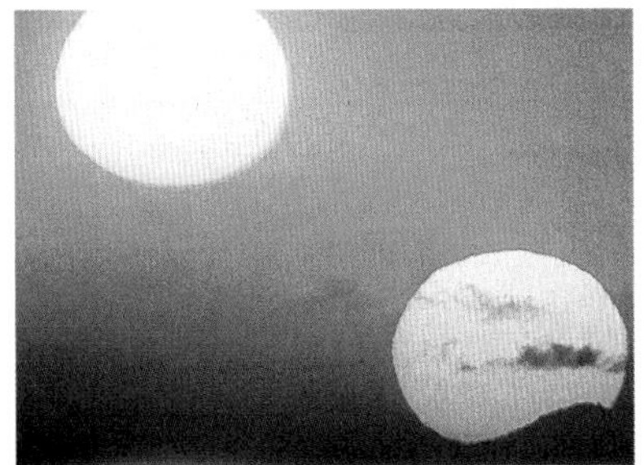

Tatoo I, Tatoo II

to destroy the Death Star, Tarkin was incredulous and refused to evacuate his glorious weapon. He paid for that decision with his life. [SW, SWCG, COF]

Tarlen, Bentu Pall Head of the Imperial Center Construction Contracts Division during the reign of Emperor Palpatine, he was in the pocket of Prince Xizor, head of the Black Sun criminal organization. Bentu Pall Tarlen delivered the latest bids on major building projects to Xizor so that the crime lord's favored companies could underbid and win the jobs. [SOTE]

Taroon system Located on the outer edges of the Rim, the system contains the planets Kuan and Bordal. [TSC]

Tarrik One of Bail Organa's most trusted aides on the planet Alderaan, he later became an aide to Princess Leia. [SWR, SOL]

Tascl, Moff Boren A large, middle-aged man with thinning black hair and a goatee, he was given the governorship of Cilpar as his reward for leading one of the TIE-fighter wings at the battle of Derra IV. Moff Boren Tascl was negotiating with the Rebel Alliance to turn over his world and supplies when he heard that the Emperor had died. Shortly thereafter, Sate Pestage, the Emperor's Grand Vizier, contacted him and promised a great reward if Tascl would make Cilpar available to Pestage if Coruscant's weather became particularly harsh. Tascl saw a power struggle ahead and decided he might get more from the breakup of the Empire than he would from the Rebels, so he used his agents to disrupt Alliance agents before Rogue Squadron arrived. [XW]

Taselda Said to be a human female Jedi living in Ruby Gulch on Nam Chorios, she is dirty and unkempt. At one point, Taselda and Beldorion the Hutt competed to rule the people of the planet's main city, Hewg Shul. She claimed that the Hutt stole her lightsaber and turned the people against her, forcing her to live as an outcast. Luke Skywalker uncovered Taselda as a fraud. A hag who eats insectoid drochs out of her arms, she is also insane. She captured Callista for a brief time to use in her ongoing battle against Beldorion, but Callista escaped. [POT]

Task Force Aster An eighteen-ship New Republic force, it was deployed above Doornik-319 to battle Yevethan forces after a Republic blockade attempt failed. [SOL]

Task Force Blackvine A twenty-ship New Republic force, it was deployed above Doornik-319 to battle Yevethan forces after a Republic blockade attempt failed. [SOL]

Tatoo I, Tatoo II The twin suns of the Tatooine system, they are binary stars. [SWN]

Tatooine A harsh desert planet that orbits double stars in the Outer Rim in the Arkanis sector near the worlds of Ryloth and Piroket, it is *far* from the galactic mainstream. Nevertheless, Tatooine occupies a strategic location at the nexus of several hyperspace routes, and it was the childhood home of Rebel Alliance hero and Jedi Knight Luke Skywalker. The Jedi Knight Dace Diath, who lived 4,000 years before the Galactic Civil War, was also a native of Tatooine.

Over the centuries Tatooine, located in the Tatoo system, has been the site of many orbital battles between rival gangsters and smugglers, and its surface is littered with ancient starship wrecks, most of which have long since been buried by the fierce sandstorms that rage across its surface. It boasts two native species: the meddlesome, scavenging Jawas and the fierce Tusken Raiders, commonly called Sand People. Animal life includes the bantha, dewback, womp rat, ronto, scurrier, sandfly, bonegnawer, gravel-maggot, dune lizard, sandsnake, rockmite, feathered lizard, sandjigger, meewit, cliffborer worm, and the feared Sarlacc, which is said to take a thousand years to digest its prey. Tatooine is also home to the terrifying krayt dragon, possibly feared more than any other animal in the sector. Although it is considered a suicidal venture, some hunt the krayt dragon to obtain its legendary and priceless gizzard stones, known as dragon pearls.

Many colonists on the planet run moisture farms, which condense water from the dry air with vaporators. Pika and deb-deb fruits have been known to grow in certain oases. Some water prospectors roam the desert searching for untapped sources of subterranean moisture. The native hubba gourd is a primary part of the diet of both the Sand People and Jawas, and other plant life includes razor moss and the funnel flower. A grove of Cydorrian driller trees, planted by the Ithorian Momaw Nadon, grows in the mountains north of Mos Eisley, and somewhere in the desert there is rumored to be a colony of alien Kitonaks. Strange mists sometimes form where the sodium-rich dunes meet the rocky

Tatooine

cliffs. Points of interest include the Dune Sea and the neighboring Jundland Wastes, Anchorhead, Motesta, Tosche Station, Bestine township, Beggar's Canyon and its Stone Needle, Bildor's Canyon, and the Mos Eisley spaceport.

Mos Eisley, the planet's largest city, has been described as a "wretched hive of scum and villainy." It is bordered by mountains on the north and on the opposite side by the decaying buildings of the southern sector. The wreckage of the *Dowager Queen*, the planet's first colony ship, can be found in the center of town. Other sites in Mos Eisley include the Lucky Despot hotel and casino (owned by the Whiphid gangster Lady Valarian), Lup's General Store, the Spaceport Traffic Control Tower, the Mos Eisley Inn, the underground Mos Eisley Towers hotel, a Dim-U monastery where ships can have their transponders illegally altered, and the infamous Mos Eisley cantina owned by Chalmun the Wookiee. After the Battle of Endor, the master chef Porcellus opened the Crystal Moon restaurant in Mos Eisley, and its fame has spread throughout the Outer Rim.

Several centuries ago, exiled monks of the B'omarr order built a huge monastery on the edge of the Dune Sea. The bandit Alkhara took up residence in part of the monastery and remained there for thirty-four years, raiding nearby moisture farms while expanding and improving the citadel. The B'omarr monastery was the home of many other gangsters and bandits until eventually becoming the palace of crime lord Jabba the Hutt, who expanded the citadel to encompass a hangar and garage. Throughout the changes, the B'omarr monks kept to their own affairs in the palace's lowest levels, trying to reach enlightenment, at which point their brains could be surgically removed by the other monks and placed in glass jars, freed from the distractions of the flesh.

Decades ago, the Jedi Knight Obi-Wan Kenobi came to the desert planet to place the infant Luke Skywalker in the care of Owen Lars and his wife, Beru. Years later, a message from Princess Leia Organa of Alderaan, whose ship had been captured above Tatooine, helped bring Kenobi out of his life as a hermit near the Dune Sea and into the service of the Alliance. After the Battle of Hoth, Skywalker returned to Ben Kenobi's house on Tatooine where he built a new lightsaber. Immediately before the Battle of Endor, Luke Skywalker and his friends returned to Tatooine to free Han Solo from Jabba's palace, which resulted in the death of the crime lord and the collapse of his organization. The B'omarr monks reclaimed the palace, persuading several of Jabba's lieutenants to join them as disembodied brains. Eight years after Endor, the Imperial battlemoon *Eye of Palpatine* stopped at Tatooine to pick up a contingent of stormtroopers but brought aboard Sand People and Jawas instead. Later that year, Luke Skywalker and Han Solo returned to Jabba's palace to investigate rumors of the Hutt's Darksaber project. [SW, SWN, SWR, RJ, RJN, MTS, GG7, LC, DLS, COJ, TMEC, DESB, DS, ISWU, TJP, SWAJ]

Tatooine A New Republic cruiser, it was lost in the battle of Almania. [NR]

Tatooine blues A musical genre, it is favored in certain casinos throughout the New Republic. [NR]

Tatoo system A star system in the Outer Rim, it consists of the twin suns Tatoo I and Tatoo II and the planets Tatooine, Ohann, and Adriana. The system is in the Arkanis sector. [CCG]

Taul A mist-shrouded, acidic swamp world in the Gunthar system, it was used by the Rebel Alliance as a training outpost until the facility was destroyed by the *Victory*-class Star Destroyer *Dominator*. [SWAJ]

tauntaun Easily domesticated reptile-like creatures insulated with gray-white fur, they are sometimes called snow lizards. Wild tauntauns roam the frozen wastes of the ice planet Hoth, where they graze on lichen. Although initially ornery, the spitting tauntaun can be tamed and ridden. The animals were used as mounts and pack animals by the Rebel Alliance when it had its base on Hoth. Although their thick fur protects tauntauns from extreme temperatures, they can't survive Hoth's brutal nights and must seek shelter. But during the day, tauntaun herds can be seen running across the plains of ice and snow. [ESB, ISWU]

Tauntaun

Taurill Industrious, semiintelligent creatures, they form a hive mind: a single organism with thousands of bodies sharing one collective consciousness. In that state, each individual creature is just a set of eyes, ears, and hands to do the bidding of the Overmind. While that can result in intense focus, it can also lead to situations that grow quickly out of control if a few sets of eyes see something disturbing. Taurill, which make good pets, have grayish brown fur, large curious eyes, and four supple arms that end in dexterous fingers. They blink their eyes a lot and constantly shift position. [DS]

Tavira, Moff Leonia A small human female with short black hair and violet eyes, she succeeded her husband as governor of Eiattu VI. Moff Leonia Tavira had been de facto moff during her husband's illness and neglected to tell the central Imperial government of his death. She was ambitious and wanted to end the system under which she shared power with a group of nobles, so she set up a complex plot that involved a pretender to the throne. [XW]

Tawntoom A frontier settlement, it is on the frozen, dark side of the planet Roon. The colony served as a base for Governor Koong and his band of thieves during the early days of the Empire. [DTV]

t'bac A plant, it is widely smoked to deliver the somewhat intoxicating drug nic-i-tain into the body. [TMEC]

Tchiery A Farnym, he was Leia Organa Solo's copilot aboard the *Alderaan*. [NR]

TDL3.5 A nanny droid sent to replace C-3PO as the minder of the three Solo children, it was part of a prank played by young Anakin to punish Threepio for refusing to read him a favorite bedtime story, "The Little Lost Bantha Cub." [NR]

TDL droid An enhanced protocol model, it was programmed to perform a majority of the functions required in the care of a young child. TDL models have been marketed across the galaxy as nanny droids for busy politicians, space military personnel, and even smugglers who have children but too little time to spend with them. The TDL droid that cared for Anakin Solo on Anoth had a silvery surface with smooth corners and no sharp edges. It had four fully functional arms, all of which were covered with warm synthetic flesh—and advanced weaponry. The droid forfeited its existence to protect Anakin. [COF]

tech dome The common name given to a combined garage and workshop structure that extends off the rest of a house, especially those built for colonists. [SWR]

Tedryn Holocron A Holocron, it was used some 4,000 years before the Galactic Civil War by Jedi Master Vodo-Siosk Baas. [TSW]

Teebo An Ewok with light and dark gray-striped fur, he is one of the leaders of the tribe that befriended Princess Leia Organa and the Alliance strike team on Endor's forest moon. Teebo wears a horned half-skull decorated with feathers. His weapon is a stone hatchet. A dreamer and a poet, Teebo has a mystical ability to communicate with nature. [RJ, ETV]

Teek Resembling both a rodent and a monkey, this mischievous creature lives in the forest of Endor's moon. Teeks have long, pointy ears and scruffy white fur, beady black eyes, and a buck-toothed mouth that's always open and chattering. They usually wear rudimentary clothing with many belts, pouches, and pockets for the items they snatch. Gifted with an enormously fast metabolism, Teeks can put on bursts of incredible speed and are nearly impossible to catch. [BFE, ISWU]

Teek

Teeko A Rodian, he was an uncle of the inexperienced bounty hunter Greedo, shot by Han Solo in the Mos Eisley cantina. [TMEC]

Teeth of Tatooine Teeth refers to fast-moving torrents of sand, rocks, and random sharp debris experienced by those left out to die in Tatooine's Valley of the Wind. [TBH]

Teilcam system Located in the Outer Rim, its only habitable planet is the watery world of Kabaira. [SWAJ]

Teke Ro A blue giant star, it is circled by Cona, homeworld of the Arcona. [GG4]

telbun A stratified class of people from Kuat, they are raised and trained by their families to excel at everything in life, whether it be athletics, academics, or manners. When they reach the appropriate age, they are tested and rated according to their stamina, intelligence, and sensitivity. They are then purchased by the upper classes of the planet for the purpose of parenting and raising a child. [WG]

telesponder A shipboard communications device, it automatically broadcasts a craft's identification profile in response to signals sent by spaceports or military authorities. [HSE]

Teljkon system The second documented sighting of the mysterious ghost ship called the Teljkon vagabond was in the Teljkon system, giving the vagabond its name. A Hrasskis monitor ship working the system spotted the enigmatic vessel. When the Hrasskis approached, the vagabond broadcast a wide-spectrum signal; thirty seconds later, it vanished into hyperspace. [BTS]

Teljkon vagabond The mysterious ghost ship called the Teljkon vagabond was sighted for only the second documented time in the Teljkon system, giving it its name. The ship kept jumping into hyperspace, sometimes after firing at approaching vessels, and finally made a getaway with Lando Calrissian and others aboard. It turned out that the ship was a key instrument in rebuilding the long-dead Qellan homeworld, which had been hit by one of its moons, iced over, and later renamed Maltha Obex. The ancient Qellan had realized the moon would strike their planet, buried themselves deep in the ground in a state of suspended animation, and constructed an organic starship, which became known as the Teljkon vagabond, to eventually return, thaw out the planet, and restore them to life. Luke Skywalker discovered how to use the ship for its intended purpose—a tool for rebuilding a destroyed world. [TT]

Tellivar Lady A transport ship, it made regular runs to Tatooine under the command of Captain Fane. [TMEC]

Telltrig-7 A type of small blaster. [TMEC]

Tels, Seggor A Quarren, he admitted to betraying his homeworld of Mon Calamari by lowering the planet's shields and enabling the Empire to invade and enslave its inhabitants. Yet Seggor Tels also helped organize his people to stand with the Calamarians to try to repel the invaders. Tels was jealous of Calamarians, yet felt shame for his actions and decided to remain on the planet while many of his fellow Quarrens fled. [SWSB]

Telti This moon was the site of a series of droid factories run by failed Jedi academy student Brakiss that Dark Jedi Kueller used to manufacture droids fitted with bombs and detonators. Kueller planned to use the droids in his campaign of terror against the New Republic. Telti has no atmosphere and no native life. The surface is covered by domed

Temple of the Blueleaf Cluster

buildings and metal landing strips; a series of interconnected tunnels run underground. Telti joined the Empire late in the Galactic Civil War, only after Palpatine threatened to destroy it if it didn't join. Telti's factories continued to sell droids to anyone whose credit was good, and except for the Imperial threat, the moon's politics remained neutral. After the truce at Bakura, Telti petitioned the New Republic for membership, which was granted, and it has remained a quiet, stable member ever since. Luke Skywalker came to Telti to find Brakiss, who told Luke of Kueller's scheme, and Luke left to confront Kueller at Almania. Later, Cole Fardreamer, R2-D2, and C-3PO also arrived at Telti to question Brakiss about the droids on Coruscant that had been discovered to be wired with detonators. On Telti they beat back a terrifying gladiator-droid group known as the Red Terror. At the last instant, Artoo disabled the master signal that Kueller beamed from Almania, which would have detonated all new-model droids in existence. [NR]

Temple of Fire A Massassi temple on Yavin 4. [DLS]

Temple of Pomojema A temple on the planet Mimban, it is a shrine to the Mimbanite god Pomojema. The legendary Kaiburr crystal was kept in this stone ziggurat supported by obsidian pillars. A stone icon representing the god—a winged humanoid with talons and a faceless head—is displayed for the faithful. [SME]

Temple of the Blueleaf Cluster An ancient Massassi temple on Yavin 4, it is pyramid-shaped and lies just southeast of the Great Temple at the junction of two rivers. [DS, GG2, ISWU]

tempter A creature on the forest moon of Endor, it generally lives in the hollows of large trees. A tempter looks like a long, blunt eel with pale, fleshy skin that is covered with a thick mucus, which allows it to slither into tight spots and then strike its prey in a flash after luring it close with a furry tongue. [ISWU]

Tendo, Liekas A Morath mining engineer, he was taken as a Yevethan hostage during the attack on the Koornacht Cluster settlements led by Nil Spaar. [SOL]

Tenloss Syndicate A criminal outfit, it has long operated in the Bajic sector, working closely with the main criminal organization, Black Sun. Its governing board is called the Leukish. Its reach extends across sixty-four major star systems in five sectors and it is involved in everything from gambling to assassination. [SOTE, GG11]

tentacle bush A low-lying plant that grows on the planet Arzid, it has grasping tentacles that snatch small creatures and deliver them to the main bush for digestion. [PDS]

tentacle cactus A spiny, semimobile plant, it waves its tentacles to capture small prey. An example is on display in the Skydome Botanical Gardens on Coruscant. [JS]

Teradoc, High Admiral An overweight warlord, he preferred to squat in his bunker behind incredibly thick shielding while his minions fought major battles. He was one of thirteen squabbling warlords poisoned by Admiral Daala after they refused to stop their internal strife and get on with the fight against the New Republic. [DS]

Terak A cruel and evil king, he leads the Marauders who prey upon the inhabitants of Endor's forest moon. [BFE, ISWU]

teräs käsi A form of hand-to-hand combat, roughly translated into "steel hands," that is taught in the Pacanth Reach, a remote star cluster in the Outer Rim. A mystical form of martial arts, it has long been practiced on the planet Bunduki, where it is taught by the Followers of Palawa. Its practitioners also study history, philosophy, and metaphysical subjects. [SOTE]

Terephon A planet with dark blue skies in the Hapes Cluster, it was the homeworld of Captain Astarta, Prince Isolder's personal bodyguard. [CPL]

Termagant An Imperial Strike cruiser allied with Warlord Zsinj, it was reconfigured from a troop carrier to a TIE-fighter carrier. The *Termagant* was completely torn in half by a volley of proton torpedoes from Rogue Squadron in retaliation for its part in the destruction of a bacta convoy in the Alderaan system. [BW]

Terpfen A Calamarian, he was Admiral Ackbar's chief mechanic—and a hidden pawn of Imperial Ambassador Furgan. While he was an Impe-

Terak

rial prisoner, Terpfen had had part of his brain replaced, compelling him to carry out secret orders and report information back to Imperial forces. Terpfen sabotaged Admiral Ackbar's B-wing fighter, causing it to crash into the Cathedral of Winds on Vortex. He also gave Ambassador Furgan information regarding the secret location of Anakin Solo, the infant son of Han and Leia Organa Solo. Finally able to overcome his programming, Terpfen stole a B-wing fighter and flew it to Yavin 4 to inform Leia of the danger to Anakin. Terpfen accompanied Ackbar and Leia to Anoth, where he fought against Furgan in one of the Imperials' MT-ATs, at last defeating the ambassador. So great was Terpfen's despair that he would have successfully committed suicide had Ackbar not interceded. Forgiven, Terpfen was accepted back as a loyal member of the New Republic. [DA, COF]

Terrafin, Kodu An Arcona, he made the courier run between Jabba the Hutt's desert palace on Tatooine and the crime lord's Mos Eisley townhouse. [TMEC]

terrain-following sensor A device that lets ships fly parallel to the ground at a fixed height, it works in conjunction with a vehicle's propulsion and flight-control systems. A terrain-following sensor automatically adjusts a ship's course to avoid obstacles and compensate for changing terrain. [HSE, HSR]

Terrik, Booster Now retired, this notorious Corellian smuggler was sought for many years by both the Empire and Corellian Security forces. It seemed there was nothing he wouldn't smuggle, and there were no tears for him when he was finally apprehended by Hal Horn and CorSec. He was sent to Kessel to serve his time, and upon his release from prison he decided to quit the business, turning it over to his daughter, Mirax. He then used his talents as a negotiator for Rogue Squadron. During the Bacta War with Ysanne Isard, Terrik was the Rogues's manager of operations at the Yag'Dhul space station. When the Imperial Star Destroyer *Virulence* arrived to destroy the station, he was chiefly responsible for getting it to surrender. After taking command of the ship, he hastened to Thyferra, where the ship's presence was essential to the surrender of Isard's *Lusankya*, ending the Bacta War. [BW]

Terrik, Captain Mod A cold, cruel Imperial officer, he supervised part of Davin Felth's stormtrooper training as captain of the Imperial Desert Sands sandtrooper unit on Tatooine. The unit was assigned to search for two runaway droids in the Dune Sea. He traced them to a group of Jawas whom he pumped for information and then killed. Next he went to the homestead of Owen and Beru Lars, and after fruitless questioning, killed them, too. When Captain Terrik was about to stop Han Solo's escape from Mos Eisley, he was shot in the back and killed by Felth. [TMEC]

Terrik, Mirax The beautiful daughter of Booster Terrik, she now runs the smuggling business her father started. Traveling in her ship, the *Pulsar Skate,* she maintains considerable contacts throughout the galaxy. Her ties with Rogue Squadron began when her father used to refuel and repair the *Skate* at a Gus Treta station owned by Wedge Antilles's parents. When Antilles's parents were killed by pirates, Booster helped to hunt down the killers. Wedge is close to the brown-eyed, black-haired Mirax and thinks of her as a sister.

Mirax wasn't aligned with the Rebel Alliance, but she found it hard to be neutral. When she was trying to deliver goods in the Chorax system, the Imperial interdictor *Black Asp* jumped into the system and held the *Skate* in a gravitational embrace, preventing its escape. However, the *Asp*'s large mass pulled Rogue Squadron out of hyperspace, and X-wings came to the *Skate*'s rescue. After the rout of the *Asp*, Mirax ferried Corran Horn's crippled X-wing to the Rogues's new base at Talasea. She then helped retrieve stranded Rebel operatives on Hensara III. Later, when the Alliance decided to risk another raid on the heavily defended Imperial base at Borleias, she again went to the rescue of Horn, whose X-wing was under attack by a squadron of TIEs and low on fuel.

When Rogue Squadron went to the prison mines of Kessel to release numerous inmates as part of its Coruscant invasion plan, Mirax used the *Skate* to bring back two dozen Sullustan political prisoners. Shortly thereafter, she ferried most of the squadron to Coruscant for their covert operation. Unable to escape from Coruscant as planned, she was forced to stay behind to help the Rogues bring down the planet's shields. When the initial plan unraveled, Mirax escaped with Horn. Later, she was part of Wedge's team when it took command of a huge construction droid. Horn was defending her team's position in the droid when the Z-95 Headhunter he was piloting crashed. Although devastated by Corran's apparent death, she went with Rogue Squadron to the Yag'-Dhul system to retrieve bacta from Warlord Zsinj, who had stolen it from a Thyferran convoy. Succeeding in that mission, she was asked to help with another bacta convoy from Thyferra. When that convoy was destroyed by Zsinj, she was thought to have perished with her ship and crew, but they were actually on a secret mission to Borleias. Later "resurrected" by Alliance Intelligence, she appeared with the very-much-alive Horn at a ceremony honoring Rogue Squadron for its role in the liberation of Coruscant. That was not the last ceremony that she and Horn would attend; the next was their marriage. [RS, WG, KT, BW]

Tervissis Homeworld of the species known as Tervigs, who sell members of the semiintelligent species known as Bandies—also from Tervissis—to the galaxy as slaves. Nine years after the Battle of Endor, the New Republic Galactic Court convened a trial of Tervig Bandie-slavers. [POT]

Tessek A Quarren, or "Squid Head," he fled his homeworld of Mon Calamari after an Imperial invasion and ended up as an accountant for crime lord Jabba the Hutt on Tatooine. At times, Tessek's conscience bothered him, and he plotted to get away with both his life and part of a secret fortune still intact. He set Jabba up to be killed by an Imperial inspection party, but Jabba learned of his plot and planned to wait him out. When Tessek heard that, he killed the messenger, a B'omarr monk whose brain was housed in a large spider-shaped droid. Tessek's plans were further compromised when Jabba insisted

Tessek

that he accompany his party out to the Great Pit of Carkoon to execute a number of Rebels. The Rebels, led by Luke Skywalker, had other plans. Tessek escaped just as Jabba's sail barge was blown up. He returned to the Hutt's palace, where some of the dead monk's associates cornered him. They turned him into a monk himself by laser-cutting his brain out of his body and sticking it into a nutrient jar atop a spider droid. [RJ, TJP, SWCG]

Teta, Empress A long-lived female warlord many millennia ago, she conquered and united the seven planets of what became known as the Empress Teta system. [DLS]

Teta system, Empress Located near the Kuar system, it contains seven carbonite-mining worlds, including Kirrek and Koros Major, and is named for the female warlord who conquered it some five millennia before the Galactic Civil War. The Tetan mines produce raw carbonite, primarily from the thick outer rings of a gas giant in the system. The carbonite is a vital ingredient in the construction of hyperdrives. The royal descendants of Empress Teta long ruled the system, sharing power and profits with the leaders of the influential Carbonite Guild.

About 4,000 years before the Galactic Civil War, the privileged sons and daughters of Tetan royalty began experimenting with the dark side of the Force, introduced to them by the royal heirs Satal Keto and Aleema. They formed a group known as the Krath, which used Sith magic and military force to quickly conquer the system. Public executions of rebellious carbonite miners were held in the central plaza of the ruling Tetan city of Cinnagar. The Krath took up residence in Cinnagar's iron citadel, which contained an inner city and an opulent palace behind its walls. Beneath the citadel were underground dungeons and a vast cavern, where the Krath hanged political prisoners.

The Jedi Knight Ulic Qel-Droma, following a Tetan attack on a Deneban Jedi assembly, traveled to Cinnagar in order to learn the Krath's dark-side secrets. In the ensuing months Satal Keto was killed and a Jedi attack force attempted to rescue Qel-Droma from the iron citadel, but he had succumbed to the dark side and insisted on remaining in Cinnagar. Qel-Droma joined forces with the Sith Lord Exar Kun, and the two implemented their plans to bring about a new Golden Age of the Sith. Some time later, as the Krath armies conquered nearby systems, the warlord Mandalore chose to strike at the heart of the overextended Tetan empire. Ulic Qel-Droma defeated Mandalore in single combat and won the warlord's loyalty and the use of his deadly armies. Later, Aleema attempted to reassert her power over the Krath forces by abandoning Qel-Droma during an attack on Coruscant, but he was rescued and eventually Aleema was killed. [DE, DLS, ISWU, TSW]

Tetsus A peaceful clan of Rodians, its members were forced to flee their planet to escape the more warlike Chattza clan. [TMEC]

Teyr A busy, crowded, and bureaucratic world located at the crossroads of three highly traveled hyperspace routes, it is thirty-four light-years from Vulvarch. The Teyr Rift, a 4,000-kilometer-long canyon slashing across the planet's face, makes the world a popular tourist destination. The increasing number of visitors has made citizens fear a huge increase in immigration. Teyr officials of the Citizen Services Corps have therefore created a welter of incomprehensible regulations and red tape to discourage anyone from staying once their tourist dollars have been spent. Huge orbital parking stations accommodate arriving traffic. The Rift Skyrail, an incredibly fast aboveground train, connects all points in the Rift Territory with each other.

The Fallanassi, religious followers of the White Current, were zealously persecuted on Lucazec. The elders sent five children to other planets, including Teyr, for safekeeping. The Fallanassi later bought a starliner called the *Star Morning*, but departed Teyr a few months before the Battle of Endor. [BTS, SOL]

Thackery A New Republic ship, it was deployed for duty at Galantos in the Farlax sector, a territory that was feared to be in danger of a Yevethan attack. [SOL]

Thanas, Commander Pter This middle-aged commander was assigned to the defense force of the backwater planet of Bakura as punishment for refusing to carry out an order. He had declined to wipe out a village to stop slave miners from complaining about lowered food rations. Commander Pter Thanas was a loyal and hard-working officer, but he could not brook such genocidal orders.

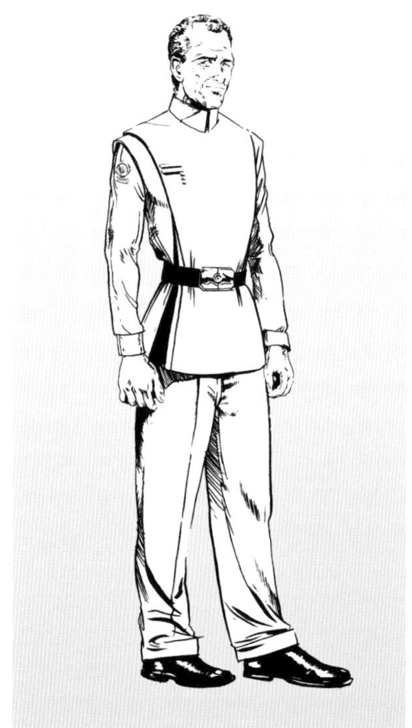

Cmdr. Pter Thanas

When the Ssi-ruuk Imperium attacked Bakura, Thanas's garrison sent out a plea for help, unaware that the second Death Star had just been destroyed along with Emperor Palpatine. The Alliance answered the call. Thanas was impressed with the Rebels, especially Luke Skywalker, and the two sides worked out a truce to battle their common enemy. When the Ssi-ruuk fled, Thanas turned on the Rebels, but his ship, the *Dominant*, blew out its lateral thrusters and was immobilized. Faced with destruction or surrender, Thanas chose the latter and defected to the Alliance. He later married Gaeriel Captison, and they had a daughter named Malinza. [TAB, SWCG]

Thanos A blue-white star orbited by Togoria, homeworld of the Togorians. [GG4]

Thanta Zilbra A name for a star, its system, and its primary planet. Thanta Zilbra was the second star destroyed during the starbuster crisis, and Wedge Antilles assisted in the New Republic evacuation of the planet's settlement. The evacuation force greatly underestimated Thanta Zilbra's population of nearly 15,000, and thousands were left behind when the star went nova. [AS]

Tharen Wayfarer A ship owned by the Pitareeze family, it was home for a while to the droids R2-D2 and C-3PO before the start of the Rebellion. [D]

Theelin A now-extinct, near-human race. Smuggler Shug Ninx of Nar Shaddaa has Theelin blood; his mother was one of the last of her kind. [DE]

Therans A group on Nam Chorios who are consulted by Oldtimers for healing and advice. Theran Listeners control the planet's ancient gun-stations and won't allow outside trade. They opposed Seti Ashgad's Rationalist Party, which wanted such trade. The Therans's original leader was a male prophet named Theras. While he slept, the planet's Force crystals entered his mind and reinforced the idea that outside contact should be forbidden. He then ordered that no ship large enough to have heavy shielding ever be permitted to land on Nam Chorios, which also prevented the Death Seed plague from escaping off-world. [POT]

thermal cape A lightweight metal-foil and spider-silk composite poncho, it retains the wearer's body heat to provide protection from the cold. Thermal capes, also called thermal wraps, are normally standard equipment in survival-gear packs. [SME]

thermal coil *See* condenser unit

thermal detonator A powerful bomb in the form of a small metallic ball, it is activated when the bearer's finger pressure is removed from a trigger, ensuring that any attempt to kill the bomber will cause an explosion. Princess Leia Organa, disguised as the bounty hunter Boushh, threatened Jabba the Hutt's court with a thermal detonator to demonstrate Boushh's nerve and impress the crime lord. She and her fellow Rebels had earlier used the miniature bombs in escaping the clutches of Prince Xizor, head of the Black Sun criminal organization. [RJ, SOTE, ISB]

thermosuit A thin, lightweight coverall worn over regular clothing, it protects the wearer from temperature extremes. [HSR, SME]

Thernbee A large, four-legged creature that lives in the mountains of Almania, it has a smallish face, short ears, a pink nose, a huge pink mouth, and blue eyes the size of small puddles. With broad shoulders and a flat back, Thernbees make even a Wookiee look small. The creature's white hair falls out with each movement, and its long, thin tail carries a lot of power when used defensively. Thernbees toy with their prey, crushing one bone at a time, giving the victim the illusion that escape is possible. The anesthetic in their saliva saps their victim's will to fight. However, they prefer eating vegetation or small creatures that resemble snakes to any other type of meat.

Thermal detonator

Luke Skywalker faced a Thernbee during his confrontation with Dark Jedi Kueller on Almania, and amid the battle he discovered that Thernbees are psychic. The Thernbee that Luke encountered had a body only a third the size it should have been; it was slowly starving to death. Skywalker helped ease the creature's pain and gained a new friend for life. When Han Solo introduced several Force-blocking ysalamiri to Almania, the Thernbee accidentally ate them, thinking they were food for it. However, the Thernbee was near enough to Kueller for the ysalamiri to counter Kueller's Force powers and gave Luke and Leia Organa Solo an advantage in battling him. [NR]

Thig brothers A notorious duo of spice-jackers, they were known to be armed with stolen Imperial blasters. [TMEC]

Thila A planet where the Rebels reorganized following their evacuation of the main base on Yavin 4. It was on Thila that Alliance historian Voren Na'al began his research into the histories of the heroes of Yavin. [MTS]

Thistleborn, Grand Moff An authoritative grand moff, he had bushy eyebrows that framed his dark, penetrating eyes. Grand Moff Thistleborn was a member of, and extremely loyal to, the Central Committee of Grand Moffs, which tried to hold the Empire together and pick a successor to Emperor Palpatine following his apparent death in the destruction of the second Death Star. [GDV]

Thobek The language spoken on the planets Thobek and Wehttam, it is closely related to the Torrock language. [SOL]

Thokos The planet from which seven ships departed 10,000 years before the Galactic Civil War to colonize the planet Ammuud. The colony eventually lost contact with Thokos and was forgotten. [CSSB]

Tholatin The location of one of the most exclusive smuggler hideaways, Esau's Ridge, which is hidden in a kilometer-long, 100-meter-deep erosion cut at the bottom of a mountain, undetectable from orbit. A network of smaller tunnels extend deeper into the mountain. The adjacent forest-covered valley has three cleared landing areas, which are disguised by camouflage nets. The remainder is uninhabited. Thirteen years after Endor, Chewbacca returned to Esau's Ridge with his fellow Wookiees to obtain supplies and information for their planned rescue of Han Solo from the Koornacht Cluster. [TT]

Tholaz An inhabited planet within the Koornacht Cluster of the Farlax sector, Tholaz is one of the primary worlds of the Yevetha and a member of the Duskhan League. Near the end of the crisis in the Koornacht Cluster, the Yevetha located a new shipyard at Tholaz. During the Battle of N'zoth, the New Republic also attacked Wakiza, Tizon, Z'fell, and Tholaz. [TT]

Tholos A Yevethan guardian thrustship for the orbital shipyard at ILC-905, it was destroyed in a battle with the New Republic fleet. [TT]

Thomork The site for top-secret Imperial construction projects including *Silencer I*, the first of the cloned Emperor's World Devastators. The Empire spread the rumor that the orbital shipyards of Thomork had been closed down due to a hive virus outbreak. Imperial agents then killed more than 450 people to add credence to this rumor, and took over the abandoned facilities for their own projects. [DESB]

Thon A continent on the destroyed planet Alderaan, it was the location of the Uplands. Once a year, the wildlife service had to cull old and sick animals who wouldn't be able to survive the Alderaan winter. [SWR]

Thon, Master A Jedi Master some 4,000 years before the Galactic Civil War, he appeared as a fearsome armor-plated quadruped whose savage countenance was balanced by his great wisdom and empathy. Master Thon trained his students on the planet Ambria; they included Nomi Sunrider and Oss Wilum. Thon was the Jedi watchman for the Stenness system. As the teachings of the dark Krath sect gained prominence, Master Thon addressed a great assembly of 10,000 Jedi who had gathered on Mount Meru on the desert world of Deneba. He spoke eloquently against straying from the light side, hoping to convince his peers of the dangers of the Krath philosophy. [DE, TOJ]

Master Thon

ThonBoka (StarCave) A sack-shaped gray nebula composed of dust, gas, and complex organic molecules, it can be entered from only one direction. Its lightning-charged interior spans more than twelve light-years. The ThonBoka has given rise to thousands of space-dwelling life-forms, ranging from intelligent, manta ray-like Oswaft to carapace-creatures and interstellar plankton that serve as the Oswaft's food. The Oswaft, ruled by a council of Elders and capable of naturally traversing hyperspace, tend to be cautious creatures who never leave the safety of their habitat. Three blue-white stars, located in the center of the nebula, surround the Cave of the Elders—the only architectural structure in the ThonBoka. This cave is constructed entirely from precious gems and is an exact replica of the surrounding nebula, but is only twenty kilometers across. After discovering the Oswaft, the Centrality Navy viewed them as a threat. They blockaded the entrance to the ThonBoka, preventing the flow of nutrients and slowly starving its inhabitants, until defeated by Lando Calrissian and others. [LCS]

Thpffftht A Bith counselor ship. [CPL]

Thrakia Homeworld of an intelligent insectoid species with genetically transmitted memories. Some 300 years ago the insectoids, who had previously communicated by scent, realized that they could also communicate by clacking their mandibles together. To this day, they view this ability as a sign that their species has been gifted by a higher power. [CPL]

thranta Great flying creatures with broad, saillike wings, they were brought to Bespin from their native Alderaan years ago. The Bespin thranta herd is now the only known surviving group of these beasts of burden, whose body cores contain a lighter-than-air bladder. Talented riders perform in "sky rodeos," leaping out into the open sky and falling until a thranta comes to the rescue. [ISWU]

Thranta

Thrasher The name of a warbeast used by fighter Oron Kira as he joined the Jedi forces in their fight against the dark-side Krath cultists on Onderon some 4,000 years before the Battle of Yavin. [DLS]

Thrawn, Grand Admiral The only nonhuman ever to be named one of the twelve Grand Admirals of the Empire, the blue-skinned, red-eyed officer of almost regal bearing nearly succeeded in accomplishing what his mentor, Emperor Palpatine, failed to: destroy the Rebel Alliance. Grand Admiral Thrawn, an intense and focused humanoid, spent most of his military career conquering the barbaric Unknown Regions and keeping them under control. He was a complex individual who had a magnificent hologram collection representing some of the galaxy's greatest art treasures, for he believed one could understand—and thus eventually defeat—a species through its art. When he linked up with ships under the command of Captain Pellaeon, he discovered that the Empire had been dealt an apparently fatal blow some five years before with the destruction of the second Death Star and the death of Palpatine.

Thrawn gathered the ragtag remnants of Imperial power and fashioned a strong military challenge to the New Republic, which he refused to accept as legitimate and still referred to as the Rebellion. He plotted meticulously aboard his Star Destroyer *Chimaera*, with backup from the loyal Captain Pellaeon. First, he figured out a way to neutralize Luke Skywalker and others with Force power by gathering rodentlike Force-blocking creatures called ysalamiri from the planet Myrkr. Next, on the planet Wayland, inside the Emperor's Mount Tantiss storehouse, Thrawn found experimental weapons, including a cloaking device, Spaarti cloning cylinders, and the Dark Jedi clone, mad Joruus C'baoth.

Admiral Thrawn also made use of the Noghri, a species that Darth Vader had tricked into feeling beholden to the Empire. The Noghri made up top-secret Imperial death squads, and one of them, Rukh, was Thrawn's personal and very deadly bodyguard. Thrawn sent a commando squad to kidnap Leia Organa Solo so that C'baoth could subvert her and

Grand Admiral Thrawn

her unborn twins to the dark side of the Force. C'baoth himself hatched a plan to lure Luke Skywalker. Thrawn also had a secret spy on Coruscant in the heart of the New Republic—his Delta Source turned out to be ch'hala trees that were living microphones and transmitters lining the corridors of the New Republic Council.

To test his fleet's readiness, the admiral launched a hit-and-run attack on the planet Bpfassh and two other worlds in the Sluis system. He also stole mole miners from Lando Calrissian's mining operation on Nkllon to use in his next attack on the Sluis Van shipyards. Later, he blackmailed smuggler Niles Ferrier into providing the location of the long-missing *Katana* Dreadnaught fleet and escaped with 180 of the 200 ships. In a move designed to trap the Republic leaders, Thrawn's ships released cloaked asteroids and confusing sensors into orbit above Coruscant.

At a climactic confrontation at the Bilbringi shipyards, Thrawn was surprised by the appearance of a fleet of smuggler ships aiding the New Republic, and his forces were defeated. In the aftermath of that failure, his Noghri bodyguard, Rukh—who had come to realize how Thrawn and the Empire had betrayed his people—assassinated him, ending a major threat to the New Republic. [HE, DFR, LC]

Thrella Well Any of a series of shafts leading from the surface of Circarpous V to a network of caverns extending deep within the planet's crust. Thrella Wells are located all over the planet's surface and are believed to be the work of a legendary race known as the Thrella. [SME]

Throgg A Tatooine humanoid and onetime spice smuggler, Luke Skywalker entrusted the moisture farm of Owen and Beru Lars to him shortly after the Battle of Yavin. The farm was later purchased by Gavin Darklighter's family. [RS]

Thrugii A desolate, rocky world located near a wide asteroid belt, it has been home to seven generations of failed miners. Present residents are considered claim jumpers by sector authorities, who assert that they control all rights to Thrugii and the asteroid belt. After the authorities locked down the planet, the Thrugii miners found themselves in desperate need of food and supplies. Smuggler Kaine Paulsen was killed while trying to deliver supplies to the miners. [SWAJ]

Thuku A male Rodian bounty hunter, he was on a mission to kill another Rodian named Greedo. Thuku worked for Navik the Red, head of the Chattza tribe. He had tracked down his prey to the spaceport of Mos Eisley on Tatooine, where he heard that Han Solo had beaten him to the punch. [CCG]

Thun, Hekis Durumm Perdo Kolokk Baldikarr The administrator of the droid production world Mechis III, Hekis Thun continually added more and more names to his title to help overcome his feelings of inadequacy. He was killed by his personal droid, Threedee-Fourex, after the assassin droid IG-88 and his counterparts arrived at Mechis III and took over the programming of all of the planet's computer systems and droids. [TBH]

Thunderflare An Imperial Star Destroyer. [CCG]

Thwim A Kubazi spy, he traded information on Tatooine. [TMEC]

Thyferra Located in the Polith system, it is the homeworld of the mantislike Vratix and is the center of the galaxy's bacta industry. Thyferra is a green-and-white world covered with rain forests; it has little axial tilt and is unbearably humid. It has two airless, uninhabited moons and orbits a yellow star. Thyferra was first contacted during the middle years of the Old Republic. Although the Vratix already had colonized other bodies in their system, contact with the Republic ushered in a technological revolution.

The Vratix soon invented the healing fluid called bacta by growing alazhi and mixing it with the chemical kavam. The remarkable fluid was extremely profitable, and powerful Vratix operations spread across many worlds. With the rise of the Empire, two large bacta-harvesting corporations, Xucphra and Zaltin, negotiated a special deal with the Imperials, allowing the companies to gain a virtual monopoly on the bacta industry. The conglomerates controlled 95 percent of the galaxy's bacta and became known as the Bacta Cartel. The human-owned companies long dominated the lives of the Vratix and ran the government. Total bacta output averaged seventeen billion liters a year.

The planet-wide government was led by two canirs (chief officers) appointed by an elected council, each canir representing one of the two corporations. Because Xucphra and Zaltin were competitors, there was frequent governmental gridlock, which gave rise to the Ashern (Black Claw) terrorist group, which viewed the corporations as a threat and attempted to topple them. In the political confusion following the Battle of Endor, Thyferra remained neutral and profited by selling bacta to both sides. Two and a half years after Endor, the New Republic, anxious to please the Thyferran leaders, recruited the human pilots Bror Jace (from Zaltin) and Erisi Dlarit (from Xucphra) into the famous Rogue Squadron.

Thyferra has three spaceports: The main one is Zalxuc City, which was renamed Xucphra City after former Imperial Intelligence head Ysanne Isard took over control of Xucphra and put the squeeze on Zaltin as she became the planet's Head of State. Foreign workers, who are hired to make the bacta runs, stay in segregated areas around the spaceport. The port's main building is a low two-story rectangle, with akonije trees growing through it and out the roof. The alazhi is harvested and kavam synthesized primarily on Thyferra, but there are dozens of colony worlds elsewhere, including Qretu-Five.

After Rogue Squadron's conquest of Borleias, Bror Jace was called back to Thyferra due to a relative's grave illness. After being tipped by a spy, the Interdictor cruiser *Black Asp*, operating near Thyferra, dragged his X-wing out of hyperspace and destroyed it, apparently killing Jace. (His presumed death became a convenient cover story.) After the capture of Coruscant, the New Republic was especially dependent on Thyferra to provide bacta for treating the Krytos virus, which Isard had unleashed as part of her plan to corner the bacta trade and become both wealthy and powerful. A deadly Bacta War ensued, with Rogue Squadron fighting Isard—but not under New Republic auspices. In the end, the Rogues were victorious. They were welcomed back into Republic service, and Thyferra voted to join the New Republic. [SWAJ, RS, WG, KT, BW]

Thyferran Home Defense Corps A paramilitary unit, it was established by former Imperial Intelligence head Ysanne Isard when she came to power on Thyferra. The THDC was composed of Xucphra Corporation volunteers trained by Isard's Imperial troops ostensibly to defend their homeworld from Ashern rebels. They were really witless pawns to be used in Isard's reign of terror against Thyferra. [BW]

Thyfonian A *Lambda*-class shuttle, it was specially modified by Fliry Vorru to be used to escape from the planet Thyferra. It was destroyed by the combined efforts of Rogue Squadron pilots Corran Horn and Tycho Celchu as it attempted to make a run to hyperspace during the Bacta War. It was assumed that Thyferra strongwoman Ysanne Isard was on board. [BW]

Thyne, Zekka A notorious Black Sun terrorist, he was taken from the Kessel prison facility by the Alliance, which hoped to use him in its operation to undermine the Imperial infrastructure on Coruscant before it invaded that planet. He had been sent to Kessel by CorSec for smuggling, but he was also tied to the murders of nearly a dozen people. Hal and Corran Horn were the most responsible for his imprisonment, and he vowed to kill Corran. They ran into each other again on Coruscant, where both were on separate undercover missions. Thyne attempted to kill Horn at the Headquarters, a bar in Invisec, but Corran made a daring escape on a speeder bike. Imperial Kirtan Loor attempted to use Thyne as an informant, but he proved mostly ineffectual. Thyne laid in wait for Horn at a secret rendezvous point, but before he could kill the Rogue, he was himself killed by his lover, Inyri Forge. [WG]

Ti, Kirana One of the Force-sensitive Witches of Dathomir, Kirana Ti helped Luke Skywalker recover an ancient wrecked space station, the *Chu'unthor*, which held records of old Jedi training. Later she became one of Skywalker's Jedi candidates and joined his other Jedi students on Yavin 4 in defeating the spirit of Dark Lord Exar Kun, protecting Luke's body and freeing his spirit. [DA, COF]

Tibanna gas A rare gas extracted from the atmosphere of Bespin, among other planets, it is processed at Cloud City. Hot air rises through Cloud City's unipod, which sucks in the gases that float in Bespin's atmosphere—including Tibanna gas. The gas is processed and packed in carbonite for transport off-planet. Tibanna gas produces four times its normal energy output when cohesive light passes through it. When spin-sealed Tibanna gas (compacted at the atomic level) is used as a con-

Tibanna gas processing center

Tibannopolis

ducting agent, blasters and other energy weapons produce greater energy yields—and therefore greater amounts of damage. Personal weapons cannot tolerate this extra power, but ship-mounted blasters benefit greatly from the use of Tibanna gas. The spin-sealing process is prohibitively expensive except on Bespin, where it occurs naturally. Nonspin-sealed Tibanna gas is used as a hyperdrive coolant. [GG2, ISWU]

Tibannopolis An abandoned city on the planet Bespin, it hangs near-empty, a creaking ghost town in the sky. The roof, decks, and sides of Tibannopolis have been picked over by scavengers hauling away scrap metal. Luke Skywalker found Streen, one of his Jedi candidates, on Tibannopolis. [JS, ISWU]

Tibor A vicious bipedal reptiloid, this Barabel bounty hunter frequents the Mos Eisley cantina and is a regular employee of Zorba the Hutt. [ZHR]

Tibrin A planet completely covered by a shallow ocean, it is homeworld to the Ishi Tib species. Tibrin circles the yellow star Cal and has one barren moon called Plah. The planet has no seasons and ocean currents evenly distribute warm water, creating a temperate zone covering most of the planet's surface. The only land masses are protruding coral reefs and sand bars, where the ecologically minded Ishi Tib have constructed their cities. Ishi Tib live in communal schools ranging from a few hundred to more than 10,000 individuals, and their organizational skills are prized by galactic corporations who often hire Ishi Tib as managers. Animal life includes the Tibrin kelp-gnat. [GG4, GG2, POT]

TIE/Advanced fighter The prototype ship used by Darth Vader at the Battle of Yavin, many of its best design features were later incorporated into the TIE interceptor and the TIE Advanced (TIE/Ad) ship dubbed the TIE Avenger.

The TIE Advanced x1 featured an original spaceframe and reinforced durasteel-alloy hull, with an elongated rear deck and matching bent wings covered with solar panels. The vessel had a solar ionization reactor and paired twin-ion engines for a more powerful drive system than the standard TIE/ln. Speed was only slightly improved due to the added mass of the vessel; a good deal of the extra power was bled off to the shield generators. While less maneuverable than standard TIE fighters, it could take a beating.

The TIE Advanced x1 had twin heavy-blaster cannons in a fixed, front-mounted position. In addition to its shields, it had a modest hyperdrive but no life support system. The Empire decided not to order the TIE Advanced x1 in large quantities, citing their excessive cost. Privately, some Imperial Navy strategists admitted that the Navy was afraid to purchase a fighter with a hyperdrive, fearing that it would give bureaucrats an excuse to slash orders for new capital starships.

The Empire instead opted for the TIE interceptor, which featured the TIE Advanced x1's drive system in a more compact ship. Although the TIE interceptor lacked a hyperdrive and shields, it was blindingly fast, incredibly maneuverable, and significantly cheaper than the TIE Advanced x1. By the Battle of Endor, the large increase in TIE interceptor production meant the end of production for the TIE Advanced x1. [SWAJ, SWSB, TSC, HE, SWVG]

TIE bomber The Empire's primary assault bomber, it is somewhat slower and less maneuverable than standard starfighters, but provides excellent surgical strike potential against ground and deep space targets.

TIE bombers have double pods and elongated solar panels. The starboard pod contains the pilot's

TIE/Advanced fighter (Darth Vader's)

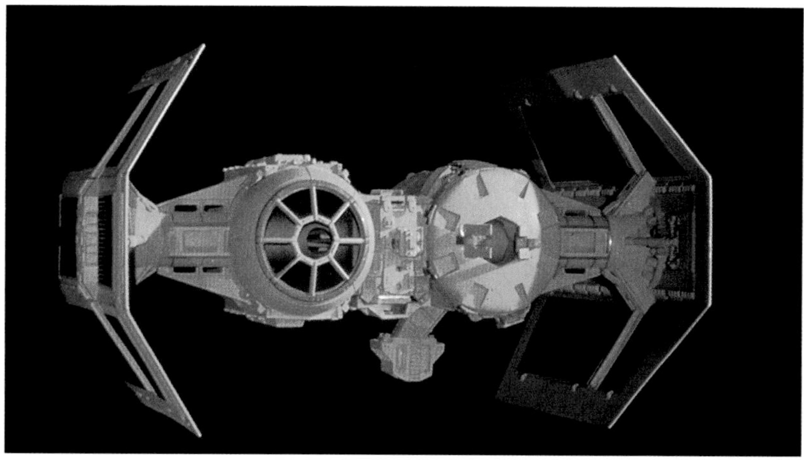

TIE bomber

compartment along with flight computers, communications, and life support. The port pod holds the ordnance bay and targeting and delivery systems. Twin ion engines are mounted between the two pods. The bomber's weaponry includes high-yield proton bombs, guided concussion missiles, orbital mines, and free-falling thermal detonators. A pair of front-firing laser cannons provide protection from enemy ships.

For space duty, the TIE bomber delivered heavy ordnance against Rebel capital ships. Normally, TIE fighters first soften up the target, followed by TIE bombers, in conjunction with assault gunboats and Skipray blastboats, which use their precise targeting computers to disable vital areas such as the shield generators or engines. When the target is crippled and unable to protect itself, Imperial boarding parties take control of the vessel or capture troops for interrogation.

TIE bombers are used to assault space stations and stardocks and to mine planetary orbits. They also are exceptionally good on ground bombing missions. Their targeting computers are precise enough to level specific buildings while leaving adjacent areas unscathed. A Star Destroyer typically carries one squadron of twelve TIE bombers. Prior to Emperor Palpatine's death, the Empire began developing a more advanced bomber prototype, which eventually evolved into the Scimitar assault bomber. [SWSB, TSC, ISB, DFR, DFRSB, SWVG]

TIE crawler

TIE crawler The century tank—which Imperial soldiers have taken to calling TIE crawler or TIE tank because of the familiar command pod taken from the TIE fighter—is a cheap, mass-produced ground combat vehicle that became popular during the revival of the Empire and the recapture of the Imperial capital of Coruscant. It is a simple combat machine, with simple controls and modular components. It requires only a single crewman, who handles both piloting and gunnery.

The TIE tank has the same central pod as the standard TIE fighter. Twin power generators are attached to each side of the pod and drive the tread wheels, giving the tank a relatively slow top speed of only 90 kilometers per hour. It can navigate through most terrain and is substantially cheaper than comparable repulsorlift craft. Weapons include two forward-firing medium blaster cannons and a retractable light turbolaser. The TIE tank has light armor plating on all surfaces, but the drive system and tread wheels are easily damaged by enemy fire. The TIE tank is entered through a top hatch, and the pilot is strapped into an automatically adjusting grav-couch. Foot controls adjust the angle of steering and speed, while the hand controls are tied into the weapons systems and the targeting computer. [DE, DESB, TSC, SWVG]

TIE defender A prototype Imperial fighter developed shortly before the Battle of Endor, it has been deployed to a small number of elite TIE wings. The TIE defender was used to defeat rogue Imperial Admiral Zaarin, who planned to depose Emperor Palpatine. The vessel is a radical departure from conventional TIE designs and features three sets of solar collection panels mounted at equilateral points around the fighter's cockpit.

The TIE defender's multiple heavy-weapons systems allow it to successfully engage enemy capital ships, while a hyperdrive allows it to operate independently of support carriers, giving the ship flexibility unmatched by any other Imperial starfighter. It is nearly 40 percent faster at sublight than the standard TIE fighter due to its new twin ion engines. Triple arrays of maneuvering jets on the tri-wing assembly make the ship capable of amazing dives and twists.

The TIE defender features four laser cannons and two ion cannons, which can be fired singly for multiple targets or fire-linked for a concentrated assault. A pair of missile launchers can be equipped with proton torpedoes and concussion missiles. [TT, SWVG]

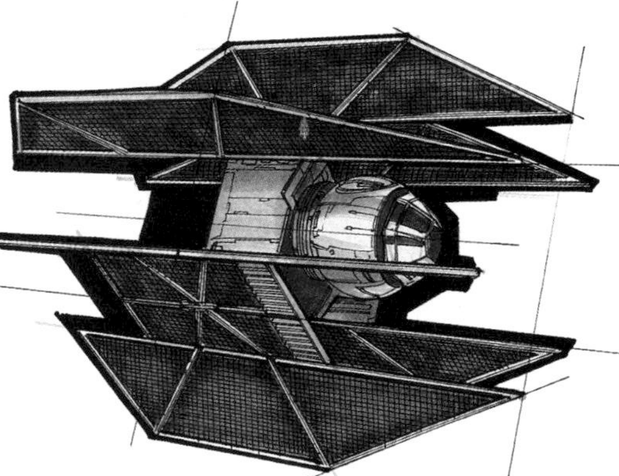

TIE defender

TIE fighter The TIE (for Twin Ion Engine) fighter was the most recognizable symbol of the Imperial Navy's control of space. TIE fighters were aboard even the smallest cruisers and were stationed at starports and garrison bases across the galaxy. They

TIE fighter

were an omnipresent reminder of the Empire's might.

A TIE fighter is a small ship; its most distinguishing feature is the pair of immense hexagonal solar array wings on either side of its small, spherical command pod. The ship presents a small profile, and its great maneuverability makes it even more difficult to target in combat.

TIEs are short-range fighters without hyperdrives to save weight and increase performance. They depend on a home base—a nearby planet or Imperial cruiser. They carry only two days' worth of supplies and often must refuel after the first few hours of combat, but their use in massive quantities makes up for any design deficiencies. The fighters were used for planetary and cruiser defense and assault against Rebel, pirate, and alien vessels. They also escorted heavily armed TIE bombers when attacking permanent planetary installations.

The TIE's famous maneuverability and speed come at great practical cost to the pilot. TIE fighters have no shields, secondary weapons, or drive systems; minuscule fuel supplies; and no onboard life support system. Pilots must wear fully sealed flight suits with self-contained atmospheres. Some claim the TIE is too responsive to piloting adjustments. It isn't uncommon for novice pilots to attempt an advanced maneuver that sends their ship out of control.

The TIE has a pair of forward-mounted, fire-linked laser cannons. The massive laser generators are in the undercarriage of the command pod and feed off the power generators and batteries. The fighter draws much of its energy from solar radiation absorbed by the array wings. The common TIE fighter is the TIE/ln, which is actually a successor to the earlier T.I.E. and TIE models, all of which were produced by the company now called Sienar Fleet Systems. The success of the TIE fighter has led to the creation of several new mission-specific designs, including the TIE/rc (a sensor and communications reconnaissance fighter), the TIE/fc (which provides fire control for long-range Navy artillery), the TIE/gt (a makeshift bomber used prior to the introduction of the TIE bomber), the TIE/Advanced (Darth Vader's ship at the Battle of Yavin was one such advanced model), the TIE bomber, the TIE interceptor, the TIE scout (a limited production, light reconnaissance starship), the TIE vanguard (a reconnaissance starfighter that, unusual for TIEs, is equipped with shields to protect the valuable information it gathers), and the fully robotic TIE/D fighter (introduced six years after the Battle of Endor.) There is also a TIE/sh shuttlecraft and a TIE boat, or sub fighter. [SW, ESB, RJ, SWSB, HESB, SWVG, GG3, GG5]

TIE interceptor Faster and more maneuverable than the standard TIE/ln fighter, it stemmed from the advances developed for Darth Vader's TIE Advanced x1 Prototype. The TIE interceptor uses the standard TIE cockpit, drive pod, and wing braces. The solar panels appear to be dagger-shaped, making the interceptor more intimidating, while giving the ship a smaller profile, making it harder for Rebel gunners to target. The TIE interceptor has more powerful drives than the TIE/1n and is almost as fast as the New Republic's A-wing fighter.

The TIE interceptor uses a new type of ion stream projector, allowing pilots to execute tight turns and rolls. Twin port deflectors can be manipulated individually for fine control and counterbalancing, making the TIE interceptor a superior choice for dogfights.

The ship has four laser cannons, one at the end of each solar panel, and advanced targeting software gives the pilot greater firing accuracy. Like other TIE fighters, the TIE interceptor has little armor plating and no shield generators. Interceptor pilots rely on their ship's maneuverability and superior numbers to survive engagements with better armed and armored New Repubic fighters.

With no onboard life-support system, TIE pilots must use fully sealed flight suits. The TIE interceptor has no hyperdrive and requires a large capital ship as a base of operations. The Empire intended the TIE interceptor to eventually replace entirely the TIE/ln, but by the death of the Emperor only about 20 percent of Imperial fighters were interceptors. As Grand Admiral Thrawn began his bid for power, he began arming some TIE interceptors with shields, knowing that the Empire could no longer consider these exceptional ships disposable. [SWSB, HESB, FP, SWVG]

TIE interceptor

Tigris

Tierfon Located in the outer Sumitra sector, it is the site of a Rebel starfighter outpost buried 250 meters into a rock cliff. The Tierfon base is relatively small, housing only eight X-wing fighters and fifty-four combat personnel (members of the Tierfon Yellow Aces Squadron), along with troops and support staff for a total contingent of 158. [SWSB]

Tigris Born the son of two parents strong in the Force, but having no Force powers of his own, he became a pawn and then a major player in a galactic drama. Tigris, with pale skin and black-and-silver-striped hair, was the offspring of two Firrerreons: Hethrir and a female healer named Rillao. Both had been students of Darth Vader, but while Hethrir embraced the dark side of the Force and even helped destroy his own world as proof of his loyalty to the Empire, Rillao's powers came from the light side and she fled with her unborn child.

Tigris grew up on a remote, pastoral planet, knowing nothing of his father. Hethrir eventually found Rillao and their son; he imprisoned her in an abandoned Imperial slaving vessel and made Tigris his personal slave. Without Force powers, Tigris could never succeed Hethrir as head of his Empire Reborn organization. Hethrir twisted the story of Rillao, making Tigris despise her. Tigris assisted Hethrir in running his worldcraft, aboard which were dozens of kidnapped children. If they showed Force talents, Hethrir tried to turn them to the dark side; if not, he sold them to slavers. Tigris, gentle and compassionate, snuck food to the captives and tried to comfort them.

Hethrir kidnapped Jacen, Jaina, and Anakin Solo, the children of Han and Leia Organa Solo. Tigris grew especially fond of Anakin and accompanied Hethrir and the boy to what he was told was Anakin's purification in the temple of the Waru on Crseih Research Station. But Rillao, who had been freed by Leia, was there and told a stunned Tigris that Hethrir was really his father. Tigris also discovered that Anakin's spirit was going to be absorbed into the Waru. He snatched the child from Hethrir's arms and took him to safety as Hethrir was swallowed whole by the imploding Waru. Tigris was reunited with his mother, and the two of them set off for Coruscant. [CS]

t'ill A flowering plant that grew on the planet Alderaan. [SWR]

timer mine A timer-activated explosive device placed by mining droids, it is typically used in ore and spice mines, but has many military applications. [CCG]

time-stream A method used by the H'drachi to interpret the Force, especially to foresee future events. [ROC]

Tinn VI An enormous gas giant in the Tinn system composed of hydrogen, nitrogen, and ammonium, it generates a powerful negative magnetic field that extends its shadow into hyperspace and can strip all passing ships of their magnetic battle shielding—forcing them into realspace and leaving them stranded in the system until they can effect repairs. Tinn VI is orbited by six moons, labeled A through F, and the domed city of Echnos is located on Tinn VI-D, often called Echnos. [SWAJ]

Timer mine

Tinnel IV Located in the Quanta sector, it contains the city of Val Denn, where the private estate of Moff Jerjerrod was located. Sometime after the Battle of Yavin, Jerjerrod's personal vault was looted by the infamous thief called the Tombat, who stole several of the Moff's priceless artworks. [SWAJ]

Tinn system Located at the border of the Outer Rim, it contains seven planets orbiting a double star. The only settlement in the system is a domed city on the moon called Tinn VI-D or Echnos, which orbits Tinn VI. [SWAJ]

Tin-Tin Dwarf Bipeds less than a meter tall, they are an intelligent rodentlike species. [SWR, NR]

Tion, Lord A member of the nobility and an officer loyal to the Emperor, he served as a task force commander charged with identifying and eradicating all Alliance personnel and Rebel sympathizers on the planet Ralltiir. Lord Tion played an instrumental role in the Rebellion when he boastingly revealed the location of the plans for the original Death Star battle station to Bail Organa of Alderaan. Thoroughly despicable, he was later killed in a scuffle with Princess Leia. [SWR]

Tion Hegemony A group of twenty-seven backwater systems in the Outer Rim on the fringes of Imperial space near Corporate Sector space, they are so remote that the Empire never bothered with direct control. As a result, the Tion Hegemony became a haven for smugglers, con artists, and other petty crooks. Common smuggling cargoes include chak-root and R'alla mineral water. Planets in the isolated Tion Hegemony, which unsuccessfully struggle to keep up with the rest of galactic society, include Saheelindeel, Brigia, Rudrig, and Dellalt. [HSR, HLL, FP]

Tionne One of Luke Skywalker's earliest Jedi trainees, she found her true

Tionne

calling in teaching other young Jedi initiates and spinning the epochal history of the Jedi Knights into haunting and evocative ballads. Tionne was one of the first dozen of Skywalker's initiates to train at his new academy on Yavin 4. What she lacked in Force powers she made up for in enthusiasm and devotion.

Tionne, a slender human female with large pearlescent eyes and flowing silver-white hair, was fascinated with the Jedi Holocron of Vodo-Siosk Baas. Even before she enrolled at the academy she had researched Jedi history and legend. With access to the Holocron, she began to weave the legends of the Jedi into songs and ballads, preserving history and using the Force to create her haunting music. She accompanied herself on a stringed instrument she had created: a shaft strung with cords separating two hollow resonating boxes, called a double viol.

Tionne was deeply involved in defending the academy and saving Skywalker when the spirit of the Dark Lord of the Sith Exar Kun came to life. Tionne found Luke's body on the top of the ancient Massassi temple, still alive, but missing his very essence. Battling against Kun, Tionne found her work in the archives very helpful. It gave her knowledge of the Dark Lord's past that aided the students in forming a strategy to defeat him once and for all.

Years later, when Skywalker had to leave on a mission, he entrusted the training of a new crop of students to Tionne. By using parables and fables, she communicated the core of the Jedi exercises—often more effectively than Luke had—and became a semiregular instructor at the Jedi academy. Tionne helped instruct the youngest students at the academy, teaching them to find their own special skills in the Force. [DA, DS, YJK, SWCG, COF, JASB]

Tiragga The Rebel Alliance had a small outpost located on this planet's second moon, but it became infected with the deadly Direllian Plague. [SWAJ]

Tiree *See* Gold Two

Tirsa An industrial planet, it is home to the Tirsa Wargear armaments company, which manufactures the Leviathan submersible carrier. [SWAJ]

Tiss'shar A reptilian species native to the humid jungle continents of the planet Tiss'sharl, they are more well known for their assassins than for their savvy in business and envirotechnology. The Tiss'shar have long necks and slender bodies covered with scales and colorful patches. Their large jaws are filled with short pointed teeth and a large pink tongue that's always in motion. They have large black eyes covered by a durable transparent film. The personal and business lives of these jungle dwellers are intertwined, and most appreciate the art of the deal. The late Uul-Rha-Shan, bodyguard for the late Corporate Sector Authority Viceprex Mirkovig Hirken, was a Tiss'shar. [GG12]

Lord Toda

Tiss'sharl Homeworld of the bipedal reptiloids called Tiss'shar, it was the birthplace of the assassin and Corporate Sector bodyguard Uul-Rha-Shan. The planet is ruled by the Tiss'sharl League. Its inhabitants are known for their shrewd business dealings. [CSSB, GG12]

Tobbra, Captain A first officer on the New Republic starship *Indomitable*, he had been the very definition of cautious throughout his career. He saw his role on the *Indomitable* as a balance to the excesses of Commodore Brand. [TT]

Toda, Lord During the Empire's early days, the gruff and surly bully called himself "overlord of the outer territories" and ruled over a major portion of the planet Tammuz-an. He dressed much like his warrior tribesmen, wearing rough canvas and organic armor. [DTV]

Togoria A world of grassy plains and rolling hills orbiting the blue-white star Thanos, it is the homeworld of the feline Togorians, tall, furry creatures who are suspicious of offworlders. The Togorians have near-complete separation between the sexes, and the males and females see each other only a few days each year. The males spend the remainder of their time as nomads, wandering the plains with domesticated flying lizards called mosgoths, used as riding mounts. The females dwell in the cities, tending animals such as the bist and etelo and maintaining their society's solar-based technology. The government is headed by the Margrave of Togoria, a hereditary office always held by male descendants. The Margrave's closest female relative, living in the capital city of Caross, rules over the cities and the day-to-day activities of females and young children. Togoria society is still relatively low-tech, although the females have proven to be an attractive market for personal technology. Togoria's vast mineral resources have yet to be tapped. [GG4]

Toklar A much-quoted Mon Calamari philosopher, he was an inspiration to Admiral Ackbar. [SOL]

Tokmia One of the planets where Imperial probe droids were sent on Darth Vader's orders to search for the new Rebel Alliance base after the Battle of Yavin. The other planets were Allyuen and Hoth. [ESBR]

Tolsk, Commander Commander of Task Force Blackvine, part of the deployment of the New Republic's Fifth Fleet at Doornik-319 during the Yevethan crisis. [SOL]

tomuon A herd animal native to Askaj, their coats are turned into a highly prized fabric. [TJP]

Ton-Falk The site of the Battle of Ton-Falk, during which two Imperial frigates and a Dreadnaught were destroyed due to insufficient TIE fighter protection and tactical advice provided by K-3PO, a protocol droid trained in strategy by Commander Narra. Analysis of this battle led to the development of the KDY Escort Carrier. [TSC, GG3]

Tonnika, Brea and Senni Identical twins and con artists, the beautiful sisters were interested in only one thing: separating men from their money. Humanoid-appearing Kiffu, Brea and Senni Tonnika were abandoned as youngsters and taken in and raised by colonists on Kiffex. Manipulative and clever, they turned friend against friend in order to squeeze credits out of the colonists. They left the planet with a bedazzled scout and continued their scams all over the galaxy. Often, only one sister would appear at a time, using the combined name Bresenni, in order to pull their intrigues. At Han Solo's instigation, they pulled such a trick on Lando Calrissian—well before either got involved with the Rebellion. Calrissian laughed out loud at the joke, but plotted to get back at Solo.

The Tonnika sisters didn't find an amused victim in Imperial Grand Moff Argon, whom they conned out of 25,000 credits. He sent hordes of stormtroopers searching for them. The sisters' infamy had spread so widely that near-identical look-alikes masqueraded as them. In fact, when the Tonnikas were attending a seven-week party at Jabba the Hutt's palace on Tatooine, the Mistryl Shadow Guards Shada and Karoly assumed the sisters' identities during an unplanned visit to Tatooine. The phony Tonnikas were at the Mos Eisley cantina and were arrested by stormtroopers searching for C-3PO and R2-D2 and their masters. Both the impostors and the real Tonnika sisters managed to get off Tatooine to work their scams elsewhere in the galaxy. [TMEC, SWCG, GG1]

Toola A glacier-covered, bitterly cold world orbiting the purple sun Kaelta, it is home to the mostly primitive species called Whiphids, who delight in hunting the indigenous caraboose, furry mastmots (also called motmots), seagoing arabores, flying snow demons, sea hogs, and ice puppies. Toola has only a brief growing season during the summer months when grasses appear and join the purple lichens on the plains. Small mining camps are scattered across the planet's surface. Whiphids have only the most primitive technology and live in loose nomadic tribes led by the best hunter, called the Spearmaster. The only significant export from Toola is ice for water-scarce planets. Whiphids can be found in the galaxy acting as trackers and mercenaries. Notable Whiphids include J'Quille, one of Jabba the Hutt's hunters, and Lady Valarian, owner of the Lucky Despot hotel on Tatooine. Four years after the Battle of Endor, Luke Skywalker traveled to Toola to inspect the ruined home of a slain Jedi Master who had once been the curator of Jedi records on Coruscant. [CPL, GG4, TJP, SWAJ]

Toorr, Jip The Yevethan primate of the warship *Devotion*, formerly *Valorous*. [BTS]

To-phalion Base A secret Imperial research facility, it was built into the hollowed-out interior of a large asteroid. Formerly used as a mining operation, the asteroid later housed a hangar bay and laboratories for the Vorknkx Project, which developed an experimental cloaking device after the Battle of Hoth. To-phalion base was surrounded by eight smaller asteroids. Just prior to the Battle of Endor, the renegade Admiral Zaarin attacked To-phalion and Grand Admiral Thrawn was dispatched to stop him. Zaarin succeeded in stealing the corvette *Vorknkx*, containing the prototype cloak, and escaped into the Unknown Regions. He was tracked and soon eliminated by Thrawn. [TSC]

Brea and Senni Tonnika

Toprawa This planet was the initial Rebel hiding place after the Alliance stole the technical readouts for the first Death Star. From the Toprawa Relay Station, Rebel operatives transmitted the plans to Princess Leia's ship, the *Tantive IV*, in the operation known as Skyhook. Later, as punishment for helping the Alliance, the people of Toprawa were forced into a preindustrial state—relying on campfires and bantha-drawn carts as their highest form of technology. Loyal Imperials began living in shining, illuminated citadels out of reach of the lowly Toprawans. Periodically, stormtroopers would ride a grain cart into village squares and watch as the peasants crawled forward on their stomachs, wailing lamentations over the Emperor's death at Endor. Grain was only given to those whose penance seemed the most sincere. Three years after the Battle of Endor, Imperial Intelligence agent Kirtan Loor spent a week on Toprawa after being ordered back from a stay on Borleias. [SWR, DS, RS]

Toq, Qrrl A Nazzar prince who lived 4,000 years before the Galactic Civil War, he was a fearless warrior and a Jedi. Qrrl Toq was also a designer and builder of Jedi armor. [FNU, DLS, TSW]

Torg, Galen A Rebel soldier, he was selected for honor-guard duty during the award ceremony for Luke Skywalker and Han Solo following the Battle of Yavin. [CCG, GG1]

Torm *See* Dadeferron, Torm

Tornik One of Jabba the Hutt's human guards. [TJP]

torpedo sphere A siege platform designed to knock out planetary shields prior to Imperial attacks, it was a precursor to the Death Star battle stations. The large 1,900-meter-diameter torpedo sphere was covered with thousands of dedicated energy receptors designed to analyze shield emissions and find weak points. When a site was selected, a rain of missiles could be fired from a group of 500 proton torpedo tubes. A hole in the shields for even a brief period allowed the sphere's turbolasers to destroy the planetary shield generators if the targeting and analysis was correct. [ISB]

Torr, Valsil A wily old Twi'lek, he was in charge of the space station at Yag'Dhul. After a brief encounter with Rogue Squadron, he and his men surrendered and allowed the Rogues to remove Warlord Zsinj's bacta from the station. [BW]

Torranix sector Twelve years after the Battle of Endor, the New Republic astrographic survey ship *Astrolabe* was diverted from this sector to Doornik-1142 by General Etahn A'baht, who was hoping to get an updated survey of the Koornacht Cluster for military intelligence purposes. [BTS]

Torve, Fynn A member of Talon Karrde's smuggling organization, the human is among the best of Karrde's freighter pilots. While not as flashy as Han Solo or as sophisticated as Lando Calrissian, Fynn Torve has adroitly handled the most important and difficult runs for his boss. [HE, DFR, LC]

Tosche Station A power and distribution station, it is located near the town of Anchorhead on the planet Tatooine. From its inception, Tosche Station served as a gathering place for Anchorhead's young people, including Luke Skywalker and his friends. Luke's friend Fixer worked there. [SWN]

Totolaya A hostage taken by the Yevetha during their attack on the Kubaz colony of Morning Bell. [SOL]

Towani, Catarine *See* Towani, Cindel

Towani, Cindel The youngest child in the Towani family, she endured a lifetime of terrifying experiences in just a few short years. Cindel and her father and mother, Jeremitt and Catarine, and her brother, Mace, were marooned on the forest moon of Endor when their star cruiser crashed. Searching for help, Cindel's parents were captured by a creature called a Borra and taken to the cliffside lair of the monstrous giant called Gorax.

Cindel and Mace foraged for food, but Cindel fell ill. They were rescued by Deej the Ewok, who took them back to his village where his wife nursed Cindel back to health. She became friends with Deej's playful youngest son, Wicket W. Warrick. Mace convinced Cindel to accompany him one night to find their parents, and they were also caught by the Borra. They were rescued the next morning by Deej's family but finally learned that their parents were in the hands of the Gorax. With help from the Ewoks, Jeremitt and Catarine were rescued.

Several months later, Wicket and Cindel returned to the Ewok village only to find it under attack by two-meter-tall marauders—humanoids who had also been marooned on Endor years before. Cindel witnessed the death of her mother and brother, but escaped to find her father. The marauder King Terak and the witch queen Charal had found him first, and he was killed warning his daughter away and trying to escape himself.

Cindel and Wicket were captured and escaped several times and were subjected to other terrors. A creature named Teek took them to his human master, a hermit named Noa who had also been stranded on Endor when his starship crashed. Cindel was captured again and taken to King Terak's castle and thrown in the dungeon with captive Ewoks. They were rescued, and a pitched battle ensued at the crash site of Noa's cruiser; Terak and Charal were neutralized forever. When Noa's star cruiser was fixed, Cindel decided to accompany him off-world, although she promised Wicket she would return someday.

Years later Cindel became an idealistic journalist on Coruscant. She received the so-called Plat Mallar tapes from Admiral Drayson and leaked the story of the only survivor of the attack on Polneye by the Yevetha. The leak was designed to garner sympathy from the public and the Senate. It worked. [EA, BFE, TT]

Towani family

Towani, Jeremitt *See* Towani, Cindel

Towani, Mace *See* Towani, Cindel

trace-breather cartridge A device used by species who require additional gases to breathe, other than those their environment provides, it releases a bit of the necessary gas at a time. [TJP]

tracomp A high-tech compass device—which can be part of a starship's sensor array or portable—it is dedicated to getting a fix on a planet's axial and magnetic poles. A tracomp then places the ship within a spherical-coordinate lattice and locks onto any transmitting navigational beacons within range. [SME]

tractor beam A modified force field, it can immobilize and then draw in any object caught in its range. An emitting tower—a tractor beam projector—produces the beams, the strength and range of which are determined by their power source. Tractor beams help guide ships to a safe landing in spaceports and hangar bays. Salvage vessels, cargo haulers, emergency craft, and engineering teams use tractor beams to

Tractor beam

help them in their jobs. Military tractor beams are used to capture enemy vessels or hold them in place to be blown out of the skies. [SW, ESB, RJ]

Trade Spine Also known as the Corellian Trade Spine, it is located near the Ison Corridor. Bespin Motors has been highly successful in selling its cloud cars to the urbanized and overpopulated industry worlds along the Trade Spine. Admiral Daala lay in wait for targets at a hyperspace node on the far end of the Spine, where ships bound for Anoat or Bespin would have to drop into realspace to recalibrate their navigation instruments. [LC, DA, GG2]

Tragett, Bogo Team leader of excavation Team Alpha, which was assigned to Maltha Obex by the Obroan Institute of Archaeology. [TT]

Tralkpha A Mon Calamari, he was navigator aboard the *Jade's Fire*. [AC]

Tralus One of the five habitable planets in the Corellian system, it is a blue, white, and green world the same size as its sister planet Talus. Both Tralus and Talus orbit a common center of gravity where Centerpoint Station is located. Together, they are referred to as the Double Worlds, and both are ruled by the elected Federation of the Double Worlds, or Fed-Dub. Beneath the surface of Tralus is a planetary repulsor, which was used in ancient times to move the planet into its current orbit from an unknown location. When a flareup in Centerpoint Station fourteen years after the Battle of Endor caused many deaths, the survivors were relocated to Talus and Tralus. When word spread of the incident, two rebellions against Fed-Dub broke out on Tralus. A group of starfighter pilots subsequently flew to Centerpoint and claimed the station for themselves until chased off by a Bakuran task force. [AC, AS, SAC]

Trammis III Famous as the home of gigantic reptiloids, the inhabitants of the planet speak Trammic, which is related to the Old High Trammic spoken by the Toka of the Rafa system. It is also home of Trammiston chocolates. [LCM, LCS]

Trandosha Homeworld of the warlike reptilian Trandoshan species, its society is based on a strict class system. Points of interest include the Lorpfan deserts. Lanish Ran, an undercover Alliance agent, once posed as an Imperial technician in a repair facility in the Doshan city of Forak. The bounty hunter Bossk is one infamous Trandoshan. [SWAJ, TBH, GG3]

Trandoshan Large, reptilian humanoids from the planet Trandosha (or Dosha), they have supersensitive eyes that can see into the infrared range and the ability to regenerate lost limbs when they are young. They also shed their skin. Trandoshans are a warlike species who allied early with the Empire, taking Wookiees as slaves. They value hunting above all else and worship a female deity known as the Scorekeeper, who awards jagannath points to Trandoshans based on their success or failure in the hunt. When hunters wish it, they return to their homeworld and mate with a convenient clutch mother; they do not form lasting relationships. Young Trandoshans hatch from eggs. They have a difficult time manipulating delicate objects with their relatively clumsy clawed hands. The bounty hunter Bossk was a Trandoshan. [COF, TBH, GG3]

transfer register An electro-optical device, it documents the sale or trade of property and merchandise. A transfer register records the thumb-prints of buyers and sellers, officially documenting a transaction. [SWR]

transparisteel A malleable metal, it is pressed and formed into thin, transparent sheets that retain nearly all of the metal's strength and durability. Transparisteel replaces glass on starships and other structures that require both visibility and protection. [HSE]

transport, Rebel The Rebel Alliance used a number of different types of ships to supply food, ammunition, and other ordnance to its troops. These transports were converted passenger liners, small freighters, and other older ships that were prone to breakdowns. Often working in convoys, their most visible effort was the evacuation of Echo Base during the Battle of Hoth. With only a couple of X-wings and a few shots from a planetary ion cannon, the lightly armed cargo ships blasted past the Imperial blockade and saved the Rebel Alliance's vital computers and equipment.

The ships used in the escape from Hoth were Gallofree Yards Medium Transports. Only about ninety meters long, they have a cargo capacity of 19,000 metric tons. Each ship's outer hull is little more than a thick shell with an open interior filled with cargo modules. Some of the ships serve as fuel tankers for long-range missions; others have been converted to passenger or troop transport duty.

A crew of seven operates from a small, cramped pod mounted above the ship's rounded hull. The ships' hyperdrives augment their standard sublight ion drives and repulsorlift drive units for landing directly on a planet. Because they aren't combat vessels—at most they have four twin laser cannons—the Rebel transports

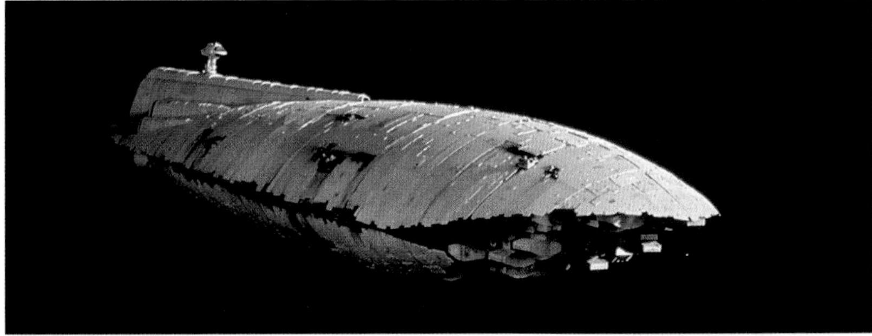

Rebel transport

make every effort to avoid Imperial entanglements. They rely mostly on starfighters for protection. [SWSB, RSB, SWVG, ESB, HESB]

Trax sector Located in the Outer Rim, it contains the planets Deysum III—site of the sector capital—and Uogo'cor and the Trax Tube—a major Outer Rim shipping lane. It was the site of a major Imperial resupply base over BissiMirus as well as a major Rebel spy network. The sector has 178 settled systems and a population of more than 500 billion. [SWAJ]

TRD An acronym that pilots jokingly use for Trench Run Disease, referring to the tactics that destroyed the first Death Star at Yavin. [BW]

treaded neutron torches (TNT) Ground vehicles, they were designed to blast through rock with their fireball-shooting cannons. Although treaded neutron torches, or TNTs, were created to open new shafts in the Kessel spice mines, they have since been used to clear jungle and forest clearings. [LCJ]

treadwell robot A multipurpose, six- or seven-limbed wheeled droid, it can be programmed to perform many forms of menial labor, including general-purpose repairs. The WED15 units are manufactured by Cybot Galactica. [SWN]

Trebela Site of a major Rebel network, it was smashed by Imperial Governor Kraxith. Most of the Rebel groups had been working independently and were not aware of the others' activities. [SWSB]

tree-botts Arboreal creatures, they are used by Rodians for meat and milk. [TMEC]

Tree of Light A mystical tree in the forest of Endor's moon, it is surrounded by a bright, beautiful glow that keeps the Night Spirit from using its powers during the day, according to Ewok legend. It is traditional for a group of young Ewoks to travel to the Tree of Light and feed it the sacred dust that rejuvenates its strength. [ETV]

Tregga An old acquaintance of Han Solo and Chewbacca, he was caught smuggling contraband and sentenced to life imprisonment in Akrit'tar's penal colony. [HSR]

Feltipern Trevagg

Treidum, Pol An Imperial officer, he was responsible for maintaining magnetic field atmosphere and security in the docking bay of the first Death Star. He was paranoid about infiltration by Rebel spies. [CCG]

Trell, Poas The executive aide to New Republic First Administrator Nanoad Engh, who urged Leia Organa Solo to buff up her public image. [BTS]

Tremayne The Imperial High Inquisitor, he sought out those who might be adept in the ways of the Force. Tremayne trained as a Jedi Knight before succumbing to the dark side of the Force. He was wounded by Jedi Corwyn Shelvay in a lightsaber duel and had to wear cybernetic reconstruction components on the right side of his face. [GG9]

Trenchant A light escort in the New Republic's Fifth Fleet, it was assigned to the blockade of Doornik-319. The *Trenchant* was destroyed during the Yevethan attack. [SOL]

Trevagg, Feltipern A male Gotal bounty hunter, he tracked Obi-Wan Kenobi to Tatooine, never found him, and never left the planet. He became a corrupt tax collector for the City Prefect of the Port of Mos Eisley. He was killed by Miiyoom Onith, a H'nemthe female, after mating with her. The killing was a common part of her species' mating ritual. [CCG, TMEC]

Trian Homeworld of the feline Trianii species, it is located far from the disputed border between the Corporate Sector and the Trianii colony worlds. The Trianii Ranger Atuarre was born on Trian. [CSSB]

Trianii An intelligent species of humanoid felines native to the planet Trian, they established many off-world colonies. The Corporate Sector Authority claimed many of the older Trianii colony worlds even before its charter over that sector of space was granted. The Trianii who lived there were forced to leave, though some were kept to labor for the Authority. [HSE]

Trianii Ranger An elite member of Trian's law enforcement legion. [HSE]

Triclops The three-eyed mutant son of Emperor Palpatine, he was banished by his father on the day of his birth and endured life in a series of Imperial insane asylums. Shock therapy and dark-side energy physically and emotionally scarred Triclops, the peaceloving son of the ultimate warlord. Nevertheless, he managed to fall in love with a nurse named Kendalina, a captured princess, who bore him a son, Ken, before she was killed. A Jedi Master spirited Ken off to be raised in the Lost City of the Jedi buried deep beneath Yavin 4.

Triclops was carted off to work in the treacherous spice mines of Kessel,

Triclops

and at one point came under the domination of another three-eyed mutant, the ruthless Trioculus, who later tried to pass himself off as the Emperor's true son to gain the throne. In his dreams, Triclops unknowingly invented weapons of destruction that were gleaned and used by the Empire. A year after the Emperor was apparently killed in the explosion of the second Death Star, the ruling Committee of Grand Moffs publicly proclaimed Trioculus as the Emperor's heir.

But Triclops managed to escape and rendezvous with Alliance leaders, who eventually discovered that he had an Imperial transplant that transmitted his thoughts to probe droids. Alliance scientists used it to send some false information and were prepared to destroy the implant. But Triclops decided he needed to be totally free, and he escaped from Alliance headquarters. He left a letter for Ken, disclosing his parentage and asking his forgiveness and trust. [LCJ, MMY, QE, PDS, SWCG]

Triitus system Located at the edge of the Corva sector in the Outer Rim, the system contains the planet Tuulab. [SWAJ]

Trillka A repair-shop operator on the planet Kalarba, she fixed the damaged face plate of C-3PO in such a way that the gentle protocol droid was mistaken for the assassin droid C-3PX. Later, when the criminal Greck tried to blow up Hosk Station, Trillka helped foil the scheme by working to undo the sabotage on the power core. [D]

Trioculus The Supreme Slavelord of the spice mines of Kessel, he came forward after the Emperor's death to claim that he was Palpatine's banished son. Trioculus was a handsome human with a third eye in his forehead. Palpatine's real son, the mutant Triclops, had a third eye in the back of his head. Trioculus had the support of the Committee of Grand Moffs, but he was revealed to be an impostor and liar. [GDV, ZHR, MMY, PDS]

Triumph One of two Imperial Star Destroyers heavily damaged during the Alliance conquest of Coruscant. If not for the tractor beams of the *Mon Remonda*, the *Triumph* would have fallen into the planet's atmosphere and been destroyed. [WG]

Trodd, Puggles A meter-tall rodent, he makes his living as a bounty hunter and often teams up with Jodo Kast and Zardra to complete high-paying contracts. Puggles Trodd feared the two, but knew that together they could earn even more credits than if they worked alone. Trodd, a Lasat, is pessimistic, unpleasant, and brooding. He loves to watch anything explode. [TM, SWAJ]

Trogan A planet located in the system of the same name, it features the famous Whistler's Whirlpool tapcafe on the coast of its most densely populated continent. At the center of the Whirlpool is the Drinking Cup, a natural rock bowl that fills with seawater six times a day due to Trogan's strong tides. The Whirlpool was a disappointing failure as a tourist attraction and has since been abandoned. Talon Karrde arranged a smugglers' meeting at the Whirlpool, which was attacked by soldiers from the nearby Imperial garrison. [DFR, LC]

Tro'Har A planet located in the Elrood sector, it is near the planet Coyn. An ice world, it is the fifth and outermost planet in the Coyn system. [SWAJ, POG]

Trommer, Ranulf An ace Imperial pilot, he was sent to the planet M'Haeli by Grand Moff Lynch to spy on Governor Grigor. When his mission was compromised, he fell in love with Mora, leader of the M'Haeli Rebels. Ranulf's sympathies shifted, finally causing him to throw in his lot with the Rebels. [ROC]

trompa A massive, three-meter high bipedal creature with long arms and sharp-clawed paws, it is ferocious and deadly. A trompa's thick fur covers its powerful muscles, and two spiral horns curve out of its head. [GQ]

Trosh One of the many planets where the Empire enslaved the native population, claiming to be protecting the rights of its inhabitants. [POT]

Troujow, Hasti A young, beautiful former mining camp laborer, she helped Han Solo and Badure reach the secret treasure vaults of Xim the Despot. The expedition, aided by Hasti Troujow, took place shortly before Solo became involved in the Galactic Civil War. [HLL]

Troujow, Lanni The sister of Hasti Troujow, she was killed after she discovered a log recorder from the legendary starship *Queen of Ranroon*. With the information stored in the recorder, Hasti was able to locate the ancient ship's lost treasures. Han Solo and Chewbacca the Wookiee helped her. [HLL]

Truchong, Brindy A female Corellian smuggler, she was on Tatooine shortly before the Battle of Yavin trying to find a quick means to provide supplies to the Rebellion. [CCG]

Trulalis A rich green planet of grasslands, forests, and oceans beneath a thick cloud layer, this unspoiled world is covered with windswept fields separated by stretches of wilderness and dotted with several small settlements. Trulalis has been set aside as a low-tech world by the Issori, and most of its inhabitants shun all forms of higher technology, using miniature banthas as beasts of burden, for instance. Nestled within a steep mountain range is the gated community of Kovit, a farming settlement dominated by a towering, buttressed theater of white limestone.

During the Golden Age of the Old Republic, Trulalis was a thriving cultural center boasting one of the finest liberal arts schools in the galaxy. Today, only a few scattered remnants testify to its former glory. Sometime before the Battle of Endor, the Dark Jedi Adalric Brandl hired the smuggler Thaddeus Ross to bring him to Trulalis, Brandl's former home. [SWAJ]

Trulalis system Located just one standard hour's hyperspace travel from Najiba, it contains the planets Issor, Cadezia, and Trulalis. [SWAJ]

Tsayv, Liat A Sullustan, he is a crew member aboard Mirax Terrik's *Pulsar Skate*. [RS]

Tschel, Lieutenant A young officer aboard the Imperial Star Destroyer *Chimaera*, he served as a member of the bridge crew under Captain Pellaeon and Grand Admiral Thrawn

Tusken Raider

during Thrawn's campaign to destroy the New Republic five years after the Battle of Endor. [HE, DFR, LC]

tsils Crystal chimney formations on Nam Chorios, they were named by the planet's Oldtimers. Small ground electrical storms that last five to ten minutes emerge from the tsils. Oldtimers are unaffected by the storms; Newcomers are sick for a day and a half if any of the charges pass through them. The tsils are sentient and are the source of the Force-sensitivity on Nam Chorios. The tsils use images in beings' heads to try to communicate, causing the Theran Listeners to hear voices. These living crystals have inhabited Nam Chorios since it was first formed. They invaded the dreams of the prophet Theras, instructing him and his followers to bar any ship large enough to have heavy shielding from landing on or leaving Nam Chorios. Their command prevented the insectoid drochs carrying the Death Seed plague from spreading from Nam Chorios throughout the galaxy. [POT]

Tsoss Beacon An automated beacon station built mainly by droids and suicide crews, it is located on a desolate planetoid in the Deep Galactic Core. The region is inundated with deadly radioactive storms and solar flares. Despite its shielding, the station was abandoned by its last human personnel several years prior to the Battle of Yavin. It was at Tsoss Beacon that Imperial Admiral Daala met with and, after futile negotiations, murdered the remaining Imperial warlords eight years after the Battle of Endor. [DS]

Tuhns, Geoff A tall, big-boned Imperial recruit with a head of flaming red hair, he was in training with stormtrooper Davin Felth. [TMEC]

Tulgah A rare species, these troll-like beings on the forest moon of Endor have an extensive knowledge of magic. Some Tulgah are great healers. Others, such as Morag, have twisted their knowledge to evil and wield powers of black magic. [ETV]

Tumanian pressure-ruby An extremely rare stone. Even a small example of this often bloodred gem could easily be worth several million credits. [SOTE]

tumnor A flying creature, it lives in the upper atmosphere of Da Soocha and its moons. These predators stalk Ixlls, hunting the small and intelligent flying species as a source of food. [DE]

Tund Located in the remote Tund system, this legendary but hidden world was home to the mysterious and ancient Sorcerers of Tund. No one is sure what species the sorcerers were, because they were always covered in heavy gray robes. Years ago, Rokur Gepta, a snaillike Croke, infiltrated the Sorcerers of Tund and learned their secrets. He then murdered his teachers and transformed the planet Tund, once an attractive world of prairies, forests, and jungles, into a blasted, sterile wasteland. The world's deadly radiation was held back in some places by force fields, so Gepta could land his ship on Tund safely. [LCM, LCF, LCS]

Tungra sector Located near the Bruanii and Javin sectors, it was home to a deep-space Mugaari cargo-loading depot. The depot in the Tungra sector was destroyed by the Empire following the Battle of Hoth. [TSC]

Tuomi, Senator A New Republic Senator from Drannik, he opposed Chief of State Leia Organa Solo during the Yevethan crisis. Senator Tuomi represents Bosch and four other planets, constituting one billion citizens. He introduced a floor challenge to Leia's credentials by claiming that Alderaan's destruction had disqualified her from Senate membership because there was no legitimate territory for her to represent. [SOL]

turbolaser A weapon that fires supercharged bolts of energy, it is usually positioned on the deck of a capital ship or as part of a surface-based defense installation. Turbolasers are more powerful than regular laser cannons, discharging hotter and more concentrated energy bolts. The weapons require constant temperature regulation from built-in cryogenic cooling units. [SW, SWSB]

turbo-skis Rocket-powered skis, they are used for sport and for rapid travel across ice regions. [DA]

Turkana This planet in the Hadar sector is circled by multiple moons. Prior to the Battle of Yavin at least five Imperial Star Destroyers discovered the Alliance fleet in orbit around the world. The Imperials engaged the Rebel fleet at Turkana but suffered severe losses. Shocked by this development, Emperor Palpatine ordered the implementation of Operation Strike Fear to crush the Rebellion. Later, Alliance pilot Keyan Farlander flew his first mission near Turkana. [FP]

Tusken Raiders A nomadic and often violent species, the Sand People of the planet Tatooine are as fierce and discomforting as their harsh desert environment. For these Tusken Raiders, even their appearance—born of necessity—gives them a terrifying mien. Wrapped in gauzy robes and strips of cloth from head to foot, they top off their outfits with breathing masks and goggles to protect their eyes. Their frightening visages make their acts of banditry easier.

The Sand People are easily intoxicated by simple sugar water, and are most dangerous during their adolescent years, when they must survive rigorous rites of passage, such as hunting the deadly krayt dragons, to become adults. Because there is no written Tusken language, the storyteller is the most respected member of Tusken communities. It is considered blasphemy—and grounds for instant death—to speak a single word of the sacred stories incorrectly. Many

Tusken Raider clans of twenty to thirty individuals return annually to their traditional encampments in the Needles, a section of the Jundland Wastes, to wait out the dangerous sandstorm season.

The Sand People possess an almost symbiotic relationship with their bantha mounts. A member who has lost his bantha is considered incomplete and an outcast among his people. Likewise, when a Raider dies, his mount engages in a frenzy that is usually suicidal, and the creature is turned loose in the desert to survive or die on its own. Tuskens maintain an uneasy and frequently shattered peace with the moisture farmers who also populate Tatooine. They attack full settlements from time to time, using their traditional weapon, the gaderffii (or gaffi) stick, a kind of double-edged ax. Targets of opportunity also include individuals or small parties roaming the desert, such as Jawa scavenging parties. Sand People subsist on a difficult-to-digest fruit, the hubba gourd, and tightly guard their hidden desert oases, the main source of their water.

Sand People rarely distinguish between their sexes, keeping records of male and female that are consulted only to arrange marriage. After bonding ceremonies in which the male and female mix their blood, as do their banthas, they adjourn to the privacy of their tent, and are allowed to unwrap themselves. This is when they see each other's faces for the first time. In any circumstance other than that, seeing another Raider's face is grounds for a duel to the death. [ISWU, SWCG]

Tuulab The second planet in the Tritus system of the Corva sector, it is a peaceful world of gentle plains blessed with abundant natural resources. It is home to a colony of 6,000 people who fled to Tuulab over the years to escape persecution under the Empire's New Order. The rural Tuulabi colonists have no form of organized government. The Gotal crime lord Mahk'khar built a three-story palace on Tuulab in an uninhabited area on the west coast of the planet's northern continent. [SWAJ]

Tuyay The Chief Operating Officer of Ororo Transportation, he was a competitor to Prince Xizor's XTS transportation company, which was a front for Xizor's Black Sun criminal syndicate. Tuyay was a fitness buff and bulged with muscles under his expensively tailored zeyd-cloth suits. Xizor's top aide, Guri, choked Tuyay, then put a blaster up to his left eyeball and killed him. [SOTE]

Twi'lek

twi'janii The Rylothan grant of hospitality to travelers. When invoked, the people of Ryloth are obliged to offer their guests the pleasures of rest and entertainment. [BW]

Twi'lek A species of humanoids with twin head tentacles, they are sometimes dismissively called worm-heads. The dual taillike appendages called lekku grow out of the backs of their heads and can be used to communicate with other Twi'lek. Native to the planet Ryloth in the Outer Rim, they speak a language that combines verbal components with subtle head-tail movements. Twi'leks cultivate edible molds and fungi and raise cowlike rycrits for their meat and hides.

The species is generally nonviolent, preferring to use cunning instead of force. Twi'leks live in vast city complexes, located on their planet's dark side to escape the heat of the planet's surface. Each complex is autonomous, governed by a group of five Twi'leks—the head clan—who jointly oversee production, trade, and other daily endeavors. The leaders are born into their positions and serve until one of them dies. Then the others are banished to die in the Bright Lands of the planet's light side, making room for the next generation of leaders.

Twi'leks depend on neighboring systems, pirates, smugglers, and merchants for their contact with the rest of the galaxy. They attract these ships with their chief export, ryll, a mineral with legitimate medicinal uses that has also become a popular and dangerously addictive recreational drug, particularly in the Corporate Sector. Near defenseless, Twi'leks also face constant raids by off-world slavers. Bib Fortuna, top aide to criminal kingpin Jabba the Hutt, was a Twi'lek, as was Oola, the dancing girl killed by Jabba. [SWSB]

Twi'lek A dry drink with a piquant bouquet and slightly sweet nose, it is ingested in abundance on Tatooine. [TBH]

twin-pod cloud car Upper-atmosphere craft popularized on Bespin, they have come into widespread use throughout the galaxy. Twin-pod cloud cars are a step up from traditional airspeeders, with top speeds of around 1,500 kilometers an hour and a top altitude of nearly low orbital height. While the cars often are used for patrol and reconnaissance duty,

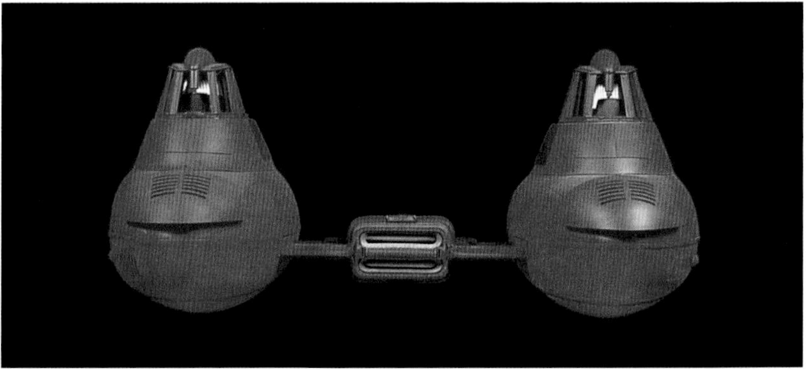

Twin-pod cloud car

Tyrann

civilians employ them as pleasure craft for long-range sightseeing and travel.

Cloud cars use ion engines for their main drives. Repulsorlift drives enhance handling along with small jets, maneuvering flaps, control vanes, and rudders. Although pressurized for high-altitude flight, they don't have life-support systems. They range in size from one- and two-passenger vehicles to large pleasure craft and cargo barges.

They can be used for personal transport, as air taxis, or as military patrol ships. Cloud City's Wing Guard pilots use Bespin Motors' Storm IV twin-pod cloud cars for patrol duty around the majestic floating city. These cars have been fitted with a blaster cannon on the outside of each pod. The hull has several clearly indicated fixture points for extra armor plating and the car's computer system is specifically designed to accept new weapons. [SWSB, ESB, MTS]

Twins Heavily modified TIE bomber variants, they belong in a class of ships known as Uglies. The Quadanium Solar panels at the front are cut diagonally to provide the pilots with peripheral vision, an essential change. The bomb delivery system has been removed and replaced with a concussion missile launching system, with two lasers complementing the weapons array. Shield generators and a hyperdrive motivator have been added to complete the package. [BW]

Tydirium An Imperial *Lambda*-class shuttle, it was used by Han Solo's Rebel strike team to covertly reach Endor's forest moon. The shuttle had been captured prior to the mission. [RJ]

Tyed Kant Homeworld of the headquarters of two corporations that supplied foodstuffs to the Empire: Nebula Consumables and Imperial Meats and Produce. This habitable gas giant with a "life zone" is the only planet in the Kantel system. It is home to giant floating creatures called iagoin. [SWAJ]

Tymmo An attractive young man whose real name was Dack, he was the consort of the Duchess Mistal of Dargul. He got the position by hacking into the central computer in Palace Dargul and sabotaging files of the other applicants. When he discovered that the Duchess was a relentless partner and that she mated for life, Tymmo fled to the planet Umgul. There, Lando Calrissian, C-3PO, and R2-D2 caught him cheating at the blob races. Rather than face death for cheating, Tymmo was returned to the Duchess. [JS]

Tynna Homeworld of the otterlike Tynnans, it is a resource-rich planet that has long been a member of the galactic community. Corporations operating under the Old Republic developed Tynna's resources but kept its natural beauty intact. The furcovered Tynnans have poor eyesight; a layer of fat beneath their skins protects them from the cold waters of their planet. Tynnan society is entirely state-run: All citizens have free access to housing, food, education, and other benefits.

For thousands of years the members of the Tynnan government have been selected by lottery. Since any citizen can be chosen to serve, the pragmatic and sensible Tynnans always stay informed on important issues. Tynnans form one of the most affluent societies in the galaxy, and they travel widely. The Empire tried to increase its control over the planet to generate greater revenue. Odumin, the Corporate Sector Authority territorial manager (also known as Spray, the skip-tracer), was a native of Tynna, and his success has inspired other Tynnans to take more active roles in galactic affairs. [HSR, CSSB]

Tzizvvt

Tyrann The Supreme Master of the Serpent Masters. [CSW]

Tyrant An Imperial Star Destroyer under the command of Captain Lennox. The starship was assigned to Admiral Ozzel's Death Squadron. Along with other starships, it attempted to capture Rebel Alliance craft fleeing the Hoth system. [CCG]

Tyrius system The system that contains the planet Rodia, homeworld of the species called Rodians. [GG4]

Tzizvvt A male Brizzit from the planet Jandoon, he hid from Imperials on Tatooine, hoping to procure

Tyrant

passage to the Outer Rim before the Empire found him. [CCG]

U2-C1 A blue housekeeping droid in the palace of Jabba the Hutt, he warned the Whiphid J'Quille of a plot against him. [TJP]

U-33 A class of orbital space boats, they are sublightspeed loadlifters that shuttle personnel and material between planetary spaceports and orbiting space stations. The U-33 is an older model and has mostly been replaced by a number of newer, more efficient classes, although some U-33s can still be found working in frontier systems, on developing worlds, and as military training ships. [HLL]

U-3PO A protocol droid, it served in the House of Alderaan's diplomatic corps. Imperials had secretly captured U-3PO and then altered his programming for espionage, making him an unwitting spy for the Empire. It was U-3PO, aboard the *Tantive IV*, who signaled the arrival of the ship carrying Princess Leia Organa above Tatooine. The Imperial Star Destroyer *Devastator* then captured the ship. [SWR, CCG]

Ubese The Ubese species comes from the Uba system. Their planet was ravaged by a preemptive strike by the Old Republic, which feared the aggressive weapons development program of the Ubese. The bounty hunter Boushh was a Ubese, and Princess Leia disguised herself as Boushh at least twice, including when she brought the prisoner Chewbacca to the court of Jabba the Hutt as part of a plan to rescue Han Solo. It is also the name of the language spoken by the Ubese species, recognizable by its metallic sounds. [RJ, TJP]

U-3PO

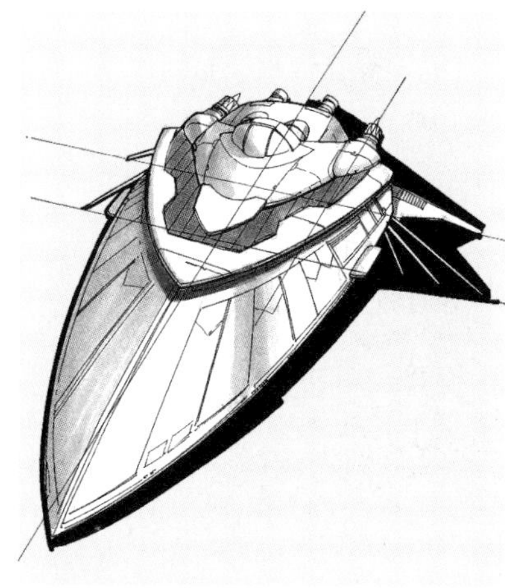

Ubrikkian space yacht

Ubiqtorate The unit of Imperial Intelligence that oversaw all of the agency's activities at the highest levels, the Ubiqtorate formulated strategies and assigned goals to the other Intelligence divisions. Ubiqtorate members were anonymous, often unknown even to the unit's subordinates. [ISB]

Ubrikkian A manufacturer of vehicles, including the sail barge of Jabba the Hutt and the Ubrikkian HAVr A9 floating fortress, an Imperial weapons platform with two heavy blaster cannons. [TJP, TMEC, SWSB]

Ucce, Lady A slave trader, she was a follower of Lord Hethrir. [CS]

Udine system An asteroid-packed system, it is next to the region called Keller's Void. Pirates sometimes bring asteroids from the Udine system to the Void to create mass shadows and force unsuspecting ships out of hyperspace. [SWAJ]

uglies A nickname that spacers give to hybrid fighters cobbled together from the salvageable parts of other craft. Uglies are frequently used by smugglers and pirates. They are a specialty of some less-than-reputable Corellian shipyards, but they do present a problem in the aftermarket because there are no specs, plans, or complete sets of manuals available. [BW, AC]

Ugmush, Captain The female Gamorrean captain of the *Zicreex*, the ship that C-3PO and R2-D2 used to escape from the planet Nim Drovis. [POT]

Ugnaught Small, hardworking, and loyal, these porcine humanoids live and work on Bespin's Cloud City, which they helped to build. They can usually be found in the Tibanna gas-processing plants or as general laborers in the bowels of the floating city. Originally from the planet Gentes in the remote Anoat system, Ugnaughts lived in primitive colonies on the planet's less-than-hospitable surface until most left the planet to work at Cloud City. [ESB, MTS]

Ugor A protozoan species, they worship garbage and treat all junk as holy relics. Ugors come from a star system they call Paradise; in reality, it is a junk-filled asteroid field. Ugors had an exclusive contract with the Empire to collect garbage jettisoned from Imperial fleet ships and store it in their garbage-dump systems. Ugors grow to about one meter in diameter and can grow up to thirty pseudopodia at a time, some of which contain visual and other sensory organlike growths that allow communication. Ugors move by oozing from place to place or by controlling specialized

Ugnaught

environ suits. Gambling and cheating are an acceptable part of their society. Other scavenger species such as the Squib are considered business rivals to be crushed and eliminated. [SH, GG4]

Ukio Located in the Abrion sector and the Ukio system, it is one of the top five food-producing planets in the New Republic and was the target of an attack by Grand Admiral Thrawn. A representative of the Ukian Overliege surrendered the planet after Thrawn seemed to demonstrate the ability to fire directly through Ukio's planetary shields, although the attack was actually an elaborate illusion. The smuggler Samuel Tomas Gillespee had bought a plot of land on Ukio, which he lost when the Empire took control. [LC]

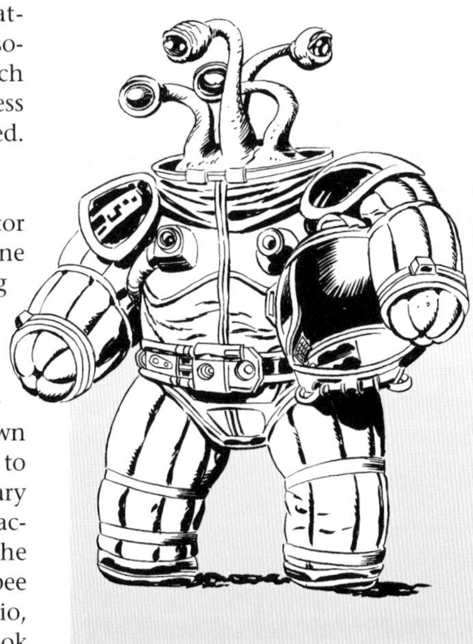

Ugor

Umboo A colony in the Roon star system, it is the site of a light station that guides ships through the hazardous dust cloud that permeates the system. Umboo was the home of Auren Yomm, a talented young athlete whom R2-D2 and C-3PO met during the early days of the Empire. [DTV]

Umgul A cool, mist-covered world in the same system as Dargul, it is a center for gambling and sports attractions. Umgul's spaceport is in Umgul City, built on the limestone banks of a wide river that attracts numerous pleasure barges. The city is covered with signs and attractions beckoning visitors; cheating in the gambling establishments is punishable by death. Tourists visit Umgul mainly to see the famous Umgullian blob races, held in an arena carved from rock and ringed with powerful fans to blow away the thick fog. The protoplasmic blobs, bred for racing, are kept in stables and monitored by the Umgullian Racing Commission for any signs of illegal enhancement. Lando Calrissian visited Umgul while searching for possible Jedi candidates for Luke Skywalker's academy. [JS]

Umwak The real name of the Dulok shaman, he often travels in disguise to trick the Ewoks on Endor's forest moon. [ETV]

Unit Zed Head of automated security on Hosk Station, it was a level-one droid. When criminal Olag Greck attempted to steal an ash ore shipment by sabotaging the station's power core, Unit Zed aided R2-D2 and C-3PO in aborting Greck's scheme, but a wrecking droid named Grozbok managed to chew up one of Unit Zed's legs during the tussle. Pursuing Greck to Nar Shaddaa, Unit Zed was destroyed by Jace Forno. [D]

Unknown Regions A name given to parts of the galaxy that remain unexplored. Certain regions within the borders of known space are also called Unknown because they don't appear on official astrogation charts. Some of these places are known to the Empire, the Rebellion, or groups on the fringe of society, but remain hidden from the galaxy at large. [HE, HESB, SWRPG2]

Uogo'cor A planet in the Trax sector near the Trax Tube, a major Outer Rim shipping lane. Outlaw stations on Uogo'cor will service any ship, including those belonging to pirates and wanted criminals. The harsh world is known for its long, frigid winters and short, intensely hot summers. It is homeworld of the Uogo, whose name for their planet translates as "home of the suffering ones." [SWAJ]

Uplands, the A pastoral region on the continent of Thon on the now-destroyed planet of Alderaan. [SWR]

urchin Also called a dandelion warrior, it is a strange, plantlike creature with heads that resemble dandelion tufts but that are actually spiked balls that can hurl sharp quills. Urchins with peculiar starred patterns are used by the Ewoks of Endor's forest moon for medicinal applications. [ETV]

Urdur A hideout world for Doc's band of outlaw techs operating in and around Corporate Sector space. Urdur, with its biting-cold winds, was the planet where Han Solo and his companions rested following their escape from Mytus VII. [HSE]

UroRRuR'R'R A leader of a Tusken Raider tribe, he is a skilled hunter and marksman and unafraid of machines. He raids moisture farms for water and roams the Jundland Wastes in search of unwary travelers. [CCG]

Ut A planet in the Hapes Cluster. As part of a series of gifts from Hapes to the New Republic, Ut sent a woman to sing a beautiful song. [CPL]

Uteens An eellike species, it is a member of the New Republic. [NR]

Utharis A world inhabited by Tarrack, it is more than 200 light-years from the Koornacht Cluster. Its main city is Taldaak Station, a full-service port. Moving slidewalks are a major means of transportation. Communications are handled by the Utharis GridLink, which offers access to two local newsgrids: Eye-On-U and Tarrack Today! The Creed is a Tarrack

UroRRuR'R'R

cult based on joy and service, and its members bear tattoos on their foreheads and cheeks. The New Republic Defense Fleet operates a small listening post in Taldaak. Twelve years after the Battle of Endor, Luke Skywalker and Akanah Norand Pell flew their ship, the Verpine Adventurer *Mud Sloth*, from Atzerri to Utharis, intending to eventually reach J't'p'tan in the Koornacht Cluster. When they arrived, they were forced to repair their ship. Luke gained access to the New Republic listening post to get information on events in Koornacht. Animal life includes the jack-a-dale and the black-winged touret. [SOL, TT]

Uul-Rha-Shan The reptilian bodyguard of Viceprex Hirken of the Corporate Sector Authority, he was a member of the Tiss'shar species. Tiss'shar are bipedal, with red-and-white patterned green scales, black eyes, a darting tongue, and sinister-looking fangs. [HSE]

Uvena system A system containing a group of planets ruled by the species called Shistavanen Wolfmen. The Wolfmen are renowned for their hunting and tracking skills, and many were employed by the Empire as scouts. Riv Shiel, a onetime Shistavanen member of the Alliance's famed Rogue Squadron, was a native of Uvena III. [MTS, RS]

uvide wheel A gambling device. [TMEC]

V-35 An older model courier landspeeder, it was manufactured by SoroSuub. It has a cargo compartment and enclosed seating. [SWVG, CCG]

Vader, Darth Though he was the personification of the evil and fear that Emperor Palpatine used to rule the galaxy, Vader proved in the end that the dark side of the Force had not snuffed out the light-side good that once filled his spirit.

Born Anakin Skywalker, he was a spirited and talented child who exhibited strong Force potential. At

V-35

an early age he became an expert pilot and was one of the warriors of the Clone Wars, along with his mentor, the general and Jedi Obi-Wan Kenobi. Obi-Wan trained him in the use of the Force, but Skywalker was impatient with the Jedi's painstaking methods. Sensing this, and noting a void in the youth's spirit, Senator Palpatine offered him a quicker path to power—that of the dark side.

By giving in to his anger, fear, and aggression, Skywalker let himself be embraced by the rapturous power of the dark side and was transformed into another individual. Kenobi sensed too late what was happening, and when he tried to draw his young friend back to the light side, they engaged in a terrible duel that led to Skywalker's fall into a molten pit. The shell of a man who emerged was Darth Vader, whose shattered body was sustained by specially built armor and a breathing apparatus. When Kenobi learned that Skywalker/Vader had survived the battle, he spirited away the Dark Sider's newborn twins.

As a new Dark Lord of the Sith, Vader was key in helping the self-proclaimed Emperor Palpatine hunt down and exterminate nearly all the remaining Jedi Knights. He commanded by terror, thinking nothing of using the Force to choke an Imperial officer who had displeased him. As the Rebellion grew into a significant threat, the Emperor put Vader in charge of an Imperial task force empowered to hunt down the leaders of the Rebel Alliance. Vader's mission became even more imperative when Rebel spies stole the plans for the Death Star battle station.

In pursuit of his goal, Vader intercepted and imprisoned the senator from Alderaan, Princess Leia Organa. Her successful rescue by Luke Skywalker and Han Solo brought Vader into contact once more with his onetime mentor, Kenobi. In another fateful lightsaber duel, Kenobi allowed himself to be struck down by his former student, and his corporeal body disappeared as he became one with the Force.

Armed with the stolen plans, Rebel starfighters began to attack the Death Star. Vader boarded his prototype TIE interceptor and proceeded to join the battle. While TIE fighters handled most of the attackers, Vader concentrated on a lone X-wing that was making a run down the Death Star trench. As he targeted the Rebel ship, he felt the Force emanating from it strongly.

Then, seemingly from nowhere, a blast caught Vader's ship and sent it spinning into space as Luke Skywalker's proton torpedoes found their mark and destroyed the Death Star.

Vader survived the battle and a further encounter with the Force wielder on the planet Mimban, where Vader lost his right arm in a lightsaber duel. But he soon discovered that the Rebel who had blown up the Imperial battle station and who had severed his arm on Mimban was a son he never knew he had. And from that day forth both the Emperor and Vader became determined to convert young Skywalker to the dark side, but Vader had his own agenda. He wanted to rule the galaxy with Luke at his side as father and son.

Using Imperial probe droids, Vader eventually tracked down the Alliance's new base on Hoth, but a commander's ineptitude made it possible for much of the Rebel force to escape. Vader hired bounty hunters to help track down and capture Princess Leia and Han Solo, and he used them as bait to lure young Skywalker to Cloud City on Bespin. There, during a ferocious lightsaber battle, Vader revealed himself to Luke, telling him "I am your father." He tried to recruit him to the dark side. Young Skywalker, who preferred death to treachery, let himself be sucked down the city's main exhaust tube. He was soon rescued by Leia Organa and Lando Calrissian.

Over the next few months, Vader had to contend with another threat: Prince Xizor, head of the Black Sun criminal organization, who had become a close confidant of the Emperor. Xizor attempted to usurp Vader's place in the Imperial hierarchy and kill young Skywalker, but he failed at both endeavors.

In the end, Luke surrendered himself to Vader's troops on the forest moon of Endor, where the Emperor had set an elaborate trap for the Alliance, centered around the second Death Star.

Brought before the Emperor and Vader, Luke appealed to his father, trying to reach the bit of Anakin he was sure remained inside. Palpatine goaded the boy about the fate of his friends until Luke attacked. Vader defended the Emperor and he and Luke were locked in mortal combat. Then, gaining control of his anger, Luke stopped fighting. But a probing Vader discovered the secret of Luke's twin sister, Leia. Luke lost control and attacked Vader again, finally beating him down and chopping off his hand with his lightsaber.

Luke then confronted the Emperor, who attacked him with blast after blast of blue Force lightning. He prepared to kill young Skywalker. Suddenly, Vader grabbed the Emperor, lifted him into the air, and threw him down the shaft of the battle station's power core. Vader knew he was dying and asked his son to remove his helmet so he could look at Luke with his own eyes for the first—and last—time. Luke, he said with his final breaths, was right. He still did have some good buried deep inside his dark spirit.

Darth Vader

Anakin's worn-out body then became one with the Force. Luke took his mask and black vestments to the forest moon of Endor and burned them on a pyre. And then, before his eyes, appeared a vision: Obi-Wan Kenobi, Jedi Master Yoda, and Anakin Skywalker—all luminous beings in the light side of the Force. [SW, ESB, RJ, SME, SOTE]

Vagnerian canapé A sweet canapé, it was favored by Leia Organa Solo and occasionally served in the New Republic Senate chambers. [NR]

Vakil, Nrin A male Quarren member of Rogue Squadron, he has a predilection for clinging to the past. Although Nrin Vakil does tend to anticipate the worst in any situation, he does not whine. Instead he accepts things with a good-natured fatalism that forms the basis of his sense of humor. He loves X-wings with a passion and takes great delight in defending them. Vakil is unfailingly brave. Far from fearless, he embraces his fears and pushes on through them, but he shies away from praise. [XW]

Valarian, Lady A large, heavy biped, her body covered with long golden and white fur, she is an imposing Whiphid crime lord. Lady Valarian's most prominent feature are her large tusks, which jut out of her lower jaw. She paints them and often wears a gold ring in the left one. She constantly changes the tint of her mane, which curls down the sides of her long-snouted face.

Valarian, the daughter of two gangsters, comes from the bitterly cold planet Toola. Her own criminal career started when she was very young. She eventually found her way to Tatooine, where she bought a battered old cargo hauler called *The Lucky Despot*, which had been refitted as a luxury hotel and then abandoned.

Lady Valarian

Tatooine's crime lord, Jabba the Hutt, wasn't pleased with the competition that he knew she would bring, but they eventually reached a truce even though they continued to spy on each other. She continually plotted to kill or otherwise dispose of the Hutt, although she was cautious, fearing retribution.

Valarian employs a large network of gambling cheats, smugglers, and other criminals to carry out her various schemes. Her wedding day ended in disaster when her mate agreed to accept a job from Jabba (to find Han Solo) and she expressed her unhappiness in the most murderous of terms. After Princess Leia Organa and Luke Skywalker polished off Jabba, Valarian set out to take over much of his empire. [GG7, TJP, SWCG]

Valdez, Shawn A charismatic leader of the Rebel Alliance, he was also an experienced evacuation officer. Shawn Valdez played a major role in the near-miraculous evacuation of the Alliance's Echo Base on the planet Hoth during a withering attack by the Empire. Also a poet and musician, Valdez had been well-trained to evacuate Rebel installations with maximum efficiency. [CCG]

Valiant This Alderaanian *Thranta*-class War Cruiser was one of three ships modified with robotic controls and slaved to accept commands from *Another Chance*, a huge armory ship bearing all the weapons banned from Alderaan but kept in readiness to return and be used in an emergency. The *Valiant* and its companions defended *Another Chance* from pirates and smugglers as it wandered through the galaxy. When a malfunction separated the *Valiant* from the rest of the convoy, it returned to its point of origin, by then the Graveyard of Alderaan. It was waiting there among the asteroids when Rogue Squadron arrived to begin a cargo transfer from Talon Karrde's freighters. The transfer was actually an ambush set up by Ysanne Isard.

As the battle raged, Tycho Celchu's X-wing received a strange signal from the Graveyard. Because Tycho's fighter was using an Alderaanian code, the *Valiant* assumed it was an Alderaanian war frigate. The ship joined in the battle, following Tycho's lead, and turned the tide of the conflict. The *Valiant* was taken back to Rogue Squadron's base at Yag'Dhul to be refitted for use by the New Republic. Aril Nunb was given command of the ship and the droid Emtrey was assigned to help her work out the robotic controls. The ship was later sent to the planet Thyferra to attack the Super Star Destroyer *Lusankya*, where it was an invaluable asset. [BW]

Valley of Royalty A site on the planet Duro, it is famous for its massive monuments to ancient rulers, including Queen Rana. [MMY]

Valley of the Wind An area on the planet Tatooine, it is located between two deserts: one high and cool, the other low and hot. Twice daily, fierce winds blow through the area, resulting in deadly sandstorms that the locals refer to as the Teeth of Tatooine. [TBH]

Vallusk Cluster The region where Admiral Ackbar attacked the Imperial fleet to create a diversion for the Alliance force evacuating the base at Yavin 4. [CSW]

Valorous An Imperial Star Destroyer, it was captured in a Yevethan raid, renamed *Devotion*, and made a part of strongman Nil Spaar's Black Eleven Fleet. Its captain was Jip Toorr. [BTS]

Valrar Located in the Glythe sector, the planet is the site of an Imperial base. The Noghri Khabarakh was scheduled to be reassigned there following his return from a failed commando mission to Kashyyyk. Valrar was also the reported port of origin for smuggler Talon Karrde's ship when his group visited Bilbringi, and the world was the destination of the Star Galleon *Draklor* after it unloaded Jedi clone Joruus C'baoth on the planet Wayland. [DFR, LC]

Vander, Jon Nicknamed Dutch, he was the male human leader of Y-wing Gold Squadron during the attack on the first Death Star. He had previously led a squadron at Renforra base, and he proudly wore the emblem of Specter Squadron on his helmet. Jon Vander was killed during the Battle of Yavin. [CCG]

Vanguard A New Republic gunship under the command of Captain Inadi, it was destroyed at ILC-905, the former Imperial orbiting shipyard taken over by the Yevetha. [TT]

Vanicus, Captain A captain in the Republic fleet some 4,000 years before the Galactic Civil War, he was in charge of the command ship *Reliance* during the battle with the dark-side Krath sect at Koros Major. [DLS, TSW]

vaporator This device gathers water on arid planets such as hot, dry

Vaporator

Tatooine, where it has given rise to the profession of moisture farmer. Standing three to five meters tall, vaporators consist of multiple refrigerated cylinders. When the hot wind blows through the open tubes, any moisture present condenses on the chilled metal surfaces and drips down into small catch basins buried beneath each unit. These in turn may be connected to larger underground tanks where the water is stored for later consumption or sale. On backwater planets such as Tatooine, most of the vaporators are programmed in the somewhat archaic binary language. [SW, ISWU]

Varl Original homeworld of the Hutts, it is a barren planet orbiting the white dwarf Ardos. Cyax is the brightest star that can be seen in Varl's night sky, and it features prominently in early Hutt legend. According to other Hutt myths, the planet Varl was once a beautiful world of green forests circling the twin stars Ardos and Evona. Evona was drawn into a black hole, causing the destruction of many planets in the system, the ruin of Varl, and the transformation of Ardos into a white dwarf. Because there are many inconsistencies in the stories, the most plausible explanation for the devastation of Varl is that the Hutts destroyed it themselves in an ancient civil war. The Hutts have since relocated to Nal Hutta in the Y'Toub system. [GG4, DESB]

varmigio This mineral is necessary in trace amounts to make most hyperdrive cores operable. [SWAJ]

Varn An aquatic planet, it is the subject of the holofeature *Varn, World of Water*. Aquatic life on the planet includes large lossors and packs of cheeb, while Varn's population of amphiboid fishers and ocean farmers inhabit its archipelagoes.

Varn is also the name of the chief scout for Tyrann, Supreme Master of the Serpent Masters. [HSR, GW]

Varonat Located in the backwater Ison Corridor, it is an isolated, sparsely populated world of jungles, plains, and mountains. A few thousand colonists live in two main settlements: Tropis-on-Varonat, among the pale yellow trees of the Great

Jungle, and Edgefields-on-Varonat, on the wide plains at the jungle's edge. About 50,000 Morodins—intelligent, fifteen-meter-long lizard-slugs—inhabit the Great Jungle. The Morodins' bodies produce a nutrient slime that when spread over crops, encourages growth and produces new strains of plant life. The berries of yagaran aleudrupe plants, when fertilized with the slime, act as a catalyst for boosting blaster firepower, much like spin-sealed Tibanna gas. Mara Jade joined up with the smuggler Talon Karrde in an adventure on Varonat. [SWAJ]

Varrscha, Lakwii Promoted from executive officer to commander of the Imperial Star Destroyer *Virulence*, Varrscha was assigned to protect the Super Star Destroyer *Lusankya*. That ship had been ordered by Ysanne Isard to destroy Rogue Squadron's operations base at the Yag'Dhul space station. When the *Lusankya* was suddenly caught in a gravitational embrace by a gravity well projector that had been secretly installed at Yag'Dhul, Lakwii Varrscha inserted her ship between the projector and the *Lusankya*, breaking the gravity grip and allowing the *Lusankya* to escape back to Thyferra. Because the projector was still on, Pash Cracken and his team of A-wings were suddenly pulled in from hyperspace. Thinking that their arrival was part of an elaborate ambush, Varrscha was tricked into surrendering the *Virulence*. [BW]

Varvenna sector The famous chef Porcellus once worked for the moff of the sector, the Imperial Governor of Bryexx, Yndis Mylore. During his tenure, Porcellus cooked meals for the Emperor himself, but he was made a slave to Jabba the Hutt a year prior to the Battle of Yavin. [TJP]

vayerbok A hot liquid drink, it is a favorite of Kid DXo'ln. [NR]

vector A popular game played in drinking establishments on the planet Bonadan. [HSR]

Veers, General Maximilian The highly capable commander of Imperial ground troops assigned to Lord Darth Vader's special armada during the Galactic Civil War, he was ordered by Vader to personally supervise the invasion of the Rebel base on the planet Hoth. Gen. Maximilian Veers's force consisted of AT-AT walkers and waves of Imperial snowtroopers. He was later betrayed by his son, Zev, who joined the Alliance. [ESB, GG3]

Veers, Zev Son of the Imperial general who commanded the ground assault against the Rebel base on Hoth, he disowned his father and went against his wishes when he joined the Rebellion. During the Battle of Calamari, Zev Veers was the chief gunner aboard the New Republic Star Destroyer *Emancipator*. [DE]

Vegnu, Jub A Sullustan, he was an aide and go-between for Jabba the Hutt on Mos Eisley. [TMEC]

Vek One of the handpicked survivors of the Dark Jedi Kueller's pogroms on Almania, he was a young man with a round face and eyes, dark reddish-brown hair, and skin still covered with pimples. Although Vek served Kueller as best he could, Kueller could never remember why he spared the boy's life in the first place. [NR]

Vekker A Quarren, he was one of the lieutenants, or Vigos, of Prince Xizor's Black Sun criminal organization. He had little ambition and was content with both his job and the status quo. [SOTE]

Velcar Free Commerce Zone (FCZ) Situated in the Velcar sector, it is a strip of corporate-run systems within the Pentastar Alignment. The Velcar FCZ, ruled by Commerce Master Commissioner Gregor Raquoran, contains many resource-rich worlds exploited by powerful corporations. They often have been allowed to bypass environmental and safety rules, and the primitive species found on such planets as Capza, Entralla, and Bextar are often forced to toil in mines or on other hazardous industrial projects. [SWAJ]

Gen. Maximilian Veers

velker V-shaped flying creatures, they have tough claws and armored wings. Velkers are natural predators of the beldons on Bespin. They attain remarkable speeds in flight and soar to extremely high altitudes. Like beldons, velkers have an electrical field surrounding their bodies, creating discharges that can damage passing cloud cars. At times, they attack small ships. [ISWU]

Velser's Ring A band of asteroids occupying the third-planet position in the Bespin system, the ring is be-

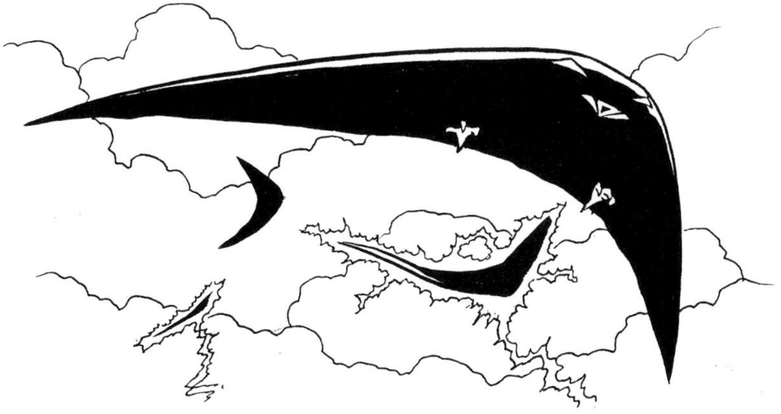

Velkers

lieved to be the debris of an unstable gas giant that exploded many millennia ago. Most of the asteroids consist of frozen gases and liquids, and the entire Velser's Ring refracts light in a rainbow pattern if seen from the proper angle. Ugnaught teams used to visit the ring frequently to obtain valuable raw materials for Bespin's Cloud City. [GG2]

Ven, Nawara This Twi'lek member of Rogue Squadron was a former lawyer on his homeworld of Ryloth. He became one of Corran Horn's friends during training exercises on Folor, before anyone had been named to the Squadron. Although an excellent pilot, it was perhaps Nawara Ven's experience in legal matters that most benefited his fellow Squadron members. When Gavin Darklighter was taken before the Alien Combine to be tried for bigotry, Nawara came to his aid, preventing Gavin's death. Later, fellow Rogue Tycho Celchu needed someone he could trust to defend him against charges of treason and the murder of Corran Horn, so he asked Ven. Captain Celchu had saved Ven's life during the first battle at Borleias, and the Twi'lek agreed to repay the debt. He enlisted the aid of others to help him combat the massive amounts of data the prosecution presented, but he was still about to lose the case. Imperial agent Kirtan Loor then offered to help them expose the real Imperial agent within Rogue Squadron in exchange for immunity from prosecution, but he was assassinated before he could testify, and Ven was seriously injured in the attack. Trial was about to be postponed, when the "dead" man, Corran Horn, showed up. [RS, WG, KT, BW]

Venaari The third planet in the Vellakiya system, this Mid-Rim world is covered with forests, plains, and mountains. The Imperial presence on Venaari has increased since the Battle of Endor in order to provide greater security for the mysterious Project Orrad research in an underground laboratory. The planet is run by Imperial Governor Vaerganth, who rules from the capital city of Ven-Kav. Around two billion humans inhabit the planet. Since the Empire's recent buildup, the New Republic has established a fledgling resistance cell on Venaari. A New Republic operative, Shandria L'hnnar, managed to steal the plans to Project Orrad and elude the pursuing Imperials with the help of the thief Sienn Sconn. [SWAJ]

Vengeance The Star Destroyer that staged the assault on the Rebels at Nar Shaddaa. [TMEC]

Vengeance Derra IV A 150-meter *Dwarf Star*–class freighter, it attempted to penetrate the defenses of the Rebel base at Borleias under the orders of Warlord Zsinj. Rogue Squadron easily put the ship to flight. Later, the ship was spotted near Mrisst, and the squadron surprised the *Vengeance* as it was making a cargo transfer. The *Vengeance* dumped a dozen TIEs from its hold and in furious battle the ship was so badly damaged that it almost fell into the planetary atmosphere. [WG]

Venjagga system Located at the edge of the Galactic Core only hours away from the Mirit and Pyria systems, it contains the planet Jagga-Two, site of a small Imperial base that manufactures concussion missiles and supplies the Imperial Star Destroyer-II *Eviscerator*. The seventh planet in the Venjagga system is a gas giant. Three years after the Battle of Endor, the Alliance staged a feint in the system to cover a simultaneous assault on Borleias in the Pyria system. [RS]

Vento system The location of an ancient Republic shipyard, it was almost the site of the destruction of the entire Republic fleet some 4,000 years before the Galactic Civil War. During the Sith War, the fallen Jedi Ulic Qel-Droma gained control of Coruscant's war room during his attack on the capital world. Qel-Droma told the war room's commander to order all Republic ships to jump to identical coordinates in the Vento system, which would have resulted in a massive collision and the destruction of the fleet. He was stopped before the order could be carried out. [TSW]

Venture A carrier in the New Republic Fifth Fleet, it was assigned to the blockade of Doornik-319. The *Venture* was damaged during the Yevethan attack. [SOL]

Venutton A scrawny, uptight human assistant to Lady Valarian. [TJP]

Venzeiia 2 Prime The planet where a Rebel spy, fleeing aboard a YT-1300 freighter, was tracked to a space station's salvage yard. A TIE Defender was dispatched to capture the freighter while the Star Destroyer *Glory* captured the space station for daring to harbor a fugitive from the Empire. [TSC]

Verachen Members of the Vratix species on Thyferra, they are the workers responsible for blending the organic ingredients that constitute bacta to give it its desired potency. [BW]

Verdanth Prior to the Battle of Hoth, the Alliance sent the droids R2-D2 and C-3PO to this jungle planet to investigate a crashed Imperial messenger drone. The drone was actually a trap set by Darth Vader, who planned to use a cybernetic Force link to read the minds of any Rebels investigating the drone and possibly learn the location of their new base. [CSW]

Vergesso asteroids These asteroids are located in the Lybeya system of the Bajic sector in the Outer Rim. The Tenloss Syndicate built a hidden shipyard in one of the larger asteroids, used by the Rebel Alliance among others. The nickel-iron Vergesso asteroid was the size of a small moon and had a surface pockmarked with craters. All types of Rebel and other vessels, from snubfighters to cruisers, were repaired and refitted at the base, right under the nose of Grand Moff Kintaro. Prince Xizor and his Black Sun criminal organization found out about the base, and Xizor presented the information to Darth Vader in order to curry favor with the Emperor and to harm the Tenloss Syndicate, one of his major rivals. Vader was ordered to eliminate the base. In the subsequent raid, hundreds of Rebel ships were destroyed, and thousands of pilots and crew members perished, seriously harming the Alliance just prior to the critical Battle of Endor. [SOTE]

Vergill A planet in the Hapes Cluster, its inhabitants have long been rivals of the water-breathers of the

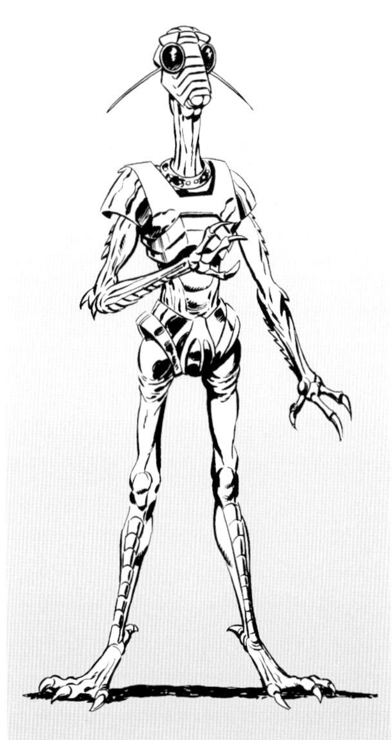

Verpine

planet Maires. Nineteen years after the Battle of Endor, the Vergills began an undersea ditanium-mining operation on the planet Hapes, next to the newly opened Mairan consulate. The Mairans filed an official protest against the noise and mining debris stirred up by the Vergills' actions, but in reality they had deliberately placed their consulate near the richest vein of ditanium in order to spark a confrontation. [YJK]

Verpine An advanced species of two-legged insectoids, this spacefaring species had colonized the Roche asteroid field before the birth of the Old Republic. Their thin, sticklike bodies have articulated joints and chitinous shells. Two antennae jut from the sides of their heads, which have two large eyes and short snouts. They communicate via radio waves using an organ in their chests, enabling a single Verpine to talk with the entire species within seconds. They have developed something of a communal mind, yet each Verpine considers itself aloof and not controlled by the hive.

The Verpine use huge repulsor shells to keep occupied asteroids from crashing into each other and to deflect other bits of space debris. They are experts in most fields of technology and have developed into expert starship builders. Their eyesight allows them to spot microscopic details, such as a hairline fracture, making them invaluable to the safety of pilots everywhere. The Verpine helped Admiral Ackbar design and build the B-wing starfighter. [SFS, GG4, DFRSB, CPL, BW]

Ver Seryan, Karia A life-bearer who lives on Leria Kerlsil, she is around 300 years old. Karia Ver Seryan had had forty-nine husbands, whose lives she had sustained for periods of time, when a potential fiftieth—Lando Calrissian—was investigating her as a possible marriage candidate. [AC]

vesuvague tree A semisentient tree, it has limbs that can strangle. [GG7, TMEC]

Veubg A being from the planet Gbu. [CS]

Vexta belt Pirates from this area attacked Delephran shipping for years, until they were wiped out by the Delephran militia during the Piracy Scouring. Former Alliance operative Col. Andrephan Stormcaller participated in the campaign against the Vexta-belt pirates during his early career. [SWAJ]

vibro-ax A handheld weapon with a broad blade, it can be deadly in fights. With only the slightest touch, an ultrasonic generator located in the vibro-ax's handle produces vibrations that power the weapon and give the blade great cutting power. Many Gamorreans carry them. [HSR]

vibroblade An ultrasonic-vibration weapon, it is a powered knife or dagger with a reverberating blade edge that produces great cutting power at only the slightest touch. It is a weapon of choice in the underworld. [HSE, HSR]

vibro-cutter A heavy-duty industrial version of a vibroblade. [HLL]

vibroscalpel A small, lightweight surgical instrument, it uses ultrasonic vibrations to excite a small wire blade in order to easily cut through most objects. Controls located in the vibroscalpel handle adjust power levels. [HSE, HSR]

vibro-shiv A small, easily concealable vibroblade. [HLL]

Victim A slang term used by Rebel pilots for a *Victory*-class Destroyer. [BW]

***Victory*-class Star Destroyer** Designed near the end of the Clone Wars by Walex Blissex, a Republic engineer, these old star cruisers still play a role in the remnants of the Imperial space fleet. When first launched, the *Victory*-class Star Destroyer was considered the ultimate combat starship design. At 900 meters long, they can carry a crew of more than 5,000. Standard Imperial armament includes ten quad turbolasers, forty double turbolasers, eighty concussion missile launchers and ten tractor beam projectors. They can carry two squadrons, or twenty-four TIE fighters, 2,000 ground troops, planetary drop-ships, troop transports, and a wide range of planetary assault vehicles, including AT-AT walkers, juggernauts, and floating fortresses.

As more *Imperial*-class Star Destroyers were built, Victory Star Destroyers were reassigned to planetary defense roles. A number have been decommissioned and sold off to planetary defense forces, including the Corporate Sector Authority, which bought 250 of the ships. They were designed for three missions: planetary defense, planetary assault and ground-troop support, and ship-to-ship combat. Their biggest weakness is in the last category, because most modern starships can outrun them. The usefulness of Victory Star Destroyers was renewed with the return of Grand Admiral Thrawn. Finding his forces lacking sufficient capital starships, he began a systematic recommissioning and refitting

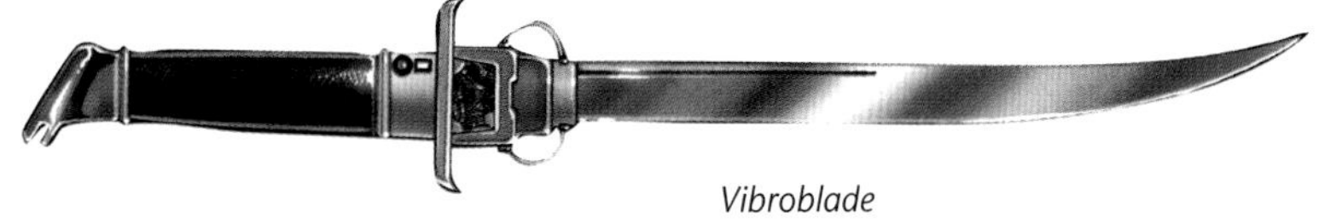

Vibroblade

of Victory Star Destroyers, gaining these ships renewed respect. [SWSB, HSR, ISB, DFRSB, HSC, SWVG]

Victory Forum A huge coliseum in the town of Dying Slowly on the planet Jubilar, it was named by the winning side of one of the planet's numerous wars. Brightly lit and with hundreds of rows of seats, the forum allowed audiences of up to 20,000 to view barbaric sporting events, most notably Regional Sector Four's All-Human Free-For-All Extravaganza. [TBH]

Victory Lake A body of water some fifteen kilometers from Imperial City on Coruscant, it serves as a reservoir for the capital. Admiral Ackbar, among others, has a waterfront home on Victory Lake. [SOL]

Vidkun, Benedict A short, thin engineer with bulging brown eyes, sharp yellow teeth, and a wispy beard and mustache, he had a younger wife with expensive tastes. Always nervous, Benedict Vidkun tended to clear his throat a lot. For a price, he appeared willing both to make maps and to lead an Alliance rescue team through a labyrinth of sewer conduits beneath Prince Xizor's palace on Imperial Center to free Princess Leia Organa. Vidkun's brother-in-law Daiv worked for the firm that built Xizor's castle. Another brother-in-law, Lair, was able to get the bypass codes for an extermination device that would have fried the rescuers. But after taking the team through the muck, Benedict pulled a blaster and shot Dash Rendar in the left hip. Dash immediately responded with a blaster bolt between Vidkun's eyes. [SOTE]

Vigilant A cruiser in the New Republic Fifth Fleet, it was deployed in the blockade of Doornik-319. [SOL]

Victory*-class Star Destroyer*

Vima-Da-Boda

Vilas A dark-haired male from Dathomir, he was the Force-sensitive companion of Nightsister Vonnda Ra. He was also Vonnda Ra's apprentice, and she wanted him to lead a new order of Dark Jedi, but a one-time street urchin, Zekk, was also in contention for that role. The two battled in the gravity-free center of the Shadow Academy space station, and Zekk sliced Vilas in half with his lightsaber and shot his body parts out an exhaust port. [YJK]

Vima-Da-Boda Descended from a long, illustrious line of Jedi, she was directly related to the legendary Vima Sunrider, the daughter of Nomi Sunrider. Vima-Da-Boda served the Force for 100 years, and raised one daughter, Neema, who turned to the dark side. The dark-side power didn't help Neema, who was abused and finally killed by her husband, a barbaric Ottethan warlord. In her rage at finding that her daughter had been fed to rancors, Vima ignited her lightsaber and cleaved the warlord in two. She then sank deep into despair over her actions and the loss of her daughter. Her retreat from the world is probably what saved her from the great Jedi purge.

At one point she was imprisoned in the Kessel spice mines and met young Kyp Durron, whom she gave some elementary training in the Force. Eventually free of Imperial shackles, she retreated to the dark lower levels of the Corellian Sector on the smuggler's moon of Nar Shaddaa.

Six years after the destruction of the second Death Star, Alliance hero Han Solo brought his wife, Leia, to the lower levels. The 200-year-old Vima could sense Leia's Jedi potential. She kissed Leia's feet, begged her forgiveness, and gave her a gift—Vima's own ancient lightsaber.

Months later, Leia and Han returned to retrieve Vima, who was on the run from Imperial Dark Siders. Vima aided Luke Skywalker with his training of Jedi students. When Luke was poisoned by Imperial scarab droids, Vima healed him. [DE, DE2, JS]

Vimdim, Bom A male Advosze, he despises beings of his own species. Pessimistic and territorial, Bom Vimdim is a lone smuggler who prefers to work for corrupt officials. He boasts about being in Mos Eisley cantina when Luke Skywalker first met Han Solo. No one believes him—or cares. [WC, CCG]

Vinda Co-owner of Starshipwrights and Aerospace Engineers Incorporated, he was once owed credits by Han Solo for work his company had performed on the *Millennium Falcon*. [HSR]

Vinsoth A planet covered by vast plains, it is home to the Chevin species. The Chevin are hunter-gatherers who follow herds of backshin as they travel the plains, and they have enslaved a native humanoid race also called Chevins. Ephant Mon, a gunrunner who spent time in Jabba the Hutt's court, is a Vinsoth native. After a life-changing encounter with Luke Skywalker in Jabba's dungeon, Ephant Mon returned to his home

Bom Vimdim

planet and founded a new religious sect that worshipped nature and the Force, though he still ran some scams on the side to finance his sect's temple. [MTS, TJP, GG12]

Vinzen Neela 5 Site of an unsuccessful Rebel attack. Following the Battle of Hoth, Rebels tried to thwart an Imperial transfer of prototype TIE Defenders to an escort carrier at a rendezvous near Vinzen Neela 5. [TSC]

Virago The personal transport and assault vessel of galactic underworld leader Prince Xizor, it was a *Star Viper*–class heavy assault starfighter with incredible speed, armor, and weaponry, custom-built at a very high cost. The ship's wings and thrust nacelles moved while in flight to enhance performance, giving it the appearance of a living creature as its wings constantly folded and adjusted.

The StarViper matched the TIE interceptor for speed and maneuverability despite a far greater mass. The rear-mounted engines provided forward thrust, while maneuverability was enhanced by a pair of microthrusters mounted on the tip of each wing. The inflight computer control system individually adjusted each microthruster. In combat, the four wings fully folded out to give the thrusters maximum effect. The well-armored wings hold reserve fuel tanks.

The *Virago's* wings folded flush against the engines and pilot compartment for standard space flight and planetary landing. The *Virago's* main weapons were a pair of double heavy laser cannons tied to an advanced targeting computer and sighting laser system. There were also two forward-firing proton torpedo launchers, each with a magazine of three torpedoes. Because the *Virago* required a large amount of energy, it needed four separate power generators. [SOTE, SWVG]

Virgilio, Captain Commander of the New Republic Escort Frigate *Quenfis*, one of the ships in Admiral Drayson's Home Guard Fleet assigned to protect Coruscant, Captain Virgilio had been part of the crew of the Alliance ship that helped Bothan spies return with the plans for the second Death Star battle station. At the time, Virgilio was a young third officer on a Corellian gunship. The ship picked up a distress call whose code identified its senders as members of a large team of Bothan intelligence agents operating in the outer regions. Of that team, only six survived—but they carried with them the plans and secret location of the second Death Star and the Emperor's schedule, which told when he would be visiting the site. [DFR, DFRSB]

Viridia system A system where Han Solo used to make smuggling runs. He had learned some of the port access codes of the Viridia system, but they were later changed by Imperials. [CPL]

Virulence A *Mark II*–class Imperial Star Destroyer, it was commanded first by Joak Dyrsso, then by Lakwii Varrscha to protect Ysanne Isard's stranglehold on the bacta trade. The *Virulence* was sent to protect Isard's bacta convoys, but this did not prevent Rogue Squadron from trying to steal the precious cargo. When the location of Rogue Squadron's secret base was finally discovered, Isard ordered Captain Varrscha to assist the *Lusankya* in its destruction. Upon their arrival at the Yag'Dhul space station, the *Lusankya* was caught in the grip of a gravity well projector and there were indications of an immediate attack. Reacting instantly, Captain Varrscha inserted the *Virulence* between the station's gravity projector and the *Lusankya*, allowing the bigger ship to escape back to Thyferra. Overwhelmed by what appeared to be hundreds of missiles and proton torpedoes about to pound her ship and the sudden appearance of Pash Cracken's A-wing group, Captain Varrscha surrendered the ship to Booster Terrik. He took command, loaded Pash's A-wings, and set off for Thyferra. Their arrival turned the tide of the Bacta War. The three squadrons of fighters brought to the fray were an invaluable asset to weary Rogue Squadron and the rapidly thinning Deathseeds. The *Virulence* poured a barrage of fire into the unprotected side of the *Lusankya*, until it finally surrendered. For his valiant effort, the *Virulence* was given to Booster Terrik, but only after he agreed to remove most of the ship's weaponry. He then renamed it the *Errant Venture*. [BW]

Vizcarra An Imperial prison planet, it was where the smuggler Tait Ransom was scheduled to be sent after he was arrested for weapons smuggling on Omman. [SWAJ]

Vjun The planet where Darth Vader built Bast Castle, a remote, heavily defended structure that became his private refuge. It was later the headquarters of dark-side Executor Sedriss and the Emperor's elite force of Dark Jedi. The planet is lashed with acidic, burning rain, and no plant life can survive on its bleak surface. Kam Solusar served as a dark-side warrior on Vjun before Luke Skywalker turned him to the light side on Nespis VIII, six years after the Battle of Endor. Soon after Solusar's conversion, three Ysanna prisoners from Ossus were taken to Vjun to serve as raw material in creating new clone bodies for Emperor Palpatine. The Ysanna were frozen in carbonite to await the future construction of a clone laboratory in Bast Castle, but Luke Skywalker and his Jedi trainees managed to storm the castle and defeat the Emperor's minions. [DE2, EE]

Vladet Located in the Rachuk sector and system, it is a blue-and-green world dotted with islands. It receives a great deal of rainfall. The Empire established a base in the lush jungle on Vladet's Grand Isle to discourage piracy in the local systems, and the garrison became the center of Imperial control for the sector. Built in the crater of an extinct volcano, the base was ringed by two steep moun-

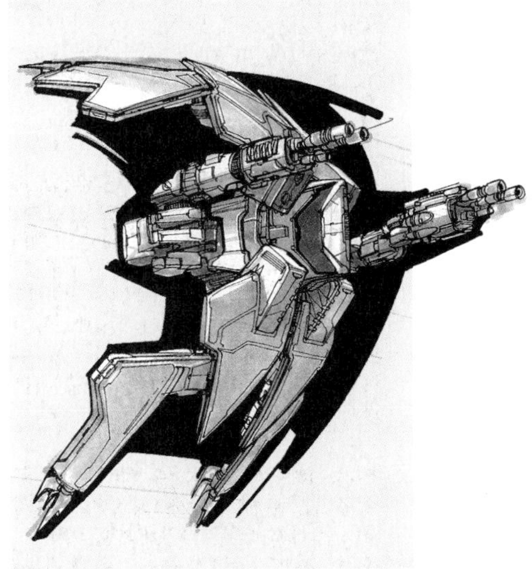

Virago

tain ranges on the west and east. To the south the crater had mostly broken down, and the base extended out to the edges of a bay. Geothermal generators powered the energy shield and twin ion cannons, while a comfortable mansion housed the command staff, including Admiral Devlia.

Three years after the Battle of Endor, an Alliance force, including members of Rogue Squadron, attacked the Vladet headquarters in reprisal for an Imperial raid on Talasea. The Alliance didn't want to capture Vladet but intended to cripple the base so the Empire would be compelled to allocate more forces to its defense. Several Y-wing squadrons blew out the northern wall of the crater, allowing starfighters to fly in under the base's defensive shield. The Alliance leveled the base in the successful raid, and Rogue Squadron pilot Corran Horn helped destroy a *Lancer*-class frigate on the way out. Admiral Devlia was presumed killed. [RS]

Vlee, Ussar One of a trio of famous Gand ruetsavii who were sent to observe Ooryl Qyrgg's life and determine his worthiness to become janwuine. Not only did they observe his activities, but they also participated fully with him during his duties as a member of Rogue Squadron. They proved to be capable fighter pilots as well as undercover operatives. [BW]

Vob A gas giant, it is famous for its perpetual atmospheric storms. [GG2]

vocabulator A device through which droids produce sounds, it is usually visible as a grille or orifice called a vocoder. A vocabulator allows a droid to produce speech. The most sophisticated vocabulators are found in protocol droids and are capable of producing the sounds necessary to converse in millions of different languages. [SWN, SWSB]

Vodran Covered with swamps and thick jungles, the planet is homeworld to the tough species also known as Vodrans, who struggle for survival against the world's huge and deadly predators. The Vodrans were enslaved by the Hutts in the early days of space travel and fought in the Third Battle of Vontor against the forces of Xim the Despot.

Rebel Alliance Lieutenant Xenon Nnaksta, an operator of the Greel Wood Logging Corporation in the Pii system, is a native of Vodran. Nnaksta's parents were killed years ago in the Thruncon Insurrection, a catastrophe in which many Vodran cities were destroyed. The planet is also home to the galactic pest known as the dianoga or "garbage squid." This seven-tentacled creature has one eyestalk and has evolved a transparent camouflage to protect it from predators. These animals are now found feeding on garbage virtually everywhere in the galaxy, and Luke Skywalker was attacked and nearly killed by one in the Death Star's trash compactor. [SW, MTS, SWAJ]

voice manipulation A frequently used Force technique, it allows a Jedi to verbally implant suggestions into the minds of others and cause the appropriate responses. Jedi employ voice manipulation to achieve their objectives peacefully. [SWN, RJN]

Voice Override: Epsilon Actual A command that immediately supersedes a droid's primary programming. The Voice Override: Epsilon Actual function is activated by a verbal code, usually delivered in the form of a word or phrase. [SWR]

Void Spider THX 1138 A light, enclosed shuttle, it is used for courier runs to large orbiting transports. The Void Spider THX 1138 is manufactured by Bespin Motors and most remain on Bespin. [CCG]

Vogel 7 The site of an Imperial Naval Academy, it was where TIE fighter pilot Ranulf Trommer was raised. [ROC]

Vondarc system Smuggler Dannen Lifehold brought a Rebel group from Rafft to this system for a rendezvous with a cargo frigate. Lifehold had joined the Alliance in the Vondarc system just prior to the Battle of Yavin. [SWAJ]

Vontor, Third Battle of The last in a series of major conflicts directed against the pre-Republic tyrant known to history as Xim the Despot. In this battle, Xim's orbital fortress and nearly all of his war-robots were vaporized by Hutt-led forces. It took place in the disputed Si'kloata Cluster. [HLL, GG12]

Vonzel A smuggler, he was an early associate of Han Solo. After being injured while making an emergency landing, Vonzel had to be attached permanently to a life-support system to keep him alive. [HSR]

Voors, Hallolar A young spice-trading entrepreneur, he was killed by Boba Fett on the planet Jubilar. [TBH]

Voota, Tho The proctor of defense for the Yevethan spawnworld. [TT]

Vorn, Liegeus Sarpaetius The pilot for Seti Ashgad, he was also a master holo-faker and a competent designer of artificial intelligence systems for spacecraft. Like Ashgad he, too, was a captive of the droch Dyzm, but through fear. He was needed to complete and then pilot the ship that would transport Dyzm safely off Nam Chorios. Later, Vorn was reunited with his lost love, Admiral Daala. [POT]

vornskr A violent, long-legged quadruped with a doglike muzzle, sharp teeth, and whiplike tail, it lives on the planet Myrkr. During the day, vornskrs are mostly inactive, but as light fades, they become nocturnal hunters. The vornskr's tail is covered with a mild poison that can inflict painful welts and stun its prey. Vornskrs display an unnatural hatred of

Vornskr

Jedi, often going out of their way to hunt and attack Force users. Smuggler Talon Karrde kept two domesticated vornskrs, his pets Sturm and Drang. The guard animals have had their tails clipped to reduce their normally aggressive nature. [HE, HESB]

Vorru, Fliry The onetime administrator of the Corellian Sector for the Old Republic, Vorru turned a blind eye to the smuggling activities all around him. The underworld's Prince Xizor betrayed him to the Emperor to curry favor, but instead of killing him, Palpatine sent him to a life of mining spice on Kessel. When Rogue Squadron liberated some Kessel prisoners to wreak havoc on Coruscant prior to an Alliance invasion, Fliry Vorru was taken along. After the conquest, Vorru attempted to ingratiate himself with the Provisional Council, offering his services to administer law to the underworld and control the black market. He was also working for Imperial Intelligence Director Ysanne Isard. Because of his faithful service, she took him along when she fled Coruscant and made him Minister of Trade when she took control of Thyferra's bacta cartel and the planetary government.

Vorru enjoyed engineering bacta price-gouging amidst shortages but was aware that the New Republic would eventually put an end to these activities. Always looking for new opportunity and worried about Isard's increasing insanity, he planned his escape. But she remained one step ahead of him. As Vorru made his way to the *Thyfonian*, Isard's Imperial guards prevented his access to his shuttle, and he was left behind to be captured by Rebel forces. [WG, KT, BW]

Vors Hollow-boned humanoids with lacy wings on their backs, they live on the planet Vortex. During the incredible atmospheric disturbances on the planet, the Vors seek shelter in half-buried hummock dwellings. [DA]

Vortex Homeworld of the hollow-boned, winged Vors, it is a blue-and-gray planet with a sharp axial tilt that causes sudden seasonal changes and severe windstorms. The Cathedral of Winds, the center of Vor civilization, is an immense crystalline structure designed to produce tones when Vortex's wind currents pass over and through it. The Vors perform a beautiful concert of ethereal music by opening and closing orifices in the building with their bodies. The Vors are an emotionless species and tend to concentrate on larger goals rather than on individuals. They refused to perform their music for off-worlders during the reign of the Empire and have only recently allowed New Republic and other dignitaries to attend these shows. All recording is prohibited, and only one concert is performed each year.

The Vors inhabit underground dwellings during the stormy season; they can be seen from above as small mounds arranged in rings in the purple, vermilion, and tan grasses of the plains. During a visit to Vortex by Admiral Ackbar and Leia Organa Solo, Ackbar's sabotaged B-wing crashed into and destroyed the centuries-old Cathedral of Winds and killed at least 358 Vors. A different, more streamlined Cathedral was then constructed by the Vors as a replacement. [DA, COF]

Vram An obnoxious young boy, he was one of Lord Hethrir's helpers. [CS]

Vratix Highly intelligent insectoid beings from Thyferra, they outnumber the human population many times over. Humans control the bacta corporations, but the Verachen, a type of Vratix, actually make the product. The Vratix, mantislike with six appendages, use their sense of touch often in social interactions, finding it to be the most reliable of the senses. They are hermaphroditic and are very long-lived. They live in modest harvester tribes within the rain forests, in dwellings made from mud and saliva. The mud is created by the Knytix, a domesticated servant species resembling the Vratix, but smaller. Each village has several high towers amid the gloan trees, with circular terraces and arching bridges connecting the towers. Vratix also can share thoughts with fellow Vratix whom they know well. The Ashern Circle was an independence movement that fought against human domination of the bacta cartels. Vratix rebel members painted themselves black. [SWAJ, BW]

Vri'syk, Peshk A Bothan and member of Rogue Squadron, his X-wing fighter was destroyed and he was killed during the disastrous raid on Borleias. [RS]

Vuffi Raa A highly polished chromium astrogation/pilot droid, he traveled with Lando Calrissian for at least a year shortly after the gambler had won the *Millennium Falcon*. Vuffi Raa was technically Lando's property, since Lando had won him in a game of sabacc. But after a few adventures together, Calrissian came to regard the droid as his friend.

Vuffi Raa stood one meter tall, with five multijointed tentacle limbs that he could move at various angles and even prop himself up with to achieve more height. Vuffi Raa was the shape of an attenuated starfish with manipulators that served as both arms and legs. These were connected to a dinner-plate–sized pentagonal torso with a single, softly glowing, deep red vision crystal.

Vuffi Raa had a complex history, from his creation as a scout by an extremely powerful being known only as the One to his ownership by Imperial spy and anthropologist Osuno Whett. The academic used a disguised Vuffi Raa in his scheme to conquer the inhabitants of the Renatasian system, a subjugation that led to the deaths of two-thirds of the system's inhabitants. [LCM, LCF, LCS]

Vultan An ancient warrior race some 4,000 years before the Galactic Civil War, one of its members was Jedi Oss Wilum. [DLS]

Vulvarch A planet some thirty-four light-years from Teyr. Twelve years after the Battle of Endor, Luke Skywalker discovered that the starliner *Star Morning*, belonging to the Fallanassi religious order, had spent the last few months in Farana, but had recently arrived at Vulvarch. [SOL]

V-wing airspeeder An atmospheric attack craft, it played a major part in the New Republic's defense of the planet Mon Calamari and in at least a dozen other battles against Imperial forces. V-wings are light combat airspeeders, as fast as standard Rebel combat airspeeders but with a much higher flight ceiling—about 100 kilometers. With a scramjet booster kicking in, the craft can achieve a top speed of 1,400 kilometers an hour,

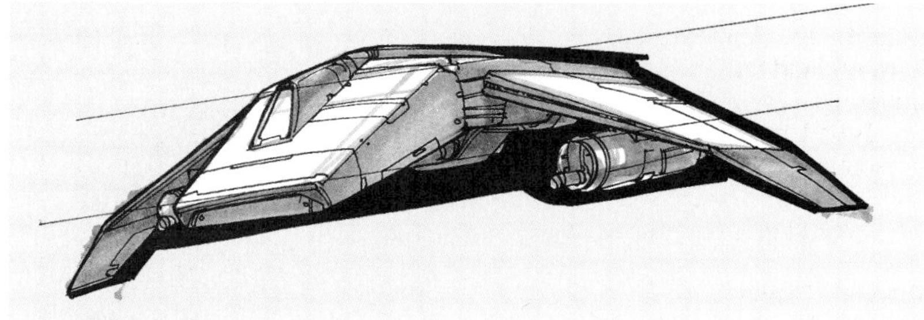

V-wing airspeeder

although sudden maneuvers at that speed can tear the ship apart.

The only weapon aboard a V-wing is a double laser cannon with an effective range of two kilometers. A pilot has minimal protection, and survivability is low despite an ejection system. V-wings can be deployed to planetary bases or capital starships. They are typically used for combat against incoming enemy fighters or in surprise raids. In the Battle of Calamari, V-wings proved devastating against the Empire's new TIE/D fighters and water-based amphibions. [DE, DESB, SWVG]

vynocks An atmosphere-breathing version of mynocks, these leathery black flying creatures are silicon-based. They evolved in the vacuum of space and feed on energy. [D]

Wadda A humanoid employee of Zlarb the Slaver, Wadda came from a species of which little is known since few of its members have become integrated into galactic society. Wadda was strong, nearly 2.2 meters tall with glossy brown skin, a jutting forehead, and protruding vestigial horns. [HSR]

Waivers List A Corporate Sector Authority register, it lists ships that are exempt from the multitude of vessel requirements usually imposed on spacecraft entering Authority-controlled space. [HSE]

Wakiza Located in the Koornacht Cluster, it is one of the primary worlds of the Yevethan species and is a member of the Duskhan League. It was the location of an orbital Imperial repair yard, code-named Black 8, serving the Empire's Black Sword Command. After the Battle of Endor, the Empire retreated from the shipyards of Wakiza, Zhina, and N'zoth, and the Yevetha were able to capture several of their capital ships. The Black 8 shipyards were later moved away from Wakiza to a clandestine location. The New Republic attacked Wakiza during the Battle of N'zoth. [BTS, SOL]

Walalla A New Republic member world in the Seventh Security Zone, it had been brutally conquered by the Empire and its inhabitants cruelly persecuted. Senator Tig Peramis represents Walalla and the other worlds of the Zone in the New Republic Senate. Twelve years after the Battle of Endor, after Nil Spaar protested the treatment of his Yevethan delegation at the hands of Chief of State Leia Organa Solo, Peramis submitted an Article of Withdrawal from the New Republic on behalf of Walalla. Nara Deega, a Bith from Clak'dor VIII, was seated in his place on the Defense Council. Peramis later passed on secret New Republic fleet movement information to Nil Spaar on N'zoth, which allowed the Yevetha to capture Gen. Han Solo. [BTS, SOL]

walker *See* All Terrain Armored Transport; All Terrain Scout Transport

wampa ice creature A fearsome and carnivorous predator, the wampa stalks the snow-packed wastes of the planet Hoth. An imposing two meters tall, the two-legged ice creature is covered with shaggy white fur. It has eerie yellow eyes and sharp claws and teeth. Solitary creatures for the most part, wampas carve their lairs out of the ice, forming huge caves in which to nest. When they hunt, they often take their prey by surprise thanks to the natural camouflage provided by their white fur. A wampa's primary source of food is tauntauns. But since life is scarce on Hoth, it's estimated that a single wampa must cover more than a hundred kilometers in search of food. Wampas never hunt when they are hungry. Instead, they capture living prey and store it in their ice caves for later consumption. Rebel hero Luke Skywalker was wounded by a wampa while he was patrolling Hoth during the Galactic Civil War and had another nasty encounter with a ferocious band years later. [ESB, ISWU, GG3, DS]

wander-kelp A cross between plant and animal, this kelp has little

Wampa ice creature

intelligence but moves under its own volition. Wander-kelp's mass of iodine-filled leaves can be sheared several times a year, distilled, and sold for medicinal purposes. The rest of a wander-kelp's biomass is often used as cheap protein fiber for animal feed. [DS, COJ]

wandrella A huge wormlike beast, it lives in the rain forests of the planet Mimban. A wandrella is an omnivore with pale, cream-colored flesh streaked with slashes of brown. The creature's blunt end is covered with eyespots and a ferocious mouth filled with sharp, black teeth. The wandrella moves by using suction organs located on its underside. [SME]

Wann Tsir This planet was placed under siege following the Battle of Endor. During the attack, Imperial commander Titus Klev discovered and stopped an Alliance agent trying to bring down the planet's shields, which earned him commendations from Imperial command. [DESB]

Warb A Corellian hyperdrive mechanic, he was assistant to Shug Ninx in his garage on Nar Shaddaa. [TMEC]

warbeast Large, ferocious flying creatures from the moon of Dxun, they first hunted and later were tamed by the outcasts of society on the planet Onderon. They were used as war machines by the beast-riders of Onderon. [TOJ, DLS]

war droid Older mechanicals designed specifically for combat, they are also called war robots. War droids have heavy armor plating, inefficient power delivery systems, and less intelligence and self-awareness than their more sophisticated descendants. Old war droids can still be found operating in isolated and remote sections of the galaxy. Later versions employ self-healing metals, point-of-impact shields, and fast-reaction servo-systems. [DE, HLL]

Warlug A Gamorrean, he was a guard for Jabba the Hutt. [TJP]

warming unit *See* condenser unit

war-mount Heavily armed, flying weapons droids, they served as battle mounts for Mandalorian warriors both on land and in space some four millennia ago. A Mandalorian rider was belted into a control seat like a horseman, and directed the droid and its weapons from a panel sporting several kinds of controls. [TSW]

Warrick, Erpham An Ewok warrior, he built the great Ewok battle wagon used to defeat the Duloks. Erpham Warrick's great-grandson is the Ewok hero named Wicket. [ETV]

Warrick, Wicket W. A hero of the Rebellion, this small Ewok helped the Rebel forces defeat the Empire in the monumental Battle of Endor while he was only a teenager. Wicket W. Warrick, a member of the short, furry bipedal species that lives in tree villages on Endor's forest moon, is the youngest son of Shodu and Deej. Wicket has always shown a greater-than-usual curiosity about the unknown, which eventually put him right in the middle of the Galactic Civil War.

In his younger days, Wicket and his friends had many skirmishes with the warlike Duloks; the evil Morag, a Tulgah Witch; giant green Phlogs; the reptilian carnivorous Froschs; and the semisentient Dandelion Warriors. When not contending with enemies, he gathered Rainbow Berries for the Harvest Moon Feast, shot arrows, went hang gliding or fishing, and rode Baga, his horselike pet bordok. Wicket and the other Ewoks also helped a stranded family of humans, the Towanis, of whom only the young daughter, Cindel, survived.

When Imperials first came to Endor, the Ewoks were alarmed. Many wanted to declare war on them, but the Ewok leader, Chief Chirpa, reminded them that their spears couldn't hurt the Imperial fortresses and that the invaders had machines that could fly through the air or burn the forests. One night, as the villagers gathered around the fires, young Wicket recounted how he had witnessed an AT-ST stumble on the rocks, fall, and explode. The Ewoks discovered they *did* have a way to fight back, and they started preparing for battle.

While on a foraging expedition, Wicket came across Princess Leia Organa, who had been thrown off a speeder bike during a chase with scout troopers and knocked unconscious. Although she initially frightened him, Wicket could sense her innate goodness. He returned with her to the village, only to find that Leia's companions—Han Solo, Chewbacca, Luke Skywalker, R2-D2, and C-3PO—had been captured in an Ewok hunting net. Even though Wicket pleaded their case to Chief Chirpa, it took some Jedi tricks from Luke to free the Rebels. Wicket then played a key role in convincing the tribe to aid the Rebels.

Wicket W. Warrick

Later, Han, Leia, and the droids were captured by the Imperials. Wicket and the Ewoks then battled the Imperials and their AT-ST walkers and helped to free them so they could shut down the Death Star's shield generator. After Alliance pilots destroyed the second Death Star in orbit above Endor, the Ewoks held a celebration for the brave Alliance members. Wicket was given the Ewok title of "lead warrior." [RJ, RJN, ETV, BFE]

Warton An inhabitant of the outpost of Eol Sha, he was among those who were evacuated to Dantooine and later killed when Admiral Daala raided the planet. [JS, DA]

Waru A powerful being, it was drawn from a parallel universe by a split in the space-time continuum created by the intersection of a black hole and a quantum crystal star. The Waru appeared to be a complex construct of gold shields covering a slab of raw, uncovered tissue much like a chunk of meat. A viscous fluid glistened between the shields and sometimes oozed out. The Waru was able to heal other beings by encasing them in this ichor, but occasionally the Waru would kill a being brought to it for healing, sucking in their strength. Lord Hethrir planned to offer young Anakin Solo to Waru as a sacrifice; in return he expected to receive great Force powers. But Hethrir himself was taken into the Waru, which then closed in on itself and disappeared, possibly returning to its own universe. [CS]

Waskiro Jabba the Hutt's henchman Bib Fortuna lied about this planet, claiming there had been an ambush in the Ampuroon mining district. Fortuna's lie was an attempt to deceive a Nuffin freighter. [JAB]

Watchkeeper A destroyer in the Bakuran task force, it was sent on an unmanned decoy mission to test enemy firepower. The *Watchkeeper* was vaporized by a Selonian planet repulsor. [AS]

watchman A title given to a Jedi Master, it connoted his or her role as overseer of a particular star system or segment of the galaxy, arranged through a loose agreement with the Old Republic. The watchman's main charge was to maintain harmony and justice. The Republic granted watchmen the authority to operate autonomously in order to right wrongs and deal with disturbances in the Force that occurred outside the purview of local laws. [TOJ, DLS]

watumba bat Gray creatures that eat primarily algae and rock dust, they serve as hosts for several flying parasitic bugs, including parfue gnats. Glottalphibs like keeping the watumba bats nearby, because they support so many "delicacies." Crime kingpin Nandreeson imported the bats to Skip Six in Smuggler's Run. [NR]

wave walker An Imperial light attack vehicle, it was designed to operate above the water's surface. During the Battle of Calamari, wave walkers were built aboard World Devastators, then unleashed upon the Mon Calamari and their New Republic allies. [DE]

wave-weapon Offensive devices, they were capable of turning their victims into smoking ash. They were developed about four millennia ago to combat the beasts of the Dxun moon during the Beast Wars of Onderon. [TOJ]

Wayland A primitive green-and-blue world located about 350 light-years from the planet Myrkr, it was home to Emperor Palpatine's private storehouse. Wayland's surface is covered with dense, double-canopied forests and grassy plains. Mount Tantiss, located in Wayland's northern hemisphere near the eastern edge of its main continent, was the hidden resting place for Palpatine's trophies, his military treasures, and an operational cloning facility.

Generations ago, when human colonists settled on Wayland, they immediately came into conflict with the planet's two native species, the Psadans and the Myneyrshi. The four-armed, blue-crystalline Myneyrshi and the lumpy, plated Psadans were driven from their land until the colonists' weapons began to fail them. When the Empire arrived, the inhabitants were forced to construct the vast storehouse in Mount Tantiss. Palpatine apparently appointed a guardian to defend his storehouse, a guardian who may have been the mad Jedi clone Joruus C'baoth—or just his imagination. C'baoth forced all three of Wayland's species to live under his strict rule in a city built against the southwest side of the mountain. When Palpatine departed with Grand Admiral Thrawn, an Imperial garrison under the command of Colonel Selid was placed in charge to help safeguard the cloning operation, which supplied Thrawn with a nearly inexhaustible stock of trained soldiers.

The Mount Tantiss complex had only one entrance, located on the southwest side. The peak of the complex held an emergency shuttle hangar, the royal chambers, and the Emperor's throne room with a twenty-meter hologram of the galaxy. The fully functioning Spaarti cloning cylinder chamber sat inside a vast natural cavern many stories high. Thrawn had hundreds of Force-blocking ysalamiri transplanted to the cloning chamber to prevent any negative side effects from the rapid

Jeroen Webb

pace of his clone growth. The cloning complex and most of the mountains were destroyed when Lando Calrissian and Chewbacca sabotaged the central equipment column. [HE, LC]

weapon detector A device that uses sensors to scan for power cells and clearly identifiable weapon profiles. The sensors feed data directly to a dedicated computer for nearly instantaneous analysis. Weapon detectors are used in restricted facilities such as military bases, detention centers, and spaceports to scan for unauthorized weapons. The Corporate Sector Authority uses them on worlds such as Bonadan to maintain order. [HSR]

Webb, Jeroen A native of the planet Ralltiir, he became a spy for the Ralltiir underground after the planet was subjugated by the Empire. A skillful starship pilot, he served with Rebel Alliance forces on the ice planet Hoth. [CCG]

webweaver A large, deadly arachnid, it lives on one of the lower ecolevels of the planet Kashyyyk. [HLL]

WED-9-M1 A unique treadwell droid, it was cobbled together by Jawas on the planet Tatooine. Now owned by the De Maals, who own and operate Docking Bay 94 in Mos Eisley, the droid is nicknamed Bantha for its slow and stubborn ways. [CCG]

WED-15-17 A septoid droid nicknamed for an insect from Eriadu, this multiarmed maintenance droid is fiercely loyal to the Empire. It specializes in extending the effective operational life of Imperial resources. [CCG]

WED-15-1662 A standard treadwell droid also known as Eye-six-six-too, it is typical of the thousands of droids that repair and maintain heavy machinery and starfighters. [CCG]

WED-1016 Also known as a techie droid, this starship maintenance droid was built by Cybot Galactica. The WED-1016 is capable of repairing more than 5,000 different on-board systems. The model was also used by Rebel Alliance salvage teams. [CCG]

Weequay A mysterious humanoid species with unusual religious rituals, they have coarse, brown leathery skin that is wrinkled and pitted, and their heads are bald except for a single braided topknot on one side. They come from Sriluur, a harsh desert planet in the Sisar Run. Weequays have a form of pheremonic communication that allows them to communicate with members of their own clan without speech. Although they are not overly intelligent, they are cruelly efficient at violent acts, and thus several were employed by crime lord Jabba the Hutt on Tatooine.

The somewhat off-kilter Weequays in Jabba's employ worshipped many gods, chief among them Quay, god of the moon (Weequay means "follower of Quay"). To contact Quay, they used a small sphere (also called quay) that were known as entertainment devices in other parts of the galaxy. The quay answered simple questions with simple answers: "It is decidedly so," "Concentrate and ask again," "As I see it, yes," and more.

One Weequay, Ak-Buz, commanded Jabba's sail barge until he was murdered by Dannik Jerriko, the Anzati. Porcellus the cook hid the Weequay's body in a garbage heap. When the corpse was discovered, the other Weequay asked their moon god to reveal the murderer, with no success. The Weequay slaughtered banthas as part of their rituals, which infuriated Tusken Raiders. Jabba put an end to the killings, then planted a dead moisture farmer next to a bantha corpse to place suspicion elsewhere. Most of the Weequay in Jabba's employ were aboard his sail barge or the accompanying skiff when Jabba planned to dump the Rebel Alliance infiltrators into the Pit of Carkoon, and most were killed in the fighting or explosion that put an end to the crime lord's long career. [RJ, TJP, SWCG, GG12]

Weerden The planet where Lord Torbin, the Grand Inquisitor, was murdered when Weerden's Imperial palace was rammed by the shuttle *Sark I*. An assassin droid is suspected of killing the shuttle's flight crew and causing the crash on Weerden. [SWSB]

Wehttam A planet located in the Farlax sector. The language spoken on Wehttam is closely related to the language known as Torrock. The chromite-mining colony of New Brigia, within the nearby Koornacht Cluster, once traded its ore along the hyperlanes to Wehttam and Galantos, until the collapse of Imperial control in the Farlax sector made commerce increasingly hazardous. Twelve years after the Battle of Endor, Leia Organa Solo decided to send the New Republic's Fifth Fleet into the Farlax sector to protect worlds such as Wehttam and Galantos from the Yevethan fleet massing in the Koornacht Cluster. Leia accepted the emergency petitions for membership from all worlds bordering the Cluster, including Wehttam. The Republic warships *Jantol* and *Farlight* were sent to Wehttam as a show of strength. [BTS, SOL]

Weequay

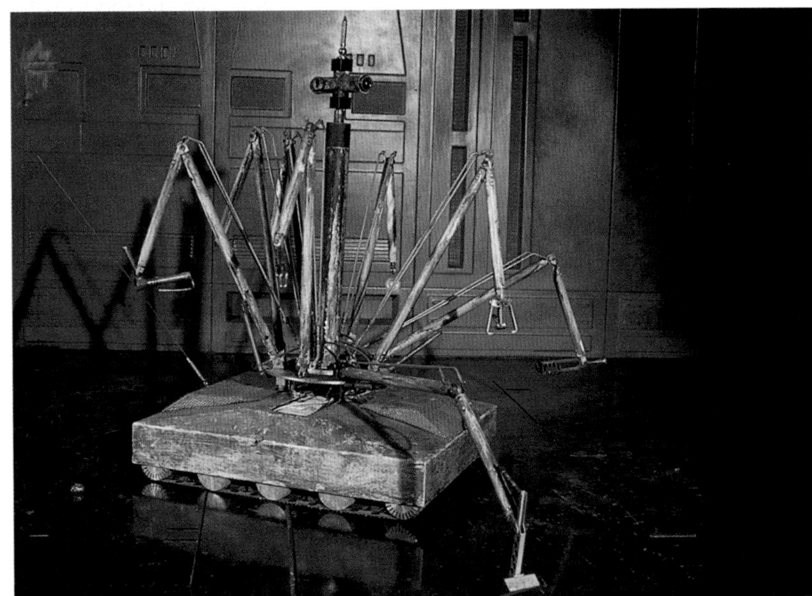

WED model droid

Wel, Tsillin A Quarren Imperial accountant, she was called to testify during Tycho Celchu's trial. During the auditing of Imperial expenditures, her staff uncovered ten million credits located in six different accounts, purportedly paid to Captain Celchu. [KT]

Wena, Master Owner of R2-D2 and C-3PO long before they became involved with the Rebellion, he auctioned them off before they went to Hosk Station. [D]

Weng, Mayli A worker with the Exotic Entertainer's Union on Imperial Center before the Battle of Endor. [SOTE]

Wermyn A tall, one-armed brute, he was in charge of plant operations at

Maw Installation. Wermyn's skin had a purplish-green cast, which left his origins in doubt. During the New Republic assault, he surrendered to Wedge Antilles after activating a meltdown in the reactor asteroid. [COF]

Wessiri, Diric The husband of Iella Wessiri, and twenty years her senior, he was from a wealthy Corellian family whose money allowed him a life of leisure. He viewed life as a collection of experiences to be studied or as a continual quest for enlightenment. When he and his wife fled Corellia, they took on false identities that led them to Coruscant. Diric was captured during an Imperial sweep, interrogated, and broken. After his imprisonment, he was forced to assist General Derricote with his Krytos virus project. Shortly after the liberation of Coruscant, he was released, then debriefed by Alliance Intelligence. Unknown to everyone, he was still working for the Empire against his will. When Ysanne Isard discovered that her agent Kirtan Loor was cooperating with the New Republic, she activated Diric Wessiri, making him an assassin who silenced Loor forever. In a tragic turnabout, Diric was then killed by his unsuspecting wife. [KT]

Wessiri, Iella Iella was formerly a member of the Corellian Security Force where she had been Corran Horn's partner. She later joined Alliance Intelligence and was working undercover on Coruscant when Rogue Squadron arrived to infiltrate the planet. She was with the squadron at the Palar memory-core factory warehouse when their first plan failed because of leaked information. On their second attempt, she was part of Wedge Antilles's team as they took command of a construction droid. Horn was flying cover for her team when his Z-95 Headhunter crashed, and he was presumed killed.

This devastating blow was made bearable only by the sudden and unexpected return of her husband Diric, after a year of agonizing separation. Iella was involved in the case charging Tycho Celchu with spying, but as the case progressed, her doubts increased. When her old Imperial nemesis, Kirtan Loor, decided to testify for Captain Celchu, he demanded that his armed escort include Iella, whom he knew he could trust. As he, Iella, and Nawara Ven made their way to the Justice Court, an assassin surprised them, killing Loor and seriously wounding Ven. Instinctively, Iella returned fire, killing their assailant, whom she was horrified to discover was her husband.

Corran Horn reappeared and was able to comfort her somewhat during the following weeks. Iella and her team of operatives were later sent to Thyferra to help overthrow Ysanne Isard's government. She joined forces with the Ashern Rebels and Zaltin security forces and, when the time was right, easily took over the Xucphra Administration Building, headquarters for Isard's puppet government. [WG, KT, BW]

Western Dune Sea *See* Dune Sea

Whaladon A species of intelligent whalelike mammals, they inhabit the deep oceans of the planet Mon Calamari. [GDV]

Whaladon hunting ship A huge submersible vessel that illegally searched the oceans of Mon Calamari for Whaladons, it was the size of a large capital ship. It was equipped with stun weapons and tractor beams to incapacitate the whalelike mammals and pull them into its recessed chambers, which could store more than a dozen creatures at a time. The ship and its crew of Aqualish hunters was under the command of Captain Dunwell. [GDV]

Whaladon Processing Center An Imperial installation inside an undersea crater where captured whaladons were taken. At the Whaladon Processing Center the mammal's meat and blubber were removed and processed for transportation to Imperial supply centers throughout the galaxy. [GDV]

Whiphid Often called "Tooth Face," members of this species of hulking, fur-covered bipeds stand about 2.5 meters tall. With prominent foreheads, long, bowed cheekbones, and two upturned tusks rising from their jaws, Whiphids are easy to spot in a crowd. They come from the bitterly cold planet of Toola in the Kaelta system. Ferocious predators with a

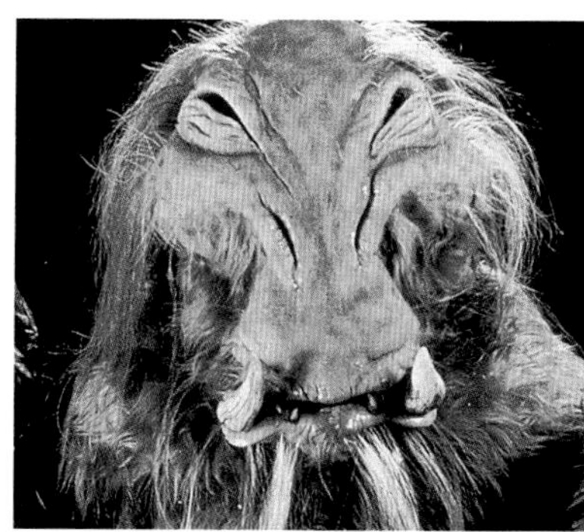

Whiphid

true love of the hunt, they also appreciate the luxuries of advanced technology and often take on lucrative bounty-hunting contracts. Lady Valarian, proprietor of an illegal gambling operation on Tatooine, is a Whiphid. [GG4]

Whistler Corran Horn's R2 series astromech droid, it navigated for the lieutenant's X-wing fighter. Whistler also came equipped with a special criminal investigation and forensics circuitry package provided by CorSec. [RS, BW]

Whistler's Whirlpool A tapcafe on the planet Trogan, it is located on the coast of the planet's most densely populated continent. This bowl-shaped rock pit is built around a natural formation called the Drinking Cup. Open to the sea at its base, the Cup fills six times every day, when the tidal shift inundates the bowl with a violent white-water maelstrom. The tables at Whistler's Whirlpool were arranged in concentric circles around the bowl, but the noise of the water made most of the clientele uncomfortable, and the tapcafe has been largely abandoned. Smuggler Talon Karrde held a meeting with fellow smuggling chiefs at the Whirlpool to discuss how Grand Admiral Thrawn's campaign against the New Republic could affect the smuggling business. [LC]

Whitebeam run A standard ore route, it crosses the Stenness systems and ends at the nearest hyperspace terminal. [TOJ]

whuffa A 250-meter-long wormlike creature, it lives on the planet Dathomir. When the whuffa's dark brown, leathery skin is dried, it can be used much like rope. [CPL]

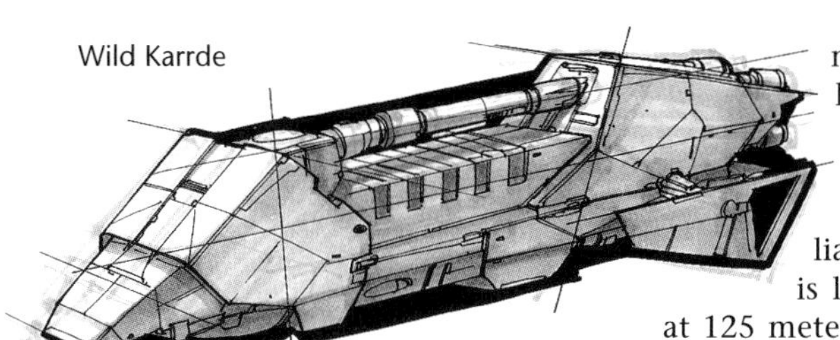
Wild Karrde

Whyren's Reserve A rare, expensive Corellian whiskey, it has an amber color and crisp, woody aroma. It is an especially attractive black-market item. [BW]

Wialu A member of the Fallanassi religious order, she was convinced by Luke Skywalker to help in the New Republic's war on the Yevetha. She used her Fallanassi gift of Immersion Meditation, which allows things to become invisible or nonexistent things to be visualized. Wialu's "phantom" fleet of New Republic ships, along with assistance from former Black Sword Command saboteurs, helped the New Republic's forces defeat the Yevetha. [TT]

Wiamdi, Vviir One of a trio of famous Gand ruetsavii, they were sent to observe Ooryl Qyrgg's life and determine his worthiness to become janwuine. Not only did they observe his activities, but they also participated fully with him during his duties as a member of Rogue Squadron. They proved to be capable fighter pilots as well as undercover operatives. [BW]

Widek Along with Joruna, it is a New Republic planet located near the Koornacht Cluster. Because the Yevetha zealously guard Koornacht's borders, all freight traffic must travel a circuitous route around the Cluster to reach both Widek and Joruna. [BTS]

wildernerf Mossy-horned herd beasts, they are native to the planet Noquivzor. From a distance they appear to be brown specks flowing together into a dark flood. They are preyed upon by prides of leopardlike taopari. [RS]

Wild Karrde Smuggling kingpin Talon Karrde's personal freighter, it looks like a beat-up Corellian bulk freighter. But beneath its scarred hull, the *Wild Karrde* is a mobile communications base for perhaps the best-informed person on the fringes of galactic business.

An unmodified Corellian Action VI transport, it is lumbering and ungainly at 125 meters long with a cargo capacity of 90,000 metric tons. It is slow, easily damaged in combat, and appears unarmed. The *Wild Karrde*, however, has three turbolasers rated for combat against capital starships, with extra shielding and reinforced hull plating. To avoid a fight in the first place, the ship has a sophisticated masking system that hides it from casual distant scans and makes it appear to be a harmless cargo ship at close range.

At sublight speed, the ship is as fast as most Imperial warships. The *Wild Karrde* has a Class-one hyperdrive, making it as fast as most starfighters in hyperspace. The ship's rear holds have been fitted with a complete life-support system, enabling it to carry passengers or animals. The forward hold contains permanent living quarters and offices. The sophisticated communications array lets Karrde keep in constant touch with all of his smugglers and spies. [HE, DFR, DFRSB, RSB]

Wild Space The galaxy's true frontier, once considered part of the Unknown Regions, this area was opened to exploration and settlement by one of the Emperor's last acts. Grand Admiral Thrawn was charged with taming this wilderness, and he declared it part of the Empire. However, with the remnants of the Empire otherwise occupied, much of Wild Space remains untamed. [HESB, SWRPG2]

Wiley

Wiley An Ewok on Endor's forest moon. [RJN, ETV]

Willard, Commander Vanden A leader of the Rebel forces at the Massassi temple base on Yavin 4, he served under Gen. Jan Dodonna. Cmdr. Vanden Willard was formerly the Suolriep sector HQ commander. As a spy he aided Princess Leia Organa and her father, Viceroy Bail Organa, in the years prior to the Senate's dissolution. [SWN, CCG]

Wilum, Oss A member of the Vultan species, he was a Jedi apprenticed to Master Thon of Ambria some 4,000 years before the Galactic Civil War. In his youth he had been an apprentice of Neti Master Garnoo, who passed on before Wilum had completed his training. [DLS, TOJ, FNU, TSW]

Cmdr. Vanden Willard

Wimateeka The Jawa leader of the Nkik clan, he was a friend to the moisture farmer Ariq Joanson. Wimateeka played an instrumental role in Joanson's attempts to make maps and peace with the Jawas and Sand People, serving as his translator and trusted adviser. [TMEC]

Windy One of Luke Skywalker's childhood friends, he grew up with Luke on the planet Tatooine. [SWN]

Winter A tall, regal, and beautiful woman with hair as white as snow, she grew up as the inseparable playmate and companion to Leia Organa and is today Leia's confidante and top assistant. Winter was on a supply run with Rebel agents when Alderaan was destroyed—a loss she still feels deeply.

Winter has a holographic and audiographic memory: She forgets nothing she has ever seen or heard. For years she worked for the Rebels' Pro-

Winter

curement and Supply division until she was reunited with Leia after the Battle of Endor. As the Alliance readied itself for confrontation with Grand Admiral Thrawn, Winter was instrumental in ferreting out Delta Source, Thrawn's main spy resource on Coruscant. She was part of the undercover operation on Coruscant prior to the Alliance's retaking of the planet.

Both Leia and Han Solo turned to Winter to help protect and raise their children. After one encounter with Imperial Dark Siders, the family found a far-off planet called Anoth, where, aided only by a TDL "nanny" droid and a GNK power droid, Winter brought up the children in secure surroundings until they were old enough to return to Coruscant. Baby Anakin Solo remained with Winter.

But an Alliance traitor discovered the location and despite Winter's valiant resistance, the Imperial Ambassador Furgan managed to snatch baby Anakin. He didn't get away, however, as reinforcements arrived. Leia and Han decided that Anakin would be just as safe on Coruscant with them, as long as Winter remained his protector. Admiral Ackbar was also pleased that Winter would not remain on remote Anoth, and the two of them enjoyed each other's company in public as well as in private. [HE, COF, BW, NR, SWCG]

Winward, Riij A Rebel spy, he was a prison guard when the Mistryl Shadow Guards Shada and Karoly were captured by the Empire on Tatooine. He released them so they could escape the planet with the Hammertong device, and in exchange he received their droid Deefour, which carried a complete technical readout of the potentially deadly device. [TMEC]

Wioslea A female Vuvrian, she owns a used-speeder lot in Mos Eisley called Spacesport Speeders. Wioslea is proud that she offered Luke Skywalker 2,000 credits for his landspeeder so he could get off-world and "save the galaxy," as she so often reports during her business dealings. [GG7, SWR]

Wistie Also called firefolk, they are tiny pixielike beings that glow brightly and can fly. Wisties, who tend to giggle a lot, live on Endor's forest moon. [EA, ETV]

Wistril Located in the system of the same name, it is the planet where the Star Destroyer *Chimaera* stopped to take on supplies. Luke Skywalker and Mara Jade hijacked a supply shuttle on the planet in order to rescue smuggler Talon Karrde from the *Chimaera's* detention block. [DFR]

Witches of Dathomir A group of Force-sensitive women, they live on the planet Dathomir and are organized into nine clans. These include the Singing Mountain, Frenzied River, and Red Hills clans. The Witches live by the *Book of Law*, which says that they should not concede to evil. Those who do must go into the wilderness alone to seek cleansing. Their main foes are the Nightsisters, a group of women who acted out of anger, were outcast, and turned to the dark side. The Witches run a completely matriarchal society; men are slaves or breeders. The Witches wear tunics made from colorful reptile skins with thick robes woven of fiber trimmed with large dark beads. [CPL]

Wioslea

Wolfman A slang term for members of the Shistavanen race. [TMEC]

womp A derogatory term derived from "womp rat," it is often directed at the ratlike Ranats on Tatooine. [TMEC]

womp rat Carnivorous creatures, they live in the canyons of Tatooine. They are vicious, hair-covered rodents that can grow to more than two meters in length. Womp rats travel in packs and use their claws and teeth to bring down prey. Luke Skywalker used to hunt womp rats in Beggar's Canyon, targeting them at high speeds from the cockpit of his skyhopper. [SWN, SW, SWR]

Womrik The planet that was a temporary base for Garm Bel Iblis's private army during its hit-and-fade attacks against the Empire. [DFR]

won-wons A Wookiee delicacy, to others they taste like franit slugs, only slimier. [NR]

Wookiee A tall, completely fur-covered species native to the planet Kashyyyk, Wookiees are widely known as ferocious opponents and loyal friends. The average Wookiee grows to more than two meters tall and lives several times the lifetime of a human. On their homeworld, Wookiees live in cities built up high in giant wroshyr trees. Although they appear to be primitive, Wookiees are comfortable with high technology. Their language consists of grunts and growls, and while they can understand other languages, their limited vocal ability makes it impossible for them to speak anything other than their own language. They also have regenerative powers that let them heal more in a day than a human would in two weeks.

From the early days of the Empire, Kashyyyk was placed under martial law and Wookiees were enslaved as laborers. It wasn't until after the Battle of Endor that the Alliance was able to finally set the Wookiees free.

Chewbacca, Han Solo's copilot and partner, is a Wookiee. [SW, ESB, RJ, SWWS, SWSB, HE, CPL]

Wookiee honor family A special bond of friendship that joins one Wookiee with a group of other Wookiees or even with members of other species. The honor family is made up of a Wookiee's true friends, who pledge to lay down their lives for each other and their extended families. [HLL, SWSB, HESB]

Wookiee life debt A sacred Wookiee custom, a life debt is pledged to anyone who saves a Wookiee's life, forming a bond that can never be broken. A life debt is a sacred act of honor, designed to repay that which is without measure. [HLL, SWSB, HESB]

Wookiee Rite of Passage This test calls for an adolescent Wookiee to perform a feat that is both dangerous and difficult. The male or female Wookiee can attempt the feat alone or with friends. If successful, the Wookiee will emerge with physical proof of bravery that can be worn or carried as a trophy. [YJK]

Wookiee-wango A drink made with Sullustan gin, it is stirred not shaken. [TJP]

woolamanders Slothlike in appearance, they are native to Yavin 4. Woolamanders have naked skin on their bellies and thick blue and gold fur on their backs. They live in family groups among the branches of the Massassi trees, feeding on flower petals, tender leaf shoots, and the rhizome seed nodules of nebula orchids. [GG2, ISWU]

Woostri Located in the system of the same name, the planet was attacked and captured by Grand Admiral Thrawn. He determined that the natives of Woostri had both a strong fear of the unknown and a tendency to blow rumors out of proportion, making them vulnerable to his seeming ability to fire through planetary shields. [TLC]

worldcraft A planetoid-sized starship created by command of the Emperor and given to a few of his cruelest officers, one was used by Lord Hethrir. [CS]

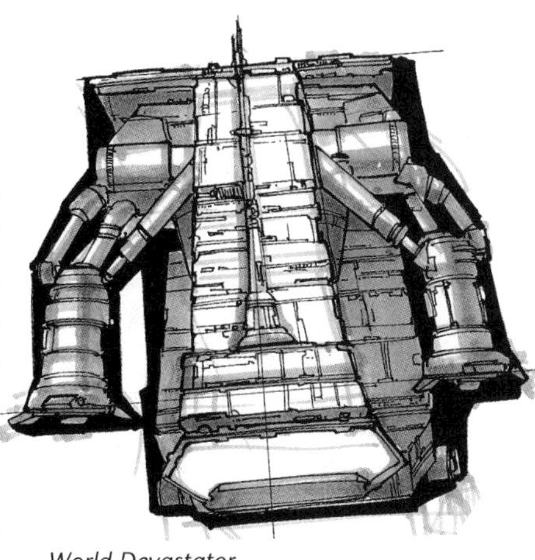

World Devastator

World Devastator Weapons of mass destruction and a symbol of the Empire's reign of terror, they are horrific planetary assault weapons ordered up by the cloned Emperor Palpatine when he attempted to retake control of the galaxy some six years after the Battle of Endor. World Devastators literally chew up a target world, using its resources to create new weapons to be used against it. Hence their many nicknames: World Sweepers, World Smashers, and City Eaters. Internal tractor beams suck a planet's surface into a molecular furnace, which breaks down the substances into useful materials with which droid-controlled factories build new weapons. Within months, a planet is virtually gone.

World Devastators have hyperdrives and ion engines for travel in deep space, but their main role is to devour a planet's surface. A central droid brain controls the onboard factories and stores plans for producing Imperial war vessels. During the Battle of Calamari, World Devastators first produced automated TIE/D fighters in large quantities. A World Devastator "grows" by consuming planets and asteroids. The droid brain can create custom additions and alterations, so no two mature World Devastators are identical.

The *Silencer-7*, the largest World Devastator, led the assault on Mon Calamari. At 3,200 meters long and 1,500 meters tall, it was larger than an Imperial Star Destroyer and had a crew of 25,000. The *Silencer-7* had 125 heavy turbolasers, 200 blaster cannons, eighty proton missile tubes, fifteen ion cannons, and fifteen tractor beam projectors. The key to the defeat of the monstrous machines was Palpatine's fear that the weapons could be turned against him. The cloned Emperor created a command and control coding system that allowed him to seize control of them at any time from his throneworld, Byss. The New Republic was saved when Luke Skywalker provided these signals to R2-D2, who shut down the World Devastators on Calamari, allowing the New Republic's forces to destroy the helpless planet smashers. [DE, DESB, SWVG]

Wormie A nickname given to Luke Skywalker by two of his childhood friends on Tatooine, Camie and Fixer. [SWN, SWR]

Wornal sector Located near the Sombure sector, it was fought over after the Battle of Endor by Imperial Moff Prentioch and Moff Eyrgen as they began expanding their individual territories. Two years after Endor, Prentioch traveled to the water world of Kaal, hoping to gain control of its aquaculture industry to help fuel his war effort in the Wornal sector. [SWAJ]

worrt This voracious predator inhabits Tatooine's wilderness areas. Worrts typically feed on insects, small rodents, and other tiny creatures, but will attack anything that passes by, whether edible or not. Jabba the Hutt had several worrts outside his palace. [SWSB]

Wor Tandell The planet where medical droid Too-Onebee made an inspection tour of medical facilities with Lord Cuvir, Imperial Governor of Firro and Too-Onebee's master. During the inspection on Wor

Worrt

Wuher

Tandell, Cuvir was assassinated by Tiree, a Rebel agent, and Too-Onebee joined the Alliance. [MTS]

Wrea A blue-and-white planet located close to the asteroid belt known as Smuggler's Run. Thirteen years after the Battle of Endor, Han Solo and Chewbacca brought a group of smugglers, injured by an explosion in Smuggler's Run, to Wrea for treatment. [NR]

Wroona A small blue world in the Wroona system, it is located on the far edge of the Inner Rim. Wroona's continents are separated by vast oceans, and their blue-sand beaches stretch for thousands of kilometers. Its seven billion near-human inhabitants are a blue-skinned species with a lighthearted and optimistic outlook on life. Their society emphasizes materialism and personal gain, and Wroonian merchants, smugglers, and pirates can be found throughout the galaxy pursuing personal wealth. The planet is run by the Wroonian Guilds, which represent trade organizations and businesses. Animal life includes Wroonian flycatchers, which hang from coastal cave ceilings by their tongues and swing down to catch their avian prey. The region of space known as Keller's Void acts as a shortcut between the Wroona and Calus systems. [SWAJ, GG2]

Wroshyr A saucer-shaped ship, it is owned by the Wookiee bounty hunter Chenlambec. [SWAJ, TBH]

wroshyr trees Giant trees of the jungle world of Kashyyyk, their separate branches meet to form one interlocked branch, which then sprouts new branches of its own. These reach out in all directions to find other branches to join with. This tendency toward unity makes wroshyr trees stronger, and is a natural symbol for the Wookiee concepts of honor and family. The wroshyr trees in the Rwookrrorro city grouping are actually a single giant plant with a unified root system. [HE, HESB]

Wuher A bulky, surly, middle-aged human, he was a shift bartender at the Mos Eisley spaceport cantina. Abandoned in Mos Eisley in his early youth, Wuher proved to be a whiz with chemicals in general and drinks and elixirs in particular. After graduating from a bartending correspondence school, he was hired by Chalmun the Wookiee. For years, Wuher hated droids, primarily because they were an easy target. But he had a change of heart when he met Ceetoo-Arfour, a processing droid capable of making new exotic drinks out of the strangest raw materials. Wuher's first concoction with Ceetoo-Arfour was a drink specially designed for Jabba the Hutt, created using the pheromones extracted from the corpse of Greedo, the inexperienced Rodian bounty hunter. [TMEC]

Wuitho Trifalls A former Alderaan landmark, it featured three spectacular waterfalls. Captain Celchu visited the Wuitho Trifalls with his family the week before going off to the Imperial Academy. It was his last visit to the famous tourist attraction. [BW]

Wukkar A heavily populated world in the Galactic Core, it was one of many planets that surrendered to Admiral Ackbar and the Alliance fleet in the years following the Battle of Endor. [DESB]

Wuntoo Forcee Forwun (12-4C-41) A traffic-controller droid, he worked at Cloud City during the time when the notorious EV-9D9 destroyed and tortured a number of droids. Wuntoo Forcee Forwun possessed elaborate circuitry that allowed certain emotions to arise, namely revenge against EV-9D9 for her evil deeds. Wuntoo Forcee Forwun eventually tracked EV-9D9 to Jabba the Hutt's palace and destroyed her. [TJP]

Wwebyls A tiny humanoid from the planet Yn, he is a New Republic Senator who was elected to the Inner Council after the bombing of Senate Hall on Coruscant. [NR]

Wyl sector Together with the Aparo sector, it forms the inner border of the Corporate Sector. It was long ruled by Moff Gozric. [CSSB]

Wynni A female Wookiee smuggler, she tried to seduce Chewbacca on his first visit to Skip One. Wynni was one of the smugglers who joined Han Solo and Chewbacca in Smuggler's Run during their investigation into the bombing on Coruscant and the rescue of Lando Calrissian from the crime lord Nandreeson. However, her amorous feelings for Chewbacca overcame her, and at one point during the trip she had to be restrained. [NR]

wyrwulf A name given to the furry young of the Codru-Ji. They have limpid liquid-blue eyes, six legs, and fangs. Wyrwulfs are intelligent but not self-aware until after they metamorphose into the upright four-armed form of an adult Codru-Ji. [CS]

X-1 Viper Automadon A recent war droid manufactured by the factory world of Balmorra, it is equipped with molecular shielding that not only absorbs the energy of an attacker's blast but also channels it

X-1 Viper Automadon

directly into its own turbolasers. Balmorra agreed to send a shipment of the X-1 Viper Automadons to the cloned Emperor's throneworld of Byss as part of a cease-fire agreement with Imperial Military Executor Sedriss. But the planet's Governor Beltrane alerted the New Republic so that it could hide stowaways inside the war droids. [DE2]

X-10D A red-and-bronze service droid, it was on board the ship of the bounty hunter Bossk, the *Hound's Tooth*. Roughly Trandoshan in shape, X-10D was brainless, receiving its commands directly from the ship's main computer. After the Wookiee bounty hunter Chenlambec tricked and captured Bossk, the Wookiee's positronic processor, Flirt, attached to Exten-dee and served as its "brain" from then on. [TBH]

X-30, X-34 landspeeders Older-model landspeeders, the X-34 was the model used by young Luke Skywalker as he grew up on Tatooine. Open to the air, it had a top speed of 250 knots per hour. Repulsorlift drives keep it suspended one meter above ground even when it is parked. [ISWU, TMEC]

X-222 A sleek high-altitude atmospheric fighter craft, it is commonly called a triple-deuce. [HLL]

Xa Fel Located in the heart of the Kanchen sector, the planet surrendered to the Empire after New Republic forces were defeated in a thirty-hour battle. Captain Harbid of the Star Destroyer *Death's Head* accepted the surrender of the Xa Fel government and handled the surface troop deployments. [LC]

Xappyh sector Jedi Master Jorus C'baoth was once named ambassador at large to the Xappyh sector by the Old Republic Senate. [DFR]

Xaverri A friend of Han Solo's from his smuggling days, after the Empire murdered her children she became an accomplished con artist who mainly swindled Imperial dignitaries. [CS]

xenoarchaeology The study of vanished off-world or alien cultures through the scientific study of the artifacts that they left behind. [SME]

Xim the Despot An ancient tyrant who conquered a vast region of space, some histories claim that he ruled thousands of star systems during his reign of thirty standard years. The conquering armies of Xim the Despot plundered and subjugated world after world, filling his coffers with untold wealth, guarded by the same war droids who guarded him. The ruthless Xim committed uncounted atrocities before the conquered star systems led by the Hutts were finally able to overthrow him and end his reign of terror. [HLL, GG12]

Xizor, Prince The top crime lord in the galaxy, he was head of the criminal syndicate known as Black Sun. Prince Xizor was also highly political and was probably the third most powerful individual in the galaxy. He schemed to supplant number two—Darth Vader—and possibly even take over the Emperor's job at some point.

Xizor was more than 100 years old, with the body of a well-sculpted thirty-year-old thanks to its crafting by myostim units. A Falleen, Xizor was tall with a slightly elevated, sharp reptilian ridge over his spine. His head was bald except for a long topknot and ponytail. Xizor exuded natural pheromones that made most humanoids feel instantly attracted to him; his skin color, normally a dusky green, changed with the rise of those pheromones, going from the cool into the warm spectrum of colors.

Xizor harbored a particular hatred for Vader. About a decade before the Battle of Hoth, Vader had established a biological weapons lab on Xizor's planet. An accident let a tissue-destroying bacterium escape, so Vader ordered the city near the lab burned to ashes, killing 200,000 Falleen including Xizor's entire family. Xizor, who was off-world, destroyed all records of the family tragedy so that no one would know of his personal reasons for despising Vader and his pledge to avenge the deaths. When he heard that Vader was seeking Luke Skywalker to convert him to the dark side of the Force—and that young Skywalker was Vader's son—he plotted to have Luke killed and Vader's plans thwarted. Xizor's huge castle on Imperial Center was only a short walk through protected corridors to Vader's palace. Every time Vader set foot outside his castle, Xizor had him under constant surveillance.

Xizor had a number of legitimate businesses into which he funneled much of the ill-gotten gains of Black Sun. The largest of these was a shipping company, Xizor Transport Systems (XTS).

Because attracting females was so easy for Xizor, he quickly tired of them. But he considered Princess Leia Organa a real challenge, although he was confident he could win her over with his pheromones. Leia initiated the contact in her attempts to find out who was trying to murder Luke. At their first meeting, Leia was indeed taken with Xizor's beauty, and she nearly let herself be seduced. But his spell over her was broken when Chewbacca interrupted their meeting and whisked Leia away. When Leia returned, she kneed Xizor in the groin, turning herself into a prisoner from a free-will visitor. Xizor had his female human-replica droid, Guri, take Leia to her locked room, then informed her that she was bait to lure Luke.

When Luke, Lando Calrissian, Dash Rendar, and Chewbacca broke into Xizor's castle through its lowest levels, the prince was at first reluctant to admit that his tight security measures could have been overcome. But Xizor became convinced that his castle had been infiltrated after Guri

Prince Xizor

was bashed by Leia. Soon, Xizor came face-to-face with Luke Skywalker and a fearsome battle ensued. When Skywalker produced a thermal detonator, Xizor let the group leave unmolested—but not before Calrissian dropped another detonator with a five-minute timer down a chute. Xizor escaped to his skyhook, *Falleen's Fist*, using his ship *Virago*. But in a final confrontation with Darth Vader, he was killed when Vader ordered Xizor's skyhook retreat blown to bits. [SOTE]

Xizor Transport Systems (XTS) The legitimate business front of crime lord Prince Xizor, the transportation company was very profitable. Much of the money from his Black Sun organization's illicit activities was funneled into Xizor Transport Systems (XTS), which benefited from Imperial contracts given personally by Emperor Palpatine. [SOTE]

Xorth system Still controlled by Imperial forces, the system bordering the Cardua system deals primarily in agricultural trade. The Xorth system produces the best farrberries in the galaxy; they are valued for both their pleasant scent and their stimulating effect. [TSC]

XP-38 landspeeder One of the most recent models, this much sought-after design emphasizes smooth lines and sheer speed over practicality. The XP-38 landspeeder, manufactured by the Sullustan company SoroSuub, has room for only a driver and passenger and is aimed at younger customers and for recreational uses. It has a snug cockpit with a retractable duraplex windscreen. The optional sensor array is mounted on a swivel so that either the driver or the passenger can run the system. Reclining and height-adjustment controls are on the seats, and a small cargo compartment is hidden behind.

The XP-38 has a rear-mounted autopilot that looks like an R2 astromech droid. As in standard landspeeders, a repulsorlift generator produces lift and provides power to the turbine engines. The XP-38 sports three rear-mounted turbine engines and maneuvering flaps fore and aft. It offers tight cornering and great acceleration, with a maximum hovering height of two meters. While engine noise is excessive by modern standards, that's a positive selling point with the target audience.

Its one weakness is a stiff repulsor generator setting that's geared for performance but isn't durable enough for rough terrain, limiting the XP-38 to travel over smooth surfaces. It can take up to three hours to recalibrate the suspension, so most owners don't bother. [SW, SWSB, SWVG]

XT-6 An ancient service droid, it was used 4,000 years before the Galactic Civil War by Jedi Cay Qel-Droma to replace the arm he lost in battle. [TOJ]

XTS *See* Xizor Transport Systems

Xucphra A major Thyferran corporation, it was one of the leaders in bacta production and distribution. A Xucphra pharmacologist discovered contamination in Lot ZX1449F. The company promoted civil war on Thyferra, aiming at complete control of the Bacta Cartel. Xucphra was aided by former Imperial Intelligence director Ysanne Isard, who was subsequently given control of the corporation and the planetary government after she fled Coruscant. After a long and bloody war, the forces of Isard and Xucphra were defeated by a free-lance Rogue Squadron. [BW]

Xucphra Alazhi One of the three Thyferran bacta tankers hijacked by Rogue Squadron during the Bacta War. Its captain and crew were reluctant to defect. When their absence was detected, their escort, the *Corrupter*, immediately backtracked to their new location. Before they were able to explain or escape, the ship was destroyed. [BW]

Xucphra Meander One of a trio of Thyferran bacta tankers hijacked by Rogue Squadron during its war against Ysanne Isard and her control of the Bacta Cartel. The contents of the freighter were sent to Coruscant to help alleviate the ravages of the Krytos virus. [BW]

Xucphra Rose One of three Thyferran bacta tankers hijacked by Rogue Squadron despite Ait Convarion's protection. The ship and its contents were sent to the colonists on Halanit to combat a disease. [BW]

Xux, Qwi From the brain of this frail and willowy woman came some of the Empire's most destructive weapons, but she found redemption in the New Republic and in the love of one of its leaders. A tall, attractive humanoid from the planet Omwat, Qwi Xux has bluish-tinted skin, long eyelashes above wide, deep-blue eyes, and gossamer hair reminiscent of pearlescent feathers. Like others of her race, she had an analytical mind that—even at the age of ten—indicated a future as a brilliant designer. At that age she was taken from her planet by Grand Moff Tarkin and forced into a tough training regimen with nine others; after two years, she was the only survivor. She was assigned to Tarkin's top-secret weapons development lab, the Maw Installation.

Qwi was placed under the tutelage of top Imperial designer Bevel Lemelisk, and she excelled at her design and engineering assignments, sharing in the design of the first Death Star and the World Devastators. Her most powerful superweapon was the Sun Crusher, an indestructible ship that carried resonance torpedoes with enough firepower to snuff out a star. Naively, Qwi Xux told herself that her plans could be used to build peaceful objects used in commerce and manufacturing.

When Han Solo, Chewbacca, and Jedi trainee Kyp Durron managed to enter the Maw, she finally let herself see the true and terrible results of her work, the death and destruction that her weapons had visited on the galaxy's innocents. When Maw chief Admiral Daala told her that she was going to use the Sun Crusher against the Alliance, Xux knew she had to act. She freed the prisoners and they escaped aboard the only working model of the Sun Crusher.

On Coruscant, Qwi was assigned Gen. Wedge Antilles as a personal bodyguard and succeeded in con-

XP-38 landspeeder

Qwi Xux

vincing the Alliance to dispose of the deadly Sun Crusher. On a trip to Ithor, just as Qwi and Wedge were beginning to fall in love, Kyp Durron—deciding on his own that Xux's knowledge of weaponry was too dangerous—used the Force to kill her memory, erasing most of her past. She traveled back to the Maw Installation with an Alliance strike force and found herself in the middle of a fierce battle with Admiral Daala, but she didn't find her lost memory. However, she started the healing process with the assistance of General Antilles. [JS, COF]

X-wing starfighter One of the Rebel Alliance's most advanced fighters, this ship played an important role in the first major Rebel Victory of the Galactic Civil War: the Battle of Yavin and the destruction of the first Death Star. The T-65 X-wing starfighter was the final design of its kind produced by Incom Corp. before the company was nationalized by the Empire. A Rebel commando team helped Incom's senior design staff defect to the Alliance with plans and prototypes of the X-wing, a devastating loss for the Empire.

The X-wing takes its name from its pair of double-layered wings, which are deployed into the familiar X-formation for combat and atmospheric flight. During normal sublight-speed space flight, the wings are closed. Each wing tip has a high-powered laser cannon. A pair of proton torpedo launchers are located midway up the main space-frame, each with a magazine of three torpedoes. In the hands of Luke Skywalker, two of those torpedoes were enough to set off a chain-reaction explosion that destroyed the Death Star.

The X-wing is a one-pilot fighter. An astromech droid housed in a snug droid socket behind the pilot handles many inflight operations, such as damage control, astrogation jumps, and flight performance adjustment. Although the X-wing has an impressive combat record, much of that is due to the skills of Alliance pilots, and that, in turn, is at least partly due to the fact that the X-wing's controls are reminiscent of T-16 airspeeders and other common sport vehicles found on frontier worlds. Bush pilots who have developed their reflexes on such vehicles easily make the adjustment to the X-wing's familiar controls.

The X-wing is also known for its durability, with a reinforced titanium alloy hull and high-powered shield generators. It can normally take minor hits without a serious loss of performance, and has full ejection and life-support systems. X-wings have hyperdrive systems, which add flexibility to its list of attributes.

Thirteen years after the Battle of Endor, a new model, the T-65D-A1, was approved by Gen. Wedge Antilles. The new design had a superb guidance system and theoretically was more efficient, because it combined its computer system and its astromech unit in one complete system, thereby eliminating the astromech droid. Luke Skywalker's X-wing was one of the first to be upgraded. However, he ordered that it be switched back to the older design, stating that he couldn't imagine piloting his X-wing without R2-D2. During the rebuilding, Artoo, C-3PO, and mechanic Cole Fardreamer discovered that the new X-wing model had been sabotaged: Each of the new computer systems contained a hidden detonator, installed as part of Dark Jedi Kueller's campaign of terror against the New Republic. An embarrassed General Antilles ordered the new design scrapped. [SW, ESB, RJ, SWVG, NR]

Xyquine Three years after the Battle of Endor, it was the site of what Han Solo called a fiasco for New Republic forces. A passenger transport was destroyed at Xyquine, and pilot Pash Cracken had to invent the Cracken Twist to disguise the escaping ships' exit vectors. [DFR, LC]

X-wing starfighter

Y-4 Raptor transport Designed as a military transport shuttle, the Incom Corp. model wasn't popularized until Warlord Zsinj expanded his own empire. Y-4 transports then became known as the ships of Zsinj's Raptors, the elite commandos Zsinj used to hold power. The main mission of the small shuttle, just under thirty meters long, is to ferry platoons of troops and supplies between starships or bases. For combat missions, the Y-4 can carry the equivalent of four AT-ST scout walkers, six compact assault vehicles, or up to eight speeder bikes.

The Y-4 Raptor has a standard array of sublight drives, a Class-two hyperdrive, a backup hyperdrive engine, and a dedicated nav computer. The crew consists of a pilot, a chief gunnery officer on the bridge, and a second gunnery officer on the dorsal-mounted quad laser cannon. The bridge has a socket for an R2 or similar astromech droid to assist in hyperspace calculations. Forward weaponry includes two fire-linked laser cannons and a concussion missile launcher with a magazine of six missiles.

Because Zsinj's Raptors are known for quiet infiltrations of planets and surgical strikes against defense grids, the commandos require a ship that can get them on a planet quickly and quietly. The Y-4 is up to the task with its streamlining and retractable swing-wings for increased atmospheric maneuverability. Han Solo used a falsified transponder code identifying the *Millennium Falcon* as one of the Y-4 transports assigned to the Raptors. The code allowed him to infiltrate the shipyards of Dathomir, but when Solo activated a new sensor and communications jamming system, he burned out the *Falcon's* nav computers, stranding Solo, Princess Leia, Chewbacca, and C-3PO on Dathomir. [CPL, SWSB]

Yaga Minor This world is the location of a major group of Imperial shipyards, with facilities on a par with those at Ord Trasi and Bilbringi. All three shipyards were extremely busy during Grand Admiral Thrawn's offensive against the New Republic. The Outbound Flight program departed from Yaga Minor. The planet is home to the Yagai species of reed-thin tripeds and to a subspecies of Yaga drones. [DFR, LC, LCSB]

Yag'Dhul A small, dense planet with three moons, which orbits a yellow star, it is homeworld of the Givin. The complex interaction of orbits and rotations between Yag'Dhul and its moons means that the planet is continually beset by massive tidal forces powerful enough to pull the water and the atmosphere to different locations, exposing large areas of the planet to hard vacuum. Although some animals on Yag'Dhul survive by traveling along with the tides, the Givin have evolved a hard, sealable exoskeleton that allows them to survive in the vacuum of space. The Givin inhabit hermetically sealed cities built to withstand the strongest tides, and their society is organized around complex mathematics due to the importance of predicting the tides. The Givin are respected starship builders.

The Yag'Dhul system contains an *Empress*-class space station owned by Warlord Zsinj. Three years after the Battle of Endor, Rogue Squadron raided the station to capture a supply of bacta, which Zsinj had previously stolen from a Thyferran convoy. They captured the station, commanded by a Twi'lek named Valsil Torr, and off-loaded the bacta onto freighters. The Rogues then resigned from the military, and Wing Commander Varth's fighters were assigned to make the station uninhabitable so Zsinj could not use it again. But Pash Cracken, newly reassigned with Varth's wing, offered Rogue Squadron the use of the station. The cramped station has fifty living levels, with a ten-level docking facility in the middle. Valsil Torr had died, so Booster Terrik was put in charge of operations. When the Imperial Star Destroyer *Virulence* arrived to destroy the station, Terrik was chiefly responsible for getting the attacking ship to surrender. After taking command of the ship, he went to Thyferra, where the ship's presence hastened the end of the Bacta War. [GG4, KT, BW]

Nevar Yalnal

Yahez The flagship of the New Republic's Fourth Fleet Task Force Apex, it was commanded by Admiral Farley Carson. [TT]

Yaka A species of near-human cyborgs, they were transformed after their home planet was invaded centuries ago by superintelligent inhabitants of Arkania, a neighboring star system. The Arkanians forced the Yakas to undergo surgery in which they implanted cyborg brain enhancers, increasing the species' intelligence to genius level. Thus, the brutish-looking Yakas are much smarter than they appear. One side effect of the implants is a twisted sense of humor that all Yakas possess. [DE]

Yak Face *See* Saelt-Marae

Yalnal, Nevar An immense Ranat scavenger from the planet Araila, he spies for anyone willing to pay his price. Nevar Yalnal is an outcast and usually works as a laborer for Hrchek Kal Fas. [CCG]

Yanee A slender man whose lined face and gray hair marked him as years older than Kueller, he became the Dark Jedi's second assistant following Kueller's disposal of Femon, his first assistant. Yanee was one of the few people who actually expressed the opinion he had rather than the one Kueller wanted to hear, which Kueller found refreshing. However, Kueller decided that the trait might soon become tiresome, so he began training a third assistant, Gant. [NR]

Yar, Senator Tolik An Oolid, he is a member of the New Republic Senate Defense Council. Senator Tolik Yar was one of Chief of State Leia Organa Solo's champions in the Senate during the difficulties of the Yevethan crisis. [BTS]

Yarar, Brimon A member of the anti-alien Human League, he was in charge of an archaeological dig on Corellia that tried to locate an ancient repulsor device. [AC]

Yasht, Ra Along with Skarten, his colleague at Beshka University, he wrote "Torture Observed: an Interview with Jabba's Cook." [TJP]

Yavaris An escort frigate, it was commanded by Wedge Antilles in the assault on Maw Installation. It is a powerful ship despite its fragile appearance, a result of the thin span that separates its two primary components. At the frigate's aft end a boxy construction contains sublight and hyperdrive engines and the power reactors, which drive not only the engines but also twelve turbolaser batteries and twelve laser cannons. On the other end of a connecting rod, separated from the engines, is the much larger command section, hanging down in an angular structure that contains the command bridge, crew quarters, scanners, and cargo bays containing two full X-wing fighter squadrons. General Antilles also used the ship to charge into the Nal Hutta system. [RSB, COF, DS]

Yavin A planet in the system of the same name, it is an orange gas giant nearly 200,000 kilometers in diameter, with a strong magnetic field. Yavin occupies the outermost position in the system and has dozens of moons, three of which (designated 4, 8, and 13) can support humanoid life. Refracted light from the system's star makes the planet seem to glow with an inner light. Yavin's atmosphere, almost 65,000 kilometers deep, is composed primarily of hydrogen and helium, and the windstorms often exceed 600 kilometers an hour.

Throughout the upper atmosphere there live several varieties of floating gasbag creatures, which breed once every century. Most are nonpredatory and feed on drifting algae, but two species (the floater shark and floater squid) prey on other animals.

Yavin

Yavin's metallic core is surrounded by a thick layer of frozen liquids under tremendous pressure. Many species of nearly two-dimensional crawlers live in this frozen layer at pressures that would crush most other life-forms. The pressures are so great that carbon and metallic hydrogen are compressed together to form quantum crystals called Corusca gems. The gems, found only at Yavin's core, glow with an inner light and are the hardest substance known in the galaxy.

The Damarind Corporation, an enormous galaxy-wide consortium of jewel merchants, had an exclusive contract with the Empire to harvest Corusca stones from Yavin. Damarind Fishing Station, in orbit above the gas giant, retrieved gems for several years until it went bankrupt due to economic difficulties.

Immediately following the Battle of Yavin, an Imperial salvage station was temporarily set up in the planet's orbit to analyze the debris from the destroyed Death Star. Seven years after the Battle of Endor, the New Republic attempted to dispose of the Sun Crusher by depositing it in the planet's dense core, but it was quickly retrieved by Jedi Kyp Durron. One year later, following an intense battle at Yavin 4, Admiral Daala's Super Star Destroyer *Knight Hammer* plunged into Yavin's atmosphere and was destroyed. Some nineteen years after the Battle of Endor, Lando Calrissian established GemDiver Station in Yavin's atmosphere to retrieve Corusca gems. The station operated by dropping a quantum-plated diving bell via an energy tether down to Yavin's core, where the largest gems can be found. Jacen and Jaina Solo were kidnapped from GemDiver Station following an Imperial attack. [SW, SWN, DA, DLS, YJK, GG2, DS]

Yavin 4 The fourth moon of the planet Yavin, it houses the temples and ruins of the now-vanished Massassi race, and once served as the primary base for the Rebel Alliance. A hot jungle world, Yavin 4 has four main continents separated by six oceans, and contains one landlocked sea. Volcanic mountain ranges and wide rivers can be found amid the thick jungles and towering, purple-barked Massassi trees. The moon has both a wet and dry season, and violent, unpredictable storms whip across its surface every few months. Beautiful rainbow storms sometimes occur when the sun rises past the gas giant Yavin and its light refracts against prismatic ice crystals high in the atmosphere.

Yavin 4's flora includes sense-enhancing blueleaf shrub, climbing fern, feather fern, colorful nebula orchids, blistering touch-not shrubs, and explosive grenade fungi. Indigenous life in its jungles includes semiintelligent simians called woolamanders, stubborn Yavinian runyips, mucous salamanders, purple jumping spiders, lizard crabs, swimming crabs, whisper birds, reptile birds, stinger lizards, crystal snakes, armored eels, stump lizards, crawlfish, ravenous stintaril rodents, tree ticks, spiderlike anglers, piranha beetles, and flying two-headed reptiles created during the time of the Sith Lord Exar Kun.

Several of the ancient Massassi ruins have been given names, including the Great Temple, the Palace of the Woolamander, and the Temple of the Blueleaf Cluster; almost all of the ruins are connected by an extensive network of underground tunnels. The pyramid-shaped Great Temple lies next to a broad, branching river. The top of the temple houses an observation deck, and below that lies the grand audience chamber. Below the chamber are housing levels, and the ground level contains the Communications Center, common rooms, and the Alliance's former War Room. The Temple's hangars are underground. Also underground was the Lost City of the Jedi.

More than 4,000 years before the Battle of Yavin the Sith magician Naga Sadow, under a death sentence

Yavin 4's Great Temple

from the Sith Lord of the time, fled to Yavin 4 with his followers so he could practice his dark-side alchemy in peace. Sadow hid his starship and his alchemy equipment beneath the Sith Temple of Fire. Sadow's alchemy helped create many monsters, including a warrior species called the Massassi, designed to guard Sadow's Yavin 4 legacy. The Massassi, the mutated descendants of the ancient Sith, gradually devolved into a primitive and dangerous people, using the dark side to augment their archaic weapons.

When the Dark Jedi Exar Kun arrived on Yavin 4, he enslaved the Massassi and forced them to construct new temples as focal points for Sith power. One temple dedicated to Kun's greatness was built deep in the jungle in the center of a still lake and featured glittering Corusca gems and a towering obsidian statue of the Dark Lord. During the Sith War, Kun brought twenty Jedi Knights to Yavin 4, where he infected them with the evil spirits of the ancient Sith. He ordered them to go out and slay their Jedi Masters, and a terrible Jedi holocaust descended on the galaxy. Soon, however, a united group of thousands of Jedi, led to the jungle moon by Ulic Qel-Droma, arrived to stop Kun.

The Dark Lord ordered the Massassi Night Beast into an isolation chamber as a surprise for his enemies and began putting his final plans into effect. Knowing that he could not defeat the Jedi fleet, Kun sacrificed thousands of Massassi lives to trap his own spirit within the walls of the temples. The Jedi attackers mistakenly ignited the moon's jungles, devastating its surface and causing the deaths of the remaining Massassi, but the Great Sith War had finally ended. Before his defeat, Exar Kun had trapped the children of the Massassi within a strange golden globe, and several desperate Massassi traveled to Yavin 8 to seek assistance from the Melodie people.

Some 4,000 years before the Battle of Yavin, the Jedi Master Ikrit discovered the golden sphere containing the Massassi children located beneath the Palace of the Woolamander and stayed with it, awaiting someone who could break its curse. Centuries later, the Rebel Alliance constructed its primary base within the abandoned temples after evacuating their installation on Dantooine. Under the command of Gen. Jan Dodonna, Alliance engineers cleared out the ancient structures and made them fit for habitation once more and also installed a turbolift and erected high lookout towers. Dodonna sealed off the nearby Temple of the Blueleaf Cluster when an eerie power crystal, containing what appeared to be trapped spirits, was found inside its main audience chamber.

The Sullustan naturalist Dr'uun Unnh took time out from his Alliance duties to begin the first modern-day studies of the jungle moon, cataloguing many of its plant and animal species. Not long after, the first Imperial Death Star discovered the secret base and moved into firing position as the Rebels counterattacked with snubfighters. The battle station was destroyed by Luke Skywalker, in what is now referred to as the Battle of Yavin, as it attempted to shatter Yavin 4 with its superlaser. During the fighting, an Imperial pilot named Qorl crashed his damaged TIE fighter in the moon's jungles and fruitlessly awaited rescue, while another crashing TIE killed Dr'uun Unnh.

In the aftermath of the battle, the Empire blockaded the moon and periodically attacked the Rebel base with TIE fighters. During one such attack, a TIE bomber that crashed in the jungle awakened the Massassi Night Beast, which had lain dormant for thousands of years. The beast, which could use the Force to shield itself from energy weapons, laid waste to much of the Rebel base until calmed by Luke Skywalker. The creature then took an Alliance ship and left the moon, intending to search for its former masters among the stars. The Alliance eventually evacuated Yavin 4.

Seven years after the Battle of Endor, the Great Temple was used as the location of Luke Skywalker's Jedi academy, and the long-trapped spirit of Exar Kun reasserted itself. After nearly killing Skywalker, Kun's spirit was finally vanquished by the efforts of the new Jedi trainees. The next year, the academy was targeted for attack by Admiral Daala's fleet. After a long, destructive battle, Daala's forces were defeated and her Super Star Destroyer *Knight Hammer* was demolished. Eighteen years after the Battle of Endor, Anakin Solo visited the academy and discovered a mysterious golden sphere hidden beneath the Palace of the Woolamander. One year later, Jacen and Jaina Solo visited the academy and were held prisoner by the TIE pilot Qorl, still living in the moon's deep jungles. [SW, SWN, DA, COF, DLS, YJK, JJK, GG2, CSW, DS, FP, ISWU, TSW]

Yavin 8 The eighth moon of the planet Yavin, it is covered with vast brown-and-green tundra between two polar ice caps and split by an equatorial range of purple mountains. Yavin 8 has few large bodies of water, although large reservoirs of groundwater lie beneath the permafrost, resulting in small marshes and swamps during the summer months.

About fifty-four million of the intelligent amphibious humanoids known as the Melodies inhabit the caverns and lakes in the warmer equatorial region near the mountains. They begin life on land, then move into water as adults, their legs replaced by tails and their lungs by gills. This transformation into adult form, called the Changing Ceremony, happens around a Melodie's twentieth year and takes place in a shallow pool coated with a unique, air-supplying algae. The Melodies are unable to leave their pools during the transformation, which can take weeks, and are thus particularly vulnerable to Yavin 8's many land-based predators.

The young Melodies perform most of the necessary functions of their primitive society because the elders can no longer leave the streams and lakes. Abundant animal life includes silver-backed fish and many species of herbivorous burrowers and their carnivorous counterparts, such as the loper and moss-hopper. Seventeen species of grazers, including the wolbak, dysart, dontopod, and songbuk, inhabit the moon's tundra and mountain ranges. Predators include snakelike reels, color-changing ursods, rodentlike raiths, flying avrils, serpentine ropedancers, and arachnid purellas.

Around 4,000 years before the Battle of Yavin, members of Yavin 4's Massassi species journeyed to Yavin 8 to seek help for their children, who had been magically trapped in a golden globe by the Dark Jedi Exar Kun. When the Melodie elders were unable to help them, the Massassi carved the story of their plight in the rocks of the Sistra mountain in the hopes that someone would eventually be able to break the curse. Some eighteen years after the Battle of Endor, Anakin Solo and the Jedi trainee Tahiri traveled to Yavin 8 to take their friend Lyric to her Changing Ceremony within the Sistra mountain. They had to battle predators but uncovered the ancient message of the Massassi and brought back a new Melodie child, Sannah, to be trained at the Jedi academy on Yavin 4. [GG2, JJK]

Yavin 13 The thirteenth moon of the planet Yavin, it is the desert homeworld of two intelligent but primitive species, the Gerbs and the Slith. The surface of the moon is covered with rocky mesas, forests of tall cacti, and shifting walls of blowing sand. A vast ocean making up most of the southern hemisphere sends patches of fog and infrequent storms across the arid desert. The nomadic Slith are intelligent serpents, traveling the desert plains at night hunting small animals with their venomous fangs. The rabbitlike Gerbs have metallic claws to aid in burrowing, and enormous, sensitive ears. Plant life includes the saldi bush and korin flower. Animal life includes a vast array of insect species, twilight lizards, solar-collecting burning snakes, and more than sixty species of scorpionlike tripions. [GG2]

Yavin, Battle of The first major engagement of the Galactic Civil War, it was also the first major tactical victory for the Rebel Alliance. The Battle of Yavin took place in the shadow of the gas giant, near its fourth moon.

The battle came about after Rebel spies stole the plans for the Empire's newest weapon of mass destruction, the Death Star. The plans made it to Rebel headquarters on Yavin 4 despite the capture and subsequent rescue of Princess Leia Organa, but the Empire had tracked Leia's rescuers to the once-secret base. With only about thirty standard minutes before the Death Star would be close enough to obliterate Yavin 4, the Rebels mustered every ship they had. The stakes were high, with only two possible outcomes: survival of the Rebel Alliance, or total destruction. The Rebel plan depended on the ability of a single starfighter to navigate the Death Star trenches—all the while avoiding laser fire from gun towers and TIE fighters—and score a direct hit with a proton torpedo on a small, unshielded thermal exhaust vent to start a chain reaction that would blow up the battle station's power core.

The battle seemed to be going badly for the Rebels. Although they held their own for a while and their superior piloting skills took many Imperials out of the fight, the sheer numerical superiority of the Imperials began to take its toll. As the Death Star started to clear the edge of Yavin and get a clear shot at the Rebel base on its fourth moon, all appeared lost. But a young farmboy from Tatooine turned off his targeting computer and—using nothing but the power of the Force—made the one-in-a-million shot that marked the beginning of the end of the Empire, for the destruction of the Death Star showed that the mighty, evil colossus was vulnerable. Soon young Luke Skywalker and his companions were known far and wide as the Heroes of Yavin. [SW]

Yavin system Far from the Galactic Core and major hyperspace lanes, the system does not appear on many astrogation charts. Yavin system's three planets—Fiddanl, Stroiketcy, and Yavin—orbit a medium orange star. Formed over 7.5 billion years ago, the system was first surveyed during the Old Republic's Expansion Era and was originally recorded as unfit for humanoid habitation. [GG2]

yayax A fierce, pantherlike beast, it lives in the forests of Endor's moon. [ETV]

Yayax

Ychthytonian A four-armed species. Bomlas, a bartender on Skip 1 in Smuggler's Run, was one. [NR]

Yemm A demonic-looking Devaronian, he excelled in saying the right thing at the right time. Yemm supervised documentation and was legal counsel at Maw Installation. [COF]

Yemm, Yarbolk A male Chadra-Fan, he is a reporter for the TriNebulon News stationed on Nim Drovis. He rescued C-3PO and R2-D2 from certain enslavement. Yarbolk Yemm's popularity is attested to by the bounty on him in seven systems, presumably paid for by Loronar Corporation, which didn't like what Yemm was writing about its operations and methods. [POT]

Yetoom Located on the edge of the Senex sector, it is the base of operations for Fargednim P'taan, a moderately large drug dealer. [COJ]

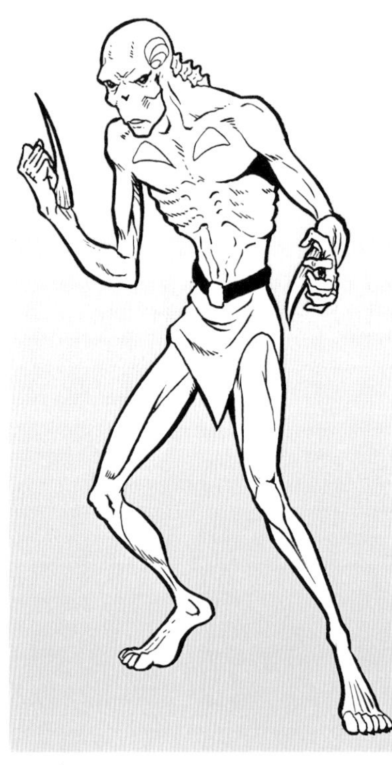
Yevetha

Yevetha The dominant species in the Koornacht Cluster, they are skeletal bipeds who evolved on the planet N'zoth. They have six-fingered hands with retractable claws underneath their wrists and bright streaks of facial color. In N'zoth's night sky, the blazing stars of the Cluster block out the light from more distant stars, and the Yevetha came to believe that their world was the center of the universe. Using spherical thrustships traveling through realspace, the Yevetha spread from their homeworld to colonize eleven other planets, forming the Duskhan League.

Little was known about the Cluster or its worlds, because the Empire kept access restricted and the Yevetha remained secretive after the Empire's departure some three years after the Battle of Endor. In fact, Yevethan policy was to execute trespassers on sight. During the Imperial reign, the brutal governor in charge of the Cluster held public executions, used women as pleasure slaves, and took children as hostages. The technologically inclined Yevetha were forced to work in the shipyards established by the Empire, repairing and maintaining its warships—and learning a great deal about Imperial technology in the process.

After the Empire left, the Yevetha underwent what they called a Second Birth, settling a dozen more colony worlds and restoring captured Imperial warships. The Duskhan League laid claim to the entire Cluster, even though it included as many as seventeen worlds populated by other species. Twelve years after the Battle of Endor, the Yevethan fleet eliminated all non-Yevethan colonies from inside the Cluster's borders, fanatically cleansing these "infestations" in a devastating series of attacks called the Great Purge. Chief of State Leia Organa Solo sent the New Republic's Fifth Fleet to the Cluster to dissuade the Yevetha from extending their actions any further, and a bitter war ensued. [BTS, SOL, TT]

Yevethan Protectorate The proper name of the Duskhan League, an alliance of worlds in Koornacht Cluster inhabited by the xenophobic species known as the Yevetha. [BTS]

Yfra, Ambassador An ambassador from the Hapes Cluster, she was really a traitor. Ambassador Yfra, with hair and eyes the color of polished pewter, went to the Jedi academy to observe Tenel Ka's studies, but her visit had to be put off when the girl's friends Jaina and Jacen Solo and Lowbacca were kidnapped. Yfra secretly planned to have Tenel Ka and her grandmother, Queen Ta'a Chume, assassinated. The plot was uncovered when Tenel Ka and her friends confronted a Bartokk assassination squad on Hapes. [YJK]

Yintal, Dr. An exobiologist at the New Republic Fleet Institute on Coruscant, he was the doctor who nursed Plat Mallar back to health. Mallar was the young Grannan from Polneye who survived the savage Yevethan massacre. [BTS]

Ylix A backwater world, it was home to the gunman Gallandro. An ancient feud existed between Ylix and Goelitz, a planet several systems away, and Ylix occasionally was attacked by Goelitz revolutionaries. As a youth Gallandro enlisted in the Ylix militia, and its forces eventually defeated Goelitz after many devastating battles. [CSSB]

Yllotat system The system where, prior to the Battle of Endor, the Imperial dreadnaught *Dargon* was transporting Rebel and Bothan prisoners to the Star Destroyer *Garret* when it fell under Alliance attack. [TSC]

Yn Homeworld of a diminutive humanoid species, it is represented by Senator Wwebyls in the New Republic government. [NR]

Ynr, Rhysati A naturally gifted pilot, her family was dislocated from Bespin by Imperial forces and she found a home with the Alliance. There was no question that she would make it into the legendary Rogue Squadron. During her training exercises, she befriended Corran Horn and began a relationship with Nawara Ven. [RS, BW]

Yoda, Jedi Master Short in height but tall in stature in the Force, this long-lived Jedi Master ensured the rebirth of the nearly vanished Jedi Knights. For more than 800 years, the diminutive green being trained Jedi Knights in the ways of the Force, but rarely did he face such a challenge as the impetuous young Luke Skywalker.

By the time Luke encountered Yoda in the bogs of Dagobah, the Jedi was nearly 900 years old and walked stooped over, leaning on a gimer stick. He subsisted on the things that nature offered him, eating plants, fruits, and fungi, and building his home of mud, sticks, and stones. Yoda had trained Obi-Wan Kenobi years before when Kenobi himself was a reckless youth.

Yoda's path to Jedi wisdom seemed simple, yet was profound. He made his students unlearn what they had been taught, guiding them instead to tune in to the world around them to learn its truths. "A Jedi uses the Force for knowledge. Never for attack," he would tell them.

When Emperor Palpatine ordered his purge of the Jedi, Yoda went into hiding on Dagobah. He used the Force and the planet's own natural defenses to discourage visitors. But he kept a watch on Luke Skywalker and Leia Organa, using the Force to monitor their growth.

It was after he had escaped almost certain death beneath the claws of a wampa ice creature on Hoth that Luke saw his late Master Kenobi in a vision. Obi-Wan told him to go to the Dagobah system to continue his Jedi training with Yoda.

Yoda lectured young Skywalker about the Force, even as Luke performed rigorous physical and mental exercises. Yoda especially cautioned him against the easy path of anger and the lure of the dark side of the Force. And when he was ordered to undertake a particularly daunting task, Luke responded that he would try. "No! Try not," Yoda said insistently. "Do. Or do not. There is no try."

Yoda

Days later, Yoda instructed Luke to open his mind to memories of old friends, and the possibilities of the future. Luke was jarred when he saw visions of Han Solo and Leia in pain on the Cloud City, and he decided to leave and attempt to rescue his friends. Yoda and the spirit of Kenobi both warned Luke that the decision could destroy everything his friends had fought for, and that he was much too susceptible to the dark side. Torn between his knowledge that Yoda and Ben were right and the visions of his friends in danger, Luke nonetheless decided to leave, promising to return to complete his training.

Shortly after the rescue of Han Solo on Tatooine, Luke did, indeed, return to Dagobah, but he found the diminutive Jedi Master dying. Yoda once again warned Luke to beware the dark side, even though he now revealed that a confrontation with Darth Vader and Emperor Palpatine would be necessary for Luke to complete his Jedi training. Finally, Yoda breathed his last and vanished, becoming one with the Force. [ESB, RJ, SWCG]

Yomm, Auren As a fifteen-year-old girl from the Umboo colony on Roon, she encountered R2-D2 and C-3PO during the early days of the Empire. Auren Yomm was a talented athlete and often led her team—which included the sleek droid Bix—to victory in the Colonial Games. [DTV]

Yomm, Nilz The father of Auren Yomm, in the early days of the Empire he ran a trading post and was a respected physician in the Roon colonies. Nilz Yomm was married to Bola. [DTV]

Yowza, Joh A Yuzzum from the forest moon of Endor, he was one of the few of his species who left his home planet to seek a more civilized future. Yowza, who was short for his species and had a deep and raspy voice, was a true ham at heart. He found employment as male lead singer with the Max Rebo Band and performed at the band's last engagment for crime lord Jabba the Hutt on Tatooine. [RJ,RJSE]

Ysanna

Yrrna system Located in the Outer Rim, it was the site of an Imperial cargo transfer area. Following the Battle of Hoth, the cargo operation in the Yrrna system was attacked by the pirate leader Ali Tarrak, using her strike force of stolen TIE Defenders. [TSC]

ysalamiri Indigenous to the planet Myrkr, these small salamanderlike creatures have the unique ability to push back the Force. Furry snakes with legs that grow to fifty centimeters long, ysalamiri live in the branches of Myrkr's metal-rich trees. Their claws grow directly into the branches, making it difficult to remove them from their perches. A single ysalamiri creates a ten-meter radius bubble in which the Force does not exist. Those who have studied them theorize that ysalamiri push the Force away from themselves like a bubble of air pushes away water. Within this bubble, a Force user cannot call on his or her powers or otherwise manipulate the Force.

Grand Admiral Thrawn's plans to destroy the New Republic included the use of the docile ysalamiri. He ordered Imperial engineers to build frames of pipes to support and nourish the creatures so that they could be removed from their branches and transported off-planet. The nutrient frames were designed so that they could be worn by Thrawn and others as a mobile defense against Jedi. The creatures also figured prominently in Thrawn's plans to rapidly grow clones in the Spaarti cloning cylinders he retrieved from the Emperor's storehouse on Wayland. [HE, DFR, LC, HESB]

Ysanna Shaman-warriors, they live on the planet Ossus and are Force-sensitive. [DE2]

Jem Ysanna

Ysanna, Jem A twenty-three-year-old shaman-warrior encountered on Ossus by Luke Skywalker, she and her brother, Rayf, accompanied Skywalker to New Alderaan. Luke and Jem shared a mutual attraction, but she was killed by a band of Dark Siders who had come to kidnap Jacen and Jaina Solo. [DE2]

Ysanna, Rayf A fifteen-year-old shaman-warrior encountered by Luke Skywalker on Ossus, he and his sister, Jem, accompanied Luke to New Alderaan where he was instrumental in saving Jacen and Jaina Solo from Dark Siders. When his sister was killed, Rayf went with the others to Nespis VIII. [DE2]

Y'Toub system Located in the center of the galactic region known as Hutt Space, it contains six planets orbiting a yellow star. A massive, radioactive gas cloud containing the hidden planet Ganath lies very close to the Y'Toub system. Four of the system's six planets are habitable. The largest and best known is Nal Hutta, with its orbiting smugglers' moon, Nar Shaddaa. Consequently, it is sometimes called the Nal Hutta system. [GG4, DESB, DE2, DS]

Yuga 2 A planet covered with dense rain forests and clinging trees, it is a popular tourist destination because of its Yuga Planetary Park. Alliance historian Voren Na'al bought passage from Yuga 2 to Tatooine on a Galaxy Tours ship to begin documenting the histories of the Heroes of Yavin. [MTS]

Yulant system Located in the Core Worlds, it contains one of the eighteen farming planets administered by the Salliche Ag Corporation. After the Battle of Endor, workers in the Yulant, Ruan, and Broest systems revolted against the Imperial-controlled Salliche Ag by burning fields and destroying hydroponics facilities. [SWAJ]

Yularen, Wulff A colonel in the Imperial Security Bureau, he was assigned to brief Grand Moff Tarkin and also ordered to ensure absolute loyalty to the Emperor. He was killed in the explosion of the first Death Star. [CCG]

Yuls, Dellis A Quarren, he was the Chief of Security for Ororo Transportation, the main competitor of crime lord Prince Xizor's own cargo company. Xizor's aide, Guri, twisted Yuls's neck until it cracked, then shot him in the base of the skull for good measure. [SOTE]

Yunkor IX In an early test of the B-wing starfighter, a single B-wing was sent to destroy a TIE fighter staging area near Yunkor IX. [FP]

Yushan sector Located in the Mid-Rim, it contains the planet Kaal. [SWAJ]

Yuzzem Humanoids with long snouts, long arms, heavy fur, and large black eyes, they are noted for their great strength and volatile, unpredictable temperaments. Yuzzem are often found as slaves in Imperial labor camps or as hired hands employed to handle physical activities like mining. A pair of Yuzzem aided Princess Leia and Luke Skywalker during their mission to the Circarpous star system. [SME]

Rayf Ysanna

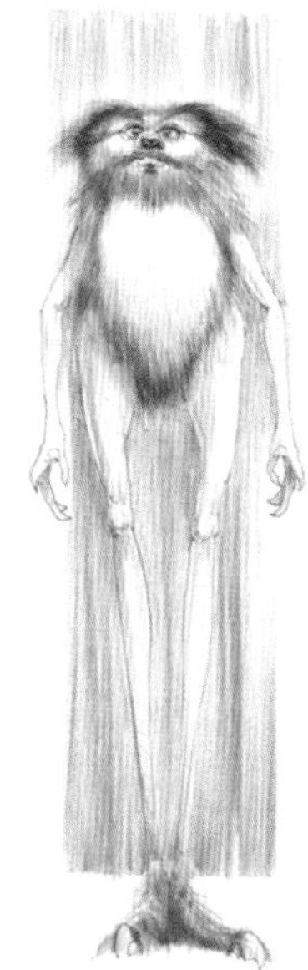
Yuzzum

Yuzzum A creature that inhabits the forest floor of Endor's moon, it has a round, fur-covered body, long, thin legs, and a wide mouth full of sharp, protruding teeth. Yuzzum are an intelligent though somewhat barbaric spear-wielding species. Traveling in groups, they flush out their favorite meal of small rodents called ruggers. Some Yuzzum, especially a few with some singing talent, have gone off-world to seek fame and fortune. They include Joh Yowza, who joined the Max Rebo Band. [ETV, RJ, ISWU]

Y-wing starfighter Despite its age, the ship has been one of the mainstays of the Rebel Alliance and saw notable duty at the Battle of Yavin, during which the Imperial Death Star was destroyed. Prior to the introduction of the X-wing starfighter, Y-wings were the flagship fighters of the Alliance.

The twin-engine Y-wing, at sixteen meters long, is a multipurpose ship that was originally designed as a compromise between a full-fledged attack fighter and a heavier bomber. The durable starfighters can give and take a great deal of punishment, but they don't have the payload capacity or the speed, stealth, and maneuverability to compete with modern Imperial attack fighters.

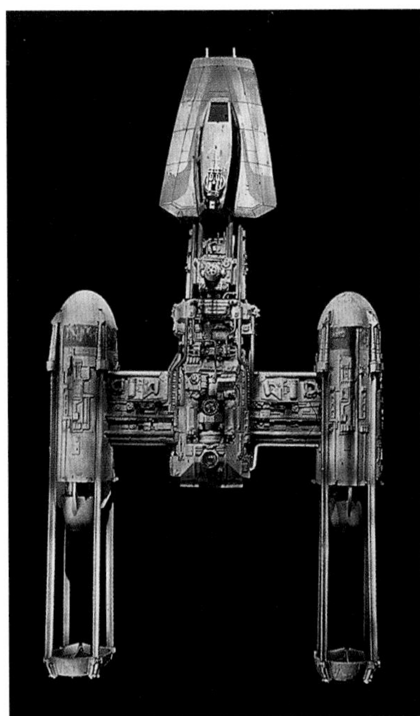

Y-wing starfighter

The Rebel Alliance has flown more Y-wings than any other fighter and has used a number of different configurations for a variety of mission profiles. It isn't uncommon for a Y-wing to be stripped down for assault runs against Imperial convoys and then be refitted by Rebel technicians for a heavy bombing run against an Imperial base. Y-wings also find use on diplomatic escort missions and for long-range patrols. The BTL-A4 Y-wing (LP), or *Longprobe*-class, has extra provisions, more powerful sensors, and a sophisticated navigation computer specifically for patrol duty.

The Y-wing has three main components. The forward cockpit module houses the pilots and weapons systems. A reinforced space-frame central spar stretches back from the cockpit module; the Y-wing's ionization reactor and hyperdrive/astrogation hardware are crammed into this narrow frame. A cross wing housing the main power cells attaches at the back of the spar, with the two powerful sublight ion drives on either end.

The cockpit module has thick armor plating. The pilot controls a pair of forward laser cannons and twin proton torpedo launchers. A turret-mounted ion cannon is directly behind the pilot. Like the X-wing, an R2 or R4 astromech droid fits snugly into the droid socket behind the cockpit and monitors all fight, navigation, and power systems. The droid can also handle fire control, perform simple inflight maintenance, and reroute power as needed. The R2 unit also stores hyperspace jump coordinates. [SW, SWSB, ESB, RJ, SWVG]

Yyrtan system A system that contains the yellow star Yyrta and several planets, including Kirtania. The Yyrtan system is positioned along a hyperspace trade route that has become more popular in recent years. [SWAJ]

Z-95 Headhunter A ship design older than most of the pilots flying it, it is one of the most common starfighters in the galaxy. The Z-95 Headhunter is both maneuverable and durable. It is used by planetary police and air defense units as well as many pirate and outlaw groups.

The original Mark I model was designed as an atmospheric fighter that could be adapted to space travel. Twin-engine swing-wing craft, they sport a bubble cockpit that gives the pilot a clear field of vision. They typically have a set of triple-blasters on each wing.

In the later Headhunters, swing wings were replaced with fixed wings, and maneuverability was maintained with the addition of maneuvering jets. The starfighter canopy was more heavily armored, and heads-up holographic tactical displays were improved. The most frequent modifications involve replacing the weapons systems or enhancing the motors for greater speed. The Rebel Alliance used a number of Z-95 Headhunters for training missions.

Han Solo flew a Z-95 Mark I when he led the defense of an outlaw-tech base against Corporate Sector Authority fighters. Solo used the Z-95's superior atmospheric capabilities to good advantage against the Authority's sluggish IRD fighters. Mara Jade has used a modified Z-95 Headhunter equipped with a hyperdrive. [SWSB, HSE, DFRSB, RSB, DA, SWVG]

Zaltin A major Thyferran corporation, it was one of the leaders in bacta production and refinement. Although its officers had no desire to become part of the Bacta Cartel, Zaltin was brought into the fold by the Empire, primarily to serve as competition for Xucphra. When Zaltin officials realized that the Empire was about to collapse, they decided to strengthen their ties with the native Vratix, for without them no bacta would be produced at all. They began an alliance with the Ashern Circle rebels, providing them with financial resources as well as hiding places. During the planet's civil war, Xucphra ruthlessly killed many officers of Zaltin. Those who survived went into hiding, fled the planet, or joined the Ashern Circle. Eventually Xucphra was defeated with the help of Rogue Squadron. [BW]

Zardra A tall, dark-haired woman, she appears strikingly sensual, with more than a hint of danger about her. Zardra carries a force pike and wears a flowing cloak. She is a bounty hunter of exceptional skill and daring and often teams up with Jodo Kast and Puggles Trodd when a particular bounty catches her interest. She enjoys personal combat and appreciates the fine things that credits can buy, but the hunt is the most important thing in her life. She fears that she will wind up dying senselessly, so she often tempts fate by taking huge risks. She killed Mageye the Hutt when the Hutt was accidentally dropped on her. As a result, the Hutts put a huge price on her head. [TM, OS, TMEC]

Zatec-Cha The grand vizier of the planet Tammuz-an during the early days of Imperial rule, he hoped to usurp the throne of Mon Julpa. In

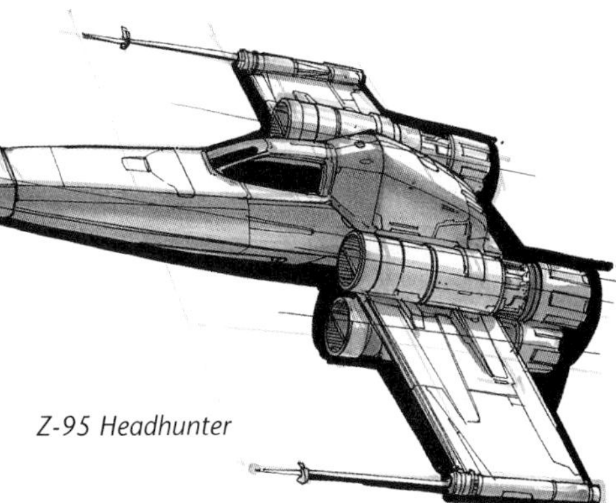

Z-95 Headhunter

Zatec-Cha

his plotting, Zatec-Cha found a way to cause the leader to suffer from memory loss. [DTV]

Zebitrope IV Located in the Zebitrope system, it is the homeworld of a species of lizard whose members symbiotically support a spongy mold growth on their backs. This mold is the only source of the addictive drug lesai, which eliminates the need for sleep. [LCF]

Zeebo A four-eared Mooka, he was the furry and feathered pet of Ken, the Jedi Prince. [LCJ, PDS]

Zeffliffl The fourth planet orbiting Markbee's Star, it is home to the seaweedlike aliens also known as Zeffliffl. They inhabit the shallow seas surrounding the smaller southern continent of the planet and must spray themselves with seawater when spending time on land. The Zeffliffl exist in close groups of several individuals, and their bodies automatically reject any outsider who attempts to join the group. [CS]

Zekk A onetime street urchin, he was taken in by old Peckhum, a supply courier and message runner for the New Republic on Coruscant. He also supplied the Jedi academy on Yavin 4. Zekk was a resourceful scamp. He spent his childhood on the planet Ennth, but when the colony there was devastated by a natural disaster, he escaped on the next supply ship and traveled from planet to planet as a stowaway.

Zekk had shoulder-length hair one shade lighter than black, and green eyes with a darker corona around emerald irises. He became friendly with young Jedi academy members but also a target for Norys, leader of the Lost Ones gang in the lower levels of Coruscant. Norys nicknamed Zekk the Trash Collector because of his uncanny ability to locate wrecks of spacecraft and other items in the lower levels.

Tamith Kai, one of the leaders of the Shadow Academy, came across Zekk, tested him, and found he had Force potential. He was stunned and taken away to the academy. There, Brakiss convinced him that his friends didn't really care for him and that he wouldn't amount to anything if he stayed on Coruscant, but that he could become a great warrior with proper training. Zekk was impressed by the respect he was shown. He was fed well and given polished leather armor, a sleek uniform that made him look dark and dashing. Brakiss trained him in the ways of the Force while indoctrinating him to the views of the Empire.

Zekk returned to Coruscant to recruit other Lost Ones gang members and encountered Jacen Solo and Tenel Ka. They were looking for him for fear he had come to harm. When Jacen tried to call for help, Zekk stunned them and he and the gang members escaped. Brakiss gave Zekk a lightsaber with a scarlet blade, and soon he was in contention with Vilas to be head of a new order of Dark Jedi. Zekk defeated Vilas in a duel to the death and gained the title of Darkest Knight. Later, Zekk was badly injured in the explosion that partly destroyed the Great Temple on Yavin 4, home of the Jedi academy. He was then taken in by the academy and cared for there. [YJK]

Zend, Salla An exotic, statuesque young woman, her hard-as-nails personality masks a softer side. Salla Zend was a technician on a corporate transport who saved enough to get a loan and buy her own ship. She quickly drifted into smuggling, where she met such rogues as half-breed Corellian master mechanic Shug Ninx, gambler-pilot Lando Calrissian, his Corellian pilot friend Han Solo, and Solo's copilot, a Wookiee named Chewbacca.

Han and Salla had an almost immediate rapport, and over the years they developed a very close relationship. But after an accident that nearly took her life, Salla decided she wanted to retire from smuggling and make a life with Solo. He wasn't ready to be pinned down and bid her goodbye in a holo-message. Over the next decade, Salla hooked up with Shug Ninx at his ship repair spacebarn on the Smuggler's Moon of Nar Shaddaa where she made a good living as a welder and occasional gun runner. In between jobs, she worked on building her own large freighter, the *Starlight Intruder*. She was overhauling the hyperdrive engines when visitors arrived: Han Solo and Chewbacca, accompanied by Leia Organa Solo and the droid C-3PO. That was the beginning of a series of adventures that got Salla Zend and Shug Ninx entangled with the New Republic, frequently rescuing some of its leaders while trying to figure out how to get Salla's confiscated freighter returned. [DE]

zenomach A powerful ground-boring machine, it looks and operates like a giant drill. [MMY]

Salla Zend

zero The point of convergence of the four laser cannons on an X-wing fighter. [RS, BW]

Zexx A fearsome, tusked species, they are most likely related to the Esoomians. [TOJ, GG10]

Z'fell Located in the system of the same name in the Koornacht Cluster, it is one of the primary large-population worlds of the Yevethan species and is a member of the Duskhan League. During the Battle of N'zoth, the New Republic attacked Z'fell. [SOL, TT]

Zhar A gas giant in the Outer Rim, one of its moons is Gall, the site of an Imperial enclave. Rogue Squadron set up a temporary base on another moon, Kile, from which they launched an attempt to capture Boba Fett and rescue Han Solo, then trapped in carbonite. [SOTE]

Zhina Located in the Koornacht Cluster, it is one of the primary worlds of the Yevethan species and is a member of the Duskhan League. It was the location of an orbital Imperial repair yard, code-named Black 11, for the Empire's Black Sword Command. After the Battle of Endor, the Empire retreated from the shipyards of Zhina, Wakiza, and N'zoth, and the Yevetha were able to capture several of their capital ships. The Black 11 shipyards were later moved away from Zhina to a clandestine location. [BTS, SOL]

Zi'Dek system A system where Han Solo used to make smuggling runs. He learned some of the Zi'Dek system port access codes, but these codes were later changed by the Imperials. [CPL]

Zilar, Senator A New Republic senator from Praesitlyn, the human is also a member of the Senate Defense Council. [BTS]

Zirtran's Anchor A trading station drifting near the Phosphura Belt Nebula, it is a hodgepodge of vessels and freighters welded together and connected by interlocking pressure tunnels. Owned and operated by tribal nests of Geelan—a short furry species that loves to barter and hoard valuables—the station continues to grow in size. Zirtran's Anchor is a haven for smugglers and other free-traders. [SWAJ]

Zlarb A slave trader, he is a tall human with fair skin, white-blond hair and beard, and clear gray eyes. Zlarb once commandeered the *Millennium Falcon* and its crew when he needed to deliver contraband to the planet Bonadan. [HLL]

Zorba The father of Jabba the Hutt, he had been imprisoned on the planet Kip for more than twenty years and didn't immediately learn of his son's death on Tatooine. Zorba had long, white braids and a white beard. All of Jabba's possessions were bequeathed to his father, including his desert palace on Tatooine and the Holiday Towers Hotel and Casino on Cloud City. Zorba made it his mission to retake whatever of Jabba's criminal empire was still left and to kill Princess Leia for the murder of his son. He put out a bounty on Leia and her husband, Han Solo. Zorba won Cloud City on Bespin from Lando Calrissian in a sabacc game and began cooperating with Imperials. Zorba got fed to the Sarlacc on Tatooine by pretender-to-the-throne Trioculus, but the creature spit him out. [ZHR, MMY, QE, PDS]

Zorba's Express An ancient, bell-shaped starship, it is owned by Zorba the Hutt, Jabba's father. [ZHR]

Zraii, Master A member of the insectoid species known as Verpine, he is in charge of the repairs and maintenance for Rogue Squadron's fleet of X-wings, as well as a number of other Alliance spacecraft. [RS]

Zsinj A warlord who, with some lesser warlords, was firmly entrenched in over a third of the galaxy, pillaging entire star systems. Zsinj and the others were, for a time, all that was left of the Empire. [CPL]

Z'trop A scenic and romantic tropical world, it is noted for its pleasant volcanic islands, wide beaches, and clear waters. Han Solo, Princess Leia, and their companions took time for rest and relaxation on Z'trop. [MMY]

Zuckuss A bounty hunter who saw a competitor get the big catch, this member of the insectlike Gand species was one of his planet's most successful findsmen. Zuckuss is from the gaseous planet Gand where people hunters—or findsmen—are highly honored. He used the elaborate and arcane rituals of his ancestors to help him in his hunts.

Zuckuss

Off-planet, Zuckuss had to wear a special breathing mask to protect him from harmful oxygen. He also wore a set of battle armor under his heavy cloak and hung a computer and sensor array on straps around his neck. He was a hard-working bounty hunter, willing to pursue his quarry in any environment. Using his often correct predictions and hunches, Zuckuss's success rate was high and he could command a top price.

He was hired by Tatooine crime lord Jabba the Hutt and paired with the rogue protocol droid 4-LOM. The droid's analytical skills perfectly complemented Zuckuss's intuition. The two heeded the call by Darth Vader and agreed to search for Han Solo and the *Millennium Falcon*, but Boba Fett beat them to the prey. Following the Battle of Hoth, he and 4-LOM severely damaged the final escaping Rebel transport, the *Bright Hope*. But they then reconsidered, and helped rescue and evacuate ninety Rebels to Darlyn Boda. [ESB, TBH, GG3]

Zuggs, Commodore A bald, beady-eyed Imperial officer, he was assigned to Trioculus, pretender to the throne of the Emperor. Commodore Zuggs was a pilot for Trioculus's strike cruiser. [LCJ]

Zut

Zut A male Phlog, he is the mate of Dobah on the forest moon of Endor. [ETV]

Zutton A Snivvian bounty hunter, like most of his species he is a tortured artist driven to live out the stories he creates. One of his stories led him to an out-of-the-way cantina in Mos Eisley on the little-visited planet of Tatooine. During his stay, he picked up the nickname Snaggletooth because of his pronounced canine fangs. He was on retainer to Jabba the Hutt. [GG12, SWAJ]

zwil A gentle narcotic, Drovians inhale it through their mucous membranes. Most Drovians are mildly addicted. [POT]

Zyggurats A terrorist group, it operated on the fringes of the galaxy. The Zyggurats were believed to have come from outside known Imperial space shortly after the Clone Wars. The new Empire quickly suppressed the group before its activities could cause much damage. [DE]

Zygian Banking Concern A bank on Tatooine, it often gave loans to moisture farmers. [GG7, TMEC]

Zythmar The temple priest of the Massassi warriors on Yavin 4 some 4,000 years before the Galactic Civil War, he emerged from twelve years

Zutton

of solitude to look over an intruder, Dark Sider Exar Kun. Kun later used Zythmar as a test subject for Naga Sadow's abandoned Sith transformation machines. [DLS]

ZZ-4Z (Zee Zee) A housekeeping droid that cares for Han Solo's long-empty apartment on Nar Shaddaa, ZZ-4Z was seriously damaged during a battle with Boba Fett. [DE]

About the Author

A writer, public speaker, and collector, Stephen J. Sansweet has transformed his love for the *Star Wars* saga into a busy career. He is the author or co-author of six books, with three more in the works; writes columns and feature articles for magazines; and has traveled the world as a Lucasfilm liaison to *Star Wars* fans everywhere.

Sansweet was born in Philadelphia and got his bachelor's degree from Temple University, where he was named outstanding graduate in journalism. He was a feature writer for the *Philadelphia Inquirer* before joining *The Wall Street Journal*. Transferred to Los Angeles, he wrote on a wide range of topics from multinational corporate bribery to the civil rights of mental patients, and covered Hollywood for three years. He was named deputy bureau chief in 1983 and served as the *Journal*'s Los Angeles bureau chief for nine years starting in March 1987.

In 1996, Sansweet joined Lucasfilm Ltd. as Director of Specialty Marketing to help promote *Star Wars* to fans both old and new. He started collecting robots and space toys in the mid-1970s and over the years that collection has been transformed into the largest private collection of *Star Wars* memorabilia in the world.

Among Sansweet's books are: *The Punishment Cure* (1976); *Science Fiction Toys and Models* (1980); *Star Wars: From Concept to Screen to Collectible* (1992); *Tomart's Price Guide to Worldwide Star Wars Collectibles* (1994, revised 1997); and *Quotable Star Wars: I'd Just as Soon Kiss a Wookiee* (1996).

The California resident also writes collectibles columns for the *Star Wars Insider* and Topps' *Star Wars Galaxy Collector* magazine, has been an editor and writer of five sets of *Star Wars* trading cards for Topps Inc., and has been a co-host on QVC *Star Wars* Collection broadcasts.